ONE BAD CARD

MURF'S FIRST LAW

Kyle Johnson

For Keri, for doing nothing more than rolling her eyes while I taught the kids how to play poker.

Contents

1

I cursed into my gag and struggled against the ropes binding me as my captors dragged me to the edge of the cliff. I kicked out with my boots, aiming for shins, but the damned nimble elves dodged my attacks easily. Something cracked the back of my skull, and I slumped as stars flashed in my vision. In that moment, the two elves hauled me up to the edge of the cliff and leaned me over it. I glanced downward, but in the darkness, all I could see was the sheer cliff below my feet and shadows yawning way, way below me. I felt one of the elves' breath against my neck as he leaned close to my ear.

"Enjoy your trip," the man whispered creepily, his lips practically touching my ear. "It's the last one you'll ever take, cheater!"

As the pair of them shoved me over the edge into the open air, and I began plummeting to my absolutely certain death, one thought flashed in my mind.

Murf's Twenty-Third Law: The bigger you win, the bigger you'll lose. Like all of Murf's Laws, it held true. I'd won plenty off the stupid elves, and in return, I was about to lose my damn life.

I should probably backtrack a bit and explain who I am and how I got here. My name's Murf. I'm a gambler by trade, and depending on who you ask, I'm also a no-good vagabond, a gutless coward, and one hell of a lover. I'm a liar and a thief, and I've taken liberties with more than one married woman. What I'm not, though, is a cheater. I never have been, and I never will be. Not for any moral reasons or anything, mind you. Cheaters just always get caught eventually, and while people will grumble over you being a lucky son of a bitch, they get mean over cheating.

Murf's Fifth Law: There's always a better cheater out there, and the moment you cheat, you'll meet them.

This all started earlier today. I'd sailed into the city of Canis on the continent of Torin with the afternoon tide, and I was more than happy to set my boots on dry land again. It's a twelve-day passage from the goblin city of Gurg up on the continent of Shuria down here to Canis. It's normally closer to twenty, but I'd booked passage on the fastest clipper I could find and shaved a week off. Plus, I might have accidentally set fire to the docks in Gurg before we left, which would make it much harder for anyone to catch up to me. I also booked passage on four separate ships and boarded mine in the middle of the night just in case anyone was in the mood to follow me.

Not that anyone would. Well, most likely, they wouldn't. I supposed it would depend on just how much that orc Chief Ragmuffin or whatever the hell his name was cared about the purity of his daughter, and how much her offering it to me hurt her marriage chances. Probably a lot on both counts. Orcs are all about family, really emotional, and not always that fast on the uptake. They aren't stupid; they just take longer to reach the same conclusions that someone else might. If she was promised to someone, they'd probably take her lack of virginity pretty personally. In orcish society, that sort of thing tends to turn into blood feuds pretty damn quickly, and because they aren't the fastest thinkers, that sort of thing could kill a lot of people before everyone realized how stupid it was.

Realistically, Chief Whats-his-name had no reason to be mad at me. I didn't know she was a virgin until it was too late to do anything about it, and the whole thing was her fault, really. She gambled more than she could afford to lose, and she was the one who offered to pay her debt in trade. She was a fine-looking woman, too—at least, for an orc—and I wasn't about to say no. I might be a liar, a thief, and a coward, but I'm no fool. Eventually, the chief would realize that and take his frustration out on the person who really deserved it, but when he'd caught me bending the girl over a bed—his bed, in fact, although I didn't know it at the time—he'd been pretty pissed at me, and he'd threatened all sorts of things that I don't even think are anatomically possible. I'm pretty sure you can't stretch a man's sac over his shoulder and nail it to itself, no matter how long you put him—and it—on the rack. That didn't mean I wanted him to try it, though, so I got the hell out of her and there in a hurry.

Wait, not Ragmuffin. Ragmaffa. That was it. Chief Ragmaffa. Not that the sac-stretcher deserves that much thought. Eh, fuck him. I like Ragmuffin better, anyway.

The point is, I had a few weeks to spend in Canis, which was perfect, because I'd come there for a reason. The city tournament was coming up, one held every three years and one of the biggest tournaments in the world, and I intended to be in it. My hope was that I could get to know the competition, win, and collect my prize before I had to get the hell out and catch a ship headed for somewhere else along the Torian coast.

That part would be easy, of course. The beast people are generally friendly and welcoming to strangers, and they always have a ton of ship traffic coming into and going out of their cosmopolitan cities. It would be easy to catch a ship heading west, toward the Kine Isles, then maybe skip across the Placid Ocean to the island of Farpoint, back in human lands. My other choice was to head inland, but northern Torin is just one huge jungle away from the coast and the Canid River. If you've never been there, the whole northern half of the continent is constantly drenched from the rains that seem to fall daily. Water drips on you pretty much all the time in the jungles, even when it's not raining, and there are at least a hundred species of bugs that like to suck human blood, some of them big enough to pick up a whole damn person and carry him off. Plus, it's not a great place for gambling. The biggest settlements there are logging towns with a few hundred people in them, and I've yet to convince the big cats or giant bugs to sit down for a friendly game of cards.

Canis is the biggest city in Torin by a large margin, and I've visited it any number of times over the years. I thanked the captain for getting us into port in one piece, then hefted my pack and walked into the city beneath an overcast sky and a steady, miserable drizzle. I considered heading to the Gambler's Hall—like any smart professional gambler, I was a member of the Guild, and I paid my dues and kept myself in good standing. That had some benefits, like a place to stay and the ability to gamble at tables guaranteed to be free of cheating. Mostly, though, I was a member because if a professional gambler didn't join, the Guild would happily explain the benefits of membership to them by way of a sledgehammer to the kneecaps until they saw the light. None of the Guilds played around, not even the damn Scrivener's Guild. You would think a society made of people who do nothing but scribe and draw cards all day would be quiet, bookish, and harmless. You'd think that right up until you saw a rogue scribe hanging from their place of business, their skin taken completely off and tacked up on the door with a note written on it explaining that a smart scribe joined the damn Guild and paid their dues. The penmanship on that note was amazing, though, I have to say.

Murf's Ninth Law: It's always the quiet ones.

The problem was, the Guild was damn expensive, and my passage to Canis had cost a lot more than I'd wanted to spend. The captain sensed my hurry to leave Gurg and bargained hard, and while I'd managed to keep him from totally ripping me off, it still cost me about half again what it should have. I had some coins in my pocket, but not enough for the Guild. Fortunately, the harbor area was lousy with drinking halls, and a gambler who can't make money off drunk sailors needs to hang up their deck and take a long walk off a short pier somewhere. The coins I needed just happened to be stuck in someone else's pocket at the moment. It was practically my duty to liberate them.

Keeghan's Fine Winery was badly misnamed. It wasn't close to fine, for one thing. Fine establishments don't have sawdust spread on the floors to catch spilled liquor, vomit, and probably piss. Fine establishments are well ventilated so that there wasn't a haze of smoke in the air that stung my eyes and tickled my throat. Fine establishments don't have tables that look like they'd been badly repaired one time too many and would probably collapse if someone farted loudly near them. Plus, fine establishments don't usually need the seven-foot-tall, muscled bouncer that stood beside the door as I entered. Like all his kind, the ursid was big, covered with hair, and had a bear-like face with small, beady eyes and a short, blunt muzzle of a nose and mouth. He growled at me as I entered, but I just rolled my eyes and ignored him. I was there to gamble, not to cause trouble.

I made my way to the bar and caught the attention of the bartender, a canid beastling. The man was shorter than me and thin, with light-brown fur covering his body and a distinctly doglike face, complete with long, drooping ears, a blunt muzzle, and a shiny black nose. The canids are the most animalistic of the four beastling species, at least in appearance, but they're just as intelligent and civilized as anyone. More than some, in fact. He walked over to me and gave me an appraising look, glancing up and down my body. I looked past him at the large mirror behind him and had to admit that I liked what I saw.

I'm tall for a human, a couple inches past six feet, with wavy blonde hair and bright blue eyes. I stayed active enough to be fit and trim but didn't have the muscles of a soldier or guard. My black coat was well tailored without looking fancy, and the wide-brimmed hat of the same color on my head was brushed but not shiny the way some nobles preferred. It was a cultivated appearance: I looked like I had enough money to be respectable but not enough to be a valid target for thieves or muggers. The heavy knife strapped to my waist, just visible beneath my open coat, reinforced that idea.

"What'll you have?" the man finally asked me in Human. His muzzle distorted the words a bit, rolling his R's and giving him a faint lisp, but all beastlings sounded like that, so it didn't bother me. I spoke a bit of Canid myself, but my mouth wasn't any better at pronouncing his language than his was at mine, so I just stuck with Human. Besides, it was what pretty much everyone spoke when dealing with a different species, and it had been since the Arnor Empire was whole, a couple hundred years ago. It was still mostly there, way to the northwest, and while it was smaller than it used to be, it was still the largest, richest, and most populous nation in the world by a large margin. Since it held most of the world's supply of coins, it could kind of tell everyone else how to speak, and the rest of the world just went with it. It was easier than arguing, especially when you'd be arguing against a massive navy and army both determined to teach you why you were wrong, no matter how many times they had to kill you to do it.

"How's the wine here?" I asked with a grin.

"Same as it is in any drinking hall," he replied shortly. "Expensive and barely drinkable."

So much for this being a winery, I thought with a silent snort. "Bourbon, neat, then."

"Four brass."

I fished four shining coins from my dwindling purse and slid them over to him, and he gave me a shot glass filled three-quarters full of dark liquid. I lifted it and turned to the room, scanning the tables. Four games were going on, and I looked over the players in each. Most were simple sailors, dockhands, or laborers, and I discarded the idea of joining them quickly enough. I was here to take someone's coins, and taking them from commoners was usually a bad idea. They typically didn't have much as it was—an average laborer made maybe five or six brass a day—and that meant they got upset about losing it easily. I didn't need to deal with some pissed-off sailor trying to stab me with a rusty dagger because he bet too big on a double set.

My eyes settled on a pair of elves at a far table. Like all elves, they had long, narrow features, large ears with small points on the ends, and angled eyes. Also like every elf I'd ever met, they were fully armed and armored, but that didn't bother me. Every elf out there considered themselves some sort of legendary warrior, even the ones who'd never used a weapon in anger in their lives. It was a cultural thing, so the fact that they had chainmail vests and sheathed swords resting against their chairs meant little. What mattered was that the armor, weapons, and clothing all looked to be in good condition, and their clothing, while travel-stained, was of decent quality. They had money—technically, they had my money, and I decided to do them a favor and retrieve it for them.

I sidled over to the table and watched for a couple hands. The sailor in front of me was playing badly. He'd drawn a 2-set of sixes and had four cards of a flush in stars, and I had to repress a wince as he put down three of the star cards and kept the sixes. Sure, the 2-set was guaranteed to be better than nothing, but there were only five suits in the deck. The man had a one-in-five chance of drawing another star card and getting a flush. His chances of drawing another of the three sixes remaining in the deck were a lot worse, especially since the goblin woman to his right had just discarded one of them. He should have folded when he drew nothing—a 2-set was the lowest hand, and with fifteen card ranks to choose from, sixes weren't great—but he stayed in, tried to bluff his way into winning the pot, and ended up losing big to one of the elves with a double set of queens and nines. He swore furiously and pushed himself back from the table a bit drunkenly, staggering to his feet.

"Fucking slant-ears," the man grumbled, staring daggers at the elf. "You should all go back to your fucking tundra." The elf just grinned at him, sliding the pot over to himself and not pointing out that the human wasn't exactly in his own homeland, either. Elves came originally from northern Shuria, but we humans originated around the Basin Sea, way off to the west between the continents of Langor and Palla, so we had no more reason to be in Canis than the elves. Of course, people like that sailor generally don't care that they're not making any sense, especially when they've been drinking.

"Go sleep it off in some gutter where you belong, flat-face," the other elf sneered. "Come back when you have more money to lose." The sailor grabbed at the knife at his belt but took a look at the relaxed, confident-seeming elves and seemed to think better of it.

"Unity-damned slant-ears," he mumbled as he stumbled away from the table. "Kill the lot and let the Unity sort them out, I say."

I ignored him as I righted the chair and settled down into it, giving the others a smile. "Well, that wasn't remotely awkward and unpleasant," I said in a cheery voice, meeting their eyes one by one and pulling out a handful of coins. "Mind if...?"

My words stumbled for a moment as I met the eyes of the elf who'd just won the hand. Usually, when I look into someone's eyes, I'm getting a measure of them. I'm learning how confident they are, how nervous they might be feeling, and seeing if they meet my gaze or look away. When I gazed into the elf's eyes, though, I saw a spark burning there, a tiny flame that radiated a little bit of power. I knew what that meant immediately, of course.

Twice-damned Holder, I thought with a sigh. I hated playing against Holders, those who'd managed to find a Unity card and attach it to their soul. The card granted them unique, magical abilities, and a person who held one could add others to make themselves even more powerful, building a soul deck. Their deck could make them stronger, faster, or more durable, and all that was fine. I didn't care if the elf could pick up the ursid bouncer and skip him across the harbor like a stone since I had no plans to wrestle with the man. The issue was that cards could also make a person luckier, more dexterous so that cheating was easier, or even let them do things like change the cards in their hands. There was no way to know just what powers a deck could give someone, and that made playing against them a lot more uncertain.

I quickly regained myself and plastered my smile back on my face. "Mind if I join you?" I said, continuing my scan and noting that the second elf was a Holder, as well. That could be a good thing or a bad thing, I decided. Holders tended to have money, after all, and even if one had a power to let them cheat, there were ways around that. Despite what most people thought, arcanum—the game they played—was a matter of skill just as much as it was luck.

"If you have the money," the woman to my right said in the husky voice that she shared with most goblins. Like others of her race, she was short and slim, with faintly green-tinted skin, delicate features, and no hair anywhere but the thick, black mane on her head. "Buy-in is twenty brass, ante is one."

I placed four stacks of five coins on the table before me with a smile. "I can handle that. Table rules?" I slid one coin into the middle to join the others who'd already anted up.

"Standard arcanum, one draw," the elf who'd just won drawled with a lazy sneer. "No wild cards in the deck."

"Sounds good to me."

The next few hours slid by in a haze of cards, clinking coins, and curses. The ursid to my left bowed out first, followed by the old canid. Others entered the game and left, until finally, it was just me, the goblin, and the two elves. I'd played carefully, losing small amounts regularly, then winning big to make it all back and then some. The woman and the elves had both added money to the table as the night went on and they ran low, and I now had a respectable stack of coins in front of me, enough that I was comfortable ending my evening. I did want to go out on a high note, though, so I played until I pulled a hand I was happy with.

"Three," I bid, tossing the coins into the middle.

"Five," the first elf replied, adding his coins as well.

"Call," the second elf said, followed by the goblin woman.

I tossed a single card on the table, as did the second elf, while the first elf and goblin both took two. I watched their reactions carefully as they examined the cards the goblin dealt them. The first elf tapped his finger against the side of his cards once; the second took a slightly deeper breath as he looked at his cards. The goblin woman crossed her legs as she set hers down. All that told me everything I needed to know.

"Ten," I bid, pushing two stacks into the middle.

The first elf hesitated, then slid his own coins in. "Call."

"Double," the second elf said, pushing twenty coins into the middle.

"Raise five," the goblin added.

I looked at the coins, then slid my entire pile into the middle. "All in."

The first elf glared at me, then shook his head. "I fold," he said in a disgusted tone.

"As do I," the goblin sighed.

The second elf stared at me, and I met his gaze steadily. "You bluff," he finally said, tapping his cards on the table.

I shrugged. "You have to pay to find out. Are you in or out?"

"I call," he said after a moment, pushing his pile into the middle and flipping his cards over with a triumphant expression. "I have a run, two to six." The cards gleamed on the table, each a hand-crafted illustration drawn by a scrivener somewhere. A run was a solid hand, five cards in a row of differing suits. It was better than a double set or 3-set and just below a flush.

"Well, that beats a double set in ladies and eights," I sighed, laying down four of my cards. The elf crowed triumphantly and reached for the pot, but I held up a restraining hand before tossing down my final card. The image of a young woman seated in a chair, staring out a window at a sky filled with four-pointed stars stared up at the others, her gentle smile somehow mocking the flabbergasted elf. "But not a full hall, ladies over eights. Sorry about that."

"You—that..." The elf sputtered, half-rising from his chair. "You cheated!"

"I never cheat," I said easily, sliding my coins over and beginning to stack them. "I just get lucky." I winked at the goblin woman, who laughed merrily.

"Well done!" she said in a surprisingly cheerful voice. "The slant-ears need to learn humility."

"Silence, green-skin," the elf snarled. "Or I'll teach you manners at the end of my blade!"

"The only thing a woman has ever learned from your blade is disappointment," she replied, rolling her eyes. "We all know that."

The elf snarled and stood, knocking his chair back, but I lifted my hands and waved them in the air pleadingly. Goblins and elves hated one another on general principle—their species shared a continent and had fought dozens of wars over the millennia, and bad blood died hard—and the last thing I wanted was a fight. In places like this, those had a way of turning into free-for-alls, after all. I just wanted to take my money and get the hell out, nothing more.

"Whoa, whoa, calm down," I said with a chuckle. "No need to go teaching anyone anything, here. It was a good game, friend, and you played well. There'll be other games and other tables. No reason to get so upset about this one."

"You cheated me, human," the elf sneered, placing a hand on the blade resting against his chair. "You are the lowest of vermin, utterly without honor, and I spit on your ancestry." He looked at me challengingly. "What do you have to say about that?" The people around us fell silent and scooted back, clearing space, and I sighed mentally.

"I say that everyone's entitled to their own opinion," I replied easily. I began collecting the cards, shuffling them into a deck. As I did, my hand darted into my pocket, and I pulled a card out, slipping it into the deck without anyone noticing. As I said, I don't cheat—but that doesn't mean I don't know how to. I could if I wanted, I just choose not to. Besides, this wasn't cheating, it was self-preservation. This wasn't going to end well, I could tell.

"That's it?" he demanded, leaning forward and placing a hand on the table. "Are you a craven coward, as well?"

"I prefer to think of it as not being an idiot," I chuckled. I gestured toward his sword. "You're wearing armor and carrying a sword. I've got a knife. Plus, you're a Holder. I'd be a fool to fight you."

Gasps spread out across the silent room, and the two elves exchanged quick, startled looks. The ursid bouncer straightened and grabbed a heavy stick from where it rested beside him. He moved closer to our table, while the bartender pulled out a similar truncheon. The people in the crowd muttered a little angrily at one another, glaring at the elves. Holders weren't popular, in general, but more to the point, common belief held that when a Holder died, their Unity Cards emerged from them. I'd never seen it happen at that point, and I was certain no one in the hall had, either, but I doubted they cared. A card could change a person's life, and most of the people in this place probably had very little to lose—and a hell of a lot to gain.

"W-what did you call me?" the elf stammered, looking around nervously.

"A Holder. You are one, aren't you?" I glanced at the other elf. "You both are. I can tell." I shrugged and pushed the deck toward the elf. "I don't really want to fight someone who might be able to toss me through a wall or set me on fire. Besides, there's no point. All you have to do is check the deck, and you'll see that there are no missing or extra cards in it. That means I didn't cheat." The elf hesitated, and I gestured at the deck encouragingly. "Go on. I don't mind waiting if we can avoid some unpleasantness." He reached out and took the deck, and as he touched it, all hell broke loose.

The thing about Unity cards is that you don't have to be a Holder to use one. I'd learned that from a cartomancer of my acquaintance. Anyone can trigger a card if they know how and have a little bit of ability. It's a talent that's inherent in every intelligent species, although 99% of people don't know that, and some people just can't use them no matter what. Loose cards don't give you a special ability, and they aren't as powerful as a card in a soul deck, but they've got power of their own. All it takes is a little bit of magic, an effort of will, and a fair bit of luck to use one. Fortunately, I had all three.

The elf screamed as the three of staves I'd slipped into the deck exploded in a blast of flame that obliterated the rest of the deck and scorched his hand. It also made a brilliant flash of light, and both elves fell back blindly as the light washed out their vision. Elves can see colors and levels of light that we humans can't, but that makes their eyes much more sensitive to sudden flashes of light, too. Screams filled the room as people panicked, and the bouncer roared in fury, swinging his stick wildly and cracking it into random patrons.

I leaped around the table and scooped up a loose chair, holding it by the back. I swung with all my might, crashing it into the first elf and hitting him in the chest. He fell backward with a loud curse in Elven, falling into the crowd behind him. Someone lashed out with a fist that took him in the back of the head, and he shoved the person back into a felid woman who hissed and slashed at the offender with her clawed fingers. The scratched man hit the woman with a backfist, and her male companion leaped on him, bearing him to the ground as a full-on brawl exploded.

I ignored all that and swung my chair again, hitting the second elf in the back. He stumbled forward, bending over, and I kicked at him, catching his face with my boot. Blood and teeth flew from his mouth, and he sprawled onto his back, screaming curses and clutching his face. I dropped the chair and spun back to the table, grabbing my still-smoking card and scooping my money into my purse. I turned to leave, then hesitated. I spun back and grabbed the goblin woman by the shoulders, pulling her in and planting a kiss on her startled lips. I let go of her and gave her a cocky wink before spinning around and rushing for the door.

The melee had spread across the room. The bartender stood atop the bar, swinging his stick at anyone in range. The bouncer had three people hanging off him, and he tossed one of them aside with a roar as he cracked his stick into another. It was pure chaos, and it was my chance to flee. I ran for the door, dodging various scuffles and ducking around wild blows. The door and safety yawned before me, and I had a hand on it when something hard slammed into the back of my skull, knocking me to my knees. Another blow to the side of my head hurled me onto my back, and I saw the first elf standing over me, grinning viciously with a metal baton in his hand. Blood ran from the side of his face, but he seemed utterly unperturbed by it as he lifted his truncheon once more.

Damn Holders. That was my last thought as the baton fell, and darkness claimed me.

I groaned as I came to, and pain flooded my skull. My head pounded like a horde of trolls performing one of their weird little drum circles inside my brain. I'd never actually seen one of those and doubted I ever would. Trolls are pretty secretive, after all, and they kill anyone they catch in their lands. I wasn't all that eager to visit them, though; trolls are also huge, bigger than ursids, and reek of old cheese and wet animal. At least the ones I'd seen did, and oddly enough, a similar taste to that filled my mouth for some reason. I pried open my eyes, but complete darkness met my vision. The world rocked and rolled beneath me nauseatingly. I tried to sit up, but my hands wouldn't move, and a bolt of panic swept through me as I tried to recall how I'd gotten this way.

"E'averith," a voice spoke, and it took me a moment to translate the Elven words. *He's awake.* The Elven jogged my memory, and awareness flooded my battered skull. I remembered the drinking hall, the game, and the elves who'd apparently been really poor losers. Something filled my mouth, which explained the taste, and my wrists burned behind my back, letting me know that I'd been bound and gagged. That meant that the blackness was probably a blindfold or mask of some kind.

Sure enough, I'd no sooner realized that then something grabbed the top of my head, pulling on my hair as it yanked upward. I protested but sighed in relief as the blackness slid away, revealing—more darkness. I glanced upward and saw the starlit sky above me. Both moons were up, the greater and lesser, and the little moon hung low in the sky, meaning it was still hours until dawn. That was good; it meant I hadn't been out for too long. I looked to the sides and saw walls of darkness around us, walls that slowly slid past, and I realized that the world wasn't rocking around me. I was on a boat, sailing up the Canid River into the continent, and the walls were the jungle looming about. At least, I hoped it was the Canid. The next closest river was the Felid, five days' travel by sea, and I seriously hoped I hadn't been out that long. If they'd hit me that hard, I'd probably have woken up dead.

I blinked as a figure moved in front of me, and it took me a second to recognize one of the elves, the one whose money I'd taken. Not that I still had it, I felt sure. By this point, he'd certainly have taken it back.

"Well, well, look who's back with us," he purred, displaying a mouth missing several teeth. "The human cheat who stole my money."

I would have protested, but there was no point what with being gagged and all, so I just looked at him a little more closely. The man's lips were swollen and cut; one eye looked ready to swell shut; a cut ran across the side of his face. What I really noticed, though, was that the fire I'd triggered had burned away his eyebrows and eyelashes, leaving him looking faintly surprised and confused when I had a feeling he was going for menacing. I couldn't help it; a chuckle slipped out of me, and rage flashed across his face. His hand snapped out, and I groaned and nearly blacked out again as the back of his hand cracked against my skull.

"You think cheating me is funny?" the elf demanded furiously, his voice rising. "I'll show you funny!" He lifted his hand again, but before he could strike, a voice spoke harshly in Elven.

"Alerion, control yourself! We don't have time for him to regain consciousness again, and I don't want to drag him down the trail."

Alerion visibly mastered himself, taking several deep breaths and clenching and unclenching his fists. "You're right, Taveroth," he said after a few moments. "Besides, if I kill him, he's off the hook. Better that he lives." He flashed me another grin that looked comical rather than frightening, and I fought to stifle another laugh. He stiffened momentarily, then relaxed.

"We could have killed you, you know," he said conversationally. "Your body would have been just another poor gambler's corpse to wash in with the tide. That would be an easy death, though." He leaned in closer to me. "I don't allow cheaters to die easily."

"We're here," Taveroth said, and the boat lurched beneath me as it ran aground with a groan. "Help me drag the boat onto the shore, Alerion. Let's just get this done."

The elf vanished, and the boat shuddered as I felt it being pulled up onto the muddy river shore. A moment later, Alerion returned, grabbing me beneath the armpit and dragging me to my feet.

"Come, cheater," he chuckled. "Your fate awaits you."

We spent an hour walking through the jungle, following a path that I could barely see but that the elves seemed to have no trouble with thanks to their superior night vision. I stumbled over roots and slipped in mud; I splashed through puddles of brackish water and staggered into bushes that grew over the path. If Alerion hadn't been holding me up, I would have face-planted a dozen times or more, but the elf seemed to be in a hurry to get wherever we were going and kept me from falling in the darkness. At last, the jungle widened into a clearing that ended sharply thirty feet or so in front of me, and the elves stopped, allowing me to collapse into a heap, sucking air noisily through my nose. Taveroth walked to the edge of the clearing and looked down, and I guessed that it ended in a cliff of some kind.

He looked back at Alerion and nodded, and the elf hauled me to my feet. He began to drag me forward, and as he did, the air seemed to thicken around me. I struggled even more to breathe as it felt like I had to work twice as hard to suck air in through my nose. The hair on the back of my neck rose up, and I could feel the hair on my arms doing the same thing. Everything out in front of me looked shimmery and wavy, like I was watching through a heat distortion, and I felt a growing sense of danger as the elf dragged me forward. I fought to pull back, but Taveroth grabbed my other arm. I couldn't fight against two elves, both of whom were stronger than me, and they hauled me forward by main force until I stood a few feet from the edge and could see down.

As I guessed, I stood at the top of a cliff. It looked like the edge was the top of a gash in the earth, one a hundred feet across or so. I could see the other side of the ravine and the top thirty feet or so of the opposite cliff face. Below that, though, the moonlight just vanished into blackness so deep I couldn't make anything out beneath it. When I looked at that darkness, the sense of danger filling me flared, and I struggled again to break free. It was in vain, though: the elves held me too securely, and they'd bound me tightly. My hands were already numb from the loss of circulation, and trying to wiggle them simply burned as the ropes or leather or whatever it was rubbed my skin off.

"You know what's down there, human?" Alerion chuckled, pointing down into the darkness. "That's one of the Unity's labyrinths, waiting for you. And not just any labyrinth. It's a virgin one." My eyes widened as fear surged in me, and my struggles redoubled. Alerion simply laughed as the pair edged me closer to the precipice.

"Good. You know what that means. A maze of monsters and traps sits below us, formed by the Unity to protect a powerful card. A death trap that no one has been able to conquer. The beasts within will have had centuries to grow strong, and they're going to be very, very hungry." He laughed, and I struggled again, lashing out with my feet and throwing my head around in a vain attempt to escape.

"We call this place our trash disposal," he continued in a happy voice. "If someone needs to disappear, we simply hurl them into this labyrinth. We've thrown over twenty people into this place, and not one of them has ever emerged—including Holders significantly more dangerous than you.

"Of course, you might hope that when we toss you in there, you'll be killed on impact, but unfortunately for you, the Unity isn't that forgiving.

Anyone entering a labyrinth, even if it's not through the actual entrance, receives a short blessing of invulnerability, one that lasts for a few minutes." He laughed again. "The Unity wants you to be able to survive in there—just long enough for the things inside to start hunting you."

"Enough, Alerion," Taveroth cut him off in Elven. "You have his money, his cards, and his possessions. Now, you'll take his life. There's no need for this melodrama."

"Fine," Alerion snapped. The pair began to muscle me forward, right up to the edge of the cliff. He leaned forward and whispered in my ear. "Enjoy your trip. It's the last one you'll ever take, cheater." The pair shoved me, and suddenly, my feet felt nothing but air beneath them. I screamed as I plummeted, plunging into the darkness below.

So, here we are, back to Murf's Twenty-Third Law. The bigger you win, the bigger you'll lose. I'd won a lot of money from the elves, and in return, they'd taken back not only the money, the Unity cards I'd collected over the years, and all my possessions but also my life. Honestly, it felt like the damn Unity might have taken my laws a little bit too seriously. I hadn't won anywhere nearly enough to justify being splattered across the ground. Of course, that would probably be luckier than landing badly, breaking a leg, and crawling through the jungle for a few hours before some big cat hunted me down and slowly ate me. Hell, if I were really lucky, I'd hit a tree on the way down and break my neck. That'd be fast and probably painless, which I supposed was the best I could hope for.

My skin tingled as I plummeted into the darkness. In an instant, everything went black and still. The wind whistling past me vanished. The stars in the sky winked out. Even the sounds of my screams cut off. It felt like I hung in a cloud of nothingness, suspended motionless in a sea of blackness. For all I knew, the damn elves were wrong, and people tossed into this blackness didn't fall into the labyrinth and die. Maybe they hung in this darkness forever, or at least until they died of thirst. That would be a bad way to go. I'd had occasion to cross the Glass Desert once, and it taught me what real thirst felt like. I'd rather get eaten by something than die like that. At least, I thought I would; I'd never been eaten before, so I didn't know how that might feel. Really, I'd have preferred to avoid either, if the damned Unity asked my opinion.

Sadly, it never did. This world would be a hell of a lot nicer place if it had.

As I hung in the darkness, something seemed to flicker in my vision. Whatever it was wasn't clear, but it looked vaguely rectangular. I only caught its edges, which sputtered in and out of my vision, like a fire in a strong breeze or an oil lantern running out of fuel. Symbols I could barely see much less read floated in the center of the shape, appearing for half an instant before vanishing too quickly for me to make out what they were. If it weren't so damn dark, in fact, I probably wouldn't be able to see them at all, but with the complete blackness pressing in on me, there really wasn't anything else to look at. The image faintly reminded me of a card of some kind, but if it were, it wasn't any that I'd ever seen before.

The hair on my neck and arms tingled as some weird energy swirled around me. That feeling grew stronger and stronger, and my skin started to itch after a few seconds. That itching grew into a burning sensation, and the burning increased steadily into actual pain. I started screaming again, this time less from fear and more from the fact that it felt like I'd been set on fire—not that I could hear my own voice there in the darkness. I could feel the sound in my throat, but it never made it to my ears, leaving me trapped in blackness with pain as my only sensory input.

In other words, it utterly sucked, and I would have rather been anywhere but there. I'd rather have had that nightmare where I show up to the Grand Tournament naked come true. I'd rather have been part of an all-male threesome with a troll and an ursid, and if you've ever seen the size of what those guys pack down below, you'll understand what I'm talking about. Not the sort of thing you just walk away from, I'd imagine.

The burning flared from pain into real agony for a moment, and I did my best to scream even louder as the feeling of fire rushed into me. It wasn't just my skin burning anymore. My bones were roasting; my blood boiled; my muscles cooked. I had a feeling that when I landed, I was going to be a perfectly seared hunk of meat for whatever monster found me first. I didn't much care at that point, though, because I was way too busy wondering if my eyeballs would explode in their sockets from the heat or just simmer a bit. The pain swelled into torment, and for a moment, I couldn't think anything at all. I hurt too much for rational thought, or any kind of thought for that matter. My whole world was pain, and I have no clue how long it lasted.

The darkness around me shattered, exploding into brilliant light that blinded me for a moment. I didn't care, though, because in that same instant, the pain just stopped, like someone had blown out a candle. Wind rushed past my ears again, and the sounds of my screams rang mercifully in my skull. A sense of warmth wrapped around me, but compared to the burning I'd just endured, it felt practically freezing, and I might have cried a little in relief. I can't be sure; I was too busy trying not to wet myself to worry about something little like sobbing like a baby.

I pried my eyes open and saw a deep, endless blue sky stretching above me. The darkness was nowhere to be seen, and I couldn't be happier. I had a feeling I'd just gained a healthy fear of the dark after that. I'd probably have to sleep with a candle burning for the next few years until I got over it—at least, assuming I lived longer than ten seconds or so. I was still falling, after all, and despite what the elf said, I didn't exactly feel invulnerable. I couldn't see the ground or anything, but I felt sure it was rushing up at me fast, and whatever that blackness had done, it hadn't slowed me in the slightest. Even as I watched, my hat tore free from my head and fluttered up into the sky, tumbling above me. I cried out as I saw it whirl away—I really liked that hat—but I quickly decided that all things considered, it was the least of my worries.

I closed my eyes, resigning myself to whatever impact waited below. I couldn't say that I'd lived a good life, really, but it was certainly an interesting one. Most people lived and died within a few miles of the place they were born. Travel was expensive, after all, and unless you were lucky enough to have a trade and be part of a Guild—or be a rich noble—it didn't really matter if you worked Lord Buttface's field or Lady Squatbottom's. Your life was probably the same either way. I'd traveled all over the world, played cards in seedy drinking halls and fancy noble mansions, and loved women of almost every species. Well, I loved certain parts of them, anyway. I wasn't really ready for my life to end, but I felt pretty good about how I'd lived it. In fact, I decided that I'd go out remembering some of the better parts of it—like that time with the two elven battlemaidens. Elven women will compete with one another over just about anything, and in that case, I was the hill they each wanted to die on. Or the pole. Whatever metaphor I chose, it was a good day…

I couldn't help but shriek in fear and pain as my back and bound arms slammed into something much harder than a human. Pain ripped through my body, and it felt like both arms shattered at the same time. A boom echoed around me, but to my surprise, I kept falling, hurtling backward through whatever I'd struck. The light dimmed instantly to shadow, but I barely had time to notice it before I crashed into another harder-than-Murf object, and pain erupted in my body again. My body bent backward, and I could have sworn that each one of my vertebrae popped like a damn grape at the same time. I screamed into my gag again—the damn thing was getting quite the workout—then fell silent as I finally hit something that didn't give way beneath me with a loud crash of shattering wood.

I lay there for a moment, dazed and quite honestly, shocked beyond belief. My whole body throbbed and hurt as if I'd broken every bone at once. My skull pounded, and my insides felt like someone had taken a hammer to them. My skin felt like one massive bruise, and I was surprised the impact hadn't knocked my eyeballs out of my skull. Everything hurt, even the damn hair on my head somehow. I could only stare upward at the hole I'd made in the ceiling, revealing the sapphire sky above. The gap was jagged and irregular, which felt wrong to me. As fast as I hit it, it seemed that it should have been Murf-shaped. A black dot danced in the middle of that hole, and for a moment, I wondered if I'd damaged my brain somehow until the dot grew larger, revealing itself as my hat. The stiff, wide-brimmed piece of felt fluttered down like a feather, twirling and tumbling down through the hole and landing brim-first directly on my nose. Despite all the pain I suffered, that one final injury, the most insulting and petty one, was the one that actually drew a sound from my dry throat.

"Ow." The croaked word echoed in the stillness, and the sound of it seemed to clear some of the fog from my brain. Speaking made me realize that the impacts had torn my gag free. Part of my battered brain dimly reasoned that if one binding was gone, the others might be, as well, and that maybe my shattered limbs would hurt less if I weren't laying on top of them. Tentatively, I tried to shift my arms and legs, and to my surprise, they all moved easily. I slid my arms out from beneath my back, utterly blown away that my shoulders hadn't dislocated from the landing—they burned as if they had been—and as I did, I thumped down onto my back on something soft and lumpy.

Heat seared my back as what felt like a burning splinter the size of my hand plunged into me. I hissed in pain and rolled away, but the splinter stayed with me. Even worse, the damn thing seemed alive; I could feel it worming its way into me, wiggling down inside me like a fucking parasite. I reached back, trying to grab it and pull it out, but my hands touched nothing; it had already slipped into my body. The fiery splinter plunged into the center of me, near my heart, then somehow continued on, sinking into an even deeper place that I didn't know was there.

An explosion of what felt like flame mingled with ice erupted in me, filling that hole in my body. The sensation poured through me, spreading out into my limbs. It rushed down to my toes and flowed up my chest, flooding my throat. The feeling washed over my brain, and for the second time in a few minutes, the world went black and silent as I lost all sensation. This time, though, it only lasted for a second before the burning sensation faded and my senses returned. I still felt stuffed full of something, as if a hole in the middle of me had been filled somehow, but the pain was gone.

In fact, I felt pretty damn good, all things considered. My head no longer throbbed, and my wrists had stopped burning. The pains I'd felt when I landed were gone, and even my throat—which I'd shredded from screaming—seemed fine. I pushed myself up to a sitting position and looked down at myself critically. The front of my coat was in decent shape, but the sleeves were shredded along with the white shirt beneath, dangling from my arms in strips of fabric. Frayed loops of thin rope hung from my wrists, the severed ends from where something in my fall had either cut or torn them drooping limply. Like my coat, my pants looked fine in the front, but the back was ripped and torn badly. The skin beneath, though, was in good shape, at least. I wasn't cut or bleeding; nothing felt sore or bruised.

It looked like the damn elf was right about being invulnerable for a bit. Too bad I still had to feel the pain of my impacts—and that invincibility didn't extend to my clothes. I pushed myself to my feet with a groan that was mostly for drama's sake and took a quick look around.

I'd crashed into a building of some sort, it seemed. At least, I stood in a large, dusty room that looked like it had once been really fancy. I stood atop a raised platform, and stairs led down to the rest of the room. Pillars flanked what was probably once a walkway leading to a set of ornate metal doors that stood closed at the moment, although I couldn't tell if they were locked or not. I glanced upward; the ceiling was high and vaulted, filled with cobwebs. The hole almost directly above me that I'd made let in a single shaft of sunlight, illuminated by the clouds of dust that flowed through it. I rubbed my nose as the dust tickled it and looked down at the floor, then rubbed my eyes to make sure they were working correctly.

I stood in the broken remains of what looked like a wooden coffin or sarcophagus of some kind. My impact had crushed the thing like an egg squeezed in a troll's fist. It had done the same to the withered, desiccated corpse inside the coffin, as well. The body was dressed in what looked like fine if seriously antiquated robes of faded purple silk. A twisted hunk of gold wire had probably once been a crown atop the thing's head, but my boots slamming into it had turned it into a warped mess, dislodging the half-dozen gemstones that lay scattered around it. My boots hadn't done the skull any favors, either, crushing it into powder and chunks of bone. I'd shattered its ribcage, crushed its legs, and crumbled its spine.

"Son of a bitch," I muttered, rubbing my head with my hand. "Looks like I'm adding 'desecrating a corpse' to the list of things I'll have to explain to the Unity one day." I looked around in amazement. "What the hell just happened?" I yelped in startled amazement as an image suddenly appeared before me, floating in front of my eyes and filling my vision. It looked like a fancy card of some sort, with a painted background that I couldn't see behind a block of strange writing.

Unity Achievement!
By killing **Ancient Lich**, you have
defeated the master of a Unity
Labyrinth. Since this Labyrinth has
never been previously completed,
your reward is improved
significantly!
Unity Points Gained: 200
Card Gained: Eldritch Hag

"What the hell?" I half-shouted, stepping back and waving a hand in front of my face. "What's going on here?" I looked around wildly, but the card hung in front of me, no matter how I turned my head. "Go away!"

The moment I shouted that last phrase, the card vanished—only to be replaced with a new one.

Hole Card Placed!
By pushing the card "Eldritch Hag" against your chest, you have placed it in your soul deck. As this is the first card in your deck, it has become your Hole Card. Examine your card to see your new benefits.

My heart sank as I read the card. I didn't know what happened, but I knew what it meant. Somehow, I'd gotten a card from smushing the corpse I landed on. With my shirt and coat in shreds, the card had pressed up against my back, and the damn Unity decided that meant I wanted to put it in my soul.

Like it or not, I'd become a twice-damned Holder—and I definitely didn't like it.

++
++

4

"Thrice-damned, fucking, son of a bitch Unity!" I swore, kicking the corpse beneath my feet and scattered its remnants even further. I reached under my shirt and clawed at my chest, as if I could pull out the card I'd accidentally stuck there. "How the fuck did this happen?" Apparently, the Unity was listening well enough to give me an answer—not that it helped much.

Warning: Entering Labyrinth boundary. Unauthorized entrance method.
Luck check successful!

You have gained: Blessing of the Unity!
Effect: Immunity to damage
Duration: 5 minutes

Warning: Lethal Impact!
Damage mitigated by Blessing of the Unity.

You have damaged: Ancient Lich.
You have killed Ancient Lich with overwhelming force!

Attempting to add Unaffiliated Wild Card. Luck requirements met!
Card added.

"Luck check?" I scoffed, reading the card. "What luck?" I looked around. "Look at this place! How lucky can I be?"

Apparently, the Unity had an answer for that, as well.

Murf

Stats

Luck: 93   Capacity: 34
Skill: 27 (+0%)

Harmonies
Coins: 43   Blades: 22
Cups: 48   Staves: 35
Stars: 37
Divine: 66   Worldly: 69
Infernal: 65

"You know that doesn't tell me shit," I muttered, waving at the card. "Go the fuck away." The card vanished, and I sat down heavily in the remains of what I guessed was once an Ancient Lich, whatever the hell that was. I was distinctly less than happy with this development.

Unity cards are pretty rare and fairly valuable. Most people never owned one in their entire lives, in fact. And of those who had them, only a small percentage were actual Holders. I didn't know why, but most people couldn't jam a card into their soul—not that I really knew why they'd want to. I'd never tried before, myself. Oh, sure, having a card in you gave you all kinds of special, magical abilities, but it also made you a target. Anyone who wants a card knows that all they have to do is kill a Holder, and the Holder's cards become theirs. Magic powers are great, but they won't save you from a crossbow bolt in the back from a hundred yards. Well, they won't unless you've got some kind of special armored skin, which I suppose might be a card power. I didn't know because, as I said, I'd never shoved a damn card into my soul, and I never wanted to.

It wasn't like I never had the chance, either. Unity cards are rare, but they aren't impossible to find, and they were often used as stakes in high-end tournaments. I'd gotten my old three of staves off a halfling noble brat who ran out of money and thought that a 3-set of knights was a lot better hand than it turned out to be, for example. I'd also won a couple cards in big city tournaments, which usually offered a draw from a Unity deck as the prize. The point is, I had the damn cards. I could have stuffed one into my chest anytime I wanted. I hadn't bothered, and it looked to me like the Unity decided to take that personally and shove one up there itself.

Murf's Third Law: The Unity is a massive bitch. I suppose I should count myself lucky that it stuck it in my back instead of going up my asshole or something. It wouldn't be the first time the Unity's screwed me, after all.

Whatever the case, however it happened, I had a card now. I supposed I'd be a damn fool not to examine it and figure out what it was and what it did.

"Okay, Unity. Show me my new card." The moment the words left my lips, a card flipped up into my vision. It was actually pretty beautiful, displaying a full scene rather than just a rank and suit. Normally, that would have meant it was a noble arcana, one of the higher ranks of cards. Cards in a deck are split into lower arcana—ace through ten—and noble arcana, the knight, lady, prince, queen, and emperor. Lower arcana have a number and picture related to their suit, like a golden goblet for cups or a wand for staves, but nobles have a drawing of a person on them, usually holding an item related to their suit. A knight of blades, for instance, is an armored guy wielding a big old sword most of the time. That made them easy to recognize. This—this didn't look like anything I knew or had ever seen before.

Eldritch Hag
Cabal Card
Greater Wild
1% Attunement

Adaptive, Needful Body,
Arcana Defense, Rootless
Hole Card Bonuses
+100% to adjacent cards/stacks, -20%
per rank removed. All abilities gain
one major upgrade.

"What the fuck does any of that mean?" I groaned. "What's an elder itch hag? A cabal? A greater wild? And one percent of what, exactly?"

The Church of the Unity holds that the Unity is an all-powerful entity of some sort tasked with creating, nurturing, and caring for the world, all the while keeping out the angels and demons that want us dead. They say it hands out blessings to those who were faithful to it—which the Church seemed to define as "people who give us lots of money"—and curses people who don't give it the proper respect. That, to me, is a load of pig shit. It isn't even good enough to be bullshit. If you're not sure of the difference, go check out a pig farm sometime. Trust me, pig shit's worse.

I didn't know anything about angels and demons, and I didn't really want to. It seemed to me that the Church's claim that "angels and demons exist, trust us, but you'll never see them because the Unity keeps them out, so thank the Unity for keeping them out and give us more money" sounded a lot like a con artist's pitch to a half-mad old widow. Whatever the case with those, though, I knew for a fact that the Unity didn't give a busted run for people, no matter how faithful they were. Good people died; bad ones prospered. Famines and plagues killed the poor, no matter how much they prayed to the Unity, and ignored the rich who basically gave it the finger. Counting on the Unity's blessings was a good way to die young, poor, and probably married to a syphilitic troll. A smart person made their own luck and didn't count on some invisible thing to take care of them.

That day, though, the invisible being seemed to be in a giving mood. That, or it knew that all these cards were really pissing me off, and it was up in its invisible palace, having sex with its invisible concubines, and laughing its ass off as it flung cards at me. That wasn't how the Church portrayed it, but I knew that if I were all-powerful and no one could see me, I'd be creating all sorts of invisible women and doing things with them that would get me kicked out of nicer brothels. But then, it might see the world a bit differently than me. Most everyone else does. For whatever reason, more cards popped up, and these gave actual answers to my questions.

The Cabal

The Cabal is the highest rank of
Unity Cards, above Arcana and
Powers. Each is unique in this world
and represents an aspect of the
greater Unity.

Greater Wild
A Greater Wild can take the place of
any Arcana or Power in a stack or
meld. Unlike the Lesser Wilds,
Greater Wilds can assume any rank,
suit, or secret.

Attunement
You are 1% attuned to this card.
Increased attunement can result in
bonuses to abilities or new unlocked
abilities.

I'd never head of a Cabal card before. Of course, I'd never heard of
Power cards, either; the only Powers I knew of were the ones the Church
said the Unity kept out. However, from what the card said, they were
unique. The other Unity cards I'd seen weren't; there could be a hundred
threes of stars out there for all I knew, or even a thousand. Even so, they
were rare enough and valuable enough that people killed one another over
them pretty regularly. It sounded like there was only one of this hag in all
of existence, and if it was the highest possible rank of cards, it was
probably pretty powerful. That meant that if people knew I had it, they'd
probably kill me, anyone near me, anyone I'd ever spoken to, and maybe
anyone I might have looked at to get their hands on it. And I'd literally
fallen onto it ass-first. I fucking hated the thrice-damned Unity.

I thought about the card again, and it popped up once more. I ignored
the Cabal and Greater Wild parts since they were mostly gibberish to me
anyway and focused on the abilities. None of them came with descriptions,
so I didn't know what the hell Adaptive, Needful Body, Rootless, or Luck
of the Draw were supposed to mean. As soon as I focused on one, though,
the card flipped over, displaying new text.

Adaptive

That was just about as clear as mud, but no matter how much I focused on it, it didn't explain any more. What did adapt mean, and how quickly was "quickly"? If I were falling after being, say, thrown off a cliff by a pair of angry elves, the ground at the bottom wouldn't really give me a lot of time to "adapt" to hitting it. On the other hand, if I were drowning and grew gills after a minute or so, that might work—except for the whole "having gills" thing, which would probably affect my romantic life. Really, this didn't feel like the sort of ability I'd expected from a super-powerful card. What if I got swallowed by some huge creature? I didn't know that I wanted to live through being digested and dropped out a monster's ass somewhere. That felt like one of those situations where death would look awfully nice.

"Go away," I finally muttered, and the card vanished. I looked at the other abilities, and one by one, their cards popped up for me to read.

Arcana Defense
You gain resistance to the effects of
Arcana. This resistance decreases
with the card's rank and increases
with exposure to its power.

Rootless
The Hag is a wanderer. You will
find it difficult to call any place your
home or to forge permanent ties.
Those around you will sense your
wandering nature.

Needful Body
All of your physical capabilities
gradually improve based on your
current needs. These improvements
fade slowly after the need has
passed.

None of those made a whole lot more sense to me than Adaptive did. I didn't feel any stronger or smarter, so I wasn't sure what Needful Body was doing for me. Being able to ignore the powers of Arcana, the lower rank of cards, sounded great, but the ability just said increasing resistance, not immunity. For all I knew, that meant that a fire card would only burn most of my face off but leave my eyebrows intact. I liked having eyebrows and all, but I'd prefer to keep my damn skin. And Rootless didn't sound like an ability; it felt like some sort of curse that would make me pick up and leave any place that I tried to settle in. Not that it sounded much different from my actual life once I thought about it. In fact, it might be nice to leave places because I wanted to instead of because if I didn't, some husband, father, or pissed-off bad gambler would try to stick a knife in me.

I couldn't help but feel a little cheated as I read through the card's abilities. For something that was supposed to be unique and presumably powerful, it didn't really live up to the hype. It might help me survive something that should kill me. It could possibly keep me safe from other Holders after they'd dunked me in acid enough times, or whatever. It may have improved my body in ways I couldn't feel and so probably weren't all that significant. That was a whole lot of "maybes" from something that was supposed to be legendary. And none of it seemed like it would help me live to get the hell out of this place.

I rose to my feet and dusted myself off. Bitching and moaning wasn't going to help me. I was still stuck in a damn labyrinth, one of the Unity's death mazes. I had no food or water. I had no weapons, and while I'd killed the lich-thing, I bet that there were still plenty of monsters out there that would be happy to snack on me if they got a chance. I needed supplies and tools. My only hope was that there'd be something in this place that would be useful.

5

I spent the better part of a half-hour searching through the remains of the room. I poked into dusty corners that made me sneeze, peeked into shadowy nooks, knocked on walls, and even stamped about all over the room, listening for vacant spaces in the floor. About the only thing I didn't do was open any doors. There were two of those: the big one I'd seen before and a smaller one on the opposite wall. For all I knew, a thousand drooling monsters waited on the other side of each. I wasn't about to find out.

I wandered all over that room and found exactly shit, so I did it again. After the third time, I returned to the stingy-ass lich and kicked it down the steps, then shoved the remains of its coffin down to crash atop it. It was petty, sure, but I was feeling petty at that point. That feeling turned into shame and embarrassment when flipping the coffin revealed the dusty outline of a trap door in the floor.

"Of course, the Unity stuck it under the coffin," I muttered. "It wouldn't want someone to be able to get the lich's treasure without dealing with the lich first, right? That might be easy." I knelt down and lifted the trapdoor, coughing and waving my hand as a plume of dust shot up directly into my face. I spat a few times to get the taste out of my mouth, then waited for the dust to settle so I could see into the hidey-hole.

The space wasn't large, maybe a foot-and-a-half square and six inches deep. A dust-coated leather pouch sat inside it, in surprisingly good shape for probably having sat there for centuries. Unless, of course, the Unity had just put it there when I killed the lich; that was a real and distinct possibility. A sheathed dagger rested beside it, along with a cloth bag tied at the top. I pulled out the bag first, smiling as I heard the clinking of metal inside. I unwrapped the string binding it and peered inside, laughing aloud at the glittering discs of gold and silver that rested within. I pulled one out and examined it closely; the silvery coin sparkled in the sunlight, displaying a six-pointed star on one side, the symbol of the Unity, and a series of symbols I couldn't decipher on the other. I didn't recognize the coin, but the edge was milled, and the coin was heavy enough that I guessed it was close to pure silver. Every country had its own coinage, and the value of each was mostly determined by weight, so I guessed these coins were fairly valuable.

I dropped the silver back in and tied the sack to what was left of my belt, then picked up the knife. The weapon slid out easily, revealing a blade the length of my forearm, almost long enough to be called a short sword. I hesitated before strapping it to my belt as well. I knew how to use a knife, more or less, but I was no soldier or sellsword. I could fight my way out of bar brawls and handle muggings; I wasn't about to go blade to blade with a trained fighter. Still, I'd rather have the knife and not need it than find myself needing it and it be sitting in this dusty crypt.

I reached down and grabbed the pouch last. Opening it revealed nothing, but I wasn't fooled. I knew what the damn thing was. It was a card holder, one that would store cards—including Unity cards—inside it. I wanted nothing to do with the thing. I figured I could probably hide being a Holder, at least until I figured out if the process could be undone. That would be infinitely harder with one of these at my hip, though. Only Holders and nobles carried them; no one else ran into enough cards in the world to need one. Sticking it on my belt would be like writing, "I'm a Holder! Kill me for my cards!" right on my forehead in big, flaming letters. With a sigh, I stuck the thing into the inner pocket of my coat instead.

I figured the Unity was probably already pissed at me for accidentally clearing a virgin Labyrinth. And calling it a bitch, I supposed. There was no need to make it worse by ignoring what it gave me.

I closed the lid and walked over to the lich's remains. I scooped up the scattered gems and the twisted wire of the gold crown. It wore a frankly gaudy ring that made it look like an elf warlord overcompensating for something, with a glittering, yellow stone and a thick, ornamented band, and I took that, too. It had a necklace of some kind around its neck, but my impact had crushed the pendant attached to it beyond all recognition, leaving the golden chain for me to scoop up. I slipped all that into the sack of coins, then sat back and considered my situation.

The money was nice, don't get me wrong, and the knife was great, but what I really needed was food and water. I had no idea if either of those could be found out in the Labyrinth, or even how big the place was. I wasn't a Delver, one of those reckless, death-loving idiots who hunted down Labyrinths and plundered them, but I knew a few. Mostly, they told stories about fights with horrific monsters and chests filled with mounds of treasure that I damn well knew weren't true since they told them while drinking cheap beer in crappy drinking halls. None of them ever mentioned anything practical, like how to find an exit from a Labyrinth or if the Unity provided food and drinks, maybe a nice upscale drinking hall or two. I'd never asked, either, but then, I never figured I'd be in one of these damn places, so it wasn't high on my list of things to know.

The fact was, I could fill a damn ocean with everything I didn't know that I suddenly needed to. Sadly, sitting there wasn't going to help with that. I doubted the Unity was going to reveal any incredible secrets if I just lazed around for long enough. No, I had to get moving and see what waited for me outside. I didn't want to, but since my only other option was to lay down and wait for death, I figured getting moving was a much better option.

The door at the end of the hall opened with a loud screech, and I shook my head as the sound echoed in the stillness of the crypt. "You'd think an ancient lich would have heard of oiling hinges," I muttered, shaking my head. I stepped through the partially opened door into a long, empty stone hallway. Torches studded the walls, illuminating the place with a flickering light that really shouldn't have been there since I doubted anyone had changed those torches out in the past few hours. The floor was paved with oval-shaped cobblestones, and the walls were decorated with elaborate carvings of animals, people, and beasts, all kneeling in worship to some guy on a throne. I assumed that guy was the lich I'd just smushed, not that it had looked anything like the man in the picture after I'd crushed it. I kind of felt bad for the guy for a moment; for all I knew, he'd spent hundreds of years ruling this place, gained all sorts of powers and abilities, only to have it all end when some random guy smashed into his coffin at a couple hundred miles an hour.

"That could be a new law," I chuckled, shaking my head. "Never pick a wood coffin if stone is available. Something to remember, at least."

I took two steps forward, then froze as the stone beneath my left foot sank an inch into the floor. A loud hiss erupted to my left, and something streaked in front of me, too fast for me to make out. It struck the opposite wall with a loud clink and dropped to the floor, and I took a step back, then carefully leaned over to pick it up. It looked like a metal dart of some kind, just an inch or so long, sharp as a needle at one end and sporting a clump of downy feathers at the other. The tip glistened with a thick fluid of some kind, and I whistled in amazement as I realized what it was.

"A poison dart," I muttered. "A twice-damned poison dart." I glanced down at the floor. "This whole hallway's trapped, I'll bet. Son of a bitch."

I tucked the dart into my coat pocket, then began walking a lot more carefully. Despite my caution, I only made it another four steps before I triggered another dart that hissed past my chest and struck the opposite wall with enough force to scratch the stone. Three more steps, and another dart flashed past me. Each time I heard that hiss, my heart almost stopped, but each time, the dart simply sailed past me without touching me. It struck me as a particularly shitty trap; wasn't the whole point of one of these things for the darts to hit the person stepping on the rock? It took a moment for realization to strike, and when I did, I couldn't help but laugh aloud.

"I'm going the wrong way!" I chortled, spinning the last dart between my fingers. The traps were no doubt designed to keep people from getting into the crypt, which meant they were set up to hit someone stepping on a stone while going the opposite direction. Since I was leaving, the darts should just flash right past me without touching me. At least, that seemed to make sense, but to be fair, I had no clue what I was doing.

I kept walking, moving slowly and carefully and still triggering traps the whole way. There was probably some trick to avoiding them, maybe a pattern of moving stones on the floor. Or maybe there was a technique that Delvers learned to deal with traps, some way to detect them and maybe disable them. That didn't help me since I didn't know it, and there seemed to be no point to working out a pattern. The traps weren't a danger to me, after all, and it was my fondest hope that this would be the last Labyrinth I ever stepped foot in.

The hallway ended in another door, and when I hauled it open, a curved, scything blade swept down across the door and slammed into the opposite wall. I froze, staring at the heavy blade in shock and awe. If that thing had hit me, it probably would have left two Murfs behind, each only half a person. The darts were one thing, but that blade drove something home for me. The Labyrinth wasn't designed to protect the card at its heart. It was meant to kill anyone who tried to get to that card. And that anyone could be me. Yes, that time, the blade had swept across the opposite side of the doorway, but I might not always be that lucky. What if opening the door had caused the whole floor to drop away, or the ceiling to come crashing down? My legs trembled, and I sat down heavily in the hall, taking a few deep breaths.

I wasn't exactly afraid of death. I figured that death would be like an endless sleep, and I really did like sleeping. In an abstract way, I knew that death would find me one day, the same way it did everybody. Nobody gets out of life alive, after all. Dying, on the other hand—I really wasn't looking forward to dying. In the past couple of hours, I'd experienced the feeling of being burned alive and having all my bones smashed from an impact. Neither had been fun, and I didn't want to feel anything like them ever again. If I kept going, though, there was a good chance that I'd get to experience something similar—or worse. Of course, if I stayed, I'd get to learn what dying of thirst was like.

Murf's Twenty-Ninth Law: Most choices are awful ones.

In this case, though, one of the choices was clearly less awful. I hauled myself to my feet and stepped through the door, edging around the crescent-shaped blade. That led me to a large, open room with doors leading in four directions, including the one behind me. I examined them all, but they just looked like doors to me. I grabbed one, pushed it open, and leaped backward at the same time. I was glad I did when a set of waist-high spears shot up from the floor before the door where I'd just been standing. I shivered at that; those wouldn't have killed me right away, but they'd probably sliced open my jewels and pinned me on them to bleed out. The law was right: the Unity really was a huge bitch.

At least I knew that door wasn't the one I wanted. The trap was on this side, after all, and had it been the way out, the trap would be on the other side. I moved to the next door, this time kicking at it instead of trying to open it. My heel throbbed as my boot slammed into the unmoving door, and I realized with a bit of shame that it opened into the room, not out into the hallway. I yanked it open and jumped back, but there was no need. A set of spikes shot out of the wall on the other side of the door, slamming into the opposite wall with the grating sound of metal on stone.

I almost slapped myself as I realized that I had a pretty easy way to find the path outside. I just had to follow the doors that opened inward. It would be stupid to set a trap on the same side that a door opened into. The door might block the trap, and the person opening it would step back in any case, probably taking them out of the way of the trap. A door that opened toward me would have a trap on the other side, meaning it probably led the way I wanted to go.

The next hall was slanted downward, and when I opened the opposite door, I heard a loud thud. I looked behind me and saw a boulder a bit large than me had dropped from the ceiling and was rolling my way. I stepped quickly through the door just in time; it crashed shut behind me, no doubt meaning to trap me in the last corridor to be turned into a bloody stain by that boulder. A huge boom echoed from the door a moment later, and dust flew from it as it shuddered from an impact. I couldn't help but shiver; getting run over by that thing would not have been a good time.

I spent the next two hours moving slowly and cautiously through the building that I'd decided to identify as a palace. That was mostly thanks to all the frescoes showing the same guy being worshipped by people and animals, leading armies, fighting huge monsters, and all the other heroic things that you think kings and emperors do. In reality, I'd only met two rulers before, and both of them were lazy, spoiled assholes, but that applied to pretty much all the upper nobility, as well. Something about money and power turned people into dicks nine times out of ten, at least in my experience. In this case, it turned a guy into an ancient lich, whatever that was. I assumed it would have been a dick if I'd given it a chance to instead of crushing it into powder with my ass. Which I guess made me the dick in that situation, but hey, I was still alive, and it wasn't. If being a dick was what it took to keep breathing, then I'd be the biggest damn one I could imagine. Besides, it wasn't like it could tell anybody, and when I told this story, I would definitely make myself out to be a hero, not a blunt object that crashed into a coffin and survived. I might be an asshole, but I wasn't a fool.

The traps never let up the entire time. I found more dart-filled hallways, of course, but those were really the nicest ones. At one point, a pit opened up behind me, and when I looked into it, I saw that someone had filled the bottom with short spears. Another place, scalding steam sprayed out into the air, and I got a little burned before I managed to jump back. If I'd been going the other way, it probably would have boiled me alive. Stones dropped from the ceiling; pits opened beneath door frames; crossbow bolts rained out of nowhere. The Unity even set up a damn hallway filled with jets of blue fire that exploded and cut off in some kind of pattern. Fortunately, that kicked in when I opened the door at the far end of the hall. If I'd been going toward the crypt, I'd have had to try to get through a maze of fire without being burned. The good thing was that as long as I kept heading out, the traps triggered in the wrong place to hurt me.

Even so, I didn't escape unscathed. My face and hands were both angry and red from the steam burns. Some sort of corrosive liquid had sprinkled on my left arm and leg, and I limped slightly from the chemical burns it left behind before I managed to wipe it off. My right cheek bled from where a ricocheting dart had scratched me—fortunately without poisoning me—and I'd lost my right boot to a patch of sticky quicksand that I hadn't quite gotten clear of when I triggered it. I still felt massively lucky. The place was a huge death trap. It had dozens of rooms with multiple passages leading away from them, all of them no doubt leading to literal dead ends.

By that point, I understood why the Labyrinth had stayed unconquered for so long. I couldn't see any way for a person to make it through the place alive, to be honest. Some of the traps were just insanely deadly, and I couldn't imagine a way to escape them—like the hallway whose walls slammed together ten seconds after I'd opened the door and left it. How was someone supposed to dodge that? Unless they were as invulnerable as I'd been when I first entered the Labyrinth, that hall was going to kill them.

At last, I staggered into a larger room than most, one that sported a pair of double doors. Most importantly, bright light shone through the cracks around those doors, illuminating the dust floating thickly through the air. I practically ran to the doors and yanked them open, blinking as bright light washed over me. I caught a glimpse of an endless expanse of sand and a sapphire blue sky before the whole scene winked out, and another card flashed in my vision.

> You have completed the Labyrinth:
> The Lich's Crypt.
> You receive:
> +2 to Luck, +2 to Skill
> 20 Harmony Points
> 200 Unity Points
> (As the first to complete this
> Labyrinth, you receive double
> bonuses)

I felt a sudden wave of elation rush through me. Not from the damn card, of course. I didn't care about that, and I didn't understand half of what it said. No, what mattered to me was that the sandy wasteland vanished as quickly as it had appeared, replaced with a pair of stone cliffs flanking a narrow path. That path had stone steps cut into it, leading upward into the jungle above. I muttered for the card to vanish and began walking up the steps, doing my best to ignore my battered body, torn clothing, and general state of exhaustion. I was free of the Labyrinth, and somehow or another, I'd make my way back to the river and to Canis. I needed to find an old friend there, one who could hopefully answer some of my questions and maybe help me give a pair of elves a much-needed knife to the throat. I reached down and patted the pouch at my belt with a smile; I also had a lot of money I needed to secure…

My smile vanished as my hand touched the cloth pouch, a pouch that felt far too light and empty. I grabbed it and looked down in horror. A long gash ran along the bottom of the pouch, and instead of being full of jingling coins, gems, and jewelry that could basically set me up for life, it looked almost totally empty. As I lifted it, three coins tumbled out to the ground, one gold and two silver, the last remnants of what had once been a damn fortune. I dropped to my knees and picked them up, holding them in trembling fingers. Two silver and one gold, all I had to show for nearly dying dozens of times.

I looked at the bag again. It looked like one of the traps had nicked it. Maybe a spear had caught it when I slipped past, or a dart bouncing off a wall had cut it open. It didn't matter; what mattered was that the thrice-damned Unity had taken back the money it gave me like the very worst of usurers. I'd earned that money—well, maybe I hadn't, but I'd claimed it, and it was mine! I tilted my head back and screamed at the sky, gripping those last three coins tightly in my fist. At last, I shoved the coins into my pocket, staggered to my feet, and started walking up the stairs.

One thing was utterly clear in my mind. My third law really needed to move to second place. The Unity was a phenomenal bitch.

6

For the second time in a week, I found myself sailing into Canis. This time, though, I came though the river gate on the opposite side from the harbor. I liked the harbor side better, personally. Over there, Canis' walls ended above the shoreline, spreading out like wings to touch the promontories flanking the harbor on each side. The main road spilled down through a maze of warehouses, shipping offices, and counting houses that wound down toward the sea. Stone quays jutted out into the ocean, with tall-masted sailing ships littering them like a forest of canvas and rope. The walls were painted golden to shine in the sun, the roads were well paved and maintained, and the buildings had all been painted over the tar covering them to protect them from the sea air. It was the face the city presented to outsiders, from common sailors to foreign dignitaries, so the canids made it sure it made a good impression.

The river side of the city, on the other hand, was the side that most of the locals saw, and apparently, the canids didn't give a shit what they thought. They'd cut back the jungles for miles along the river for the farms, lumber mills, tanners, and other less desirable but necessary parts of society to live. They'd also dug irrigation canals to help water all of those, and that left the river shallow, slow, and muddy as it flowed toward the city. In the city, the canids had built stone walls to funnel the river and keep it from eating away the foundations of nearby buildings, but here, the shorelines were muddy, brown, and totally unimpressive. The rickety wooden docks, water-powered mills, and fishing shoals running along the shore didn't exactly help, either. Beastling men and women stood in the shallows, doing laundry, fishing, cleaning, and bathing—while at the same time, half a mile upstream, some farmer's cattle plodded along the muddy banks, dropping their waste into the river.

I shuddered at the thought that those people probably drank from that river as well—unless they had wells to tap, of course. I didn't know; I did my best to avoid farming villages whenever possible. They didn't have any money, and their idea of a good time rarely involved gambling. You might have heard the legends of perpetually horny farmgirls ready to hop on the staff of any man who crosses their path, but I can assure you, it's far from the truth. Living and working in a place like a farm or mill requires a strong back and a wide streak of practicality. Those farmgirls don't have the time or inclination to bother with strange men who roam into town for a day or two. Plus, they're just too tired to worry about it. I suppose spending all day buried waist-deep in turnips or whatever will do that to a person.

The point is, it wasn't a pretty sight. Plus, the whole thing stank to the high Powers. Without the ocean breeze to carry it away, the stench of rotting vegetation, dead fish, animal droppings, and who knew what else hung heavily on the water. Tiny, biting insects buzzed all over the place, flying into eyes, ears, and nostrils in search of a meal of blood, making it even more miserable to be up on deck.

Which was exactly why I was safely ensconced in a cabin with the windows shut. I'd come this way before. It wasn't exactly the kind of experience I needed to have again. I was more than content laying on my too-thin cot in clothing that didn't quite fit right with my arm draped over my face. The riverboat I'd booked passage on didn't rock all that much, and the sailors weren't as loud and vulgar as seafarers tended to be, so it was actually kind of relaxing to just rest there and wait for the wind and current to get us into the city.

I lifted my head as someone pounded on my door, followed by a gruff voice shouting, "Arriving in the city!" through it. I sighed and sat up, looking down sadly at myself. My clothes had been utterly ruined, of course, forcing me to buy some new ones in the logging village I'd found on my way back to the river. The village had a few men my size, and their clothes were mostly coarse fabric meant for cutting wood in, not anything for show. One man had a set of seven-day finery that he'd worn twice in his life, once to his wedding and once to his daughter's wedding, and it still had stains in the armpits from where he'd sweated through it. It was the best I could get, though, so I'd bought it, a new carrying pack, and a ride to the nearest place I could catch a boat from for ten brass. The man ended up having to go around to his neighbors to scrounge up change for my silver coin, but in the end, at least my ass wasn't hanging in the breeze when I walked, and I'd gotten quicker and more comfortable transport to the city than shank's mare.

I adjusted the clothing as best I could, fixing my hat on my head and tilting it at what I considered a jaunty angle. I grabbed my mostly empty pack and opened the door, stepping out onto the lower deck of the riverboat—which was really just a narrow walkway right next to the hull that led up to the main deck above. Unlike some of the fancy passenger boats cruising the Apilnee River way over in Langor, this boat was meant for hauling cargo, not people. I'd been lucky enough that the boat's boatswain had gotten sick with one of the nasty fevers that came out of the jungle, meaning his cabin was available. Otherwise, I'd have been bunking with the crew or just spreading out in a nook somewhere on deck.

The shoreline still slid past us, but the road running along it was far busier than it had been the last time I'd come out. Ox-drawn wagons trundled along it, with smaller pony carts zipping past in both directions. On the edges of the road, men and women hauled wheelbarrows and handcarts, some empty, others laden with sacks of grain or flour, fruit, or vegetables that they probably intended to sell in the city. The sheer number of them told me that we had to be close to the gates, and as I watched, the riverbank shifted into stone walls and the boat began to slow in preparation for entering the city.

I walked up on deck and did my best to stand out of the way as the sailors hauled the boomsails, reefed the hindquarters, shanked the midshaft, or whatever the hell things sailors did to slow down a boat. I wasn't a sailor and had zero interest in learning to be one. Whatever they did, it made the boat slow down significantly until it was drifting with the current alone. We slid through the arched river gate past the walls, floating beneath a barred portcullis that could probably be dropped to bar entry to ships as needed. After twenty minutes or so, the boat turned to dock at a pier, and I watched as a felid woman flanked by two canid soldiers came aboard and spoke quietly with the captain. A few coins changed hands, and the woman strode off the boat as quickly as she'd arrived.

As soon as the woman got off the boat, I wove my way to the gangplank myself, stopping to thank the captain briefly before I stepped onto the pier. I knew that the crew would be unloading their cargo, and once that started, I'd be stuck on the boat for an hour or two, minimum. It was a nice enough boat, really, but not so great that I wanted to spend half a day on it.

I had places to go and people to see, but first, I needed to do some shopping. The problem was, while gold and silver coins are pretty to look at, they don't spend that well. They're simply too valuable, and a lot of places don't have that kind of change. I needed to shift them into smaller currency, and the best place for that was the Gambler's Hall. I wound through the city, crossing one of the tall bridges spanning the river splitting the city, heading toward the harbor. In Canis, being close to the harbor but still in the walls meant you had money and influence, so the biggest, fanciest Guilds had their halls there. The Usurers were not one of those. Their Hall lay in the eastern-central portion of the city, a part that was well maintained and had plenty of Watch activity to keep it safe but that was easily accessible for tradesmen, artisans, merchants, and nobles alike. The Usurers don't care about the social status of the people they lent money to, only about their ability to pay it back plus hefty interest. There's always interest, and it's always more than you want to pay.

That should probably be a law, really, but I've already got enough of the things.

One of the great things about the big guilds is that their halls always look the same. No matter what city you go to, for example, the Gambler's Hall there is a red, three-story building with the eight-pointed star of the Unity painted above the door, flanked by paintings of cards. Every Sage's Hall is a one-story black building with four towers on the corners, usually with all kinds of weird smoke and noises coming out of it. The Shipper's Hall is always near the harbor and is five stories tall, shaped like an upside-down ship hull, and painted white.

That made it a lot easier to find the Lender's Hall, home of the Usurer's Guild. They called themselves lenders, but most people just called them the Swindlers. Those who'd worked with them often called them demons from hell, as tenacious as a hungry goblin after a steak, as single-minded as a troll berserker in battle, and as vicious as an elf battlemaiden who thinks she's been insulted just because you said her armor makes her ass look big. Even if it happens to be true. The lenders were happy to dole out money at what seemed like reasonable rates until you actually figured out how compound interest works. Then, you'd realize that you were paying back two brass for every one you borrowed, and if you were late with a payment, boom went the penalties. Only merchants, nobles, and the terminally stupid ever visit a Lender's Hall unless they're planning on burning it down—or unless they've got money to change.

I stepped through the doors into a large, semicircular room about twenty feet across. The room ended at a stone wall pierced every four feet with an arch protected by a steel mesh with squares too narrow for an arrow or bolt to slip through. It being late afternoon on a three-day, the place was mostly empty except for the ubiquitous guards standing throughout the place, and only a single one of those arches was manned. A line of three people stood before that arch, and I stepped into the back of it with a sigh. It wasn't a long line, but transactions at the Lender's Hall tended to take a while. Most people only visited during the middle of the week if they knew they weren't going to be able to make their six-day payment and wanted to beg for some forgiveness—which they never got—or some emergency came up for which they needed coins in a hurry. Those usually had their hopes dashed since the lenders didn't like to give money out to people unless they felt they had a good chance of getting that money back somehow. Sure, the Guild had pressured every kingdom in the world into passing debtor's laws letting them toss delinquents into jail, but people in jail didn't make the lenders coins.

As I feared, it took nearly an hour for me to get to the front of the line. Before it was my turn, I had to stand and listen to the woman in front of me beg and plead for a loan to get a healer for her sick kid, who apparently was dying of one of the jungle fevers.

"Please, good sir, I'm desperate!" the woman begged. "I just need two silvers, that's all!"

"But you admit that you have no collateral to secure those silvers," the lender said in a deep, rolling voice that marked him as one of the halflings, the diminutive species from southern Palla. "And you have no income of which to speak. How would you make your payments?"

"My husband—when the *Frozen Stag* returns to port, and he gets his pay, I can pay it back in full!"

"And when is that scheduled to happen?" the man asked interestedly.

She hesitated. "S-six months."

The halfling tsked sadly. "In six months, the interest will have accumulated to quite a bit more than two silvers. Would you be able to pay it all back then?"

"I—no," she said in a defeated voice, then paused before messing with the front of her shirt. "However, I'm sure I could find another way to repay you, good sir. We could come to an arrangement…"

I could have told her that particular tack wouldn't work. First, halflings tended to view "tall folk", as they called us, with a certain amount of disgust. I'd never gotten the details on exactly why, but we simply weren't attractive to them. Second, everyone knows that Swindlers are soulless monsters whose hearts are the only things in them that harden. I expected the man to refuse; I didn't expect his actual response.

"Yes, that could work," he cut her off in a thoughtful voice, either ignoring or oblivious to her real meaning. "Were you to take up employment on the Avenue of Roses, with your ample assets, you could certainly make your payments until your husband returned. Would you be willing to do that?"

The woman froze and remained silent for a few seconds. I guessed that while she'd been willing to trade her body to one man in exchange for the coins, she hadn't really considered the idea of doing it in a professional manner.

"But—my husband! He would find out…"

"Do you think he'd be angry that you did what you had to in order to save his son's life?" the lender asked in what sounded like honest curiosity.

"If so, then you'll have to decide what's more important to you: his anger or your son's health."

The woman's shoulders slumped, and her head hung forward. "I—my son is everything to me," she whispered. "I'll do it."

"Excellent!" he clapped his hands together. "I'll give you the name of a madam who'll take you on…"

I sighed and stepped forward, putting a hand on the woman's shoulder. She jumped and jerked her head toward me, and I got a good look at her. She was a felid, one with pale white fur, attractive features, and a slim face. She also had large breasts half-revealed by how she'd opened her shirt and wide hips; she'd do well on the Avenue of Roses, to be sure, but it would probably wreck her family. I wasn't a nice guy, but I wasn't quite that heartless. Besides, this was the one place that I could do this without being a sucker.

"Good Lender, would the Guild be willing to lend her a single silver?" I asked in a tired voice.

The halfling looked down and consulted his notes. "Yes, she has the collateral for a single silver, sir."

"I don't know who you are," the woman spluttered, "but this is a private matter, and…"

"Would the Guild also be willing to oversee a personal loan?" I said, ignoring her. "Say, of a silver coin without interest?"

"Of course. That's one of our primary functions, after all. You will have to have an account with us, though."

"I do."

"Excellent! In that case, we can also accept payments for that loan, and for a small fee, guarantee repayment just as we guarantee payment of our own debts."

"I don't think that'll be necessary." I pulled out my remaining silver and held it up, looking at the woman. "If I lend you this, when your husband returns, you pay it back here. No interest. Deal?"

She stared at me, and her eyes narrowed suspiciously as she pulled her shirt closed. "What's the catch?" she demanded.

I leaned closer to her. "The catch is that if I find out that you don't have a sick kid, I'm going to come and get it back personally—with plenty of interest," I said ominously, then leaned back. "But that won't be a problem, will it?"

Her eyes widened, and she hesitated. I could practically see her thoughts churning as she wondered if I was really the lesser of two evils, here. The fact that she had to think about it meant she knew exactly zero about the Usurer's Guild. I'd heard that the current Lender King, head of the whole damn guild, had gotten his position by selling his own mother into slavery when she was a day late on a payment. I didn't know if it was true, but the fact that it realistically could have been said all that needed saying, really. Eventually, I guess she decided the same.

"N-no," she shook her head. "It's not a problem. I—thank you." She gave me a grateful smile.

"Let's just get this written up," I sighed. "I've got some money I want changed, and I'd like to get it done while the stores are still open."

"Of course, sir," the halfling said, much friendlier now that a transaction was taking place. "May I have your account card?"

"I recently lost my card," I sighed. "Stolen, actually. I probably should have reported that, shouldn't I? I don't want someone else using it."

"That's not possible, sir. Those cards are bound to their owners and won't work for anyone else." He pulled out a flat piece of wood with cards attached to it facedown in a strange, diamondlike pattern with a gap in the middle. He slid the plank up to the semicircular hole in the bottom of the screen protecting him. "Simply place your hand in the center of this layout, sir, and I can verify your account and get you a new card."

I reached through and placed my hand on the empty spot in the center of the layout. I felt a tingle rush through my body as the magic of the cards placed on the wood ran through me, running up my arm into the center of my chest and back down. The halfling flipped over one of the cards and smiled.

"Thank you, Mr. Murf. Give me a moment, and I'll write up the contract between the two of you."

It took another twenty minutes for the short man to produce a contract by which the woman—whose name turned out to be Neeana—agreed to pay me a silver coin in six months. The man had added a penalty clause for late payment, but he emphasized quite firmly that the Guild wouldn't be guaranteeing the contract's enforcement, and that while the law was on my side, I'd be in charge of enforcing it myself. I handed my coin to Neeana, who gave me a grateful and slightly fuzzy kiss on the cheek, letting those assets I'd noticed before rub against my arm in the process, then scampered out with her two coins hugged tightly to her chest.

"I just hope she makes it back to her home without getting mugged for those," I sighed. A lot of thieves made a point of staying near the Lender's Hall and following anyone who looked like they came out carrying more than they entered with.

The halfling shrugged. "Not the Guild's concern," he said briskly. "Now, you said you had money to change, sir?"

I pulled out the gold coin and slid it over to him. "I'd like this in brass and silver," I told him.

He lifted the coin and examined it, and as he did, I got a good look at him for the first time. Like all halflings, he had a wide face, heavy features, sharply pointed ears, and a solid frame. I couldn't judge his height, but most of his species never got near five feet, being even shorter than goblins, so he probably stood on a block or sat on a stool of some sort to be at my eye level. His skin was lightly tanned, pale for his species, meaning he probably spent most of his life indoors when most of his kind lived outdoorsy sorts of lives. His clothing was rich, with a powder blue coat over a black silk shirt, and hair the color of his shirt gleamed with oil that kept it slicked back away from his face. His eyes widened as he placed the coin down where I couldn't see for a moment, and he glanced up at me a little nervously.

"How…" He stopped and cleared his throat. "What currency would you like this in, sir?" he asked in a suddenly respectful voice.

I frowned. "I was thinking local currency, of course. Why?"

"Because this is…" He cleared his throat again. "Ah—many people who change Unity coins prefer Imperial currency, sir. The coins are more valuable and will spend anywhere."

"Does it matter?" I shrugged. "It's just worth its weight, right?"

He stared at me with a puzzled expression, then shook his head. "Not precisely, sir. Unity coins are worth quite a bit more than their weight might suggest. For one thing, all Unity coins are 100% pure and can't be adulterated. For another, their inherent magic makes them useful for more than just spending. This coin is worth three Imperial gold crowns or four Canid gold marks in fair trade."

I stared at the coin, suddenly pissed off beyond belief. I'd had over a dozen of those damn coins. Plus, I'd just given one away…

"Would a silver Unity coin have a similar value?" I asked in as mild a tone as I could manage.

"Of course, yes. All Unity coins are far more valuable..." He glanced up at the door, then at my face. "Oh. Oh, dear. Did you just give her...?"

"Assuming that I wanted this in Imperial currency," I cut him off before my growing urge to hit something got me in trouble, "how much would I get?"

"As I said, three Imperial crowns," he said promptly. "As each crown is worth twenty silver wands and each wand is worth twenty brass discs, it would be 1,200 Imperial brass in total. Keeping the coins close to even, it would be..." He paused for a moment. "Fifty-seven wands, sixty discs. I might suggest fifty-four wands and 120 discs, though. The exchange will cost twenty discs, leaving you with precisely 100. That would be easier to track expenses."

"That..." I took a deep breath. Worrying about what I'd lost was just going to make me angrier, not get it back. For the first time, though, I sort of understood why Delvers were willing to risk their lives heading into those death traps. If I'd come back with everything I'd found, I would have been set for life!

"That will be fine," I finally said. "Could you put half the brass and five silvers in a purse and add the rest to my account here?"

"Of course, sir! I'll also get you your new card, so you can withdraw from any of our Guild Halls!"

The halfling vanished and returned fifteen minutes later with a leather purse that I slipped into my pack and a glossy, black card with the Guild symbol, a silver hand with gold circles in the palm, emblazoned on it. He placed the card on a different layout and had me touch it, and I once more felt a tingle of power rush up my arm and back down.

"Done, sir," he said with satisfaction, handing the card back to me. "Your new card is attuned to you, and no one else can use it. Will there be anything else?"

"No, thank you," I shook my head. I hesitated for a moment before slipping the card into the card holder in my pack, then hefted it. "Enjoy your day."

"You as well, sir, and we hope to see you again soon!"

I hoped not to, personally, but I didn't say that. I turned and walked out the door, heading for the market square. I had a wardrobe to fix. There was no way I was going to meet Azara dressed as I was.

There was a decent chance she'd want to kill me as it was. There was no need to make it worse.

7

Canis, like most cities, could be split up into sections. The river bisecting it helped with that, dividing the city into eastern and western halves. The eastern half was typically slightly nicer and wealthier, mostly because it was the side of the river that had been settled first, while the western bank was newer and thus not quite as upscale. As I mentioned, the closer a person lived to the city wall facing the harbor, the wealthier and more influential they usually were, while the closer they were to the river gate, the poorer they were. That made the southwest corner the dirtiest, smelliest, poorest place in the city, while the northeast corner—where the palace and most guild halls were—was the richest, most extravagant, and snootiest.

Most people, though, lived somewhere in between those places. The southeastern section of the city was where most of the unskilled workers who still managed to make a living made their homes, which meant the bulk of the people in the city. Rich merchants, successful artisans, and lesser nobles filled the northwestern corner. And all the people in between—craftsmen, mildly successful merchants, scholars, and so on, lived in the middle. These were the people that everyone needed but no one remembered, not poor enough to be scorned the way the southerners were, but not rich enough to have influence the way the northerners did.

Azara's shop was there, in the middle western section, tucked away down a side street. I stood down the street from it for a bit and examined it; it looked mostly the same from the last time I'd seen it, seven or eight years ago. It was two stories tall, narrow and pinched between a travel house and a glassmaker's shop. The front was painted bright yellow but the door was black, as were the windows. A sign hanging above the door read simply, "Azara's Cartomancy" along with an image of four facedown cards beneath it. The sign was a bit faded since I'd last seen it, and the building's paint looked worn and chipped in places, but the building still seemed to be in decent shape. Apparently, Azara had been doing okay for herself.

I took a deep breath and crossed the street. I placed my hand on the door and hesitated for only a moment before I pushed it open and stepped inside to the jingle of a bell conveniently placed above the door.

The room beyond was dark, dusty, and small. It was only ten feet or so across, with most of that space being occupied by a flat, oval table covered with heavy red fabric. A single oil lamp hung above the table with the wick pulled short so it barely gave out any light. Images of cards, arcane symbols that I was pretty sure didn't mean a damn thing, and occasional ravens that could barely be seen in the dim light dotted the brown walls. A door in the far wall was the only way into the deeper parts of the shop, where Azara worked on her cards and layouts.

"A moment!" a voice called from the back, one that was almost painfully familiar. It was high and airy like that of most avians, with a distinct nasal tone. I still reveled in it since I was fairly sure that it was going to get a lot more unpleasant in just a few moments. I remained silent and braced myself as the back door opened, and the shop owner stepped through.

Azara was a raven beastling, one of the avians, and it showed. Black feathers jutted from her head in place of hair like an ebony crown, and shorter, downier ones covered her arms. Her face and chest were free of the feathers, displaying her half-human ancestry—which meant that the low black vest she wore showed plenty of her cleavage. Her eyes were bright blue and as fierce as any raptor's, and her slightly hooked nose was black, the effect oddly striking in her otherwise tan face. She was beautiful, smart, and one hell of a cartomancer. And from the way her eyes flattened and her jaw clenched when she saw me, she was also royally pissed.

"You!" she spat, taking a step into the room with her head forward like a predatory bird. "How dare you step foot in this place after all these years, you lying, cheating, son of a ragged whore?!" Like most avians, her voice had a slight raspy hiss to it, and her anger amplified that so she sounded like a spitting snake.

"Azara," I said calmly, tipping my hat toward her. "You're looking well."

"And you look far too healthy for my tastes!" she snarled, reaching into her vest pocket and pulling out several cards. "Something I intend to fix!"

"Easy, now," I said, taking a step back and holding out my hands in a placating fashion. "I'm here in a professional capacity, not a personal one. I just need…"

"You think that I'd ever work with you?" She barked a sharp laugh filled with contempt. "You want my cards? Here, take them!"

Her hand flashed forward, and one of the cards in it sailed out, spinning in the air toward me with frightening accuracy. I swore and dove sideways as the cards struck the door with a loud bang and the smell of burning wood. I scrambled to my feet and jumped back as another card hit the floor in front of me and exploded in a flash of bright light. I covered my eyes, turned my head away, and felt a third card hit my chest. A buzzing sound arose from it, and something started tickling the skin of my chest and throat.

I opened my eyes and saw a three of stars stuck to my shirt, flashing with arcs of electricity that crawled across my chest and throat. I grabbed the card and yanked it away, feeling it tingle in my grasp as the lightning crawled across my fingers. While it hadn't hurt, it had scorched my shirt, leaving blackened marks along the collar and upper breast.

Azara wasn't a Holder; in fact, she hated them and held them in contempt. Most of her cards weren't even Unity cards. That didn't mean they weren't dangerous. She made them herself, and as a cartomancer, she could channel power through them the way I could a Unity card. Mind you, only she could; for anyone else, they were just fancy-looking cards. According to what she'd told me back when she looked at me with something other than naked hatred—something very different from that, in fact—her cards weren't as powerful as true Unity cards by a long margin. They weren't exactly a gentle caress, either. I'd seen her fell a seven-foot-tall ursid who thought he could rob her with a card like the one stuck to my chest. Either she'd lost her touch over the years—which wasn't likely—or something odd was going on.

"Damn it, Azara," I swore, tossing the card onto the floor, where it quickly sputtered out. "This was a new shirt! I ought to make you buy me another one!"

"You..." I looked up to see her staring at me with a shocked expression. "You should be twitching on the floor right now. And screaming. I wanted lots of screaming." Her head cocked sideways in a birdlike expression I knew meant she was curious. "Why aren't you screaming, Murf?"

"I was kind of hoping you could tell me," I said with a shrug, feeling a stirring of hope. That was one of Azara's weaknesses: she hated an unsatisfied curiosity, and she was endlessly curious about anything to do with cards. If I could get her thinking rather than reacting, I might be able to talk to her.

"You must have an electricity ward," she muttered, her eyes going distant. Her hand swept forward again, and I slapped the card out of the air before it hit me. It stuck to my palm, radiating an icy chill that was uncomfortable but not painful, and I glanced at it.

"Seven of cups," I muttered. "That's a strong card, Azara. Are you really trying to kill me?" I shook my hand, dislodging the card, and it quickly lost power as it dropped to the floor.

"Amazing," she whispered. "Wait—what about...?" Her hand flashed again, but this time I dodged, leaping sideways away from the attack. It didn't matter; the moment the card struck the wall behind me, a blast of wind exploded from it, slamming into my chest and knocking me onto my ass. My chest ached and throbbed, and I rubbed it, glaring balefully at the woman.

"Damn it, Azara, cut that shit out!" I bellowed. "I'm here for your help, but if you do that again, I swear I will punch you in the mouth!"

"Greater effect from a noble arcana," she muttered, apparently ignoring me. "It must be a Power. No other answer." I glanced sideways and saw a card lying on the floor displaying an armored man on horseback holding a spear in one hand, a bag of coins in the other, and looking to his left.

"A knight of coins?" I half-shouted. "You could have blown this whole place to hell, woman!"

"The building's safe," she said dismissively, waving a hand and walking toward me, her head cocked sideways and her upper body leaning forward. "What did you do, Murf? How did you get your hands on a Power? And which one is it?"

"I'm not saying shit until you promise to stop attacking me, woman."

"Fine, fine. I won't attack you again—at least, not unless you do something else to piss me off." She drew close and looked into my eyes, peering deeply into them with her ice-blue raptor gaze, then reached out to touch my chest. She hissed and pulled her hand back as if I'd burned her, and she took a step back from me. "You're a Holder!" she hissed.

"Yeah, but it wasn't my idea," I sighed.

"Not your idea? What are you talking about? How was it not your idea to defile a card by placing it in your soul, Murf?"

"Short answer: I got tossed into a damn Labyrinth, managed to kill the final monster on accident, and fell onto the card it dropped. Next thing I know?" I shrugged. "I'm a damn Holder. I was hoping you'd know how to undo it."

"I could kill you," she flashed me a wicked grin. "That would take the card from your soul."

"Yeah, I was looking for something slightly less lethal." I sighed and lifted my hat to rub my hair. "I've spent my whole life avoiding Holders, Azara, same as you. I dislike them almost as much as you do, and suddenly, I've become one. I was hoping you could help me figure some of it out."

"Why come to me?" she asked suspiciously, her eyes hardening again. "You know I'm not happy to see you, Murf. The Sage's Guild could tell you what you want to know. Go see them."

"Or they might slit my throat for the card, and we both know it. Look, Azara, I know you've got reason to think poorly of me…"

"Good reason?" she echoed, her voice rising in both pitch and volume. "You left, Murf! No goodbye, no letter explaining anything, not even a damn card message! I told you I loved you, and you vanished!" The cards in her hand began to crackle with power again, and a dangerous light grew in her eyes.

"Yes, I did. I'm an asshole, Azara. A selfish, thoughtless, asshole, and the thought of you loving me scared the shit out of me." I shook my head. "You don't love halfway, and we both know it. It's all or nothing for you—and I couldn't give you that. So, I ran. I figured it was better to hurt you once than to keep doing it for years. I'm sorry."

She glared at me, then lowered the cards in her hand, slipping them back into her vest. "You didn't explain why you came to me," she said shortly.

"It happened just south of the city, so I was nearby. Besides, you know more about cards than anyone I've ever met, including those dicks in the Sage's Guild. If anyone can help me, it's you." I took a step closer. "Please. I just need to know what I got myself into and if there's any way out of it. Then, I'll go, and you'll never see me again."

"That sounds familiar," she muttered, then sighed. "Sit. I'll be right back." She vanished back into the back, and I sat warily into one of the chairs. As I did, I looked down at my chest, rubbing the burns on my shirt.

"What the hell just happened?" I mumbled, not really expecting an answer. To my surprise, the Unity decided to give me one.

Arcana Defense Activated!
Skill check versus lesser arcana
passed!

Arcana Defense Activated!
Skill check versus noble arcana
passed! Effect mitigated.

"What the hell is a Skill check?" I asked with exasperation as I waved the card away.

"You'd have to ask a Holder that." I looked up as Azara re-entered the room carrying a folded square of black cloth. "I know cards, not Holders. You know I loathe them."

"Yeah, I remember," I nodded. "You're not a fan."

"No. However, as you already disgust me, that doesn't change things." She sat down and began unfolding the cloth to reveal a pattern of card-size rectangles, each numbered from one to thirteen. The rectangles were in the shape of a cross, with a card in the center and four T-shapes of three cards each jutting out in each direction. She smoothed the cloth down, then carefully fastened it to the table beneath with brass tacks. She pulled out her card deck and began shuffling it, her eyes closed and her lips moving soundlessly as she did. After a minute or so, she placed the deck in front of me.

"Cut," she instructed, and I lifted part of the deck up and placed it on the table. She touched the top card of the remaining stack and opened her eyes. The blue orbs glowed with an eerie power that always unnerved me when she did this, as it seemed to look beyond me into something much deeper. Of course, according to her, that was exactly what she did. Azara was a true cartomancer, not one of the charlatans cold-reading people from a booth in a shady alley. She had power, and while I didn't understand it, I respected the hell out of it.

"You wish knowledge of your card," she said in a hollow voice that echoed in the room, her face utterly expressionless. "This is the Unity layout, the tableau of understanding." She lifted the first card and placed it in the middle, slowly and carefully lowering it so that it rested perfectly inside the framed rectangle on the mat. An old man seated in a palanquin stared up at me, six-pointed stars hovering around his head and a crown on his brow. His head pointed toward Azara, and his feet pointed at me.

"The Emperor of Stars," she intoned. "The symbol of control and command over the essence of the universe. Inverted, it shows that the universe guided you to this result, and that your destiny may not fully be your own any longer. This is the base card, the card from which the rest of the layout will draw power. It is a potent card, the greatest in the deck; you will gain great knowledge from this if you have the wit to understand."

She began to turn over cards, flipping them one at a time into position. The first card went below the Emperor, its top touching his crown. The next went above it, touching his feet, while the third went to the left and the fourth to the right. She didn't bother to explain what the cards were, but I knew that was because they didn't matter. Only the base card did; everything else would pull off it. Until the tableau was complete, the other cards were simply decoration. I wasn't a cartomancer, but I'd spent enough time around Azara to know the basics.

Her hands moved smoothly and surely as she carefully placed each card, one by one in the proper order. Most cartomancers took their time and went a lot more slowly since a mistake could lead to anything from a failed tableau to cards getting destroyed to an explosion. Azara had spent decades honing her skills, though, and every movement was precise and perfect. At last, she laid the final card, then reached down and touched the upside-down Emperor.

A flare of power rose from the cards, crawling along my skin and making my hair stand on end. I could practically taste the energy filling the room, the sense of it metallic and bitter on my tongue. It rolled over Azara, and her feathers fluttered and danced in the unfelt breeze of it. Her head rolled back, and she inhaled deeply before turning to look back at me, her expression grave.

"You hold the Hag in your heart," she intoned in that same hollow voice that rang in the room. "The unwanted mother of the Cabal, greatest of the cards. She is the Cabal of Change and Protection, most malleable of the cards, able to bond with any other and make them part of her. Her magic protects you but also drives you as she seeks her wayward children. As her vessel, you will go places that others dare not tread, whether you wish to or not, and you will emerge from them, greater than you entered. No place will be your home, and those who follow in your path will wander forever, never knowing what drags them down the endless roads. Beware the power of the Hag, for it is great and unpredictable. It will draw her children, like calling to like, bringing them ever closer and drawing you into greater danger. Hold your heart close, or the Hag will snatch it away."

The woman shuddered as the eerie energy drained from the room. Her eyes faded back to their normal color, and she blinked them several times, wincing as she did.

"I never get used to my eyes drying out," she muttered, gathering the cards and collecting them. She stacked them up and stared at me, her expression grave. "You're in a lot of trouble, Murf."

"It sounded like it," I nodded. "I didn't get all of that, though."

"You took a Cabal card into your soul, Murf. Do you even know what the Cabal is?"

"Not really," I admitted. "I'm a gambler, not a Holder. I only care about the cards in a deck."

She sighed. "The Cabal is the name we give to the most powerful rank of cards in existence. They're so rare that I don't know their names or even how many there are, to be honest. What I do know is that they're above the Arcana and Powers both, they rule the deck of the Unity, and their Holders rarely live long or happy lives."

"I had a feeling it would be something like that," I muttered, putting my face in my hands. "So, what in the hell is this Hag?"

"I don't know," she shrugged. "She's mostly hidden from me. I could barely make out what little I got. The reading called her the Mother of the Deck and the Cabal of Change. That's all I can tell you—that and the fact that the Hag in your heart is *the* Hag, the only one in existence, so anyone who wants it will come looking for you to get it."

"Great," I muttered, laying back in my chair. "Someone's going to put a bolt in my head for this card. Can I just take it out?"

"Of course not, and you know that. It's your hole card, Murf. The only one that can't be removed. At least, not without your death—but that's not going to be as easy as you seem to think."

"What do you mean?"

"The Hag—she's not like other cards, Murf. Every card is an expression of the Unity, as you know, and they speak to us who know how to listen, but the Hag seems to be much more than that. What little I read of her, I got because she allowed it."

"Allowed it?" I asked dubiously.

"Yes. I told you. She's not like other cards. She chose you and made you her vessel. I get the feeling she won't give you up so easily. She'll protect you from harm as best she can, the way she protected you from my cards."

"So, wait, I'm invulnerable now?" I asked in amazement.

"Hardly," she laughed bitterly. "The Hag isn't all-powerful; no card is. You won't die as easily as you used to, though. Like a damn roach. It's fitting, really."

"What about the card's abilities? How can I use them? How do they even work?"

"I'm no Holder, Murf. You heard what the Hag let me find out. Anything else, and you'll need to ask a Holder—although I'd be careful there. Any Holder alive would give their soul for that card."

I sighed and rubbed my face. "Anything else?"

"Yes." She hesitated. "The Hag's children are drawn to her, Murf. She'll call them to you, and she'll make sure you find them, whether you want to or not."

"What does that mean? Her children? How does a card have babies?"

"The deck, Murf. The arcana and powers. Maybe even the rest of the Cabal; I don't know. Like the reading said, like will call to like." She shook her head. "You're going to attract danger and death everywhere you go, now."

I rubbed my eyes for a few moments, considering her words. I didn't know exactly what she meant, that like would call to like, but I assumed it meant that other Holders would be able to tell when I was around—or maybe I'd be able to sense them. I'd be fine with that since if I knew someone like that was nearby, I'd happily get myself as far from them as possible. For everything else, I'd need to talk to a Holder, and I only knew two or three that I remotely trusted—none of them in this city. That would just have to wait.

"Thanks for the information, Azara," I finally said, sitting up and reaching to my purse. "What do I owe you?"

"Nothing," she said flatly. "I don't want anything to do with this card—or you. This finishes us, Murf." She rose to her feet, her eyes both angry and sad at the same time. "Don't ever darken my doorstep again, or by the Unity, it'll be the last thing you do. Not even the Hag will protect you from me." She turned and strode out of the room, slamming the door behind her, and after a moment, I rose to my feet.

That was a bridge I'd well and truly burned, no doubt about it. Part of me felt regretful. Azara was an amazing woman, gifted with cards, extremely intelligent, and one hell of a lover. My time with her had been special, and I'd occasionally wondered what might have happened if I'd stayed and tried to make it work with her. I shook my head; there was no point to worrying about that anymore. She'd made herself clear. I wasn't welcome here, and it was time to leave. This time, though, I could do one thing differently.

"Goodbye, Azara," I called out, reaching down and touching the table. "For what it's worth, I'll always treasure what we had."

I turned and walked out of the room into the cool of the evening. It had been a shit day, and the only thing that could make it better was a night of gambling, and maybe a little whiskey. Or more than a little, depending on how the night went. It was time to head to the Gambler's Hall.

8

I stopped and breathed deeply as I entered the main floor of the Gambler's Hall. I closed my eyes and listened to the shouts of triumph, the muttered curses, even a few quiet sobs as someone realized they'd gambled something they couldn't afford to lose. I opened them and watched as a felid woman wearing barely enough fabric to be called decent brought a drink of some light green liquid to a goblin with a pile of coins in front of him, then leaned over and whispered something I was sure was indecent in his ear. People tossed down cards in frustration, raked in coins by the handfuls, and pulled at their hair as good hands lost to better ones.

There was nothing quite like the heady aroma of cheap whisky, stale tobacco, and despair to make a man feel like he was home.

The main floor was, quite obviously, a gambling den. There was a bit more to it than that, of course. One wall held a bar since drunk people gambled more and lost more money, and thanks to scantily dressed servers—both male and female—a person didn't even have to stop playing to get a drink. There were rooms off to the side that a group could rent to play a private game, whether that be cards, dice, or "fondle the server", assuming they had the coins for it. Most of the room, though, was dominated by gambling tables. The predominant game was arcanum, the most commonly played card game anywhere, but there were a couple tables playing noblesse, the game of the wealthy. Dice rattled in a wooden cup to my left as a group of people played pips, each trying to roll the dealer's mark without rolling a seven first. To my far right, a few people played a game of bust out, where they tried to draw as close to the sum of the dealer's three cards as possible without going over.

Personally, I stayed way the hell away from those games, as any smart gambler would. In arcanum and noblesse, I played against other players, and my skill mattered as much as luck. In pips and bust out, people played against the hall, and the hall always won in the long run. The games offered odds that seemed to mitigate the extra risk, but they didn't. Pips paid out 3:2, for example, so a bet of two coins would win three, but the odds were stacked so that you'd spend sixty-two coins to win fifty-seven. That was why pro gamblers avoided those games and stuck to cards.

I walked past the main tables, lingering for a moment at a table of noblesse where some well-dressed people played a higher-stakes game than most. I only hesitated for a moment, though. The real players weren't out here, and neither were the real stakes. The dilettantes didn't get to partake of the true action. That happened in the back rooms, in the members-only section.

A pair of heavily armed and armored ursids flanked the rear door, and when I glanced into their eyes, I saw the odd flicker there that marked them as Holders. The Hall didn't play around with its security. Being a successful gambler meant that you'd probably pissed off a bunch of people who thought they were good at cards only to discover that in reality, they had no clue what they were doing. Rich and clueless people were great sources of income, but they could also afford to hire people to go after someone who pissed them off. As I approached the door, I pulled out a glossy green card and placed it in the center of a tableau of cards attached to a square column beside me. The tableau flashed a bright green, and one of the ursids nodded to me, allowing me to pass.

I gazed contentedly at the card before returning it to my pouch. It had the Guild's symbol, a fan of three facedown cards, emblazoned on it but was otherwise blank. I'd had to jump through the same hoops getting into the Hall that I had with the Swindlers, thanks to those damn elves stealing everything I owned, but it was worth it. That card held pretty much every bit of important information about me on it if a person knew how to pull it up. It told my rank in the Guild, the number of tournaments I'd won, and the fact that I'd never been caught cheating. Those three things more or less defined me, which I suppose is probably kind of sad, all things considered. Good thing I never gave a shit, I guess.

The room beyond was smaller and significantly quieter than the main hall. The men and women here were professionals, and when they won and lost, they did it quietly, if not always with good grace. The liquor here was higher quality and more expensive, but fewer people partook of it. The servers also dressed more conservatively since no gambler worth the name could be lured away from the table by a pair of tits, no matter how fine they were.

The games here were different, as well. Pips and bust out were gone; nobody in the Guild was dumb enough to play them. Whereas in the main section, arcanum was the most common game, in the back, more people played the higher-stakes noblesse. As well, no one played with coins in the private hall. The Guild provided chips that could be cashed in or deposited in the Guild for credit at any time, although most of us kept our chips unless we were traveling away from the Hall for a long time or needed some coin quickly, as I had when I got the hell out of Gurg.

I walked over to a goblin woman seated behind a low counter with the word "Cage" on the front. Once, this had been an actual cage, the way the

Swindlers' hall was, but as the Guild got more civilized, the bars went away. The name stuck, though. The woman smiled at me as I walked toward her, and I flashed a rakish grin of my own at her. She had the typical greenish skin and small stature of most goblins, but her cheeks were rounder than normal, and the shock of hair on her head was dark green rather than black.

"Good evening," she said in the usual husky voice of a goblin. "Cashing in or out?"

"In," I said, holding out my card and three of my silver coins.

"Of course." She took the lot, placed the card on a tableau I couldn't see, did the same with the silvers, then slipped them into a slot in the desk before handing me back my card. "Three Imperial wands are worth seventy-five chips. How do you want them?"

"Two tens, six fives, the rest singles."

"As you'd like." Her hands moved beneath the counter for a minute to the clacking sound of hardened wood striking together. At last, she lifted up a tray and held it out to me. I took it and looked it over; it had five stacks of white-painted wood discs worth one chip each, a stack and an extra blue-painted circle, and two red-painted circles. A quick count confirmed that she hadn't short-changed me—it was rare but it happened, even in the Guild—and I tipped my hat to her.

"My thanks, Eegla," I smiled at the girl. "How're the pickings tonight?" Eegla played the role of a simple cage girl, but as a rank nine Gambler, she was actually fairly high up in the local Hall, just a couple steps below Guild Master. I'd known her long enough to know that she liked to slum it in the cage sometimes to keep in touch with the members and make sure everything ran smoothly.

"Not bad, Murf," she shrugged. "There's a tournament coming up in a couple weeks, so people are playing hard to try to win enough to get invited. It makes for bad decisions."

"Why do you think I'm here?" I grinned, then paused. "Hey, you know anything about a couple of elves, names of Alerion and Taveroth?"

"Never heard of them, sorry. They must not be in the Guild. Why?"

"They took offense to losing to me recently. Knocked me out, stole everything I had, and left me for dead. I'd like to get my stuff back."

Her eyes hardened, and she looked down at her desk to the sound of a metal pen scratching on paper. "Alerion and Taveroth, you say? What can you tell me about them?"

"I met them in Keeghan's Fine Winery," I shrugged. "They looked like typical sellswords with some money to me. You know how elves are. Armor this, sword that, 'Oh, look at how I sneer at you! I'm so great!' Alerion is blonde; Taveroth has light red hair. Oh, and they were both Holders."

She froze and looked up at me, her expression slightly stricken. "Holders? Are you sure?"

"Sure as I can be, yeah."

She sighed. "You know that means the Guild won't go after them for you, Murf. We look after our own, but Holders are a different story."

"I can handle my own affairs, Eegla, but if you can maybe track them down for me, it would make things a lot easier."

"That—that, I can do." She paused. "By the way, you should know: Ferdi's in town."

I winced and looked around nervously. "Is she in the outer hall tonight?"

"No. She's never been much for gambling, as you know, and I don't know that she's in town for you. She got in four days ago, went to the halfling hold in the southeast, and hasn't budged from there since. She's made sure that the posters went up all over the city, though, so my guess is she's anticipating you'd come." The woman grinned at me. "You know, she's upped the bounty to three silvers. She really wants you, Murf."

"Not all of me," I grumbled, shifting around uncomfortably to shield my crotch. "The bounty's only for part of me."

"The only part of you that's worth anything, as far as I can tell. At least, if the stories are even halfway true."

"I'm sure we could arrange a demonstration," I flashed her another grin, and she laughed warmly.

"You're worse than an orc in their first mating season! Go on, get out of here. Give me a day, and I'll know all there is to find out about your elves."

"Thanks, Eegla. You're the best."

"I know. Now, go play. I want to see your ass in the tournament!"

I've always felt like goblins have a bad reputation. Most people think of them as coarse, blunt, and maybe a little lax about hygiene, and well, that tends to be true—mostly for the males. However, they're also intelligent, clever, and dedicated. Their crafters are the best in the world, and while part of that is their nimble fingers and the fact that their society ranks crafting highly, it's also because a goblin blacksmith will spend sixteen hours a day, every day, mastering their craft. They tend to be like that in whatever they do: they pick something to focus on, and they make that their entire life. That focus means they don't always have the best social skills or time to bathe regularly, sure, but if you can get beyond it, they're friendly and easy to get along with.

Eegla's focus was gossip. She knew every rumor in the city, and she knew everyone of any importance. She knew who liked to talk, who could be bribed, and how much it would cost. She'd find out who the elves were, assuming there was anything to find, and unless they'd left the city, she could find where they were staying, as well. That was what mattered to me. As much as I wanted to pay the two back, what I really wanted was everything they'd taken from me, and if I could liberate it from their room while they were gone—along with a little extra for my trouble—that would probably be for the best.

I walked away from the cage and stood to the side, scanning the tables. I preferred arcanum to noblesse, but I knew that the desperate players, the ones who had to win big to get into the coming tournament, would be a lot more likely to be at the noblesse tables. The stakes were higher there, after all. Stifling a sigh, I made my way to the nearest table with an open seat and settled in.

"Good evening," I smiled at the dealer, an avian man with grayish feathers and wide yellow eyes. "Game rules?"

"Straight noblesse; spread, cross, and fool; no wilds," he said without looking at me as he shuffled the deck in his hand. "Ante's three, blind's five."

"Isn't it the rule that the newcomer always pays the blind?" a red-haired human woman three seats down from me asked, flashing me a smile. She was pretty in the way that the sun is bright or a brick to the crotch is painful, with brilliant green eyes, smooth skin, and hair that hung in ringlets from where she'd coiled it atop her head. She wore a shoulder-less dress the color of her eyes, cut low enough to show off her womanly assets, which a few of the men at the table seemed to be avidly noticing. I couldn't help but chuckle at that. I would have bet gold to silvers that she knew exactly what she was doing. A gambler with his mind in his pants doesn't have his mind on the cards, where it belongs.

"I don't know what you're talking about, Millie," an orcish man beside her grunted in a gravelly voice. "Blind's on you this hand." Like most orcs, the man had gray-green skin, small eyes, and a severe underbite that made his speech sound like he was chewing his words. He wore a simple green shirt with a gray vest over it that oddly complemented his skin tone. Also like most orcs, he seemed to be a little slower of thought, no doubt totally missing her joke. She didn't seem to care as she looked past him and smiled at me.

"My name's Millie," she said in a friendly tone.

"So I gathered," I chuckled. "Murf. It's nice to meet you, Millie"

"Yes, yes. We're all good friends, now. Let's play cards," the orc grumbled, glancing at me. "Ante up, human."

I tossed three chips into the center, then waited as the dealer dealt us all three cards. I lifted the corners of mine just enough to see the cards, noting as I did that most of the others did the same. No one wanted to give anything away, after all. I had a decent hand: an emperor of coins, the highest rank of that suit, a queen of cups, one below an emperor, and a ten of stars. With a knight, lady, and prince, I'd have a court run, the highest run possible, but that wasn't very likely.

"Bid's on you, ma'am," the dealer said to Millie, who sighed dramatically.

"Check," she said, indicating that she wanted to stay in but didn't want to bid higher. That was a pretty standard first move in noblesse, when you only had three cards to base your chances of winning off of. The orc checked, as well, tossing two more coins into the pot to stay in since his ante hadn't met the blind minimum of five. The black-furred canid to my right did the same. I folded immediately, not wanting to toss good chips after bad; while my hand had lots of potential, nothing had materialized yet. The avian man to my left, though, bid a chip, raising the bid to six, at which point half the table followed me in folding.

I watched as the dealer laid down a card faceup on the table, called the spread card, a six of cups. Millie, who'd stayed in, checked again, and the avian bid another chip, causing everyone but the two of them to drop out. The dealer put down a second card, the cross, a ten of staves that would have given me a nice 2-set if I'd stayed in. A 2-set wasn't enough to keep me in a game, though; the odds were good that at least one of Millie and the avian had a 3-set or better. I suspected the bird of bluffing, personally, but I couldn't be sure, and I wasn't ready to risk chips on it. That suspicion grew when the bird bet a fiver; Millie called, and I saw a wince in the man's eyes, one that passed quickly but was enough to tell me he'd hoped to drive her out. It was a dumb move, really. It was possible that he had a seven, eight, and nine, but not likely. It was more likely that he had a 2-set of sixes or tens and another of the other card to give him a double set, but as only the second-lowest possible hand, that was no reason to bid so high.

The dealer placed the last card, the fool card. Legend held that it had that name because only a fool stayed in long enough to see it flip, but no one really knew. The card came up a five of cups, and Millie tossed a ten into the pile, forcing the bird to fold instantly. I was glad I'd stayed out; I didn't know what she had, but I felt sure she'd had at least a 3-set to hang in that long—either that or she'd learned to read the bird well enough to know when he bluffed.

I tossed three more chips into the middle and picked up three more cards. This time, I had a 2-set of twos with a three of stars on the side, not a great hand but enough to actually stick around. I hung in until the cross card dropped, a two of cups that gave me a 3-set, then bet a little larger, forcing the others to fold. That was the way noblesse tended to go; most people dropped out in the first or second round of betting, but the high antes and presence of the blind—a player who had to bid the minimum on the first round, in this case five chips—meant that even if everyone folded, the last player in would win a decent pot. I pulled twenty-six chips from my win and didn't even have to finish the hand.

The game moved on, and I played fairly conservatively as I got a feel for the others. Bird-man was one of the desperate, betting big in the hopes of winning big, but at least a couple of the others had learned enough to know when he bluffed them. The orc was just there to play, seemingly unconcerned about his wins and losses and just enjoying the game. Millie was there to win, and she was a sharp player who won infrequently but made a good haul when she did. A couple hours slipped past, and as they did, I began to win more often as I learned about the others. I still lost more hands than not just from the luck of the draw, but as the play went on, winning grew easier and easier.

A familiar sensation stole over me as the night passed. My awareness seemed to spread out over the whole table, as if I could see everything happening at once. I could practically feel the cards the others held— Millie had a 2-set with a strong kicker; the orc had nothing; the avian held a hand with high potential that was going to disappoint him. The dealer was going to put down a decent layout, one that would help me and Millie and hurt everyone else. I didn't know how I knew this, but I did, just as surely as I knew that in the end, my hand was going to beat Millie's.

I had no idea where that feeling came from. It was something that happened to me every so often when I was really into my play, and I didn't know if anyone else felt the same thing or not. I'd never been able to adequately explain it to anyone in a way that didn't sound like I was cheating or using some sort of cartomancy. I couldn't even control it; it just sort of happened sometimes. I fell into a place where the cards became my best friends and told me all their secrets, and when it happened, I knew I could win big.

I won the pot, then tossed in the blind while waiting for the others to ante. The cards came down, and I barely had to glance at mine to know that I had a 2-set of fours and a six off-suit, meaning it was a different suit from either of the fours. A glance around the table told me that the orc had a small 2-set that would get swamped during the layout. The canid beside me had three of the same suit and would probably hold into the cross for the chance at a flush draw. The avian had a potential high run, maybe even three court cards, and he'd hang on until the fool for the chance to make a 2-set out of it. Millie had middling cards, nothing great, but she had a chance during the layout to make something from it. The others had nothing, and I discounted them.

"Check." Technically, I didn't have anything, and while I felt that wouldn't remain true, I couldn't bring myself to bet on a hope like that. The avian tossed two chips into the center, which made three of the others with nothing drop out instantly. That was fine; they would have dropped out the moment anyone bid, anyway. The others called the avian; I didn't have to, as I'd already met his wager with my blind.

The dealer turned over the first card, a four of cups. I checked again, and the avian once again bid two. Millie called, as did the canid, but the orc dropped out at that point. I went ahead and raised the avian one more, and to my surprise, the canid tossed his hand in, leaving me, Millie, and the bird in the game to see the cross.

The cross came, an eight of blades that I knew helped Millie but hurt the avian. I still checked, and the bird hesitated a moment before tossing a five in, obviously hoping to scare us out. Millie raised that to a ten, and I called her. The avian sat for long seconds before laying down his cards with a sigh and leaning back in his chair. I was surprised but not shocked; he'd wanted to stay in, hoping for a high 2-set, but at that point, he had to know that we wouldn't be bluffed, and his 2-set wouldn't hold up. It was a smart move, one of the smarter ones he'd made that night.

And then, there were two.

The fool dropped, and I didn't even bother to look at it. I stared directly at Millie as I tossed a five into the pot. She did the same with a smile, hesitated, and slid two tens in to match it. I glanced down at her pile and mine, then matching her grin, shoved everything toward the center.

"All in," I said calmly.

"Holy shit," the canid muttered. "All in on a low layout like that? How much have you been drinking?"

"He's bluffing," the orc shook his head. "Look at those cards. He can't make anything from them!"

"Is he?" Millie murmured, still staring into my eyes. "He might be. I suppose I'll have to pay to find out. I call." She slid her pile forward as well, and the others broke out muttering to one another loudly enough that the dealer had to raise his hands for quiet.

"The bet's been called," he said. "Show your cards."

"Happily," Millie smiled. "I've got a 2-set of eights." She turned over an eight, then laid down her second card, a four of coins. "And a 3-set of fours. Full hall."

"Ha!" the avian laughed, smacking a feathered hand on the table. "She's got you, human! What do you have?"

"I've got a double-set," I sighed. "Fours…" With a grin, I laid my two fours down next to the fool card, the four of staves. "And fours. 4-set. Sorry, Millie."

"Son of a bitch!" the canid howled, tapping his hands on the table in a staccato rhythm. "That's all five fours! Who the hell shuffled this?"

I expected Millie to be upset, but she flashed me a wide grin and laughed cheerfully. "Well played!" She rose from the table and nodded at everyone. "And I can't think of a better note to end the night on."

"I agree," I said, looking at the dealer. "Can you have these arranged and deposited in the cage for me?"

"Of course, sir," the man nodded. "And congratulations. It was a well-played hand."

I stood, and Millie walked over to my side, taking my arm and leading me from the table. "Well, if you're done as well, Murf," she said, "you can buy me a drink. It's the least you can do after taking all my money."

"The very least," I smiled at her, leading her toward the bar. "And perhaps, in return, you can tell me a little bit about yourself."

"There's not much to tell," she said self-deprecatingly. "I'm not exactly anyone special."

"I'm afraid I'm going to have to disagree with you there," I chuckled. "You seem pretty special to me, and you're a much better gambler than most people here."

"But not you," she said dryly.

"We all get lucky sometimes," I shrugged.

"Why yes, Murf," she smiled at me, giving me a smoldering look. "Yes, we certainly do."

9

My dreams that night were strange. Azara was in them, flinging cards at me that turned into ravens that pecked at my face and clawed at my hair. Eegla showed up with a pair of shears, laughing merrily as she told me she was going to collect Ferdi's bounty. A dusty corpse ran after me, demanding that I give his card back and screaming that I'd crushed his face with my ass. Alerion and Tavethor put in an appearance, as well, laughing as they wore my clothing and used my membership cards to rob me blind. They chased me into a rotting crypt, wielding huge sticks the size of tree trunks, and I barely made it inside and slammed the door before they reached me. Still, they pounded on the door, shouting my name and trying to bust their way in, the thumping so loud that it actually woke me up.

I jerked awake, and to my amazement, the thumping from my dream still rang in my ears. I stared at the ceiling of my room in confusion for a few moments before the pounding sounded again, followed by a gruff voice calling my name.

"Murf! Wake your ass up! Come on, I haven't got all day!"

I blinked the last of the sleep from my eyes as I realized that I wasn't still dreaming. Someone was really pounding on my door and calling my name, and they sounded annoyed.

"Wuzzat?" a mumbled voice said in my ear, and I looked to my left to see Millie curled up on my arm, wearing nothing but a sleepy expression. I reached out and touched the bare skin of her arm, sliding my fingers up to her shoulder and down her side, and she murmured contentedly. "Mmm…'s nice. Do that again."

I rolled sideways, intending to follow her instructions, when whoever it was at my door slammed their fist into it again, loudly. "Damn it, Murf, if you don't get up, I'm going to break the fucking door down!"

"Make them go away," Millie murmured. "Then come back."

"Your wish is my command," I sighed, kissing her gently on the lips— then dropping lower to favor a couple of even more enticing spots with my attention, making her gasp—before slipping out from under her and rising to my feet. I stamped over to the door, muttering under my breath about cock-blockers and the special place the Unity held for them in hell. I undid the bar holding the door shut, slipped the lock, and yanked the door open.

"What?" I demanded irritably. An orc man I didn't recognize stood there, his face showing mingled irritation and surprise as he stared at me. His gaze drifted lower, and it suddenly occurred to me that I was naked as the day I was born, and thanks to what I'd just done to Millie, I looked pretty happy to see the guy. A second after that, it suddenly occurred to me that I didn't give a shit.

"I—why are you naked?" he asked in a low, guttural voice.

"It's my secret weapon. Distracts other players, plus I can hold more cards with an extra limb. Why the hell do you think I might be naked in my own room early in the morning?"

He opened his mouth, but before he could speak, Millie called out from behind me, "Whoever you are, go away and come back in an hour." She paused. "Make it two."

"You heard the lady," I shrugged, starting to close the door, but he slammed his meaty hand into it and shook his head.

"Can't, sorry. You're wanted."

"I know. And I'm about to go take care of that if you'll give me a while, thanks."

He blinked at me in confusion. "No, not by—I mean, you're wanted by the Guild Master!"

I frowned. "He's not really my type, sorry. Tell him I appreciate the offer, but I'm going to stick with Millie, here."

"Unless he wants to join us!" Millie called out.

"I call the backdoor!" I said quickly, glancing back at her with a grin.

"No, not—the Guild Master and Mistress Eegla asked for you to come immediately," the orc sputtered. "I mean, right now!"

"And that's what I was trying to do before you interrupted me," I explained patiently. "Although probably not immediately. A lady needs some attention, after all."

"I—you…"

"Why don't you think about what you're going to say for a bit," I suggested. "While you do that, I'll follow the Guild Master's excellent instruction. When I'm done, I'll follow you to see them—although I might be too spent to do it again, if that's what they want."

The orc looked utterly perplexed, and I did my best not to roll my eyes. Despite the stereotype, orcs aren't stupid. They just take a while to get to the same place as someone else, is all. Personally, I've always thought it's sheer laziness: they don't want to think when they can have someone else do it for them. That's probably why they've been so happy letting the goblins rule over them for the past few centuries. The goblins think so the orcs didn't have to, and in return, the goblins get all that extra muscle. It was a solid arrangement that lasted for as long as anyone could remember.

Of course, all that mattered to me was that while he was thinking, I had some time to kill, and I knew exactly how I wanted to do that. I gently shut the door in his face, locked it, and turned back to Millie. She gave me a wicked smile as I crawled onto the bed and over to her.

"You aren't really going to leave the Guild Master waiting, are you?" she asked breathily.

"If I go up there right now…" I kissed her gently on her lips. "…he's just going to make we wait for him for an hour or so." I kissed her again, between her breasts, and she gasped at my touch. "I'm just doing him a favor and getting that waiting part out of the way." I moved down and kissed her even lower, and her gasp turned into a moan.

"You—you're just being a—oh, shit—a good Guild member!" she panted.

"Exactly. And speaking of a good member…" I kissed her again, and all conversation ended.

Almost exactly an hour later, I walked out of the room, fully dressed, leaving Millie snoring contentedly on my bed. I closed the door gently and shifted my pack on my shoulder—I wasn't stupid enough to leave anything that I wanted to continue owning in the room with the girl, after all. I found the orc sitting slumped on the floor with his arms across his knees. As I closed the door gently behind me, he rose to his feet, his face angry.

"Finally!" he snapped. "It took you long enough!"

I looked at him with an arched eyebrow. "You really thank that was long enough?" I asked with a chuckle. "I feel bad for whoever you're with, friend."

He blinked at me in confusion for a moment, then shook his head with a growl. "Come on. The Guild Master's waiting."

"You really think so?" I asked as I fell into step beside him.

"He summoned you over an hour ago!"

"Well, yes, but do you really think he's been sitting in his office for the past hour, chin in his hand, drumming his fingers on his desk, thinking,

'Where is that Murf? He should have been here by now!'?" I laughed. "I'm pretty sure he's busy with a hundred things, and I'm going to be five minutes out of his day."

"I—maybe," the orc grunted. "Still, it's rude to make the Guild Master wait."

"It's rude for the Guild Master to pull me out of bed at..." I paused. "What time is it, anyway?"

"Almost the tenth hour."

"Seriously? What gambler is up this early?" I shook my head. "If he wanted me to hurry, he should have asked for me at a decent hour." My stomach growled noisily, and I glanced down at it. "And he should have sent you with some food. That would have gotten my attention."

The orc gave me a strange look but didn't say anything as he led me up to the third story, where the Guild offices were. I looked around a bit as we walked since I rarely went up past the second level, where the living quarters for Guild members were. The top floor was nothing but offices and the Guild's vault. That second part probably sounded interesting, but it wasn't. The vault was just a steel safe locked inside a steel-lined room heavily guarded with card tableaus and guards who would not take kindly to someone popping their head in just to look around. They'd probably pop that head right off as a way to express that unhappiness, in fact. Sure, there were a hell of a lot of coins in the vault, but there were easier ways to get to them. Like winning them from other Guild members, for example.

The Guild Master's office was, predictably, at the very end of a long hall. The orc knocked, waited for a female voice to say, "Enter", and opened the door, ushering me in less than gently. I stepped into a small room maybe six feet by ten feet with a second door opposite me. The only furnishings were a pair of chairs to my left, directly under a window that let sunlight shine into the room, an oil lamp burning overhead, and a desk to my right. A human woman sat behind the desk, her graying black hair pulled back severely to expose her round, slightly sagging face. Her thin lips pressed together in a line, making the lines beside her eyes stand out. Her expression screamed that my very existence annoyed the shit out of her, and the wrinkles around her mouth could never be called laugh lines.

"This is Murf?" she asked in a reedy voice that grated on my nerves for some reason, looking at the orc as she spoke. She looked back at me, not waiting for a response. "You are very late."

I shrugged. "I prefer to think that the Guild Master was very early, personally. If he'd sent this guy to get me five minutes ago instead of an hour, I'd be right on time." I looked around the office, noting that everything was different from the last time I was here. "What happened to Alina?"

"Alina?" the woman asked sharply.

"Yeah. The person who did what you're doing, but before you started doing it. Pretty felid, golden fur, fantastic tits—that Alina."

"The Guild Master decided that her services were no longer needed," the woman said crisply. "I am now his assistant."

"That's a shame," I sighed. "Your tits aren't anywhere near as nice as Alina's."

"The Guild Master didn't hire me for my—attributes," she snapped. "I'm here to perform a service, not to be put on display for people like you."

"Alina could do both," I sighed. "Ah, well. I'll go see what he wants and get this over with."

"You will sit down and wait until he summons you," she corrected me haughtily. "He'll be with you shortly."

"He's not ready to see me?" I asked incredulously. "Why would he send for me, then?"

"The Guild Master is a busy man," she said acerbically. "He has many demands on his time, and most of them are far more important than you. He'll see you when he's ready."

I glanced at the orc with a grin. "See? Told you." I looked back at the woman. "That's fine. In the meantime, then, I'm going to go get some breakfast. When he's ready for me, send this guy to find me."

"Excuse me?" she said, her voice astonished and angry as she half-rose from her seat. "How dare you? You will sit there and wait on the Guild Master's pleasure, or you'll be expelled from the Guild!"

My eyes narrowed, and my voice lost its jovial tone as I spoke next. "No, I won't, lady," I said in a flat, icy voice. "You can't expel a member without cause, and you've got no cause."

"Every Guild member is required to obey the orders of the Guild Master…"

"Yep. Section 2 of the charter requires every member to obey the direct orders of the Guild Court, including the Master. And I am. He wanted to see me, and I'm here to see him. But the Guild laws don't say that I have to sit on my ass, waiting on his pleasure. If he wants to see me, he can damn well be ready to see me when I arrive. Otherwise, I'll come back at a better time."

"You can't do that!"

"Obviously, I can, or the charter would stop me. It's not just a piece of paper, you know. It's card-linked. If it could stop me, it would." I paused and grinned at the woman. "In fact, technically, I don't even know that he wants to see me in the first place. For all I know, this is an elaborate prank you're pulling on me. Without hearing from him directly, I don't have to do shit, lady."

I turned toward the door, ignoring her outraged splutter, when a voice stopped me in my tracks. "Get your ass in here, Murf!" The deep voice echoed from behind the closed door. "Now!" I sighed, both at his words and at the tingle in my chest that accompanied them. That had been a direct order, and I could feel the charter's magic forcing me to obey it. It wasn't urgent yet, though, so I had a few seconds of grace before I had to listen. I turned back around to see a triumphant gleam in the woman's eyes as she sat down, and I favored her with a smile. I wasn't going to let her get away with thinking she'd won, after all.

"You should have told me he was ready to see me right away," I admonished her. "I can't believe you were going to make him wait! He's the Guild Master, for Unity's sake! Have some respect for him and his office, woman!" Her mouth gaped open, but I strode past her and opened the door, stepping into the office beyond before she could say a word.

The next room was as large as the last was small, and as opulent as the antechamber was bare. The floor was thick, green carpet decorated with the Guild symbol, and the walls were polished mahogany that gleamed in the light of three separate oil lamps. Books stood in shelves along one wall, and a waist-high safe rested in a corner, no doubt bolted down and shielded with a tableau or five. A small liquor cabinet stood to my right, the half-filled crystal bottles in it gleaming with various deep red, pale gold, and amber liquids. Paintings adorned the walls, all of various gambling scenes. There were no windows, which made sense to me—why would the leader of a Guild make it easy for thieves, spies, and assassins to break into their office, after all—but the room was big enough that it didn't feel dark or closed-in. A large desk of ebony wood dominated the center of the room, elaborately carved with images of cards, dice, and coins. Several padded wooden chairs stood before that desk, and a man sat behind it, glaring hard at me as I walked into the room.

The head of the local Gambler's Hall was a canid, of course. The rulers of the city had what they called a "meritocracy", the idea being that the most gifted and talented people ruled. Somehow, those always turned out to be canids, and those canids really preferred to deal with others of their kind whenever possible. Unlike elves, beastlings didn't generally look down on non-beastlings, but canids considered themselves to be the most practical of the intelligent species. Simple pragmatism suggested that if everyone in a position of real power in the city was of the same species, it would cut down on all sorts of cultural misunderstandings. It wasn't a law that only canids could be in charge or anything, but since anyone assuming a position of authority had to be approved by the meritocrats, all of whom were canids, it just seemed to happen that only other canids got approved. Fancy that.

The Guild Master had a wide face, with drooping jowls and a slight underbite. Mottled brown and white fur covered his face, everywhere but his pug nose and squinty eyes. His red coat looked fancy, with gold buttons on the front and cuffs and matching embroidery tracing the lapels. His slim fingers drummed impatiently on the table, and his dark eyes glared at me with what I hoped was just irritation.

"Get over here," he instructed gruffly, and I closed the door behind me, pulled out one of his chairs, and flopped down into it. He glared at me. "I didn't say sit, Murf."

"You didn't say stand, either, Jerrick," I pointed out with a grin. "You should know that if you want me to do something, you have to be specific. The charter doesn't require me to read your mind, after all."

He snorted and leaned back in his chair, his expression easing into a rueful grin that spread wide across his canine face. "Is that why you took so damn long to get here? I wasn't specific enough?"

"I don't like being woken up early," I shrugged. "Especially not when someone soft and warm is filling my bed." I jerked a thumb back toward the door behind me. "By the way, what's the deal with grumpy-face? What happened to Alina? I liked her better."

"You always like felid ladies, Murf. I liked her, too, but the wife started taking umbrage over her. Something about my staying here late too often. It was easier to ship her to Felis than to keep explaining I was busy handling the Guild, not my assistant."

"As if anyone believes that," I chuckled. "Felids are the horniest people in the world, they don't believe in monogamy, and they don't much care about consequences. Nobody hires a felid assistant unless they're planning to boink them, Jerrick."

"I did. Hire her, I mean. No boinking. Alina was good at her job. If she'd asked you to sit out there and wait, you would have, and you'd have thanked her for letting you do it. You know how many problems she solved just by getting people too turned-on to remember why they were pissed at me in the first place? Hundreds, that's how many." He sighed. "Aggie out there is a competent organizer, but she's as friendly as a knife in the crotch, and her idea of diplomacy is barking out orders and expecting to be obeyed."

"You need a male felid. Someone easy on the eyes and friendly enough that they can talk the assholes down before they reach you, and someone your wife won't have to worry about."

"No, then I'll be the one worrying about her. She's got the same thing for felids you do, you know. She'd be stopping here every hour or so with some made-up errand or other just to ogle him."

I laughed at that. "Sounds like you're stuck with Aggie, then."

"So it seems."

"So, what's going on, Jerrick?" I asked curiously. "Why did you call me here?"

"I'll tell you once Eegla's here." He glared at me again. "If you'd come when I called for you, she'd have been here, and you wouldn't have to wait."

"If you'd waited until a reasonable hour, I would have come right away," I countered. "I assume there's a reason for the rush?"

"Of course, there is." I turned as the door behind me opened and Eegla walked in, wearing a long emerald dress and looking somewhat tired. "You think I want to be up this early? I worked the cage until the third hour this morning, Murf, while you were snuggled up in your bed—doing whatever you were doing." She grinned wearily at me. "I assume that you and Millie...?"

"Stayed up late to share gambling tips? Absolutely," I chuckled.

"Is that what you're calling them these days?"

"Only in polite company." I glanced at Jerrick. "I don't think the boss called us here to talk about that, though."

"Not in the slightest—although you might want to be careful around Millie," he warned. "She's sharper than she lets on, and she's richer than all the meritocrats combined thanks to her family."

"Her family? She mentioned that her father was a merchant..."

"And a very successful one, but it's her grandfather who's horrifically rich—the kind of man who can afford to hire Black Roses if someone were to, say, impregnate his granddaughter and try to run for it after."

I shuddered slightly at the thought of that. The Black Roses weren't an official Guild; they were an organization of professional assassins spread out across the world. Rumor had it that they were all Holders, and that their cards gave them powers like invisibility, flight, and the ability to walk through walls. No one knew if any of that was true, of course. Officially, they had no standing in any city and existed under a death penalty, but realistically, no ruler wanted to make a real effort to stomp them out. The tale held that the last one who tried was Emperor Beren the Eighty-Fifth or whatever, then-ruler of the Empire of Arnon. The day after he posted the decree, he choked to death drinking his breakfast wine. His son, Beren the Whatever-Plus-One, quickly rescinded the decree and lived to a ripe, old age. I really didn't like the idea of having someone like that hunting me, needless to say.

"I'll be careful," I promised.

"Good. Now, as to why I brought you here—an hour ago, I might mention." He glanced at the goblin woman beside me. "Eegla?"

"I did some checking on the elves you mentioned, Murf," she said, instantly all business as she pulled a folded piece of paper from a pocket of her dress and opened it up. "It wasn't really that hard, as it turned out. A couple questions in the right place, a few coins in the right hands, and the information flowed like cheap wine."

She held the paper up before her and cleared her throat. "Alerion and Taveroth, both of House Eledar," she said. "They came to Canis six months ago, sailing directly from the city of Maewith on the southern tip of the island of Elleagar. They've been hiring out their services as mercenaries through the Sellsword's Guild to make a living, and they're doing fairly well for themselves. They're considered rude and condescending even for elves, but they have a reputation for getting whatever job they're hired for done."

"That's all great," I chuckled, "but what I really need to know is where they're staying, Eegla."

"It's not that simple, Murf," Jerrick grunted.

"Why not? I find them, take back what's mine plus a little extra for making me go through all this trouble, and it's over. Sounds simple to me."

"It isn't," Eegla confirmed. "After I heard all this, I got curious. These two get paid in silver for each job, Murf. Why would they get so upset about losing some brass? Upset enough to try and kill you? It didn't make any sense to me, so I did a little digging, asking around, looking more deeply into them, and when I did..." She gestured toward Jerrick. I looked at him curiously, and he sighed and picked up a folded piece of paper, one that had a broken seal whose remains displayed a sigil I didn't recognize.

"This came this morning at first light, hand-delivered by a messenger from the Meritocracy." He unfolded the paper, cleared his throat, and began to read. "'Esteemed Guild Master Valgrac, of the Gambler's Guild. I hope this letter finds you well. As always, my compliments to your excellent leadership and management of the Gambler's Hall, whose continuing profitability enriches us all...'" He paused and scanned down the page. "It goes on like that for a bit, hold on. Ah, here go." He cleared his throat again and continued.

"'It has come to my attention that one of your Guild officers, a certain Eegla Maalla...Malaga...'" He looked up at the woman. "How the hell do you say that again?"

"Mallaagalash," she said fluidly, making it sound like, 'My-khah-gal-osh', only with a throat full of phlegm that never quite came up. Goblin names are all like that, by the way, nice and easy first names but last names that you need an extra tongue to say correctly. I didn't blame Jerrick; I still can't say it right.

"What she said," he agreed, glancing back at the paper. "'...has been making inquiries into certain elven mercenaries. I feel that I should inform you that these two are currently engaged in a mission of minor but still significant importance to me, the details of which are unimportant. I therefore strongly suggest that you encourage your officer to cease all such inquiries. If you have further questions or concerns, you may of course direct them to my office, and I will answer them as I am able. With all regards...'" He looked back up at me. "Meritocrat Grodvulf."

My face must have shown my surprise and confusion. "A meritocrat? Wait, those two are working for a meritocrat?"

"Who knows?" Eegla sighed. "Maybe. Maybe they work for someone who's paying Grodvulf enough money to get his protection. I'd have to dig more to find out..."

"Which obviously won't be happening," Jerrick said firmly. "Sorry, Murf, but someone trying to kill a Guild member—even one I like as much as I like you—isn't worth the hassle of an angry meritocrat. I told Eegla to let it drop, and as far as the Guild's concerned, that's the end of the matter."

"Can I see that?" I asked, holding out a hand. He obligingly handed the letter to me, and I read it through somewhat casually. As I suspected, it said exactly what he'd told me. There was even a signature at the bottom, a large, looping one with lots of swirls and flourishes. "Nice signature." I tossed the paper back on the table. "Does this mean you're ordering me to drop it?"

"If I do, will you?" he snorted.

"Probably not, but since I'll have to work around the charter, it'll be harder—and probably messier."

"It's just money, Murf," Eegla said soothingly. "You'll win more."

"It's not just money, Eegla!" I replied forcefully. "It's principle! If I let them get away with stealing from me, pretty soon, every thief, cutpurse, and priest of the Unity out there will look at me as easy pickings!"

"You know, they also tried to kill you," Jerrick reminded me.

"Well, yes, but that happens fairly often," I shrugged. "Someone else tried that just yesterday, in fact. If I start getting upset about that, I'll never get anything else done." I hesitated. "Plus, there might have been some Unity cards involved."

"They stole Unity cards from you?" Jerrick asked in a surprised voice. "How many?"

"Three or four. Maybe five." I paused, thinking. "No more than eight."

"You had eight Unity cards?" Eegla demanded, punching me rather painfully in the arm. "Where the hell did you get those?"

"I won most of them, obviously. Tournaments, high-stakes games, nobles who should have known better but didn't—the usual." I grimaced. "And a few just sort of—made their way into my possession somehow."

"So, you stole some Unity cards, and you're upset that someone else stole them from you?" Jerrick chuckled. "Sounds like the Unity's balance to me."

"If the Unity's balanced, I've never seen it," I scoffed. I shifted a little uncomfortably. "Besides, I kind of need a couple of them back. I technically borrowed them from someone and never got a chance to return them, and she hasn't been very understanding about it. I'd really like to get them back to her before she realizes I'm in the city."

Eegla's eyes widened as she understood what I meant. "Ferdi? Is that what that's all about? You stole cards from Ferdi? What the hell's wrong with you?"

"Borrowed," I corrected with a pained wince. "She loaned them to me willingly, and through a series of unfortunate incidents—that were totally not my fault, by the way—I wasn't able to return them. Then, one thing led to another, until she decided I'd stolen them and put a bounty out on me."

"You might try explaining that to her," Jerrick suggested.

"Ha!" Eegla snorted. "Ferdi's a halfling, a delver, and one of the oath-bound—and the bounty's for Murf's lower staff."

He winced. "Then it sounds like you need to find some way to repay her, Murf—or get out of town."

"I'm not leaving until after the tournament, Jerrick," I said adamantly. "Which means I at least need to get Ferdi's cards back." I glanced over at Eegla. "So, where...?"

"Nope," Jerrick interrupted, shaking his head. "The Guild's not getting in the middle of this one, Murf. As far as we're concerned, you've been told to leave those elves alone and let the matter drop, and we won't be offering you any help."

"And definitely stay away from the Royal Lamb, up in the northeastern part of the city," Eegla added. "Don't go anywhere near that place, Murf!"

Jerrick glared at her, his expression exasperated. "Eegla!"

"What? I'm not telling him that those elves are staying there. Besides, it wouldn't help if he knew, Jerrick. The Lamb's one of those exclusive places that will only let you in if you've got money, connections, or both." She winked at me. "You know, like if you knew someone who came from a family that could buy and sell a meritocrat or two."

"*Eegla!*" His face darkened as he half-shouted her name, and the goblin woman clamped her lips shut. He glowered furiously at her for several seconds before relaxing his scowl and turning back to me. "Murf, you need to be careful, here. People have been disappearing around those elves recently—a lot of people, and no one seems to be looking for them. This is bigger than some lost money or even missing Unity Cards. Sometimes, being a good gambler is all about knowing when to cut your losses and walk away from the table."

"Thanks for the advice, Jerrick," I nodded, rising to my feet and tipping my hat toward the man.

"You aren't going to listen to it, are you?"

"I just did listen to it, didn't I?"

"Are you going to take it?" Eegla asked.

"I'll answer that with Murf's Seventh Law, Eegla. Only dead men keep secrets, and even then, not well."

"I hate those damn laws," Jerrick muttered, rubbing his face.

"Don't feel bad, Jerrick," I chuckled. "They hate you, too."

As I suspected, Millie wasn't there when I returned to the room I'd been given for my stay here in Canis, but a folded note lay atop my pillow. I sat down on the bed and opened it up, reading it with a smile.

"Murf. Last night was amazing, and I hope to do it again soon. The sex wasn't bad either. I'll see you at the tables tonight. -Millie."

I laughed and tossed the card onto the wooden table beside the bed, then lay back down. I took a deep breath, relishing the faint scent of the woman that still lingered in the rough blankets, and closed my eyes. I was tired, to be sure, but at the same time, my brain was far too active to let me drift back off to sleep.

Jerrick's warning had been a lot more dire than it seemed. I'd known the man for over a decade, ever since we'd gone head-to-head in the finals in a tournament in the human city of Floodgate. He'd won, but I'd expected that since he was the Guild's golden child at the time. What no one had expected was that I'd push him as hard as I did, staying neck-and-neck with him until a final all-in round where he beat my flush with a full hall. He'd kind of taken me under his wing—or ruff, I suppose, since he was a dog instead of a bird—for a couple years, showing me how the Guild worked and how to rise swiftly in it. I knew him as well as I knew any person, and one thing I knew was that he wasn't given to caution or overstating danger. He'd gotten to his position by taking risks, not avoiding them.

That meant that Alerion and Taveroth were even more dangerous than he'd made them out to be. As I thought about it, I should have realized that. After all, while Keeghan's place, being outside the main walls, wasn't exactly a pinnacle of grace and sophistication, it was still part of the city. A brawl would have attracted the Watch, and they would have been curious about a pair of elves dragging an unconscious human away from the place. The gate guards would have been even more curious when the two left with me trussed up on the deck of their boat. Somehow, the elves had gotten me past all that, and while I'd assumed they'd just been really sneaky about it, now I wondered otherwise.

If the pair had the connections and clout to ignore the Watch and guards, I'd have to be more than careful dealing with them. Right now, they probably assumed I was dead, and that was likely for the best. If I marched over to this Lamb place and confronted them, not only would they know I was alive, they'd probably just drag me outside, finish the job they'd started, and leave my body for the Watch to find, and no one would say a word to them. I wasn't anybody, after all, at least not as far as the city was concerned, and I didn't think too many people would get upset enough to raise a fuss if I were found facedown in a gutter somewhere.

Part of me—the smart part—suggested that I just stay in the Gambler's Hall and forget the whole thing. The place had everything I needed: food, drinks, gambling, attractive women—I stopped and sniffed at myself and winced—and baths. I could stay here until the tournament, practicing my skills, learning about the players who'd be my biggest rivals, and cozying up to the dealers. It wouldn't be the first time I'd gone to a city and never left the Hall the entire stay. The last time I'd visited the elven city of Dornangar, for example, I'd gone from the harbor to the Hall, stayed there for two weeks, then headed back to the harbor and gotten the hell out. Of course, Dornangar is up on the north coast of Shuria, just south of the line where the ground stays frozen all year long. It's cold, dark, and rainy two days out of three, so not going out isn't much of a loss. Canis was a lot more fun, but with the two elves in the city—and Ferdi, apparently, although she'd yet to show herself—a wise man would go back to bed, sleep until dinnertime, and pretend this whole mess never happened.

I sighed and sat up with a groan. Apparently, I wasn't close to a wise man. Also, I needed a bath, badly, and maybe some food. If I was going to be up this early, I might as well indulge in some breakfast.

An hour later, bathed, clean-shaven, and dressed in fresh clothing, I walked down the hall to the Guild dining area. This early, it was mostly empty, although a few people sat wearily at the tables, most of them looking like they'd been up all night rather than that they'd risen early. Millie wasn't here—not that I expected her to be—and while I sort of recognized one or two faces, I didn't really know anyone. That was fine. I wasn't feeling particularly social at the moment anyway. I sat down, ordered a simple breakfast of ham, gravy, and bread with a mug of strong tea to help me wake up a bit, then turned my thoughts inward.

My problem, I decided, was that I had a lot of problems and not a lot of information on them. The elves were obviously being employed by either this meritocrat or someone paying them for protection, and I had no clue who that was. Millie came from a rich and seemingly vengeful family, but I had no idea who or how dangerous they really were, either. Ferdi was somewhere in the city, apparently laying low, and I didn't know where or why. Plus, I had a card stuck in my soul that I barely knew how to use, and the person I'd hoped might be able to help hated me so much that she'd rather burn me to a crisp than see me again.

Not that I probably didn't deserve it.

My food came, and I munched it half-heartedly. The food here was better than it was downstairs, but it wasn't exactly good. The Hall knew that most of us ate here for convenience or safety, neither of which motivated them to hire top-quality chefs. As I munched on bread that was somehow already slightly stale despite it being so early, using it to wipe up the grease that dripped from my too salty and overly fatty slice of ham, I wondered if Jerrick and Eegla ate any better. I wouldn't put it past the man to reserve the best chef and thus the best food for himself and his officers. Not that the best damn food in the world could have enticed me to do his job for a single day. He had an office with a desk for a reason, and that reason was paperwork. I'd rather get tossed into another Labyrinth than spend a day handling paperwork.

As I considered my problems, I realized that there wasn't much I could do about most of them. The elves were out of my reach, at least for the time being. I could ask around about Millie's family, but that would probably have to wait until later in the day, when more of the Guild woke up. At that point, I could just ask her directly. I could also head down to the southwestern section and snoop around for Ferdi, but if she caught me, she'd probably happily collect her own bounty. I wasn't even going to consider risking that.

My card, though—I could probably do something about that. The real question was if I could without outing myself as a Holder or at least giving away just how rare a card I held. I finished up my meal, left a few brass to pay for it, and rose to my feet. There was no real choice. I needed to visit the Scribblers.

I stepped outside into far too much sunlight for my tastes. The morning sun had cleared the walls and shone down almost directly onto the main door of the guildhall, blinding me for a moment before I tipped my hat forward to shield my eyes. I blinked a few times to adjust to the light, then stepped down into the cobbled street, heading toward the damnable sun.

The Scrivener's Guild—generally known as the Scribblers—was one of the oldest and largest Guilds in the world. It predated every Guild but the Sage's, and it held a ton of power and influence. That meant that it was across the river in the northeastern part of town along with the Sage's Guild, the other "respectable" major Guild. The Gambler's and Merchant's Halls were both in the northwestern section, although the Gambler's Hall was right at the southern edge to make it easier for anyone to come lose money there. The Usurers and Sellswords had places more centrally located, and the Shippers had their Guild beyond the walls, near the harbor.

There were other Guilds, of course, but those were lesser ones. Groups like the Healers, Carters, Chandlers, and Blacksmiths all had Guilds, but they weren't as big or as universal as the major ones. Some of them weren't even real guilds as much as groups of people who decided that working together was safer than standing alone. The major Guilds had presences in every city and large town in the world; they owned their own estates; their upper echelons held patents of nobility in their nations. Jerrick, for example, had some sort of official rank in Canis, and that rank came with estates and servants and income and everything—which meant even more headaches, as far as I could tell. The big Guilds were powers that even nations had to cater to.

There were a lot more people out than I'd expected. I suppose I should have known better; we gamblers liked to play late and sleep late, but most people were up with the sunrise. In a way, the moderate crowd was nice since it helped me to blend in, but it also hid the inevitable pickpockets, cutpurses, and muggers that infested any big city. Thievery was so ubiquitous that I sometimes wondered why the thieves hadn't banded together and created a guild for themselves. Then I reminded myself that if they had, they wouldn't exactly go around announcing it, and I wasn't really on close speaking terms with any pickpockets I could ask. Then I reminded myself that I had a lot better things to worry about than some imaginary guild—like keeping its not-so-imaginary members from stealing everything I carried.

I walked with a hand touching the coin purse tucked inside my coat, crossing the tall, wide Firstford Bridge that spanned the Carid River. As the name suggested, the bridge was the oldest one in the city, built to connect the eastern and western banks since the river here was deep and swift, with dark blue water that rushed north to spread into the harbor bay. The bridge was wide and heavily traveled, and I stayed to the side out of the way of the carriages, litters, and rickshaws that moved swiftly back and forth. Most of the occupants of those would be noble, rich, or both, and none of them would much care if they happened to run over a down-on-his-luck gambler. They probably wouldn't give a shit if they crushed a group of orphans and a Unity priest or two, realistically, although they might toss the priest a coin as they rolled over his spine, just to ward off bad luck.

The Scrivener's Hall was easy to recognize since the Scribblers always built the same building in every city. It was light blue, blocky, wide, two stories tall, and decorated with the six-pointed Unity star flanked by a pen on one side and a quill on the other. Its windows were high up in the walls, wide, and rectangular, letting light inside without letting casual passersby see into the building. Its main doors were fashioned to look like a furled scroll, with each door being one side of the scroll. I paused for a few moments before the steps leading up to it, then walked quickly up before I could change my mind and yanked the door open.

Most people thought of the Scribblers as a bunch of scribes sitting in dusty nooks, bent over desks and scratching at pieces of paper until their eyes gave out. I was one of those people, for the most part. I'd never had much occasion to use the Guild's services since I could read and write on my own, and I bought my card decks from merchants, not from the Guild itself. Sure, Scrivener decks were pretty and all, but they worked the same way any other deck did. So, I'd really never had much call to come visit the Scribblers—or any call, really. My first step into their Hall didn't let me down.

The entrance chamber was large, quiet, and dusty. Shafts of sunlight illuminated by the dust streamed from the high windows, not quite fully lighting the place and leaving a lot of it in shadow. High tables set at an angle to face the person sitting at them filled most of the room, and men and women in loose clothing sat at those, busily scratching away. A low, constant buzz of sharpened feathers and metal nibs scraping on paper and parchment mingled with the smells of dust, preservative, and ink to utterly fulfill any stereotypes about the Scribblers I might have held.

It was glorious. I love when the world justifies my cynicism.

"Can I help you?" I turned toward the quiet voice that spoke and took in a few features of the room I hadn't noticed before. The door opened toward a long but low desk, and a wooden railing about waist height ran from the sides of that desk, spreading out about fifteen feet total before turning sharply to connect with the wall to my right and left, essentially funneling me toward the desk. A canid woman with cut ears that stuck up like points from her head and pale orange fur covering her face and hands stared at me through large, liquid purple eyes. I walked over to her and flashed her my best smile.

"Good morning," I said, taking a cue from her and speaking quietly. "I'm here to inquire about the Hall's services."

"Of course," she replied with a professional smile. "Here at the Scrivener's Hall, we offer many services. Are you looking for copying, scribing, translation, restoration, drawing, or binding services?"

"Actually, I..." I paused. "Wait, binding? You mean, people pay you to tie them up?"

She gave me a slightly frosty stare as she answered. "No. Book binding. We can bind loose papers into book form, repair damaged bindings, and even restore faded leather and parchment to like-new condition. For that other binding, I suggest the Avenue of Roses."

"Oh," I said, faintly disappointed. I'd suddenly had a vision of all the dusty, quiet scribes dressed in shiny black leather corsets, tying half-naked people to walls. The reality was a major letdown. "Well—that sounds useful, too, I guess."

"It is. So, what are you looking for?"

Of course, just because the Hall didn't offer leather and bondage as a service didn't mean they couldn't practice it privately, I realized, ignoring the woman. For all I knew, the moment this place shut down, the scribes went wild. There could be nightly drunken orgies. They were probably quiet, dusty ones, but orgies nonetheless. As I said, it's always the quiet ones.

"Sir?" The woman's annoyed tone jarred me from my ruminations, and I refocused on her. "Is there something you need?"

"Sorry about that. Mind wandered. Dusty orgies. You understand." She looked both shocked and confused, and I cleared my throat, speaking in an even lower tone than before. "I'm actually here about—cards."

"Of course," she nodded. "We offer various standard decks for sale, and all Scrivener decks are guaranteed to be complete and accepted at any legitimate gambling establishment. We can also create decks with customized backs if you prefer. Our 'Ladies of Felis' line is quite popular."

"No, I…" I paused, then shook my head. I couldn't possibly show my face at the Gambler's Hall with a deck of naked felid lady cards. Not unless they were really good quality, of course. That was a consideration for later, though.

"I'm talking about Unity cards," I said in a tone just loud enough for her to hear. "I understand that you provide services related to them."

She frowned, looking me up and down critically. "Yes, the Guild is capable of producing certain low-rank Unity cards—but the cost is prohibitive. Producing a card of the lowest rank, an ace, costs five gold crowns and requires two weeks to complete, and higher ranks are considerably costlier. We require either payment in advance or a letter of credit from the Merchant's or Usurer's Guild stating that you have the funds for such an endeavor, as well."

I stared at the woman in surprise for a moment. I knew that cards were expensive, but it sounded like all the treasure I'd found in the Labyrinth— and lost—might have bought me a mid-rank card or so. "Why are they so expensive?" I asked in genuine curiosity.

"Creating a Unity card isn't a simple matter of grabbing a blank card and tracing one out, sir. Unity cards aren't just paper; they're an expression of the Unity itself, the force that created and governs our entire world. They're condensed magical energy given solid form. The art of crafting them is a secret of the Guild, and only a very few people even possess the ability to do so, much less the training. The Guild is the only reliable source of arcana cards outside of finding and conquering a Labyrinth." She flashed me a flat smile. "Of course, if the cost is too high, you can always try that, sir."

"I'll pass," I snorted. "What if I've already got a card, and I want to learn how to use it? Can you help with that?"

"No, sorry," she shrugged. "We do buy Unity cards, if you're looking to sell one, though."

"Hold on," I said, confused. "You offer cards for sale—but not instruction on how to use them? What do you tell people who buy a card from you when they ask how it works?"

"To visit the Sage's Guild," she said shortly. "Or the Unity Cathedral. We simply sell them. We don't offer any training. Is there anything else you might need?"

"No," I shook my head, then paused. "Wait. Maybe. Those felid lady decks—how much are they, and do you deliver them?"

She just managed not to roll her eyes. "A standard deck costs one silver wand, and we can have them delivered within the city walls for a fee, yes sir."

I winced at the thought of losing a whole silver, but I pulled one out with a sigh and handed it to her. "I'll take one, then."

"Of course. Delivery costs two brass. Where should we send them?"

I gave her the address and coins. "Can you include the message, 'To my magnificent beast. Love, Alina'?"

"I..." She stared at me strangely. "Yes, I suppose."

"Perfect. That'll be all, thank you." I turned and headed out, whistling a jaunty tune, ignoring the irritated looks the quiet scribes gave me. Jerrick's wife was going to be furious when she saw that deck. As far as I was concerned, it was fitting payback for dragging me away from Millie so early in the day. As I stepped outside and headed across the street, I decided that it was turning out to be an okay day, after all. I realized that I should have known better than to tempt the Unity as something hard slammed into the back of my skull, knocking me to my knees and filling my vision with stars.

I really hate when that happens—and it's more often than you might think.

11

Strong hands grabbed me beneath my armpits and hauled me into the nearest alley. I groaned as I felt myself slammed up against the side of a building—a stone one, because of course it was—and held upright against it. Something sharp and cold pressed against my throat, and a guttural voice growled, "Don't move." As the sharp thing pressed a little harder, I wisely decided that was advice I could take.

"Is it him?" another voice that sounded like someone was gargling gravel spoke.

"Looks like him," a higher but huskier voice answered.

"Are you sure?" the first voice asked. "All humans look alike to me."

The stars in my vision disappeared, and the ringing in my skull faded enough for my brain to start working again. I blinked and focused, looking around without moving my head. An orc woman had my left shoulder pressed against the wall. She wore plain leather armor, her only hair a dark blue topknot that flowed down the back of her head. She had the muscles of a trained fighter, but then, all orcs did, so that didn't mean much. The point of the spiked hammer she held to my throat was a little more suggestive. Most people didn't use a weapon like that if they didn't know how to use it. A male orc held my other arm and wore metal armor made of overlapping scales that looked both heavy and hot. He also had a dagger in his hand. It took me a moment to recognize it, and I felt a flash of possessive anger as I realized it was mine, the one I'd gotten from the Labyrinth. I didn't say anything, though. Both orcs were bigger than me, better muscled, and had weapons. I didn't really want to find out how well they could use them.

A third figure stood in front of me, peering at a large piece of paper that covered their face. After a moment, they lowered it, and part of me wondered if I could ask him to hold the paper back up again. The last guy was a goblin, and while goblin women could actually be quite attractive despite their lack of eyebrows and eyelashes, goblin men were not. The man's skin was almost as green as an emerald, and like all goblin men, he was totally hairless, even on his head. His nose jutted out from beneath a sloping brow and above a weak chin that made his whole face look like someone had grabbed his chin and forehead and squashed them together.

Honestly, I've never understood how goblins managed to survive as a species considering the way their males look, but they have. In fact, not only do they survive, they thrive. Goblins as a whole make more babies in a month than the elves do in a whole year. It takes all kinds, I guess, and for whatever reason, goblin women seem to look at their hairless, squashed-face men and think, "I have got to get some of that!" It works for them, which I guess is all that matters.

The man flipped the paper around to face me, and I forced myself not to sigh as I saw a poorly drawn caricature of my face on it above the word "Bounty". I glanced over the sign a little curiously, reading what it said.

BOUNTY

Human Gambler known as "Murf" is wanted alive for lying, theft, and oath-breaking.

Reward: 5 Silver Wands (Imperial)

Present Murf or his genitalia with proof of origin to Ferdi Oath-Bound at Clan Baargoth's holdings in the southeastern section to claim the reward.

That was a pretty serious reward, really. It was enough that I was tempted to turn myself in to Ferdi for the coins. If it made its way to ten, I might have to give it serious consideration.

"This you?" the female orc growled, glancing between me and the paper.

"Idiot. He won't say that it's him if it is," the goblin sighed.

"Look, friends, I think there's been a..." I paused as the woman pressed the spiked end of her hammer against my throat, and my voice went up half an octave or so. "A misunderstanding," I squeaked. "I'm not that person, whoever he is. You've got the wrong guy!"

"It says he's a liar," the woman suggested. "He might be lying now."

"I still can't tell them apart," the male orc grunted. "We should bring him just in case."

"I'm not about to bother a halfling oath-bound warrior over a possibility," the goblin shook his head.

"I wouldn't either," I agreed. "I hear that they're somewhat unforgiving of people wasting their time."

"It's just a halfling," the orc male spat. "Who cares?"

"She's a halfling who could kill all of us without so much as breaking a sweat, Urgik," the goblin snapped. "The oath-bound spend their lives training and fighting. Killing people is a pastime for them. She won't hesitate to slaughter us if she thinks we're trying to trick her. The oath-bound are—touchy." He grunted. "I think it's him, though." He looked around. "Not sure how we're going to drag him through half the city without raising a fuss, though."

"Why not just take his cock, then?" the woman asked, lowering the hammer spike to point at my crotch.

"I'd really rather you not," I said nervously. "Besides, I should point out…"

"Because the bounty requires proof of origin, Dagiza," the goblin cut me off, ignoring my protests. "We have to bring him either way."

"Or we could just bring his head," she shrugged. "It's a lot more portable, after all."

"Again, not really a fan of this idea," I said gamely. "Also, I feel that I should mention…"

Once again, the goblin ignored me. "The bounty says that he has to be alive, though."

"How else can you show proof of origin, Ongru?" she demanded angrily, flaring up quickly in typical orcish fashion. "Hire a Scrivener to paint a picture of us cutting off his sack? She has to know what she's asking for."

Actually, Ferdi probably never thought of that, I realized. She was totally honest and never bent or twisted the law to suit herself, and it probably never occurred to her how someone else might. If these three showed up with just my head when she asked for me alive, she'd definitely kill them. Not that I'd be able to enjoy that fact, of course.

"As interesting as this is," I said loudly, interrupting the burgeoning argument and forcing all three to look at me, "I just wanted to mention that all the noise seems to have attracted the City Watch. I thought you might be interested."

I looked past them meaningfully at the alley entrance, and all three whipped their heads around almost comedically to stare at the street beyond. There was no Watch, of course, but that wasn't the point. In that moment, none of them were looking at me, and I took my shot.

My right knee shot up and slammed into the crotch of the male orc with a loud crack. At the same time, my left hand swept down and grabbed the woman's hammer, shoving it backward so that the butt spike on it stabbed into her thigh. The orc man dropped to his knees with a loud squeal, folding up around his crotch and doubling over, while the woman grabbed her leg, where a thin stain of greenish blood began to spread from the hole I'd left in her armor. As the two orcs fell back and released me, my right hand whipped out and cracked into the goblin's skull with a loud thunk. The goblin simply stepped back and shook his head, while my hand felt like I'd punched the wall behind me, and I cursed as I remembered too late that goblins had exceptionally hard skulls.

Everything sort of paused for a moment, at least until I yanked with my left hand, jerking the hammer out of the woman's grip. I swept it sideways and cracked it into the side of the male orc's skull, not even bothering to change my grip on it. His eyes rolled up as the top spike pierced his temple, and he dropped to the ground, senseless and possibly dying. I shifted back toward the woman, who I guessed was now the greatest threat.

I'd barely moved when she crashed into me, shoving me against the wall. She slammed a fist into my stomach, knocking the wind from me, while she reached up and grabbed my hair. She slammed my head backward into the stone wall with a loud thwack, and my knees turned rubbery as stars flashed in my vision once more. They faded quickly, but she yanked my skull forward and slammed it back again, cracking it into the stone a second time. Blackness shrouded the edge of my vision, and she bashed my skull a third time, knocking my hat off in the process.

Anger flared in me at that; I liked that hat! She pulled my head forward, but my vision cleared instantly, and strength returned to my muscles. Before she could smash my head a fourth time, I swung the hammer in my hand blindly upward. It plunged between her thighs, butt-spike first, and her eyes widened as the haft tore through whatever undergarments she wore and kept going. She staggered back, clapping her hands between her thighs with a stunned expression. I flipped the weapon around the right way, wincing and nearly dropping it from the slipperiness on the end of the haft.

"You bastard!" the goblin roared, and I turned toward him to see him produce a short sword from somewhere and lunge for me. As he dove toward me, his blade aimed at my stomach, the whole world seemed to slow down around me for a moment. The odd sensation almost made me freeze up, but self-preservation kicked in, and I quickly twisted sideways, away from the blade. The world sped back up, and he swore as his blade struck the stone wall with a clang. I whanged the hammer down on his outstretched arm, and the bones snapped with a muffled crack. He cried out in pain and dropped the sword, taking a step back, and my foot whipped out into his midsection. He folded up around my kick and flew backwards, smacking into the opposite wall, and I stared at him as he slumped to the ground, curled up in a ball. I hadn't kicked him that hard; hell, I *couldn't* kick him that hard! What the hell was happening?

A scream of rage tore me from my stunned paralysis, and I spun to see the woman rushing at me, her eyes wide, her face darkening in anger, and blood trickling from between her thighs. She crashed into me, wrapping her arms around me, but rather than falling onto my back, I took two steps backward and remained upright. I brought my knee up, hard, and I felt it sink into the spot between her thighs. She screamed again, this time with mingled pain and fury.

"Why?" she shrieked, twisting her body in an attempt to hurl me to the ground. "Why do you keep hitting me there?"

"You were going to take mine first," I grunted, somehow catching my balance and staying erect. Despite her muscles, the woman's struggles barely moved me, as if she were a child trying to shove me around instead of a warrior. I yanked my right arm outward, and to my surprise, I tore it from her grasp easily. I doubled up my fist and cracked it into her head, and she tumbled backward, the blow tearing her arms from me with ease. She fell onto her ass, her face looking dazed, and shook her head. The spot where my fist landed was already starting to swell up, and she moved unsteadily as she scrambled back, her eyes unfocused. I took a step toward her, hefting the hammer, and she looked at me fearfully.

"G-go a-ahead," she mumbled, the words practically drooling out of her mouth. "K-kill m-me. M-might as w-well."

"I don't want to kill you," I told her. "I don't much like killing people." I reached down and grabbed my hat from the ground, sticking it back on my head and glaring at her. "The question is, can I afford to let you go?"

"W-we'll f-find you," she mumbled. "P-pay you b-back."

"Pay me back? For what? For defending myself when you attacked me?" I stared at her in mingled amazement and irritation.

"T-took it," she said, grabbing her crotch as she spoke. "V-virgin. P-pay f-for th-that."

I looked up at the sky, silently swearing at the damn Unity. "You're telling me that you don't consider yourself a virgin anymore—because of this hammer?" I lifted it up and shook it. "Trust me, it's not remotely the same thing!"

"K-kill y-you," she muttered, collapsing to her elbows. The lump on her head kept swelling and growing, and her eyes refused to focus. One side of her face looked strange, her mouth turning down in a frown that slurred her speech, and that eye kept sliding shut on her, as if she couldn't keep it open. I was pretty sure my punch had damaged something important in her skull. Even if I let her live, I didn't know if she'd make it past the end of the day.

"She—she won't kill you," a voice gasped from behind me, and I looked back to see that the goblin had pulled himself up to a sitting position with his back against the wall. "None—none of us will."

"Yeah, I'm sure I can just take your word," I scoffed, hefting the hammer.

"It's not..." He shifted and hissed in pain, grasping his ribs as he moved. "It's not about words. Urgik's dying—if he's not...not dead already." He jerked his chin toward the orc male, who lay slumped and unmoving in a heap, blood trickling from a hole in his temple where the hammer spike had caught him. "And Dagiza's got—got a hurt brain." He sighed heavily. "Seen it in the wars, up by Tungin. She'll be gone within a day."

"That leaves you," I said ominously.

"Me?" he laughed, coughing and grasping his ribs with a moan of pain. "I've got—a bunch of busted ribs. I'm gonna find somewhere in the low—low section to heal, then I'm getting..." He grunted again. "Getting out of this city. Not cut out for—for bounty hunting. No one—no one tells you about—about damn H-Holders."

I stared at him, wondering if I could risk leaving him alive. I hadn't lied to the woman. I really didn't like killing people. I didn't even like fighting, really. Sometimes, though, they both had to be done. I did my best to avoid both, but when I had no choice, I would do what I had to. This time, though, it wasn't my only option.

I hefted the hammer, then smashed it down on the goblin's leg. He screamed as the bone crumbled beneath the blow, leaving his leg oddly twisted below the knee. I figured that along with his ribs would keep him from going anywhere soon. I flipped the hammer upside down and slammed it into the road beneath me, driving the butt spike between two paving stones. I stomped on it a couple times to drive it in deep, then did the same with the goblin's fallen sword. I retrieved my knife from the fallen orc and slipped it into its sheath, picked up the poster and rolled it up, then left the alley and walked back to the Scrivener's Hall. As I walked in, the woman behind the desk looked up at me, her eyes wide and confused.

"Welcome back," she said uncertainly. "Is this about your order? I can't cancel it, but if you need..."

"I need you to send a messenger to the Watch," I cut her off.

"The—the Watch?" Her eyes grew even wider as she took in my newly unkempt appearance. "W-why?"

"I got attacked by three people in the alley across the street and one block north. Two orcs and a goblin. I left them there for the Watch to pick up."

"You..." She looked me up and down again and swallowed hard. "I'll see to it right away, sir!"

"Thanks."

I turned and headed back out, my good mood ruined. The woman had given me two suggestions, and I'd been planning to head to the Sage's Guild before my—unfortunate episode. Instead, I turned my steps toward the Unity Cathedral. I had a few things I wanted to say to the Unity, and I figured its own house was as good a place to say them as any.

12

Just like the Halls of the big Guilds, the Church of the Unity didn't go for creative expression when building its cathedrals. Each was built of brick and laid out like a perfectly symmetrical eight-pointed star, the symbol of the Unity, only with rounded tips. The roofs of the building arched steeply up about three stories overhead, meeting in the center at a tall, sixty-foot belltower with another star set atop it. The whole thing was sheathed in golden granite and had to have cost the Church as much as all the commoners in this city made in a year to build. Of course, after building it, the Church went to those same people and asked them to give 20% of their income to the church "for the Unity's blessing" without even blinking. The kicker was that the people most likely to give were the ones who could least afford it. Nobles didn't seem to care about the blessings of the Unity, most likely because they probably considered their entire lives to be one.

You might guess that the Unity and I have issues. You don't know the half of it. The Unity—and its damnable Church—took my mom from me, and I'd never forgiven it.

The doors to the cathedral stood open as usual, but not too many people were walking up and down them. I hadn't expected the place to be busy. Services to the Unity were traditionally held at sundown on three-day and an hour after sunrise on seven-day, as I recalled. Not that I'd been since I was a kid and my mom dragged me to them. All I could remember about them was that there was lots of singing, lots of thanking the Unity for things, and lots of the priests begging for money. My mom always gave, even though as a simple weaver and "reformed" gambler, she couldn't really afford much. I can still recall her telling me why she did.

"The Unity deals us all our lot in life, Murf," she explained. "And you always, always tip your dealer."

When the sickness hit her, she'd gone to the Church even more often and gave even more coins to them. If she'd saved those coins, instead, we might have afforded a healer, but that wasn't her nature. She might have left the games behind her, but she was a gambler, through and through, and she'd bet everything on that final hand. In the end, she'd lost that bet and left me busted, without a coin to my name. I'd come up with my first law at the pauper's funeral the Church provided after taking all her coins, looking down at her wasted and sunken face and wanting nothing more than to punch the priest who droned on about the Unity's blessings and balance directly in the face.

Needless to say, the Church and I had never really gotten along after that, and I wasn't expecting anything to change from this visit. I just needed to vent a bit, and who better to vent to than the damn thing that seemed to be screwing with my life? It wasn't like the Unity was listening. I didn't even know if it could listen. For all I knew, the Unity was a machine of some kind, running mindlessly and doing whatever it had been designed to do. Maybe it was a mystical balance of some sort that reacted whenever it shifted too far in one direction or another. Hell, it could be that the Unity was a giant cosmic pig that ate our lives and farted out Labyrinths in return. One explanation was as good as another, really.

I practically stomped up the stairs, ignoring the young felid priestess standing just inside with a silver plate, begging for collections. It was kind of funny when I thought about it: if she'd been a commoner standing on a street somewhere doing that, the Watch would have arrested her. As a priestess doing it in a church, though, not only was she safe pleading for alms, but people seemed happy to give them to her. I swept through the outer gallery and marched into the main chapel, barely glancing around as I tromped up the center aisle. The pews, I noticed, were mostly empty. The stained-glass windows depicting the cards of the noble arcana along with a few I didn't recognize didn't merit the slightest glance from me. I walked directly toward the huge, ornate star adorning the raised dais at the far end, stopped before it, and plopped down into the very front row of pews.

"Listen up, Unity," I growled in a low voice, not bothering to keep my "prayer" silent the way most people did. "Let's be realistic, here. I know you don't much care for me, and honestly, the feeling's mutual. I'm fine with that. I've never asked you for a damn thing, and in return, you've never given me anything. I've always considered that to be a fair relationship between us, and I kind of thought we had an understanding."

I leaned forward and stared hard at the star. "So, why the hell have you been screwing with that lately?" I demanded. "I'll happily admit I'm not a good man, but I'm not a bad one, either. So, what's with all the punishments? First, those asshole elves, then that Labyrinth, and now Ferdi? What did I do to piss you off, and how the hell can I undo it?"

I sighed and rubbed my face, closing my eyes as I continued. "Look, Unity. I'm not asking for your help. I'm not asking for mercy, or blessings, or whatever. We both know that I don't want any cards you might be dealing. I just want to be left the hell alone, to play the hand I've got and make the best of it. Is that so much to ask? Don't give me anything, good or bad, and in return, I won't cause you any problems. That's how we've lived so far, and I'd really like to get back to it."

I looked back up at the damn gleaming golden star, trying to ignore the fact that the very sight of it turned my stomach a bit. "So, what do you say? Can we agree to let bygones be bygones? I won't expect you to pay me back for all the shit you've pulled recently, and in return, you stop giving me more of it. Deal?"

"That's quite the prayer, my son."

I jumped and glanced sideways to see an older male halfling dressed in the white and gold robe of a priest sitting about six feet from me. White streaked his lavender hair, and his face had just started to gain deep wrinkles around his mouth and eyes. His expression was calm, but I felt a sudden twinge of guilt as I looked at him.

"Sorry," I muttered. "I didn't mean any offense."

"Why would I be offended? You weren't talking to me," he said easily.

"No, I meant, I'm sorry if what I said offended your religion. I didn't think anyone was listening."

"You'd be surprised at how many people come in here angry at the Unity," he chuckled quietly. "Something unfortunate has happened to them, or maybe several somethings in a row, and they come in here, demanding that the Unity fix it."

"Does it ever work?" I asked a bit bitterly.

"It's hard to say," he shrugged. "After all, who can say what's the Unity and what's sheer dumb luck? Or is all luck just an expression of the Unity, the way the Absolutists believe? I can tell you, though, that the people coming in here demanding, pleading, or bargaining for the Unity to undo all the bad things in their lives don't really understand it and how it works."

"And you do?"

"More than most, I think. The Unity is all about balance, you see. It's not a purely benevolent force. That means that its blessings have to be accompanied by some curses. Those people forget that."

"Or they understand it perfectly, but they're tired of always getting the curses while the nobles get the blessings," I countered a little heatedly. "Maybe they're tired of seeing their loved ones die of hunger, or disease, or just plain sadness while watching rich merchants ride around in carriages.

Maybe, priest, they just want their own blessings and curses to balance out."

"I suppose that's one way of looking at it," he nodded thoughtfully, seemingly unperturbed by my outburst. "I hadn't considered that, and it does make sense. However, that's just a different form of misunderstanding, isn't it?"

"What do you mean?" I asked waspishly.

"The Unity isn't responsible for everything in our lives. It can't be, or we wouldn't have free will, would we? Some things are no one's fault, like being born into wealth or poverty. Other things are the fault of the imperfect creatures ruling us, like how that wealth and poverty is perpetuated. And some things are simply the result of our own poor decisions—of which we tend to make quite a few."

"Murf's Fourteenth Law," I muttered. "Given two choices, you'll take the dumber one."

"I like that," he laughed. "I might have to incorporate it into my next sermon. It does seem to capture the living condition, doesn't it?"

"That it does," I sighed, rubbing my face. "Thanks for chatting, priest. I appreciate it."

"Well, I wasn't quite finished yet, if you've still got some time to spare," he said encouragingly. "I'd like to talk to you about that prayer you just gave."

"It wasn't really a prayer," I admitted. "It was more of a rant. I'm not naïve enough to think that the Unity's listening—or that anything I say will matter."

"We never know, do we? But prayers aren't just about asking the Unity for things. They're more like conversations. You offer your thoughts to the Unity and hope it responds. That makes that a prayer and a very interesting one."

He tapped on his chin as he gazed at the icon towering over us. "You know, I've been here for a very long time, my son. I've seen every sort of person come in and offer their prayers to the Unity. Most are just mouthing the words they think they're supposed to say, of course. Some thank the Unity for something good that happened; others curse it over something bad. Many plead with it for something they'd like." He looked back at me. "But you're the first person I've ever heard ask just to be left alone, and that intrigues me."

"Like I said, I wasn't trying to be offensive or anything. If it bothered you, I'm sorry."

"I said I was intrigued, not offended. Your prayer actually showed some understanding of the nature of the Unity. You asked for nothing and offered nothing in return. You were willing to accept whatever trials you've endured recently without expectation of some form of balancing repayment, and all you wanted was for the Unity to treat you like you don't exist. To be frank, it was one of the more well-thought-out and balanced prayers I've ever heard uttered." He smiled and looked back at the star. "However, it, too, contains a rather crucial mistake."

"Oh?" I muttered. "And what's that?"

"You were speaking at the Unity, not to it." He smiled as he spoke. "That's a rather common failing, I'm afraid. People talk at the Unity, but they never expect to hear an answer. They never think that the Unity might have a reply for them."

"Has the Unity ever replied to anyone?" I scoffed.

"Oh, yes. It happens all the time. The problem is that most people aren't really listening. They want the answer that they came to hear, and if the response is anything other than a thunderous voice from the clouds giving them that answer, they ignore it." He chuckled. "Most of the time, the answer is a lot more subtle, and you have to be paying attention to notice it—and be willing to take 'No' as an answer." His smile faded into a more intent look. "Are you willing to hear the answer, my son—whatever it might be? Even if it's not what you want? Or did you just want to rage against the universe like a child?"

I stared at him, then up at the altar. I hadn't really come here expecting anything, and I still didn't. That wasn't how the Unity worked, after all. It just did what it wanted, regardless of the people it might be helping or hurting. It didn't respond to people's wants or desires. How could it? There were so many people, and there was just no way to keep them all happy. Some people had to suffer for others to excel. That was simply the way the world worked.

At the same time, it really did feel like the Unity was trying to tell me something the past few days, and if it was, maybe I needed to stop and listen so I could get the message. Otherwise, it might just keep on sending me signals until I finally broke down and paid attention—or I was too dead for it to matter. With a sigh, I lowered my head.

"Fine. I'll listen."

"Not to me, my son." The priest gestured toward the altar. "Go up there and ask it what you want to know. Touch the altar and listen. Maybe it'll answer you."

I grimaced, torn between following his instructions and just getting up and walking the hell out of there. I loathed the Church, hated its priests, and wanted nothing to do with the Unity, after all. Only—he wasn't acting like a normal priest. He hadn't hit me up for money once. He wasn't telling me how benevolent the Unity was and how I just had to trust it. He admitted that the Unity blessed and cursed in equal measure, something I'd never imagined dropping out of a priest's mouth before. And the Unity did seem to be shouting at me lately, trying to get me to listen.

With a sigh, I got up and walked to the huge star. *"Okay, Unity,"* I thought silently, reaching my hand out to touch it, *"what are you trying to tell me?"*

And yelped as something reached up my arm, through my chest, and yanked me down into the very center of my being without so much as a "How are you?" The world vanished, and darkness flooded my vision for a brief instant before the light returned.

I shouted in alarm and jumped backwards, away from the altar—but it wasn't there. I looked around wildly and realized the cathedral was gone. Instead, I stood in the middle of a dark, twisted forest. Leafless trees surrounded me in all directions. The sounds of crows and frogs echoed in the still, moist air. A miasma of rotting vegetation and stagnant water filled my nose. The ground beneath my boots squelched, and my heels sank into soft earth and a carpet of dead leaves with each step.

Not to mention, the whole damn place glowed a greenish-blue color, from the tree trunks to the ground below me and the scudding clouds above. Teal light bathed everything, washing out all other colors. It was eerie as hell, and I wanted to do nothing more than to get the hell out of there.

"Where the fuck am I?" I shouted aloud, spinning around to see nothing but more trees. "Hello?"

"This is your soul," a rich, mellow voice replied, shimmering in the air and seeming to come from everywhere at once. "Or should I say that this is the place you've made for me in your soul? That's somewhat more accurate."

I froze as the shadows left the trees and ran like quicksilver across the ground. The shadows flowed toward a spot about ten feet from me and pooled there, swelling impossibly into a bubble that stuck up away from the ground. The shadows thickened and rose into a solid, inky cone that stood as tall as me. I could only stare in stunned amazement as the cone compressed into a vaguely feminine shape. Colors erupted from within the shadow and spread out to cover the figure, and in a moment, a woman stood before me. She wore a fine if archaic black dress with frills at the neck and sleeves and a tall, pointed hat with a wide brim, again something centuries out of fashion.

She was also the most beautiful woman I'd ever seen. Her face was utterly perfect, with a petite nose, high cheekbones, and a strong chin. Almond-shaped eyes that glowed with turquoise fire peered out at me beneath flowing, wavy locks of hair of the same color. Her figure was a curving hourglass that made my heart beat faster, and I swallowed as her full lips shifted upward into a smile.

"It's nice to meet you, Murf," she purred in the same rich voice I'd heard before.

"Who—who are you?" I managed to stammer even as a dreadful suspicion dawned within me.

"You know who I am, Murf," she laughed pleasantly. "But do you need me to say it? Fine. I'm the Eldritch Hag. Welcome to my card."

13

"Wait, what?" I demanded, taking a step back from her. "You—that can't be! You're just a card. Cards aren't real!" I shook my head, trying to focus my spinning thoughts. "I mean, they aren't people!"

"For the most part, you're right," she nodded. "The Arcana have no awareness to speak of. They simply exist, physical representations of their concept and nothing more. They communicate only in the most basic, fundamental sense, and very few people can understand them." She took a step toward me, and I had to force myself not to retreat.

"There are greater cards than the Arcana, though. The Powers, those above the Arcana, are aware in a sense, and they know who's using them and for what. For some, like the Performers or Supplicants, their consciousness is less than a person's, closer to an animal's. The greatest, the Rulers and Avatars, though, have the same level of intelligence that you do."

"I—what?" I asked, still too confused to follow her. "What the hell are you talking about? Performers? Avatars?"

She sighed and gestured, and the ground between us began to shudder and shake. The earth bubbled upward as roots rose from the soil, and I jumped backward, fearing some sort of attack. The woody tendrils just stretched upward, though, twisting and writhing around as they formed three shapes. I watched in amazement as the roots braided themselves together into what looked suspiciously like a round, flat-topped table flanked by two chairs. When the plants stilled and settled, the woman walked over and sat delicately in one of the chairs, gesturing to the other.

"Come, sit, Murf," she said encouragingly. "We have a great deal to discuss."

"Wait—how did you do that?" I asked suspiciously, looking around. "Do you control all these trees?"

"I'm the Hag, Murf," she laughed merrily. "All magic is within my purview—at least in a limited sense."

"You don't much look like any sort of hag I've ever seen," I muttered.

"You can't blame me for that," she chuckled, looking down at herself. "I look like this because you want me to. If you want me to look old, wizened, and ancient, I can." She patted the table with her hand. "Sit, Murf. I don't bite—at least, not hard—and you have many questions. I have the answers, but you need to stop and get your bearings before you're ready to hear them. That was the point the Unity was trying to make in the cathedral."

"The—the what? You mean, that priest...?"

"The one who just happened to appear the moment you needed him?" she laughed. "Who happened to know the exact words to say to get you to touch the altar? Who never asked you for money and admitted the Unity's ambivalent nature? That priest?" She laughed again, shaking her head. "For someone as perceptive as you are, Murf, you're being awfully obtuse. Yes, he was the Unity—at least, he was a small aspect of it. The Unity sent him to deliver a message that you needed to hear."

"I—the Unity talked to me..." My brain refused to process that information, and I walked almost in a daze over to the table and slumped heavily into the chair. I'd expected it to be hard and lumpy, but the woman—the Hag had made it soft and fairly comfortable. My brain noted that in passing. It was much too busy trying to understand what I'd just heard. It was even too distracted to notice the steaming tea kettle and teal porcelain cups that appeared in the middle of the table.

"Have some tea, Murf," the woman cooed supportively, lifting up the pot and pouring the steaming liquid into the cup in front of me. A plate stacked with sugar cubes appeared as she set the pot down, and she delicately dropped one into my cup. "It'll calm you down."

I lifted the cup and took a sip without thinking, noting absently that the tea was my favorite blend, just the right temperature and perfectly sweetened. "The Unity actually spoke to me!" I breathed in awe. "It—wait a minute." My eyes narrowed as suspicion filled me, and I set the cup down. "Why me? I've never bothered it before. Why would it pick me to talk to?"

"The Unity talks to a lot of people, Murf. Most don't realize it, any more than you did." She made a sour face. "Of course, it doesn't usually take a physical form to do it. It's typically a lot more subtle. You're a special case, though."

"No, I'm not," I shook my head. "At least, I don't want to be! I just want to live my life and play my cards as they're dealt me. I don't want any extra attention!"

"Unfortunately, that choice was taken from you the moment you took me into your soul," she sighed.

"I didn't mean to do that!" I replied heatedly. "It was an accident! I didn't even know you were there until you'd stuck yourself inside me!" I pounded a fist on the table, spilling some of my tea in my sudden pique. "Besides, I'm not the only Holder out there! Why can't the Unity go bother someone else?"

"Because you aren't just a Holder, Murf. You hold a Cabal card, and you have it as your hole card. You literally hold a large chunk of the Unity's power in your soul, and it'll stay there until your death. That means that the Unity's taken an interest in you, whether you like it or not."

"Why does that matter?" I demanded, realizing as I did that I was being petulant. "It wasn't like I asked for this!"

She sighed again and set her cup down. "This is part of what we need to discuss—a big part of it, in fact. For all your talent with mundane cards, you've never bothered to learn a thing about the Unity's deck, have you?"

"No," I shook my head. "I don't care about it."

"Well, now you have to care, Murf, so I'm going to have to teach you." The tea set vanished—although my half-empty cup remained—and instead, a swatch of green felt unrolled across the table. The Hag lifted a hand that suddenly held a deck of cards in it and began to flip them faceup, laying cards out in a row.

"The Unity Deck," she said as the cards from ace through emperor appeared in order. "The physical expression of the Unity's will on this world, and its primary method of enforcing and maintaining balance. Each card is a tiny fragment of the Unity's power, an expression of some truth of the universe given physical form…"

"Truth of the universe?" I interrupted skeptically. "That sounds awfully dramatic."

"It's true, though." She drew a card from the table and held it up to display a card with nine golden goblets on it. "Take this lowly arcana, for example. The nine of cups. As a cup, it represents emotion, connection, adaptability, personality, and the powers of water, ice, and other fluids. As a nine, it grants its wielder the ability to generate an aura that affects and controls some aspect of those things. As a card, it represents the truth that everyone and everything in the Unity is connected, and that the actions of one can generate ripples that spread outward, affecting far more than they intended. A truth of our universe, solidified into this innocuous card."

I stared at the card in utter amazement. "I—I thought they were just magic!" I muttered.

"Most people do. Only some sages and cartomancers truly understand the nature of the Unity's Deck—well, and the few Holders who've taken the time to learn all this. Most don't." She set the card back down.

"The Arcana Deck," she said. "Ten low arcana, ace through ten, and five noble arcana: the knight, lady, prince, queen and emperor. Five suits: coins, blades, cups, staves, and stars. Each suit stands for a set of concepts, and each rank represents a truth within those concepts." She made a face. "Of course, truth is a somewhat flexible concept, and one person's version of truth might vary from another's. That's why the same card can manifest different powers depending on who's holding it."

"The same card can do different things?" I reached down and picked one up, the ace of staves. "Like what? What can this do?"

"Staves represents knowledge, understanding, the power of the mind, and the strength of fire. An ace stands for improvement of its concept. This card for one Holder might make them more intelligent; for another, more perceptive. A third might gain flashes of intuition. A fourth might gain resistance to fire, while a fifth might be able to make flames burn hotter." She shrugged. "The arcana can have widely varying effects, and the lower the rank, the more those can shift. Even two people who gain an intelligence boost from that card might get it in different ways. One might become better at reasoning while the other at making connections or calculating."

She held a hand out over the tableau. "The Arcana Deck is the low deck because the powers it grants tend to be singular, specific, and focused. Even the highest cards, the emperors, merely allow control of a specific part of their suit's domain. An emperor of coins could give someone power over precious metals or the wind, but it'll only give one of those, not both."

She swept up the cards, quickly stacking them, then began to deal them again. This time, though, each card held a different image on it. The first showed a woman kneeling before an angelic figure, while the second showed a winged figure blowing on a trumpet. She laid out nine angelic figures, then began a new row. The first of these was a man dressed in rags, holding out a plate for alms; the next showed a woman dressed in the silks of a dancer. Nine cards, each depicting a person of some sort, and she began a third row. This time, the first card showed a masked figure holding a knife and a bag of coins, while the next displayed a dark figure standing over a woman stretched out on a rack. Seven cards fell after that, each showing something dark, demonic, or evil, and I shuddered as I looked at them.

"The higher deck," she said at last, holding her hands out over the cards. "The Powers. The deck is split into nine tiers—the Supplicant, the Performer, the Guide, the Sage, the Pair, the Priest, the Warrior, the Ruler, and the Avatar, in order of strength—and three secrets: Divine, Worldly, and Infernal. As with the Arcana, each rank denotes some aspect of the greater secret it's part of. However, rather than being concepts of our world, the secrets represent all worlds."

"All worlds?" I echoed, confused. "What do you mean? Is all that pig shit the Church says about angels and demons...?"

"True," she confirmed with a nod. "At least, the core of it is. There are other worlds, divine and infernal, worlds above and below. Divine worlds are ones where the power of creation is stronger than here, where life abounds, and death doesn't exist. Infernal ones are places where the forces of destruction are greater. They're worlds of pain, misery, and death for the most part."

She reached out and touched a card showing a map that looked like our world on it. "This world—our world—is the place where those forces balance out. The Unity maintains that balance between creation and destruction, life and death, and what you'd probably call good and evil, although the forces themselves aren't really moral."

"I don't know." I picked up one of the infernal cards that showed a demonic warrior in spiked plate armor, wielding a jagged-edged sword and surrounded by slaughtered bodies. "This looks pretty evil to me."

"Is war evil?" she asked with a shrug. "Is killing evil? Or is it necessary sometimes? Wouldn't the goblins fighting to keep elves out of their lands think that battle is a good thing?" She leaned toward me. "You killed today, Murf. Those orcs are both going to die without magical healing, and the Watch won't give them that. By now, Urgik is certainly dead, and Dagiza will be within a day. Was it evil of you to kill them, or were you just protecting yourself?"

"I..." I sighed. "Okay, fine. Sometimes, killing is necessary. I get it."

"Exactly. Creation isn't inherently good; destruction isn't inherently evil. Too much of both can be evil, and so can too little of either. That's why the Unity exists: to protect this world from too much or too little of either."

"Why?" I demanded, leaning forward. "Why not, say, less death? Less despair? Wouldn't that be a good thing?"

"Death is a necessity, Murf. In a very real sense, without death, life would become an unending horror. Imagine people too injured to ever heal but unable to die. Suffering from endless starvation because plants and meat both grow inside you when you eat them. The world overrun by every type of living thing because everything grows but nothing dies. That's the reality of a world without death."

I opened my mouth to argue, but I realized that I couldn't. She was right. If nothing died, we could never eat. People would keep being born, but we'd run out of space to live. Plants and trees would overrun the land, destroying anything we built. The whole world would be filled with hunger-maddened beasts and probably people attacking each other savagely but unable to kill or die. It would be nightmarish. If some death was necessary, then there had to be a balance between life and death, and I guessed that was the whole point of the Unity.

"Okay, I get it," I grunted, unhappy but unable to argue. "So, the Unity is about balance."

"Yes, and as I said, the cards are its way of doing that. The Arcana aren't really important and don't add much to the balance overall, but the Powers do. They each represent a fundamental force of creation, destruction, or the balance between. A Holder of one of these cards matters to the Unity. It takes a minor interest in them. Their actions can have profound effects on the world around them and can disturb the balance the Unity has to keep."

She swept the cards up and laid a single one down, the card I'd seen displayed as being my own. "And above the Powers, we have the Cabal," she said with a smile. "Of which I'm a member."

"What about the others?" I asked curiously. "Aren't you going to lay them out, too?"

"I can't," she shrugged. "As Mother of the Deck, I have authority over the Arcana and Powers, so I can show them here. The rest of the Cabal are my equals, though, and I have no power over them. I can't even tell you their names. I can say that we're seven in number, though."

She picked up her card and turned it to face me. "The Arcana are minor truths of this world. The Powers are greater concepts of all worlds. The Cabal, though, are the facets of the Unity itself. Each of us holds some measure of the Unity's power. In my case, I'm the avatar of change and chaos. I'm the expression of the forces of growth, of motion, of randomness and luck." She laughed. "In other words, you and I are rather perfectly suited, Murf! You're a lucky man!"

"I don't feel lucky," I sighed, leaning back and rubbing my face. "In fact, I've had nothing but bad luck since I found you."

"Have you?" she asked, grinning at me with twinkling eyes. "Think about it, Murf. You got dropped into one of the deadliest Labyrinths in the world, and you pretty much just walked out. Sure, you lost some coins in the process, but everyone else who's entered there lost their life. Is that all that unlucky?"

"Well…"

"While Azara tried to hurt you, she didn't really try to kill you," she pressed on. "And despite how mad she is at you, she gave you a reading—and a really impressive one. She's extremely skilled, you know. Most cartomancers couldn't even detect me, much less divine as much as she did about me. She got more than I meant her to. That seems lucky to me."

"I suppose, but…"

"Today, you got attacked by three trained fighters who wanted to kill and mutilate you, Murf. You beat them easily. Now, you've got some experience as a brawler, but fighting three warriors and ending up without a scratch?" She chuckled. "That seems lucky to me."

I frowned. "That—how did I do that? I was hoping to nut the orc, get the other two off me, and run like hell. Instead, I beat them like an orphan in a Unity church. At the end, the woman couldn't even move me around. That shouldn't have been possible!"

"That's the power of being the Holder of the Cabal of Change, Murf," she laughed. "You adapted to that fight. You became resistant to blunt trauma. Your strength grew to the point that was needful. Your perceptions and reflexes sped up to avoid being disemboweled." She leaned back. "You're welcome."

I just stared at her, a little stunned. "So, you did all that?"

"Technically, you did all the fighting. I just gave you the ability to do it. I changed the situation until it was in your favor." Her grin widened. "Still don't think you've been lucky lately?"

"I…" I just looked at her, totally nonplussed for a long moment. "I don't get it. Why me? I'm nobody. Why is this happening to me?"

"First, you aren't nobody, Murf," she said firmly. "You're my Holder. That makes you somebody. The Holder of any Cabal card is powerful and important, and a person with one of the Cabal as their hole card is even more so. Other cards in your deck may come and go as you add, remove, and replace them, but your hole card becomes an integral part of you, and its power reaches out around you whether you like it or not. The Holder of an Arcana affects things near them, usually within their touch; the Holder of a Power changes things in a wider area around them. The Holder of any member of the Cabal can affect the entire world—and I'm the oldest of the Cabal."

I stared at her in disbelief, and her lips thinned. "Don't believe me? Have you heard of the Age of Heroes, Murf?"

"Those legends?" I scoffed. "Of course, I have. Everyone has. The story says that the Unity created champions and gave them the powers of gods. They used those to save the world from some ancient evil and rescue us all. Everyone knows they weren't real, though."

"Well, the stories have been altered over time, but the people were real, and so were their abilities. There was no ancient evil, only a plague of monsters unleashed on the world by a desperate and foolish man. To save the peoples of this world, the Unity created the Cabal and gifted us to exceptional individuals. Those were the heroes of your legends."

"Wait, what?" I gaped at her. "So…Amalis the Elf Mother? Shurmerik the Warleader? Bardona the Huntress? They were real?"

"Yes, but not the way the stories portray them. Amalis wasn't the first elf and mother to the race; she had a Cabal that let her take command of them—all of them, from the smallest babe to the eldest warrior. She forged them into a fighting force, the first true army ever, and used them to slaughter the beasts of ice and snow. Shurmerik the orc wasn't a mighty general; he was a smith and inventor. He gave the orcs, goblins, trolls, and hobs better weapons and armor and discovered how to smelt metal from ore, changing the entire world in the process."

"Hobs? I've never heard of those."

"The elves killed them all," she said simply. "And Bardona was a halfling hunter who fought and killed two extremely powerful beasts, Kewan the Earth Tiger and Garud the Sky Eagle, monsters that threatened to obliterate every living thing on this world. The others existed, too: Tobonoo the Lord Monkey, who accidentally killed off all the beastling species except the avians, canids, felids, and ursids; Gunti the Great Sage, who created the first of the Labyrinths to trap the ravening monsters and ultimately saved the world; Karzak Stormrider, the gobliness who tamed the first horses, cows, and oxen and used them to build the highways that still stand in the goblin lands. All of them held a card of the Cabal, and with our power, they changed the entire world."

She leaned forward and reached across the table, poking me in the chest. "That's why the Unity has taken an interest in you. And that's why you're in terrible danger."

"Because if someone kills me, they can steal you," I sighed, shaking my head as I realized I was basically doomed. "And any Holder can probably sense you, can't they?"

"No, they can't. The Cabal is hidden. No one can sense us except another Holder of a Cabal card, and even then, it's a faint and ephemeral thing. And like Azara said, you aren't so easy to kill anymore, Murf. I can help you survive an awful lot. Besides, while it's true that if someone were to kill you, they'd have a chance to take me, it's not a certainty, and really, the chances are incredibly slim. I can't just be taken, you know. I have to choose to go with someone. Otherwise, I become just another card—and anyone who knows about my existence knows enough not to risk that.

"Which is why that's not the real danger." She leaned back. "Remember those other worlds I talked about, Murf? Well, the Unity doesn't just maintain the balance between them. It shields this world and everyone in it from the forces of those worlds."

"Then the priests really are right. The angels and demons are out there, and they want to kill us."

"They want to consume you," she corrected. "At least, they want to consume this world, and they have agents here working toward that end."

"Agents?" I asked in a guarded tone. "You mean, actual angels and devils walk around the world?"

"No, the Unity locks them out. However, there are always people who covet more power than they have, and the other worlds offer that to them, giving them abilities that don't stem from the Unity but can be just as dangerous and deadly. Zealots are those who draw from the worlds above; warlocks draw power from the worlds below. Both can be as deadly as any Holder, and both would see you as a great prize."

"Why?" I asked a little plaintively.

"Because you hold a piece of the Unity in your soul, Murf, and the other worlds crave the energy the Unity holds. This is a place of magic and great power, far more than the other worlds possess thanks to the balance here. The worlds above and below covet that power. If one gains enough of it, they can use it to destroy the other. Zealots and warlocks are driven by their divine and infernal masters to feed them power, primarily by offering them souls and cards to devour. The Unity in turn works to root them out and shields its power by hiding cards inside Labyrinths, places where divine and infernal power can't reach and thus zealots and warlocks are close to powerless. That's the real reason for Labyrinths, Murf—well, that and to contain the beasts within them so they don't overrun the world."

She shook her head. "We're getting off track here, though. The point is, the other worlds want the Unity's power, and the Unity works to deny them. So long as the balance holds, the divine and infernal have no power here—at least, not enough to matter—and the Unity keeps that balance. That's one reason a Holders of the Cabal is so important. You hold a fundamental aspect of the Unity in your soul, Murf. You can use that power pretty much any way you want. You could help the Unity keep things balanced and shut the other worlds out, or you could work to lean that balance one way or the other. Whatever you choose may change the entire world, and because of that, the agents of the divine and infernal will seek you out and try to bring you to their side. They'll try to get you to shift this world's balance, hoping that you'll deliver the world into their hands."

"What if I don't want anything to do with any of this?" I protested, knowing as I did that I was being kind of whiny but unable to help it. "What if I just want to gamble, meet loose women, and win money in new and exciting places?"

"Those agents won't care what you want, Murf," she said, reaching across the table and resting her hand on mine comfortingly. "They won't care that you just want to gamble, or that you prefer to be left alone. They'll try to bring you to their side—and if they can't, they'll kill you to free me. If they can, they'll take me and give me to someone who's more amenable."

"Fuck!" I screamed, pushing myself up from the table in a sudden rage. "I didn't want this shit! I don't want it! I don't want to be somebody! Go find someone else to fuck with!"

"I can't," she said quietly, her face downcast. "You put me here, even if it was on accident. I can't leave—not without killing you, that is, and the one thing I can't do is harm my Holder. No card can. You can't take me out. Your hole card becomes a part of your soul, and it can't be removed safely any more than your heart and brain can. I'm sorry."

She took a deep breath. "However, you aren't helpless, here, Murf. You're the Holder of a Cabal, and the oldest of those. You're a force to be reckoned with—or you will be one day. You have power and the ability to gain much, much more. If you learn how to use it, you can avoid those agents—or destroy them. You can grow strong enough that the other worlds will leave you alone out of fear of what you might do if they piss you off, knowing that it's smarter to let you die of old age and try to find me when I pop up again. If you get strong enough, you can have your dream: to live the life you want, unbothered by the struggles between the worlds, dying peacefully one day."

"In the arms of a girl a third my age," I muttered.

"I'm sorry, what was that?"

"You forgot part of it. I want to die peacefully in the arms of a girl a third my age—I'm assuming I'll be old by then, obviously." I sighed, taking several deep breaths. I didn't want any of this shit. I didn't want to be stuck in a damn fight between up and down, or left and right, or whatever the hell they were. I didn't want to be the Unity's middle finger jammed up the nostril of those other worlds. Sadly, I'd learned long ago that the world—and the Unity—didn't give a shit what I wanted. I hadn't wanted to be left alone when my mom died, and the Unity hadn't listened then when I'd begged it to keep her around for me. It wasn't about to listen now.

Murf's Thirty-Ninth Law: You'll never be given anything worth getting. The point being that anything you want, you have to make happen yourself. Yeah, there are a lot of laws.

"Okay," I finally said, sitting back down at the table. "So, I have you, now. There's no point in fighting that. The question is: how do I use you? How do I get stronger? And how do I keep people from taking you?"

The smile returned quickly to her face, and I saw the relief flash across it for a moment. "That's the whole reason you're here, Murf: so I can explain that. Everything I said before? That was just background for the real lesson. What you really need to know is this: what makes a Holder, and how do you become a stronger one?" She knocked a fist on the table. "So, let's teach you how to be a Holder!"

14

The table and chairs vanished, but before I could fall on my ass in the mud, a set of vines reached down from above and grabbed me, lifting me gently to my feet. I shook my arms, and they let go quickly, allowing me to stand up and brush myself off a bit. I wasn't really dirty—hell, I didn't know if I was really here—but I was confused, uncertain, and more than a little pissed off, and the simple act made me feel a little better.

"First things first," the Hag said, and I looked over to see her standing about five feet from me, her hands at her sides and her mischievous smile back in place. "What do you think makes a great Holder, Murf?"

"Great cards, I assume," I shrugged. "The better the cards, the better the Holder, right?"

"Actually, that's backwards," she laughed. "Or maybe sideways. A great Holder doesn't always have better cards, but they can—and they can use the ones they have more effectively. And that all comes down to stats."

She waved her hand, and a card appeared in the air before me, as big as a large pillow and easy to read.

> ## Murf
> Rank o None (400/500)
> ### Stats
> Luck: 95   Capacity: 54
> Skill: 29 (+1%)
>
> ### Harmonies (20)
> Coins: 43   Blades: 22
> Cups: 48   Staves: 35
> Stars: 37
> Divine: 66   Worldly: 69
> Infernal: 65

"I remember seeing that before," I said slowly, reading through the card. "Right after I found you, in fact. I didn't get what the hell it was talking about."

"It's not very self-explanatory," she admitted. "The Unity isn't big on explaining. It prefers people figure things out on their own. In this case, though, that's dangerous, so I'll explain it all to you."

She walked over to stand beside the card and laid a hand on top of it. "Every person, Holder or not, has stats like these, Murf. Most people simply go through their lives never knowing what they are or even that they exist. Holders, though, gain the ability to see their stats—and more importantly, to improve them. Higher stats allow a Holder to bind more and better cards to themselves, to create stacks of cards to increase their power, and to meld stacks together to create entirely new cards unique to them."

"Okay, you lost me," I sighed.

"I know. This is all still just the introduction. I'm getting those terms out there so that later, when I mention them, you'll recall that I said them. First, let's go through these stats and what they mean."

"I think I can figure most of them out," I shrugged. "Luck is a measure of—well, of how lucky I am. Capacity is how many cards I can hold, and Skill is—how good I am, I guess?"

"Not really," she laughed. "Although you're close. Luck isn't really about how lucky you are. It's how connected you are to the Unity, and how much you act in accordance with it."

"Then this thing's screwed up," I snorted, pointing to Luck, my highest stat. "Because I am not at all in accordance with the damn Unity! I can barely stand it!"

"Actually, you really are, Murf," she shook her head. "People who worship the Unity, asking it for things, are the ones out of accord. You've always been good at accepting that bad things will happen, and that complaining about them is pointless. What do you always say? You're fine playing the hand that's dealt you. That's a perfect definition of the Unity's existence. The upper and lower worlds deal it a hand, and it does its best to play it in a way that harms the world at large the least.

"Think back to when that priest said that he'd never heard someone just ask to be left alone to live their life without the Unity's help. That priest *was* the Unity. He heard your prayer, and it impressed him enough to actually answer directly. The Unity would like nothing more than everyone in the world to do the same thing: just accept that it's doing its best and stop pestering it for things. Just like you, it has to play the hand it's given."

Her words rocked me, and I considered them silently for a bit. I hadn't made that connection, really. The Unity itself had come and told me it liked my little tantrum. And if its entire job was to keep the other worlds from taking a massive shit all over this one, then not only didn't it care about our little day-to-day problems, it probably couldn't. It couldn't do whatever it wanted, or everything would go to hell—maybe literally. With that being the case, having to listen to people constantly beg it for things it couldn't do had to be beyond annoying. I'd bet it did wish that people would just say, "You go your way, I'll go mine, and let's not talk again."

"I can see that you get it," she nodded. "And you understand why your Luck is so high."

"I do—but why call it Luck? Why not 'Connection' or something?"

"Because the more connected you are to the Unity, the more important you are to it, and thus the more likely it is to use you to affect the balance. People with high Luck are more likely to have unusual things happen to them, especially positive things. Your high Luck and your connectivity to the Unity sometimes combine to give you that sense of how the cards are going to fall and encourage the card you want to be the one drawn. That's the Unity reaching into your life and changing it, Murf." She made a face. "Of course, so was the orc chief walking in on you and his daughter, most likely. The Unity offers blessings and curses in equal measure, you see—if not equally to every person, as you pointed out.

"However, that's not truly why this stat matters to a Holder," she shook her head. "Luck determines in part how powerful a card you can bind to yourself. The more powerful a card is, the more in tune with the Unity you have to be to use it. That's why I said before that someone killing you only has a chance to take me, and not a very good one. If they don't have the Luck that you do, I won't even appear for them."

"In part?" I repeated. "What's the other part?"

"I'll get there, I promise. Let's do this one stat at a time and not get ahead of ourselves, okay?" I nodded reluctantly, and she went on.

"Good. Okay, Capacity is next. In a sense, you're right that Capacity does affect how many cards you can add to your soul deck, but it's not a direct thing. Capacity is a measure of how easy it is for you to add new cards to your deck, not a hard limit. For the average person, adding one card is easy. Adding a second isn't much trouble. A third is painful but doable. It takes a lot of will and pain tolerance to handle more than that. Your Capacity is high enough to easily fit half a dozen cards into your deck, although it'll get harder after that.

"However, what you put in as a hole card can affect that, as well. A low hole card or one that you aren't really suited for will make adding more cards a lot harder. A strong hole card or one that suits you well makes adding more cards easy." She grinned at me. "Like I said, you're a lucky man, Murf."

"Unless I have zero interest in adding more cards," I pointed out. "Which I do. Less than zero, really. Negative one interest, if you want to be precise, since I'd prefer to take you out and go back to my old life. No offense."

"None taken, but the fact is, you're going to have to add more cards if you want to go back to that life one day. That's the surest and best method of getting stronger." She shook her head. "But we're getting ahead again.

"So, Luck is how powerful a card you can handle. Capacity is how many cards you can handle. Skill, therefore, is how good you are at handling cards." I opened my mouth, but she reached out and put her hand over my mouth, stifling me. "Unity cards, Murf. I know. You're great with regular cards." She took her hand away.

"Skill is a measure of how well you can use the powers a card or cards give you. The higher the Skill, the more you'll get out of any given card. A person with a low Luck might have no cards over a three or four, but if their Skill is high enough, those can be as effective as a seven or eight."

She lowered her hand to point to the bottom section of the card. "Which brings us to Harmonies. Luck measures how in accord you are with the Unity overall. The different Harmonies measure how well each suit of Arcana or secret of Powers suits you. If your Harmony in that suit or secret is low, its cards won't work as well for you—or at all, in extreme cases."

"So, wait, you can bind a card that you can't even use?" I asked in disbelief.

"Yes, you can. If the card's Harmony requirements are too far above your stat for its suit or secret, it can work imperfectly, have a totally different effect than intended, or even fail completely." She shrugged. "The Unity doesn't promise anyone anything, after all, and it's not its fault if you don't know what you're putting in your soul deck. Fortunately, you can remove any card other than your hole card from your deck if it turns out you can't use it."

"And if you bind a hole card you don't have the Harmony for?"

"Then you're generally screwed. The hole card affects every other card in your deck, even ones not stacked with it. If the hole card's unstable or nonfunctioning, it could stop the other cards from working. That's why intelligent people don't add a card to their soul deck without knowing what it does, first, Murf—especially their hole card."

"I keep telling you, it wasn't exactly my idea," I reminded her.

"So? Do you think the Unity cares whose fault something was?"

"Not in the least," I sighed. "So, I'll have to have each card I find checked out before I can add it. Any clue how I can do that?"

"Not really. I know the deck, Murf, not how society works." She gave me a friendly smile. "Besides, for the most part, you won't need it. I can tell you the Harmony and Luck requirements for any non-Cabal card in your possession, so you'll never have to worry about binding a card you can't use. That's part of being the Mother of the Deck. I know my own children."

I grunted, slightly mollified. "That's something, I guess. That way, I can ignore cards I can't use—or sell them."

"You could, but just because you can't use a card today doesn't mean you won't be able to eventually. Your stats and harmonies are all somewhat malleable and can increase or decrease with time, practice, and luck. Your Luck and Skill both went up for completing my Labyrinth, and that's one way to improve them. Skill can go up from using your cards, especially if you use them well. Capacity can go up with special types of training. Luck can go up by acting more in accord with the Unity, and Harmony can go up if you're getting more in tune with the concepts of that suit or the powers of that secret."

"So, if I act greedier, my Coins Harmony might rise?"

"More or less, yes. Train with weapons, and your Blades Harmony will go up. Study or hone your mind to improve Staves, and learn cartomancy to boost Stars."

I supposed that meant my Blades Harmony was doomed to stay low, then. I was a lover, not a fighter, as the saying goes. It occurred to me, though, that having a low Harmony in a certain suit wasn't necessarily a bad thing. After all, if that Harmony was low, it was because I wasn't all that interested in whatever that suit represented, so I probably wouldn't want cards from that suit in my soul deck. I'd much rather have a card that helped me read or affect someone's emotions than one that let stab a person in the face a little better.

"What about Rank?" I asked after a moment, pointing to the staggeringly unimpressive zero beneath my name. "What does that mean?"

"It's sort of a way of telling how accomplished you are," she replied dismissively. "It increases when you do something the Unity thinks is important."

"Wait, if I increase it by helping the Unity, why do you sound like it doesn't really matter?"

"I didn't say helpful, I said important. If you do something the Unity thinks really matters, it'll give you Unity Points. The Unity determined that you completing my Labyrinth was important, for example, so it gave you 200 Unity Points for it." She waved a hand before her face like swatting bugs. "Honestly, at the moment, trying to get points is probably the worst thing you could do, so don't worry about it."

"Why? Is being a higher rank a bad thing?"

She made a sour face. "Yes and no. When you increase your Rank, your stats will increase a bit, as well, and your Harmonies may shift slightly. However, it'll also increase card requirements for you—and for the cards you're likely to find."

"That doesn't make sense," I protested. "Why should a card be harder for me to use because I completed a few Labyrinths?"

"Because the higher your Rank, the more you're affecting the world around you," she sighed. "And thus, the more attention the Unity's paying to you. It doesn't want people who are that influential to go around acting against their own natures."

She touched the floating card again. "Assuming nothing else about you changes, Murf, when you go to Rank 1, your Blades Harmony is likely to drop. You just aren't interested in fighting, metalwork, or other things that matter to that suit. The Unity will notice that and make Blades cards harder for you to bind, raising their Luck requirements. It might also make you less likely to run into a Blade card at the same time since you just don't seem to have a need for them.

"On the other hand, your Cups Harmony will probably go up, meaning those cards will be a little easier for you to bind and might pop up around you a bit more. The higher your rank, the more you affect the world, and the more the Unity alters the world to better suit you."

"So, as I rank up, it'll be easier for me to find cards that I can use more effectively? That doesn't sound like a bad thing!"

"It's not. It's a limiting one, though. Just because you aren't a fan of fighting doesn't mean you won't have to do it, Murf." She made a little gesture, and suddenly a card with five gleaming daggers on it appeared in her hand. "Five of Blades. Rank five cards are always about diminishing their suit's effects. In your deck, this card would probably give you a resistance to being injured by weapons. In a set of fives attached to me, that could grow to a near-immunity. Imagine how much easier that fight in the alley would have been if Dagiza's hammer couldn't have hurt you."

She wiggled her fingers, and the card shifted, another dagger swimming into view on its surface. "Sixes, on the other hand, are all about controlling their suit. With this, you might have been able to call your dagger into your hand, freeze Ongru's short sword, or turn Dagiza's hammer back on her." She shifted her fingers again, and all but one of the daggers vanished. "Even with this lowly ace of blades, that punch you gave Ongru might have been extra-powerful and might have knocked him out, or you might have found the hammer easier to use. If that happened, you might have been able to get out of there without killing anyone."

She lowered her hand, and the card vanished. "Eventually, you'll want to specialize, Murf, but first, you need a solid base from which to grow. If your entire deck is nothing but cups, you'll be a master at reading and controlling emotions, but a random bandit with a crossbow could kill you in a heartbeat."

"Can't you just adapt to the crossbow bolt?" I asked archly.

"Absolutely, but I need time to do it. Right now, you and I are about 1% attuned, meaning we're just barely linked, and the frailty of that linkage limits how much power I can send your way. As you use me, our bond will grow, and you can call on more of my power. Eventually, I'll be able to adapt to a sword thrust or arrow the instant they touch you."

"So—I'd be invulnerable?" I asked with a mixture of skepticism and awe.

"No, I'm afraid not. No matter how close we are, there will always be forces out there that can harm you before I can adapt to them. Some of the abilities of the Powers, for example, could cripple or kill you, especially when wielded by someone with much higher rank and stats than you. I can adapt to them, but that won't happen if someone uses the Reaver to rip your heart out of your chest from half a mile away."

I blinked and swallowed hard, and when I spoke, my voice was hoarse. "Someone can do that?"

She nodded. "They can. The Warrior-type Powers all grant incredible combat skills, as the name implies, and they're powerful enough that I'll always need a bit to adapt to them. And I'll never be able to fully adapt to the other members of the Cabal, just as no one of them will ever be able to fully shield against my abilities.

"The point, Murf, is that other cards will help. If you had a defensive power in your deck, something like a Priest or Supplicant, it's likely that

Reaver's attack would only cause you a bit of pain and some minor damage because I could use it to counter the Reaver rather than having to do it all myself. When you add another card to your deck, you see, you link their power to mine, and it's much easier for me to boost and adapt another card's existing power than to create an effect out of nothing. If you've got a five of blades, I don't have to adapt your body to crossbow bolts; I just have to empower the five to get the same effect. The same goes for any card you add: I'll empower every card you bind to me because every card you bind is another power I can use to help you adapt. That's why you need to build out your soul deck; then, you can worry about ranking up and specializing it."

"Fine," I sighed. "Okay, so that tells me what these stats are in general. What exactly do mine mean? Are they good? Bad? A little of both?"

"It depends on what you're comparing them to, really. Stats and harmonies can go as low as 0 with no technical upper limit. Most people have scores at or near zero in just about everything, in fact. That's why they can't bond even an ace: with zero Luck, no cards will connect with you; with zero Capacity, there's no room in your soul to add cards; and with zero Skill, you can't even guide a card into your deck. Harmonies aren't the same; you can still bind a card with which you have no Harmony, it just won't work well for you." She laughed. "Of course, since most people never even see a Unity card, much less touch one, that doesn't matter to them.

"So, yes, compared to the average person, your stats are good. Great, even. Compared to a Holder with moderate rank, though, only your Luck is impressive. Your Skill would be considered decent, but while you've got Harmonies with every suit and secret, they're too low to use the strongest cards."

"Can you be more specific? Like, with a Harmony of 3 in Coins, what rank of cards can I safely bind?"

"That's not how it works, I'm afraid. Each card has its own Harmony, and your Luck and Skill play some part in it, too. You're likely to have lower Harmony with threes or eights, for example, than with fours or sixes. Threes and eights are more combat-oriented in general, while fours are about sensing and feeling, and sixes are, as I said, about control. Even if you struggle to use that three of blades, though, your Skill might overcome that difficulty."

"So, there's just no way to tell if I can use a card until I use it?"

"Not until you actually hold it in your hand, I'm afraid." Her voice turned faintly regretful as she spoke. "As a Cabal card and the Mother of the Deck, I have some control and authority over my children, but it's not unlimited. They're wayward and don't like to cooperate. If you hold a card in your hand, I can tell you how likely it is to work for you and some possible abilities it will grant, but until it's actually in your deck, nothing is certain. I'm sorry."

I sighed. "Fine. So, what's this number '2' next to Harmonies?"

"You gained two Harmonies by completing my Labyrinth. You can add those to any of your existing Harmonies to bump them up by one. It's up to you, but I'd recommend leaving that until you need it." She smiled. "Which brings us to our final topic: stacking cards."

"You mean, putting them on top of each other?" I snorted. "I'm good at that. Shuffling, too."

"Not exactly, no." She gestured, and my stat card disappeared. A moment later, an image appeared instead, one that looked like the surface of a poker table with a single card in the center and four blank spaces surrounding it.

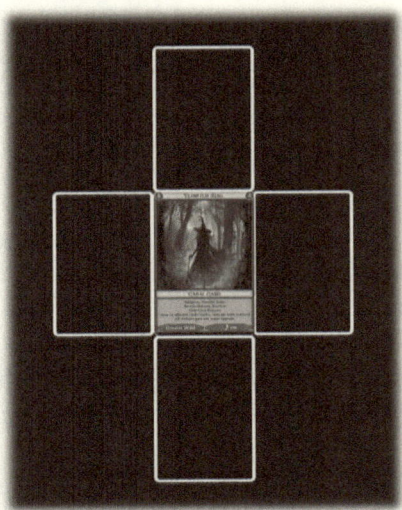

"What's this?" I asked, peering closely at it. The five spaces visible formed a symmetrical cross shape, with the top, bottom, left, and right all empty white rectangles. The center card was definitely familiar; the Hag card stared up at me from the middle of the table, seeming to mock me somehow. The whole thing reminded me of one of Azara's tableaus, except that this one was extremely simple and small. Apparently, that wasn't just a weird coincidence.

"This is your tableau, Murf. It's the layout of your soul deck—at least, the part that you can see. You've actually got an excellent potential layout here."

"It doesn't look like much to me," I scoffed. "It's only five cards!"

"So far, it is. That's because you can't see the farther parts without filling the nearer ones—or learning more about your soul." She touched one of the empty card slots. "Whenever you find a Unity card, Murf, you can add it into a blank slot. When you do, the slots beyond will open up and show you what options you have beyond that card. You might have a single slot beyond it; you might place a card and find that nothing opens; you might unlock two or three more card slots. There's no way to know until you place a card, although the higher your Capacity, the more likely you are to have multiple slots open up—for obvious reasons.

"The reason this matters," she continued, "is that cards placed next to one another can stack together, creating a more powerful effect." She smiled at me. "This part should feel familiar to you. An Emperor is nice to have in your hand, but a 2-set of aces is better, and a run or flush are both much better."

My eyes widened slightly as I got what she was saying. "You mean, if I put a run of cards all together, that's different than just putting random cards into those spots?"

"Not just different; better. You're not just building a deck; you're building hands within that deck, and those hands can play off one another—and off me. You aren't limited to five cards, either, or to just the cards in a normal deck. You can build a run that's ten cards long, or a set of seven or eight of the same rank. There are even wild Unity cards out there that you can use to extend your stacks or even link them together." She shrugged. "You can build any hand you like, but the better the hand, the more powerful each card in it will be, and the stronger your deck overall will become.

"And that isn't just for the Arcana," she added. "You can match ranks of Powers together, too; build a hand made up of all one secret; or make a run of Powers, and they'll all be stronger than randomly mixing Powers together."

"So, basically, the idea is to gain cards that can match together and add them to my soul deck," I said slowly. "Wait, what about the Cabal? You aren't an Arcana or a Power. Can you stack with anything?"

"I can stack with *everything*," she laughed. "We Cabal are wild cards of a sort, Murf. We can attach to any stack and make it stronger. Plus, I have a unique ability: I can take the place of any Arcana or Power in the stack, of any rank, suit, tier, or secret. If you find two avatars, one divine and one infernal, for example, I can take the place of the Worldly avatar to give you an alliance of avatars, a very, very powerful stack."

"Does it have to be three cards?" I asked.

"You can make a 2-set, but it's not much better than having the original cards. Runs have to be at least three cards long, though, flushes four, and flush runs five. For Powers, it's different: Powers can only be stacked in sets of three for balance."

"What about stacking Cabal cards?" I asked curiously. "Can you do that?"

"I'm afraid I can't answer that, as it's a question about the rest of the Cabal," she sighed. "If you find more of them, though, you can always try and see!"

I snorted. "Right. Like I'm going to find another card as powerful as you—or even one of those Powers. I've never seen a Unity Card that wasn't an Arcana before."

She grimaced. "That's the last thing we need to talk about, Murf. This is something that Azara told you but that you've kind of ignored. As the Eldritch Hag, not only do I have a role in the Unity Deck, I have one in the Cabal, as well. There, I'm the Mother of the Decks, the matriarch of all the cards. I drive my children to leave the nest and wander the world, but they always return to me eventually."

"I remember she said something like that," I nodded. "I'm not sure what it means, though."

"It means that I draw other cards to me. The weaker ones, the least of my children, flock around my skirts, often so thickly I have trouble moving about." She laughed. "Even my greater children will find their way to me, though, one way or the other."

"Okay, but what does that mean?" I pressed. "Exactly? Without all the metaphors about being a mommy?"

She sighed. "It means that cards will find their way to you, Murf. Their Holders will feel drawn to you without knowing why. Labyrinths will appear around you, and even ones that are constantly farmed for cards might drop a higher-ranked one, or even a Power when you complete it. You might even find yourself being drawn toward those places, especially if no one's completed them in a while."

"Wait, you're going to send me into Labyrinths?" I half-shouted, taking a couple steps back from her. "Not only no, but hell-fucking-kiss-my-ass-Unity-no!"

"I can't control you, Murf. None of us can. The Unity gives all people free will, and as part of it, I have to respect that. However, it's my nature to nudge you toward my children." She made a sorrowful face that I didn't buy for a second. "I can't help it, any more than I can keep them from finding me. It's going to happen. You're going to find yourself at odds with other Holders. You're going to stumble over Labyrinths. You're going to attract cards like a carcass attracts flies. You might even encounter more of the Cabal."

"That's not likely, though, is it?" I ran a hand nervously through my hair. "I mean, you're the only one of your kind, right? And I'll bet the other Cabal cards are the same. I'm sure people snatched them up centuries ago and keep them hidden away in their soul decks—or locked up in some king's treasure vault or something."

"It doesn't work that way," she shook her head. "You can lock up Arcana like that, yes, but Powers and the Cabal aren't just objects, Murf. We have our own awareness and our own needs. We exist to be used, not squirreled away in a dusty vault somewhere. People have tried to lock me up before, and when they do..." She shrugged. "I leave."

"What do you mean, you leave? You're nothing but a card!"

"Nothing but a card?" she echoed, her eyes flaring brilliant teal for a moment. "I'm a piece of the force that guides all creation!" She rose into the air as a sudden wind whipped around us, tearing at my clothes and threatening to rip the hat from my head. The trees began to wail and moan, thrashing their limbs about madly, and turquoise lightning streaked from the sky in blazing forks. The earth shook and rumbled beneath me, vibrating so hard that I fell onto my ass. I scrambled back from the woman as fire exploded from her body and swirled around her like a blue-green tornado.

"I AM THE PRIMAL FORCE OF CHAOS," she said, her voice booming in my ears and forcing me to cover them to keep from going deaf even as she grew and swelled into immensity, towering high above me like a pillar of fire. "I AM THE BRINGER OF CHANGE, THE MISTRESS OF GROWTH, AND THE MOTHER OF THE DECKS! I AM THE ELDRITCH HAG, ELDEST OF THE CABAL! NEVER DISMISS MY POWER, FOR I CAN DESTROY WITH A THOUGHT!"

"All right!" I shouted over the wind. "All right! I won't! I promise!" The piss had been quite thoroughly scared out of me. I was definitely taking her seriously at that point!

"Good." Instantly, the wind died, the earth stilled, and the trees fell silent. The fire around the Hag winked out, and she shrank to normal size in an instant. Her roguish smile reappeared as she walked over to me and offered her hand. I hesitated before taking it, then let her haul me back to my feet. She laid her hand on my chest, looking intently into my eyes.

"I and my brethren of the Cabal will not be used however someone wishes, Murf," she said quietly. "We have our own desires and needs, and our Holders have to respect those or suffer the consequences. I chose you because I felt the compatibility of your soul. I sensed the Harmony between us. We can do wonderful, magnificent things together—but I won't be disrespected, and I won't be ignored. In return, I'll respect your free will and never ignore your needs, either. Is it a deal?"

"Yeah," I panted, my heart still hammering in fright. "It's a deal."

"Good. Then go, find cards, and get stronger. Just accept that those cards will find you, as well—and there's nothing either of us can do about it."

She shoved me, and I took a step back, blinking as the teal light vanished and I found myself back in the cathedral, standing a couple steps back from the star. My hand tingled from where it had touched the icon, but I seemed otherwise unharmed. I looked around quickly. The halfling priest was gone, leaving my pew empty. A woman in somewhat ragged clothing a few pews back was looking at me a little strangely, but no one else seemed to be watching me. I assumed that meant I hadn't been standing there for too long.

"Did that even happen?" I wondered silently, staring at my hand. *"Or did I have some kind of hallucination? Maybe that orc slammed my head into the wall harder than I thought."*

I stared at the star, then shook my head. If it had been a hallucination, it was an especially vivid one. More to the point, it was an awfully explanatory one, and it gave me a ton of information I seriously needed. I had to assume it was real, and that all it had told me about what my stats meant, how to stack cards, the other worlds out there, and how to use my card...

I froze as it occurred to me: the bitch hadn't told me how to use her! I still had no idea how to use my own damn card! I stepped forward and placed my hand on the star again, intending to hop back into myself and give her a piece of my mind. Of course, nothing happened, and I found myself standing there, touching the damn Unity star and looking like an idiot. Apparently, the hag had said all she intended to say. Maybe if I hadn't pissed her off, she'd have given me more instructions, but as it was, I could only think of Azara's advice. If I wanted to know more about being a Holder, I'd need to talk to one.

I wiped my suddenly sweaty forehead as I considered my choices and spun quickly, striding out of the cathedral as fast as I could without risking running anyone over. I needed a Holder, and the Hag wanted cards. Fine. I knew a couple elves who had quite a few of them, some of which were mine. I wanted them back, so we'd both be getting what we wanted. The problem was, even with my new card, I didn't think I was a match for two professional sellswords who were Holders themselves. I needed a warrior of my own, one I could sort of trust, one who had a stake in getting those cards back, and one who was also a Holder and could maybe give me some advice.

That left me one very unpleasant option. I needed to go see Ferdi. But first, I needed a thrice-damned drink.

15

"You're an idiot, Murf, and you're going to get yourself killed!"

Eegla's words rang in my skull as I headed south through the city, winding about a bit and keeping a sharp eye out around me. She was probably right. I was kind of an idiot. And one day, it was probably going to kill me. About all I could do was my best to make sure today wasn't the day. Tomorrow might be a different story, but that was a problem for tomorrow's Murf. Today's had a mission: keep my genitals firmly attached to my body. That should have been a low bar, but all things considered, there was a good chance it was out of reach.

Eegla hadn't wanted me to go find Ferdi, for obvious reasons.

"I have to get those cards back, Eegla," I explained. "And I don't want to go messing with two Holders—sellsword Holders, at that—without some muscle on my side. They don't get much more muscular than Ferdi. She eats worse things than those elves for breakfast. I should know. I've actually seen it happen."

"Fine, but she'll be having you for dinner," the goblin pointed out. "Why not just hire some sellswords of your own?"

"Because I can't afford to hire Holders, and non-Holders wouldn't take the job. Plus, they're sellswords, Eegla. By their very definition, they can be bought. I don't want the elves buying them right out from under me."

"The Guild wouldn't allow that, and you know it."

"Assuming I was alive to tell the Guild about it, which I wouldn't be, would I?"

"…Good point."

"Anyway, the elves have Ferdi's cards. She wants them back." I shrugged. "Hopefully, she wants them back more than she wants to emasculate me."

"What if she decides that she wants both?"

"Then I'll quit gambling and join a soprano choir, I guess."

"I can't wait to hear you sing."

Despite Eegla's rather gloomy predictions, she gave me directions to the Baargoth hold down in the southeastern section of the city. I headed out—after three shots of bourbon, just for confidence, mind you. To my surprise, while the liquor got me faintly tipsy, within ten minutes or so, the feeling vanished. I muttered under my breath as I walked, grumbling about cheating bartenders handing out watered alcohol—at least, until a card popped up in my vision.

> Adaptive Ability
> Your body has adapted to the mild
> toxin "alcohol" and will suffer no
> further ill effects from it.

After I slapped the card away, I switched from complaining about bartenders to complaining about treacherous chunks of the Unity that stole my buzz. I didn't complain too loudly, though. I remembered the Hag's unleashed power just fine. I had no intention of pissing her off. At least, not too much.

The southeastern section of Canis isn't the nicest place in the world, but it's not the worst I'd ever been, either. That was a little section in the orcish city of Grosh affectionately called "Hell's Taint". It smelled like the name, and I'd only gotten a hundred feet or so into it before three orcs burst through a wall in front of me, stabbing each other with knives and rolling into the muddy, shit-covered street. I was pretty sure that all that crap wasn't good for knife wounds, but the orcs didn't seem to care. Neither did the crowd that rushed out after them, screaming bets on the outcome. I didn't see how it ended since I turned around and walked the hell out of there, then out of Grosh completely when I heard later on that the knife fight turned into a full-on riot that left a large chunk of the city looted, destroyed, and burned to the ground. Orc cities leave a lot to be desired. Goblin ones are nice, though, so when you're in southern Shuria, I highly recommend sticking to those.

Canis, though, was a pretty nice city, all things considered, and its poorer sections weren't as bad as they could have been. The ever-practical canids had put the river running through the city to good use by digging a sewer system that emptied into it, so at least the place didn't smell horrible. I didn't want to go around sniffing the gutters or anything, but it wasn't awful. The houses were small, wood, and built closely together. Trash littered the alleys and piled up in the side streets, but the main roads were mostly clear. The people walking by were mainly common laborers, people who made enough to be able to afford a room but not to be able to move farther north, and at this point in the day, they trudged along tiredly. That made the streets fairly quiet.

There were also a surprising lack of thieves, pickpockets, and whores, but after a bit of thought, that made sense. The people here didn't have any money to steal or spend on women. Those folks probably plied their trades a bit north, in the mid-city areas. Too far north, and the Watch became more vigilant, potential victims carried weapons and had bodyguards, and they'd be likely to kill a thief rather than have them arrested. Plus, the men there could afford actual mistresses and didn't need prostitutes. In the mid-city, though, people had money but not much power. A tradesman whose purse was snatched would chase and call the Watch, but if they caught the thief, they'd just give them a beating and turn them over to be arrested. And there were plenty of lonely artisans looking for brief and affordable companionship. If I were a whore, that was certainly where I'd be.

Baargoth Hold was something of an oasis in the section. If you've never seen a halfling hold, the important thing to know is that the halflings came from western Palla, which is a hot, fetid jungle filled with disease, poisonous frogs and snakes, and bugs that burrow under a person's skin to lay eggs. I'm not kidding; that's a real thing, there. There's a bug called a fleshtunneler that creeps up under your clothing, numbs you so you can't feel what it's doing, then digs its way under your skin to eat and lay eggs. The only way to get them out is to cut out the bug and burn the wound; otherwise, you'll end up with fleshtunneler larvae hatching inside you and digging deeper into your body. At that point, the safest way to get rid of them is to amputate the affected appendage.

Needless to say, having a fleshtunneler in your underwear is not a happy circumstance. Not that it's happened to me, but I can't imagine it's a good thing. Healing cards can only do so much.

All of these are good reasons why instead of trying to live in those jungles, the halflings got the hell out of there and headed up the western slopes of the Pallor Mountains. Sadly, the monsters of the jungles tried to follow them, so the halflings cut stone from the mountains and built walls and towers to protect themselves. Elves say that they have a warrior culture, but most of that is for show. The halflings spent the first couple millennia of their existence fighting daily for their survival as a species, and it shows. Even elven warlords and orc berserkers walk carefully around an oath-bound halfling warrior.

From these holds, the halflings slowly pacified the jungles, avoiding fleshtunnelers in their various crotches as much as possible, working their way out to the sea. They never lost their love of walls and towers, though, and halfling cities are always tall things built of stone with very little exposed wood. This does tend to make them hard to burn down, which is a good thing. Of course, since most of them are built on marshy shorelines close to rivers where the ground is soft, those cities are all slowly sinking into the earth. That doesn't bother the halflings, though, since they can just keep hauling stone from the mountains and building higher as each layer of their city vanishes beneath the mud.

Stubborn people, halflings. Once they get an idea in their heads, it can be very hard to get them to let it go.

Thanks to this stubbornness, in the midst of short, rundown wooden buildings crammed together and looking like a major fire hazard, a stone tower rose high above the ground. A ten-foot wall of the same material surrounded it, with a wide street running around the exterior of the wall so that people couldn't just climb off a roof into the compound beyond. Smaller watchtowers stood at the corners of the wall, overhanging the street so that the archers inside could target anyone huddled against the wall. A bronze gate pierced the wall, and two armored halflings stood beside it, carefully watching everyone who passed. The Hold was an armed compound, for all intents and purposes, a fortress in the middle of the poorer part of the city, and the guards looked like they suspected everyone around of being potential invaders. Which, considering how much wealth that gate alone represented, might have been a realistic possibility. A ten-foot wall wasn't really that high, and desperate people do desperate things.

For example, what I was doing right then.

I stood in the shadows of a nearby alley and gazed at the compound, wondering what the hell I was doing. I didn't technically have to do this, after all. Maybe the Sage's Guild could tell me more about how to use my card without needing to know what it was or killing me to get it. Maybe I could win enough to buy some cards from the Scribblers, including replacements for Ferdi's, and she'd never know the difference. And maybe the sky would open, and gold crowns would start raining on my head, dumped from the clouds by a pair of beautiful women who found me irresistible and didn't mind sharing. All of those things seemed equally likely.

I sighed and took a step forward, only to freeze as something sharp jammed into my back, just behind my heart.

"Don't move," a cold voice said in a tone that brooked no argument. "Lift your hands and place them atop your head."

"That'll mess up my hat!" I protested.

"If you don't, your hat will be by far the least of your worries." The sharp object poked me again. "And this lance will be the greatest. Lift your hands, now."

Sighing, I lifted my hands and placed them as gently as possible on my hat. A moment later, strong hands grabbed me and shoved me against the closest wall before ruffling through my coat. As the hand slipped down into my pockets, I jumped slightly.

"Hey! At least have the courtesy to buy me dinner, first! A man likes to be wooed!"

"I have no interest in your genitals, human," the voice said emotionlessly. "Ferdi has prior claim on them, in any case." The hand slid my knife from its sheath and took the deck I always carried around from my pocket.

"Those are just regular cards," I protested.

"We'll see." The hands released me. "You can lower your hands, now, but move slowly, human. Very slowly."

I dropped my hands and felt the man behind me grab them roughly and bind them tightly together. Once my wrists were secure, he grasped my arms and pulled me ungently away from the wall, turning me around to face a halfling woman with pale orange hair pulled into a braid that rested atop her head in a cone-shaped spike. She held a long, heavy lance tucked under her armpit with a sharp, piercing spike at the end pointing directly at my chest. I swallowed as I saw her mount; halfling cavalry rarely rode horses or ponies and had instead domesticated giant jungle cats for use as mounts. The striped creature's head came up to just below my chin, and its powerful fangs looked like they could rip off one of my limbs without trying. In case that didn't kill me, it had claws as long as my middle finger as well. Even if I'd had a mind to run, this thing could catch me in no time and turn me into a light snack at its leisure.

"You are the human named Murf?" the woman said in a cold voice, her features flat as she looked at me.

"Aren't you sure?" I asked curiously, flexing my arms slightly. "You've already assaulted me and tied me up. It seems like you should have asked that first, shouldn't you?"

"Your identity is known, human. You've been watched and followed since the moment you entered this city. I'm simply trying to extend you the most basic courtesy." She lifted her lance suggestively. "Your presence is demanded within the Hold. You will come with us quietly and calmly."

"What if I don't? I think Ferdi will be upset if you kill me."

"She would, which is why I won't kill you. If you cause trouble, I'll remove your feet, and Garris will drag you." Her voice was ice as she spoke, and I swallowed hard in response.

"That seems a little unnecessary."

"You've been declared an Oath-breaker by one of the Oath-bound. You deserve worse. Now, walk."

The man behind me shoved me forward, gripping my elbow, and I stumbled to keep from falling. I let the man push me across the street, waited as the door guards signaled for the gate to be opened, then staggered inside. I almost fell as I found myself face-to-face with another of the tiger-mounted warriors, this one a man holding a wide-bladed spear.

"This is him?" the man asked as the guy behind me shoved me through the gate.

"So Elima says," my captor replied. "She's been following him, so I assume she knows."

The mounted warrior grunted. "They all look alike to me." He glared at me. "You are the human known as Murf?"

"You people keep asking that as if you're not sure," I muttered. "I really wish you'd figure out who you're kidnapping before you do it."

"We're certain. At least, Elima is, and she was posted to watch you." The mounted man leveled his spear at me. "Within this Hold, human, you will follow all orders and remain docile. If not…"

"Yeah, yeah, I know," I sighed. "Off with my feet. Look, I actually came here looking to speak to Ferdi. This isn't necessary."

"You think to turn yourself in to claim the bounty?" His eyes narrowed. "While that would be unorthodox, technically, the offer doesn't forbid it."

"No, I…" I paused. "Wait, you think that I'd come here to get my nuts cut off for a few silvers? Seriously?"

The man shrugged. "Humans are often foolish and greedy. I wouldn't be surprised." He spoke a few words in the high, trilling halfling tongue that reminded me of birdsong, and my wrists suddenly came free as the man behind me cut through my bindings. I lifted my hands and rubbed at my wrists, wincing as feeling began to return to my fingers and giving the mounted man a questioning look.

"You came here of your own free will to face your fate. That shows at least some honor. In turn, I'm giving you the chance to show your intentions by letting you walk freely." His face darkened. "Don't abuse my offer of trust, human, or you'll be thanking Ferdi for what she intends to do to you. Understood?"

"Yeah," I said. "I got it."

"Good. Follow Garris. Cause no trouble, and don't try to escape."

"This way, human," the man who'd been shoving me said in a flat voice, stepping in front of me and walking through the gate. I followed him quickly, not wanting the halfling to think that I might be considering trying to get away.

The gate opened into a small courtyard that encircled the main building. Halflings moved through it, some armed and armored. Others dressed in typical halfling fashion, with brightly colored layers of thin, almost gauzy clothing. Men and women both wore long sleeves and pants that clung tightly to their bodies, almost like a second skin of clothing. I didn't know much about fashion, human or halfling, but I had to admit that seeing a bunch of women wandering around in translucent clothing wasn't the worst thing in the world. Of course, the men wore the same thing, which I didn't find quite as enjoyable. Plus, I wasn't exactly a welcome guest here, so I did my best to keep my eyes where they belonged. If I just happened to glimpse a few female posteriors barely hidden beneath a few layers of fabric, well, that was simply accidental. Absolutely.

My guide led me through another wall, this one flanked by a pair of towers, and into the stone building beyond. I had to duck slightly as we stepped into the Hold proper; the ceilings were made for halflings, not for me, after all. The hallways inside were short, narrow, and turned often, which I supposed made them easier to defend. Oil lamps hung in every corner to light the passages, and some sort of rush matting covered the floors, muffling our footsteps. I followed the silent man through the halls, squeezing past halflings that gave us curious looks but didn't ask questions as we passed. At last, we trudged up a flight of circular stairs that I assumed led into one of the towers. The steps ended at a wooden door banded with iron that looked like it'd be hard to break down but that had a lock so simple I could probably pick it with my fingernail. The man knocked on the door, and a voice from the other side spoke in the trilling halfling tongue for a moment before the door opened.

A young woman with dark brown skin framed by thin lavender braids stood in the doorway. She looked up at me with an expression of barely concealed contempt, then looked at my guide and spoke in Halfling for a few moments. He answered her tersely, and she stepped back, pulling open the door.

"Enter, human," she said in a cold voice, gesturing to the room beyond. I stepped past my guide and tried not to wince as the woman slammed the door shut behind me. I looked around and realized that this was some sort of antechamber or receiving room. It was small, only about fifteen by fifteen, and the only decorations were two sets of halfling-sized wooden chairs placed around an oblong table. The narrow end of the table had the most ornate chair and faced another door, and the woman walked ahead of me toward that. I couldn't help but admire the way the thin, sheer fabric barely covered her ass as she moved while concealing practically nothing, even though I knew staring at her backside was probably a bad idea. It occurred to me that it might be the last ass I ever got the chance to see, so I resolved to get as good a look as possible. Plus, the sight helped me ignore the rising panic growing inside me.

The woman stopped at the door and knocked, calling out in her language. A slightly deeper voice replied, and the woman pushed open the door, revealing a larger room beyond.

"Enter, human," she said in the same frosty voice, and I swallowed as the fear bubbled up inside me. I took a deep breath, then quite deliberately looked down at the woman, examining her barely hidden body in careful detail. She stared at me with a flat expression, ignoring my wandering eyes.

"Get in here, Murf," the deeper voice spoke from the next room. "Dawdling will only make it worse."

"Not sure that's possible," I muttered. I swallowed hard and stepped forward into the room beyond and whatever fate awaited me. I seriously hoped the hag had been right about my luck. I was absolutely going to need it.

16

The door shut firmly behind me with a loud click that might have been ominous if I didn't know how crappy the locks were. The room beyond wasn't precisely what I'd been expecting. I'd figured Ferdi's personal space would be neat, tidy, and organized. I assumed it would be filled with the tools of her trade: racks of weapons, stands full of armor, practice dummies for training, and the like. I also would have guessed that she slept on a hard, wooden cot to keep her tough, perhaps even a bed of actual nails or broken glass. If you knew Ferdi, you wouldn't have been surprised to see that, either.

Instead, the room was rather messy and surprisingly feminine. Curtains of pale green sitria, the same fabric that halflings made their clothing from, hung from the walls, unevenly framing paintings of various flowers and brightly colored birds. A thick green rug covered the floor instead of rush mats, rumpled and stained with what I hoped was gravy. Clothing lay tossed in piles all about, and an actual bed stood off to one side, soft-looking and with emerald-colored blankets strewn carelessly across it. It looked like no one had cleaned this place in some time; fortunately, thanks to the open window off to the side, it didn't smell like it. At least, not much.

I got a solid glimpse of all that before what felt like a sledgehammer wielded by a troll on horseback smashed into my stomach. I literally flew back, knocked off my feet by the blow, and crashed into the door behind me. Vomit sprayed from my mouth as the impact disgorged the drinks I'd had earlier, and my head swung back to crack loudly against the wooden frame hard enough to fill my vision with stars and make my brain decide that maybe it needed to step back for a second or two. I slumped toward the floor, but before I could reach it, something grabbed my throat and slammed me back into the door, pinning me solidly in place.

"You're braver than I thought, Murf," a voice said calmly. "Or a lot stupider. I can't decide which."

"Definitely stupid," I muttered, trying desperately to focus my eyes. At the moment, they seemed to want to work independently of one another, one drifting to the left while the other kept turning toward the floor. As I spoke, the hand around my throat tightened, and I coughed as a steel band seemed to cut off my breath.

"That's most likely," the voice agreed. "Not that it matters." The arm tensed, and I suddenly felt myself flying through the air. I arced up like a tossed stone, soaring for a full second or so before I slammed into something much harder than my poor back. My head cracked into something again, but this time, the impact didn't jar my brain quite as much. I crashed in a heap to the ground, but I managed to scramble to my hands and knees. Unfortunately, that just made it easier for the monster attacking me to smash something into my ribs and launch me back into the same way-too-hard surface. Something grabbed me again, and I once more found myself floating in the air for a blissful moment before I crashed into the floor and rolled across the room.

The landing this time barely even fazed me, though, allowing me to push myself up into a sitting position. My eyes regained their focus, and they settled on a figure standing across the room. Ferdi was tall for a halfling, only a few inches short of five feet, and built like a stone wall, with calloused hands and broad shoulders. Light blue armor made of overlapping plates covered her body, leaving only her hands and tanned face exposed. Her blue eyes glared at me like twin sapphires below the blonde braids of hair coiled atop her wide head. The wooden haft of her battle axe jutted up above her left shoulder where she could easily grab it.

A strange sensation flowed over me as I looked at her. I'd seen Ferdi hundreds of times, and I knew her pretty well—at least, I used to. She was a delver, a person who ran Labyrinths for a living. She was tough as nails, had literally no sense of humor—I'd never met a halfling with one, in fact—and was loyal to a fault. She was also a Holder, as most delvers tended to be. I'd always known that in an abstract way, but now, as I took in the sight of her, I could feel the cards within her. They practically screamed in my sight, and as I gazed at her, a new card flashed into my vision.

Ferdi
Rank 2 Delver
Luck: 41   Capacity: 53   Skill: 57
Hole Card: 6 of Blades
Likely Powers: Weapon Skills,
Animate Weapon, Earth Control

"Hey, Ferdi," I groaned, rubbing my aching ribs and waving away the card, which was surprising but just a distraction at the moment. "Nice to see you, too. Been a while, hasn't it?"

Her response was to blur slightly. I'd always known that Ferdi was strong and fast, but I don't think I'd ever really realized just how strong and fast she was. I realized it at that moment as she just kind of appeared beside me. My vision spun as her fist slammed into the side of my skull, knocking me down. Fortunately, she wasn't using her full strength, or that hit would probably have fractured my skull.

Instead, I crashed to the floor, spitting blood from busted lips, but before I could pick myself up, her foot knocked me into my back and pressed against my neck and throat, once more cutting off my wind.

"You betrayed me, Murf," she said in a voice like stone. She bent down and crashed her fist into my stomach, the blow curling me up and making me groan loudly. "You lied to me." Another hammer-like fist blow dropped, this time into my side, making my ribs creak. "You stole from me." Wham! "And worst of all, you broke your oath to me!" Wham!

As her fists fell, I couldn't help but notice that the pain of each blow lessened substantially. The kick that had greeted me literally knocked the liquor out of me and unfocused my brain. Her second one stunned me a bit. The punch to the face hurt, but it probably should have cracked my jaw and dislodged a tooth or two. Her last punch certainly hurt, but Ferdi hit like a blacksmith working on a stubborn piece of metal. My ribcage should have collapsed beneath her blows or at least cracked in a few places. It creaked and groaned, but it felt intact, and in fact, the pain of her earlier blows slowly drained away as the seconds passed. I wondered for a moment if that meant I was passing out—part of me hoped that was the case—but my brain quickly reminded me that this was probably my adaptation thing. As soon as I thought it, the Hag apparently felt the need to confirm it by flashing a card in front of me.

> Adaptive Ability
> Your body has adapted to blunt trauma damage and will receive less injury from this damage type!
>
> Needful Body
> You have gained temporary additional strength and healing.

Part of me wondered if that adaptation was permanent. After all, the ability said the more exposure I got to something, the longer it lasted. This beating felt like at least a year or two worth of regular pummeling. Would I always take less damage from, say, a bottle to the skull from now on? That was an ability I could have used a few times in bar fights. Someone in those always decided to pick up a bottle and start cracking people in the head with it. I think they expected the bottle to break in some dramatic fashion, but in my experience, it was usually the skull that gave way first. The same was true for getting hit in the back with a chair. Unless the chair was built really badly, it usually held up fine, and my spine was what suffered from the impact.

That was a concern for the Murf of a later time, though. The Murf of that moment was taking less damage from each of Ferdi's blows—although they still hurt, unlike that orc woman's attacks that I'd been able to totally shrug off—and soon, she'd realize that. At that point, she'd probably switch to her axe. I needed to get her to stop hitting and start talking, and the first step was to get her to stop standing on my damn throat.

I reached up and grabbed her ankle with both hands, then lifted and shoved, twisting my upper body to try and get some extra power. Ferdi was stronger and faster than any person had a right to be, but she was also a halfling. No matter how solid she was, she wasn't all that heavy, even with twenty or thirty pounds of armor strapped to her body. She'd braced herself well, but she just didn't have the mass to hold me in place if I really wanted to get out. All I had to do was lift her foot up a couple inches and shift her balance, and I'd be able to scramble out from beneath her boot and hopefully stand up. Maybe then, she'd actually listen instead of punching me. Although that felt like a big, big maybe.

That wasn't exactly what happened. When I shoved Ferdi's foot, I hadn't really taken that extra strength the Hag mentioned into account. Instead of her tipping a little backwards, her foot flew up in the air. She was probably flexible, but I'm sure her armor put limits on that flexibility, and as her leg shot up, she fell backwards. She windmilled her arms to try to keep her balance, but I pushed a little harder, and she toppled backward. She curled up acrobatically as she hit the floor with a muffled clang and rolled backwards, coming to her feet in a couple seconds. When she rose, instead of attacking, she stared at me, her eyes wide. That gave me the chance to scramble to my feet. I stood slightly hunched over, my left hand wrapped across my stomach and ribs, panting as I held up an imploring hand, but she didn't leap forward and kick me in the face or anything. She just stood, watching me.

"Hold…" I coughed up the last of the nastiness in the back of my throat, spat it and a glob of congealing blood onto the already stained carpet, and took as deep a breath as my groaning ribs would allow. "Hold up, Ferdi. I'm here to…"

"You're a Holder," she cut me off, her eyes flat and her face colder than the elven forests in winter. "You took my cards and made them yours, Murf. How dare you?"

She blurred again, but this time, my eyes managed to track her as she rushed toward me. That meant I saw clearly as she snatched her way-too-huge double-bitted axe from her back and slashed it at me. I let out a sound kind of like a cross between a yelp and a choked gurgle and fell backward, tripping over the carpet and landing hard on my ass. Her axe whistled through the air where I'd been, but the halfling whipped it about and redirected it at me. I scrambled back just in time, and I felt the breeze as the blade whiffed past my nose.

"I didn't steal your cards!" I shouted, pushing myself backward. "Damn it, Ferdi, stop this shit and just *listen* for a second!" I rolled sideways as the axe hissed through the spot where I'd been and pushed myself back to my feet. "You owe me that…"

I screamed as I dodged too slowly, and the axe slid across my stomach. The blade seemed to move in slow motion, and I could feel the steel blade parting my skin and cutting into my muscle. The moment felt like it lasted at least a minute or so as the wickedly sharp edge cut me open like a pig to be slaughtered. Warmth spilled down the front of me, and as the blade exited my body, pain exploded from the wound. I dropped to my knees, clutching my stomach in pain and disbelief. She'd done it! She'd actually cut me open!

She stepped forward and grabbed my hair, yanking my head back, and rested the axe blade against my throat. "I'm sorry, Murf," she said with what sounded like actual regret. "I always liked you, but this is what oath-breakers deserve."

In response, I spat another gobbet of blood directly into her face. She didn't even flinch as it struck her cheek and began to slide down. "Fuck you," I groaned. "I didn't break any damn oath."

"I don't believe you. Goodbye." Her shoulder lifted slightly, as if tensing, and in that moment, I knew I was going to die. She'd cut me open like a fish, gutted me, and now she was going to slit my throat. I was pretty sure the Hag couldn't adapt to something like that, and I didn't know if I'd want her to if she could. Could I adapt to having my head separated from my body? Would I have to walk around carrying my head under my arm, like some weird purse? How would I eat? Or talk? Or have sex ever again? Even if my body could make it work mechanically, I couldn't imagine any woman being cool with taking a decapitated guy to her bed.

"When I said I'd give you a little head, Murf, this wasn't what I meant!"

As that ridiculously inane thought popped into my skull, though, a surge of energy rose up inside me and poured into my body. Strength flowed down my muscles, and warmth spread into my stomach, cutting off the pain there. Ferdi seemed to freeze, her face frozen in a mask of regret and determination. The gobbet of blood I'd spat hung at the edge of her chin, dangling in midair, waiting to fall off. The whole world took a breath, waiting for me to either do something or accept my death. I decided to do something.

My fist whipped out and slammed into the halfling's face, and the world sped up to normal once more. As it did, several things happened at once. Ferdi shouted in pain and alarm as my fist smacked into her chin. Her feet left the floor as the impact lifted her off the ground and hurled her backward the same way she'd tossed me about earlier. Her axe whipped forward, but it swept over my head harmlessly before her nerveless fingers let go of the weapon. It hit the wall behind me and bounced off. The wooden haft smacked into the back of my skull, adding insult to my existing injury. And my stomach began to scream once again that it had been sliced open like a ham, causing me to curl back up in a ball and moan.

Ferdi hit the opposite wall with a crash of steel and the thunk of her skull slamming into stone. Her body collapsed to the floor in a heap, and she lay there, groaning but not getting back up. The pain in my stomach had flared once that weird moment of stillness ended, but it seemed to be ebbing now, enough at least that I managed to uncurl my body. I tried to push myself to stand, and as I did, my hand came down on the haft of Ferdi's axe.

I gripped it and looked at the woman lying barely conscious on the floor across from me. I could end this, I realized. She'd probably shake off the blow in less than a minute, but that was more than enough time for me to stagger over there. She hadn't bothered to wear a helmet, so her neck was exposed. I wasn't much with an axe and had never learned to fight with one, but it would be like chopping wood. One big swing to the back of her neck, and the threat she posed to me would be over.

I used the axe to push myself upright, then slowly stumbled over toward her. My stomach burned and throbbed, but the pain seemed to be easing as the seconds passed, allowing me to stand upright by the time I reached her. I hefted the weapon, surprised that while it was heavy, it wasn't anywhere nearly as heavy as I'd imagined. I tested the edge with my thumb, not that I had to since I'd felt that edge inside my stomach just a minute ago, then gripped the thing with two hands and looked down at the halfling.

Ferdi lay on her stomach, her face toward me. Her half-lidded eyes stared vacantly at my boots. Her jaw where I'd hit her was already swelling and darkening, and I suspected I might have broken it. I rested the blade of the axe on the side of her neck, gripped it in two hands, lifted it— and lowered it until the top spike was under her closer arm. I lifted, flipping her onto her back with a grunt of effort—she wasn't heavy, but that armor wasn't light, either—then crouched down and carefully began removing her weapons, watching her eyes as I did.

The woman was a veritable armory. A short, broad-bladed sword hung from one hip, while a heavy dagger hung from the other. A small axe the size of a hatchet was strapped to her right thigh, while a long, pointed knife gleamed on the other. Each boot yielded a small knife, and lifting her up revealed another hatchet strapped to the small of her back. I assumed she also had weapons hidden beneath her armor, but no way was I messing with that.

Her gaze cleared as I finished my inspection, and she reacted instantly, lashing up at me with a foot. I caught it and held it firmly as she tried to yank it back, barely managing to keep my grip on it.

"Damn it, Ferdi, calm down!" I said sharply. "Stop it!" She kept thrashing, and anger surged in me. "I just spared your damn life, woman! Is this how you repay that? Is that your honor?"

She froze instantly, and her eyes narrowed for a moment as she glanced past me to see her weapons piled up behind me. She looked back up at me, her gaze questioning, and I nodded.

"That's right. You were out, and I could have killed you without even trying. I didn't, and that means you at least owe me the common courtesy of listening to me, don't you think?"

Her face took on a thoughtful expression for a moment before she nodded once, wincing as she did. I released her foot, then stepped back. She pushed herself slowly to a sitting position, grunting with pain several times, then leaned back against the wall and gazed up at me. I couldn't help but sigh with relief. She was finally listening, and all it took was nearly dying and not killing her when I had the chance. Damn halflings are ridiculously stubborn sometimes.

"Finally." I took a deep breath, wincing myself as the motion caused my stomach to twinge. I glanced down at the wound, noting as I did that my clothes were ruined again. My coat and shirt hung open from where the axe had sliced through them, and blood stained the bottom of both and flowed down onto my pants. No amount of laundering was going to get that out.

"Damn it, Ferdi, why'd you have to go and ruin my clothes?" I said petulantly. "You're going to buy me a new set, you hear me? These things aren't free!" I looked up at her and saw the hardness in her gaze and sighed. Halflings. Stubborn as hell, and no sense of humor.

"Fine," I sighed. "Right to business, then." I squatted down beside her. "First of all, I came here to talk to you, not to get my cock cut off—or to kill you. We go way back, you and I, and I thought that maybe—just maybe—that friendship would have counted for enough for you to give me a chance to explain."

She shook her head vigorously, wincing as she did, and I sighed again. "Yeah. So I see. It's a damn shame that we had to go through all this, but here we are, and at least you're listening." She made an impatient gesture, and I grimaced. "Yeah, I'll get on with it."

"First of all, I never broke my oath to you," I told her. Her face went flat, but I shook my head. "No, you said you'd listen, so just sit there and actually listen with an open mind. What I'm about to tell you is the truth, so help me Unity. When I'm done, hopefully, you'll understand, and you'll be a little less inclined to kill me."

She looked at me for several seconds then nodded slowly. I took that to mean that she agreed to at least hear me, which I supposed was the best I could possibly hope for. Better would be for her to just take my word for it, but I knew that wasn't going to happen, not for a long time. Maybe not ever. Halflings don't trust easily, and when they do, they don't forgive someone for breaking that trust.

"I assume you remember the day you loaned me those cards," I began. "Lord Clearford's tournament in Lakeholm. The entry fee was two Unity cards, and the winner got to take all those cards as the prize. It was a massive prize, bigger even than the Guild's Quinquennial. You said it was too big, too good to be true." She nodded again. "Yeah, well, you were right and wrong at the same time, it turns out.

"The tournament ran normally enough. Three rounds, with the winner of each meeting at the high table. It was me, Lord Clearford—who was pretty clearly cheating, but no one wanted to say much since his guards were everywhere—and some guy named Bloodfane. I think he was cheating, too, but I never actually saw it happening, so I couldn't make any accusations."

I sighed and rubbed my face in frustration. "Clearford went out first," I said. "High run that lost to Bloodfane's flush. I expected him to raise a stink, maybe declare the tournament over or something, but he took the loss with good grace and bowed out. Bloodfane and I played back and forth a bit, neither of us winning much or losing much, and for a bit, it seemed like the game might go on all damn night."

I gazed into her eyes as I spoke, hoping she could read the sincerity there. "I guess that was too much for Bloodfane. He didn't want to wait all night. He'd just lost a small hand, nothing big, a couple hundred coins or so when my 3-set beat his. He pushed away from the table, looked at me, and said, 'Well, Murf, this has been fun, but I'm out of time, I'm afraid.

Maybe we can do it again sometime.' And that's when all hell broke loose."

She gazed at me questioningly, but I shook my head as I recalled that night. "That's the best way to describe it, Ferdi. One second, I was collecting the pot. The next, the air caught on fire all around me, and I fell out of my chair. I banged my head on the way down and ended up under the table somehow. A bunch of people started screaming, and guards began shouting and calling out to each other. The air filled with smoke, and I could smell burning wood and blood. Lots and lots of blood."

I shuddered. "I crawled out from under the table, intending to get the hell out of there. You know me, Ferdi. I'm a lover, not a fighter." She glared at me and pointed fiercely at her jaw, and I had the good grace to look embarrassed for a moment. "That's—a recent development, and one I'm not happy with. Back then, though, all I wanted was to get out of there with my skin intact, and that seemed like a tall order since a bunch of people in black armor were spread out all over the room, killing everyone they saw, including Clearford's guards. The place was on fire, and the doors seemed to be locked since people were banging on them and they didn't open.

"I guess Bloodfane had somehow hidden a bunch of guards in the place, ready to kill everyone if he didn't win. I don't know how—the room was pretty well lit, and there weren't any places to hide that I could see—but he managed it somehow. And the man himself was up on the main stage, unlocking the safe that Clearford had stuffed all the cards into. He pulled them out and began to make his exit, and when I saw that..." I grimaced. "Well, I got a little stupid, I guess. I didn't want him getting away with all those cards—all MY cards since I would have won the whole, damn thing, I was pretty sure. I didn't have any weapons, and if I did, I wasn't going to last any longer against his warriors than anyone else had, but I had to at least try to get them back.

"So, I just kind of charged him," I sighed. "It was dumb, but I just ran at him. Somehow, I made it across the room and grabbed the bag of cards. I meant to pull it away from him, but he held on, and as we yanked, the bag ripped open, and cards fell everywhere. We both kind of looked at each other, then dropped down and started scooping up all the cards we could grab. I made sure to get yours, Ferdi, plus a few extra.

"Before I could get more, though, something exploded in the room, and the fire got a lot hotter. I backed up, but another explosion smashed me backward right into a window. I busted through it, cutting my face in the process, and fell. Fortunately, the window looked out over the lake. Unfortunately, there was a log a few feet under the surface, and I cracked my head on it. I sort of drifted for a while, and when I came to, Clearford's place was burning to the ground. Even worse, more of those people in black armor were roaming the lakeshore, and I guessed they were looking for me. I swam downstream and got out of the water, but they were still looking, and I knew I had to get the hell out of there and hide. I found a fishing village, paid a widow to let me sleep in her attic for a few nights, then made my way back to Lakeholm.

"I looked for you, but by then, you were gone," I sighed. "Old Butterman at the travel house told me that you'd decided I'd run off with your cards and set out to find me. I tried to catch up to you, but there were more of those black-armored guys around, and I knew that I had to leave Lakeholm. I caught the next ship I could out of there, figuring I'd look you up later and give you your cards back.

"Of course, I never did," I shrugged. "The cards took me one way, and you went another. Every time I looked for you, you'd moved on somewhere else. Eventually, you set up that damn bounty demanding my cock, and at that point, I just figured it was better to stay way the hell away from you. I never got rid of your cards, though. I kept them with me the whole time, just in case."

She frowned, then reached into the front of her armor and pulled out a card. I tensed up, but she just touched it to her face. A moment later, the swelling in her jaw visibly shrank, and after half a minute or so, she wiggled her jaw around, testing it out.

"Better." She slipped the card back into her armor and rose to her feet, looking at me with an expression that had only thawed somewhat. "I followed you to that game, Murf. Did you know that?"

I shook my head. "No, but I suppose I should have. You probably wanted to make sure that I didn't just run away with your cards."

"No. The cards weren't that important. They were two low cards that I couldn't use well, to be honest. I went because I suspected something was wrong. That many cards in one place? It's too big of a target. I knew things would go badly, and when they did, I wanted to be there to help you."

She shook her head, her face sorrowful as she spoke. "When the building went up in flames, I knew I was right, and I wished I hadn't been. Once the flames died down, I went through the wreckage, hoping to find you from that stupid hat you always wear, but I couldn't. Then, I got suspicious. You're clever for a human. What if you started the fire so that you could steal the cards and get out of there? I asked around, and two of the bystanders swore they saw a man wearing a hat like yours jump out a window into the lake. That's when I knew. You'd stolen all those cards. You'd lied to me. You'd caused all those people to die. Worst of all, you'd broken your oath that you'd give me the cards back—and that was what really hurt.

"I looked for you, hoping for another explanation, but I never found you. I went hunting for you, going from Gambler's Hall to Gambler's Hall, but you'd always left a step ahead of me. Eventually, I had no choice but to post the bounty. Oath-breakers must be punished—even ones who used to be my friend."

I winced a little at that, but I understood. No matter what I said, the friendship between Ferdi and I was gone, years ago. I'd become her enemy, and I couldn't just undo that.

"I don't know if you're telling me the truth," she continued. "I don't know if that story is just a clever lie you've spent years making up, or if it actually happened. However, you did spare my life, and in return, I'll accept your tale. You say that you still have my cards; give them back, and we'll call it even. I'll rescind the bounty, and we can go on with our lives. Deal?"

"I'd love to," I replied slowly. "Only it's not quite that simple."

"Why?" she demanded. "You said you had the cards. Did you lie about that, too?"

"I didn't lie about anything," I snapped back with a little heat. "I said I never got rid of your cards, and I didn't. I never sold them, never traded them, and never used them as a stake in a game. I always kind of hoped that I'd get the chance to give them back to you, and maybe you'd forgive me."

"So, where are they, then?"

"Stolen. A couple elves jumped me when I first came to the city, stole everything I had, and tried to get rid of me. That didn't work, but they still took everything I had—including your cards."

"Then go get them back," she said flatly.

"They're Holders, Ferdi," I sighed. "Both of them."

"So?" she shrugged. "Obviously, so are you—and with a powerful card, judging from how you hit me. Go do the same thing to them and get my cards."

"I'm barely a Holder. It happened by accident, and I have no idea how to use my card. Sometimes, things just happen, usually when I'm about to die." I grimaced. "I need help, Ferdi."

What little warmth her face held vanished instantly. "So, that's what this is all about. You didn't come here out of honor, or to make peace with me. You came here because you need help getting your things back. Is that it?"

"I came here hoping for both, really," I admitted. "I need your help, but I was also hoping this would make peace between us." I stood up, hesitated for a moment, then handed her axe back to her. She took it slowly, her face slightly startled as she hefted it.

"You were my friend once, Ferdi," I said. "We looked out for each other. I know those days are gone, but I don't want us to be enemies, either. If I could just give you the cards, I would. I can't, though, so this is the only way you can get them back. We work together, one last time. You get your cards; I get my stuff. Afterward, we part ways with everything evened up. Fair?"

She glared at me, then lifted her axe and reattached it to her back. "One last time," she agreed. "For the sake of our old times, and for you sparing my life. We do this, and then we're done. You never come to me for help again. Understood?"

"Understood," I nodded. I couldn't help but compare her words to Azara's. *"You never come to me again."* That was what the avian had said, too, more or less. Apparently, this was just one more bridge I was about to leave burning behind me. I couldn't help but wonder if one day, I'd torch so many that I had nowhere left to go.

That was for another day, though. For the moment, I'd done the impossible. I'd met Ferdi and survived. Whether I'd keep living through the next few days, though—that remained to be seen.

17

"3-set of ladies," I proclaimed grandly, laying down the pair of ladies in my hand that matched the lady of staves down on the table already.

"Fuck," the male elf sitting four chairs down from me swore, tossing down his hand to reveal a double set, queens and tens. "The pot is yours."

I nodded, sliding the pile of chips my way to add to the growing stack before me. "Nice hand," I complimented him.

"Not nice enough, obviously. The Unity's luck is on your side tonight, quite clearly."

Despite the elf's complaints, he really wasn't having a bad night himself. He still had a respectable stack in front of him, one that was larger than he'd started the night with, so he couldn't really complain. This was the third time we'd gone head-to-head, though, and all three times, he'd come out the loser. I got why he wasn't happy.

After my last time playing with elves, part of me had been hesitant to sit down at the table with this guy, to be honest. Fortunately, we were playing in the Hall rather than a gambling den somewhere, and the Hall didn't tolerate foolishness or poor losers. You played your hands, accepted your losses, and moved on with life. Maybe drowned your sorrows in a drink or a romp in the sheets, if needed. You didn't draw steel, though, and you definitely didn't try to kidnap and rob fellow Guildmembers. The first would get you kicked out of the Guild, and the second would get you dead, fast.

The inner hall was crowded that night, as more and more professionals flocked to Canis in preparation for the tournament. Most people here would be entering, and while most would also be out in the first round, the best players had finally taken to the tables to secure their invite. Elf-boy was one of those, a solid player who won more than he lost and probably would have walked away the big winner at most of the tables in the place. That was why he was frustrated: he was playing well, but he kept losing out to me when it mattered. That frustration just made things worse, amplifying his tells and making him more prone to bad bluffs and overbidding.

And hey, if I happened to take advantage of that, well, that's just how the damn game works. If you don't like it, leave the table so someone else can play.

That should probably be a law, now that I think about it. I'll have to see if I can squeeze it in somewhere.

It had been three days since I'd spoken to Ferdi. She'd agreed to set her people to watching for the elves to see if and when they might be vulnerable, and since then, she'd sent me daily reports about the two. They weren't anything exciting. Apparently, as Eegla said, the elves were holed up in the Royal Lamb, up in the fancy section of town. What they'd been doing slumming outside the walls was beyond me, but they weren't doing it now. They stayed in the Lamb and never left, as far as Ferdi could tell. Her halfling scouts were good enough that I'd never realized they were following me through the city, so I assumed she was right.

The problem was, if the elves never left the Lamb, we couldn't easily get to them. The place wasn't just another travel house. It was a super exclusive one, at least according to Eegla. Every room was a full suite with a sitting chamber and private bath. The place served meals fit for the meritocracy, multi-course deals, and the alcohol was included. The place combined a travel house, gambling hall, drinking house, and house of ill repute; apparently, the employees would happily bring your meals to your room, feed them to you, join you in the bath afterward, and warm your sheets at the end of the day, all for just a ridiculously large extra charge. About the only thing they wouldn't do was wipe your ass for you, and I guessed that could probably be arranged if you wanted.

A place like that wasn't just guarded, it was incredibly well guarded. It housed visiting nobility, political dignitaries, extremely wealthy merchants, and other people with lots of money and influence, and it didn't just offer luxury. It promised security. I felt sure the place was guarded by Holders at all times, and it probably had cartomancer tableaus all over the place shielding it. I wouldn't be surprised if they had actual cartomancers there doing readings on everyone inside to make sure no one was an assassin. It wasn't a place you could break into or even sneak into, at least not unless you were a master thief of some sort, which I wasn't.

We couldn't tell what was going on inside, either. Ferdi was a talented Delver, and I considered myself a damn fine gambler, but neither of us was important, at least not as far as the Lamb was concerned. They didn't let in people they considered riff-raff, and we were definitely that. Without a letter of introduction, sponsorship by someone powerful in the city, or just gobs of money, we weren't getting past the front door.

As it turned out, I knew someone who fit that last bill. I just had to convince her to help me out.

I watched the cards fall again almost mechanically, riffling the corners of mine to see that I had a nine, six, and five, all off-suit. It was a shit hand, and I folded without even seeing the layout. Sure, it was possible that a seven and eight would fall, but it wasn't likely. Trying to make the inside of a run was a fool's game, especially when I needed two cards to make my run instead of one.

Instead, I let my eyes wander over to the table two from mine. Millie sat there, dressed in a low-cut light blue dress that prominently displayed her natural assets. She smiled as she talked animatedly with an avian man beside her, ignoring the way his eyes kept dropping down to her cleavage. Her stack was impressive—and so were her winnings—and I was sure that the dress wasn't making things any harder for her. Or more to the point, it was making several things just hard enough to distract their owners, who probably kept thinking about the wrong kind of staves for some reason. She was quite beautiful, really, and she knew it. Not only that, she leveraged it, using it to her best advantage to keep her opponents too distracted to play well.

I refocused as the cards fell again—the last hand had gone to the human male two seats to my left, with a double set of princes and eights—then flipped through my cards. Ace, six, and prince, all of cups—ironic, considering the two objects I'd just been admiring—a good enough hand for me to stick around. I checked the first round, matching the blind and nothing more, then waited for the first card to drop on the layout. It was a six of coins, giving me a 2-set, and I checked again, glancing almost nonchalantly at the others. No one had a great hand, but my elf buddy had something better than my 2-set from how conservatively he was bidding, and the felid lady to my right probably had a strong 2-set of her own or even a double set of sixes and something judging by how her tail twitched.

The cross dropped, a three of cups that I quite carefully didn't react to. I checked my bet again, then watched as the elf raised three and the felid upped that to five. I considered my cards without looking at them. I had a four-flush, one of those hands that looks tantalizingly good but was worthless in reality. I had a one-in-five shot of getting what I wanted—well, not really, as it was likely that the cards that had fallen so far weren't all evenly distributed among the suits, but close enough. The question was: was that good enough to push it? I could fold at this point, and I wouldn't be out much. The elf and felid both had better than my 2-set. The smart play would be to hold back and be patient, waiting for a more certain hand.

"Twenty," I said instead, pushing four stacks of chips into the pot. The felid folded immediately, dropping her cards with a hiss of dismay, but the elf simply stared into my eyes as if trying to get the measure of my soul.

"I think you're bluffing," he finally spoke.

"It'll cost you twenty to find out," I replied casually. "That's not that much, right?"

"No, it's not." He glanced down at his chips. "Raise to fifty." He pushed the stacks in while the others muttered in amazement, and I met his raise without hesitation. "Call."

The final card dropped, and I stared at it for a moment before tapping a finger on the table. "Check."

The elf grinned at me. "As I thought. You were bluffing." He pushed two stacks of red chips into the middle. "One hundred."

The others scoffed as they looked at the tableau. The dropped cards didn't really support that big of a bid, and everyone knew it. He'd bet about half of his stack on what would probably at best be a low run. He was overbidding again, hoping to drive me out and force me to fold. With just what the pot held, if he won it, he'd probably have high stack at the table, and he'd definitely have the momentum moving forward. Noblesse isn't just about luck and skill; it's a mental game as much as anything. The elf's losses had him rattled, and he was taking bad chances in the hope of a win. A victory would settle him down and return him to his regular conservative play. A loss here would probably break him, maybe sending him to another table or even finishing him off for the night. Even when he came back, that loss would burn in his mind, changing his play until he won enough to regain his confidence.

"I'll see that," I finally said, sliding my chips into the middle. "And raise you—one." I pushed one extra chip into the pot.

"One?" he echoed, staring down at my lone white chip. "What do you mean, one?"

"I mean, if you want to see my cards, you have to pay one more chip, elf. That's all. Just one more. Can you handle that?"

He glared at my chip as if it had insulted him somehow, which I supposed it might have. What it really did, though, was kill his bidding momentum. He'd laid down this massive bet, expecting me to either fold or call. Maybe I'd even go all in, at which point, if he were smart, he'd have dropped out. He'd been ready to see an end to the hand, though, one way or the other. Instead, I'd raised him the smallest possible amount and thrown him off his stride.

"I raise fifty," he said almost challengingly, sliding two stacks of blue chips that he couldn't afford to bet into the middle.

"You forgot to see my one," I reminded him, and he angrily tossed a single white chip into the center, knocking down a stack. "Hey, don't spill the pot, now! This is a friendly game, here! I'll see your fifty and raise you—two." I added two more chips to the middle, and he ground his teeth as he glared at them. My play didn't match his expectations, and it was messing with his head. His experience told him if I'd been bluffing, I would have either gone really big or folded. If I had the cards, I'd have bet larger and larger amounts, drawing as many coins from him as possible. His big bets were designed to force my hand, but they weren't, and he couldn't quite figure out what it meant. He glanced down at his dwindling stacks, and I could see him debating whether or not to go all in. If he did and won, he'd have high stack at the table and would probably walk away at that point, feeling like a winner. If he lost, not only would he be done for the night, but there was a good chance that he wouldn't recover for the tournament. Finally, he made the smart play.

"Call," he said, tossing two more chips into the middle and spilling the pot even more. He laid down his cards with a grin of triumph. "Run, three to seven."

I just slid my cards over to him without expression. He stared at me, his face startled, and I gestured at him. "Go ahead and look at them," I said encouragingly. He slid the cards over to himself, lifted the corners, and groaned. His shoulders slumped, and he pushed them away from himself, staring in defeat at his incredibly small remaining stack of chips.

"What did you have?" the man beside me asked curiously.

"If he wanted you to know, he would have showed his cards," the felid woman answered. "This was between the two of them." I nodded at the woman as I collected my chips, stacked them neatly, and slid them over to the dealer, handing her a five as I did. "Can you get those checked in?" I asked.

"Of course, sir."

"Thanks." I looked at the others and slid my chair backward. "I'm gonna take a bit of a break, friends. I've got something else to take care of." No one seemed particularly upset as I rose, but I wasn't really paying attention to them. My eyes were fastened on the gleaming lady of cups that had fallen, the fool card that secured my flush. The card showed an elegant, beautiful woman with coppery tresses, seated on a chair, holding a goblet in her hand, and I couldn't help but meet her gaze as I stood.

The priest had told me that the Unity spoke to people all the time, but that they usually didn't bother listening. Normally, I would have brushed off that card as a coincidence. After all, it was just a card, and it had as much chance of coming up as any. The only problem with that was that as the man to my left had tossed his cards in when he folded, he'd lifted them too high, and I got a glimpse of them before they hit the table. I was willing to believe that the lady might have fallen by chance—but not when I'd just seen it in someone else's hand. That card had no business turning up where it did, flipping over as the fool, falling at an angle so that its heavenward gaze looked directly at me.

I was a fool, but not that big of one. I couldn't ignore that message. I walked to the bar, ordered a drink, and walked over to Millie's table, where a seat happened to be available.

Apparently, the Unity's as subtle as a fist to the face. Another good candidate for a law, really.

I waited until the current hand was finished and took the open seat. As I sat, I met Millie's gaze and flashed her a smile. She returned it with a shy smile of her own that held a slight edge to it, one I wasn't sure I understood.

"Murf, how nice to see you again," she said pleasantly.

"Millie," I replied. "A pleasure as always." I looked around the table. "How's everyone's evening going?"

"Well enough, Murf," an older avian woman with dark blue feathers going gray at the tips replied with a more relaxed smile.

"Aela," I nodded to the woman. "Good to see you! It's been, what, two years?"

"Three. The tournament in Tarrish."

"That's right. How've you been?"

"Well enough that I'm still here," she laughed. "A woman can't ask for more than that."

"Maybe not, but a man can ask for a peaceful table," a rather scruffy-looking man halfway between Millie and me said in a sour voice. "The way it was before you sat down. I happen to think it'd be better if it went back to that way."

"Now, Ephan, that's hardly a way to behave," Millie chided. "Besides, Murf here is a friend of mine, and I love when my friends play with me." Her eyes sparkled as she looked at me, and the man's sour expression deepened. It wasn't hard for me to understand why; he obviously had some designs on playing with Millie that didn't involve me in the slightest. Unfortunately, I had plans of my own, and he didn't factor into them, either.

"And I'll bet your friends love playing with you," I replied with a grin before looking at the dealer. "Standard noblesse?"

"Spread, cross, fool, no wilds, sir."

"Works for me." I tossed in my ante and settled in to play, watching the others as I did.

Millie had done a good job charming this table. Of the five other men playing at it, four were so busy staring at her tits that they forgot to ante half the time. She kept touching the ones beside her, brushing her hand against their arm or shifting so her hip touched theirs, and every time she did, their bets got larger and more outrageous. Only Aela and an older ursid man with graying fur seemed unimpressed by her antics, and both of them were playing conservatively. Millie had quite the hoard of chips from her admirers, none of whom seemed terribly upset to be losing to her.

Murf's Twenty-Fourth Law: Any idea that comes from your pants is a terrible one. Really, that one should be a lot higher, all things considered.

I sat back and let the cards fall, bidding small and checking a lot as I got a feel for the table. Millie's admirers weren't even trying, really, and taking their money wasn't even an effort. Aela was a smart gambler, losing small, winning slightly larger, always staying in the game and just ahead. The ursid was competent, as well, but he had a tendency to overplay his bluffs, leading him to larger losses than he should have had. I'd already gotten a good feel for Millie—several good feels, I might add—but she was playing smarter tonight, no doubt planning to clear the table and all but guarantee herself a spot in the tournament. I understood at last where the odd edge to her smile came from. She was going all out tonight, hoping for a big win, and I was a potential disruption to that plan.

As the night drew on, the cards fell, and the chips shifted around the table. The man to Millie's left dropped out first, tapped when he overbid on a 3-set that lost to Millie's run. He smiled at her as he pushed his chair back and gave her a hopeful look.

"Perhaps, Millie, you'd be willing to buy me a drink with some of the money you won from me?" he asked with a complete lack of guile.

"Oh, but I'm on a winning streak, Delthon," she pouted. "Could I get a rain check on that drink, maybe?"

"Of course," he sighed, no doubt realizing at last that she'd never intended to leave the table with him. He glanced down her cleavage one last, wistful time before wandering off toward the bar—and probably a nice cold bath.

One by one, the other players dropped out, sometimes to me, sometimes to Millie. A canid man lost when my 3-set of knights beat his of sevens. The avian man fell to Millie when her run beat his double set of Queens and Princes. Scruffy went all in on a bad bluff, and I called it, beating him with nothing more than a 2-set of tens. He simply stared at the coins, his expression lost, then up at me.

"You—you cheated!" he stammered. "You saw my cards!"

"Ephan, what a terrible thing to say!" Millie gasped. "You never accuse another player of cheating just because you lost!"

"But—but he..." He looked back and forth between us. "How'd you know I was bluffing?"

"Lucky guess," I shrugged, not wanting to tell him that he tapped his foot when he bluffed just in case I wanted to win more money from him. "Sometimes, that's just the way the cards fall, friend."

"Exactly," Millie nodded. "No use getting upset. It's just money, after all."

"I..." He looked at Millie, then back at me, and his shoulders slumped in defeat. "Yeah. I guess that's the way the cards fall. Well played, ma'am." He nodded to Millie, then rose from the table, moving toward the bar like an arrow toward its target. I had a feeling he'd be getting angry drunk soon, and he'd probably wake up in the morning with something to regret. None of that was my problem, though, so I dismissed the man and promptly forgot about him.

As the game played on, I could feel that sense of understanding slowly steal over me. I could sense the cards; I knew what the other players had without having to more than glance at them; I could tell when they'd turn well and when they'd bust me. As we kept playing, more and more of the players lost to me rather than Millie, with Aela being the last to bow out, folding her low 3-set, not knowing that she'd lost to a 2-set of twos. My stacks grew, while Millie's stayed more or less the same, and I could feel the woman's frustration building.

The cards fell, and I riffled through mine, barely glancing at them before looking at Millie. "Check."

She smiled at me, but I felt the brittle edge beneath her forced friendliness. "I'll bid, oh, let's say five," she said, tossing a blue chip into the middle.

"Call." I slid a chip of my own, then watched as the spread fell. It was an eight of coins, and I could feel Millie's exultation with it. I checked again, and she seemed to hesitate before reluctantly bidding ten. I called her, then waited as the cross flipped over. I didn't even have to glance at it to know that it didn't help me and did help Millie, who made as if to fold before sighing.

"Oh, what the hell. It's just money. I'll bet—fifty." A murmur rose around us, and I glanced about to see that we'd picked up quite the crowd of onlookers. Nearby tables stood empty as people flocked around to watch us play, and dealers stood a bit forlornly at their tables, waiting for the spectacle to end so they could get back to work—and make the tips that they relied on.

"I call your fifty," I agreed. "And raise you another fifty." More muttering echoed around us, but I ignored it as I stared into the woman's eyes. I could see the hesitation there. She had a good hand, one worth betting big on, but she wasn't sure it was that good. At last, she called and slid the chips into the middle, and the fool fell. I glanced down at it and wondered if it was a sign: the lady of stars lay on the table, her face turned toward Millie as she sat at a window, looking out at a starry sky.

"The lady is the fool. Poor Millie," I thought with a touch of amusement.

"Check," I said as usual, but this time, Millie barely hesitated.

"A hundred," she bet, sliding two red stacks into the middle.

"I'll call that," I smiled, then looked down at my chips. I had more than her, no doubt, but she still had a respectable amount. "All in." I slid my chips forward as the people around us gasped and murmured appreciatively, some wondering what I had while others speculated what Millie held. As the noise grew, the dealer held up his hands.

"Quiet, please," he instructed, and the chatter immediately dropped to a reasonable level. "Ma'am, to stay in, you'll have to bid all your chips."

Millie stared at the layout, worrying her lip, and I knew she was about to fold. She couldn't risk losing everything to one hand that might be good but might not. Before she spoke, I lifted up a hand.

"How about this?" I offered. "Forget the pot. Let's play for something much better than money."

"Why Murf," she gasped, her hand going to her chest but not, I noticed, actually covering her cleavage. "What a wicked thing to suggest!"

"Not that," I grinned at her. "Dinner. I win, and you have dinner with me." People laughed nearby, and more than one person expressed their admiration for my bet—not all of them, I noticed, strictly males.

"And what if I win?" she asked archly.

"Then I have dinner with you. Winner chooses the place, loser pays."

She stared at me, and a smile spread across her face. "Deal," she said firmly, flipping over her cards. "Full hall, emperors over eights." A pair of emperors and an eight of stars lay before her, combining with the eight spread and the emperor cross to form a full hall. Amazed murmurs rose around us as she flashed me a grin. "Can you beat that, Murf?"

"That's a good hand," I nodded. "Fortunately for me, I've always had a way with the ladies." I laid down my cards, revealing the three ladies I'd picked up, giving me a 4-set that beat her hall.

"Holy shit!" someone muttered as the crowd broke out in cheers and applause. "Did you see that?" someone else asked. "A way with the ladies!" a man laughed loudly.

Millie just gazed at me, and I saw the relief in her eyes as the dealer split the pot back between the two of us. She'd done well that night, and while she hadn't for sure earned herself a place in the tournament, her play—and that hand—had come close to guaranteeing it. If she'd lost it all, though, there was a good chance that she'd have blown her shot, and we both knew it.

"How about we go have that dinner, Murf?" she asked me, leaning forward to display her assets even more fully, her eyes half-lidded and her lips slightly pursed. "I find that I'm suddenly—very, very hungry."

"I can't wait to eat, personally," I grinned back at her. "But maybe we should have dinner first."

"Tease," she said playfully, reaching out to cover my hand with hers. "Where did you have in mind?"

"A little place I've heard about," I shrugged. "Up north of here. It's called the Royal Lamb. Ever heard of it?"

"I have, in fact. It's wonderful." She rose to her feet and pulled me to mine. "Believe me, everything there is delicious."

"So is something right here," I replied, pulling her close to me. "Now, come on. Let's get out of here. I'm in the mood to try something new tonight."

She had the courtesy to blush slightly as I led her past the quickly dispersing crowd toward the door, and I shoved down a tiny bit of guilt. I was using her, plain and simple. Of course, she was using me, too—I just didn't know what for. It could have been the sex, but I doubted that. I was good, but Millie probably could have picked and chosen any man in the Guild that night, and even a few of the women. She had some other game in mind, just as I did.

Part of me couldn't wait to play it. Sometimes, the Unity dealt me a fantastic card.

18

The night was cool when we stepped out, at least compared to the warmth of the Gambler's Hall, and I pulled my coat closer to myself. As I did, I noticed Millie clutching her arms and rubbing them. Her dress wasn't exactly made to keep its wearer warm, after all. It did a good job of warming other people up, but at the very least, her exposed shoulders and arms had to be chilly. If I were a gentleman, I'd have given her my coat despite the fact that my purse and the card holder I'd gotten from the Labyrinth were in it. If I were a suspicious bastard, I'd have buttoned it up to make sure Millie's swift hands couldn't slip inside it. I was a little of both, though, so I compromised. I subtly slipped everything valuable out of my pockets, slipping them into the much smaller and more vulnerable pockets of my pants, then took off my coat and draped it around her.

"Why thank you," she smiled at me, taking my arm and pulling it against her, incidentally pressing something soft, warm, and round up against it. Then again, it was probably totally deliberate; Millie struck me as a woman who never did anything incidentally.

We strolled through the darkness beneath the flickering light of oil lamps and the gleam of the big moon overhead. It was still early enough that Little Moon hadn't cleared the horizon to catch up to her big sister, but the silvery orb still provided a decent amount of light on its own. It wasn't enough to illuminate the darker alleys that lacked lamps, though, so I kept an eye out, just in case. I knew that Ferdi had people watching me, but I didn't know if they'd get involved if someone attacked me. Probably not, unless I was in danger of being killed; Ferdi had no real love for me, after all. She wouldn't risk her people just to protect my belongings.

"So, you've been to the Lamb before?" I asked her nonchalantly.

"Once or twice," she agreed.

"Isn't it awfully exclusive? How'd you get in?"

She gave me a rather scornful look. "You know how, Murf. You obviously know about my family. Otherwise, you wouldn't have mentioned the Lamb in the first place, would you?"

"I know that they're merchants, sure, and that they're ridiculously rich. I don't know who they are, though, just that they're rich enough to buy a meritocrat or three if they wanted."

"My grandfather could buy the whole damn meritocracy," she sighed. "With money left over to buy the felid Matriarchs and the avian Nestmothers, as well." She shot me a sideways glance. "Is that what this is about? You're hoping to get to my family's money through me?"

"Not in the slightest," I laughed.

"Why not? Is my family not good enough for you?" she demanded, shifting gears almost quickly enough to throw me off. Almost, but not quite.

"It's possible," I shrugged. "I don't know them, remember? That's not the point, though. Even if I knew who they were, I'm not really all that interested in money."

"Really?" she asked sarcastically. "You know that all those chips you won tonight represent money, don't you?"

"Of course, but if you're gambling to try and get rich, you're likely to be an unhappy gambler," I chuckled. "And a terrible one. I gamble because it's fun and I'm good at it. The money is just a way to measure how well I'm doing, not an end in and of itself."

I gave her a slightly more serious look. "Money can do strange things to people, Millie. Most people who chase it say that they're only after the things it can buy—security, luxury, comfort—but they never seem to spend it on those things. They either hide it away, or they use it to get more money and more money. It's never enough for them, and your entire life becomes about getting more of it. For some people, it gets to the point where nothing else matters, and gold is the only happiness they have in life."

I shook my head. "I like my life the way it is, thank you. I have enough money to do the things I want to do, and that's all I need. If I want to pick up and hop a ship to the Kine Isles tomorrow, I can. If I need new clothes because some honor-bound ass of a halfling cut mine all up, I can afford them. Having too little money limits your choices, but having too much does, as well, since you have to worry about protecting it and making more. I'm happy right here in the middle."

"Then, I suppose you wouldn't mind giving me your winnings from tonight?" she asked slyly, grabbing my arm in both hands. "Since you're so happy with what you have and everything."

"You wouldn't take it if I offered," I laughed. "If all you cared about was having more money, you could probably just ask your family for it." I flashed her a grin. "I think you're like me. You like the game, not the prize. You like beating people and showing you're better than them—and if you can make them look like an undersexed idiot in the process, even better. Am I right?"

"You seem to have quite the read on me," she said primly.

"That's what I do, isn't it? It's what all good gamblers do. We read people, so we know when they're bluffing and when they've really got it."

"True." She pressed against me again. "So, what else have you discerned about me, might I ask?"

"That you're a beautiful woman who's used to using that to her advantage. You're smarter than you let on—and a lot more dangerous." I gave her a suggestive grin. "And you become extremely devoted to the Unity when you're really excited."

She blushed slightly but held my gaze, giving me a smoldering look. "Perhaps later, then, you can help me with my devotions?"

"I'd be more than happy to, Millie. As many times as you need."

I didn't spot anything unusual on the way to the Lamb. I didn't see any of Ferdi's people, either. That didn't mean they weren't there, of course, just that I didn't see them. I hoped they were following me, and that they'd get word to Ferdi that I was going to the Lamb. She'd figure out what I was doing, and hopefully, she'd be there to provide me with backup. I had a feeling I was going to need it eventually.

The Lamb didn't look like any travel house I'd ever seen or stayed in. It looked like a damn palace, except nicer. The building stretched six stories above me, behind a stone wall topped with metal spikes to keep out people like me who might try to sneak in. It was bigger than the Gambler's Hall, taking up half a damn block. The whole place was either made of golden marble or covered in it, which had to have cost a shitload since golden marble could only be found on Farpoint, an island far to the west near Palla. It was rectangular in shape, with carved spires stretching from the top, the sculptures too shadowed for me to make out in the darkness. Glittering gold traced its doors and windows, and an image of a lamb made of sparkling gemstones decorated the highest spire, illuminated by what looked like a card tableau rather than lamps. The whole placed screamed wealth and luxury, as did the dozen ursid guards walking the perimeter of the walls and manning the gold-painted gate leading inside. As I looked at the place, I couldn't help but whistle in appreciation.

"Holy shit," I muttered, rubbing my eyes as if they might be deceiving me. "Is this place real?"

"It is," Millie laughed. "And if anything, it's nicer inside."

"I don't know how that's possible," I shook my head.

"You should see the Divine Lily in Morningstar," she snorted. "It makes this place look like a dump." I gave her a dubious look, but she simply shrugged. "Canis isn't really all that big of a city, Murf—or that wealthy. There are more people living in and around Morningstar or Floodgate than there are in all of Torin. This place is kind of a backwater compared to the Empire."

"Canis is the trading center of this whole continent," I argued, even though I knew she was right. "There's a lot of money changing hands, here."

"No, there's a lot of credit changing hands," she laughed. "But I'll bet that Morningstar and Harborage handle more money in a month than all of Torin does in a year." She pulled me forward, toward the gates. The guards there stiffened instantly, but she reached into her bodice and pulled out a golden card embossed with an image of a balance on it. She held it out toward the guards, and one produced a board of smooth golden wood decorated with facedown cards. She placed her card in the center, and the card closest to the guard glowed dully. He picked it up and looked at it, then bowed his head to Millie.

"Miss Deepwater," he said in a low, growling tone that was also oddly respectful. "Welcome back to the Lamb." He made a gesture, and the gate behind him swing silently open a moment later.

"Thank you," she smiled, pulling me forward. The guards didn't even give me a second glance as we swept past them onto a marble walkway framed with splashing fountains lit from within by glowing lights that I assumed were card-formed. Low trees spread out past the fountains, shadowing the ground beyond the light, which seemed like a bad idea to me. After all, if someone made it over the walls, they could hide in the foliage pretty easily. Of course, that was only if the trees extended more than a dozen feet or so. It was possible that the owners of the place let the trees grow just thickly enough to give the illusion of walking through a jungle but left everything beyond open.

Another pair of guards stood atop a set of marble stairs leading to a pair of mahogany double doors with elaborate golden handles molded to look like shepherd's crooks. The guards pulled the doors open as we approached, and Millie led me into one of the single nicest rooms I'd ever stood in. The room was large, as big as one of the gambling rooms back in the Hall, but everything here gleamed with golden marble. A set of semicircular stairs swept down to a lush red carpet that led between two sets of fluted columns. The ceiling overhead was vaulted and decorated with elaborate paintings that were honestly hard to see past the hanging crystal lamps descending from them. A handful of very well-dressed people occupied the room, standing around in small groups and talking quietly to one another, none of them looking our way. Felid men and woman stood off to the sides in somewhat revealing costumes, almost hidden between the pillars, and as we descended the steps into the room, one glided elegantly toward us, his fur bright orange and his green eyes bright as he bowed to Millie.

"Miss Deepwater, sir," he said. "A pleasure to have you joining us tonight. I am Kikoum, and I have the honor of serving you this evening. How may I assist you?"

"Good evening, Kikoum," Millie said pleasantly. "This is my friend, Murf. We're here for dinner, perhaps some gambling…" She gave me another smoldering look. "And a special suite for the night, I believe."

"Of course, Miss," the felid replied. "Would you prefer to dine first, or would you like to whet your appetite at the tables?"

"Dinner, please."

"Follow me, then."

I followed in stunned amazement as the man guided us along another carpeted path, through the columns, and into a room filled with tables. Heavenly scents assaulted my nose as we entered, making my mouth water. Nearly nude felids wandered about, carrying wooden trays piled with steaming food and glistening drinks. Men and women sat about the tables, talking and laughing quietly but earnestly with one another, all dressed in clothing that I couldn't afford even if I had all the coins I'd found in the Labyrinth. I gazed over them, looking for familiar faces, but my elf buddies were nowhere in sight, so I followed Kikoum to a vacant table, where he pulled out a chair for Millie and held it for her to sit. I handled my own. Apparently, I didn't rate a chair-holder.

"Would you like to start with drinks?" the felid asked.

"Sparkling wine for me, please," Millie answered. "Teshean Vineyard."

"Bourbon, neat," I added.

"Which kind, sir?" he asked. "Elvish, human, or halfling?"

"You have halfling bourbon?" I asked dubiously. "Wabanagan Select, by any chance?"

"Five or ten years?" he asked.

"Ten."

"Excellent choice, sir." He bowed his head. "For dinner tonight, we have a choice of braised lamb in golden apple glaze, Kurrdish steak with mushroom sauce, or silverdeer medallions prepared in the elven fashion."

"I'll have the lamb," Millie smiled.

"Steak for me."

"Very good. I'll return with your drinks in a moment." He turned and walked away, and I stared around at the place with thinly veiled awe before turning back and giving Millie an arch look.

"Deepwater, eh?" I asked her. "As in, rulers of the Free Kingdom of Deepwater? Those Deepwaters?"

She made an unhappy face. "My grandfather is Plutarch Deepwater," she admitted.

"So, you're some kind of royalty?"

She snorted rather indelicately for a princess. "Hardly. I'm nowhere near the line of succession. My father is the youngest of eight, and I'm the youngest of five. I barely qualify as a Deepwater." She made a sour face. "I don't at all, according to my father."

"But your family does rule that entire kingdom," I pressed.

"It's not a kingdom, officially, because my grandfather's not a king. Its official name is the Plutarchy of Deepwater."

"How is that different from being a king?"

"It isn't, really, except that since we aren't a kingdom, the Empire doesn't see the point in trying to swallow us back up after we broke free of them in the Rebellions. Plus, grandfather gives them a ton of money each year to encourage them to leave him alone." She paused as Kikoum returned with our drinks and a wooden tray covered with various loaves of steaming bread and blocks of cheese.

"Do you need anything else at the moment, miss, sir?" he asked.

"No, thank you, Kikoum," she smiled. The felid bowed again and vanished, and she took a long sip from her drink. I watched her as she did;

she looked tense and unhappy, and I guessed that the subject of her family was an unwelcome one.

"Well, it doesn't really matter to me," I shrugged. "I don't much care who your family is."

"Right," she said heavily. "I'm sure you don't."

I reached out and took her hand, covering it in mine. "Seriously, I don't. I'm here with you, not them."

She stared into my eyes for several seconds, and I could see a subtle tension flow out of her as she relaxed. At last, she gave me a soft smile. "Thank you for that," she said quietly. "I can't tell if you're being honest or not, but I appreciate the thought—and I think I'll choose to believe you are." She took another sip of her wine, a smaller one this time, then gestured at mine. "What is that?"

I lifted the small glass filled with a dark brown liquid that moved thickly, like warm honey. "Halfling bourbon," I pronounced. "The finest in the world."

"What makes it so good?"

"Mostly the grain used and the barrels it's aged in. All bourbon is made of corn and other grains, and most are aged in oak barrels. Halfling corn is much sweeter than most, though, which gives the bourbon more flavor and higher alcohol content. They also age it in wood taken from their jungles—they don't tell anyone what kinds—and that gives it a slightly spicy flavor." I took a sip of the drink, feeling it coat my tongue and enjoying the mild burn as it rolled over my tongue, mingling with a smoky and sweet taste.

"They also only release two hundred barrels of it per year," I added. "Which means this little glass here probably costs five or six gold crowns, easy." I looked about the room with a disapproving gaze. "That seems about right for this place."

"Most of the people here would consider that downright cheap," she laughed, holding up her glass. "This probably costs double that."

"For a glass of wine?" I scoffed.

"For a glass of Teshean sparkling wine," she corrected. "It's a goblin vintage, made from a blend of grapes that they've cultivated for a thousand years. Their wine is more aromatic than any other kind." She took another sip and giggled slightly. "And much stronger."

"To excellent alcohol, then," I laughed, lifting up my glass.

"I'm always willing to drink to that," she agreed. She sipped her drink, then looked around at the room a bit distastefully. "You know, I've never liked this place—or any place like it."

"No?" I asked, also looking around. "Seems nice enough. A bit quaint, if you ask me—but then, I have very discerning tastes." I arched an eyebrow at her, and she laughed lightly, taking my hand in hers.

"Or very poor ones," she countered.

"I suppose that's possible." I looked around again, not really paying attention to the people but scanning for my elf friends. "Actually, this place seems to take itself far too seriously for me. I prefer something a little livelier. Where's the music? The dancers?" I shook my head. "It's kind of a disappointment."

"That's all in the gambling areas, not here. That's the fun place; this is where business happens." She glanced around again. "That's really the whole point of this place, you know. It's here to help people with money and influence get even more of it."

"Oh?"

"Absolutely," she nodded, gesturing around with her drink. "That's what all these people are doing. They're negotiating for something. Land, goods, power, sex—it's all for sale, and someone in here is probably buying and selling it as we speak."

"I thought that's what the Merchant's Hall is for. Or the Avenue of Roses."

"People here aren't buying whores, Murf," she laughed. "They're buying mistresses or multiple wives. Young, untouched daughters of excellent breeding, raised and trained to serve them in whatever capacity needed." Her words were once again bitter as she spoke.

"That sounds like a moderately awful existence." I said with a shudder.

"I agree, but for some, it's everything they hope for." She seemed to shake off her annoyance. "And only lesser merchants actually do any business in the Hall. There's no privacy there, and anything said there gets spread around the city as a rumor within the hour." She gestured at a pair of older men at the table to our left, one a canid and the other a human. "Take those two. The canid's no doubt a local landowner of some importance, and he has something to sell, either goods or information. Perhaps this year, the rains were light, so the sugarcane harvests were small; or maybe the soil is especially fertile, and the tobacco yields were excellent. He's brokering a deal with the human not only for his goods but for that information."

"Why would that matter?" I asked, confused.

"Because if the sugarcane harvests are low this year, next year, the prices for things like wines, confections, and baked goods will all go up as sugar becomes dearer. The human can invest in those things now, promising to buy a few tuns of, say, sweet wine at the current market price next year. Then, when the price goes up, he can turn around and sell those tuns to a winery for a hefty profit. And all he had to do to get that information was purchase a bunch of sugarcane."

She gestured around again. "That's what's going on here. Perhaps that elf over there is an emissary from Bardara, sent here to conduct diplomacy with the canids, but she just happens to know that the elves have a silver-wood surplus this year. She's selling that information along with her contacts to that avian. He'll get to buy that silver-wood at a lower price than the market value but more than it'll be in a year and resell it before the news gets out. She makes some money as a go-between; he makes some profit; her contacts make more than they would have otherwise. Everyone wins."

"Except the people buying the wood for too much this year," I noted.

"Yes. Except for them." She took another swallow of her drink. "Of course, all of that would be pointless if the information got out, and if they tried to do this deal in the Hall, it would. So, they meet here, make their arrangements, then send a runner to the Hall to have them finalized and marked in the records. That's the real point of the Merchant's Guild."

"What? Recording sales?"

"And guaranteeing them," she said solemnly. "The man offering to buy sugarcane, for example, could just promise the canid to do so, get the information he wants, then back out of the deal. The Guild prevents that. The human will have an account with the Guild and plenty of crowns on credit with them; the canid will have had a Guild assessor come out to verify that he has the sugarcane promised. Once they enter that arrangement into the Guild's ledgers, they're both locked into honoring it, and the Guild will send a card-locked agreement to them both verifying it. Then, the canid can give the human his information, and the human can act on it immediately through another runner."

"It sounds awfully complicated," I noted. "You seem to know a lot about it, though."

"It's very complicated, and of course, I do. I was raised to do this, after all. I wasn't supposed to become a gambler, Murf. I was supposed to be another merchant, spending my days in places like these and using these..."

She gestured at her chest. "…to convince some perverted, old man to part with his goods cheaply for a chance at mine."

"Instead, you use them to convince perverts not to pay attention to their cards," I chuckled.

"Yes, and that's much more fun than all this—stuffiness." She gave me an arch look. "You know, Murf, you would do very well as a merchant, yourself. You can read people, and you're quite easy to look at. There are just as many rich old female merchants as males, and if you unbuttoned that shirt a bit—maybe took them somewhere dark and let your hands roam— they'd probably sell you their children at a nice discount. Why don't you try it?"

"No, thank you," I shuddered. "I don't want money that badly. Besides, gambling's more fun."

"Exactly. It's almost the same thing as being a merchant, in fact. You and the other player are each trying to trick the other into believing you don't have something you have, or that you have something you don't, and to give you coins for it. The difference is, if I swindle some old merchant out of a few thousand crowns, he's not the only one hurt." She made another unhappy face, and I could see her tensing up again. "Enough of that. Tell me a story, Murf. Make it an interesting one."

I flashed her a grin. "As her royal Highness demands," I chuckled.

"Stop that."

"As you wish, milady." She gave me another angry look, and I laughed, waving my hands in front of me. "Okay, okay, I'll stop. Let's see—a story, and a good one. How about the time…?"

Our food arrived soon, and it was amazing. The steak was tender enough that I felt like I barely had to chew it, and so flavorful I wondered if anything would ever taste good again afterward. This meal wouldn't be worth it if I never wanted to eat anything again. I glanced up at Millie, daintily nibbling her lamb, and realized that wasn't going to be a danger, at least as long as I played my cards well.

We chatted amiably as we ate, keeping the topics light and steering away from her family or merchanting. After we finished, Kikoum brought us two plates of some frozen, fruity thing. I swear that it tasted like eating a frozen rainbow while butterflies danced on my tongue. The whole meal was better than anything I'd ever eaten, and I'd dined in a couple palaces over the years. I didn't even want to know how much it cost—or how Millie was paying for it. I assumed that card of hers would take care of it, which meant that Fancypants Deepwater or whatever the plutarch's name was was buying our meal. I was fine with that; apparently, so was Millie. In fact, she was so okay with it that she also had him pay for the chips we purchased for gambling. These were much fancier ones than at the Hall, but basically served the same purpose except that ten was the smallest denomination available.

The gambling hall was just as fancy as the dining room had been, but I felt a lot more comfortable in it. Millie seemed to, as well, as a predatory gleam appeared in her eyes the moment we stepped inside. We agreed to split up and go to separate tables, as we didn't want to take one another's chips. Every game was noblesse, of course. I couldn't imagine the fancy folk wanting to play something as common as arcanum. That was fine; I had no real qualms about exactly how I took coins from rich people, as long as I did. The ante at the table was ten, with a blind of fifty, and most people were betting hundreds of chips on double sets and 3-sets. I was practically drooling as I sat down. I was going to clean up in this place.

I'd given Millie a great line about money not mattering, but the fact is, it does. It's not money that's terrible in my deck; it's hoarding it away so that no one else can have it. Money, to me, was meant to be spent, and I intended to have a good time spending whatever I could get from these people. It wasn't like any of them would miss it, after all.

The merchants, nobles, and diplomats around me weren't exactly novices at cards, I could tell, and most of them were used to covering their tells. They were good, but they weren't quite good enough, and in less than an hour, I had a solid feel for the table. My stack of chips slowly but steadily grew as I won enough to stay ahead but not so much that I'd anger the powerful people around me who could probably buy half the Sellsword's Guild to give me a beating if they felt like it. People grumbled, but no one openly complained as I won more and more, and a couple of the ladies at the table even seemed relatively happy to give me their chips. One was so happy that she accidentally slipped a small, brass-colored card in with her chips as she pushed them over to me, along with a number written on it. I gave her a winning smile and pocketed the card that I felt sure unlocked her room. Not that I was going to do anything about it later, but refusing it would have hurt her feelings.

I glanced from time to time at Millie's table and wondered how many of those cards she'd been slipped during the night. She was doing as well as I was, but the men at her table seemed almost happy to lose to her. One of them, a male halfling with pure white hair, stared openly at her cleavage the entire time, not even pretending to be discreet about it. That was odd because usually, halflings didn't find what they called the "tall folk" all that attractive. At least Ferdi never had with me, which I assumed meant it was an inter-species thing. I know I'm irresistible, after all.

At last, the woman caught my eye, and I slid my chair back, stacking my chips almost gleefully. I'd come to the table with a few hundred chips and left with over ten thousand. I'd gone all in on people several times, and after each one, they simply bought back into the table. That gave me a new stack of coins to take from them.

All in all, it had been a good night.

I met up with Millie, who had a similarly sized stack, and flashed her a grin.

"What say we cash these in, toss the coins on a bed, and roll around on them naked?" I asked her. I'd always wanted to do that, but I'd rarely had enough coins at once to make it a possibility, and when I did, I was usually too busy avoiding whoever had lost them to me to have the time.

"What happened to not caring about money?" she asked archly.

"Well, I don't want to keep it. I just want to roll around on it a bit."

"Naked."

"Naked, with you. It wouldn't be fun without you."

She laughed, her eyes twinkling mischievously. "Sadly, that's not possible, I'm afraid. You can't cash these in."

"What do you mean?" I asked plaintively, feeling my dream shatter just as it seemed in my reach.

"When we return these, they'll go on my Merchant's Guild account—which means they'll go to my grandfather."

"Could we put them on a Gambler's Guild account?"

"Only if we used it to get in here—which we didn't since without the family's account, we wouldn't have been let inside."

I made a face. "Then, if I turn these in, it'll make your family richer?"

"Only by a tiny fraction, but yes."

I sighed, then turned and walked back to my table, setting the coins down on it. I looked at the dealer. "Go ahead and distribute these out," I said mournfully.

"Sir?" the felid woman asked, giving me a surprised look.

"I don't..." I took a deep breath. "I don't want them. I was just here to play the game." I wanted to sob as I said that, but I forced myself to take a deep breath and remind myself...

Murf's Sixth Law: The only good money is spent money.

I walked back over to Millie, who stared at me with wide eyes. "You actually gave all that up?" she asked in surprise. "Isn't that against the Gambler's Code or something? Never give back what you've won fairly?"

"I'd rather they have it than your family," I shrugged. I gave her a quick glance. "Like I said, I can read people, and from what I've read, I don't think I want to help your family."

She blinked rapidly, then walked over to her table and placed her chips down as well. She walked back over to me and grabbed my face, pulling me down and kissing me fiercely. The kiss was deep and passionate, and it lasted for several seconds. At last, she let go, and I came up for air, staring into her gleaming, emerald eyes that gazed back into mine.

"We may not have the coins," she murmured, "but I think we can do the rolling around naked on the bed thing—maybe a few times in a row if you're up for it."

"I'm willing to give it a try," I smiled at her.

As we left, Kikoum stopped us and gave Millie a brass-colored card similar to the one I'd received from my admirer earlier. "Room 411, Miss," he said, bowing low. "A bath is prepared, and glasses of both your preferred drinks are waiting for you."

"Talk about service," I murmured. "I could get used to this."

"We aim to please, sir," the felid assured me. "Follow me, and I'll guide you."

The man led us back into the main entry and down the hall across from the entryway. A double set of spiral stairs rose from there, and he led us up the leftmost one. We took the stairs to the fourth floor, then followed him down a hallway to a door with the number 411 emblazoned on it with gold letters.

"Here we are," he said, gesturing to the door. "Will there be anything else, Miss, sir?"

"No, Kikoum," Millie said. "You've been amazing. Please add 20% to our charges for yourself."

"Twenty?" I asked. "Why not thirty?"

"Make it forty," she agreed. "It's grandfather's money, after all."

"Miss is very generous," he bowed his head, holding out a golden card. "Please touch this to verify the amount." She did so, and he bowed low once more. "My thanks, Miss. I will see you both sometime tomorrow." He turned and walked away, and Millie touched her card to the door to our room, which opened instantly. She pulled me inside, and I barely got a look around before she wrapped her arms around me and pulled me in for a kiss.

"The drinks and bath can wait," she murmured, pressing her body against mine. "We have something much more important to do."

"Yes, you do." We both spun at the strange voice, and my eyes widened as I recognized a familiar, elvish face staring at me, his mouth spread in a leer. I opened my mouth to protest, but before I could, he held up a card, one that I recognized as one of the ones he'd taken from me.

"That son of a bitch is going to get me with my own damn card!"

That was all I could think before a brilliant light flashed before my eyes. The light seemed to sink down into my brain, grabbing my consciousness and pulling it with it, leaving only darkness behind as I tumbled to the floor.

19

Darkness swirled about my vision, dragging me down into its depths, but even as it clawed at my mind, I could see the edges of it starting to tatter. Gray peeked around the corners of my thoughts, and ragged holes appeared in the dark blanket smothering me. Those holes grew as their edges frayed, shivering into wisps of nothingness before my eyes. The darkness faded into gray that quickly brightened to white, and a moment later, my awareness swirled back over me in a rush of sound and sensation.

Coming to from the card wasn't like coming out of being knocked unconscious or even sleeping off a night of too much whisky. One moment, whiteness covered my brain; the next, I was totally awake and aware. It was more like someone yanked a hood off me than rising from sleep. That was a good thing since without that moment of fuzziness and confusion, my brain realized right away that being visibly awake was probably a bad idea at that moment.

I must have only been out for a few seconds at most, I realized, since I still lay on the floor, and from the smell of the room, it was the suite that Kikoum had prepared for us. I was facedown on the floor with something hard and heavy pressing against the small of my back, holding me in place. Strong hands had mine locked behind my back, and I felt a cord of some kind pulled tight around them, binding my wrists in place. For a moment, I considered fighting back. After all, my card gave me all kinds of strength when I really needed it, and while I was no warrior, if I moved quickly enough and caught the elf by surprise with a shot to the chin the way I had Ferdi, I could probably take him. That thought quickly died as a second voice spoke in the room, uttering the flowing, musical Elven tongue.

"We should just kill him, Taveroth," a voice I recognized as Alerion's spoke. "I don't know how he survived the Labyrinth, but he won't survive having his head cut off."

"That wasn't the arrangement, Alerion," the elf atop me said firmly. "The masters of this place agreed to let us take these two, but only if no violence was performed here. If you kill him here, you'll not only anger them, but you'll have breached our employer's word. Do you want to explain that to him?"

"No," Alerion replied, and I heard a tiny undercurrent of fear ripple through his voice before it settled into a far more recognizable tone of mild lust. "What about the woman? Do you think he'll let us have her?"

"Unlikely. He's angry enough at us as is that we let this one live."

"We have some time," Alerion said speculatively. "He won't know exactly when they came up here, after all. She's ready, Taveroth. It would be a shame to waste that."

"He'll know, Alerion, and then, we'll have failed him twice." Taveroth's hands paused on me for a moment. "I don't think you understand the situation. Our continued existence depends entirely on how well we perform this task. Our reward at the end is likely to be survival and nothing more. If that's the case, neither of us has room to complain. Now, tie the woman, and do it without taking liberties."

"Fine."

During the conversation, Taveroth finished binding my hands and proceeded to do the same to my feet. I did my best to remain limp and unresisting, but it wasn't easy, especially not when he pried open my mouth and stuffed a hunk of cloth in it. He tied something to hold the gag in place, then pulled what I assumed was a bag or hood of some kind over my head. That was actually welcome since it meant I could safely open my eyes and blink; they itched a bit, and blinking helped. The bag looked to be some kind of rough, dark cloth, and it tickled and scratched the tip of my nose. That made me want to wriggle my nose and shift around to make it more comfortable, but I knew that would give me away, so I did my best to ignore the irritation.

From the sound of things, Alerion tied Millie up in silence, and while I hoped that he did it without copping a feel or two, I was pretty sure that hope was misplaced. I'd gotten a bit of a feel for the elf, enough to know that he took elvish arrogance to an extreme. Millie wasn't a person to him; she was a thing that he found appealing. I was an annoyance that had the gall to beat him at cards. I felt pretty sure that killing us—or raping Millie—would bother him about as much as stepping on a bug.

Every species has its sociopaths. The elves just seem to have more of them, and they don't seem to care.

It wasn't easy staying limp and unresponsive as the elves hauled me over to an open window, tied a rope beneath my armpits, and lowered my body down to the ground. I had to fight not to panic as my feet hung in space, held up only by whatever knot the elf tied around me and a rope whose strength I didn't know. I had trust issues naturally; you can imagine how much worse those were with people who'd already tried to kill me. I wanted to thrash and kick, but I forced myself to stay still as they lowered me to the ground. I heard Millie land next to me with a soft thump a couple minutes later, then I was lifted and carried a short distance before being tossed onto something hard and flat. Millie joined me, and I felt us start to move in a bouncing fashion that told me I was inside a cart or wagon of some kind. I'd wondered how the elves moved me through the city before without alarming anyone; it looked like I had my answer.

Millie didn't stir as we spent the next hour being bounced and shifted around in the wagon bed. I just focused on trying to figure out where we were. I heard the creak of a gate at one point early on, which I assumed was the servant gate Taveroth mentioned. We went over a bridge, meaning we were now in the western part of the city. The wagon turned and twisted quite a bit, so I guessed that the elves were taking a roundabout route that avoided the main roads. I couldn't hear the river, so we'd gone closer to the walls, and as we traveled, I began to smell the stink of the slums in the very southwest, the poorest part of the city. We never got close enough for that smell to really sink into my nostrils, though, so we had to be in the western part of the middle city, toward the southern end.

That narrowed it down to a thousand or so businesses, homes, warehouses, and storefronts. Not much help, really. Not that it mattered anyway. Assuming I escaped this somehow, I'd be able to figure out where I was in the city easily enough. Canis wasn't big enough to really get lost in. And once I had, I could make my way back again if I wanted. Of course, if I didn't escape, then I'd probably be dead, and nothing would really matter anyway.

The wagon stopped at last, and a few minutes later, I felt myself hoisted up onto a shoulder. I was carried for several minutes before being tossed onto another hard wooden surface, adding more to my growing list of bruises. I heard Millie hit the floor beside me, and I lay still, just listening. I got the impression of being in a large, open space. I heard the sounds of boots shifting on wood, and the stink of unwashed beastling bodies drifted into my nose, a funk of mingled sweat and damp fur that was particularly unpleasant. Everything was silent for almost a full minute before a voice spoke, shattering the stillness.

"I'm surprised, elves. You actually performed the task I set you. It looks like you might get to live another day after all."

"We performed the last task, as well, sir," Taveroth replied in an even tone. "We disposed of the gambler into the Labyrinth, as instructed."

"I instructed you to kill him, then toss him in, and it wouldn't have been necessary if the two of you hadn't been slumming at the waterfront, hoping to impress some serving wench enough that she'd agree to satisfy your partner's—appetites."

The speaker was obviously male but spoke without inflection or accent. He felt mature—someone who was used to being in charge and had been for a long time—but I couldn't be sure of that. His voice sounded oddly flat, lacking any sort of defining characteristics I might use to work out his identity. He didn't fumble his R's the way avians did or roll them as felids tended to. His speech wasn't as thick as a canid's or as deep as an ursid's. It wasn't as musical as an elf's or as rolling as a halfling's, and it lacked the hissing S's that goblin speech tended to have. That suggested that he was human, but he didn't speak with any sort of accent I could have used to identify him, which typically implied that the speaker was non-human, and Human was their second language.

"It shouldn't have been necessary, sir. No one survives being forced into a Labyrinth like that. Anyone who tries to get in anywhere but the entrance vanishes and is never seen again."

"Obviously, then, you must have failed to put him into the Labyrinth—either that, or you're wrong, and Labyrinths can be entered from outside their entrances. We'll have to see which it is. How were they incapacitated?"

"Five of staves, sir. It negated their consciousness. It should last for a day, at least."

"Is that accurate?" the unknown speaker asked. I expected Taveroth to answer again, but to my surprise, a different voice spoke, one I recognized.

"Not precisely," Azara's sultry hiss spoke, and I had to force myself not to jump as I heard her. "The five of staves, wielded by skilled hands, can shut down higher functions, placing the subject into a deep, dreaming state ruled by their subconscious. How long it lasts depends on the will of the individual and the skill of the card wielder."

"Can you undo it?" the man asked.

"Easily. A simple one of staves applied to the subject will stimulate their mind…"

"Then do so for the male," the man cut her off.

"And the female?"

"Is unimportant. Leave her."

"As you wish." I heard the swishing of the woman's feathers as she neared me. "I'll need to remove the mask, though. The card has to touch his forehead."

"Proceed," the speaker said after a momentary hesitation.

I closed my eyes as the mask came away, but I didn't need to see to hear Azara's sharp intake of breath as she saw my face. I felt a little gratified about that; I'd been worried about her working with the elves and what that meant. She knew about the card in my chest, after all, the only person other than me who did. If she was pissed enough at me to knowingly work with the people trying to kill me, I was in big trouble. If she didn't know I was involved, though, maybe she wouldn't give me up.

Although she did sort of promise to kill me if she saw me again. That put a damper on my enthusiasm.

I felt a card touch my head and a brief surge of energy tingle through my skull. For a moment, everything seemed sharper and clearer, but that faded quickly. Whatever the card was supposed to do, either Azara didn't put much oomph into it, or my card's Arcana Resistance worked against it. Whatever the case, I knew what I was supposed to be doing, so I snapped my eyes open and immediately began to struggle, stopping only when something sharp and cold pressed against my chest. I looked up and saw Taveroth standing over me, his sword resting on me, and I gave him a fierce glare that he ignored. As I looked at him, a card with his name on it tried to rise up and block my vision, but I mentally waved it away before it could. It would be a distraction at a time I didn't need one, and I didn't much care what the elf's stats were. If I had to fight him, I was probably a dead man no matter what.

"Welcome back to the world of the living, Mr. Murf," the voice said, and I quickly turned to get a glimpse of my real captor. As I did, I noticed that I was in what looked like an empty warehouse of some kind. An oil lamp hanging overhead provided enough light to see the edges of the room dimly, showing me the source of the shuffling feet I'd heard and body odors I'd smelled before. Nine or ten people stood around the edge of the room, a curiously mixed lot that included members of every major intelligent species.

As my eye glanced over them, I picked them apart without really trying. A pair of ursids, one in chainmail and one wearing armor of overlapping scales, both carrying large, heavy weapons were obviously heavy warriors; a felid woman in scuffed black leather with knives festooned across her body appeared to be an assassin; two orcs in hardened leather armor wielding wicked polearms looked like soldiers; a halfling man in heavy armor holding a short spear was probably an oath-bound like

Ferdi; a goblin dressed in regular clothing but with card holders strapped to his body had to be a card-wielder of some sort; an elf woman dressed in gray with an unstrung bow and a quiver of arrows slung to her back was obviously an archer and hunter. All of them looked well trained, and as I met each of their gazes, I saw the sparkle in them that marked them as Holders. I couldn't help but shiver as I came to a conclusion.

Whoever these people were, they were dangerous as hell, and I wanted to be as far from them as possible.

I looked at last toward the voice and was met with disappointment. The dim light in the room didn't seem to reach that part of the room, leaving the man shrouded in shadows. I couldn't see anything about him, not even an outline that might help judge his species. I guessed that was quite deliberate: the flat voice and darkness were both contrived to keep the man anonymous. I guessed that the people here probably didn't even know who they worked for. I supposed the secrecy could have been for me, but I figured I wasn't supposed to live out the next hour or two anyway, so that didn't make much sense. That meant that trust between these people was probably bought with gold, and that sort of trust could be broken—assuming, of course, I got the chance to do it.

"Remove his gag," the boss instructed, and Taveroth's sword slipped along my cheek. The cloth holding the gag in place parted at once, and I pushed the cloth out of my mouth quickly, spitting and coughing as I did.

"What the hell did you use for that, Alerion's underpants?" I demanded, looking back at the impassive Taveroth. "It tasted like troll ass!" I looked back at the other elf, who watched me through narrow eyes. "It's called bathing, Alerion. Learn to do it, for all our sakes."

A couple of snorts rose from the others, and Alerion's eyes blazed as he took a step forward, but he froze as the hidden man spoke.

"Stop, Alerion," he instructed. "He's trying to bait you, and he'll probably keep doing so. If you can't control yourself, leave." Alerion took a step back and set his jaw, and I flashed him a grin before turning back to face the darkness.

"You look awfully shadowy back there," I noted. "I'm not sure what the point is, though. What's my reaction supposed to be? Fear? Curiosity? Should I be secretly turned on? It's hard to tell, really."

"Yes, you're very amusing," the man said in his flat voice. "But your life hinges on my word at the moment, so I suggest…"

"Ah, the shadowy overlord," I nodded. "Got it. The hidden figure in darkness, pulling all the strings, using his little toys to—what? Take over the world? Conquer Canis? Maybe there's this one serving wench you just really, really like…"

A sudden flash shot from the darkness as a streak of electricity slammed into my body. It burned and tingled as it raced through me with a lot more power than Azara's had, but it didn't seem to be damaging me all that badly. I still fell back, writhing and shaking for a few seconds until it cut off. I had to pretend it hurt, after all, or he might switch to something that really would, like thumbscrews or hooking me up with the ursid woman. Even I had standards, and they didn't include seven-foot-tall women with bear faces covered with fur. At least, not unless I was really, REALLY drunk.

"Do you understand your situation better, now?" the man asked.

I groaned and sat up, nodding my head. "Yeah, I get it. No wenches. Let me guess: it's a felid man, right? An orc? A troll? Hey, I don't judge, but that sounds like it'd be painful…"

I dropped again as the lightning arced out and slammed into me once more, thrashing and jerking about like it was frying me. It lasted longer this time, but the more I was exposed to it, the less it seemed to affect me until by the end, it was like having ants crawling on my body. Not something I enjoyed, really, but nothing more than an annoyance. I was fine with enduring it, though, because I still had hope. Ferdi's people would have recognized the elves bringing me through the city, after all, and they'd have followed us here. For all I knew, halflings were ringing the building as we spoke, planning how to come in, kick some ass, and get Ferdi's cards back. And free me in the process, hopefully.

The lightning cut off, and the voice spoke again. "For the moment, Mr. Murf, I need you alive. I have questions, and you have answers. However, I don't need you whole for that. I'm not sure how long that lightning would take to burn off part of your body, but if you don't cooperate, we'll find out."

I shifted back to where I could look at him and shook my head, giving him a disappointed expression. "You know, this whole evil torturer thing is really cliché. You should try something new. Why not dress as a felid woman and dance for me, instead? You know, seduce me to talk. Hell, since you're probably back there to hide the damage deep-throating that troll did to your face, I might talk just to get you to stop!"

"Perhaps you're right," the voice said. "Maybe I'm going about this the wrong way. Obviously, you've got a decent pain tolerance, and while there are ways around that, I don't have the time. What if, instead, I did this?" The arc of electricity shot out again, but this time, it flashed past me and tore into Millie's still form. The woman's body convulsed immediately, and she began screaming and thrashing as the power raced through her. Apparently, that was another way to wake her up. I did my best to keep my face confused rather than angry as I watched her, even though I wanted to rip off my bindings, run up to the guy, and punch him in the crotch a few dozen times. The more I showed that it bothered me, I reasoned, the more likely the man would be to keep torturing her to get me to cooperate.

The electricity ended, and Millie collapsed, sobbing and wailing into her gag. I ignored her and looked up at the darkness.

"What was the point of that?" I asked curiously. "Is that supposed to bother me? I barely even know the girl. She just looked like a fun ride, really. If you want to zap her to get your jollies, be my guest."

"I think she's more than that," the voice chuckled in a flat, dry tone. "But I could be wrong. Perhaps this would serve better, instead."

A commotion rose behind me as a wooden door slammed open, and I glanced backward, twisting my body to see what was happening. A pair of humans, one male and one female, both dressed in loose, charcoal clothing and wearing masks that concealed their features entered the room, dragging a weakly struggling figure. The captive was short, not even five feet tall, covered from shoulders to toes in blue and silver plate armor that only left her head exposed. My heart sank as she lifted her head, and her eyes met mine, eyes that were blackened and swollen.

They'd gotten Ferdi. That made these people even more dangerous than I thought—and it meant my chances of getting out of this had dropped to practically zero.

✦ ✦

20

"This one was skulking around the outside of this building," Hidden Man said. "I understand that she and you have a history of sorts—at least, judging from the bounty posters she's put up all over the city." He looked past me at the pair. "Was she alone?"

"No, sir," the woman growled in a scratchy, gravelly voice. "She had six halflings with her. They were trying to surround the place."

"And now?"

"They're dead. Their bodies are in the wagon, waiting for transport."

"Excellent." He looked back at me. "What about her, Murf? Are you willing to see her tortured? Humbled? Humiliated? I can do all of those to both of these women—or you can answer my questions. It's that simple, really."

I struggled to a sitting position and spat in his general direction. "What do you want to know?" I asked bleakly, letting my anger show a bit at last.

"It's simple. The two elves behind you threw you into a Labyrinth some time ago. That should have killed you. Obviously, it didn't. How did you survive?"

"Labyrinth?" I asked in a confused voice, letting my doubt show on my face. "I don't know anything about a Labyrinth. At least, I don't think I do." I jerked my head backward. "These assholes threw me off a damn cliff, is what they did, and just because I beat them at cards!"

"And how did you survive that?"

"I hit a tree on the way down that softened the fall," I shrugged. "Got scratched the hell up and dislocated my shoulder, but it slowed me enough that when I landed in the mud, I only blacked out. It's not my fault that they're incompetent."

"He's lying," Alerion snapped from behind me. "We threw him directly into the Labyrinth!"

"Sounds like you missed it," one of the orcs chuckled. "Can't trust an elf to do anything right."

"He could be lying," the felid woman suggested in a languid voice. "He could also be telling the truth. In either case, though, it sounds like there's no job for any of us, here."

"I beg your pardon, Fisya?" the shadowed man asked in a calm but dangerous voice.

"I mean no offense, sir, but if these elves are telling the truth, then that means that this man—not a Holder and with no training—walked out of the Labyrinth unarmed. If he could do that, it's not truly a virgin Labyrinth, and it won't have the rewards you promised us.

"On the other hand, if the human is telling the truth, then there is no Labyrinth there at all. Either way, I'm not sure what the point of our being here is."

The others grumbled, most of them echoing the felid's thoughts, while the elf woman shook her head in negation.

"This man wasn't the first body we've thrown down there for disposal," she said harshly. "If there's no Labyrinth, where are all those people?"

"You mean, the half-rotted corpses all over the jungle floor in there?" I snorted. "I'm guessing they didn't land as nicely as I did, obviously."

"There's another explanation," the goblin suggested. "Perhaps the human fell into the Labyrinth, survived—and completed it."

The others burst into frenzied conversation at that idea, but I just kept my expression confused as I looked at the diminutive, green-skinned man. As the arguments began to rise, I felt a little spark of hope. If they all quit this job—or even better, turned on one another—I could try to break my bonds, free Ferdi and Millie, and the three of us could get the hell out of there in the chaos. Unfortunately, that wasn't to be.

"SILENCE!" the hidden man thundered, and the arguments quickly ended. That surprised me. Some of those people seemed really angry at one another, and all of them looked and felt dangerous enough that it seemed like they wouldn't take kindly to being yelled at. I saw the fear in their eyes when they looked at the shadows, though. Whoever this guy was, he scared the shit out of these people, which meant that maybe I should start taking him a bit more seriously.

"There's a simple way to find out the truth of this matter," the man said. "Cartomancer, is it possible to divine if he's telling the truth?"

I glanced at Azara, who looked at me and hesitated. "Yes," she finally nodded. "It's possible. It will take some time to set up, though. I didn't bring the correct layout for that."

"And is it possible to see if he's holding a card?" the man pressed.

"Yes, of course. A simple divination will reveal that. I'm prepared to perform that."

"Then do what you need to. That should answer everyone's questions."

"What if he's telling the truth?" the felid pressed.

"Then it's obvious these two idiots failed to put him into the Labyrinth, and we proceed as planned, of course."

"And if he's lying?"

"If he's lying, and he's not holding a card, then I'll give him to you to get the truth from him, one way or the other. A combination of torture and watching these others be tortured and humiliated should loosen his tongue. Once we know the truth, we'll know how to proceed."

The felid purred happily, gazing almost hungrily at me. That unnerved me a bit, I admit. Felids were usually horny things, and apparently this one got off on hurting people. I really didn't want to end up in her hands, or claws, or whatever she had.

The others seemed less enthusiastic. They grumbled a bit, but no one seemed ready to argue with Shadow Man. As Azara set to work, I tried to catch her eye, but she studiously avoided looking at me. I supposed I'd burned that particular bridge rather permanently. After a few minutes, she rose from her work and looked back over her shoulder.

"I'm ready. I can tell you if he's telling the truth or not, now."

"How accurate can you be?" the goblin broke in, his voice curious. "Cards can't compel a person, after all..."

"I can read his emotional and mental state as he speaks," she cut the man off coldly. "If he knowingly speaks a lie, I'll sense it." She made a slight face. "However, the cards will only tell me what he believes to be the truth, so if he believes he's correct but isn't, I won't know that."

"That should be sufficient for our purposes," Shadow Man said. "You understand the situation, don't you, Mr. Murf?"

"I think I have an idea," I muttered.

"Then you know that the truth is your only chance. Tell me the truth, and your death will be painless—and the only one that needs to happen today."

His voice turned colder at he spoke. "Lie to me, though, and not only will your death be incredibly painful, you'll first have to watch these other two suffer and die as well. I can make your deaths last for days, Mr. Murf. No one is looking for you; no one will come to save you. Do you understand?"

I nodded; I did understand. He held all the cards, and I had nothing worth playing. If we'd been at a table, I'd have folded in a heartbeat. We weren't, though. This was the only hand I had to play, and I didn't have shit. That left me one choice.

Murf's Nineteenth Law: When the Unity deals you shit, bluff, and make it good.

"Good. Mr. Murf, did these two elves capture you?"

"Why yes, they did," I answered. "Because they're assholes."

"Truth," Azara proclaimed, lifting a card from the tableau before her.

"See?" I chuckled. "Even the cards know that they're assholes."

The goblin and orcs all laughed quietly, but the Hidden Man ignored my jibe.

"Did they take you to the edge of a cliff and throw you off?"

"They did. Like I said, assholes."

"Truth."

The orcs and goblin laughed again, while Alerion looked pissed, but Shadow Man pressed on.

"Was there a Labyrinth below that cliff?"

I mentally crossed my fingers, said a little prayer to the Unity, and bluffed.

"I couldn't tell you," I said with a shrug.

Azara lifted a card and frowned at it. "Unclear."

"What do you mean, 'unclear'?" Alerion demanded. "Of course, there is!"

"He didn't answer the question, that's why," the goblin pointed out. "He didn't say yes or no. He said he couldn't tell us."

"If he can tell us, then that would be a lie," the felid said drily. "And if he can't, it would be the truth. I'm not sure…"

"All of you, be silent!" Shadow Man commanded. "Mr. Murf, is there a Labyrinth there?" I remained silent, and the silence stretched out. "Mr. Murf, refusing to answer is the same as lying and will result in these others being punished."

"But you told me to be silent," I protested. "Which is it?"

Ferdi hissed as lightning arced out and slammed into her. Her body shook and spasmed, but she clamped her lips together and refused to make a sound. After several seconds, the power ceased flowing, and she sagged in the grip of her captors. She snarled and glared at the darkness, her eyes promising all sorts of terrible vengeance to whoever was behind it, but he ignored her.

"I'm done with these theatrics, Mr. Murf," he said. "From now on, you'll answer my questions simply, without attempting to confuse the issue, or these others will pay."

"It's not my fault you're asking bad questions, buddy. Ask better ones, and you'll get better answers."

He seemed to pause for a moment. "What do you mean?"

"You asked if there's a Labyrinth below that cliff, but how could I know that? I've never even seen one. For all I know, I walked right through one and never knew it."

"That…" He sighed. "Could be correct. Fine. What happened after you were thrown off the cliff? Exactly, and in detail."

"I fell," I shrugged, crossing my fingers and hoping the Unity wasn't being its normal bitch self at the moment. "I was pretty sure I was going to die, but I hit a tree, instead. It hurt. After that I hit the ground and blacked out. I woke up with a dislocated shoulder, a ton of scratches, and some bruises I can't show in polite company. I fixed my shoulder, followed the cliff out of the ravine, found a fishing village, and came back to Canis." I shrugged. "Pretty simple."

Azara frowned as she looked at her cards, and I had to refrain from holding my breath. "Mostly true," she finally proclaimed. "The last part is incomplete, but not untrue."

Only all my years at the tables kept my jaw from dropping. Either my card had somehow kept Azara from reading me, or she'd just lied for me. Fortunately, I'd bluffed enough over the years to roll with it without showing surprise.

"Fine," I said, rolling my eyes. "Some of the bodies down there had purses that weren't hidden anymore once their owners exploded on impact. I helped myself to them since these assholes stole my stuff, and I needed a new stake if I wanted to win enough to enter the tournament."

"Truth," Azara confirmed.

"There's not even a fucking Labyrinth down there!" the male ursid roared. "You lied to us!"

The big bear lifted his heavy hammer and rushed toward the darkness with a scream of fury. He made it all of two steps before a lance of dark purple fire shot from the shadows and slammed into his chest. The flame seemed to slice through his armor without touching it and bury itself in him. His eyes exploded into flares of violet fire, and liquid flames poured like blood from his mouth. He fell like a puppet with its strings cut, collapsing in a heap on the floor. Flares of purple flame erupted from his back, burning fiercely but swiftly for several seconds before guttering out and dying.

"Harvest his cards—or what's left of them," Shadow Man commanded. I watched as the other ursid flipped the dead man over and touched his chest, pulling out a handful of cards, some of which looked blackened and burnt and quickly fell to ashes. I swallowed hard, and even Ferdi looked ashen-faced as she glared at the shadows.

At least I knew now why the others were so scared of him.

"Now, for the other matter. Does Mr. Murf have a card bound to him?" the man asked. I watched as Azara took her cards back up, shuffled them, and unrolled a new layout. She placed these cards quickly and easily, touched one to my chest, and put it into the center. She flipped it over and shook her head.

"No, he doesn't," she said firmly.

"Excellent. Mr. Murf, it seems you were telling the truth, which means that you and these others will die swiftly. Congratulations."

"I suppose I should say something like, 'But you promised!' but we all knew you were going to do this anyway," I snorted. I glanced at the Holders standing around looking half-pissed, half-terrified. "Might want to remember how he keeps his word for when it's time to get paid."

The warriors looked a little concerned, but the Hidden Man chuckled.

"Oh, I'll keep my word, Mr. Murf. I promised not to kill them, and I won't. In fact, I won't kill you, either. I'll let the Unity do it." He laughed, the sound oddly dry and emotionless. "Bind the halfling, and place all three of them in the Ochre Forest. Let the Unity deal with them." He paused. "The cartomancer, too."

"What?" Azara squawked, reaching into her vest and pulling out a card. "Treacherous snake! I'll…"

Her words cut off as the felid woman seemed to float across the room and swarmed all over her. The assassin grasped Azara's upraised hand, yanking the card from it. Her other hand slipped around the avian's throat and squeezed. A few seconds later, Azara crumpled in her grasp, her eyes sliding shut, and the felid proceeded to bind and gag her.

"See?" I said contemptuously, looking at the others. "This is what you all have to look forward to, as well. He'll use you, then toss you aside."

"To the contrary, Mr. Murf. I have an agreement with these others to reward them well for their services, and I always honor my agreements. The avian was employed for a single job, and now, that job is done. I have no further need of her. Fisya, relieve her of her cards."

"She might be able to help find that Labyrinth, sir," the goblin suggested. "If the human didn't enter it, it could be hidden or sealed, which would explain why it's never been plundered."

"I know the Labyrinth is there, Zeric. As I told you, you aren't the first team I've sent inside—but you'll be the last…"

He stopped speaking as Fisya gave a yelp and jumped back from Azara, shaking a hand that smoked furiously. "Her cards are trapped!" she said, putting her burned fingers in her mouth and glaring accusingly at the darkness.

"It's no matter. They aren't Unity cards, anyway. Leave them." He paused for a moment, and when he spoke again, despite the flat, emotionless tone of his voice, I could swear I heard some glee in it. "Mr. Murf, I would say that it was a pleasure, but I'd be lying. Goodbye."

As Taveroth stepped in front of me and held up a card, part of me felt I should probably say something back. Maybe something along the lines of, "You haven't seen the last of me!" or, "I'll be back, Shadow Man!" Those seemed ridiculously clichéd, though, so instead, I glanced at the others.

"You guys are next."

I didn't get to see their reactions as the white flash erupted in my vision and once more smothered my thoughts, dragging me into darkness.

21

The darkness didn't last long this time; it barely wrapped around me before it flared back to white and vanished. My senses returned instantly, just in time for me to feel my gag being retied and the bag shoved over my head again. I was lifted and carried once more, then dumped onto something both hard and yielding at the same time. It took everything I had not to let out a yelp of disgust when touching something warm, wet, and sticky made me realize that I'd been tossed into the wagon with the halfling bodies. A loud clang beside me told me that Ferdi had been tossed in, as well, and I couldn't help but wince at the thought of her being forced to lay on top of her dead companions. That seemed cruel and morbid even for Shadow Man, and I just hoped that they'd knocked her out, first.

The wagon ride lasted much longer this time. I heard it as we passed through the city gates and exited into the countryside. The wagon picked up speed at that point, suggesting that horses were pulling it instead of a pair of card-buffed elves. I could hear the two of them talking as we traveled, but over the muffling effects of my hood, the clanking of the bodies around me, the clopping of the horse's hooves, and the rattling of the wagon, I could only make out occasional words and phrases. From the sound of it, Alerion was ranting loudly, and Taveroth kept trying to calm him down. I realized that I wasn't going to hear anything important and settled down to try and relax during the ride.

That turned out to be impossible.

As it turns out, armored halfling bodies don't make for a great mattress. They shifted with every bounce and sharp turn, flopping me about. Metal-clad elbows jammed into my ribs and spine; my face smacked against breastplates; what I think was an armored knee even shoved its way into my crotch at one point. That was much less than comfortable, believe me. And to make it even worse, the bodies quickly began to smell, as some of their biological processes apparently kept going after they died. Hearing dead halflings fart isn't the creepiest thing in the world, but it's right up there, and when that fart is accompanied by something else—well, suffice it to say that it wasn't the most pleasant ride I've had.

I spent the time trying not to breathe, shifting to get as comfortable as possible, and working on my bonds. I couldn't tell what Taveroth tied me up with, but it felt like leather, and apparently, it still had a little stretch in it. By twisting my arms behind my back, I managed to work out enough slack to slip a hand free. With my face covered, I couldn't tell if the elves were watching me or not, so I slid my hand back into the loop and began to work on my feet. I wasn't going to get enough slack to pull a boot free, that I felt sure, but I didn't have to. My legs draped over an armor-covered corpse, so I found a metal edge and began rubbing the tie back and forth across it. It was probably rounded so the wearer didn't cut themselves on their own armor, but after an hour or so, the friction built up enough that the thong parted. Again, I left my feet together and relaxed, unsure what the elves might notice or not.

At least a few hours passed as we traveled, enough time that I actually got bored and dozed off here and there. I couldn't sleep since every bounce jammed cold metal into me somewhere, but I managed to drift off enough that the time didn't drag interminably. At last, the wagon slowed to a halt, and I heard a new voice speaking.

"What's this?" a woman's voice with the throaty liquidity of a canid spoke, her tone flat and not particularly friendly.

"Just a delivery to the Forest," Taveroth replied. "A bit of garbage that needs tossing."

"The Forest isn't a waste disposal service, elf. There are places for that."

"Of course, but this is special garbage. I understand that it's allowed, but that there's a fee for doing so. It's a silver, right?"

Silence reigned for a moment before the woman growled. "Two, actually."

"Of course, my mistake. Two silver it is. Here you go."

"Dispose of your trash and be quick about it, elf. Remember that the entrance is only open for a few minutes. After that, you're in trouble."

"Thank you." The wagon began to roll again, but this time, it only drove for a minute or so before stopping. I heard the two elves jump down from the wagon and begin walking toward the rear.

"We're not going to be able to carry all these in before the entrance closes, Taveroth," Alerion said in a low voice, speaking Elven.

"I know, Alerion. I think that's supposed to be the point. He sent us here to be trapped in the Forest ourselves as punishment for screwing up."

"So, why don't we just abandon the wagon and run for it?"

"Because we'd have knives in our backs before we made it out of here. I'm certain he sent those two human assassins to trail us and make sure we followed his orders."

"Fuck," Alerion swore. "I say we forget the wagon, unhitch the horses, and run for it."

"That's not a bad idea, actually. Not running for it—we'd be killed—but unhitching the wagon. We could pull it into the Forest, leave it there, and take the horses back. We've done what we were ordered to, so we don't have to run, and we survive."

"Good idea," Alerion sighed. "Let's get to it."

The wagon shifted a bit as the two untied the horses from it, then I felt it moving much more slowly as they apparently pulled it into this forest they were talking about. Half a minute later, my skin tingled and burned slightly as I felt a weird energy flow over me, and a new card popped up in my vision.

Labyrinth Entered!
You have entered the Labyrinth of
the **Ochre Forest**!
Labyrinth Type: Escape
Recommended Rank: 3-5
Probable Rewards: Low

I immediately began to struggle, yanking my hands and feet free and tearing off my hood. I did NOT want to be in another Labyrinth! I most certainly didn't want to get stuck in one and have to actually work my way out of it instead of getting to cheat my way through it!

As my sight returned, I silently swore a little bit. The elves had draped a covering of some kind over the wagon bed. I supposed that made sense once I thought about it. They wouldn't want the city's guards or some passing merchant to see our bodies, after all, and that canid woman from before probably wouldn't have been okay with it, either. My guess is that she suspected what was in the wagon, but suspicion and knowledge are two different things. The point was that I could have gotten free of my bindings and made myself more comfortable a long time ago, and they never would have noticed.

"This should do," Alerion said after a few seconds.

"No," Taveroth replied. "Last time, we left that human and assumed he'd die. I won't make that mistake again." I heard his sword sliding from its sheath. "We kill all four, then run for the entrance before it closes."

"Fine." A second sound of steel on steel echoed in the quiet. "Let's be fast, though."

I quickly looked around for something that I could use as a weapon and came up distressingly short of options. The halflings had all been disarmed, apparently, or if they had any weapons left, I couldn't see them. I wasn't about to go searching Azara for a card—I remembered what happened to Fisya when she did—and Ferdi was too far away to check. That left me with only one possibility that I could see, and while I doubted it would be terribly effective, it would certainly have surprise on its side.

The cover flew up, dazzling me for a moment, which meant I didn't get to see the elves' faces as 150 pounds of armored halfling corpse flew from the wagon bed and smashed into them. Both of them swore loudly and fell backward, and I heard a crash as at least one of them uselessly attacked the dead body. I didn't wait for them to recover before leaping out at them and knocking down the closer one, who turned out to be Alerion. The elf stared at me in confusion for a moment as I landed astride him, pinning him down. In that second, I cracked my fist down onto his nose as hard as I could.

I didn't really expect much to happen from my attack, to be honest. I hadn't forgotten that entering a Labyrinth granted people a short period of invulnerability, which meant that my punch probably wouldn't hurt the elf. At least, it wouldn't damage him. I knew from past experience that invulnerability didn't mean immunity to pain, and getting punched in the nose hurt. Trust me. It doesn't matter if the fist comes from a jealous husband, an angry father, or a bitter gambler who hates losing. Having your beak whacked hurts like hell and makes your eyes water, which might have been enough for me to wrestle his sword away from him and hopefully stab him somewhere important with it.

As I expected, his head snapped back, and his eyes flew open in pain. I hadn't expected the blood that exploded from his face as his nose crumbled beneath my fist, and I don't think he had, either. We both froze for a second, startled by the sudden spray of crimson. Sadly, as a supposedly trained warrior, Alerion regained his bearings first. His own fist flew up and knocked me in the side of the head, and his blow was a lot more serious than mine. For one thing, he was strong, as strong as Ferdi. For another, he'd had the foresight to wrap his hand in steel, which was a decidedly unfair advantage.

At least, it should have been. I should have been knocked out cold, or at least flung from his body. Instead, my head whipped to the side from the impact, which otherwise hurt about as much as a slap from an offended barmaid. The blow knocked me out of my stunned paralysis, and even more, it pissed me off. As I looked down at Alerion, that anger turned into fury. This was the man who'd started all this. He was the one who started the fight in Keeghan's; he was the one who shoved me into the Labyrinth; he was the one who wanted to rape Millie and kill me. This man didn't deserve to be on this world anymore, as far as I was concerned, and I intended to make that happen.

My fist crashed into him again, and his eyes glazed for a moment as his head whipped sideways. As his body went limp, I snatched the sword he held out of his hand. I had no idea how to use a sword. I'd never swung one in anger in my life. That didn't matter, though. I wasn't planning on dueling Alerion with it. I sat up straight and placed the tip against his throat. His eyes widened, and he reached up to grab it, but I leaned forward and shoved down, as hard as I could. The weapon dimpled his throat, but it refused to penetrate, and I could feel the power of a card at work, protecting him.

It didn't matter. Whatever card he had wouldn't keep him safe from me—and from the Hag. I didn't know how to use her, but I didn't care. I simply demanded that she help me, and she responded at once. A surge of fury boiled up in me, and power accompanied that rage, flowing into my arms and down the blade. The barrier around the elf's throat collapsed beneath the power of a Cabal, and the weapon punched through his trachea and kept going, tearing past his spine and plunging into the ground below. His eyes widened in terror for a moment before they went distant and unseeing as the blade cut his brain off from his body.

Something slammed into the side of me, and I flew off Alerion and crashed into the ground. I rolled with the impact, but before I could come to my feet, a blade whistled toward my head. I felt a spike of panic, but as the weapon descended, the world slowed around me for a moment, giving me just enough time to roll away. The weapon barely touched the earth beneath me before thrusting forward, and a shimmering line of energy whipped out from it and sliced into me. I hissed in pain as the attack cut my skin deeply enough to draw blood. The elf slashed with his sword, and a crescent-shaped, almost-invisible blade leapt from it and hit my stomach, again drawing blood and making me swear with pain. He lifted the sword one more time, but before he could swing it, a stone spike suddenly burst from the top of his leading foot, punching through his armored boot and sticking six inches up into the air. He screamed and leaped backward, but the spike flattened out, trapping his foot, and he fell with a loud pop that came from his ankle.

He roared in pain and anger, lifting his sword to cut himself free, but I charged at him and slammed my foot down on his arm, pinning it and his sword in place. He strained to lift it, but I pushed down, and I saw a look of shock on his face as his arm stayed immobile, the Hag's strength overwhelming whatever lesser card he had. I lifted my other foot high and slammed it down on his stomach, and the armor beneath my boot crumpled with a groan of steel. Vomit erupted from his mouth, and he curled up around the blow, trying to grab my foot. I yanked it free and crashed it down again, feeling the steel bend beneath my heel. I stomped once more, this time aiming lower, and the elf screeched in a high-pitched voice as my heel crumpled his codpiece.

"You took some cards from me," I growled, tearing the gag from my mouth. "When you fuckers tossed me off that cliff. Where are they?" I stamped again, and he shrieked as my heel dug deeper into his crotch.

"Gave—employer," he groaned. "Always—cards—him."

"SHIT!" I roared in sudden fury. I'd been hoping to end the whole thing with Ferdi, but apparently, that wasn't quite over yet. In a fit of anger, I lifted my foot and slammed it down once more, this time into his stunned face. My heel crunched his nose, and his whole body spasmed as his skull crumbled under my foot. I stomped again, and my foot squelched into the ground as his head flattened around me. As his head collapsed into paste, a flicker of a card tried to pop up in my vision, but I pushed it away before I even caught a glimpse of it. My entire focus was on my boot and the ruin of a man that had once been Taveroth.

I stared at my foot buried in his skull for all of three seconds as the rage drained away from me. Taveroth's head was a bloody mess, with brains spread out everywhere. His eyeballs had popped at some point, and one of them clung to my boot, along with smears of brain matter and clots of blood. It was the most gruesome thing I could remember seeing, and I had done it. Me. Not the Hag, just me. I had inflicted that kind of savagery on the man.

"What the fuck am I turning into?"

The question echoed in my head as I stumbled backward. I took a few steps away from the dead elves, spun, and dropped to one knee as vomit sprayed from my mouth. I'd killed before, when I had to, but I'd never done anything that brutal in my life. I'd never been able to, for one thing, but I'd never had the urge to, either. Now, apparently, I could—and I'd stomped a man's skull into paste in anger. My stomach clenched again, and I coughed as more of the meal I'd eaten at the Lamb spilled onto the ground.

A hand touched my shoulder, and I spun quickly, thinking that maybe somehow, one of the elves had survived. Instead, I saw Azara, standing over me, looking down at me with sorrow and compassion.

"It's a terrible thing to kill a person, Murf," she said quietly. "Even one who deserved it, as these two did."

"Yeah," I breathed, spitting out the nasty taste from my mouth. "They did. Just—I can't believe I did that, Azara. I can't believe I was that vicious."

"There's darkness in all of us," she shrugged. "More in you than most. It was bound to come out eventually."

"Me?" I scoffed, shaking my head. "I'm the opposite of dark and brooding, Azara."

"Yes, you cover your shadows well with wit and sarcasm," she nodded. "But they linger deep within you. There's an anger there—a deep and abiding one, born of pain and betrayal." She shivered slightly. "And it's gained strength since last we were together."

I opened my mouth to protest, but the simple fact was, I didn't have the strength or inclination to argue. Besides, after what I'd just done, I wasn't completely sure she wasn't right.

"Well, that's fun," I sighed. I rose to my feet, and her hand fell away. I glanced over at her as something occurred to me. "How long have you been awake?"

"Hours," she shrugged. "The elf was a fool to think that a simple arcana would hold a cartomancer for long. I burned through my bindings and waited for my chance. I knew it would come eventually, especially considering that the card must have barely affected you."

"You figured that out, huh?"

"Of course. Little in the cards is hidden from me, as you should know. Plus, I'd seen the limited effect my cards had on you—and if I'd forgotten, I was reminded when my truth-finding tableau had no effect on you whatsoever."

"Really?" I laughed. "I thought you were just lying to cover me."

"I was. It wasn't hard to decipher the actual truth from what I'd seen already. I confirmed the story you wanted them to hear." She gave me a thin, brittle smile. "The cards warned me that there would be treachery of some sort. I chose to believe it wouldn't come from you. Not again."

"If you knew that, why work for that guy?"

"You assume I was given a choice in the matter." She turned and looked back at the wagon. "I'll wake the others. We should make our way from this place quickly, Murf." She looked around and shivered again. "There's something here that makes the cards nervous."

"Well, we don't want that," I sighed. I had no clue what that meant, and I didn't think I wanted to. Sadly, I was pretty sure the Unity was going to make sure I did before too long. It had just been that sort of day…week…life, to be honest.

I walked over to the wagon and pulled both women out, laying them on the ground well away from the halfling corpses. I didn't really want either of them waking up on a pile of dead bodies, after all. I figured things were bad enough as they were. Plus, having Ferdi wake up like that felt like a good way to get myself hurt in a hurry. I grabbed a dagger from Alerion and used it to cut their bindings, then stepped back as Azara knelt beside the halfling. That same card kept trying to flutter up into my vision, and with a sigh, I finally let it. It seemed pretty damn insistent, and the Hag had helped me a lot during that fight. I really didn't want to piss her off.

Card Attunement!

You have increased your Harmony with your hole card, the Eldritch Hag, from 1% to 10%, giving you Minor Attunement with this card.

Benefits

Adjacency Bonuses +25%
All abilities are +25% stronger
Adaptive and Needful Body abilities last 50% longer.

Unity Achievement!

You have defeated your first Holders in single combat! For this Achievement, you receive:
100 UP per rank of the Holders
100 RP per rank difference
+50 UP per Holder
+1,300 UP

Rank Up!

You have reached Rank 1!
You receive:
Luck +1, Skill +1, Capacity +1

Harmonies:

A sudden flow of warmth rose up from within me and washed through my body, relaxing my muscles and healing some of my lingering bruises. I read the cards again in mild confusion, wondering what the hell they were talking about. Profession? Was that what I'd seen in Ferdi's card, when it called her a Delver? I had no clue—but I knew who to ask. I swiped the cards away and turned back toward Azara, who'd produced a card from her vest and was just touching it to Ferdi's forehead.

The halfling's eyes fluttered open, and a look of confusion spread across her face. That shifted to mingled fear and anger a moment later, and her body bucked as she whipped a fist at Azara hovering over her. The avian had time for a quick squawk before the blow crashed into her stomach, knocking her onto her ass. She groaned but managed to pull out a card and hold it up, pointing it toward Ferdi. This was about to go bust in a hurry.

"Wait!" I shouted, stepping up between the two women. That turned out to be a pretty stupid idea, as a blast of force hit my right side from Azara's card at the same time that Ferdi's foot cracked into my left side. About the only good thing about that was that the two impacts sort of held me up instead of knocking me sprawling. The bad part was that I got a personal introduction to how grapes feel in a wine press, and that definitely outweighed that tiny positive. I let out a sound that was probably a fair imitation of goat being kicked by a troll and wondered how my ribs managed to hold out against that one.

"Ferdi," I managed to wheeze, holding up a restraining hand and trying to inflate at least one of my lungs, "she's with us!"

"Murf?" the halfling asked, taking a step back and looking around as her gaze cleared. "Where are we? Last I remember, we were in that warehouse..."

"I'll explain in a minute," I said, taking a deep breath and rolling the shoulder I could have sworn had popped right out of its socket but apparently just hurt like it had. "Azara, can you wake up Millie? It's probably better only to go through this once."

"She struck me, Murf!" the cartomancer said shrilly, still holding her card.

"It was an accident. Ferdi doesn't react well when she's startled. Or angry. Or hungry, for that matter. In fact, she rarely reacts well at all."

"That's not true," the halfling replied calmly, still looking around. "I react appropriately to different situations. You simply don't like how I react sometimes."

I let that go, not wanting to mention that just about anyone would say putting out a bounty for a man's jewels was a bad reaction—unless he'd forced himself on someone, of course. I suppose it might have been appropriate then. Instead, I did what I probably should have a while ago and followed Ferdi's lead, looking around to see where we were.

The Ochre Forest had come by its name honestly. We stood in the middle of a leaf-strewn clearing about fifty feet wide surrounded by a veritable sea of trees. There were tall trees and short trees, trees with spiky needles like pines and ones with big, wide leaves. Some were straight while others bent and twisted. Seriously, the place simply reeked of trees.

And every damn last one of them was orange. Just an unrelenting, unnatural, and probably unhealthy wall of orange that wrapped around us in every direction. They weren't all the same shade of orange, not exactly, but they were close. Every trunk looked like someone smeared muddy clay all over it. The leaves fluttered like tiny pumpkins or tangerines, with a few carrots and persimmons thrown in for good measure. A glance upward confirmed that the sky overhead was a pinkish orange that reminded me of a peach, while the ground below the mat of leaves was the color of an actual orange.

Apparently, all that orange also made me hungry, which was weird.

"We're in a Labyrinth, aren't we?"

I stopped my examination of the terra cotta thicket or whatever it was called and looked at Ferdi as she spoke. The halfling's face was grave, and her whole body looked tense. One fist clenched and unclenched spasmodically, and her jaw was clenched tightly.

"Yeah," I said quietly. "The Ochre Forest, I guess. How's you guess?"

"There's a feeling to them that you get used to." She rolled her head around on her neck. "And I've heard of this one, at least a little. How long have we been here?"

"I'm not sure. A few minutes, maybe?"

"Then the entrance is closed." She sighed. "The only way out is through the Labyrinth." She turned back and looked past me, and I glanced back at the bodies of the two elves. "Your doing?"

"Yeah." I shuddered as I looked at the pair.

"Good. They deserved it."

"I'm not sure anyone deserved that, Ferdi."

"You don't know these two. I've had people asking around about them. Taveroth was just a common sellsword, but Alerion was twisted. He liked hurting people. You did the world a favor." She walked past me and stood over the mangled remains. "Did you claim their cards?"

"I didn't think about it," I admitted. "I don't really want them, to be honest."

"What do you mean, you don't want them?"

"I…" I took a deep breath. "I'm not really proud of this, Ferdi. Profiting off of something like this seems—wrong. Evil, even."

"That's just stupid, Murf. We're in a Labyrinth. We need to use every available resource to survive. The Unity will provide, but only if we take what it offers. Now, get over here before I drag you over." She knelt beside the corpses, seemingly unfazed by the gore splattering them and surrounding them, and yanked Alerion's sword from the ground, pulling hard to slide it free of his body. "You didn't have to stick it so deep, Murf. A few inches would have been enough."

"That's what she said," I muttered almost without thinking as I slowly walked toward the bodies.

"She who? The bird-woman?"

"No, I…" I paused, realizing Ferdi wouldn't get the joke, no matter what. "Yeah, let's go with her. That's what she said."

"Then you should have listened." The halfling grabbed a handful of leaves and began wiping down the blade, then busied herself with the elf's belt.

"What are you doing?" I asked her curiously.

"Stripping the body, of course. We need weapons, and you might be able to fit into their armor. It'll probably be too heavy for the others, though." She looked at Taveroth's crushed body and made a face. "Well, not his, obviously. Why'd you crumple it up like that?"

"It seemed like a good idea at the time," I sighed. "Ferdi, I've never worn armor in my life, you know."

"Everything has a first time." She slipped off the belt, removed the scabbard from it, and began attaching it to her own belt. She pulled off a dagger in its sheath and handed it to me. "Here. They took yours, it looks like. You can use this, right?"

"Sharp end in the other guy," I nodded.

"It's more complicated than that, but that's a start." She began stripping the elf's armor off, and as she did, I remembered the cards I'd been reading earlier.

"Hey, Ferdi, you've been a Holder for a while, right?"

"Obviously. You've known me for a while, Murf, which makes that a stupid question."

I winced. "Yeah, it was. What can you tell me about professions?"

She glanced at me sharply. "You reached Rank 1?" I nodded, and she grunted. "That was fast. How long have you been a Holder, Murf?"

"A few days," I shrugged. "Why?"

She snorted. "You know that it takes most people a year or more to get enough Unity Points to become ranked, right?"

"Nope. I don't know anything about any of this, Ferdi, and now I've got to make choices that I have a feeling will affect me more or less the rest of my life."

"Not necessarily. You can change professions if you try hard enough." She stopped yanking at the elf's armor and looked at me. "For professions, the rules are simple. First, choose something that matches your stats. If your Capacity's shit, don't choose a profession with high Capacity. Second, choose something that sounds like it's what you do already. It's easier to rank up a profession that you enjoy."

"That makes sense," I nodded. "What do 'Common' and 'Uncommon' mean, though?"

She stared at me, her eyes flat. "You got offered an Uncommon profession? What was it?"

"Something called 'Wilder'."

"You must have a wild card as your hole card," she grunted. "That could be a good thing or incredibly idiotic depending on the card." She shook her head. "Remember those rules I said earlier? Well, forget them. Always choose the least common profession you can."

"Why?"

"Because the less common it is, the more you get for ranking it up. You'll get about 10% more stats and 25% more Harmonies per rank from an Uncommon profession."

"What about that whole, 'it's easier to rank up when you enjoy it' bit?"

"That's for Common professions. Rarer ones are harder to get, so they're always more specialized toward you, and that makes them easier to improve. I think that Wilders rank up by creating stacks linked to their hole card, which shouldn't be hard for you."

"Okay." I looked at the card again, reading the Cabalist profession. "Are there other rarity ranks besides Uncommon?"

"Yes. You'll probably never see them, though."

"What are they?"

She sighed. "Common, Uncommon, Incredible, Singular, Murf. At least, that's what the sages say. I've never heard of anyone actually having an Incredible or Singular profession. They're incredibly rare and more or less unique, obviously." She shook her head. "Just choose Wilder, Murf. Trust me; you won't regret it."

I looked back at the options I'd been given. She'd said to pick Wilder, but it wasn't my rarest profession. The thing was, I wasn't sure if I wanted to pick something that might paint an even bigger target on my back. Gambler sounded simple and easy; I could gamble and rank up, and that suited me just fine. However, the Hag's admonition still tugged at my thoughts. She'd told me that if I wanted a life of peace and ease, I'd have to get so strong that the people who'd covet my card would decide it wasn't worth the trouble annoying me. Gambler seemed like an easy profession to follow, but Cabalist was probably a lot more powerful, and the stronger I was, the better.

I sighed and chose the rarer profession, and as I did, another card popped up before me.

Profession Chosen
Cabalist (Incredible, Arcana)
A Cabalist holds one of the Cabal as
their hole card. This gives them
great mastery over all lesser cards.
Benefits
All Harmonies +10%
Ability: Suppress Cards
Per Rank: Luck +3, Skill +2/1,
Capacity +2/1, all card abilities +5%

Suppress Cards
By activating this ability, you make
other cards harder to use around you.
All cards within 10' have their Luck
and Harmony requirements
increased by 5% and are 5% less
effective.
This ability affects an additional 10'
and inflicts an extra 5% penalty per
Rank of Cabalist

"All done?" I jumped as Ferdi reached up and grabbed my sleeve, hauling me down toward her. I stumbled and fell to one knee, and she pointed at the elf's chest. "Good. Time to claim his cards."

I stared at the man's chest with a sense of disgust and repulsion. The slash the sword had left gaped like a crimson grin above his clothes. The blade cutting his throat had soaked his undershirt in blood that was slowly coagulating and thickening. My stomach fluttered a little again, but I swallowed hard and did my best to ignore it. I didn't think Ferdi would appreciate me puking all over the body. More to the point, I knew that covering Alerion in vomit wouldn't stop her from making me claim his cards, and it promised to be nasty enough as it was.

"So—where are they?" I asked hesitantly. "Aren't they supposed to pop up when a Holder dies or something?"

"People think that. They're wrong. Cards stay in a Holder's soul until they're claimed." She pointed at the man. "Claiming a card is simple. All you have to do is put your hand on his chest and pull like you're drawing from a regular deck."

"That's it? I just do that, and I get his cards?"

"Maybe. Maybe not." She shrugged. "It depends on your Harmonies, his cards, and the Unity. You might get all his cards. You might get a few of them. You might get none. You might get something totally different. You never know until you do it."

"Something totally different?" I echoed in confusion. "Like what?"

"Like a card that he didn't have. If you've got low Harmonies with his cards and high Luck, the Unity might give you a card or two that's more appropriate for you. Or it might give you nothing at all. There's no way to tell what card you'll draw until you've drawn it."

"That should be a law," I muttered.

"A real law, or one of your made-up ones?"

"Mine are real," I protested. "And a lot more useful than most laws."

"A lot stupider, too. Stop stalling, Murf. Claim his cards and see what you get."

I took a deep breath and reached out toward the elf's chest. I reminded myself that I'd touched blood before, even this much. I'd carried my mother's blood-soaked body to the church after she'd finally coughed her lungs out. Compared to that, this was a damn breeze.

My fingers touched the man's chest, and I ignored the warm stickiness of his shirt. I pinched my fingers like I was drawing a card, and I felt the tips tingle slightly. I hoped that was the man's cards and not some sort of weird elf venereal disease that I was about to catch. I wouldn't have put it past Alerion to frequent the sorts of places where the ladies didn't regularly see healers, after all. I doubted he could have gotten a woman any other way.

I closed my eyes and lifted, and as I did, I felt something flat and hard between my fingers. I pulled my blood-smeared hand away from the elf and opened my eyes, gazing at a card showing an armored warrior riding a horse, carrying a lance and a golden goblet. As I looked at it, a different card flashed in my vision, blocking my view of the ones I'd taken.

Cards Gained!
You have claimed the cards of
another Holder.

I held the card up, admiring the noble arcana displayed before me. It looked like an armored man in the middle of a press of unarmed peasants all wielding wine bottles like clubs, far different from the normal knight on horseback carrying a golden goblet that I was used to. I turned to Ferdi, who stared at the card with an astonished expression. She looked at me, and her eyes narrowed suspiciously.

"What's your Luck, Murf?" she demanded.

"That seems awfully personal, Ferdi," I chided her. "I don't think we know each other well enough for that, yet. If you want that information, you're going to need to woo it out of me, I'm afraid."

She glared at me, then shook her head. "You're right. It is personal, and I'm not that interested. That's a good draw, though. And there's no way that elf was holding that."

"What do you mean?"

"He was a warrior. His highest Harmony had to be blades, which means his hole card must have been a blade, too." She gestured at the cards in my hand. "If you get anything from a draw, the hole card's always part of it. See any blades on that knight?"

"He's wearing armor. Doesn't that count?"

"No, it doesn't. I doubt he even had a noble arcana in his whole deck, though, much less his hole card. You're a lucky fucker, Murf, no two ways about it." She shook her head again and resumed rifling through the man's clothing.

"What the hell's going on?"

I glanced up to see Millie sitting up, rubbing her head and peering around curiously as Azara moved quickly away from her, obviously having learned her lesson with Ferdi. The redhead stared at the orange sky, her face blank and confused. "Where the fuck am I?"

"Labyrinth," Ferdi said shortly, not looking up from her work. "Same as the rest of us."

Millie looked our way, and her confused gaze fell on me. It quickly hardened as she pushed herself to her feet. "You! Murf!" Confusion gave way to anger as she stomped her way toward me, holding her dress up away from the leaves underfoot.

"Yes, me Murf," I said nervously, standing up and backing away from the corpse nervously. "You Millie. Are we talking like trolls for a reason?"

"Don't you dare try to charm me!" she fumed, storming up until she stood in front of me, glaring up into my face. "I heard what you said!" Her face twisted as she deepened her voice. "'She looked like a fun ride.' 'If you want to torture her, go ahead.'" Her hand whipped up, and my skull rang with the force of her slap.

"Wow," I muttered, rubbing my cheek. "You're stronger than you look."

"You're damn right I am, and don't change the subject!"

"He was trying to save you, obviously, foolish human," Azara said coldly from where she stood.

Millie whipped around to face the avian, her eyes blazing. "Excuse me? Who are you, and who asked for your opinion?"

"She's right," Ferdi agreed, rising to her feet with full arms. "The bird-woman, not the overly dramatic human. He was trying to protect you by pretending that you didn't matter to him." She paused, her face thoughtful. "Either that, or you really don't matter to him, and he took advantage of that. With Murf, I could see it going either way."

"Gee, thanks, Ferdi," I sighed as Millie whirled back to glare at me. I took a step back and held up my hands defensively. "Whoa, whoa, lets calm down, here, Millie. This really isn't the time or place for this. Maybe we can have this discussion when we're not all in danger of, you know, dying?"

"Dying?" the redhead repeated, lowering her hands and looking around nervously. "What do you mean, dying?"

"You're in a Labyrinth, human," Ferdi answered seriously. "We all are."

"A Labyrinth?" Millie gasped, stepping back from me. "How did we...?" She paused and sighed. "Never mind. Dumb question. A better one is: how do we get out?"

"That is better," the halfling nodded. "We're at the very start. The only way out is through the Labyrinth."

"Can't we just go back the way we came in?"

"Not anymore. When you enter a Labyrinth, there's a couple minutes where the Labyrinth can't hurt you and you can leave if it looks like it's too much for you. We missed that window."

"I was going to ask about that," I said as her words jogged my memory. "I thought you were supposed to be invulnerable when you enter a Labyrinth, at least for a bit."

"In a sense, yes," the warrior nodded.

"Then, why did the elves think they could kill us?" I pointed at the body to my side. "And how did I kill them?"

Millie glanced down, seeming to see the dead elves for the first time. Her face blanched, and she took several steps back, her hands going to her face. "They—they're dead!" she gasped, then turned to look at me. "Wait. You killed them?"

"They were intending to kill us all and leave our bodies for the beasts here," Azara spoke up. "Although the one he nearly beheaded spoke frequently of using your body before killing you, human."

She looked at Azara, then back at me, and I shrugged. "I couldn't hear what they were saying, but it wouldn't be the first time he talked about doing that."

"They deserved death," Ferdi proclaimed, moving over to Taveroth's body and beginning to strip his corpse, as well. "And as for why you could kill them, Murf, you only gain protection against the Unity when you enter one of its Labyrinths, not other people. The Unity doesn't shield us from our poor choices, and entering a Labyrinth with someone you can't trust is as poor a choice as you can make."

"Apparently, not as poor as going to dinner with you," Millie told me accusingly.

"Hey, I didn't exactly plan on being ambushed and kidnapped," I protested. "Besides, I wasn't the one who let them into our room. That was Kikoum. Blame him."

Her eyes narrowed. "You're right. He must have let those—those *elves* into our room! I can't believe he did that!"

"And after you tipped him so well," I encouraged her.

"I did! And he…" She broke off. "Don't try to distract me, Murf. I'm still angry at you!"

"We could hurl recriminations for some time," Azara broke in, her voice frosty. "And in another place, human, I'd join you in finding fault with Murf quite happily. For now, though, we should focus on escape. The cards are whispering that danger approaches." She looked at Ferdi. "Halfling, you seem to know these places. How can we escape this?"

Ferdi paused her looting and looked at the avian. "There are two types of Labyrinths: inbound and outbound. Inbound Labyrinths start you at their edge, and your goal is to reach the center. Usually, that's where the guardian is, and you have to ether fight it or get past it to exit. Outbound ones start you at the middle, and you have to find an exit at the edge somewhere." She looked around thoughtfully. "This seems to be one of those. I think we're in the center, and we need to find our way out."

"That's it?" Millie asked dubiously. "We just have to find an exit, and we're fine?"

"Of course not," the warrior snorted. "What kind of a challenge would it be if it were that simple? Labyrinths are designed to kill the weak and unwary, and they use monsters, traps, or both. This one is probably a monster type—most natural settings are. That's a good thing for us, really."

"I'm not sure I'd call being surrounded by things that think of us as food good, Ferdi," I pointed out.

"That's only because you don't understand the situation, Murf." She looked at the others. "Do either of you have any sort of skills with finding traps? Disarming them?" Both women shook their heads, and she looked at me.

"I can pick a lock," I said helpfully. "Does that count?"

"It could be useful. It won't help much if a spike-filled pit opens up underfoot, though, or a noose drops around your throat and chokes you to death. Labyrinth traps can be ridiculously deadly, almost impossibly so, and if you don't have any practice in finding and disabling them, they'll kill you in a heartbeat. You won't even see it coming. One moment, you're walking along normally; the next, the ceiling drops on you, and you're nothing but a red smear and some crushed armor."

"There's no ceiling here, Ferdi," I pointed out.

"Which is why I'm hoping this is a beast type." She lifted Taveroth's sword. "I can fight creatures. Murf sort of can. You, avian, you have attack cards, yes?"

"Some," Azara admitted. "Not many, and I haven't trained much with them. I mostly use them to deter thieves or people who try to force me to give them a reading."

"You'll get plenty of practice soon enough. The point is, we can fight monsters. We'll need to, in fact. We're critically undersupplied for this, and we'll need the drops from those kills."

"Drops?" I asked in confusion. "What are you talking about?"

"You'll see soon enough. We need to get moving. The bird-woman's right; I can feel danger getting closer."

"You want me to claim his cards, too?" I gestured at Taveroth.

"Yes. You'll get more cards you can use—and maybe some for the screechy human."

"Screechy?" Millie protested shrilly, apparently ignoring the concept of irony entirely. She paused as the rest of the halfling's words seemed to register. "Wait, what do you mean, cards? I'm not a Holder!"

"You will be soon—at least if you want to live through this." Ferdi rose to her feet and eyed us each in turn. "This isn't going to be easy. It might even be impossible. I don't know much about this Labyrinth, and knowledge and preparedness are the most essential keys to defeating one. However, another is the willingness to use the tools the Unity gives you. These cards are the Unity's gifts. If we don't use them, it can and will kill us for it." She eyed Millie dubiously. "Can you do anything other than complain and look pretty, human?"

"She's a fair gambler," I offered gamely.

"Not a very useful skill in here," the halfling shrugged, once again missing my sarcasm. "You need something combat-oriented. I can't protect you if you can't protect yourself."

Millie's eyes hardened as the warrior spoke, and she stomped over to Taveroth's body, yanking free the man's dagger. She lifted it, seeming to test it for a few moments, then began to spin it across her fingers. I watched in amazement as the dagger rolled across her knuckles, flipped to her other hand, spun in her palm, then leaped back to her right hand. She caught it by the tip, and her arm snapped down. The blade streaked forth and slammed into the ground between Ferdi's feet, quivering slightly from the force of impact.

"I can handle myself," the redhead said coolly, folding her arms over her chest and glaring haughtily at the halfling.

"Not bad. Of course, the ground's an easy target." Ferdi reached down and pulled the knife free, then tossed it back to the redhead. "Next time, aim for something useful, like the heart. Murf, claim his cards."

I knelt beside Taveroth, doing my best to ignore the mangled mess that had been his skull, and once again pinched my fingers over his chest and pulled. It was a lot less awkward this time since crushing his head had caused most of his blood to pool on the ground around and beneath him, leaving his shirt relatively clean. Two cards came away in my hand, and I lifted them up and fanned them out, ignoring the card that tried to pop up in my vision. I didn't need the Unity's help to tell me what I'd gotten, after all.

"A 2-set of threes, coins and blades," I told Ferdi.

"Decent draw. Not as good as your first one." She looked at Millie speculatively. "Good for her, though. A gambler who's good with knives? You should give them to her and keep the knight—assuming you have the Harmony to add it to your deck."

"I don't want any cards," Millie protested.

"Then you'll die in here," Ferdi replied calmly. "And quickly. Without a card, you don't stand a chance."

"Why?" the redhead demanded. "I'm good with knives and daggers—better than Murf, I'll bet!"

"It doesn't matter. Being a Holder of any card, no matter how small or weak, makes you stronger and tougher. It lets you heal faster and keep going longer than you would otherwise. The card's energy strengthens your mind and body, and you need that."

She gestured at the woman. "Despite your training, you're soft, human. In addition, you've got a short-bladed weapon, no armor, and you're wearing a dress that'll slow you way down. That makes you weak compared to the rest of us."

"What about her?" Millie demanded, pointing to Azara. "She's not a Holder!" She glanced at the avian. "Are you?"

"No," the woman shook her head. "Holders corrupt the purity of the cards and taint themselves with the Unity's touch."

"See?" Millie said triumphantly. "She's not a Holder, either!"

"She's a cartomancer, and a strong one—strong enough that I can feel her power from here," the halfling shrugged. "The beasts will, too. They can sense strength—and you don't have any. They'll come for you first."

She looked thoughtful for a moment. "That might be for the best, actually."

"What?" Millie's face purpled in anger, and I wisely took a step back, staying well out of the conversation.

"That dress is going to slow you down in these woods. We'll all move faster without you. Plus, once you die, we won't have to share any drops with you."

Millie looked down at her rather voluminous dress, then at the trees. She made a dissatisfied face, then lifted the back of her dress. She wiggled her hips as her hands busied themselves behind her, and in a few moments, the underskirt that held her dress in shape slid down her legs. Part of me immediately noted that without that, it was pretty likely she was naked under that dress. Another part of me pointed out that we were in a damn Labyrinth, and thinking about things like that was probably inappropriate. The first part didn't give a damn, especially when Millie lifted the hem of her dress, which hung on the ground without the underskirt, and began cutting it off with the dagger, revealing flashes of her white thighs. At last, she dropped the fabric, leaving a ragged hem that hung to about the middle of her calves.

"There. Is that better?"

"Yes. You're still going to die, though," Ferdi shrugged. "You know, if you aren't going to take a card, it'll probably be kinder if I just kill you now. You'll prefer that to being taken down by the beasts and eaten. The choice is yours, though."

Millie's face paled as she looked at the sheathed sword in Ferdi's grip, the one she'd taken from Taveroth. She looked pleadingly at me, but I simply shrugged.

"She's the expert on Labyrinths, Millie. She'd know if you need a card to survive one."

The redhead glared at me, looked nervously at Ferdi, then slumped in apparent defeat. "Fine. Give me the damn cards, Murf." I wordlessly handed the two threes to her, and she snatched them from my hand. She glared at me as if it were all my fault, then at the cards in her hands. Her gaze softened to confusion, and she looked at Ferdi. "So—now, what?"

"Take one of the cards and press it against your chest."

"Which one?"

"Whichever one speaks to you. Don't think about it, human. Go with what you feel. That's your Harmonies telling you what to do."

"I don't know what that even means," Millie replied, her voice defeated sounding. She looked up at me, her gaze pleading. "Do I really have to do this?"

"I don't know," I said honestly. "This is all new to me, too, Millie."

"Wait, why doesn't Murf have to become a Holder, too?" she demanded suspiciously. "Or the avian?"

"He already is, and the best cartomancers are never Holders," the halfling replied. "Quit dawdling. Choose one and get it over with."

Millie looked at the cards for a moment, took a deep breath, and lifted the three of coins to her chest, pressing it against the bare skin between her breasts. As the card touched her, her eyes shot open, and she gasped in pain.

"Catch her, Murf," Ferdi instructed, and I stepped forward to grab the woman as her body went limp. Her eyes began to flutter as the card slipped slowly into her flesh, seeming to dissolve into her skin, and she slumped against me, seeming to be barely aware.

I looked over at Ferdi questioningly. "What's wrong with her? Did she choose the wrong card?"

"Nothing's wrong. The first card always hurts. She'll be fine in a moment."

I remembered that the Hag had burned going into me, but it hadn't almost knocked me out the way this card had Millie. Of course, I'd been in the middle of the absolute worst pain I'd ever felt in my life at the moment. Maybe I was already so close to passing out that I just didn't notice the extra. I glanced down at the shuddering woman, and as I did, a sudden card flashed in my vision.

Millie
Rank 0 ???
Luck: 24   Capacity: 28   Skill: 34
Hole Card: 3 of Coins
Likely Powers: Wind Strike, Rapid
Attack, Blinding Attack

The card was interesting, especially the part with the question marks after Millie's rank. For Ferdi, that part had said what she did for a living. Ferdi was a delver, and the Hag's card recognized that. For Millie, it came up question marks. I had exactly zero clue what that meant. Was "delver" something recognized by the Unity, while "gambler" wasn't? Did it mean that I knew for a fact that Ferdi was a delver while I couldn't really say what Millie did for a living? I didn't know, which wasn't all that surprising. The list of things I didn't know about Unity cards just seemed to grow with every passing hour. One of those was how to stop the damn things from popping up whenever they damn well felt like it, and I made a note to ask Ferdi about that later.

Millie groaned and shifted, resting her head against my chest for a moment. "Oh, that sucked," she muttered. "That was just awful. It felt like my heart caught on fire! Why would anyone do that to themselves?"

"Power. Greed. Lust," Azara answered crisply.

"Survival," Ferdi added.

"Well, I'm never doing that again."

"Yes, you are," the halfling said flatly. "And Murf, you'll be adding that knight to your deck, too. And hurry. I'll need all the help I can get."

"Help with what?" I asked.

"Those." She lifted Taveroth's sword and slid it from its sheath, discarding the scabbard as she pointed toward the more distant treeline. I almost asked her what she was pointing at when I noticed the trees there shifting and moving around. Fear spiked in me as something burst from the trees, racing toward us, followed by a half-dozen of its brothers and sisters.

Apparently, the Unity was sick of our standing around and decided to get the party started.

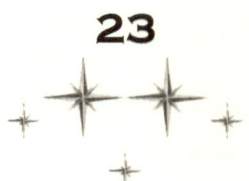

23

The things rushing toward us weren't anything I'd ever seen or heard of before, and I'd been around a bit. Depending on who you ask, I've been around a lot. According to some people, I've been around way too much. Of course, those are mostly people I'd once been around with, so I'm not sure how reliable you can consider them.

The monsters were utterly hairless and mottled orange in color, of course, which made them a little hard to see as they raced toward us on all fours. Their front legs were much longer than their back ones, giving them a weird, stooped appearance, as if they were all squatting in preparation to unleash a massive shit on the ground as they ran. All four legs ended in clawed hands or talons or whatever. Their heads were what really caught my attention, though. Their heads were huge compared to their four-foot-tall bodies, at least a foot wide and about eight inches tall. A massive, single eyeball that glowed scarlet dominated their face, with a long mouth stretched beneath that ran from one side of their skull to the other. It made it look like their heads could flip open on a hinge, and for all I knew, they could. Rows of sharp, pointed teeth filled that mouth, and a long, tangerine tongue that tapered to a point hung from their mouths as they ran. I stared at the things in horror and awe, not even aware that Azara and Millie were doing the same.

Fortunately, Ferdi responded faster than the rest of us. "Bind those cards!" she shouted loudly. "I'll hold them!" She let out an inarticulate shout that I supposed was a battle cry as she launched herself forward. She ran faster than I could easily track, reaching the closest of the creatures in less than a second. Her sword flashed, and one of the things let out a piercing shriek as the blade thrust through its chest. She jerked the weapon free in a spray of blood and slashed at another, but that one jumped backward, letting the sword swish past. Another leaped at her, snatching with its front claws while its mouth gaped wide, but she smashed it aside with an armored fist and stabbed down into it.

The violence held me spellbound for a moment, but that moment passed as a blast of lightning flashed out and caught one of the creatures, sending it twitching and spasming to the ground. "Move, fools!" Azara hissed as she stepped forward, pulling out another card. "There are more coming!"

I looked beyond Ferdi and saw the trees shifting again. A moment later, three more of the things burst forth, running toward the halfling. That made seven of them to only one of her. Ferdi was good, but I didn't know if she was that good. I shook off my amazement, shoved my fear aside to deal with later when I could afford to be a gibbering mess, and held up the card I'd drawn, looking at it. I had no idea how to put it in my deck, or if I could choose where to put it. As I thought that, the image of the tiny poker table I'd seen before popped up in my vision.

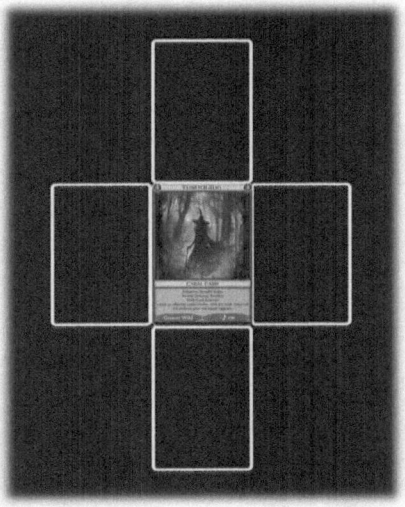

I had four possible places to put my card, and I had no idea what to do with that. I didn't even really know what the damn card did—or if I could bind it. As I thought that, though, it appeared in my vision, floating above the table with a label attached to it.

Knight of Cups
Likely Power: Combat Debuff
Requirements:
Luck: 49 Harmony: 44
Compatibility: 10%

I stared at the layout and the card, completely confused about what to do. Did it matter where I put it? Was one spot better than another? I had no idea, but I could hear the shrieks and snarls of the creatures getting closer and knew that I had to decide. I grabbed the card, pulled down the collar of my shirt, then looked at the tableau. As I touched the card to my chest, I concentrated on the left blank spot. I didn't have any reason for it; I'd just heard once that when you're stuck in a maze, you should always go left. That seemed good enough for me. I pressed the card to my chest, concentrating on that spot.

Pain flared in me as the card dissolved into my skin. I hissed as it burned its way into me, burrowing like a red-hot needle toward my heart. The card wormed its way inside me in seconds, and I felt it settle into place with a sudden heaviness. The pain ebbed, leaving me with a slightly full feeling that wasn't uncomfortable but wasn't quite comfy, either. It almost felt like I had to burp but couldn't quite get it out. The pressure eased a moment or two later, and a pair of cards flared in my vision.

Knight of Cups
Drunken Combat
Noble Arcana
11%
8/73
Hostile creatures within 20' of you become increasingly intoxicated. This is a mind-altering and physical effect.

I blinked in surprise; I could feel the new power pulsing inside me, ready to be tapped. I felt stuffed, as if the power was a waterskin I could squeeze out if I wanted. The thing was, I'd never felt anything like that with the Hag. Part of me wondered what that meant, but as another arc of lightning crackled out, I decided that could wait. I yanked out my dagger and looked toward the combat, which was still in full swing.

While I'd been fooling around with my card, Ferdi had managed to kill four of the nightmarish monster things. Two more lay on the ground with smoking holes covering their bodies. In that same time, though, five more of the things had apparently joined the pack, and they were pushing Ferdi back. Her armor had long scratches in it, and while her sword still thrust and danced, the things looked like they were getting better at dodging it. Azara held up her card again, but I could see the paleness in her face as she hurled another bolt of lightning. She couldn't keep that up for long. She was a diviner, not a warrior. If something didn't change, Ferdi would be overrun, and we'd all get killed. I glanced sideways and saw Millie on her knees clutching her chest and shuddering. Apparently, her second card went down even harder than the first. That just left me.

Fuck, I really wished it hadn't. I could think of a thousand things I'd rather be doing than getting gnawed on by a monster. Hell, ten of those things I'd already done with Millie and kind of hoped to do again. Sadly, that wouldn't be possible if we both got eaten in a Labyrinth. For the sake of my future sex life, I had to do something.

I ran toward the combat, holding back and watching for a moment. A creature leaped at Ferdi's side, its claws grasping at her armor and trying to drag her back, and I darted forward. The dagger leaped out, plunging into the thing's back and sinking deep into it. It screeched deafeningly, making my damn ears ring, and I wondered what the fuck I was doing. I wasn't a fighter. I hated fighting. I'd done a fair bit of it, but only when talking, bluffing, and running didn't work. It was the last resort of last resorts, at least for me.

Of course, a Labyrinth was about as "last resort" as you could get, so I yanked out the knife, grabbing the back of the thing's neck so it couldn't twist around and slash at me, then stabbed it again. It yelled again, and I pulled out the knife and cracked the hilt onto the back of the thing's head.

"Just shut the hell up!" I shouted, yawning to pop my ringing ears. "Do me the favor of dying quietly, ass!"

"Just kill it, Murf," Ferdi shouted. "Don't play with it!"

I stabbed the dagger into the back of the thing's neck, then spun as I caught movement in the corner of my vision. Another of the things raced at me, its claws outstretched. I reared back and let fly with a boot, catching it right under its chin. It tried to shriek, but the kick kind of cracked its jaw as it flew backward, crashing into a pair of the things and bowling all three over. I jumped back from another set of claws and kicked again, this time catching the thing in the stomach. As it doubled up, I jammed the dagger into the back of its neck, and it died quickly. Despite my assistance, though, Ferdi continued to give ground as the creatures kept lashing at her with swift, darting attacks, barely giving her a chance to respond. As she stepped back, she glanced at me, her face a little desperate.

"What did you get, Murf? Anything good?"

"What are you talking about?" I asked in confusion. "Get from what?"

"From the card, idiot!" she shouted. "Did you get a combat power?"

"Well, yes, but..."

"Then use it!"

I dodged another slashing claw a bit too slowly, feeling it slide along my side and rip my jacket. "Are you sure? It's a bit—odd."

"Will it kill us?"

"...probably not?" I guessed.

"Then use it!" She cut down another of the monsters. "Because these things will!"

I took a deep breath, mentally preparing myself. I still had no clue how to use the Hag, but the Knight sat inside me, and I could feel its power pulsing within my chest. I could sense the energy inside of me, soft and yielding. Activating it would be easy. I just had to squeeze, and it would happen. The problem was, I didn't really want to do it. Before this, I could pretend I wasn't really a Holder. Somehow, using a card deliberately felt different. It would make me a Holder, a real one, not just a guy with a card.

Ferdi's cry pulled me from my thoughts. As I stood there, dodging claws and being all angsty, one of the things had gotten hold of her leg. It was doing its best to pull her off balance, and if she fell, I was pretty sure she wasn't getting back up. Yeah, using this card would change things, but things always changed. I would just have to suck it up and get used to it.

I squeezed, and power exploded from me in a wave.

I'd used card powers before. I had a handful of Unity cards, after all, and Azara had taught me how to activate them a long time ago when she could still stand looking at me. I wasn't good at it or anything, but I could do it. So, I kind of had an idea what a card power was supposed to feel like and what they could do. Using a card felt kind of like having ants crawling inside the veins of your arm, then leaping out of your fingertips. It wasn't painful, but it wasn't comfortable, either. I'd never used a noble arcana before, but I figured it would just be a stronger version of the same thing: bigger ants, maybe, or beetles of some kind.

I was wrong.

The surge of energy rolled up from the middle of my stomach, feeling almost like some really bad fish coming back up on me. Instead of pouring up my throat and out my mouth, though, when it reached my chest, it raced outward toward my skin. For a moment, I had an image of my heart and lungs being crushed against my own ribcage and wondered if I'd just killed myself. That would be the Unity's ultimate way of saying, "Fuck you, Murf," now, wouldn't it? Dying to the power of the card it gave me that was supposed to save my life. There was definitely a law in there somewhere.

The power didn't crush my organs. It flowed past them and burst out of me, washing over the little stab-monkeys. The creatures stumbled and hesitated as the card's energy hit them, and about half of them just stood stupidly, looking around in confusion. The rest recovered quickly and charged us again, but their movements were clumsy and unsure. They tripped over their own feet, lashed wildly at blowing leaves or one another, or ran the wrong way entirely. One even climbed onto the back of one of its fellows and started going to town on it in some monstrous version of romantic seduction. I decided I kind of liked that one. Anything that got drunk and immediately tried humping things couldn't be all bad.

The battle shifted instantly. Ferdi kicked out, and the creature holding her leg just let go, allowing itself to be flung several feet away. Her blade whipped out, spearing one of the things in the center of its chest. It didn't even try to dodge; it just stared down at the sword in its heart with a look of surprise before she tore it free, and the thing died. Her slash decapitated another monster, and her return cut took the front legs off another.

One of the things lumbered drunkenly at me, batting with its claws. I stepped to the side and jabbed my dagger into its back, just behind its heart. It slid off the weapon and fell to the ground in a heap, and I whirled back to kick another in the face, then punch a third as it grabbed at my coat. I stabbed that one, killing it, then slashed at a beast trying to claw my face but actually just pawing at my chest. It fell back with its huge eye ruined, but as I stepped forward to finish it off, a heavy weight crashed into my back, making me stagger forward. Ragged claws swiped across my chest and dragged at my face, tearing my shirt and knocking my hat off. I tucked my chin and closed my eyes to shield them, but a moment later, the weight fell away, freeing me. I turned and saw the thing lying on the ground with a dagger protruding from its back. It still twitched and thrashed—at least, it did until I slammed my boot on its neck with a muffled crack. I yanked the second dagger free and looked up to see Millie running toward me, holding her dress up with one hand, her hair a mess and her eyes a little wild.

"Nice throw," I said, holding the blade hilt-first to her.

"Shut up, Murf," she snapped, snatching the knife from me and brandishing it. "I'm not happy right now!"

"Well, there's a whole bunch of things to vent on." I jerked my thumb over my shoulder. "Go to town."

"I will. And I'm pretending they each have your face when I stab them." Her eyes glittered dangerously as she ran past me. I started to warn her about the monsters, but apparently, she didn't need it. She ducked under a claw swipe and slashed upward, her dagger opening a gash up the thing's body. She spun around another clumsy attack and buried her dagger in that creature's lung, then cut the back of a third's knee so that it fell to the ground.

I couldn't help but stare in amazement. I mean, I wasn't a slouch with a knife, but my skills were haphazard, things I'd picked up here and there because I'd had to. I'd learned from losing fights and surviving them, mostly, which isn't the best way most of the time. Millie, though, had obviously gotten real, honest-to-Unity training of some kind. She moved like a jade breeze through the monsters, slashing and cutting, rarely killing them but leaving them crippled and bleeding behind her. She was deadly, swift—and beautiful.

Shit, I was in a lot of trouble.

I shook myself from my stunned admiration and followed behind the woman, stabbing and stomping. The wounded, drunken creatures barely put up a fight, and I killed them more or less effortlessly. Millie's advance finally stopped as the monsters faced her in numbers she couldn't simply slice her way through, and we both retreated to Ferdi's side, Millie moving to one flank while I guarded the other. It wasn't really all that necessary at that point, though. The battle had become a slaughter.

My card's energy continued to flow forth, and as it did, its effects on the beasts seemed to worsen. Their attacks turned sloppy and half-hearted, not even cutting through my clothing. They stumbled, fell, and struggled to get back up. They struck at one another as often as us, and a few fights broke out between the creatures. Several just dropped to the ground without being touched, apparently passed out and snoring peacefully. Between the three of us, we cut through the almost incapacitated creatures without too much effort. By the end of the fight, all we were doing was stabbing slumbering creatures that weren't even awake to fight back. I kind of felt bad about it, really.

Ferdi flipped over the last of these, looking at the corpse almost disapprovingly. She shook her head and glanced up at me, her eyes hard and questioning.

"What in the blood of Kewan kind of power did you get, Murf? And what's your damn hole card?"

24

Rather than answering, I turned around and scanned the clearing, wincing as I did. I hadn't gotten through that battle unscathed, apparently. The stab-monkeys had ruined another set of my clothes with their damn claws, and some of their blows had drawn lines of blood along my skin. I pulled open a gash in my shirt to confirm that the wounds weren't too deep and were already clotting. The first ones I'd gotten were the worst; the last few times the monkeys clawed at me, they hadn't even broken the skin. That, I assumed, was thanks to the Hag adapting my body to their claws, or maybe my Needful Body ability toughening me up. I wasn't sure, and while I could ask Ferdi, that would require me telling her about the Hag. I wasn't sure I wanted to do that. Ferdi had weird ideas about cards, and I could see her deciding I wasn't worthy of something so powerful and deciding to cut it out of me.

My eye finally spotted what I was looking for, and I walked stiffly over to where my hat lay tumbled on the leaves. I picked it up, brushed it off, and examined it critically. It had been stepped on at least once, it looked like, and one of the stab-monkeys bled on it. The left brim was crumpled, and it smelled a bit. I was going to have to have it cleaned and repaired when I got back to civilization, assuming I did. I really liked that hat, and if the Unity had its monkeys destroy it, I was going to be pissed.

"Are you done?" I looked back over my shoulder to see Ferdi looking at me with disapproval and mild annoyance. "Put your stupid hat on and answer my question."

"Why?" I asked, slipping the hat onto my head.

"Why, what?"

"Why should I answer your question?" I shrugged nonchalantly. "Don't Holders usually keep those sorts of things to themselves? You've never told me what sort of abilities you have, and I've known you for years, Ferdi."

"We weren't in a Labyrinth, then, Murf," she replied shortly. "We are now. It's important that we know what one another can do. Suspicion and mistrust will kill us as quickly as the monsters in here."

"Then I think we're all dead already," Azara muttered, walking over to join us. "None of us have much reason to trust one another." She glanced at me, her eyes cold. "And good reasons not to."

"That may be, but if you want to live, you'll have to put all that aside," the halfling sighed. She stabbed her sword into the ground and gave us all a serious look. "What we're doing here isn't just dangerous, people. It's deadly. Probably fatal. I don't know this Labyrinth, but I've heard stories about it. It's the most infamous Labyrinth of the three known to be near Canis. It's got a bad reputation, and most delvers won't go near it. From what I've heard, I wouldn't willingly enter it without at least a team of eight Holders, all of whom I know and trust, and all of whom have some experience."

She gestured at us as she spoke. "There are four of us, and I'm the only one who's ever stepped foot in a Labyrinth before. The pretty human is a brand-new Holder, and Murf is probably pretty close and has no combat training to speak of. The bird-woman's the only one I trust to have my back in this. We've got no supplies, no shelter, and no information on this place. The odds-makers in the Sellsword's Hall would probably give us a one in a thousand shot of getting out of here alive, and that's being generous.

"Our only chance is to rely on one another," she continued. "We'll either survive this together, or we'll die together. That takes trust, and if you want to get trust, you have to give it." She looked up at me. "So, I will. My hole card's a six of blades. The power it gives me is called Weapon Mastery. It makes me more skilled with any weapon I pick up, even if I've never used it before. I've also got improvements to strength, speed, and durability, plus minor resistances to mental manipulation and lesser card abilities. There, now you know what I can do. Your turn."

I hesitated. Ferdi had shared with me, true, but it wasn't the same as asking me to share with her. My card was a bit more valuable than a six of blades, after all.

"The knight gave me a power called Drunken Combat," I finally said. "It makes hostile creatures within twenty feet or so of me get more and more intoxicated the longer I use it."

"That's a potent ability," she said, her eyes widening. "Stronger than I'd expect from a knight, really. What kind of cooldown does it have?"

"It didn't say anything about one," I shrugged.

"Does it feel like you could use it again right now?"

I paused and felt inside myself. The pressure I'd felt before I activated my card was still there, but it felt soft and depleted. It was spent, as if it had spent the night frolicking in the Avenue of Roses. And like a cock after a night like that, I got the feeling I could use it if I had to, but it wouldn't be very effective.

"I'm not sure about a specific amount of time, but it does seem to be recovering right now," I admitted.

"Try to track when it feels recovered. Knowing that is useful." She frowned. "It spread farther than twenty feet, though. It covered most of the clearing."

"My hole card boosted it," I said uncomfortably. "It also gives me improved strength and an ability to adapt to things that are dangerous or damaging to me, so I become resistant to them."

"It—it does what?" Her face paled as she spoke. "What kind of limits does it have? What kind of cooldown?"

"Well, I haven't found anything it can't adapt to, yet, but it does take time to adjust to things. That's why you hurt me when you started knocking me around back at the hold. The more you pounded on me, though, the less it hurt, until I barely felt it. That didn't help when you cut my stomach open with your axe, though."

"You did what to him?" Millie gasped.

"It was deserved," Ferdi said absently, her face thoughtful. "At least, I thought it was. I'm not so sure anymore." She rubbed her chin and looked at me. "How long does the adaptation last?"

"No clue," I shrugged. "I've never…OOF!" I crumpled as Ferdi's foot slammed into my stomach, hurling me back several feet to crash into the leaf-strewn ground. I rolled onto my knees, clutching my abdomen and staring at her in mingled shock and anger. "What the fuck?" I gasped, struggling to regain my breath.

"Looks like it weakens over time, but it lingers a bit," she mused. "That should have at least had you dry heaving, if not passed out completely."

"You could have just punched me lightly," I groaned.

"I could have. I didn't want to." She looked around. "Everyone spread out. Look for the drop from this fight. We need the supplies."

"Or you could tell me what we're looking for," Azara suggested. "I can probably find it in a couple seconds."

"Good point. You're useful to have around. It'll be a chest or container or some sort, probably hidden but not too deeply."

"That should be simple enough." The avian knelt down and produced a square of cloth that she unfolded on the ground. She smoothed it out as best she could, then placed several cards on it in a circular pattern. She lay a card in the middle, and as I watched, the card trembled and shook, then twisted until it pointed toward the spot where the things had entered the clearing. "It's there, just past the trees. It's buried under something."

Ferdi gazed at the woman respectfully. "You're good, avian. Most can only get a direction on an object."

"Yes. I am."

Ferdi looked at me. "Come on, Murf. Let's go find it. You should open it."

"Why him?" Millie protested, falling into step beside me as Ferdi led us toward the trees.

"Because his Luck stat has to be exceptional, and that means better drops."

"You know, you never explained what a 'drop' is, Ferdi," I reminded her.

"Treasure, obviously," Millie said, rubbing her hands together excitedly. "It has to be if it's in a chest. Murf, if we get through this, we could be rich!"

"You already are rich, Millie."

"No, my family is. I'm not. I want to be rich on my own, not through them."

"Not to disappoint," Ferdi interrupted, "but drops aren't always coins. In fact, I hope that our first several drops aren't."

"What? Why would you hope that?" Millie gasped.

"Because we don't need coins. We need waterskins, tents, food, and weapons. You both need better clothing and armor."

"And you think we'll find those things?" I asked dubiously.

"It's possible." She led us into the edge of the underbrush and looked around. "Now, spread out. Look for anything that could be a container or trap door. Remember, if you find it, let Murf open it. It'll be better for all of us."

Millie actually found the "drop", which turned out to be a large wooden box buried under a thicket of thorns and brambles. Ferdi pulled those off, unaffected thanks to her armor, and hauled the box out into the clearing, where Azara joined us. The halfling, set it down, stepped back, and motioned for me to open the lid. I pried it up and looked inside.

I wasn't immediately impressed with what I saw.

A dusty leather waterskin lay atop what looked like moth-eaten blankets. A rolled-up bit of leather unrolled to reveal a shoulder pack, and beneath that lay a half-dozen cubes of what looked like dried beef tucked next to a rusty metal pot. It looked like an out-of-business dry goods store vomited into the box, and we got what was left. Ferdi, though, seemed quite happy with it all.

"Good enough," she said, reaching past me and dragging out the blankets and waterskin. She examined them critically, then shrugged. "Not the best, but it'll do. Good work, Murf."

"I literally just opened a box," I pointed out.

"Yes, but if I had, it would probably be full of weapons, and we don't really need those yet. If the pretty human had, we'd have had coins that we don't need at all. And if the bird-woman had…" She paused. "I have no clue what we'd get. More cards that only she can use, maybe?"

"Wait, I might have gotten money if I opened it?" Millie protested shrilly.

"Yes, and you'd have regretted it in the morning when you realized that you can't eat coins, human."

"No, but you can buy food with them! Really nice food sometimes, that other people cook for you!"

"I don't see any restaurants nearby, Millie," I pointed out as I helped Ferdi empty the box. As I removed the pot, I froze, then reached inside, chuckling. "Besides, you got what you wanted." I held up the single brass coin that lay in the bottom and flipped it to her. "Here you go. Coins, just as you asked."

"I—you—why…" Millie snatched the coin effortlessly from the air and stared at it, her face growing red.

"We should probably get moving," I said nervously, eyeing the knife at Millie's hip. "Before more of the stab-monkeys return."

"Stab-monkeys?" Ferdi asked in a puzzled voice.

"Those things we just killed."

"The guwatri," she corrected. "That's the name for them."

"I'm calling them stab-monkeys. It's a lot more appropriate, I think. They kind of look like hairless, one-eyed monkeys, after all, and you stab them. Perfect name."

"But that isn't their name, Murf. They're guwatri."

"Stab-monkeys is better," Millie volunteered. "That other word sounds too pretentious for these things."

"The annoying human is right," Azara agreed. "'Guwatri' means something similar to 'killers among the trees.' Stab-monkeys is far more prosaic."

"Wait, you speak Lurgesh?" Ferdi asked, her face surprised.

"Obviously."

The halfling rattled something off in her tongue, a trilling sort of language with lots of vowel sounds in it, then looked at Azara expectantly.

"How I learned is my own business," the avian replied coldly. "And if you refer to me that way again, you'll regret it, Holder or no."

"Stab-monkeys it is, then," I interjected as the two women glared at one another. "Sorry, Ferdi, you've been outvoted."

"There's no voting," the warrior protested, turning her focus back to me. "That's their name!"

"Not anymore. Now, come on. Let's pack all this stuff up and get moving before the stab-monkeys come back. I think we all want to get the hell out of here as quickly as possible."

25

The next several hours, quite frankly, sucked beyond belief.

Before leaving, we rifled through the remains of the two elves, hoping to find something else we could use. There wasn't much, but there was a little bit left of them that was useful. We got a second sword, a couple of small knives, two coin purses, and the five of staves that the elves had been using to knock us out. Ferdi took the blade as a backup; Millie grabbed both purses, glaring at me as if daring me to ask for one; Azara took the card since neither Millie nor I had any interest in adding it to our decks. According to the Hag, the card probably would have given me some sort of resistance to mental effects, but I figured the Hag was doing that already. Ferdi suggested that I take Taveroth's armor—what pieces I could—but the breastplate didn't quite fit me, and I didn't see much point in armoring my legs and arms but not my chest.

With the looting done, we explored the edge of the clearing and found three paths leading away from the center into the Labyrinth. Azara did a quick divination that suggested that they were all equally dangerous, so I picked one at random and led us down it. The path was leaf-strewn and muddy, and orange clay covered the soles of my boots in minutes, making the footing slippery. The trees crowded overhead, shading whatever light came from the sky overhead. They were spaced far enough apart that we could see for a fair distance through them. That also let tangles of bushes and brambles grow beneath them, all covered with orange leaves, of course, providing more than ample hiding spaces for anything that wanted to attack us.

And there seemed to be no lack of those.

The next group of stab-monkeys swung down on us less than an hour after the first. I mean that literally: the damn things swung from the trees with their long front legs and dropped on us from above. Fortunately, Azara's cards warned her that danger was near, so we were all more or less watching and spotted the creatures before they landed. I still ended up with two on my back, clawing at me, and I roared in pain as I felt one's teeth sink into my left shoulder. I reached back and stabbed that one in the eye, then grabbed the other, tore it off my back, and flung it into a tree with a loud crack.

My power hadn't really recovered yet, but I activated it anyway, and a much weaker wave of power rolled out over the monkeys. Instead of debilitating them, it slowed them down and made their attacks less accurate, but apparently, that was all that we needed. Ferdi's sword chopped through the things with ease, while Millie's knives slashed and cut them. I stabbed the ones I could and threw and kicked the rest, crashing them into tree trunks hard enough to break bones. Without their full speed and agility, the things just weren't that dangerous to us.

Apparently, the Unity agreed and decided to reward us appropriately. This time, the drop was a leather sack stuffed into a fallen log, and opening it revealed another waterskin, a length of fraying rope, a belt knife, and several more meat cubes. Plus, of course, another brass coin I tossed to Millie, who glared at me but pocketed it anyway.

My only concern was that I didn't know if using my power when it was still recovering like that was a good thing or not, so I actually took a second after the battle and asked Ferdi. She shrugged in response.

"If you let it build up longer, it'll have more effect," she told me. "That might be important if we face something stronger than the guwatri..."

"Stab-monkeys," I corrected.

"I'm not calling them that. As I was saying, if—no, when we face something stronger than the guwatri, having your full ability might be useful. Of course, we have to live to reach that point, as well, and your power certainly makes these battles easier."

After that, I decided to hold off on using my power until I knew how long it took to recover or unless we really needed it. That resolution lasted right up until the next time the monkeys swarmed over us. Over a dozen of the damn things popped out of the bushes and leaped at us, and after ten seconds or so, it became clear that they were going to overrun us. Azara couldn't use her lightning or fire safely in the woods, meaning she stuck to stabbing the things with stone spikes or hitting them with blasts of force. The brambles caught in Millie's dress, keeping her from dodging effectively, and there were too many of them for Ferdi and I to deal with alone. I squeezed that inner muscle again, and once more, the stab-monkeys slowed down enough that we could kill them pretty easily.

We came to a fork in the path, and Azara determined that the one to the left eventually dead-ended, so we went right. Ten minutes after that, the ground beneath my feet suddenly shifted and crumbled, and I felt myself falling. The trip wasn't a long one, but the ground beneath me was hard and covered with long thorns that tore at my face and hands and ripped my clothes. The landing hurt, but as I sat up, nothing seemed broken. My back stung, and I guessed my clothes had taken another hit, but nothing warm and sticky trickled down my back. My head swam a bit, and I felt woozy, but that was about all.

"You okay, Murf?" I looked up to see a dirt wall maybe ten feet high beside me, with Ferdi's head peeking over the edge and peering down.

"Fine," I groaned, rising to my feet. I tripped as I stood, almost falling, and I looked down to see what grabbed my feet. I winced as I saw the sharp, inch-long roots jutting up all over the floor, each gleaming wetly. As I noticed them, a card popped up in my vision.

> Adaptive Ability
> Your body has partially adapted to
> the toxin Xanthous Resin and will
> suffer reduced effects from this in
> the future.

"Although, I guess I got poisoned a bit," I added, shaking my still-foggy head.

"Poison?" I saw Millie's head poke out into the air. "Is it bad?"

"My ability adapted to it, at least a little. I'll be fine in a few minutes, I think."

"You know..." The redhead hesitated. "If it's really bad stuff, maybe you should try to collect some?"

"What? You want me to try to scoop up this stuff?" I wondered if the poison was starting to affect my brain and making me hear things. "Why?"

"Because if we smear it on our weapons, maybe it'll poison the stab-monkeys," she suggested.

"Guwatri," Ferdi growled.

"You know no one's going to call them that."

"You should. It's their name. And if you play with poison, you're likely to end up poisoning yourself instead of the guwatri."

"But Murf will be the one handling it, and it sounds like he can't really get poisoned from them," Millie pointed out. She looked back down at me. "Do you think that you can collect some?"

"If you toss down your knife, I can rub it on these roots," I sighed. "Just don't scratch yourself or anything."

"I'll be careful."

I wiped the dagger she threw down against a bunch of the roots until the blade gleamed with poison, then did the same with my own. When I finished, Ferdi tossed down our rope, and I laboriously climbed out of the pit. Athletics have never been my strong suit, after all. I'm a lover, not a climber. When I reached the top, I brushed myself off and gave Millie her sheathed knife back.

"So, now we know there are traps, too," Ferdi said grimly. "That means we'll have to watch out for them." She looked at Azara. "Any chance you can sense them?"

"Only if they present an active threat to us," the avian shook her head. "Something like this pit isn't an actual danger until someone steps in it. I felt it as Murf stepped on it, but not before then." She gave me a thin smile. "Which just means that you should walk in front, Murf."

"Me? Why me?"

"Because you and the halfling are the most likely to survive a fall like that, and she is by far the more valuable of the two of you. You simply have to be able to use that ability of yours, nothing more. Even if you're badly hurt, we could simply drag you along, and you'd be as useful."

"Damn," Millie muttered. "That was brutal. True, but brutal." She made a face. "She's right, though. You should go in front, Murf. Just in case."

"Fine." I gave Azara a glare that she met with a steely gaze. "If I break something, though, you're the one carrying me. I'm riding piggyback on you the rest of the way."

"You will never be riding me in any fashion again, Murf. Of that, I can assure you."

"That's even more brutal," Millie laughed. "I think I like her."

"I don't much care," Azara shrugged. "Once we're out of this, I hope never to see any of you again."

"And on that happy note," I sighed, "let's get going."

Being in front of the group was definitely not entertaining. Exciting, yes; entertaining, no. I was the one the stab-monkeys targeted first when they swarmed us; I was the one who fell into the two other pits we found; I was the one the tree rigged to come crashing down landed on top of. That one was especially fun since I managed to dodge most of it, and it only pinned my legs. Of course, that was when the damn stab-monkeys appeared, and there I was, stuck under a fucking log, slashing wildly at every monkey that came close. The tree squashed my legs down into the muddy ground, the others ended up having to dig me out, and I walked with a limp for the next hour as my body healed my bruised calves and throbbing knees.

About the only positive was that the drops started to include clothing. That was useful since my own shirt hung in rags by that point, shredded by claws, teeth, and sharp roots, and my coat wasn't in much better shape. Millie's dress was in tatters below her thighs, and she'd lost her fancy shoes hours ago. When a simple lime-colored blouse and pair of emerald trousers appeared, she snatched them from me almost instantly.

"About time," she muttered, clutching the clothing to her chest. "I'm almost indecent." She gestured to her dress, which still covered everything important except her calves, knees, and a few spots on her stomach. She turned and walked toward the nearest thicket when Ferdi stopped her.

"Where are you going?" the halfling asked.

Millie looked at her as if she'd grown another head or three. "To change," she said in exaggerated fashion, as if speaking to a particularly young child. "In the bushes. Where no one can see."

"And where you could fall into a pit, get crushed by a tree, or dragged down by guwatri before anyone could help you," the warrior shook her head. "No one goes off on their own."

"What about when I need to—see to nature's call?" I asked.

"Go in the bushes beside the path. That's what we'll all do, and it'll be a lot more awkward for us than you. Not that it matters; these two have obviously seen you naked before, you've seen them, as well, and I have no real interest in any of you."

"Murf, look away," Millie commanded, her face turning red.

"You know, I've seen it all already," I pointed out.

"Yes, but that was because I wanted you to. Now, I don't. Turn around, or I'll try to collect Ferdi's bounty on you, Murf."

I quickly spun, using the time to strip off my coat, remove my ragged shirt, and slip on the one the Unity provided. It was coarser than I preferred, off-white instead of white, but it was at least intact. As I dressed, I heard the rustling of fabric behind me, and I had to force myself not to imagine what was happening. Sadly, Ferdi seemed determined to make that impossible.

"Impressive," the halfling said after a moment.

"What?" Millie asked, her voice surprised.

"Your breasts. They're quite impressive. Don't they get in the way when you fight, though?"

"I really would rather not have this discussion right now."

"Fine. I won't discuss your breasts." She paused. "I see that your hair color's natural." I couldn't help but snort at that.

"Ferdi!" Millie snapped. "And Murf, stop listening!"

"I've never understood why humans have hair down there," Ferdi continued. "Doesn't it itch? Do you have to cut it the way you do your hair?"

"Just—please just stop talking," Millie begged.

"If you prefer." Silence reigned for several moments.

"Could you also stop staring?"

"I could. I won't."

I was chortling by that point, and even Azara had a thin smile on her face. I waited until Millie told me I could turn back around, then looked back at her. I looked, then looked again, then looked once more just to be sure I was seeing what I thought I was.

"Not a word, Murf," Millie said through gritted teeth as she did her best to try and maintain her dignity. "Not a twice-damned word, you hear me?"

I wondered if maybe I shouldn't have been the one to open that box after all. The Unity had provided clothing for Millie of a sort, but it didn't look like anything comfortable or concealing. The shirt and trousers were both a size or two too small but fortunately seemed to be made of a fabric that stretched well. That was necessary since her shirt pulled tightly across her breasts, and her trousers hugged her legs and body like a second skin, revealing her ankles and lower calves. It almost looked like someone had painted clothing onto her body rather than actual fabric, to be honest, and I couldn't help but be appreciative.

"Not a word," I finally agreed with her, give her a reassuring smile. I hesitated. "If there were a word, though, it would probably be 'Wow'."

She gave me a little smile and sighed, letting her hands drop. "Thank you." She swung her arms and moved her legs around a bit with a grimace. "At least this should be easier to move in and won't get caught in thorns as much."

"You'd better hope not," I laughed. "If you rip either of those, they're likely to give way entirely."

"Shit. I hadn't thought of that." She sighed. "I hate this damn place, Murf."

"Me too, Millie. Monsters, pits, and not a single gambling table in sight." I spread my arms and looked around in mock disbelief. "Who builds a place like this and forgets the gambling tables? Sometimes I wonder what the Unity's thinking."

"Exactly," she grinned at me. "Although I'm not sure if bluffing a stab-monkey would work." She looked hesitant for a moment, then stepped toward me, stood on her tiptoes, and kissed my cheek lightly. "Thank you for trying. I know this isn't your fault. I'm just scared, and I want to be out of here."

"I'm terrified, myself," I agreed.

"Really?"

"Absolutely." I tapped my chin thoughtfully. "You know, I think today is the first time I've ever run toward a fight. Away seems like a much smarter direction."

"It does. Think if we run fast enough, the Labyrinth will give up and leave us alone?"

"I think we'll both end up trapped in the same damn pit," I laughed. "Which could be its own sort of fun, really."

"It could." She smiled at me. "Come on. Let's get moving. The faster we go, the sooner we're out of here."

I turned back to the front, but as I did, I saw Azara's eyes watching us. I met her gaze for a few moments, feeling a stab of guilt as I did. I really shouldn't have flirted with Millie, at least not right there in front of the avian. If she felt any jealousy, though, it didn't make it into her eyes as she gestured toward the path.

"You're first, Murf. If anyone is going to fall into a deep pit, after all, it should be you."

Yeah. Definitely no jealousy and anger there. I needed to pull my head out of my pants and focus on getting out of here alive. Azara could hate me all she wanted. I'd prefer she and I both be alive as she did it.

26

"I—I need a break," Millie panted, sitting down heavily on the leaf-strewn ground. "Just for a bit." As she sat down, her stomach gurgled, and she made a face. "And maybe something to eat."

"I'm tired, as well," Azara agreed from behind me. "Some rest would be welcome."

I didn't need to look at the two women to know that they were right. They both needed a rest. I'd seen the signs of it for the past few hours. Azara stumbled more frequently over roots and slipped on leaves. Her warnings came slower and later. Millie's knife had slowed significantly as her body tired, doing less damage and missing as often as not. Her idea about the poison had been a good one and made even her small cuts dangerous, but even with that—and me renewing it every time I fell into a pit because the poison wore off after a battle or two—she was still struggling to keep up. Her new clothes had tears in them revealing long, deep scratches covered with bandages we'd gotten as drops as she just got too slow to keep up with the things.

I was doing somewhat better, but I was feeling the pressure, as well. My stomach ached from hunger, and while we'd found enough water to keep thirst at bay, it didn't help with the gnawing feeling in my center. Using my new ability so frequently seemed to slow its recovery, and in the last few battles, it barely affected the stab-monkeys at all. My body felt mostly fine, but fatigue tugged at my thoughts. My brain felt foggy, and not from poison but just from sheer exhaustion. I needed food and sleep, and the others did, as well.

"We can't stop," Ferdi shook her head. "We'll just get swarmed by the guwatri."

"Stab-monkeys," Azara muttered.

"Whatever you call them, we can't stop."

"We have to, Ferdi," I told her, shaking my head. "In another hour, my ability is going to stop working entirely. Azara will be too tired to use cards, and Millie is having trouble standing right now."

"No, I'm not!" she protested

"Be silent," Azara hissed. "He's making our case!"

"Oh. Yeah, then, I can barely stand up."

"You think I'm not tired?" the halfling sighed. "I am. I've been as active or more so than the rest of you, and I'm starving. My own abilities are weakening, as well, and I've trained them a lot more than you have yours, Murf. If I'm tiring, then you all must be close to exhaustion. I understand—but do you really think that sitting for a few minutes is going to help?"

"I just need an hour or so," Millie said with a yawn. "And maybe a bite to eat."

"Don't start that," I scolded, fighting not to yawn myself. "You'll have us all doing it!"

"In half that time, we'll have a swarm like the one we faced in the first clearing on top of us," Ferdi shook her head. "That was the biggest group we've faced so far, and I think it's because we were still for so long. Do you want to face that again? Do you think we can?"

"We still need to rest. Even a fifteen-minute nap is better than nothing," I told her.

"Not if you wake up from that nap dead." She gestured at the trees. "Besides, where would we rest? Here on the path, where everything can find us? In a bramble thicket, where anything can sneak up on us?" She shook her head. "We can sit for maybe ten minutes, no longer."

"If you can give me ten minutes—and clear ground to work with," Azara said slowly, "I think I can give us a few hours to rest." My tired mind took a second or two to process her words, and as it did, my eyes widened.

Ferdi looked at the avian skeptically. "You can shield against the guwatri? Then, why haven't you been?"

"Not a shield," she shook her head. "That would take far too much power. I can hide us. It's a tableau that makes us look like part of the background, so that others don't notice us." Ferdi looked skeptical, so I stepped in.

"It's true, she can. I've seen it. It's hidden us from people in the middle of the city before."

"Oh?" Millie asked archly. "And what were you doing in the middle of the city that you needed to hide, exactly?"

"Something that we'll never do again," Azara said shortly. "But that's not the point of the tableau. I originally made it when I first started as a cartomancer before I joined the Sage's Guild. They were—less than happy that I was practicing without paying my dues to them, and they sought me out to make that clear." She eyed Ferdi. "They never found me, not even using other cartomancers to divine my location. They knew where I was, but when they arrived, they couldn't see me and assumed I'd tricked their cards somehow. If it can hold against hunters from the Sage's Guild, I think it should keep us safe against the stab-monkeys."

"Gu..." Ferdi sighed. "Whatever. What if you're wrong?"

"If she's wrong, then we're dead either way," I said grimly, turning to Azara. "What do you need from us?"

"A circle, one large enough to enclose us all, with no leaves or sticks inside it, and time without interruption."

I nodded. "Millie, you and I can clear a spot. Ferdi, you keep an eye out for us."

"Fine," the halfling said resignedly. "I want it to be noted that I'm doing this under protest."

"I'll keep that in mind. That way, if we all get eaten in the next hour, you won't have to say, 'I told you so.'"

"I won't have to. I will, though."

Azara led the rest of us off the path toward a clearing she said her cards told her was there—it was—and Millie and I spent most of ten minutes clearing all the leaves and sticks from it, including pulling up rocks that the avian said were in the way and then smoothing over the holes left behind.

"I don't remember going through all this before," I muttered as I dug a finger into the muddy clay to pry up a large rock. "You just drew a circle with chalk, and that was it."

"That was on a floor, an artificial surface," Azara answered as she carefully lay down another card on the unfolded blanket in front of her. "One designed for people to occupy. This forest floor is natural and not meant for us. We have to claim it as ours first. Now, stop bothering me."

We finished the circle to Azara's satisfaction, and she knelt before her tableau, taking a deep breath. I walked over and squatted beside her, my voice quiet as I spoke.

"Are you going to be okay to do this?" I asked softly. "I know this is complex and takes a lot of power from you..."

"Don't," she cut me off. "Don't start acting like you care, Murf. Not now."

"Hey." I grabbed her chin and turned her face until she looked into my eyes. "I do care, Azara."

"It's easier on us both if you don't." She jerked her chin from my hand and took a deep breath. "I'm fine. Go entertain your new friend, and don't worry about me."

I watched her for a few moments before I rose to my feet and stepped back. She lowered her head for a moment, then raised her hands, and I felt power flowing out from her. That energy plunged down into her cards, which shivered and shuddered before her. I caught myself holding my breath. I didn't know much about cartomancy, but I knew it was a tricky thing. A single misplaced card could make a tableau fail, and that could be explosive. Azara was good—one of the best, as far as I'd seen—but she was also tired. A mistake would be disastrous for all of us.

The power rippled out through the cards, and I felt it flow beneath my feet. The few scraps of leaves and twigs we'd left behind danced and trembled along the ground as the energy flowed outward, jumping off the clay with a faint buzzing sound. As I watched, smoke rose from those fragments, and one by one, they all smoldered into ash that fell on the ground. I understood now why Azara was so finicky about the ground being clear; if we'd left the leaves in place, the tableau might have used up all its energy obliterating them. The energy rolled outward in a visible wave leaving tendrils of smoke behind until it reached the end of the cleared area and stopped.

Azara suddenly slumped, and without thinking, I ran forward and caught her before she hit the ground. I scooped her up gently and examined her with mild concern. Fortunately, she seemed fine. Her breathing was strong and regular, and while her skin was pale, it wasn't ashen and white. Exhaustion had finally caught up to her, and that last tableau had been a bit too much for her.

I glanced back at Millie, who watched me with a curious expression. "Can you lay out a blanket for her? I think she just needs to rest."

"Before you do that—did it work?" Ferdi asked, looking around. "Looks normal to me."

I shrugged. "I don't know. You'd have to step out to see, I think."

"Good idea." The halfling strode to the edge of the clearing, hesitated for a moment, then stepped outside it. She turned and looked back at us, her face confused for a few seconds, then stepped forward again. "That's pretty good," she admitted as she reentered the circle. "I knew that you were here, so I could sort of see you, but I couldn't focus on you. If I didn't know, I'd have walked right past." She paused. "Does it work against sounds?"

"Yes. That I know for certain."

"Do you, now?" Millie asked dryly as she unfolded one of the ratty blankets we'd gotten and spread it on the ground.

"Some people are noisier than others," I shrugged, arching an eyebrow at her as I lowered Azara to the ground gently. The redhead had the good grace to look embarrassed for a moment, although I was fairly sure that she was faking it.

She cleared her throat. "What about odors?"

"Odors?" I lowered my head and sniffed myself. "I'm not that bad yet. Ferdi's armor stinks worse than me."

"Armor stinks. That's its nature," the halfling shrugged.

"I was thinking about food," Millie rolled her eyes. "I'd like to build a fire and cook something—assuming those meat cubes we got are food, that is."

"They are," Ferdi nodded. "They just have to be boiled, and they make a sort of stew. It's not very good, but it's nourishing." She looked at me. "Well? Odors?"

"I—don't really know. I mean, no one ever mentioned smelling anything, so—probably? I didn't go around after asking people if they smelled something, though, and I was a little too distracted at the time to watch their faces closely."

"I think we should chance it," Millie volunteered as her stomach rumbled once more. She grimaced. "I mean, obviously."

"You're probably right. Ferdi, can you get a fire started?"

"Not without wood. You two fetch some, and I'll dig a pit and work up some tinder."

We stepped out of the clearing, and as we did, I glanced backward. I frowned as my eyes just seemed to slide away from the clearing behind us. When I forced them to focus, I could see the forest behind our impromptu camp, and I could sort of tell that there might be something in front of me, but I couldn't seem to focus on it.

"That's a little scary," Millie said, shivering as she looked back as well. "I know that Ferdi and Azara are there, but I can't see them."

"It's weird," I agreed. "I've never seen it from this side before."

She smacked my arm. "Enough about that. I don't need that image in my head, thank you very much. I keep picturing the two of you in the Unity Cathedral, or in the Gambler's Hall…" She shuddered.

"I never thought of the Cathedral," I mused, rubbing my chin. She punched my arm this time, and I laughed. "Okay, I'm done talking about it. Let's find some firewood."

Fifteen minutes later, the three of us sat around a cheery campfire with our rusty pot propped up over it on a ring of stones. Ferdi poured it about half-full of water and dumped one of the meat cubes in, then sat back to let it heat up. She leaned back, looking around the clearing with satisfaction.

"This is handy," she said approvingly. "If it works, I'm bringing a cartomancer on all my delves from now on."

"You don't usually?" I asked. "Seems like they'd be useful."

"Not really. Most of them focus on divinations, not actively using cards the way bird-woman does."

"That still seems like it would be helpful," Millie volunteered. "Isn't more knowledge about one of these places a good thing?"

"Of course, but typically, we have all that knowledge before we step foot inside." She shifted and looked at the two of us. "Usually, when I'm planning a delve, I hit up the local Sage's and Sellsword's Guilds and buy all the information I can on the Labyrinth first. Sage's Guilds usually have maps and descriptions of local Labyrinths for sale, while you can learn about the Labyrinth's monsters and traps at the Blade Hall. If you can find other delvers willing to share, you can even learn more."

"Like what?"

"How numerous and dangerous the monsters are. The difficulty level of the traps. Even what rank you should be to have a reasonable chance of success."

"Rank?" the redhead asked. "What's that?"

"Something all Holders have. The higher your rank, generally, the more cards you can bind, the stronger your abilities, and the more often you can use them. Different Labyrinths are appropriate for different ranks." She looked around. "I'm guessing this one's about rank 3, which makes really dangerous for us.

"However, the fact is, I don't know. If these guwatri are the main monsters in here, we'll be okay as long as we can rest to reset Murf's ability and Azara's cartomancy. If they're just the introduction, we're in trouble."

I felt a little stab of guilt at that, and I picked up a nearby stick and poked the fire with it. "Uh, about that—I might be able to help, there."

She looked at me sharply. "Help? You mean, you've heard more about this place?"

"No, not exactly. It's more like..." I paused, wondering how much to share, then grimaced. We were counting on one another for our lives, here. It would be stupid if we all died because I was keeping secrets. "When we entered the Labyrinth, a card popped up in front of me that told me a bit about it."

"What?" she half-shouted, rising to a crouch with an angry expression.

"Shh," Millie said as Azara snorted and rolled over onto her side, where she began to snore loudly. I winced as I remembered that sound; it was something about her nose, as far as I could figure, and it made her snore like a sawmill. I walked over to her and reached down, gently pinching her nose shut. Her mouth popped open, and the snoring halted instantly.

"Sorry," I said to the others. "She's not a side-sleeper."

"Obviously," Millie said a little sourly.

I walked back over and sat down, looking at Ferdi. "Before you say anything, Ferdi, stop and think for a bit. First of all, I know exactly shit about being a Holder. For all I knew, you got the exact same information that I did. I still don't know that you didn't, in fact. Second of all, once I realized that you didn't, I didn't really want to overshare with you. You've already tried to kill me over cards once, after all, and if my card can do things that yours can't, well..." I held my hands out with a shrug.

"Wrong, Murf," she said in a flat voice. "I didn't try to kill you because of the cards. I don't give a damn about those cards. I gave you two that I have no Harmony with, so I can't even use them and was planning to trade them or sell them anyway." She leaned toward me. "I tried to kill you because you made an oath to me, and you broke it. I had to, or I'd be breaking my own oath. I'm still not sure if I can let you live or not, to be honest. I didn't find my cards on those elves."

"No, they gave them to their boss," I shrugged. "We'll have to find him to get them, I suppose—not that I think that's a good idea."

She grimaced. "No, probably not," she sighed, then looked up at me a little sadly. "Did you really think that I'd kill you over a card, Murf?"

"You cut my stomach open, Ferdi. If I didn't have the card I have, I'd have bled to death right there in your hold, and you've have stood back and watched, wouldn't you?" I glared at her. "So, yeah, I might have had that thought."

She stayed silent for a few moments, then looked down at the fire. "I might—I might have handled that badly," she admitted. "I should have talked first. I was angry, and I let that control me." She looked back at me. "I'm sorry, Murf. You have my vow: I won't harm you in any way for your cards. This, I swear on the spear of Bardona." A little pulse of energy rippled out from her, and I sat back, shocked. That was the same oath she'd made me take, so long ago, and I knew it held religious and real significance for her.

"I—thank you, Ferdi," I said quietly. I glanced at Millie, who held her hands up defensively.

"I don't even want the cards I have," she said quickly. "I'm certainly not interested in yours!"

I watched her closely, but her body language wasn't giving away any tells. That didn't mean much, as she was an excellent gambler, but I'd read her plenty before. Besides, Ferdi had said it earlier: if I wanted to get trust, I had to give it. No matter how hard that was.

"Fine. My card is called the Eldritch Hag. It's—it's one of the Cabal."

Ferdi hissed in surprise, leaping to her feet, while Millie looked confused. "The what?" she asked.

"The unaffiliated powers," Ferdi said in a low voice, stunned amazement and even fear written across her face. "Part of the Deck of Fate."

"That means nothing to me, you know," the redhead said helplessly.

"They're the most powerful cards in existence. No one even knows for sure how many of them there are. Wars have been fought and kingdoms broken over one." She gave me the most serious look I'd ever seen on her face. "Murf—you can't tell anyone about this. Ever. Nobody."

"I was trying," I pointed out.

"Try harder." She shivered. "Even with my vow, part of me wants that card, Murf. With it, I could probably tear through this whole Labyrinth alone."

"It's that good?" Millie asked.

"Put it this way. What abilities did you get from your cards, human?"

Millie looked suspicious for a moment, and Ferdi sighed. "Three of blades, three of coins. Probably an improved cutting ability with knives since you seem to favor them, and maybe a speed boost or wind-based attack. Am I right?"

The redhead's eyes widened. "I—how did you know that? Yes, I got something called Keen Blades that makes my dagger cut deeper, and one called Ride the Breeze that makes me faster and more agile."

"And for having the 2-set, you probably got a pretty weak sensing ability, most likely precious metals considering your personality."

"That—how are you doing that?" Millie demanded.

"I'm not doing anything. Those are lesser arcana, and everybody knows what they do. The Sage's Guild's documented thousands of abilities linked to each of them and have even worked out ways to predict what abilities you're likely to get from any given card before you bind it. That's what most people do before taking their hole card: they get a reading from the Guild and decide if that's what they want, but you can still make a solid prediction based on the card alone. Threes are always attack-based; blades deal with metal, earth, and battle; and coins are always about air, wealth, and the body. A 2-set of threes gives you an extremely weak sensing power, which is usually an ability you'd get from a four.

"You got those two small cards, and you probably feel like they made you a lot stronger. They did, but Murf?" The halfling looked at me. "He got an ability that can protect him from practically any danger and that might eventually make him immortal."

"Immortal?" I chuckled. "Hardly, Ferdi. Remember your axe in my belly? I can still die."

"Think about it, Murf. Right now, your card is new, your Harmony with it is low, and your rank is probably zero. Cards get stronger as you bond with them, especially your hole card. What if, as you rank up, it adapts more quickly, or even instantly? What if the adaptations last longer or indefinitely? You hold your hand in a candle, and you're immune to fire forever. Stab yourself with a knife, and no blade can ever cut you again. Get punched once, and you could jump off a cliff without getting hurt."

She shook her head. "And that's just physical damage. What if it helps you adapt in other ways? If it helps you draw the cards you need in a game of arcanum? Teaches you any language you hear so that you can speak and read it? Makes you good at anything you try to do? Lets you walk on water or air to get places?" She leaned forward. "What if it adapts to aging, Murf? You could literally live forever, impossible to harm, a master at anything you try!"

I sat back, stunned by what she suggested. I admit, at that point, I hadn't really put any real thought into the Hag's ability, at least not long-term. I considered her an annoyance, to be honest. My life had been so much simpler before her, and some part of me hoped that maybe someday, it would go back to being simple. If things happened the way Ferdi suggested, though, nothing would be simple again. I'd be someone like the heroes from legends—exactly the way the Hag suggested I could be.

The real question was: would I want all that? I knew the answer to that right away. Hell no, I wouldn't. Life is a game, and games are only fun if there's risk involved. What's the point of playing if you know you can't lose?

I shook off those thoughts; after all, Ferdi could be wrong, and even if she wasn't, all I had to do was avoid gaining ranks or Harmonies, and I'd be fine. The way the Hag worked now was great, as far as I was concerned. Of course, that assumed that I was going to have that option. Somehow, I doubted the Unity would let me.

"That—wow," Millie breathed. "That's a hell of a card, Murf!"

"It is, but you'll forgive me if I'm hoping that you're wrong, Ferdi," I sighed. "That—that's all a bit too much for me. Anyway, as I said, when we entered the Labyrinth, I got a card that told me about it. I think I remember most of it..." As I said that, the card in question flashed in my eyes. "Never mind. It came back."

"On its own?" Ferdi asked quizzically.

"That's how it usually happens." I frowned. "It isn't like that for you?"

"No. I have to call up my card to see if it's got anything to tell me."

"I can call up my card?" Millie asked.

"Yes. Reach down to it and think about seeing it, and you will. When you do, it'll tell you anything you need to know about it. It's a good habit to check regularly; otherwise, you could miss things." The warrior glanced at me. "At least, most of us might. So, what does yours say, Murf?"

I glanced over the card again, rereading its contents.

"It says that this is an escape type Labyrinth, whatever that means," I said. "Recommended ranks are 3 to 5, and the likely rewards are low."

"Damn," she said, spitting into the fire. "I hate escape types."

"Why?" Millie asked. "Doesn't it just mean that you have to find a way out?"

"No. It means that the moment we entered, the guardian started hunting us. We either have to kill it or find an exit before it catches us—and with those ranks, that's what we'll want to do, especially with low rewards. The guardian's usually higher than the recommend ranks for a Labyrinth, and we can't handle a Rank 6 monster."

"So, no getting rich?" the redhead sighed.

"Nope. We probably won't even see gold. Maybe a low arcana or two for killing the guardian." She spat again. "It's no wonder no one else was running this thing. High risk, low rewards, the worst kind of Labyrinth there is—and we're stuck in the damn center of it." She looked at me. "That sounds like one of your stupid laws. Got one about this?"

"Law number three," I sighed. "The Unity is a massive bitch."

Ferdi stirred the boiling pot in silence for a few moments. "That one—that one might have something to it," she finally admitted. "Look at that, Murf. You finally got one right. Took you long enough."

27

Ferdi's stew was, as she promised, not particularly good. In fact, it was just this side of awful. Pools of grease floated on top of it, the hunks of meat in it were still tough and stringy, and the greenish bits I assumed were supposed to be vegetables felt like chewing on rubber. It was filling, though, and a couple bowls quieted my stomach nicely. With full bellies, Millie and I laid out two of the tattered blankets and went to grab some sleep. Part of me considered asking her if she'd like to share my blanket, but the much wiser part of me knew that wouldn't be a good idea. Ferdi probably wouldn't care, but if Azara woke up—well, I couldn't see any way that would go well and lots of ways it could end up with Millie and me on fire.

It turned out that restraint was probably a good idea since I dropped off almost the moment my eyes closed. No woman appreciates a man falling asleep when he's supposed to be enjoying other things, a fact I learned years ago thanks to a night containing far too much alcohol and far too little sleep. I slept hard and woke suddenly, jerking awake with no real recollection of time passing. I glanced up at the orange canopy that looked exactly the same as it had when I closed my eyes, stretched, and considered whether or not I should lie back down. I felt mostly rested, honestly. My head was clearer, for sure. The pressure in my stomach from my ability wasn't as strong as it had been when I first got it, but it was somewhat close. A headache I didn't even know I had was gone, and while I could still feel a touch of fatigue lingering in my brain, it was easy to ignore. It would have been easier with a cup of coffee.

"Hey, Unity, maybe you could include that in our next drops instead of another damn waterskin," I thought silently.

Movement caught my eye, and I looked up to see Ferdi still standing near the glowing embers that had been the fire. That it had burned down told me I'd been out for a while, at least, but we hadn't put that much wood in it in the first place, so it probably wasn't too long. Millie slumbered a few feet away from me, while Azara still lay quietly on the other side of the fire. I rose to my feet, stretching as my back and neck twinged a bit. Sleeping on the ground was awful, I decided. Beds were infinitely better, and I resolved to enjoy one as quickly as possible, maybe with Millie's help, if she was interested. I considered asking the Unity for that as well—

the bed, not Millie's help—but realized if it listened, I'd have to drag a damn bed through this forest. I decided to stick with the coffee for now.

I walked over to Ferdi, pausing to glance into the mostly empty pot of stew and deciding that I wasn't hungry enough to try that again. Instead, I sat beside the halfling and stared at the glowing coals of the fire.

"How long was I out?"

"About two-and-a-half hours. Not that long."

"How can you tell?" I asked, glancing up at the unchanging canopy overhead. "Did the light change at all?"

"No. It never does in a Labyrinth. If it's daytime, it's always daytime; if it's night, it's always night."

"So, how do you judge the time?"

"Counting," she shrugged.

"Counting?"

"Yes. I started counting when you went to sleep. I count to 120, which is about two minutes, then start over. I did that seventy-eight times since you fell asleep, so about two-and-a-half hours."

I stared at her in amazement. "That—are you serious, Ferdi? That has to be the most boring thing I've ever heard in my life!"

She shrugged. "It's an old delver's trick. It passes the time while you're on watch, and it helps to keep you focused and alert. Of course, most of us only sleep for an hour at a time."

"Sorry for keeping you up," I grimaced.

"It's fine. I don't need as much sleep as the rest of you, and thanks to this thing…" She gestured at the edge of the clearing. "We can afford a longer rest. Usually, you're given an hour, but you rarely get all of it before your camp gets attacked. It's hard to sleep through something like that."

"You know that sounds like a terrible way to live, right?"

"It is. Exciting, though."

I looked up at her curiously. "Is that why you do it, Ferdi? Why you delve? The excitement?"

"No," she shook her head. "No one delves for the excitement, Murf. At least, they don't for long."

"Why not?"

"Because people who do this for the thrill don't last long. They throw themselves into battles, embrace danger, take greater and greater risks, until eventually, the Unity decides to give them one they can't handle."

"Seems like the Unity would love people like that," I snorted. "More meat for its Labyrinths, right?"

"That's how most people think. They see Labyrinths as death traps, places the Unity creates to guard its cards and kill anyone who wants to claim them. It's an idea that several of the Guilds promote, especially the Sage's, Scrivener's, and Sellsword's, as it makes them money if people are terrified of the Labyrinths."

She sat down beside me, curling her knees up and wrapping her arms around them. "That's wrong, though. That's not the point of Labyrinths at all. They aren't meant to kill; they're meant to test, to make sure that those who are claiming the Unity's powers as their own are worthy of them. Failure means death, but the point is to succeed. The Unity wants its Labyrinths to be conquered, not to be left untouched out of fear."

"If that's so, why is the damn thing trying so hard to kill us?" I scoffed.

"Is it, Murf?" she asked, looking at me seriously. "If the Unity just wanted us to die, why send guwatri after us? If this place is for ranks 3 to 5, they have to be about the weakest things in here. Why give us breaks to recover between battles? Why not just send waves of creatures against us until we're slaughtered?"

She shook her head. "And why would it give us what we need to survive? Without food and water, rest wouldn't have helped us much. Why would it give you a card that's perfectly suited for leveling the battlefield with the guwatri?

"It did all that because it wants us to have a chance. We just have to be smart enough to use what we're given intelligently and not waste our opportunities." She looked back out into the distance. "And the fact is, you're currently our most valuable resource, Murf."

"Me?" I asked dubiously. "I'm barely holding my own, Ferdi!"

"That ability of yours and your Luck stat—whatever it is—have kept us all alive. The problem is, you don't know how to use either of them very well."

"Hey, I'm doing pretty good for someone who's never had a damn card before!" I protested.

"You are, but 'pretty good' will get us all killed. You need to do better." She sighed. "And that will only happen if I help you. If I leave you to work it out on your own, we'll all be dead before you do."

"Actually, that was one of the reasons I came to see you," I admitted. "I don't know shit about being a Holder, and I was hoping that you'd help me if we could put our past behind us." I chuckled weakly. "Looks like it took a damn Labyrinth to make that happen, though."

"Nothing's behind us, Murf. For the moment, survival just trumps justice." She turned toward the fire and poked it a bit with her sword, stirring the ashes. "Take a look at your card again. The knight, not the other one."

"How?"

"Just think about it. It'll happen."

I dutifully turned my thoughts toward the knight and focused on seeing it, and it popped up in front of me once more.

Knight of Cups
Drunken Combat
Noble Arcana
12%
9/81
Hostile creatures within 20' of you
become increasingly intoxicated.
This is a mind-altering and physical
effect.

"Hey, the number things changed," I said, reading over the card.

"Number things?" she echoed tiredly. "What in Kewan's blood are you talking about, Murf?"

"There are three numbers on the card. One beside a music note, another by a single jagged slash, and the last beside two slashes. The first one went from 11% to 12%, the second from 8 to 9, and the last..." I frowned, not able to remember what it had been, just that it had been lower. "Went up," I finished lamely.

"That's your attunement," she sighed.

"You probably think that means something, Ferdi. It doesn't."

"No, it does, you just don't know what it is, Murf." She reached out and dug in the firre a bit with her stick. "This is stuff that most Holders learn before they even get a card. That, or they go to the Sages or Church and pay to learn it."

"Yes, but they don't have you to explain," I chuckled.

"True. Fine. Attunement is how well you're linked to your card. It's based on the card's power—you have to be higher ranked to have high attunement with a more powerful card—your Harmony for that suit, which I assume is high for cups for you to have even that much attunement to a noble, and how much you use it. You've been using yours a lot, so the attunement went up a percent."

She tossed the stick down and sighed. "The other numbers are base power and max power. You've got a base power right now of 9."

"And the crown means the type of card, right?"

"Yes. That's its rank. What's the max power, the other number?"

"81," I answered after only a brief hesitation.

Her head whipped up to stare at me, her eyes wide. "It's *what*?" Her voice rose sharply in volume, and I quickly shushed her, motioning toward the others.

"81. I take it that's not normal."

She stared at me for a moment before seeming to regather herself. She let out a snort and looked back at the fire. "No, Murf. That's not normal. A card's max power depends on your rank and Harmony with it. I haven't seen it before, but I'd expect a knight to have a max power in the twenties or thirties at most for a new Holder."

"What about that base thing? Is that high, too?"

"For a new card? A bit, yes." She gestured at the slumbering form of Millie. "I'll bet your pretty friend there is just squeezing a base power of 1 out of her cards, which is pretty normal for a new Holder. If you gave her the knight, that might go up to a 2 or 3." She shook her head with an expression of disgust. "That hole card of yours is absurd."

"Okay, but what does it mean? What's base and max and whatever power? Is it how much I'm using each time I activate the card? And why is it only 9 out of 81?"

"Enough," she said, waving her hands. "Just shut up, and I'll explain, Murf. Stop asking so many damn questions!" She stopped and took a deep breath. "Okay. Power. Power is kind of like—it's like a measure of the potential strength of your ability. Max power is how strong your ability could be; base power is how strong it actually is right now, and that's low because you aren't attuned to the card or high-ranked enough to use it well. As for what it really means…"

She picked up her stick again and began poking the fire as she continued. "What most people don't realize is that every monster, person, and even rock has some inherent resistance to card abilities. For Holders, it's a lot higher based on your rank and profession, but everybody's got some level of resistance. Your ability's power is your chance to get through that resistance and affect someone or something."

I pulled up my status card again and read it with a frown. "I don't see anything about resistance on here, Ferdi."

"You don't, no, because resistance isn't constant. It changes based on the rank of the card being used against you, the rank of the Holder using it, and your Luck and Harmony stats. I could use two different cards against you, and your resistance to each would be a little different. If the pretty human used the same two cards, your resistance would change again.

"What matters is that the higher your base power is than your target's resistance, the more strongly it affects them."

"So, higher is better, basically."

"Yes." She grimaced. "However, that's only if you know how to use it, and you don't. Those guwatri are probably rank 1 or 2 creatures, Murf. While they're unintelligent, which gives them a higher resistance to mind-affecting abilities like yours…"

"The card says it's mind-affecting and physical," I supplied helpfully.

"It is? That's useful."

"Why?"

She glanced toward me with a resigned expression. "Because like I said, everything has resistance to card abilities, and some things are more resistant to some types. Unintelligent monsters like the guwatri have higher resistance to mind-affecting abilities just because they don't have enough minds to work with. At the same time, things like undead or plant monsters are usually resistant or immune to physical effects like poison. Your ability is both, though, so something would have to be resistant to both to ignore it."

"So, that means I can get plants drunk?"

"Probably not. Plants don't have minds, after all. You might be able to get undead drunk, though, at least intelligent ones.

"What's important is that the guwatri probably have a resistance in the low teens to your card. If you could use even half of it, you'd drop them in seconds, not over a minute or more, and these battles would be nothing more than going around and slitting their throats while they slept. You can't, though, because you're barely touching what your card can do. That's why your attunement's so low, and it's why you're getting a ninth of the power you could be from that card."

She looked back at the fire, her face thoughtful as she spoke. "Being a Holder's not just about having power, Murf. It's about knowing how to use it. It's like…" She paused, obviously trying to think of a comparison, and I just sighed.

"It's like the difference between having a great hand and knowing how to play it," I finished for her. "Anyone can win with a great hand, but a good gambler keeps people in the game and betting, so they win more. I get it, Ferdi. I do. I just don't know what to do about it."

"That's where I can help. Maybe."

"Maybe?"

"Everyone's different," she shrugged. "I can tell you what works for me, but in the end, you have to turn it into what works for you."

She rose to her feet and held out a hand. I took it, and she hauled me effortlessly to my feet. She took a step back and drew her sword. I looked at it a bit nervously, but she simply held it up in front of her.

"Everyone's different," she repeated, "but some things are the same. Every ability, no matter how powerful, has its own energy pool, and using it draws on that pool. The higher the base power rating, the higher the draw, and the more control you need over it to make it useful." She whipped her sword around, and I could almost see a shimmer of energy surrounding it. "This is Weapon Mastery. It's got a base power of 12, mostly because I've got some bonuses to it from the cards I've got and how I've placed them. Against you or the pretty woman, it's closer to a base power of 50."

"She has a name, you know, Ferdi," I chuckled. "It's not even a hard one to say. 'Millie'. Give it a try."

"I know her name. I'm not sure that she's going to live through this, though. If I don't name her, I won't get attached to her."

"She's not a pet, Ferdi."

"All you tall folk are like pets, Murf. You're needy, hard to understand, and you always need me to take care of you." She shook her head. "We're getting off the subject.

"As I said, this is Weapon Mastery. When it's waiting to be activated, it feels like a ball of ice in the pit of my stomach that pushes outward. To use it, I let that ice flow upward into my weapon, and..." She spun, and the blade whizzed past my face, close enough that I felt the breeze of it against my nose.

She quickly sheathed the blade. "Using an ability is easy. Controlling it is harder. At first, at least, most Holders just squeeze out every drop of power they can manage every time, the way you're doing. They exhaust their ability, then they have to wait for it to recover before they can use it again."

She gestured at the still-slumbering Millie. "For her, that's not a big deal. Her base power ratings are probably 2 or 3 at most, so her abilities don't take much power and don't take long to recover. That knight of yours, though, needs a lot of energy. That means it takes longer to recover it, and the more you drain it, the slower that happens. That's why your ability kept getting weaker and weaker the longer you used it, and why it's not at its maximum power now. It needs to rest longer to regain full effectiveness."

"That makes sense, really," I mused. "I mean, it's like going all in on every pot and losing. It's harder to build back up from just a few chips than it is to grow a big stack. You can't bet as much, you have to fold more often, and you can't afford to take risks."

"If that helps you understand it, sure. The point is that you have to control the outflow of your power. You have to use only the amount you need, not everything you have. What's left will recover faster, and your body and mind will both be less tired."

"Seems reasonable," I nodded. "How do I do it?"

"That's where everyone's different. When I'm using Weapon Mastery, I have to reach into that well of ice and draw some up. I've practiced enough that I can draw up smaller amounts, now. How does it feel for you?"

"Like..." I paused. "Like a pimple that needs popping."

"That's disgusting, Murf."

"It's accurate, though," I chuckled. "When the power's ready, I feel full, like there's a place inside of me that's overstuffed. I squeeze it, and the power comes out. Just like popping a pimple."

"Or squeezing a full waterskin," she added. "That's a lot more pleasant to think about."

"But it doesn't bother you as much as the pimple thing seems to."

"Which is why it's less likely to get you stabbed for saying it." She shook her head. "Actually, the waterskin is a better visual for a more practical reason, as well."

"Which is?"

"When you—do what you were saying, it happens all at once. It's all or nothing. You can't do it partway."

"It's not that hard to say, Ferdi," I laughed. "The word is 'pimple'. We all get them."

"No, all humans get them. We don't. And they're disgusting." She shuddered.

"Seriously? I've seen you disembowel something and step in its intestines without flinching. Why do pimples bother you so much?"

"Because..." She grimaced. "The first time I saw a human with one, I asked about it. He told me that it was a blessing from the Unity, and if I looked closely, I could see the star on it. I was young, naïve, and didn't understand that talk folk lie sometimes because they think it's funny. So, I did, and—he squeezed it."

"That's both mean and hilarious," I chuckled.

"As far as I can tell, it was simply mean. Some of it..." She paused. "It got in my mouth, Murf."

"Oh, that is nasty," I agreed, laughing harder. "Still funny, though."

"I don't understand you tall people and your humor. How is it amusing that I fell violently ill and nearly died, Murf?"

"Wait, you what?" I asked, startled enough that my laughter died instantly.

"Yes. Whatever's in those things, it's not meant for us, I can tell you. I developed a fever within a day. I couldn't keep anything down, not even water. I had chills and tremors for three days, and the healers thought I would die." She shivered. "I don't know why that would amuse you."

"Okay, so that's not funny," I admitted. "Fine. No more pimples. Waterskin it is."

"Thank you." She took a deep breath and seemed to regain her focus. "The point is, you have to envision it in a way that you can easily control and limit. For me, I picture my abilities as packed snow rather than solid ice. I scoop out what I need and leave the rest. As I get better, I'm hoping to have even finer control, until eventually, I can handle individual snowflakes.

"That works for me. Others have their own methods. You simply need to work out a way to visualize what you happen that you can control. It doesn't have to be a waterskin if that doesn't appeal to you. It needs to be something intuitive, something you can do without really thinking too much about it. If you have to think in the middle of a fight, you're probably dead already."

I frowned as I considered her words. She was right about the pimple popping thing. That was an all-or-nothing deal. A waterskin would work, I suppose, but really, I'd never used a waterskin like that, squeezing it to spurt out a bit of water. I needed something intuitive, something I could limit without too much thought. I could think of something that I rather enjoyed that involved spurting, but I didn't think that imagining that in the middle of a fight would be all that productive. Fortunately, I came up with another possibility.

Instead of picturing a boil in the middle of my stomach that needed lancing, I imagined that the pressure was a deck of cards, flexed in my hand. It was a trick I'd practiced plenty, a fancy shuffling method where I sprayed the cards from one hand into the other. With enough practice, it was even possible to deal cards that way, shooting one at a time out, although it was a lot harder to get them to land facedown. I relaxed the edge of my mental grip, imagining letting a few cards shoot out, then clamping back down to stop them.

A ripple of power rolled out of me as I practically felt the cards slip from my fingers. More slid free than I'd wanted, and my mind's grip seemed clumsy and unsure compared to my nimble fingers. Of course, my fingers weren't always that skilled, either. They'd needed practice. I assumed the same would be true of this. As the energy flowed away and dissipated since nothing nearby wanted to kill me—at least, not at that precise moment, what with Azara sleeping—I checked my internal pressure again. It was down, but not by all that much, and I felt like I could probably do the same thing a couple more times. I was pretty proud of it. Sadly, it seemed I was the only one.

"Still too much," Ferdi shook her head. "You have to do better."

"It was my first try," I protested. "No one's good at anything on their first try!"

"True, but you don't get time to be a baby." She gave me a hard look. "Your ability might be the only thing that lets us get out of this place alive—that and the bird-woman's tableau. Try harder, and get better. If you don't, we'll probably all die."

"You know, Ferdi," I gritted, doing my best to ignore my sudden spike of anxiety, "you could at least try to be a little nicer about these things. You know, say something positive and soften the blow."

"I could. I won't." She turned and walked away from me, toward the blanket I'd vacated. "I'm going to sleep. That gives you an hour or two to practice. Do better."

"You know what? Screw you, Ferdi. You don't like what I'm doing, go fight the damn things yourself," I snapped with sudden heat. She kept putting pressure on me, and I was doing my damnedest already.

"If I could, I would. Honestly, the three of you make this harder because no one of you know what in the hell you're doing." She gave me a flat look. "If I had that hole card of yours, with my experience and cards, I'd clear this whole Labyrinth solo in a couple days. With that and the knight, that would be a few hours. I'd go hunt the guardian, knock it out with the knight, and cut its throat. I can't, though, so I need the three of you—well, you and the cartomancer. Not the pretty one. She's just baggage." She paused. "And I told you. I'm not interested in sex with you, Murf. No screwing."

"Was that an actual joke?" I asked her disbelievingly, feeling my irritation starting to ebb.

"Was what a joke? That I don't want to have sex with you? No. I really don't."

"Well, the feeling's mutual."

"Good. That makes it easier."

As she lay down on the blanket, still wearing her armor, I stared at her for a few seconds. "Hey, Ferdi, I've gotta ask. Why snow?"

"What?"

"Why snow? You know, to control your abilities."

She lay there quietly for long seconds, and I sighed as I realized she wasn't going to answer. To my surprise, though, her voice spoke quietly just as I turned away.

"I grew up in one of the high mountain villages. We got snow there every year—feet of it sometimes. I used to have snowball fights with my siblings when I was young. I'm comfortable with it, and it's easier to use an image you're comfortable with."

"Ferdi, that's downright adorable," I chuckled, feeling some of my irritation slip away. "You've never mentioned them before. You have brothers and sisters?"

"Had," she corrected. "They're gone."

My smile dropped from my face. "I'm sorry to hear that, Ferdi."

"So am I. A Labyrinth took them. They thought it would be easy, went in unprepared, and never came out." She looked over at me. "That's why you have to do better, Murf. Do better than my siblings. For all our sakes."

There wasn't much I could say to that, so I simply turned away from her, waiting for my reserves to refill a bit. I wasn't going to get good at this in an hour, and Ferdi knew it. I could get better, though. I had to.

I was not going to die in this damn Labyrinth. I promised myself that.

28

I swore as fangs clamped onto my boot, digging into the leather. I kicked, dislodging the attacker, and a long, orange, hairless body flew through the air. It slammed into a nearby tree with a sickening crack as its spine wrapped around the trunk, then dropped into a weakly moving heap at the base. As the next beast leaped at me, I jumped sideways and kicked again, this time catching a monster under its ribs and lofting it several feet away to crash near Ferdi. The halfling lashed out, striking not with a sword but a long spear and stabbing the beast in its throat.

Another of the wolflike creatures loped toward me, its overlarge head held low and its single huge eye fastened on my throat. It howled as stone spikes suddenly burst from the ground beneath it, stabbing into its wide, clawed paws. The spikes flattened out, pinning it in place, and I darted forward, slashing with the short saber I now carried. The wolf snapped at the blade as I cut and took the edge across its face, blinding its single eye. It yelped and jerked its head away, and I took that opportunity to stab it in the throat, stepping out of the way so that its blood spray didn't ruin another set of clothes.

True to Ferdi's prediction, the Unity had provided for us in the past two days we'd spent traveling the Labyrinth. I'd ruined the first set of clothing I'd gotten from it less than an hour after we broke camp, when we got attacked again, and found more in that drop. Those lasted a few hours until they had to be replaced again. I was currently on my fifth set of shirts and pants and my second coat. Only my hat was the same. Millie hadn't fared much better, and even Azara had to replace her black dress at one point.

Fortunately, the Unity kept replacing what we lost. Apparently, it wasn't a big fan of naked people wandering its Labyrinths. I mostly approved of that. I'd found that quite often, the people most eager to be naked were the ones you least want to see naked. And there were a whole lot more of those people in the world than the other kind, by a large margin. I didn't need to see some orc running through the forest naked as the day it was born, its junk flopping every which way and probably catching on brambles. It probably didn't want that, either, and since it seemed the Unity agreed, we were all on the same page.

Not that we saw anyone else. It might have been nice if we had; if nothing else, we could band together for protection. The Forest was empty of intelligent life, though, and every creature we met seemed dedicated to tearing apart our clothing to get to the tasty flesh beneath.

Unfortunately, as I was the one who kept collecting the drops, it also seemed that the Unity was favoring my tastes in clothing. The scarlet dress that it gave Azara to replace her black one was far more form-fitting than the last had been, with a long slit up one leg. Millie's clothing continued to be a size or two too small, something she complained about every time she had to replace her wardrobe—which was regularly. For whatever reason, though, my clothing was always comfortable and loose-fitting.

Apparently, the Unity's a pervert as well as a bitch. Who knew?

We'd gotten more than just clothing, of course. We kept finding the disgusting food cubes; we now had a grate we could set over our fire for cooking; we'd even gotten a hunk of flint we could use to start fires. We got weapons, too. Ferdi had her spear, Azara had an iron-banded staff, Millie had another dagger, and I had my saber. Ferdi also grabbed a small shield about as wide as her forearm was long, Millie took a hardened leather vest that she happily used to cover her too-tight shirt, and I now wore a vest of steel links under my coat that gave me at least a little protection against getting stabbed in the heart. It did not, however, stop monster blood spray from soaking through it and drenching my clothes, which I'd learned the hard way the day before.

And of course, we'd gotten a single brass coin each time, each of which went to Millie. She pocketed them with low mutters that I swore involved the Unity doing things to itself I didn't think were anatomically possible. Apparently, the Unity was also kind of an ass, which I hated, because that made me want to like the thrice-damned thing.

Whatever the case, I was glad for the new equipment because the Labyrinth kept making shit harder on us. After our first rest, the stab-monkeys disappeared, and the stomp-foxes emerged. Those were shorter than the stab-monkeys, only eighteen inches tall or so, but faster as well. They had long muzzles that were better for biting, and they loved to dart in, bite at our legs, and dart back out, hoping to cripple us. They also liked to target Azara whenever possible for some reason, and one of their attacks had been what ripped up her dress to the point she had to clutch her vest shut to keep things from spilling out. We figured out how to deal with those by keeping Azara in the middle of us, making them go through us to get to her, and kept going until we had to stop and rest again.

That was when the ass-wolves appeared. Ferdi really didn't like that name, but the fact was that not only did the three-foot-tall and six-foot long things kind of look like one-eyed, orange-skinned, hairless wolves, they smelled like ass. And not good ass. Nasty ass. The kind that you want to dump down a well to get rid of the stink, only you know you'd poison the water supply. The things reeked, and while they weren't quite as fast as the stomp-foxes, they were a lot stronger and more dangerous. Their howls actually chilled our blood, making it harder for us to fight, and they blended in so well with the foliage that they could pretty much disappear while you were watching them. About the only reason we were still there fighting was my ability—and Ferdi's insistence that I keep practicing with it every chance I got. That practice saved us fairly often since sometimes, my ability firing off triggered an ambush before the creatures were really ready, making it much easier to deal with them. In fact, that was how I'd accidentally drawn the current group to attack us.

As more of the creatures erupted from the nearby brush, I flexed the imaginary cards in my center and let a few spray out. A rush of power washed over the wolves, who stumbled and crashed into one another as my power turned them into drunken idiots for a bit. I clamped down on it at once, conserving as much power as possible. The power would wear off in a minute or so that way and wouldn't affect the ass-wolves as deeply, but I'd found that keeping the ability going made it recover a lot slower afterward.

Another of the things howled as Millie leaped out and slashed with both daggers, cutting it across the face while also slashing a leg. The monsters' giant eye turned out to be a serious weak point for them since they couldn't close it. Blinding them didn't take them out of the fight completely, but it did make them much less dangerous. Ferdi's spear slid out and took that one in the throat before it could recover, and Millie jumped back into place before the creatures could move to flank her.

While the ass-wolves were a lot more dangerous than the monkeys and foxes, there were never as many of them, and we dispatched them quickly enough. As the last one died on Ferdi's spear, silence settled over the forest once more, broken only by Millie's gasping, panted breaths.

"Nice work, everyone," I said grandly, wiping the saber off with some leaves before I sheathed it rather awkwardly.

"Except for you," Ferdi replied. "You need to learn how to use that thing, Murf. It's not just a longer, curvier knife, you know."

"So you keep saying, but my way keeps working, doesn't it?"

"Barely, and then, only because they're drunk." She looked back at Azara. "Drop?"

"That way, half-buried in a leaf pile," the cartomancer replied with closed eyes, pointing to her left.

"I think I should open this one," Millie declared, looking down at the small tears marring her overly tight clothing. "I'll bet if I open it, Azara and I will both get something we could be seen in public wearing." She glared at me, and I held up my hands defensively.

"Don't blame me," I shook my head. "The Unity's the lecher handing those things out. Yell at it if you don't like it."

"If you open it, human, it's unlikely you'd get clothes at all," Ferdi said calmly. "We've only been getting what we need because of Murf's Luck, and I'm fairly certain yours is much lower. You might get something random—or even dangerous."

"Dangerous?" I asked. "The Unity might reward us with something that could hurt us?"

"Blessings and curses in equal measure, as the churches say," she shrugged. "It's rare, but it happens. Let Murf open the drop, human, and accept whatever blessings the Unity deigns to give us."

"Millie," the redhead said in a frustrated voice. "I have a name, and it's Millie! It's not difficult to say!"

"I'm aware." She turned back to face me. "Get on with it, Murf. Human, go with him."

"I'll go when you learn how to say my damn name, *halfling!*"

"I know how to say it. I prefer not to."

"I will go," Azara said in a cold voice that cut off the argument. "Anything to end this bickering. Come, Murf. I can guide you to the drop."

I followed the woman into the forest as she deftly slipped around tangled brambles and stiff bushes that would catch on her dress. My coat, on the other hand, kept catching on everything, which meant I had to hurry a bit to catch up to her as she stood before a pile of leaves.

"Here," she said, waving almost apathetically at the leaves.

"You know, that was a lot faster than us wandering around searching for it," I said suspiciously as I knelt down and cleared away the leaves to reveal a box not much bigger than my head. "I suppose there's a reason that you never did this before?"

"Of course, there is. I didn't want to. Plus, it's entertaining to watch you all scratching around in the thorns looking for it." She grew quiet for a moment as I began digging the box out of the muddy ground. "Why did you leave, Murf?" she finally asked, her voice quiet and not as cold as it usually was.

I froze. I hadn't wanted this conversation, hadn't been looking forward to it, but there it was. "I told you that, Azara."

"That was bullshit, and we both know it. Why did you leave? You loved me; I know that you did. So, why vanish in the middle of the night?"

I sat back on my heels, adjusting my hat and closing my eyes. It looked like we were doing this, one way or the other.

"It wasn't bullshit. I ran because I was scared."

"Scared of what?" she demanded. "Stand up and look at me, Murf! Give me the courtesy of looking me in the eye when you lie to me!"

I rose slowly to my feet, staring down at the furious woman. Her face was flushed with anger; her eyes were narrow enough that the whites were barely visible, leaving a pair of ice-blue slits staring up at me. Her hands were clenched and kept drifting up toward her chest, where she kept her cards. She was on the edge, and I knew that a single wrong word would set her off.

"You're right, Azara," I said after a moment. "I did love you. Hell, part of me still does."

"Then why did you LEAVE?" She shouted that last part, and I suppressed a wince. Shouting struck me as a bad idea. We were being hunted, for one thing. For another, I didn't need the others knowing that we were over here fighting.

"Because I knew I was going to, Azara," I admitted heavily. "I always do. I stayed with one woman until the end—just one—and you know who she is."

"Your mother," she said softly.

"Yeah. And you know how that turned out." I lifted my hat and rubbed my hair. "I don't want to go through that again, Azara. If I never get close enough to anyone for it to matter, it won't. So, I leave before that happens." I looked directly at her. "You were the first person who made me want to stay."

"You should have," she said softly, her stance softening slightly. "Losing once doesn't mean you'll lose again, Murf."

"Everyone loses, Azara," I laughed quietly. "That's the Fourth Law: Everyone busts eventually. Avians don't live as long as humans, and we both know it. If I stayed with you, I'd probably have to watch you grow old and die—assuming you lasted that long. The Unity's a bitch, after all, and making me happy with you, then taking you from me is just the kind of thing it would do." I shook my head. "The thought terrified me, and when I get scared enough, I run."

"So, you left." She straightened, and her eyes hardened a bit. "The cards told me you would, you know."

"They did?" I asked, surprised. "When?"

"When we first slept together. I took a piece of your hair and did a divination. I knew that I was falling for you, and I wanted to know if we had a future." She looked down again. "The cards said you'd betray me. I knew then that one day, you'd hurt me."

I stared at her, stunned. "Then—then why didn't you leave then? If you knew, why did you stay?"

"Because sometimes, the cards are wrong," she sighed. "They tell what might be, what's likely to happen, but they can't tell what *will* be, Murf. We have free will, after all. And I had hope that they were wrong." She shrugged. "Besides, everything ends. Your silly law is right. We all lose eventually."

She put a hand on my chest. "I lost that night, Murf. That night when you went out for a walk and never came back, I lost hope. I lost faith. I've never managed to find either again. I've tried to love since then, but it never lasts. Maybe I never will." She looked up at me, her eyes sad. "I think you lost, too."

"I did."

She lowered her hand and stepped back. "I'm still angry at you, Murf. I think I always will be. But being around you—it reminds me of the good times. I don't..." She took a deep breath. "I don't want those to be gone forever."

"Azara, I can't..."

"No, you and I as we were are gone, Murf," she said heavily. "You left, and when you did, that died. It won't come back. It can't come back. I don't want it back." She blinked rapidly, her blue eyes bright with tears. "But maybe—maybe we don't have to hate one another."

"I never hated you, Azara. Not once."

"I know." She wiped her eyes and looked back at the trees behind us. "So, your friend, the gambler. You seem to like her."

"Millie?" I shrugged. "She's interesting."

"She is. There's something about her, Murf. The cards say she's more than she seems."

"Aren't we all, Azara?"

"Sometimes." She looked back at me. "She seems to suit you."

"For right now," I chuckled. "In a month, we'll hate each other. Not that it matters. I don't think either of us are looking for anything serious."

"That's a shame." She pointed down at the box. "You should get that and open it. The others are waiting for us." She paused, then looked up at me. "Something to consider, Murf. Every game you play ends, too. Eventually, you walk away from the table, or everyone else does. Does that mean it's not worth playing?" She turned and walked away, and I stared at her for a moment before snatching up the box and hurrying after her.

I knew her words had meaning, but I didn't really want to think about them. We had to survive this Labyrinth first. Anything more than that would have to wait. And once we got out, introspection would have to take a back seat to all the terror and panic still lurking at the edged of my brain, waiting for their turn to take center stage. I figured dealing with all that would take no more than a year or six. I'd consider Azara's thoughts then.

I opened the box and frowned as I pulled out what looked like a round, smooth, white orb about as wide as my thumb was long. The ball felt cool in my hand and looked smooth and seamless. It was oddly heavy, as if it were solid inside, and I tossed it up and down in my hand a few times before slipping it into my coat pocket. Besides the ball, the only thing in the box was a single brass coin that I gleefully picked out to give to Millie.

I emerged onto the path to find the others waiting for me. Azara studiously avoided look at me, while Ferdi seemed amused. Millie, though, looked back and forth between me and the avian several times, her eyes hard and narrow. At last, she marched over to stand in front of me, her chin jutting out aggressively and her back straight.

"I am NOT going to be part of any harem, Murf," she snapped. "Do you hear me?"

I stared at her, blinking in surprise. "What the hell are you talking about, Millie?"

"I can count." She pointed at me. "One man." She pointed at the others. "Three women. This is how harems start. I'm not doing it!"

"I told you, I'm not interested in any of you like that," Ferdi spoke up.

"Yet. Give it time." She glared at me. "He grows on you. Like fungus."

"I've known Murf for years, human. He hasn't infected me yet."

"That's the operative word. 'Yet'."

I opened my mouth to defend myself, planning to point out that I had never once mentioned having a harem, or even considered it. Well, not seriously. Sure, I'd fantasized as much as any man, but the closest I'd ever gotten to a harem was a wild night with a pair of elf sisters who lost a really fun wager, and that had nearly crippled me. Elf women are strong, and they aren't shy about taking what they want. After that, any fantasies I had of multiple women remained just that: fantasies.

Before I could say a word, though, Azara's eyes widened, and she whipped around to face the path behind us. "Danger!" she hissed, pointing toward the trail. "Extreme danger! That way!"

At the same moment, a mammoth screech rang through the forest, loud enough to shake the branches and send leaves cascading down on us.

"What the hell was that?" Millie demanded, her voice high and fearful.

Ferdi's eyes widened, and a look of fear crossed her face. "The guardian," she whispered.

"What?" the redhead asked.

"The guardian. Run." She looked at us. "Everyone, RUN!" She turned and raced off down the path, and after a moment of stunned amazement, the three of us did the same. Another titanic scream shook the trees as my boots pounded the muddy ground, and the fear that had been hiding at the edge of my mind suddenly rushed into the very center of it, lending strength to my muscles and dramatically weakening my bladder.

Whatever that thing was, it was huge—and it sounded pissed. This was not going to be good at all.

29

We raced down the path, our boots clomping on the soft ground, not even trying to be quiet. The guardian screamed again behind us, shivering the trees, and I couldn't help but keep glancing back to try and catch a glimpse of it. I wanted to see my death coming, after all, and I was pretty sure this thing was going to kill us all. Within a few seconds, my heart raced in my chest, and my breaths came in heaving gulps, but fear gave my legs all the strength they needed, and it seemed the others agreed as no one suggested slowing down.

The trees flashed past us. Millie slipped and skidded in a wet spot but quickly recovered, putting on a sudden burst of speed as she used her ability. Branches reached out and caught at my coat and Azara's dress, dragging on us, but we tore free and pushed on. We ran as if our lives depended on it because we were pretty sure they did. When another screech rang out, sounding a bit farther away, I felt a little surge of hope that maybe we could outrun this thing, and if we did, maybe the Labyrinth would count that as a success and let us the hell out.

As I glanced at the others, though, that hope quickly died.

Ferdi was well out in front. Even carrying all her armor and weapons, she was simply stronger and faster than us, and she was running hard. She'd leave us behind soon as the rate she was going. Millie wasn't too far behind. The woman ran well—and was fun to watch in her skintight trousers, let me tell you—and every so often, she sped up for a second as she triggered her power. I was doing okay, as well. My breathing was starting to even out a bit as I guessed the Hag helped me adapt to the exertion, and my Needful Body ability gave me plenty of strength and stamina. Plus, my legs were longer than the women's. Azara, though…

The avian was struggling. A single look at her showed me that. Her dress wasn't meant for running and tangled around her legs. Her low shoes slid on the mud more than my heavy boots. Plus, she didn't have a card the way the rest of us did, and I'd never realized just how much that had been helping us. One hand clutched her side, and her breath came in heaving gulps. It hit me all of a sudden: Azara wasn't a Holder. She was so skilled that I hadn't really thought about it, but she didn't have the natural advantages that Holders did. She only had her own energy to draw on, and that was quickly running out. She'd never been terribly athletic.

She wasn't going to make it.

Part of me, the asshole part of me, wanted to keep running. If we got away from the guardian, I had a feeling the Labyrinth would open an exit for us. Leaving Azara behind would be awful, but I'd be alive to feel guilty. Enough bourbon—and time—would ease that guilt, and eventually, all this would become a distant memory, and when I retold the story, Azara probably wouldn't even be in it. The only people who'd know wouldn't say anything, after all, since they left the woman behind, too.

Azara squawked as I dropped back behind her, ducked low, and scooped her up onto my shoulder. "Murf!" she half-shouted, half-panted. "Put...me...down!"

"Nope," I said grimly as I adjusted her on my shoulder so her stomach lay flat on me. "I'm not leaving you this time."

She fell silent for a few seconds. "Can you at least take your hand off my ass?" she finally asked, and I suddenly realized where that hand was.

"Oops. Sorry." I slid it down to the back of her thighs.

"Are you, though? Really?"

"No," I laughed weakly. "Not at all."

I ran on, carrying the woman as best I could. The others quickly outpaced me, though. Her weight pulled at me, and I had to adjust my gait a bit to stay stable. I slipped more often on muddy spots, and I staggered into bushes that grabbed at my coat and slowed me down. Another screech echoed behind me, this time closer, and I realized that carrying Azara, I wasn't going to get away from the thing. I just tightened my grip and ran on. I was a liar, a thief, and a coward, to be sure—but I wasn't going to be the asshole who murdered a woman I once cared about to save his life. That was a little far even for me. At least the others would get away...

I should have known better than to tempt the Unity like that.

The trees suddenly opened up around me as I burst into a large clearing similar to the one we'd first found ourselves in. Ferdi stood in the middle of it, looking around wildly, while Millie stood to my right, hacking at a thicket of brambles with her knife. I looked around, wondering why they'd stopped. It only took me a moment to realize the reason. The path ended here.

"Damn you, Unity," I swore, spinning around and looking at the trees for an exit.

"What's wrong?" Azara asked from my shoulder.

"There's no way out of here!" I looked at Ferdi. "Is there?"

"Not that we've found. The brambles are too thick even for me to push through."

"I think they're poisoned, too!" Millie shouted, slashing again at the thicket. "And the damn things won't cut!"

The thought that I could probably get through those thorns never crossed my mind. Well, not really. Fine, so I realized it right away. The Hag would adapt my skin to the thorns and my body to their poison. It would hurt at first, but I could probably shove my way through them. The problem was, if they were thick enough, I doubted the others could follow. Even Ferdi's armor wouldn't completely shield her from being buried in a tangle of thorns, and if the poison was nasty enough, a few scratches might be all it took. Millie and Azara wouldn't stand a chance.

"Put me down, Murf!" Azara snapped at me, smacking my back and jarring me from my introspection. "Maybe I can burn them, or find a path out!"

I quickly set the woman down, noting the dark look Millie gave me as I did, and stepped away from her. I yanked out my saber and ran to the nearest tangle of thorns. I slashed as hard as I could, but the springy bushes simply gave way around my blade, twining around it and forcing me to yank it back. I stamped on a tendril, pressing it to the ground, and slashed at it again. The sword bounced off the rubbery wood, leaving only a faint slice in the bark. I tried sawing at it instead and quickly realized that while I could probably cut through the thing, it would take several minutes, meaning cutting open a path would take hours. We didn't have hours. In fact, we barely had seconds.

Millie screamed as a shadow swept over me, and I spun around just in time to see a huge shape about the size of a small house land with a heavy thump in the center of the clearing. I stared at the thing in mingled shock and terror, caught between wanting to laugh and piss myself. I could only look at the thing, unsure how exactly to respond, at least until Millie broke the sudden silence.

"Shit, it's a damn bunny!"

She was right. The guardian was a massive rabbit at least twenty feet tall and forty long. Thick, dappled orange fur fluffed out from the mammoth creature. Its single large eye peered at us as it nonchalantly reached down and ripped up a sapling from the edge of the clearing, chomping it down with a sound like a sawmill running. Its feet ended in claws as long as my hand, and its ears flicked in the air with a whump that whipped air past me. And just in front of those ears, a pair of long, spiraling horns jutted out, sticking from its head like some sort of twisted antelope or gazelle.

"It's not a bunny," I shouted back. "It's a bunzelle!"

The huge thing lifted its head as it swallowed down the last of the tree, its mouth gaping to display teeth as long as my forearm. Another trumpeting scream rang out, and I realized why its cry had rocked the trees. The blast of sound rolled out with a visible ripple and crashed into us, flinging us all backward. That hurled me into the thicket of brambles, and I nearly bit my tongue as I tumbled through them. Thorns scratched my face and neck, dug at my hands and arms, and even ripped through my pants. My armor didn't help much since the thorns slid right through all the little holes in it, and I ended up getting stabbed just about everywhere. I couldn't keep from shouting in pain as I sat on top of at least a dozen of the thorns and felt them stabbing into my ass and thighs.

Even worse, a dreamy sort of feeling spread over me as I lay tangled up in the bushes. The pain slowly faded, and as it did, I decided the thicket was a perfectly comfortable spot. It might even be nice to take a little nap there. I was hidden, and the place seemed safe enough. I doubted anything in the Labyrinth would dig through the thorns to come get me. Of course, I was wrong.

Screams rang out as a huge shape crashed into the bushes, heading straight at me. I was having a little trouble focusing, and I wondered who was bothering me as I was about to take a nap. Confusion turned to irritation as whoever it was grabbed me around my chest and tore me out of the thicket, lifting me high into the air. My captor was squeezing my chest and back tightly enough that I was having trouble breathing, and the pressure of my armor against my ribs was really starting to hurt. More screaming erupted somewhere below me as I felt myself being swung side-to-side in the air, tweaking my neck and making my head wobble around.

"Hey, cut it out!" I shouted, smacking whoever held me with a fist. "I'm not a fucking toy!"

Suddenly, the pressure on my chest and back exploded into pain, and as it did, my head cleared almost instantly. Clarity burned away the fog in my head, and I screamed as I realized I was in the damn bunzelle's mouth, and its teeth had just torn through my armor. Its bite had missed my ribs and ripped through my stomach, and the pain of that was almost enough to knock me out. It whipped its head about again, and I screamed once more as the movement tore the wound wider. Darkness shrouded the edge of my vision as the pain tore through me, and cold seemed to spread through my body, sapping my strength.

I was about to die. Part of me recognized this and wanted to relax and let it happen. I'd had a pretty good life, after all. Plus, dying would definitely make the pain stop, and I really wanted the pain to stop. The Fourth Law still held. Everyone busts sometime, and it felt like this was my time. It wasn't how I wanted to go—who'd want to be chewed to death by a giant bunzelle—but the Third Law was right, too. The Unity really was a massive bitch.

And that thought stirred me from my growing resignation. The Unity was an asshole. Not only was it trying to kill me, it was denying me the one thing I'd always wanted. My life's goal was simple: I wanted to die peacefully in a bed with a woman a third of my age, although I'd settle for half. The Unity was giving me none of those. No bed, no peace, and certainly no woman. Anger roused me from my lassitude, and as the rabbit lifted its head to shake me again, I managed to reach down with my left hand, yank free the saber at my hip, and stab it at the bunzelle. The blow wasn't very powerful, and my aim sucked, but then, my target was enormous, and it was almost impossible to miss.

The rabbit screamed and flung its head back as the blade plunged through the lower part of its eye. It probably didn't blind it, but I'll bet it hurt like a son of a bitch. The force of the scream tore me from its mouth and flipped me up into the air, yanking the saber from its eye in the process. I flew upward, twisting and turning in midair, then landed hard on something soft and furry. The surface beneath me moved, flinging me into a pole jutting up from it, and I grabbed the pole, wrapping my arm around it to hold myself in place. It took me a moment to realize that I was splayed across the top of the thing's head, gripping one of its antlers for dear life.

"MURF!" a roaring voice echoed from far below me. "YOUR ABILITY! USE IT! HARD!"

In my pain and confusion, I'd totally forgotten about my card power. I quickly flexed the deck, not bothering to restrain the cards as they sprayed out. Energy surged up through me, rolling up into my chest and lungs before bursting out of me and spreading over the clearing. The bunny lurched beneath me as the power wrapped over it, and only my grip on its antler kept me from flying off.

That antler was growing warm beneath my hand, though, making it harder to hold. The heat increased steadily, becoming painful, and my hands tingled and burned. That burning spread into my chest and legs. A flash of light suddenly exploded before my eyes, blinding me, and a massive boom flung me backward. My whole body shook and spasmed as I soared backward, my muscles totally out of my control. I crashed into something soft and yielding that flung me forward to crash back into the antler again. I managed to fling an arm around it once more, blinking and shaking my head as I tried to regain control of my body and keep control of my bladder. A massive dark spot filled my vision, blotting out everything, and I heard nothing but a loud ringing that drowned out all sounds. The world lurched and shuddered beneath me, and I barely managed to keep my grip to avoid being hurled into the darkness in my vision.

Fortunately, my senses returned quickly, and as they did, my head began to clear a bit. The pain in my stomach and back still burned, but even that slowly ebbed, and my scattered thoughts started piecing themselves back together. As my focus returned, though, another scream ripped the air, and a heavy impact crashed into my chest, tearing me from the antler and flinging me backward. I smacked into something soft again, but this time, I was aware enough to realize it was the damn thing's ear. Before it could flick me back into the antler, I stabbed out with the saber still clutched in my left hand. The weapon slashed into the bunny's ear, punching through it. Apparently, that was a sensitive spot.

The rabbit shrieked again, the impact of its cry flattening me against its ear. Its skull suddenly rushed up to meet me, tearing a long gash in its ear as I realized it had just jumped into the air. It shook its head, trying to dislodge me, but I grabbed a handful of fur and jabbed the saber down into the earhole leading into its skull. I guess that was even more sensitive since the bunzelle screeched again, which just drove the blade deeper. My body flew up in the air as we descended, and I slammed into its skull again as it launched itself forward once more.

I glanced around, seeing that we were above the treetops and that the forest seemed to stretch below us like a lumpy orange sea. It was kind of pretty, really, although I was really sick of the color orange by that point. A spot of blue would have been nice, or maybe some green. Hell, I'd have taken a real yellow at that point instead of the occasional yellow-orange. Really, the Unity could have spiced this place up a bit with a little splash of color.

The trees disappeared as we hurtled downward, but this time, when we landed, the rabbit stumbled and almost fell. As it did, I pulled out the saber and stabbed it again. I knew I wasn't doing any real damage it, but I didn't want to. I just wanted to hurt it enough that it would leave us alone. Surely, the Unity would count that as a win. It screamed again, once more driving my hand and the sword deeper into its earhole, then leaped once more.

I nearly fell off the damn thing as its jump flung it directly into a fucking tree. It tumbled through the air, landing hard, and the jerky movement almost flung me off it. It did pull the saber from its ear, and in a panic, I jammed the blade down hard to catch myself. It crunched into the bunny's skull and wedged itself inside, and I grabbed it with one hand and a handful of fur with the other.

The next few minutes were one hell of a ride. The bunzelle kept trying to escape the pain in its skull, but its movements grew clumsier by the second. It smashed through trees and rolled through brambles. It slid on mud and tumbled when its legs splayed out on landing. It launched itself in random directions that took us all over the place. It screeched every so often, the impacts buffeting me and occasionally tearing my sword free of its skull. That forced me to stab the damn thing again to stay in place, which made it scream all over.

During that time, I also got to learn what had blinded me before. At one point, the thing's antlers started to crackle and glow, and arcs of electricity snapped and danced between them. I jammed my eyes shut just in time to keep from being blinded again as ropes of lightning exploded from its horns, several of them crawling across my body and making my muscles dance and seize. The lightning scorched trees all around us and set leaves on fire, but it didn't seem to do too much damage to me other than setting my limbs to jerking and twitching and making my clothes smoke crazily.

The rabbit threw itself forward but stumbled as it jumped. Its spring turned into a chaotic tumble, and it rolled across the ground. Its skull slammed me into the mud, pressing me down into the soft ground, and as it continued past, it tore my sword from my grip at last. I found myself lying on the muddy ground, pressed into a Murf-shaped indentation in the ground, while the bunny slammed into a nearby tree. It tried to stagger to its feet but collapsed, its chest heaving and its limbs splayed out around it. It tried once more, then fell heavily to the dirt. Its head dropped to the ground, and a loud snore rolled out of its mouth.

The damn thing had passed out.

I knew that was my chance to get up and end it, but I just couldn't bring myself to do it. Not for any sentimental reasons or anything. That bunny wasn't remotely cute, and I would have happily made its fur into a couple hundred coats for myself if it weren't so damn orange. No, the problem was that I hurt way too damn much. My stomach and back still burned, although the pain was a lot better than it had been. My head pounded like Ferdi was taking a hammer to it. Every muscle in my body screamed at me, and the skin of my face, hands, and chest felt burned. The entire front of me was bruised and sore. And really, that indentation in the ground was pretty soft and comfortable. I could lay there for a bit, let myself heal, maybe catch a few winks…

"He's this way!"

I silently cursed Azara as I heard several bodies crashing through the bushes nearby. I tried to sit up, but I couldn't. I tried again, but my body refused to move. Panic swept through me for a moment as I wondered if the damn bunny crushing me had snapped my neck, and if that was the kind of thing the Hag could even fix. I tried to flex my arms and bend my knees, and to my relief, my leg came up with a nasty sucking sound. I sighed as I realized that I wasn't paralyzed; I was suctioned into the damn ground. I could probably work myself free, but to be honest, I didn't much want to. I just lay there and waited for the others.

Ferdi appeared above me first, staring down at me with a worried expression. Her braids were loose, and chunks of her hair were missing with the ends scorched. Black marks marred her armor, and burns lined her face.

"Murf?" she asked, looking down at me.

"Hi, Ferdi," I croaked. "You look like hell."

"Same to you. Can you move?"

"Yes. I don't really want to, though. It's kind of nice down here."

"Too bad." She reached down and grabbed my armor, tearing me from the earth with the sound of someone sucking a fart back in. She hauled me to my feet, and I staggered, grabbing the burning wound in my stomach and fighting to stay upright.

"Ow," I whispered. "Too rough."

"There's no time for nice." She pointed to the fallen rabbit, and I turned my head to watch it slumbering peacefully. "It must have knocked itself out, but it'll be awake soon. We need to..." She froze as the rabbit took a deep, shuddering breath, then a few shallow ones—and fell silent. Instantly a set of cards appeared in my vision, and I couldn't help but grin as I read them.

Unity Achievement!
You have solo-killed a Labyrinth
Guardian 3 ranks above you.
Luck +1, 750 Unity Points
All drop values are doubled for you
in this Labyrinth.

A warm feeling spread over me, washing through my body and easing the pain of my injuries significantly. Another warm feeling of a totally different sort filled me as I read the first card again.

"Hey, Ferdi, I just solo-killed a Labyrinth guardian. You ever done that?" I flashed her my best shit-eating grin as she stared at the creature's inert form.

"What? How—did it bleed out internally? How did it die?" She whirled on me. "And why did you get credit? It almost ate you!"

"Alcohol poisoning." We both turned to look back at the rabbit and saw Azara standing beside it, her eyes closed and with a card pressed against it. "That's how it died. Its heart and lungs shut down."

"Wait, I thought your ability just got things drunk!" Ferdi protested.

"It does. However, one of the hole card effects is that it can eventually be lethal. I've had it running ever since you reminded me to use it. Good call, by the way."

"I—I thought it would give us the chance to avoid it and escape," she said dumbly. "Maybe to drop you, as well. Not that it could kill it!" She locked back at me, her eyes narrowing. "And not that you'd ride the damn thing all over this forest! By Kewan's blood, how are you even alive?"

"I'm not entirely sure that I am," I admitted. I looked around, realizing who was missing. I swallowed hard as fear spiked in me. "Millie. Is she...?"

"Recovering back in the clearing," Ferdi sighed. "The lightning strike caught her hard. She's hurt, but she'll be fine." She smiled a little thinly. "That's part of being a Holder, you know. If it doesn't kill you, you can eventually heal from it."

"The drop is also back in the clearing," Azara announced, walking over to stand by the two of us. "Perhaps we should return there."

"Good call," I nodded, looking around. "So—where the hell is it? And how did you two get here so fast?"

"About two hundred feet that way," Ferdi said, pointing back behind me.

I turned slowly, my whole body protesting at the movement. "That can't be," I shook my head. "The bunzelle was jumping hundreds of feet at a time."

"The what?"

"Bunzelle. That's what that thing was. Half bunny, half gazelle."

"It works," Azara nodded.

"No, it doesn't," the halfling protested. "That creature already has a name. It's a terakwid!" Azara snorted, and the warrior gave her a flat look. "That word amuses you?"

"Yes." She looked at me. "In Lurgesh, the halfling tongue, 'terakwid' means deer-rabbit."

"Damn. I forgot that you speak Lurgesh." The warrior made a face. "You never explained how you learned it, by the way."

"No, I didn't. However, if you need to know, I spent a few weeks hiding out in the halfling hold in the southern part of the city back when I was trying to avoid the Sage's Guild," she shrugged. "I picked up the language. It wasn't difficult when it was all I heard."

"So, wait," I chuckled, wincing as pain flared in my side for a moment. "Ter—terk—what she said. It basically means...bunzelle?"

"Yes," Azara nodded, giving me a half-smile.

"Then it's unanimous. Bunzelle it is!"

"First, there's no voting, Murf. Things have names, and you can't just change them. Second, it's not unanimous. The pretty human hasn't agreed."

"You really think Millie is going to agree with you?" I snorted. "She still hasn't forgiven you for threatening to kill her when we first got here, Ferdi."

"That wasn't a threat. It was an offer. I was being kind."

"It was still a threat, even if it was meant to be a nice one." I stretched, wincing as pain still radiated from my wound, even if it wasn't as bad as it had been. The bunny had gotten me good, but apparently, Ferdi was right. If I lived through it, I could heal it. That didn't stop it from hurting while I did, though.

"As far as names," I continued, walking slowly in the direction she'd pointed, "a name is nothing more than a construct that people agree on to refer to an object or concept, Ferdi. It's a convenient label we use so that we don't have to say, 'The giant rabbit with horns on its head back in the Ochre Forest Labyrinth' every time we want to talk about it. That means that for something to be a name, it just has to be understood by a majority of the people to refer to that specific object." I pointed to myself, then to Azara, then toward the forest ahead of us. "One, two, three. That's a majority. That means it's a bunzelle."

The halfling stared at me, her face confused. "What are you talking about, Murf?"

"Names, Ferdi. And why you're wrong about the bunzelle."

"Terakwid!"

"You can say that all you want, Ferdi. It doesn't make you right."

30

The walk back to the clearing didn't take long, even with me moving slowly thanks to my still-healing injuries. Ferdi wasn't really in all that much better shape and limped along beside me, her left leg stiff and dragging a bit. Azara seemed mostly okay, though, and I gave her a curious look.

"How did you keep from being hurt by the lightning?" I asked.

"I avoided it, Murf, as the rest of you should have done," she said loftily.

"The terakwid's force attack flattened her every time it triggered," Ferdi corrected with a snort. "After the first couple times, she just stayed down and covered up. The lightning went right over her head."

"I believe its cry flung you into a tree," the avian replied calmly. "Twice. And then, as you tried to charge the bunzelle, its lightning tossed you back into the same tree. I think we can all agree that my method was better."

"Safer, maybe. Not necessarily better. It could have stepped on you, you know."

"And you could have been the one in its teeth instead of Murf. Which method of death would you have preferred?"

Ferdi tapped her unwoven braid thoughtfully. "That's a good question." She looked at me. "Murf, it squashed you and bit you. Which was worse?"

"The biting," I said fervently. "Definitely the biting. The squashing was kind of nice, actually. I was about to take a little nap in the mud there when you people showed up and spoiled it."

"You see? Better," Azara said triumphantly.

Our path back led through a scorched hole in the brambles surrounding the thicket. I examined the charred, still-smoldering branches around us and looked over at Azara. "Your handiwork?"

"The bunzelle's lightning started the fire," she shrugged. "I simply accelerated and focused it with some wind."

"Nice job."

"Of course."

I lurched back into the clearing and took a look around. I hadn't really seen any of the fight despite my high perch, and I was a little astounded by how much of the place we'd torn up. The rabbit's feet had ripped long furrows in the ground. Fallen trees ringed the clearing's edge, some of them snapped low to the ground, others torn from the earth entirely. Scorch marks seared the grass, and small fires burned here and there, sending plumes of smoke up into the air. More than one tree smoldered fitfully, looking to be on the edge of bursting into flames. I looked around a bit worriedly.

"Should we put out those fires?" I asked nervously. "This seems like a really bad place for a forest fire."

"It's all too wet to spread," Ferdi shook her head. "And even if it did, it would take hours for it to really get going. We'll be gone from here before then."

"So, we're just leaving it for the next group to deal with." I nodded. "I'm fine with that."

"Once we leave, this whole place will return to the way it was, Murf. That's how people farm Labyrinths. Once you've cleared it, it resets, and you can do it again. It changes a bit each time, but never in a fundamental way."

Azara frowned. "That doesn't make sense," she said slowly. "Creating things like the stab-monkeys and bunzelle takes energy, not to mention the drops we received. Surely, the Unity can't simply restore them instantly each time someone defeats them."

"You're right, cartomancer. It's not instant, and if we finish this one, then turn right back around and do it again, there'd be a lot fewer creatures, worse rewards, and a weaker guardian. The longer you leave a Labyrinth alone, the stronger it gets, and the better the rewards. Of course, leave it too long, and it'll get too dangerous for the reward to be worth the risk. You have to leave it just long enough to restore the rewards, but not so long that it gets too powerful. There are teams that do nothing but run all the Labyrinths in an area, moving from one to the next to give each time to recover, and then starting back at the beginning, over and over again."

"That seems like a horrible lifestyle," I shuddered. "Not only because you spend it inside Labyrinths, but because I imagine it would get boring as hell after a bit."

"I agree. That's why I don't do it. Plus, the rewards are terrible. You're only guaranteed to get a Unity card the first time you complete a Labyrinth, and the more frequently you run the same one, the worse your rewards are. They're supposed to be challenging tests, after all, not ways to get rich quickly."

"Did someone mention rich?" I turned as a groaning voice spoke and saw Millie laying on the ground near the edge of the clearing, her arm flung over her face. I just stared at the woman in surprise for a couple seconds. It looked like she'd taken a bolt of lightning to the chest, and the skin on her stomach and over her ribs was burned and blistered. The bolt had also burned away most of her shirt, leaving her impressive assets proudly displayed, if somewhat reddened and tender-looking.

"That's—quite the look on you, Millie," I chuckled. "Want me to get a blanket to cover you up?"

"Murf. You're alive. Good. Don't you dare put anything over me. I hurt too much to cover up, and I'm too damn tired to care. Besides, that's not what matters. Did we beat the bunny? Are we rich now?"

"Murf killed it," Ferdi said sourly. "We haven't found the drop yet, though. It's in this clearing somewhere, according to the bird-woman."

"I'm not looking for it, before anyone asks," the redhead said quickly. "In fact, I'm just going to lay here for a bit longer. A day or two at the most. Lightning really hurts."

"You're lucky to have survived it at all. If you hadn't been hiding behind that tree…"

"Taking cover," Millie corrected.

"What?"

"I wasn't hiding. I was taking cover." She uncovered her face, revealing cheeks that had been reddened but not blistered by the blast she'd taken, and glared at the halfling.

"Were you planning to come back out and attack the terakwid?"

"The what?"

"The bunzelle," I supplied.

"Oh. That's a better name. And no, I wasn't going to try to stab a forty-foot bunny with my little knives, Ferdi, because I'm not an idiot."

"Then it was hiding."

The redhead sighed and covered her face again. "I hurt too much to argue. The point is, someone else will have to find the drop. I'm busy being miserable."

"It's not necessary," Azara volunteered. "I can locate it easily enough." She closed her eyes and held up a hand, then pointed toward the center of the clearing. "It's that way."

"Wait, you can just concentrate and find it?" Millie demanded. "Then why have we been crashing through thorn bushes all this time?"

"For my entertainment, and I appreciate the effort you all put into that for me."

"If I weren't about to die, I would stab you in the face right now, Azara."

"You aren't going to die," Ferdi corrected. "You're looking better already." She gazed intently at Millie's breasts. "Much better, in fact. Your nipples have nearly returned to their normal coloration."

"That is so damn creepy, Ferdi," Millie groaned. "Murf, make her stop staring at me."

"I'm having trouble with that myself," I admitted.

"Murf!"

"Come on, Ferdi," I chuckled, walking toward the center of the clearing. "Let's go find the drop. Millie obviously needs her beauty rest."

"I could stab you, too, Murf!" the redhead called out as we walked away. "But a lot lower than the face!"

Azara guided us unerringly to a wooden door buried beneath the mud in the center of the clearing. The trap door was about six feet long and three across, made of old, gray wood planks with a rusted handle on the top. Crossing my mental fingers, I pulled open the lid and stared inside for several seconds, then looked back over my shoulder.

"Hey, Millie! I think we might be rich!"

"That—look at this drop!" Ferdi gasped, kneeling beside what honestly looked like a short coffin buried in the ground and reaching inside. She pulled up a gleaming, double-bitted axe with ornate silver scrollwork on the blades and oddly white edges. The shaft was mahogany inlaid with more silver tracing, and a heavy steel spike jutted from the bottom. She held the axe almost reverently. "This—Murf, do you know what this is?"

"It's an axe, Ferdi," I replied with a grin. "You chop things with it. Did you forget that after using a spear for a couple days?"

"No, I remember. It's not just an axe, though. The edges—they're whitesteel!"

"What's that?"

"A somewhat rare metal alloy forged by the elves," Azara answered. "Lighter, stronger, and more durable than steel by a significant margin." I looked at her, and she shrugged. "What? I read."

"What she said. This axe—it's worth at least a gold or two, Murf!"

"Are you planning to sell it?" I asked.

"No, of course not!"

"Then how much it's worth doesn't matter."

"How rich are we?" I looked back and grinned to see Millie tottering toward us, her red face puffy and her hand pressed across her chest to cover it. "What? Don't give me a look, Murf. Just answer the question! How rich are we?"

I reached wordlessly down and pulled out a leather satchel about the size of my head. I bounced it a couple times, and the bulging sack jingled loudly. "I haven't counted yet. You want to do the honors?"

"Yes!" She snatched the bag from my hand, grunting at the sudden weight of it, then stepped back and set it on the ground, pulling coins from it. "Silver," she breathed. "If this is all silver…"

"Do you really trust her with that?" Ferdi asked in a quiet voice. "She's likely to try to steal all of it instead of sharing."

"Where would she hide it?" I asked with a chuckle.

"Do you really want me to answer that question, Murf?"

I winced and shook my head. "No. Feel free to keep an eye on her."

"I will."

Beside me, Azara reached into the pit and pulled out a length of tightly rolled felt. She unrolled it and stared at it with wide eyes. "A layout," she breathed.

"What?" I glanced down at the dark green fabric and saw rectangles drawn on it in silver, each marked with a card rank and suit and laid out in a dizzyingly complex pattern.

"A layout, Murf. One I've never seen before. I'll need to experiment with it…find the order…a reading on it…" Her voice fell off to mumbles, and I chuckled as I looked back into the pit.

Several items still lay in the hole, even after removing the axe, satchel, and felt roll. I took out a small wooden box with a hinged lid and set it aside, then pulled up a long, flat leather bag and laid it aside, as well. A flat metal case about the size of my hand was next, followed by a stiff leather box about two feet to each side and a foot high. I placed them all on the ground and looked around. Millie was busy counting coins with Ferdi standing over her like a hawk waiting to pounce. Azara knelt over her new layout, touching the spaces where cards would go and muttering too softly for me to hear. I shrugged. I guess that meant I got to open everything else.

I started with the flat metal case. I lifted the lid, revealing a leather card case. I sighed. The elves had taken the case I'd gotten from the Hag's Labyrinth, but apparently, the Unity thought that I really needed one. Either that, or it was meant for Ferdi or Millie. I held it up in the air.

"Anyone want a card case?" I asked.

"I've got one," Ferdi said, glancing at my hand. As she did, I noticed Millie slip a few silvers behind her back before the halfling's gaze darted back to her. "That's a nice one, though. You should keep it. You'll probably get enough cards to need a case eventually, if you keep running Labyrinths."

"Yeah, I'll pass. If I never see the inside of another Labyrinth, I'll have already seen one too many." I laid the case down as the start of what I decided would be the 'sell' pile. That would probably include my saber, Ferdi's spear and swords, most of the camping equipment we'd found, and maybe Millie's daggers. I sincerely hoped that I'd have no more use for any of them once we left the Labyrinth. I wasn't planning on stepping foot in another for at least a lifetime. Maybe two, just for good measure.

I opened the long, flat bag next and pulled out a fancy, green dress decorated with tiny, sparkling crystals, cut low in the front. I looked over at Millie and held it up.

"Hey, I'm guessing this is for you, Millie."

"What?" she asked. "Murf, I'm counting. Don't disturb me."

"Even if it means being dressed in normal clothing for the first time in days?" I asked archly.

She glanced up at me and the dress, then back down at the coins, biting her lip. "I'll put it on later," she finally said. "I'm busy here."

I laughed and laid the dress back down on the bag, watching for a moment as she deftly sorted and stacked the coins. A strand of her hair hung over her face, and she blew at it absently, her expression a mask of concentration. She had her bottom lip between her teeth, and her eyes sparkled as she worked.

In other words, she was utterly adorable, and she wasn't even trying.

I turned back to the loot, opening the box next. I stared for a moment in satisfaction before I pulled out a long, black coat of thick wool. Beneath that was a white, long-sleeved shirt with ivory buttons, a pair of black trousers, and black leather boots. Unlike Millie, I was much more interested in being dressed and comfortable than getting presents, so I quickly began stripping off my coat and pulling the torn, bloody chainmail off over my head.

"Murf, what are you doing?" Azara asked uncertainly.

"Changing. I got new clothes, and I want to put them on."

"Is this—is this really the time? Or the place?"

"I am not going another minute in metal armor and bloodstained rags." I tossed the armor on the ground and pulled off the ripped, padded shirt beneath. I only hesitated for a moment before slipping out of my battered, bloodstained and fang-pierced boots, then stripping my pants off, as well.

"Impressive," Ferdi observed, and I looked up to see both her and Millie staring at my naked body.

"Um…thanks," I said, turning away from her to conceal my more masculine features. I suddenly understood why Ferdi's comments bothered Millie so much. I wasn't exactly shy, but the clinical way she complimented my package was a bit—unsettling.

"Oh, and it goes all the way through to the back?" she added, confusing me for a moment. "Very nice. How are you not dead, Murf?"

Oh. She meant the wound. Actually, that made a lot of sense, considering Ferdi.

"I got better," I shrugged, pulling the new pants on and covering my shame, assuming I had any. I hadn't found any yet.

"Obviously."

"You should keep watching Millie," I advised. "She's got about a dozen silvers tucked into the back of her pants already."

"Murf!" the redhead said in a hurt voice. "How could you?"

"What, watch the back of your pants? That's easy. I don't even have to try."

"Put them back," Ferdi instructed, and with a pout, Millie reached back behind herself, producing a handful of silver coins and dropping them into her pile. "All of them."

"That is all of them."

"Do you really want me to search you? I will, and I promise, I'll look everywhere."

Millie's face paled. "No, that's not necessary." She produced another handful of coins. "This is actually all of them."

"We'll see," Ferdi grunted.

Millie glared at me, her expression promising all sorts of retribution, but I ignored her and slipped on the shirt and coat, then went through my old clothes, taking everything from them and slipping it all into my new pockets. I stopped as I looked at the round stone, wondering again what it might be, but I just stuck it in my pocket. I'd ask Ferdi later—or have Azara do a reading on it. Hell, I might even take it to the Sage's Hall and let them identify it. If it was worth something, they'd probably even buy it from me, along with some of my extra cards.

As I buttoned my coat, I sighed with contentment. The new clothing was much nicer than what the Labyrinth had been providing before. I luxuriated in the feel of the fine fabric against my skin. Granted, that skin was sweaty, grimy, covered with dried blood, and in dire need of a bath, but it was still nice. I sat down and pulled on the boots, lacing them up. I felt like an actual person for the first time in days.

There was no question about it. I was never stepping foot in another damn Labyrinth again. At least, not without a complete wardrobe, a portable bathtub, a horse-drawn carriage to pull me around in, and an army to do all the fighting for me. And even then, it was iffy.

The wooden box was last, and I opened it to reveal a small stack of facedown cards. Power tingled in the box as I reached my hand in, crawling over my fingers. The cards felt misty and fluid as I touched them but solidified quickly beneath my fingertips, and I somehow felt the edges of them sticking up, begging to be drawn. I pulled the cards from the box, and as I did, the feeling of power faded, and the box crumbled to dust in my hand. A handful of cards rested in my grip, and I flipped them over to see what I held.

"How many cards is that, Murf?" Ferdi asked, walking away from Millie and looking down at the crisp rectangles in my grip. "Did we get more than one?"

"Four," I said, spreading them out so that she could look at them.

"Four," she breathed. "That's amazing for a low reward Labyrinth! What did we get?"

"Eight of blades, two of coins, five of staves…" I held the last card up. "And lady of cups." As I looked at that last card, an image of it popped up in my vision, and I gazed at it to read over what the Hag had to say about it.

> **Lady of Cups**
> **Likely Power:** Emotion Control
> Requirements:
> Luck: 47   Harmony: 61
> Compatibility: 25%

I stared at the card in surprise and suspicion. The lady of cups usually showed a pretty human woman holding a golden cup. The Unity version displayed an even prettier elven woman with golden hair who seemed to be blowing a kiss at a group of cowering savages. She'd gotten me into this mess, and ironically enough, she seemed to be my reward for surviving it. Somewhere, I knew, that damn halfling priest was laughing his tiny ass off just then, and I swore that if I ever saw him again, I'd choke the shit out of him, and damn the consequences.

31

"Kewan's blood," Ferdi swore as she saw the card. She reached slowly out to it and took it almost delicately from my hand. "The knight and the lady! That—we shouldn't have gotten this, Murf. Not in this Labyrinth. Maybe not in a damn lifetime!"

"Is it really that big of a deal?" Millie asked, pausing her counting. "I mean, yes, it's a noble arcana, but…"

"I've run dozens of Labyrinths over the years, human," Ferdi cut the woman off in a quiet voice. "I've found one noble arcana in all that time. One. None of us had the Harmony for it, so we sold it to the Scriveners for more gold than we made off ten lesser arcana."

"Wait, it's worth that much? Maybe we should sell it, then!"

"Only if no one can bind it. You never sell a card someone can bind." She handed it back to me. "I can't. I have no Harmony with cups. Can you?"

I read over the card description, then examined my stats again. "I have the Luck for it, but I'm a few short of the Harmony I need."

"How do you know that?" the halfling asked, her face confused.

"When I hold a card, I can tell the Luck and Harmony needed to bind it," I said cautiously. "I take it you can't?"

"No. I've never heard of such a thing," she sighed. "That hole card of yours—you should still bind it. Being a little short on Harmony isn't too bad. The card will still work, you'll just take a hit to attunement and power."

"Wait, maybe I can bind it!" Millie protested. She turned to Azara. "Can you tell me my Harmonies?"

"Of course," the avian nodded with a thin smile. "I charge ten silvers for that sort of divination. I assume you'll be fine if I take it from your share of the coins?"

"You're going to charge me for it?"

"Why wouldn't I? My services don't come for free."

"Here, just take the damn card," Ferdi snapped, taking the lady and handing it to Millie. "Don't try to bind it. Just hold it." Millie took the card a little hesitantly, her eyes uncertain, as if she suspected some sort of trap.

"Okay, now what?" the redhead asked.

"How does the card feel? How does it make you feel? Does it feel welcoming? Uncomfortable?"

"It feels—slippery," Millie said after a few moments, frowning. "Like it's trying to slide out of my hand."

"That's its way of telling you that you're not suited for it. Not that I expected you to be."

"Why not?" Millie demanded irritably.

"Because most beginner Holders have their highest Harmony in the twenties or thirties. That's good enough to bind most of the lesser arcana, but it's not enough for the nobles. I still can't believe that Murf bound the knight." She took the card from Millie and handed it back to me, then took the two of coins from me and gave it to Millie. "Here, put this one next to your three of coins in your layout if you can."

"Why?" She took the lesser arcana and looked at it distastefully.

"Because if you can also find the ace or four, you'll have a short flush run in coins. That'll make all the cards in the stack a little more powerful. You'll need five for the full effect, but even three will help." She looked back at me. "You should do the same with the lady. Try to put it next to the knight if you can. Find a ten—or, Unity help us all, a damn prince— and you'll have a short flush run into the nobles." She shook her head.

I picked up the card, but as I did, I glanced over my stats once more.

Murf
Rank 2 Cabalist (2,925/3,250)
Stats
Luck: 103   Capacity: 56
Skill: 35 (+3%)

Harmonies (40)
Coins: 48   Blades: 19
Cups: 58   Staves: 32
Stars: 38
Divine: 66   Worldly: 68

Infernal: 65
Infernal: 10

The number 40 after the word Harmonies grabbed my attention. Could I add some of those to my cups Harmony? If I could, I'd be able to use the lady without any problems. The only issue was, I didn't have the faintest idea how to do it. I opened my mouth to ask Ferdi about it, but as I did, another card popped up in my vision.

> You have 40 Harmony points to add. Would you like to add 3 to the Cups Harmony? This will bring this Harmony to 61.

I thought, *"Yes,"* and the card vanished. Looking at my stats again, I saw that my cups Harmony had gone up to 61. I didn't feel any different, though. I'd expected something big, like a surge of power or a sudden rush of emotions. The whole thing was honestly anti-climactic. Or maybe I was just getting spoiled for drama lately. I could see it going either way, really.

I unbuttoned my new shirt and touched the lady to my chest, concentrating on the card slot to the left of the knight. The burning began instantly, worse than the knight had been, and I bit my lip to keep from swearing. A flaming shard of glass seemed to dig its way into my body, slowly working its way inside me. The burning lasted for several seconds, growing in intensity until it felt like I'd swallowed a handful of hot coals. I bit my lip hard enough that I was shocked I wasn't bleeding, and my legs trembled from the strain of remaining upright against the pain. As quickly as it came, though, the pain ended, and once more, I got an uncomfortably full sensation in my lower chest, like a bit of bad meat trying to find its way back out. I sighed with relief as a new set of cards appeared in my vision.

☩ LADY OF CUPS

☩ FLOOD OF EMOTION

You cause a single emotion to slowly grow in a group of creatures within 25'. This can be allies, hostiles, or neutrals, at your choice.

♛ Noble Arcana ♪28% ⚡23 ⚡⚡81

Lady of Cups
Flood of Emotion
Rank: Noble Arcane
Attunement: 28%
Base Power: 23 **Max Power:** 81
You cause a single emotion to slowly grow in a group of creatures within 25'. This can be allies, hostiles, or neutrals, at your choice.

Hole Card Boost!
Your Flood of Emotions power gains a 105% bonus to effectiveness, ignores lesser resistances, and can become debilitating!

At first, that power seemed really underwhelming. After all, I'd used my knight power to kill a damn giant bunzelle. What could I have done to it with this power, make it happy? The more I thought about it, though, the more I saw the utility in it. I could use it to calm down a barfight or a jealous husband. I could make a mugger scared enough to run away. I could even keep people playing at a table longer, although I couldn't see myself doing that, any more than I'd use my knight's ability on other players to make them play poorly. That would be cheating, and I never cheated. The lady's ability wouldn't be as bad, but I could still misuse it. If I made everyone at the table apathetic, for example, they'd all fold too quickly; if I made them eager, they'd stay in when they shouldn't. Controlling your emotions is paramount in a game, and if I was in control of other people's emotions, then I had a major advantage.

In fact, realistically, the lady's power was a lot stronger and more useful to me than the knight's would be in the long run. After all, I wasn't Ferdi, running from fight to fight, clearing out Labyrinths and wondering which monster's brains I just spat out of my mouth. Definitely not for me. I wanted to gamble, to drink, to explore, and mostly to have fun, and the lady's power would help me do all those. I didn't know just how effective it would be or how slowly the emotion would grow in someone, but the Hag's boost promised it could be powerful. Crippling fear was nothing to sneer at, and neither was extreme ecstasy. An angry father might have trouble holding onto that anger while writhing on the floor in pure joy, I imagined.

I waved the cards away and looked over to see Millie on the ground, shuddering and writhing as she clutched her chest. Ferdi stood over her impassively, mostly making sure her thrashing around didn't spill the stacks of coins the redhead had carefully placed.

"Is she okay?" I asked in mild alarm.

"Fine. She's getting close to her limit for cards, though. One or two more will probably be it, at least until she increases her Capacity." She looked up at me consideringly. "You didn't seem to have any trouble."

"It hurt like hell, Ferdi. Trust me."

"Like this?" she asked drily, gesturing at the spasming Millie. "She's writhing in agony, Murf."

"Well, no, not like that."

"I didn't think so. You'll probably be able to get five or six cards in your deck in total, more if you train your Capacity."

I held up the other two cards. "You want either of these?"

"I'll take the eight. I've got no Harmony for staves, either." I handed her the card, then turned to Azara. "You…"

"Yes," she said, reaching out and taking the final card. "I can use this."

I handed it over willingly. I didn't much care about the card, to be honest, except maybe as something to sell. I looked down at Millie, still writhing on the ground. "About how long will she be out?"

"Probably a couple minutes," Ferdi shrugged. "The pain goes away quickly. Although she seems kind of soft, so who knows?"

I wanted to make a comment about her being soft, and the parts that were extra soft, but I remembered Azara just in time and bit my tongue. Instead, I looked down at the remaining coins. "I suppose I should finish this, then. No point in waiting for her, really."

I settled down beside the coin piles, and as I did, Ferdi moved to stand over me. I glanced up and gave her an irritated look. "Do you really think that I'm going to steal from you, Ferdi?"

"I know you, Murf. I'm sure that you'll try."

Damn me if she wasn't right. I sighed and went to work. Fortunately, Millie had done a pretty good job of organizing them, separating the brass from the silver and piling each into neat stacks of ten. I'd had plenty of practice handling and stacking coins and chips myself, obviously, so it didn't take me too long to finish the job. At the end, I rose to my feet and stretched my aching back, idly touching the few coins I'd managed to pocket beneath Ferdi's gaze to make sure they weren't too visible. I'd only taken brass, and I hadn't done it to steal from the others as much as to prove that I could even while Ferdi was watching. Of course, that didn't mean that I intended to put them back, either.

"Well?" Ferdi asked impatiently.

"It looked like more than it was," I said deprecatingly. "It's mostly brass, no gold at all."

"Numbers, Murf. We want numbers."

"271 brass, 48 silver." The halfling stared at me, and I shrugged a little uncomfortably. "As I said, it looked like more than it was. Lots of brass in that bag."

"That's—do you know how many golds that is, Murf?"

"Three," Azara answered instantly.

"What she said," I nodded.

"Three in coins, plus four cards, plus items for each of us. All told, we probably made almost ten golds from this run!"

"Is that good? I've never finished one of these before." The lie came easily enough, although I caught Azara giving me a look and had to keep from wincing. I'd told her that I'd been thrown into a Labyrinth before, after all, so she knew I was lying. Fortunately, she didn't say a word.

"For a low reward Labyrinth? It's amazing, Murf. We shouldn't have gotten half of this." She looked uncertain as she hefted her axe. "Plus, I got enough UP to rank up. I—I don't know if we should take all this."

"Why not?" I asked, unconsciously clutching my coat around me. She was taking my new clothes over my dead body. Well, maybe over my somewhat battered body. "What's the matter with it?"

"The Unity doesn't just give blessings like this without a balance, Murf. I expected a slightly larger than normal reward because it was our first time running it and we really shouldn't have survived it, but this—this is way more than it should be. Four cards? Three gold in coins? Another seven in items? 300 UP?" She shook her head. "I would have predicted half that."

"Oh. Well, I might have an explanation for that, actually. When I killed the bunzelle…"

"Terakwid."

"Bunzelle," I repeated with emphasis. "Accept it, Ferdi. That's its name now." She grumbled but didn't argue, and I pressed on. "Anyway, when I killed it, I got a card saying that as a reward, all my drops for this Labyrinth were doubled. That's probably why we got more than you expected."

Her eyes widened, and she stepped forward, grabbing my arm. "For how long?" she asked in a hoarse whisper.

"How long what?"

"How long are they doubled?"

"It—it didn't give a time limit. Just that they're doubled. Why?"

"Murf—do you know what this means? Every time you run this Labyrinth, you'll get double the rewards! Double the UP! Every time, forever! We could run this, over and over…"

"Nope," I cut her off, gently pulling my arm from her grip. "Not only nope, but hell no. Hell fucking no, Ferdi. I never want to step foot in another Labyrinth again."

"But…"

"And I don't think the others will disagree with me. Azara, do you want to keep doing this again and again?"

"I'd rather be set on fire," the avian answered calmly.

"What about you, Millie?" I glanced down at the woman who'd slowly sat up during our conversation.

She looked up at me, her gaze determined, and shook her head. "You would have to drag me, Ferdi, and I'd do my best to kill you in the process. This was beyond awful."

"I could find a team…" the halfling protested.

"No means no, Ferdi." I pulled my coat around me and shifted my shoulders in it. "I want to get out of here, rest for a bit, and get ready for the tournament. After I win it…"

"Excuse me?" Millie scoffed. "You mean, after I do."

"Tell yourself whatever you need to," I grinned at her. "But after it's over, I'm going to hop a ship the hell out of here and head in a random direction." Azara gave me a troubled look when I said that, but I ignored it. There was no way I was staying in Canis, and she had to know that. There was no point pretending otherwise.

"Speaking of getting out of here," Millie said, groaning as she pushed herself to her feet. "How do we? Do we have to go all the way back through the forest to where we started? Do we have to fight all those things all over again?"

The halfling glared at me for a few seconds, but I returned her look as evenly as I could manage.

"Ferdi, you're a delver," I said quietly. "I'm not. I don't want to be. Ever. I don't like pain and fear and fighting and running. I'm going to have nightmares about this as it is. I'm sorry, but you're out of luck."

She sighed and shook her head as she looked at Millie, her voice glum as she spoke. "No, we don't have to fight anything. Killing the guardian always causes all the beasts in a Labyrinth to disappear. And we won't have to go far to get out." She pointed toward the far side of the clearing. "The exit's that way. There's always an exit opposite the entrance to the final area."

I froze as her words sank in. "Wait, what?" I asked a little hoarsely.

"I said, there's always an exit opposite the entrance to the final area."

"Always? In every Labyrinth?"

"Every one I've heard of," she shrugged. "I've never heard anyone mention anything different."

"So, when you kill the guardian, an exit just—appears opposite the entrance to their room?"

"Well, it's not usually visible until you get close to it, but yes. Why?"

I stared at the woman, then closed my eyes and took a deep breath, cursing the Unity as I did. If she was right, the other door in the tomb—the smaller one I'd ignored—was probably the way out. Instead of backtracking through that infernal maze of death traps and nearly wetting myself a dozen times in the process, I could have just—left. I screamed silently for a few seconds, then recovered myself.

"Murf, are you okay?" Millie asked, her voice both concerned and confused. "What's the matter?"

"Nothing," I sighed. There was no point to railing at the Unity. It wasn't its fault that I knew nothing about Labyrinths and took the hard way out. In fact, I supposed I should have been grateful since at least it made leaving possible instead of killing me instantly. I couldn't blame the Unity for my idiocy. Besides, there were plenty of things I could blame it for. I didn't really need more.

"Before we leave, you should change," I reminded her, pointing to the dress still lying on the ground. "Unless you want to walk out of here hanging out like that, of course."

She blushed and looked down at herself, quickly covering her breasts as she remembered that her shirt was ruined. "Yes, I should." She bent down and snatched up the dress. "Just give me a moment." She began to walk away, and to my surprise, Ferdi started to follow her. The redhead paused and looked back at the halfling.

"What are you doing, Ferdi?"

"Going with you, obviously," the warrior shrugged.

Millie took a deep breath. "Okay, but why are you going with me? I can change alone, after all."

"Yes, but it'll be easier to search you if you're already naked anyway."

Millie's eyes went wide, and she clutched the dress against her chest. "You—you don't need to do that, Ferdi. I don't have any coins…"

"I don't have to. I will, though."

The redhead glanced pleadingly at me, and I sighed. "Ferdi, leave her alone, okay?" I said tiredly.

"You know she's got some coins hidden away somewhere, Murf," the halfling said, turning to look at me. "Unless you were planning to search her yourself, I should probably do it."

"Do you plan to search her, Murf?" Azara asked in a deceptively idle tone.

I ignored Azara and tried not to picture performing an adequately thorough search of the lovely redhead. "It's fine, Ferdi. A silver or two isn't worth someone's dignity, is it?"

"It is to me."

"Just let her change," I said firmly. "You got your axe, a new rank, and a new card. Don't be greedy."

"Fine," the halfling muttered, walking away from the redhead, who flashed me a grateful look.

The exit, it turned out, was a hidden path into one of the thickets that ended after a few feet in a wall of mist. Millie wanted to run through it, but Ferdi and I ended up going first. We didn't really know what waited for us out there, after all, or even what time of day it was, and the halfling and I were the most durable of the four of us. The mist tingled on my skin as I passed through, and I blinked as a sudden flare of light washed out my vision for a minute. It passed quickly, and I looked upward. The sun was high in the sky, making it close to midday and lighting everything brilliantly. I gazed at the sky with a contented sigh.

"What?" Ferdi asked grumpily.

"Look," I pointed into the air. "Blue."

The halfling glanced up, her face confused. "Yes. The sky is blue."

"It's just so—not orange."

"You're weird, Murf."

"You're one to talk, Delver."

I looked away from the sky and took a good look around. As I scanned our surroundings, I got a good look at this place for the first time. We stood in the middle of a clearing that actually looked a lot like the one we'd just left, except the trees here were green and brown the way trees were supposed to be. The broken remains of what must have been a truly enormous dead tree stood behind us, and we'd stepped out of a gash in its trunk that led into darkness. A path worn into the grass of the clearing led to a dirt road that curved out of sight into the woods. It was a prosaic enough sight, and all the colors felt like a balm to my eyes.

"Murf—that drop," she whispered. "The one that you got right before the guardian came, when you were flirting with the bird-woman…"

"That was not flirting, Ferdi," I said firmly. "And if you think it was, I feel bad for your next partner."

"Whatever. What happened to that drop? What did you do with it?"

I frowned, trying to remember, then chuckled. "I dropped it, ironically enough. When I picked up Azara. Why?"

"Your doubled drops, Murf," she groaned. "You could have gotten one more!" She spun around. "Maybe if I hurry…" She stopped as Azara and Millie appeared a moment later, both looking around with relief at the sunlit clearing. Behind them, the gash in the tree shimmered, the darkness turning into a misty gray fog. "Damn you, Murf. We could have had another drop!"

I started to laugh as relief at being out of the damn Labyrinth flooded my brain. The laughter grew as all the fears and terrors I'd pushed aside while we were inside reminded me of their presence, turning into a full-blown belly laugh. Tears streamed down my cheeks, and I doubled over, clutching my stomach as I expelled all the stress I'd built up in one cathartic moment of hilarity.

Millie and Azara just stared at me in confusion, but a moment later, a grin creased Millie's face, and she began to chuckle, as well. Even Azara's icy mask slipped for a bit as she let a wide smile spread across her dark lips, and I saw her chest shuddering with quiet, concealed laughter. Millie's chortle grew into a laugh, as well, and she flung herself into me, wrapping her arms around me and clinging to me fiercely.

"We did it," she crowed triumphantly. "We got out! Suck on that, Unity!"

Even Azara had to laugh a bit at that, leaving Ferdi glaring at us all in incomprehension.

"Tall folk are all idiots," she muttered, stamping past us. "Come on. Stop your foolishness, and let's get out of here. It's a long walk back to Canis."

32

Darkness had fallen over the city by the time we returned to it. The Ochre Forest, it turned out, wasn't all that far from the city. The walk back had taken us mostly past farms and small villages, one of which we stopped in to buy some actual food at a travel house before continuing on. The trip was uneventful, and the worst part was going past the pig farms. Pigs, if you don't know, stink. I mean, they really, really stink.

The gate guards didn't want to let us through since officially the gates closed at sunset, but a couple brass coins changed their minds, and they opened a small door beside the gate to let us in. As we entered the city, we all stopped and looked at one another a bit uncertainly.

"Well, it was fun," I finally said to the others. "We should do it again some time."

"No," Azara shook her head firmly. "We absolutely shouldn't." She gave me a serious look. "Murf, you saved my life. I consider any disagreement between us settled. Feel free to call on me if you need a reading done. Otherwise, good luck in your tournament." She turned and walked away, heading for her shop, no doubt.

"I'm heading back to the hold," Ferdi added. "I need to arrange for rites for the ones those assassins killed."

"How did they get you all, anyway?" I asked her curiously.

"They're Holders, obviously, with some sort of hiding or disguising power," she snorted. "Damn coins suit and its shadow magic. They took us out, one at a time and silently. I fought back, but there were two of them, and…" She shrugged. "I need to tell the others' families the bad news, but I'll be in touch soon."

"Ferdi, I told you, I'm not going back to that Labyrinth…"

"I know. I heard you. You still owe me my cards, though, and the person who did this to us has them. I'll see if I can figure out anything about him, and when I do, I'll come get you for help." She gave me a hard look. "Don't leave the city, or I'll have to reinstate the bounty. Neither of us want that." She turned and stalked away, and I sighed.

"What bounty?" Millie asked.

"She put a bounty out on my…" I froze and shook my head. "It doesn't matter. I doubt she'll find anything, and she can't blame me for that." I looked at the redhead. "To the Guild Hall?"

"By the Unity, yes," she sighed, taking my arm and resting her head against my shoulder. "I need a bath. So do you."

"I could wash your back," I volunteered. I expected a smack or at least a snappy reply, but to my surprise, she gave me a soft smile.

"I'd like that," she said quietly.

A hot bath and some vigorous exercise later, I lay quietly in my bed in the Hall, staring at the ceiling. The bed was welcomingly soft, and I was utterly exhausted, but I couldn't drift off to sleep. Millie slept fitfully beside me, but I wasn't sure how long it would last. Our lovemaking had been especially tender and intimate, and when it ended, she broke down into sobbing, clinging to me fiercely. That was the kind of thing that a man might take as a pretty heavy-handed critique if he were so inclined, but I got it. We'd all lived the past few days in fear of our lives, always just a step or two away from death. She'd had to rely on strangers to survive, and she'd had to kill more times than any of us bothered to count. That wasn't the kind of thing that a person just shook off, and the storm of weeping was Millie's way to deal with it. Honestly, I didn't much blame her.

That same stress was what kept me awake—that and a sudden realization about my mortality. Oh, sure, I knew in an offhand way that someday, I'd die. After watching my mom's decline, how could I not? The fact didn't occupy too much space in my brain, though. It was always there, a reminder to live my life as well as possible because I never knew when it could end.

That sort of hazy, ephemeral concept that sure, one day I was going to die, though, didn't hold a candle to the past couple weeks. I'd come incredibly close to death any number of times, especially when the giant bunzelle was chomping on my insides. I'd been lucky and more than lucky, starting from the moment I entered the lich's tomb. I'd thought it was just a maze of traps, but what if it wasn't? What if it had monsters like the lich in it as well as the deadly traps? That would explain why it lay unbeaten for so long. Even if you knew how to spot the traps and deactivate them somehow, how could you do that while you were busy fighting a bunch of walking corpses? As big as the reward for that Labyrinth was, its monsters had to be way stronger than the ones in the Forest. What if each creature in the tomb was as dangerous as the bunzelle, or worse? If I'd landed even fifty feet away from where I had, I'd have been dead, period.

A chill rose up my spine as the fear I'd been suppressing suddenly broke free of my control and washed over my brain. All the ways I'd nearly died flashed through my brain, replaying themselves in terrifying detail. I felt the pain of claws and teeth piercing me, the hammering of my heart and the labored bellows of my lungs gasping for air. Exhaustion clawed at me, but I knew that if I gave into it, even for a moment, I'd be dead. I could practically feel the grim specter hovering behind me, its claws reaching for my back, just waiting for me to make a misstep. I couldn't help but wonder if Mom had felt the same toward the end, and what that skeletal touch felt like…

I shuddered as silent sobs wracked my body. My chest heaved and my stomach clenched, and I felt tears stream from my eyes. Millie had cried out her anguish already; it was my turn, apparently. I didn't even try to fight it as I wept quietly, both in celebration of escaping death's grip and from the knowledge that being in the Labyrinth had changed me, and that I wasn't the person I'd been before I'd met that damn Hag. I would never be that person again.

Sleep was long in coming, but at last, exhaustion won out over stress, and I passed into a nightmarish slumber filled with darkness and shadows that chased me through an endless orange forest dripping crimson blood.

I started awake to see sunlight streaming into the room. Millie gasped and shot up the moment I moved, her eyes wild and frantic and her hands clenched into fists. My own heart hammered in my chest, and I dimly recalled dreaming about watching everyone I loved being eaten by a giant purple rabbit that shot lightning from its single horn while talking about how it was going to make delicious food out of all our corpses. It was a disturbing dream, and it took me a few seconds to realize that's all it had been. Millie also seemed to come to her senses, and she lay slowly back down, nestling into the crook of my arm as I held her close.

"I slept like shit," she said after a few moments.

"Me, too," I agreed.

"I had nightmares all night long. Things kept chasing me, and when I ran, the ground grabbed my feet…" She shuddered. "That place was terrible, Murf."

"Worse than terrible. What say we pick another place for our next night out? Or you pick the place next time. I'm apparently shit at it."

She snorted in laughter, but I felt her tense up. "Kikoum," she said darkly. "You know that he betrayed us. He let those elves in our room."

"Probably, yes. What can we do about it?"

"We could…" She fell silent and sighed. "We can't really do anything, can we? He's safe inside the Lamb, at least from us. Of course, I could message my family, they'd lodge a complaint, and he'd probably be killed—but if they found out I'd been attacked and kidnapped…" She went quiet again, and I gave her a quick hug.

"I take it you and your family aren't on the best of terms, then?" I asked lightly.

She snorted. "That's an understatement."

"Just because you'd rather be a gambler than a merchant?"

"That wouldn't be a 'just because' to my family, Murf. It's sacrilege. But mostly, it's because I'm an investment that went sour on them."

I looked down at her dubiously. "I can't imagine that, sorry. There's not a single thing wrong with you that I can find—and I've been looking very, very closely."

She laughed. "Yes, you have, but it's not that. They spent a lot of time and money trying to make me into who they wanted, and that wasn't a gambler. They tolerate it because they still hope to bring me back into the fold, but if they thought I was in real danger, they'd have their agents in Canis bundle me up on the next fast ship to Deepwater."

"Or try to," I corrected. "You're a Holder, now. It might not be that easy for them."

"That's worse," she shivered. "If they found out about that, they'd grab me even faster. The family has uses for Holders, Murf." She shook her head as if banishing an unpleasant thought. "Enough of that. We have the whole day ahead of us. How should we spend it?"

"Well, I'm thinking breakfast, then the Swindlers," I said, stretching.

"The Usurer's Hall? Why?"

"Because those Unity coins we got from the Labyrinth are worth more than you might think. Apparently, each Unity silver is worth three Imperial wands, and I assume the same is true for brass. We can get them changed at the Swindlers."

Her eyes widened, and her head popped up, displaying her chest. "That's over forty wands," she breathed. "Two gold crowns!"

"Thirty-six, officially," I chuckled. "Unless, of course, you managed to sneak a few extra for yourself."

"Of course, I did. So did you, didn't you?"

"Well, yes, but mostly because Ferdi was standing there as if she'd be able to stop me."

The woman sighed contentedly and lay her head back on my chest. "It's not a fortune, but it's a start," she said. "With seed money like that and the right games, I could win enough in a year to buy out of the family and be on my own."

"Buy out?" I asked, startled.

She made a face. "I told you. I'm an investment that went bad, and the Deepwaters didn't get to where they are by not recouping those investments. Once I pay them back, I'm free of them, and I can live my own life."

"Would the money that we won in the Lamb have helped with that?"

"No. Grandfather would have said that it was his money we gambled with, so the winnings were his no matter what." She smiled at me. "Don't worry. I have a plan to handle it, and this tournament is part of it. I don't even need to win; I just need to make a good enough showing to place in the top tier, so that I get invited to the high-stakes games and the private invitationals. That's where the real money is, after all."

"True." I pulled her closer. "And you've got the skills to get there. You just need a little more practice at hiding your tells."

"Oh, really?" she asked archly. "And what are those?"

"Well, if I tell you, then they aren't tells anymore," I grinned at her. "And I've still got to play you in the tournament."

"That's not very fair," she pouted.

"No, it's not. Life tends not to be." I leaned down and kissed her forehead. "I'll make you a deal, though. You make it to the finals of the tournament, and I'll teach you what I can while I'm still in the city. Deal?"

She pouted for another moment, then made a sour face. "Deal," she said at last, then leaned forward and kissed me on the lips, her kiss much deeper and more intense than mine had been. She pulled back and stared into my eyes. "And in return, I'll teach you what I can while we're here in the bedroom."

"I think you've showed me most of that already," I chuckled.

"We haven't even scratched the surface, Murf," she murmured. "For example, let me show you a little something I learned from an elf prostitute in Maewith…"

She was right. She really did have a lot more to show me. And I really needed to find that brothel in Maewith she was talking about.

We missed the Hall's breakfast service but grabbed a midday meal, then headed south to the Usurer's Hall. I realized as we walked along that the Labyrinth had changed me even more than I'd thought. My eyes scanned everything, constantly checking every window, doorway, and roof for possible threats, even as Millie and I chatted companionably. Whenever I looked at the woman, I saw her doing the same, looking everywhere for possible danger. In the Forest, that had been necessary for survival, and now, it seemed we were both having trouble putting that habit behind us.

The Swindlers changed our money for a nominal fee, and we both left with smaller purses than we'd entered with but much larger accounts in the Hall's books. As we stepped outside, still looking around for danger, Millie took my arm again.

"Where to, next?" she asked.

I had to think that one over a bit. I wanted to sell my saber at some point, and Millie probably wanted to do the same with her daggers, but I doubted we'd get much for those, so it wasn't really worth a trip to either the marketplace or the ironworks, down in the southwest where the blacksmiths mostly plied their trade. I did have one thing that I thought might be worth some money, though, and I pulled it from my pocket, holding up the white, smooth orb for Millie to see.

"Ooh, what's that?" she asked curiously. "Did you get that from…" She stopped herself and looked around; we'd already realized that talking about the Labyrinth would mark us both as Holders and put targets on our backs. "The Forest?" she finished.

"Yep. Right before the bunny, when you were talking about being in a harem."

She had the good grace to blush at that. "Well, it seemed like a real concern at the time," she laughed weakly. "Ferdi likes you, Murf, and Azara obviously still cares for you."

"Ferdi and I were friends, once. We've never been anything more. In fact, I've never seen her with anyone like that, to be honest." I frowned. "I'm not sure if she's even got the right equipment for it. I've never seen her out of armor.

"And as for Azara..." I took a deep breath. "Obviously, we were close, once. She wanted us to be more than close. That scared me, so I left. She hasn't forgiven me, and she probably never will. I don't even think I'd call us friends anymore, really. Just two people who happen to know one another."

"She doesn't feel like that," Millie shook her head. "I can see it in her eyes. For someone so good at reading people, Murf, I think you're pretty blind about Azara."

"Maybe. It doesn't matter. I won't see her again while we're in the city, I'm sure, and then, I'll be leaving." I paused. "I think I'll stop by and say goodbye this time, though. It's the decent thing to do."

"It's the minimum requirement for decent, yes. Better would be to have a meal or drinks with her and say goodbye properly."

I glanced at her skeptically. "You're actually asking me to go to dinner with Azara?"

She laughed lightly. "Come on, Murf. We both know that you and I are only going to last until the tournament. Once it's over, we'll go our separate ways. I'm fine with that; you're a lot more interesting than any other man I've met in this city, and except for the mind-numbing terror, we've had a lot of fun together." She kissed my cheek lightly. "Plus, you've got great stamina. That's always a plus.

"I'm not saying you should go have dinner with her today, though," she clarified. "Like I said, I don't want to be part of any harem. But maybe right before you leave. Or you could wait until I've left the city, when it won't matter anyway." She shrugged. "That seems like the kind thing to do. At least you can leave her with one last fond memory."

"I'll think about it," I sighed. "You're assuming she'll even say yes."

"She will." She looked back at the sphere. "So, what is that thing?"

"No clue," I shrugged. "I was going to ask Ferdi, but we all kind of got distracted by the giant bunny, and then I forgot until this morning."

"You should take it to the Sage's Hall. They appraise things like this."

"That was the plan," I nodded. "Now that we've got the money for an appraisal, that is. I'd like to see what we can get for it. All that silver was great, but I'm really hoping for gold."

"Murf, you are amazingly sexy when you talk like that," Millie murmured, nuzzling up against my ear.

"I'm amazingly sexy all the time, woman."

"But you're even sexier when you talk about gold. Maybe we'll get enough for that naked rolling in the bed thing you wanted to do."

"Now, that is the best idea I've heard in days," I laughed. "Come on. Let's go see if the Brainies can make both of our days."

33

The Sage's Guild set up shop in a large, squarish black building with four towers, one jutting from each corner. I'd only been in them a few times in my life—usually to appraise something I'd won in a game when I didn't know for sure what it was—but all of them were the same. We entered through a pair of doors shaped like unrolled scrolls and entered into an open, brightly lit space. Desks stood around the room, each of them with a sign hanging above them and most with a line formed up before them. A fair number of people bustled around the room, mostly moving from line to line as they reached the front of one only to find they'd been in the wrong line the whole time.

The main reason for that was that the Sages—or the Brainies, as some people called them—didn't have the clearest and best-defined labeling system. The main desk in the center had a sign above it that read "Information", so most people assumed that was where they went with generic questions. It wasn't, though. Information was where you went to buy current information: rumors, gossip, trends, and the like. If you wanted to know what the meritocrats had for dinner last night, what horse was favored in a race, or who some noble was boinking on the side, you went to the Information desk. If, on the other hand, you wanted to know where a specific place was located in the city, you went to the desk labeled "Guides". The system only made sense to the Brainies, and I suspected that was deliberate. I guess maybe someone who's spent their whole life gaining odd and esoteric knowledge just likes seeing other people wander in ignorance. Some people are like that.

We ignored most of the lines and joined the one leading to the desk labeled, "Acquisitions". I suppose the idea there is that if the Brainies are going to buy something from you, first, they need to be sure what it is. Whatever the logic, though, that's where you want to go if you need something appraised. They'll tell you what it is, and if they want it, they'll offer to buy it from you for a decent chunk of its actual value. Unlike merchants, the Sages aren't looking to resell what they buy; they want to use it, so they don't care about making a profit off it. Of course, the downside is they'll only buy things that they think they can use. That means they're probably not the best people to go to with your Aunt Myrtle's antique teapot with the paintings of the naked felid ladies on it. Now, if those ladies do a sensual dance when the pot's full of hot water, the

Sages might just be interested. After all, all that studying probably isn't great for their sex lives. Hell, I might be interested, as well, so feel free to bring it to me first.

We waited for a bit until we got to the front, where a young elf man with cinnamon hair tied back in an elaborate braid looked at us with a bored expression.

"Welcome to the Hall of Sages. How can I assist you today?"

"I have an item I'd like identified and appraised," I said.

"Well, at least you're in the correct line," he sighed. "That shows you have at least half of a brain—or got lucky. An identification costs three brass for standard items, a half-silver for exotic ones, and will only include a proposed value if the Hall wishes to purchase it. If that is the case, and you agree to sell, the appraisal fee will be waived. Do you understand these extremely simple rules?"

"Not really," I shook my head. The elf's attitude annoyed me, as elven attitudes often did, and in my book, annoyance is an emotion best shared. "Could you go through that one more time?"

He rolled his eyes. "If your item is a simple one, with no special properties, we'll charge you three brass to identify it. If your item has unique or special properties, we'll charge you ten brass. If we want to buy it, we'll also tell you what we think it's worth, which will also be the amount we're offering to pay for it. In that case, we won't charge you for the identification as long as you agree to sell it. Is that clearer?"

"Almost. What's the cost for a regular item again?"

"Three. Brass."

"And that's what you'll pay me for it?"

"No, that's what we'll charge you to identify it!"

"And what makes something exotic?"

"Exotic items have special features," he spat.

"Would a picture of a naked felid lady count as regular or exotic?" I pressed. "I mean, if the lady's got some pretty special features?"

"I—what?"

"Her features. They're very special. By which I mean her breasts. They're simply enormous." I held my hands way out in front of me. "Like, out to here. That seems pretty exotic."

"Is—is that what you're bringing to have appraised?" he asked, and I swore his voice sounded kind of hopeful. "Do you have a painting of a nude woman like that?"

"No. I was just curious. Wouldn't that be nice, though? Well, unless she was your mother or something."

"My—my mother?"

"Yes. You wouldn't want to see a picture of your mother's enormous breasts, I imagine."

"My mother doesn't have enormous breasts!"

"That's not a nice thing to say about your own mother," I said severely. "Saying that she has no breasts!"

"I never…" He let out an exasperated sigh. "Look, just show me the item. I'll tell you how much an identification costs, and you can decide if you want to pay it. I'd really like to get this over with."

"That sounds fair. You should have said that to begin with, instead of giving me all these fancy rules and talking about naked lady paintings and your mom's breasts."

"I—you were the one talking about that!"

"That's not how I remember it." I raised my voice slightly to make sure everyone around me could hear. "I distinctly recall you asking me if I had a naked lady painting for you to look at. You sounded really excited to see it. Then you went off on how small your mother's breasts are." I heard Millie snort beside me, and I had to work to keep a straight face.

"That—no—I didn't mean that!" he hissed, his face turning bright red as people around us turned to look curiously. "Just show me what you've brought, damn you!"

"No need for that kind of language," I admonished him, pulling out the orb. "What will you mother think of you? Swearing and talking about her breasts?" I held the ball out, and he practically snatched it from my hand, pink all the way to the tips of his ears. He examined the sphere for a moment, and the blush faded as curiosity filled his eyes. He pulled out a wooden tray covered with facedown cards, placed a card and the ball in the center, then gazed down at it. A moment later, his eyes widened, and he picked up the orb with trembling fingers.

"I—I'll need to take this to a specialist appraiser," he said, his voice shaking slightly. "It's beyond what I can tell."

I eyed him suspiciously, reading the hunch of his shoulders, the way his eyes flicked about, and the gentle but possessive way he held the orb. "I don't think so," I shook my head, holding out my hand. "I'll take it back now, thanks."

"But—this—I..."

"If you disappear through a door with this, how do I know I'm getting it back?" I cut him off. "Bring the specialist here."

"I..." He stopped, then seemed to come to a quick decision. "Actually, sir, perhaps you and your companion would like to come with me, instead? We have a room that we use to perform appraisals for guests of the Hall, and you're welcome to wait there."

I glanced at Millie, who gave me a nonchalant shrug. "That sounds fine," I said at last. "But I'll take that back, first, thank you."

"Of course, sir." He handed the sphere back to me, and I slipped it back into the pocket inside my coat. "Please, follow me."

As we followed the young elf through a doorway into a carpeted hallway, Millie leaned close to me. "Quite the shift in attitude, don't you think?"

"I noticed," I nodded. "Do you think he realized I was making fun of him and stopped before it got worse?"

"I think that if you kept going, he'd have tried to stab you with his own ears, Murf. That was mean."

"He annoyed me, what can I say?"

"I didn't say you were wrong, just that it was mean."

As it turned out, there really was a special room in the back near the end of the hallway. It had padded leather seats, a thickly carpeted floor, and a table with carafes of what looked like wine, ale, and water sitting on it. The elf held open the door and gestured for us to enter.

"Please, take a seat. I'll go inform the specialist, and they'll be with you shortly. In the meantime, feel free to avail yourself of our refreshments." We stepped inside, and he closed the door softly behind us.

"This is nice," I noted, looking around the room. "Not that nice, but nicer than standing in line out there."

"And they offered us refreshments," Millie noted, walking over to the table and sniffing at the wine pitcher. "Think they're poisoned?"

"That would be one way to acquire interesting items," I chuckled. "Bring the owners back here, poison them, then claim they sold it to you and disappeared with the money."

She paused in the process of picking the carafe up. "That sounds far too plausible, Murf," she said, setting it back down.

"Not really. Only people with wealth and power are likely to have items worth bringing back here."

"We don't, and we're here."

"We're special," I winked at her. "The point is, they don't know that. This ball seems to be pretty valuable, which means we might be rich and important. They wouldn't risk it."

She stepped back from the table, shaking her head. "It's not worth it for a glass of wine." She walked over and sat down in a chair, and I settled in beside her. "This thing seems to have caused an uproar, Murf."

"It does. Let's hope that means that it's worth a lot of money. If it is, you might be rich after all."

We sat for a few minutes before the door opened, and a slim, female halfling with pale blue hair stepped into the room. Her wide, lightly tanned face was dusted with freckles, and her dark eyes peered almost myopically at us. She wore a black robe with a crossed pair of rolled-up scrolls on the breast in gold and a similarly colored line running from her shoulder to the cuff of her sleeve.

"Good morning," she said crisply as she entered. "I'm Senior Sage Gertla, and I understand you have a valuable item to be identified."

"Nice to meet you, Gertla," I nodded. "Although it's well past morning."

"Is it?" She looked out the window curiously. "So, it is. It doesn't change the intent of the greeting, which was to place you at ease and make you feel welcome. Did it work?"

"I suppose."

"Then your clarification was trivial and unnecessary." She walked in and sat down at the table, pouring herself a glass of water and sipping it. "May I see the item in question?"

I hesitated for only a moment before I pulled out the orb and placed it on the table. Gertla picked it up, examined it carefully, then set it down.

"This came from a Labyrinth," she said. "And quite recently, yes?"

"How would someone know that?" I hedged.

"I can feel the energies still seeping from it, but it's slowly bleeding them out. Within a day or two at the most, it will be inert, I judge." She placed it on the table, then pulled a card holder from her robe's pocket. She sat up on her knees so she could see well over the table and began pulling out cards, shuffling them, and arranging them.

"You're a cartomancer?" Millie asked in surprise.

"Yes. An object such as this requires a full divination. Tableaus are insufficient."

"We actually know a cartomancer," the redhead continued. "Her name's Azara, and she's in this city."

"Yes, I know of her. Quite skilled." The halfling paused. "You could have gone to her for this, you know."

"She would have charged us ten silvers for the reading," Millie said bitterly.

"Ah. Then by 'know her', you don't mean that you're friendly."

Millie's eyes narrowed. "Why do you say that?"

"She usually charges a silver for this sort of thing, and she'd probably give you better information than that tableau would have."

"A *silver?*" Millie spun toward me. "She was going to charge me ten, Murf!"

"She can be touchy sometimes," I nodded solemnly.

"Only if by 'touchy', you mean similar to an alchemical explosive on the verge of eruption," Gertla said without missing a beat. "I can give you the same information, though, and perhaps some advice if this is what I think it is."

"What do you think it is?" I asked.

"Best not to say it aloud. Preconceptions can taint the cards. Now, be silent and let me work." We watched as the woman deftly laid out cards, placing them in an elaborate pattern. Energy built in the room as she worked, making the hair on my neck tingle and stand on end. The power crested and fell, rising higher and higher each time, swirling around the table until at last, it reached a peak and plunged down into the table, swirling around the orb before it vanished. Gertla took a deep, shuddering breath, her back straightening and her head lolling back. Her body shook for a moment before her head rolled forward, her body slumped, and a shiver seemed to pass through her. Millie and I simply sat watching her in silent awe. Azara had never looked like that, and I'd never felt that level of power in one of her divinations. I suddenly realized that maybe this halfling woman was a "Senior Sage" for a reason.

"It..." the woman said in a croaking voice. She paused, grabbed the glass of water, and took several large swallows. When she spoke again, her voice was back to normal.

"Much better. Such divinations are quite taxing and always leave me parched." She took another swallow before setting the glass down. "It is as I thought. This is a Unity seed."

Millie and I exchanged blank looks, and I looked back at the woman. "A what?"

"Your ignorance is understandable. These are quite rare. Even worse, most who find them don't have them evaluated until after they've bled their power and it's too late. Smart of you to come here quickly." She nodded.

"That doesn't actually answer the question, you know," I pointed out.

"Hmm. You're right. It doesn't. Of course, to do that, I simply have to repeat what I already told you, but I presume that your intended question is, 'What is a Unity seed?', correct?"

"That is what I was wondering, yes," I nodded. "And maybe how valuable it is."

"Oh, its value is incalculable. Quite literally, as that value varies from person to person. Once I explain what it is, you'll understand. Or possibly not, depending on your native intellect, which young Nerennyn suggested might be lacking."

Millie let out a little snort beside me, but I ignored her and kept my focus on the halfling. "How about you give it a try, and we'll see how it goes?"

"That was my intention, yes." She picked up the ball and examined it carefully. "A Unity seed is called such because many believe that it is a solidified piece of the Unity itself, separated from the main body. This is, quite obviously, impossible, as the Unity can't by its nature be divided that way."

"What about the cards?" I asked.

"They are manifestations of the Unity, yes, but not actual, separate pieces of it. At least, not as our current theories stand, which I must admit involve a large quantity of belief and assumption. The Unity does not easily lend itself to experimentation, after all."

"I've heard people say that cards talk to them, though."

"I've also heard a woman say that pigs speak to her and tell her to burn things. While that's possible, I find it highly unlikely. I presume that anyone who hears cards speaking to them suffers from similar delusions, although I have no proof."

She shrugged. "Whatever the case, I believe that a seed like this contains a tiny spark of the Unity's potential, not the Unity itself. I like the name 'seed' because it is an apt analogy. Like a seed, it can be planted, and it grows something. And like a seed, how well it grows depends on the planter and the fertility of the field—although at this point, we belabor the metaphor somewhat."

"So, you plant it, and something grows," I nodded. "But—what?"

"That's the issue. What grows depends on the individual, and there's no way to predict it. Your soul is the field in which it's planted, and its fecundity can be difficult to determine. The only constant is that whatever is produced is something living. The Guild keeps records, and there have been all sorts of outcomes. One person was inflicted with a wasting illness that killed them slowly over the course of a decade. Another received a sapling that, when planted, grew quickly into a tree that dropped silver coins as fruit before crumbling to the ground. Another produced a beast that slaughtered her and her family. One even received an eternal potato."

"I'm sorry?" Millie broke in. "Eternal potato?"

"Yes. Quite a useful thing, really. You can cut it up, cook it, and eat it, and so long as you save one piece, it will regrow into a full potato in hours. Such a thing could theoretically feed entire villages if used wisely— although I understand the flavor left something to be desired."

"So, let me see if I understand this," I said slowly. "If I plant this—in my soul—it will grow...something? But there's no way to know what?"

"It doesn't seem to be completely random. There's some evidence that the more in accord with the Unity you are, the better your results will be. It's not absolute, but Holders with high Luck stats—meaning they're more favored by the Unity—generally get better results than those with low Luck stats. Most average people who use one have terrible outcomes, but the average person isn't really much favored by the Unity."

"But I could get a terrible disease from it," I said.

"Or a silver tree," Millie said eagerly.

"Or an eternal potato," Gertla added. "Personally, I would root for the potato."

"Was that a deliberate pun?" I asked with a scowl.

"Hmm? Was what?"

"Never mind." I sighed. "You said you had some advice?"

"Yes. The Hall will certainly buy this, but you'll get a much better price from a Holder. They know their Luck stats, after all, while most of us do not since even a diviner can't discern it unless you have a card in your soul. A Holder with a high Luck stat will likely pay you ten to twenty gold for it." She hesitated. "However, if you happen to be a Holder and know your Luck stat—and it's sufficiently high—I would use it myself. As I presume that only a Holder would have one of these, especially fresh from a Labyrinth, that would be my advice to you. Plant it, and beg the Unity for a potato."

She paused again. "Normally, a reading such as this would cost two silver wands," she said. "Instead, should you choose to sell that to us, we will pay you five gold crowns and waive the fee. However, should you choose to plant it and do so here, allowing me to watch, I will pay you as if we had purchased the item."

"Why would you do that?" I asked curiously.

"Murf," Millie hissed. "Never question the dealer on a pat hand!"

"While that's good advice, and I may choose to repeat it, the answer is simple," Gertla shrugged. "If we purchased it, we would have one of our Holders plant it and observe the results. I would gain the same way if you were to plant it with me watching and answer some questions about yourself and the experience."

"What sort of questions?" I hedged.

"Simple things like your stats and Harmonies, and any information that the Unity gives you about whatever is produced. Assuming, of course, that we all survive the process." She hopped off the chair and stood beside the table. "I will, of course, give you some privacy to discuss it. Obviously, an action that could result in the potential death of you both is a matter of discussion. I will return in five minutes, and should you still be unsure, the offer will remain for up to twelve hours."

She slipped out of the room, and the moment the door closed, Millie turned and looked at me, her face intent. "Murf, you have to do this!" she hissed.

"I don't think I *have* to," I protested.

"Maybe not, but you should! A silver tree, Murf! You could get a silver tree!"

"Or a deadly illness," I said firmly, enunciating each word. "Deadly, Millie!"

"Wouldn't your ability just adapt to it, though? The way it did the poisons?"

"I have no clue. What if it only partially adapts, and I spend the rest of my life fighting the disease?" I shuddered.

"What if you get a tree that sheds gold?" she countered, her voice turning dreamy. "Or that sheds actual golden apples? Do you know how much a golden apple would be worth?"

"Not a clue."

"Neither do I, but a gold crown only weighs about a tenth of an ounce, and an apple would weigh a lot more than that. One gold apple would probably make you rich; with a whole tree, you'd be as wealthy as grandfather!"

"Or I'd be dead from a disease that killed me over the course of a year or two. You keep missing that part."

She frowned. "You're very fixated on the disease, Murf. Are you afraid of getting sick?"

"No. Yes. I..." I sighed, took off my hat, and swiped my fingers through my hair. "When I was young, only twelve, my mother got sick. She was a gambler, like us, but she gave it up when she got pregnant with me. I never knew my father, so we only had each other. The disease took her from me slowly, over a year or so, so I got to watch as she coughed her lungs out and couldn't stand up without losing her breath. When she died..." I fell silent, then shook my head. "So, yeah, I guess I'm a little afraid of that sort of illness, Millie."

"I'm sorry, Murf," the woman said softly. "I don't blame you. It's fine; you don't have to. I can do it."

I looked at her in surprise. "You'd do it?"

"Yes," she shrugged. "It's just a gamble, right? Like drawing to a four-flush, except I'll bet the odds are better."

Guilt surged in me as she spoke. "Do you happen to know your Luck stat?"

"That's personal, Murf. Isn't that what you told Ferdi?" She laughed. "I don't care, though. No, I don't know it, but Ferdi guessed that it was probably in the twenties or thirties since I couldn't bind that lady of cups..."

"Mine's over a hundred," I cut her off with a sigh, and she froze, staring at me.

"It's—it's what?"

"103. Apparently, that's really high."

"That—how unfair is that?" She held her hands up to the air, as if beseeching the Unity. "Seriously, how is that okay?"

"I told you, Millie. The Unity's a massive bitch. There's no point in arguing. It's not remotely fair."

"Easy for you to say. You've got a damn 103." She made a face. "Still, I'm fine doing it. Or we can sell it to them. But Murf, with that kind of luck—imagine what you might get! You're not drawing on a four-flush; you're drawing for a flush run in a deck where half the cards are the one you need, and the rest will give you either a run or a flush!"

"Except that one that'll leave me with nothing," I sighed. "You're asking me to go all-in on a hand with a card I haven't seen yet, Millie. Would you do that in a game?"

"In a real game? No. In one where the dealer stacked the deck in my favor? Absolutely." She took a deep breath, calming down quickly. "I can't tell you what to do, Murf, but I don't think visiting the Sellsword's Hall to find a Holder with high Luck is a good idea. I'll bet those elves that kidnapped us came from there, and they might have friends. If you won't do it, then sell it to the Sages, and we'll still have the gold—which is better than getting attacked by some monster."

We sat in silence for several moments when the door opened and Gertla stepped back inside. "Sorry, I know it hasn't been five minutes, but you stopped talking, so I thought perhaps a decision had been made."

Millie glanced at me, then leaned forward. "Yes, Gertla, we're going to sell..."

"I'll do it," I said heavily, slapping my hat back on my head. "So, how do we do this?"

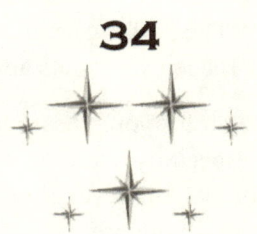

34

"Murf, are you sure?" Millie asked quietly. "I don't want…"

"No, you were right, Millie," I shook my head. "This is just a gamble, and the deck seems pretty stacked in my favor. What kind of gambler would I be if I didn't go all in?"

I knew the answer to that question, of course. I'd be a scared gambler, and fear is a gambler's enemy. Caution is fine; caution is smart, in fact. Knowing when to fold is important. But fear will keep you from taking risks, even ones likely to pay off big, and once a gambler starts listening to fear, it's a slow spiral down into dissolution. A gambler has to be willing to bet it all when he thinks he has it but isn't sure, or he'll always end up losing.

"Very good," Gertla said, her voice perking up as she whipped out a piece of paper and a metal pen. "First, do you have a next of kin or beneficiary you'd like to will the five gold to?" She looked up at us. "You know: in case of the worst?"

"I…" I glanced helplessly at Millie, then back at the halfling as an idea popped into my head. "Actually, yes. If we both die, give my share of the money to Azara."

"Very kind of you, considering she obviously doesn't feel the same way about you both," the halfling said, writing swiftly on the paper. "And you?"

"Royal family, Plutarchy of Deepwater, family accounts, care of the Merchant's Guild," she said promptly.

Gertla looked up at her, her expression both impressed and suddenly cautious. "You—you're a member of the Deepwater royalty?"

"The Plutarch is my grandfather, yes."

"Perhaps you should leave the room, then, Miss," she said respectfully. "If something were to happen to an heir of such a powerful family…"

"I'm not an heir," Millie corrected. "I'm the heir's first cousin, once removed. I'm nowhere near the line of succession."

"Oh. That's fine, then." The halfling scratched on the paper once more, then looked at me. "I'll need your stats and Harmonies, please."

"I can just write them down for you," I said, glancing at Millie. I knew my stats were kind of high, especially some of my Harmonies, and I didn't want to annoy her even more than the revelation about my Luck had. Gertla handed me the paper, and I quickly scratched them down, then returned the sheet to her.

"Hmm. You have decent penmanship. Wide letters, though." She frowned, then gave me a flat look. "I need these numbers to be accurate. Inflating them to impress me will just skew our data."

"Those are accurate," I assured her. "I know. My Luck's a little ridiculous. I swear to you, though, on—on Bardona's spear, those are correct." I wasn't sure if I'd gotten that right, but Ferdi had insisted on it, so hopefully, it would convince the woman.

"As you likely don't practice the traditions of the oath-bound, and neither do I, that vow is meaningless," she scowled, then sighed. "However, I have no choice but to take your word, as I'm not prepared to do a full reading on you to verify the information. Hopefully, you understand the gravity of this situation. If your Luck is truly what you say it is, then this result could greatly affect all our theories on Unity seeds in the future."

"Why?" Millie asked.

"If he has such a high Luck, he's likely in great accord with the Unity. If he then has a poor result, or even a mediocre one, it pokes a large hole in our existing theories. If, on the other hand, he has an exceptional result, it's strong evidence in favor of them."

"If that's just evidence, what would you consider proof?" I asked curiously.

She shrugged. "Truly? Nothing short of the Unity manifesting and saying that yes, we are correct would count as proof. No matter how much supporting evidence we collect, all it says is that we haven't yet found a convincing counterexample, just one of which could destroy the theory." She made a face. "And in fact, the example of the Unity I gave wouldn't be evidence unless we could first prove conclusively that it was the one and only Unity, which we can't."

"It sounds complicated."

"Science is complicated. If it weren't, we'd already understand everything there is to understand." She shrugged again. "And if it were easy, everyone would do it."

She looked down at her paper. "How many cards do you hold?"

"Three."

"All arcana?"

"Yes," I lied easily. I was definitely not about to tell the Sages that I had a damn Cabal in my chest. "Nobles, to be precise."

"Impressive, although that would track with your Luck. We've found that a higher Luck usually leads to people drawing better cards." She paused and tapped her pen against her mouth. "Actually, if we survive this, I may have another proposal for you."

"Does it also pay gold?" Millie asked eagerly.

"It might." She shook her head. "Let's finish this, first. Are you currently experiencing any of the following symptoms: lethargy, chest pain, bowel irregularity, fever, hunger, thirst, internal bleeding, difficulty urinating, or erectile dysfunction?"

"Excuse me, what's that last one?" I asked, honestly confused.

"Erectile dysfunction. Are you having difficulty achieving and maintaining an erection during intercourse?" Millie laughed loudly, and I knew my cheeks were beet red.

"Why do you need to know all that?" I demanded.

"There's a theory that the desires and needs of the individual can affect the outcome of the planting. If that's so, your inability to become physically aroused would likely motivate you to wish for something to aid with that."

"Such as an eternal potato of masculinity," Millie offered with a laugh.

"Something like that, yes. A powerful aphrodisiac, perhaps, or a tree that grows in erotic form to stimulate you."

"An erotic tree? Really?" I scoffed.

"Tall folk have strange tastes," the halfling shrugged. "I try not to judge. So, any symptoms?"

"No. I'm fine."

"Excellent." She gestured toward me. "You may proceed."

I nervously picked up the ball and held it. "Proceed how?"

"It needs to be planted in you, obviously."

"Planted how, though? How does it get in me? There are ways it's definitely not going."

"The same way you place a card in your soul. Place the seed against your bare chest and see what happens. It may help to concentrate on a desired outcome, but that's not certain."

I unbuttoned my shirt and pulled it open. As I bought the orb toward my bare chest, I heard Millie beside me whispering, "Golden apple tree. Golden apple tree!"

To my annoyance, right before it touched my skin, the halfling muttered, "Come on, potato…"

I ignored them both. In my mind, a single mantra repeated itself over and over.

"No deadly illness. No deadly illness. And none of that erecting stuff the halfling was talking about."

I took a deep breath, then pressed the seed against my chest.

The moment it touched my chest, the inflexible sphere softened and ruptured, spilling frigid liquid onto my skin. The temperature of my skin plummeted, going from cool to freezing cold in instants. I hissed and hurled the orb away, but the empty shell of it faded into vapor before it hit the floor, leaving a puddle of thick, clinging liquid stuck to my chest. The cold began to burn, and I gasped in pain. I reached up to try to wipe it off me, but the goopy mess vanished before I could touch it, sinking down into my body.

Ice rushed through my veins, pouring into my heart and flooding my body. My limbs thrashed and curled up in a vain attempt to warm myself, flinging me from my chair. I dimly heard Millie calling my name and felt the pressure of her hands on my body, but my nerves were too numb to feel her touch. The ice rushed up my chest and poured up my neck. My jaw chattered uncontrollably as my lips and tongue went numb. The frozen feeling washed over my eyes and filled my ears, and the world went black and silent. At last, it flooded my brain, and all sensation vanished.

I hung there in blackness for some indeterminate amount of time. There was no more cold, no more heat, no more anything. There was just darkness, and honestly, it was kind of nice. Peaceful, even. No pain, no fear, no stress—just lots and lots of darkness. Sadly, it didn't last long enough before a card shimmered into view, destroying my nice, quiet moment.

I tossed the whole idea of Power out the window instantly. I didn't want the power I'd gotten, much less more of it. If I could, I would have gotten rid of it all and gone back to being regular, old Murf again. It had brought me nothing but unhappiness, pain, and misery. No, Power was out.

Skill didn't seem too bad. I was great at cards, but I could always be better. The problem was, it didn't say skill in what. Would I become a better gambler? Great! A better street sweeper? Less great. A better Holder? Not interested. Again, I didn't even want what I had, much less more of it. The problem was, I was pretty sure that was exactly what I would be getting. The Unity had no real motivation to make me a better gambler, after all, but it seemed to delight in making me a more powerful Holder.

Companionship—actually, that sounded kind of nice. I was alone in the blackness, and while it was kind of comforting, it was also a little lonely. Someone to talk to sounded just about like what I needed. I focused on that, and a new card appeared.

The cold flowed away from my brain as the card vanished, and sensation returned in a rush of light and sound. The ice sucked down into my chest, drawn out of my limbs and shoved into a small ball just behind my heart. That ball rushed up out of me and flowed across my chest, leaving me lying on my back, panting and heaving, luxuriating in the lack of pain and the quickly returning warmth in my limbs.

"Hi, Dad!"

"What the fuck?" My eyes snapped open, and I looked up to see a small, black and white face peering into mine. A tiny animal, maybe half the size of my forearm, stood on my chest, gazing down at me. Its face was triangular shaped, mostly black with a white ring around its pink nose, white marks above its eyes, and white tips on its round ears. It took me a second to recognize that the thing looked like a baby ferret. An adorable baby ferret—that glowed bright blue and had a misty, wavering quality to its translucent form.

And apparently, it had just called me "Dad".

"Murf!" I looked sideways to see Millie kneeling above me, her face tear-streaked and red. "Murf! Are you okay?"

"I'd say yes," I croaked weakly, "but I'd be lying."

"Oh, shit, is it the disease? Are you dying?"

"We're all dying." I took a deep breath, and the ferret moved up and down with my chest. Its presence was a chill pressure on my bare skin; it wasn't unpleasant, but it was odd. "Not today, though. Hopefully. Do you see this, Millie?"

"See what, Murf?" she asked, her voice confused. "Fuck, I'm so sorry! You were screaming, and then you stopped moving, and now…"

"I'm not dying," I cut her off. "For a bit, I kind of wished I was, though." I pointed at my chest. "Can you see this?"

"What? Your chest? Yes, I see your chest, Murf…"

"Do you want them to see me, Dad?" a tiny, adorable little voice said in my brain, somehow bypassing my ears entirely. I decided that whatever the seed had done, it had damaged my brain. I was seeing things and hearing things, and it wouldn't be long before they tossed me into an asylum. Which, really, might not be that bad. I wouldn't have to worry about cards, or Holders, or halflings out for my testicles. Plus, I hear that you get to eat lots of pudding in those places, and I do like pudding.

"Oh!" Millie lurched back away from me, her eyes wide and one hand pressed to her chest. The other, I noted, rested on the dagger hidden in the pocket of her dress. Labyrinth-earned habits didn't die in a day, after all. "What is that?"

"You see it, now?" I sighed, looking back at the ferret. Its form wasn't misty and glowing anymore; it looked like a normal baby ferret, just sitting happily on my chest for some reason. "Can you hear it, too?"

"I—I don't hear anything," she said slowly. "Murf, is that—is that a ferret? Where did it come from?"

"Fascinating!" I turned my head to see Gertla standing a short distance away, writing furiously on her papers. "An actual, living animal! I've never heard of one of those coming from a seed before." She took a step closer and reached out her hand. "Does its fur feel natural? Is it warm? Does it have a heartbeat?"

Instantly, the ferret flashed back to misty blue, and I felt its frosty claws scrabbling against my skin as it climbed under my arm—flowing directly through my shirt as it did.

"I don't like her, Dad!" the tiny voice said in my brain.

"Where did it go?" the halfling asked, her voice disappointed. "Was it only temporary? An unusual result, but not particularly powerful…"

"It's still here," I sighed, lifting up my arm. "It just didn't want to be touched. It's hiding under my arm right now." I forced myself to sit up, and as I did, I felt the animal clamber up my shirt, its chill toes running up my back until it sat on my shoulder. "And now, it's sitting right here."

"Astounding!" the halfling breathed. "It can turn invisible? That's an amazing ability!" She shook her head. "Please, tell me everything you can about the planting."

"Well, first, it hurt like a mother fucker," I said sternly. "It felt like something colder than ice filled my entire body, from my toes to my brain."

"That would explain the initial shivering and screaming," she nodded, writing furiously. "Please, continue."

"When the cold hit my brain, everything went black. I don't really know how long it lasted…" I looked at Millie. "How long was I out?"

"Maybe half a minute," she said quietly.

"I couldn't tell. I couldn't see, hear, or feel anything. A card appeared in my vision, telling me to pick between power, companionship, and skill…"

"An aspect of choice?" Gertla's voice sounded surprised. "Another thing I've never heard of before! Fascinating! And what did you choose?"

"Companionship." I reached up toward the tiny ferret. To my surprise, not only did it not scurry away from my hand, its body felt solid beneath my fingers. I petted it gently, noting that it felt soft, furry, and cold all at the same time, and it pressed its head upward, pushing into my fingers.

"That's nice, Dad. Do that more."

"When I made the choice, all the cold flowed out of me and pooled on my chest—where this little guy appeared. Assuming he's a guy, that is. I don't know how to check on ferrets—or anything that isn't a person, really."

"Male ferrets have exterior penises," the halfling noted absently. "Check beneath it for one. What more can you tell me about it?"

"Just that it can appear and disappear as it wants to—and apparently, it can talk to me. It's calling me 'Dad'." I didn't want to share the part about the animal being part of my soul, or sharing it, or whatever. I'd given the woman plenty of information, enough for her to know that the little guy was special. That was all she really needed.

Millie giggled. "Congratulations, Murf. You're a daddy!"

"He's better behaved than most babies," I shrugged, continuing to pet the little guy.

"Can—can you have him appear again?" she asked. "It looks weird with you petting the air above your shoulder."

"Mind coming back, little guy?" I asked. "Don't worry, I won't let them touch you." The cold beneath my fingers vanished, replaced with the warmth of a normal animal. Millie drew in a surprised breath, both hands flying to her mouth at the same time.

"Oh, Murf, he's *adorable*!" she swooned. "Look at his little face—and his teeny paws! He's so beautiful!"

"I like her, Dad."

"Yeah, me too," I thought with a chuckle.

"Good. Can I play with her?"

I froze. *"Wait, you heard me think that?"*

"Yes. I can hear you. Can I go play with her?"

"Um...I guess, but it's really up to her. I'll ask." I looked at Millie. "He—he says he likes you, and he wants to know if he can play with you."

"Of course, he can," she crooned. "Come here, little…oh!" She yelped as the ferret shifted to his misty form and flowed through the air, turning solid again as he reached her. He scurried across her chest, up her shoulder, and clambered onto her hair. "Wait—he—wow, he's fast! How did he do that?" She winced as the little guy started pawing at her hair. "And he's pulling my hair."

"Be nice, buddy," I chuckled. "You have to ask a woman before you pull her hair."

He clambered down onto her shoulder, and she reached up to pet him, cooing softly at him. His large, black eyes closed as he leaned into her caresses. I didn't blame him. I'd felt those fingers myself, and they were not to be underestimated.

"Does it have any other abilities?" Gertla asked, still scribbling. "Other than becoming invisible and, apparently, insubstantial."

"Not that I know of," I lied. "I think those are pretty good, though, don't you?"

"Extremely, yes." She looked up from her notes with a smile. "You've been quite helpful, and this information will be very useful in our future theories. I'm also naturally relieved that none of us died in the experiment, something that might have been in greater doubt had we used a Holder with lesser Luck." She shook her head. "I'll go get your reward, and as I said, I might have another proposal for you."

"Make sure it pays gold," Millie said firmly.

"That will depend entirely on him. I'll be back in a moment." She turned and left the room, closing the door. The moment she vanished, Milie flung herself onto me, clinging to me tightly.

"Murf, I'm sorry," she whispered in my ear. "I pushed you to do that, and when you fell down and started screaming…" I felt her body shake as she sobbed. "I'm sorry!"

"It was my decision, Millie," I said firmly, stroking her hair gently. "If I didn't want to do it, I wouldn't have." I paused. "Well, if I didn't think it was a good risk, I wouldn't have. I'm glad I did, though. I got this little guy out of it, if nothing else."

She pulled back, sniffling and wiping at her eyes and nose. "He needs a name," she told me.

"What?"

"A name. You can't keep calling him 'little guy'. You don't even know if he's a guy."

"I don't know if he can be a guy. He's not a regular animal, obviously. He might not have any of those parts at all."

"He still needs a name," she insisted. "If you don't give him one, I will."

I looked at the ferret, perched on her shoulder, nuzzling her hair with his nose the same way I'd just been stroking it. "He kind of looks like a 'Charlie' to me," I finally said.

"Why?" she asked, turning her head to look at the ferret.

"I don't know. He just does. What do you think, buddy? You want to be called Charlie?"

"I'm Charlie, Dad. I like it."

"He likes it, so Charlie he is."

We paused as Gertla returned and placed a small pouch on the table. "Here you are. I know we agreed on five gold, but I added another. The data was extraordinary, and quite frankly, I'm immensely grateful. Plus, I'm hoping that the generosity will encourage you to consider my second proposal."

"What is it?" I asked a little wearily. "If you've got another seed, I'm not interested."

"No, of course not. I'm not even sure if planting a second one would work, to be honest, but we certainly don't just have them lying about, waiting for someone to plant them. No, this is a much simpler task, one with far less risk to you—if perhaps a bit more morbid."

"Just spit it out," I sighed.

"Well, every so often, the body of a Holder is brought to us," she explained. "Usually to perform a divination on the corpse to determine what cards it holds and if they can be liberated."

"Can't help you there," I shook my head.

"Of course not, and we need no help making those sorts of determinations. However, if the Holder was a criminal, died in the commission of a criminal act, or simply placed the instructions in their will, the body is given to us, and we are able to draw the cards from it."

"You want Murf to help you draw those cards," Millie guessed. "Because his Luck's so high."

"Precisely. There's significant evidence that the cards you draw from a Holder's body are not always the cards they held. A person with a higher Luck stat can draw better and more powerful cards. If you were willing to do this, we would reward you."

"How much?" I asked.

"Half the difference in the values between the drawn card and expected card," she said promptly. "That will usually work out to at least a gold per two elevated rank per card."

"Three-quarters of the difference," Millie countered. "It's something that only Murf can do, after all, and it's not like you'd be reselling the cards for a profit, would you?"

"Occasionally, yes. I could go as high as sixty percent."

"Seventy, and no lower. I'll bet that even thirty percent of the improved value is a significant amount."

"Shall we meet in the middle at sixty-five?" the halfling sighed.

"I said seventy," Millie shook her head. "Again, this is something only Murf can do—unless you can find someone else with his ridiculous Luck." She reached up and touched the ferret on her shoulder. "I've known Murf for a while, and I can tell you that things like this happening are normal for him. You're probably thinking he'll draw sixes instead of fours, but it'll probably be more like nines and tens—or nobles. Trust me. You'll be happy with thirty percent of the increase."

Gertla's eyes narrowed as they fastened on the ferret, but at last, she nodded. "Very well. Seventy. However, if it's not worth it, we'll simply end the arrangement."

"Fair enough," I agreed, rising to my feet and rebuttoning my shirt. "Well, Millie, I've had quite enough adventure for today. What say we head back, grab a few drinks, and take a nap before the serious gambling starts."

"You're both gamblers?" the halfling asked. "Are you staying at the Hall?"

"Yes, to both," I nodded. "Although we're only in the city for the tournament. We'll be leaving afterward."

She made a face. "That takes some of the value out of our arrangement, but I suppose I did forget to set a termination date. Very well. That makes it easier to send word to you if there's a body that needs your attention."

"We'll see you soon, Gertla," Millie said, taking my arm and half-pulling me toward the door. She leaned close to me. "There's a body that needs your attention right now, after all."

"And that examination is worth more than all the gold in this place," I murmured back quietly with a sly grin.

"I'm certain that you will," the halfling said absently, waving her hand at us with her nose stuck in her notes. Apparently, she's been too engrossed to hear our byplay. "Go and enjoy your copulation."

Oh. She had heard, after all. Well, the least I could do was follow her parting advice.

We exited the Hall without issue, although the elf I'd first spoken to did give us a nervous look as we passed him. No one else gave us a second glance, though, which I suppose I should have realized was a bad thing. After all, how many people in the city were walking around with a baby ferret on their shoulder? That realization didn't hit until we'd stepped outside into the afternoon sun and stood in the sweeping shadows the towering buildings drenched us in.

"Well, that was interesting," I sighed, glancing at the woman. "Charlie, we're..." I paused and looked around. "Wait. Where's Charlie?"

"I—I thought he just went invisible again," Millie said, also looking around vainly. "He was on my shoulder, and then he wasn't. I assumed he went back to you!"

"No," I sighed, tugging the brim of my hat in frustration. "He must still be back in there. Come on, let's go find him."

We turned and headed back toward the doors, but I stopped as a misty, blue figure flowed through the crack between the doors, heading in our direction.

"There he is," I sighed with mingled relief and irritation as the tiny ferret scampered across the stone portico toward us. "Charlie, where were you?"

The ferret scampered up my leg, his icy claws sending shivers down my back, then ran up my chest and leaped across to Millie. The woman let out a small yelp as he appeared on her shoulder, his nose extended out toward her—and a single gold coin clutched in his mouth.

"What—what's this?" she asked as he nudged her chin with the coin.

"Charlie, where did you get that?" I asked with a growing suspicion.

"The nice lady likes these, Dad, so I got one for her. Tell her that it's hers."

"He says you like them, so he found one for you," I sighed, rubbing my forehead. "He wants you to take it."

"For me?" She reached up and slipped the coin from his mouth, holding it in her hand with a growing smile. "Good boy, Charlie! What a good boy!" She reached up and petted his head, and he practically hummed with pleasure as he pressed up against her.

"Don't encourage him, Millie!"

"Why not? You really think that the person he took this from needs it all that badly? No one walks around with gold in their purse unless they can afford to lose it, Murf." She gently grasped the little monster and cradled him in her arms, holding him close to her chest.

"So soft," the animal purred in my thoughts.

"Yeah. They really are soft," I sighed, and Millie blushed a bit, giving me a sideways grin. "Come on. Let's get back to the Hall."

Great. I had a little thief on my hands, one who could turn invisible, flow through cracks, and...

Actually, it really was kind of great, the more I thought about it. In fact, I could think of a thousand ways that Charlie could be really, really useful. I reached over and stroked his soft fur with a finger.

"Good boy, Charlie," I said with a wide smile.

Charlie
Soul Familiar
Abilities: Immaterial, Air Walk,
Ability Leech

35

I told Charlie to hide again before we entered the Hall, but instead of simply going all foggy and blue, he actually climbed down into my chest and slid back inside me. I shuddered a bit as I felt the tiny ball of ice that was my ferret sink down into my chest and settle just below and behind my heart. It wasn't a painful feeling, but it was unnerving. Still, I was glad that he'd vanished when no sooner had we stepped inside than a familiar orc face walked over and stood in front of us, holding up his hand.

"The Guild Master wants to see you," the man who'd fetched me for Jerrick the first time said, his voice gruff. "No, let me say that differently. He insists that you come to his office immediately to speak with him. In person. This instant. At his command."

I grinned at the man. "That was much better," I congratulated him. "You've been practicing for this moment, haven't you?"

He simply grunted and looked at Millie. "He wants you, as well."

"Well, that's flattering, but from what I hear, he's married," she said in a shocked voice. "What would his wife say about that? Still, tell him that I'm appreciative of his interest." I chuckled as she began to walk away, but he moved to block her.

"No. You are ordered to go to the Guild Master's office immediately to speak with him. By the Guild Master himself." He pulled out a piece of paper. "I have it in writing with his signature." The man gave me a hard look. "I think he knows you."

"We go back a while," I agreed with a sigh. I could see ways to weasel out of Jerrick's orders, but if the orc showed me that piece of paper, I was probably screwed. The Guild charter did require me to follow all reasonable orders of a member of the Guild Court, and I knew Jerrick's signature well enough to know if he'd written the note or not. Once I looked at it, I'd have to go see him. I was sure that he'd left me no loopholes. It was easier just to go along.

"Fine. Let's go see what the Guild Master wants. I've got much better and more important things to do today."

"More important than seeing the Guild Master?" the orc scoffed.

"Much more important." I gave Millie a meaningful look that she returned with a ridiculously false shy smile. "And much more fun."

The orc rolled his eyes. "Come with me," he said shortly.

"Hold on, friend, that wasn't an offer for you to join us," I laughed.

"I do have standards, after all," Millie sniffed imperiously.

"What? I..." The orc growled and stomped off, not even trying to reply. That was probably the smartest thing he could have done, really.

Aggie the uptight assistant sat primly at her desk when we arrived, and she fixed me with a cold glare. "Mr. Murf. And you must be Millie. The Guild Master will be with you in a moment. Take a seat."

Millie moved to sit down, but I grabbed her elbow and stopped her. "Are we really going to do this again?" I asked Aggie. "Fine. Tell him that, as ordered, we came to his office to speak to him. He wasn't available. We're going back to my room, and we'll be back in an hour."

"Make it two," Millie suggested. "We might want to bathe afterward." She gave Aggie a suggestive look. "Or during. You know how hot that sort of thing can get, right?"

"Actually," the orc interjected, "the note does say something about waiting..."

"I note I haven't seen," I cut him off, turning toward the door with Millie in tow. "And have no intention to look at, so it doesn't matter." I gave Aggie a hard look. "Or you could just say please."

I—what?" she asked, looking startled.

"Try asking. I'm much nicer to people who are nice to me."

"I..." She stopped and took a deep breath. "Mr. Murf, would you please take a seat? The Guild Master will be with you shortly."

"Of course," I nodded. "See? Isn't that easier?" I let a smile spread across my face once more as I walked to her desk and leaned one hand on it. "Something you should know if you're going to last in this job, Aggie, is that we gamblers tend not to take rules and authority very seriously, and the best of us are usually pretty good at riling people up enough that they can't focus on their cards. Since I'll bet most of the people who come to this office are in a bad mood when they do, you're going to get people taking it out on you all the time."

"And?" she asked primly.

"And if you get angry back, you're going to go gray early." I glanced at her hair. "Well, grayer, and you'll end up with an ulcer or worse. You'll also end up making pissed off people even more unhappy, and that makes the Guild Master's job harder—and if that happens, you aren't going to be here for very long."

Her eyes looked panicked for a moment, and she flicked her gaze toward the closed door to Jerrick's office. She cleared her throat and straightened. "And what would you suggest, Mr. Murf, since you seem to be so knowledgeable?"

"Relax. Don't take this all so seriously. Be polite. And maybe do something with your hair."

"My hair?" She reached up and touched the side of her head. "What's wrong with my hair?"

"Nothing, but as tightly as you've got that pulled back, I'll bet it's giving you a headache. That can't make this job easier. Maybe relax it a bit, or even try doing something nice with it. That would probably put you in a better mood right there." I shrugged. "Up to you, though, really, but if you don't change something, you're not going to be here long."

"Murf!" Jerrick's voice called from the other room. "Get in here!"

"Gotta go," I told Aggie, leaning forward and touching her hand. Her expression had softened from anger to something more thoughtful, and she didn't pull her hand away as I figured she might. I leaned closer to her. "Mind if I make one other suggestion?" I asked in a soft voice.

"I—no, I don't mind. What is it, Mr. Murf?"

"I've found that nothing relaxes me more than a nice roll in the sheets. You should give that a try sometime."

Her face went instantly pink. "Mr. Murf! I—I'm not that kind of woman! Propositioning me like that..." Despite her protestations, she did not, I noticed, remove her hand from under mine.

"While I'm flattered, I'm afraid I'm a little busy right now." I jerked my head toward Jerrick's office. "Shouldn't keep him waiting, after all. However..." I glanced at the orc still standing by the door, whose face quickly grew alarmed and confused. "He probably doesn't have anything to do for the next ten minutes or so."

"Ten minutes?"

"It doesn't take long to be bent over a desk," I shrugged, straightening and taking my hand away. "And you've got a nice one, right here."

"Murf!" Jerrick's voice sounded annoyed, and I flashed the woman a grin.

"Just a suggestion, of course. I just want you to find joy in your work, Aggie, nothing more." As I turned away, I noticed that the woman's eyes darted toward the trapped-looking orc, and while she flushed even brighter, the look she gave him was oddly speculative. I wondered if maybe beneath all the bluster and ice, Aggie was a bit of a demon in the sheets. It wouldn't be the first time I'd seen that.

Murf's Ninth Law: It's always the quiet ones.

Jerrick rose from his desk as Milie and I entered, which confused me for a moment until he gave her a respectful nod.

"Miss Deepwater," he said politely. "Thank you for coming to see me."

"Guild Master," she inclined her head. "It's a pleasure to meet you—and my duty as a member of this Hall, I might add."

"I still appreciate it." He looked at me and pointed to a chair. "Murf. Sit. Now."

"Hi Jerrick," I said amiably as I took one of his chairs and held it for Millie, then settled into one of my own. "Great to see you, too. How's the wife and kids? Seen any good plays lately?"

"Cut the shit, Murf," he growled, sitting back down. "I told you to leave those elves alone."

"No, you suggested it," I shook my head. "That's not the same thing. And I did leave them alone."

"You went to the Royal Lamb, where you knew they were staying." He pointed at Millie. "You used her connections to get inside. And then you both vanished for days. You're telling me that it had nothing to do with those elves?"

"A man can't want to take a beautiful woman out for the fanciest meal in the city?" I asked, feigning a hurt expression. "Jerrick, I feel so bad for your wife…"

"What happened, Murf?" he growled, cutting me off. "Where were you the past few days?"

I shared a look with Millie, who shrugged helplessly in return, then looked at Jerrick with a sigh. "You want the short version, or the long version?"

"Start with the short one. We'll go from there."

"The elves ambushed and kidnapped Millie and me, then tossed us into a Labyrinth called the Ochre Forest. It took us a few days to get out."

He stared at me, his eyes wide and his muzzle hanging slightly open. "Bullshit," he finally said, shaking his head.

"Really, Jerrick. That's exactly what happened. Well, the short version of it."

"No way, Murf. I know a little about the Ochre Forest. There's no way you both could have survived it."

"It really is the truth, Guild Master," Millie assured him.

"Begging your pardon, Miss Deepwater, but it's just not possible," he said adamantly. "Look, I know Murf. I've known him for a long time. He's a decent brawler and okay with a knife, but he's no fighter. He runs from fights."

"It's true," I agreed. "I do tend to do that."

"It seems like a sensible reaction," Millie smiled. "What's the point of fighting, anyway?"

"I happen to agree, but the point is, he's no fighter, and begging your pardon, Miss Deepwater, but I don't think you are, either."

"You might be surprised, Guild Master," she said a bit coolly. "And I prefer Millie, by the way."

"Millie, then." He glared at me. "Tell me the truth, Murf. Consider that an order from the Guild Master."

I grimaced as his words tingled and burned in the center of my chest. That was a command, and the Guild charter was enforcing it. It was simple to obey, but I really hated being compelled like that.

"I did, Jerrick," I said flatly. "That was the truth."

"I…" He turned to Millie. "Tell me exactly what happened to the two of you after entering the Royal Lamb, Miss Deepwater."

Her eyes flashed as the compulsion settled into her, but her face remained calm and unruffled as she spoke. "Well, we were greeted as usual by a felid escort—a male since the card we used to enter is in my name, obviously—then settled in for dinner. I had sparkling wine and lamb in apple glaze; Murf had bourbon and steak. The meal was excellent. We talked for a bit, mostly about my family…"

"Can we skip the trivialities?" he interrupted with a sigh. "Please?"

"But you ordered me to tell you exactly what happened, Guild Master," she protested. "I'm just doing what you said! You really should make up your mind."

He glared at her, then scowled at me. "You've corrupted her," he accused.

"I've certainly done my best," I chuckled. "She was pretty corrupted already, though. She does this thing where she tucks her ankles…"

"Stop!" he said, waving his hands. "Stop!" He took a deep breath, then gave us both a serious look.

"Let me explain what's happening, and then you'll understand how grave the situation is. After the two of you went into the Lamb and disappeared, half the city seems to have gone up in flames, and all those fires are being blamed on me—well, on the Guild, but mostly on me."

"What kind of fires?" I asked cautiously. "Are you being metaphorical, Jerrick, or did the city actually catch on fire?"

"A little of both," he snorted. "Seriously. It's the metaphorical fires I'm worried about, though. You see, Murf, there's been a slew of disappearances all over the city. The Sellsword's Hall reported a half-dozen missing people, all Holders. The Scriveners lost one of their Makers, the people who create Unity cards for them, and they're demanding that the meritocrats take the city apart looking for her." He glanced at Millie. "And the Merchant's Guild was in a minor uproar to hear that a member of the Deepwater family—and of their Guild, I might add—was one of the vanished."

He gave me a frosty look. "Less than an hour after you stepped foot in that place, I had a meritocrat here, bitching at me for not prohibiting you from going near it. Not their messenger or associate; Grodvulf himself stood in my office and chewed me a new asshole. The next morning, the Master of the Merchant's Guild was here doing the same. Then, I got a message from the Sage's Guild that one of their cartomancers had gone missing, and that a divination revealed that you'd visited her just before she vanished.

"Needless to say, none of that reflected well on the Guild," he said heavily. "It reflected so poorly, in fact, that the meritocracy called me to an audience the next day, where I was told in no uncertain terms that the upcoming tournament wouldn't be held here in the Hall, as it always is, but would be in their own audience chamber, where they could keep an eye on things. I, I was told directly, can no longer be trusted to handle something like that if I can't even control and safeguard my own people—never mind the fact that the other Guilds lost people, too."

He slammed a hand down on the desk. "Do you have any idea how much that will cost us in revenue, Murf? What kind of a loss we're taking? Hundreds of crowns, minimum! I'd planned our whole budget around that income, and without it, we're fucked." He glared at me. "So, tell me, Murf. Where the fuck were you two, and why did you do exactly what I asked you not to?"

"Damn," I said, shaking my head. "That—I'm sorry, Jerrick. That's a lot to have to deal with. I told you the truth, though. We've been in a Labyrinth for the past few days. I'm pretty sure that's where everyone's disappeared to, too." He opened his mouth to protest, but I held up a hand. "Hold on, now. You asked me a question, and I'm going to answer it. You got the short version. Here's the longer one."

I quickly went over the events of the last few days, leaving out only the fact that Millie and I were Holders. I upsold Ferdi's skills and abilities and mainly suggested that those had seen us through the Forest, along with Azara's card skills. I did my best to give the impression that Millie and I had only helped here and there, just enough to be considered useful and not left behind. I did mention the Shadow Man, though, and the Holders he'd employed.

"My guess, Jerrick," I finished, "is that Shadow Man is the root of your problems. He thinks that there's an untouched Labyrinth south of the city, and he's trying to create a team to take it. He wants them to be as strong as possible, so he probably took those Holders and that Maker for their cards. He might have used some of the Holders to replace his losses, as well."

He looked at Millie. "How accurate is that story?" he asked her in a tired voice.

"Fairly, Guild Master. I wasn't awake for part of his meeting with the Shadow Man, and I was dazed from the lightning for the rest, so I can't tell you about that, but the gist is all true. Those two elves ambushed us in our room at the Lamb, knocked us out with a card, interrogated Murf, then tossed us into that Labyrinth along with Ferdi and Azara when Murf didn't know what he wanted. We fought our way out—well, Ferdi did most of the fighting—and came back to the city."

"Why not go to the Watch?" he demanded. "Or me?"

"And say what, Jerrick?" I laughed. "You didn't believe me even after you compelled me to tell the truth—which was a dick move, by the way, and I'll be remembering that."

He winced. "Sorry about that. To both of you. I'm just desperate. We need that tournament, Murf."

"Then insist on it, Guild Master," Millie shrugged.

"It's not quite that simple, Miss Deepwater."

"Millie, please. And yes, it is." She leaned forward. "In fact, really, the Meritocracy doesn't have much choice."

"What do you mean?" he asked in confusion.

"The city isn't holding a tournament, Guild Master. The Guild is. We're providing the cards, the chips, the tables, the dealers. We're the only ones who can. The Meritocracy doesn't have any of those, and even if they stripped every non-Guild gambling den in the city to get them, who's going to trust a dealer from a dive near the waterfront? One who wasn't good enough or honest enough to get Guild certification?" She shook her head. "No one reputable."

"Plus, all the top gamblers are part of the Guild," I added. "If you told them what was happening, they'd drop out. I know I would. Without them, there's no draw, no crowds, and no money."

"And I'm fairly sure the Guild is staking the prize," she finished smugly. "No prize, no tournament." She leaned forward and tapped a fingernail forcefully on the table. "You've got all the bargaining power, here, Guild Master. Without the Guild's cooperation, there's no tournament, and they can't force you to cooperate."

"Tell them where to stick it, then ignore them," I chuckled.

"I…" Jerrick stared at the woman, his eyes wide, then groaned and rubbed his face. "I need sleep. How did I not see that? You're right, Miss Deepwater. I simply have to tell them that the tournament will be held here, period. What can they do?"

"Well, technically, they could lock down the city so that no one can get in," I pointed out. "Or place the Watch around the Hall, so that no one can get inside."

He glared at me, then made a face. "You're right. They could. Which means I can't just tell them where to stick it. I'll probably have to make a concession or two. Maybe let them station some guards in the place, or have the Sage's Guild run a divination every so often to make sure it's safe."

"Just make sure they pay for that," Millie said. "This is something they want, after all, not something you need. If they want it, they have to pay for it."

"Miss Deepwater, I can't thank you enough," Jerrick sighed.

"Seriously, Guild Master, please call me Millie," she said a bit exasperatedly. "I really prefer not to use my family name."

"Millie, then." He glanced at me. "You're too good for this one, you know. I could tell you some stories about the women he's been with in the past—including that orc grandmother."

"Grandmother?" she repeated, turning and giving me an arch look. "Really?"

I shrugged. "I was young, she was lonely—and very experienced. She taught me an awful lot, and older orc women can do some freaky things with those tusks of theirs. Don't knock it until you try it, Jerrick."

"I'll pass, thanks. So, Millie, you ever thought about getting a rank in the Guild? Eegla's great, but I could use another Lieutenant with better bargaining skills."

"I'll consider the offer," she said with a smile. "How does it pay?"

"Poorly. Just like all Guild positions." He gave me a sour look. "By the way, Murf, I owe you."

"Owe me, Jerrick? What do you owe me?"

"I owe you for that prank with the cards. 'Magnificent beast'? My wife yelled at me for two days straight!"

"I don't know what you're talking about, Jerrick," I lied blithely. "However, if I had pulled some sort of prank on you, it would only be fitting payback for waking me up my first morning here."

"I was just doing my job, Murf!"

"Well, I was doing something much more pleasant." I gave Millie an arch grin.

"He did interrupt us, didn't he?" she smiled back. "Twice, now."

"Twice?" Jerrick asked.

"Did you think we came back here early for the atmosphere, Jerrick?" I laughed. "She's right. That's twice. Sounds like you're getting another present from Alina."

"For the Unity's sake, no," he growled. "Or I swear, I'll nominate your ass to the Guild Court, Murf! You know that half the Guild would vote for you just to piss you off. See how much fun you have being a damn Lord, handling all the problems for this whole continent!"

I gasped in mock shock. "Jerrick! You wouldn't!"

"Screw with my marriage and find out," he said. "Now, go on you two. Go do whatever you were going to do. Just do me a favor and stay in the damn Hall until the tournament, okay? Both of you!"

"I suppose we could find ways to occupy ourselves," I shrugged.

"Many, many ways," Millie added.

"Good. Go, and send Aggie in here as you leave. I've got some messages to send."

As we rose and walked toward the door, something he'd said earlier tugged at my curiosity. I stopped and turned back to face him, and Millie paused, looking at me wonderingly.

"Hey, Jerrick."

"Yes, Murf?" he sighed. "How are you going to make my life harder, now?"

"Nothing like that. I just have a question for you. You said that there were actual fires in the city, too. Were there?"

He looked at me, his face puzzled. "Yes. Why?"

"Well, it seems like the kind of thing Shadow Man would do to the warehouse where he interrogated me. You know, burn it down to conceal all evidence. That might be a good place for someone like Eegla to start looking for him."

"Oh. Well, no, nothing like that," he shook his head. "It was down in the southeastern part of the city. A fire broke out in the halfling hold down there. Most of them died, I guess." He shrugged. "Quite the tragedy, really."

I froze and shared a look with Millie, one that she instantly returned. We both understood. We weren't going to be going to the room and staying there until we passed out from exhaustion.

Jerrick was going to be so pissed.

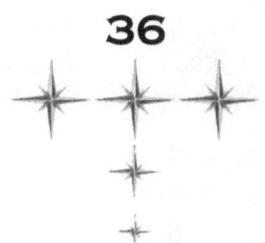

36

"Holy shit," I muttered, staring out at the wreckage of what had once been Baargoth Hold.

We'd smelled the smoke from the hold before we even entered the southeastern section of the city. It was faint but detectable, a lingering scent of burnt wood on the air that made me think of campfires and fireplaces. I had a feeling the reality wouldn't be quite so prosaic. I'd never seen the aftermath of a big building fire before—I hadn't gone back to Clearford's estate after it burned down for obvious reasons—but I'd never heard anyone joyfully reminiscing about one. No one told stories about how they gathered around the burning orphanage to roast sausages on sticks because burnt kid added a special flavor to the meat. Whatever we were going to see, it probably wasn't going to be pretty.

We saw the smoke next. Thin plumes of it rose above the low buildings of the poor section and pooled into wispy clouds. Gray tendrils of it floated up, vanishing into the breeze as they crested the height of the city walls. It didn't blot out the sky or darken the lowering sun or anything, but it did add a faint haze to the air, a hint of gray that would probably only last until the next big rainstorm.

The hold itself didn't look too bad at first glance, at least not from the outside. The walls still stood, as did most of the towers, although a couple had collapsed and crumbled. Ash and soot blackened the stone of the central keep, and smoke poured from the highest windows, creating the thin streams we'd seen before. The gates were warped and hung freely open, barely standing and providing plenty of room for someone to slip inside. The fact that no one currently seemed to be suggested that either some of the halflings were still inside, defending the place—which seemed unlikely—or it had already been as looted as it was going to be.

We walked slowly toward the gates. I didn't really want to see what was inside, and I was guessing Millie didn't, either. I was hoping that it wouldn't be necessary. I wasn't here to see dead halflings, after all. I was here to find Ferdi.

"Ferdi?" I called out, pausing before I could a good look inside. "Ferdi, are you in there?" I waited for several seconds, then repeated my call. Silence was again my only answer.

"She's probably not here, Murf," Millie said quietly. "Maybe she went to the Sellsword's Guild to get help."

"Maybe," I sighed, taking another step forward. "I kind of have to see, though. Feel free to stay back here if you want."

"Yeah, I think I will," she said, wrapping her arms about herself. "I don't really want to see what's in there."

"Neither do I, but I owe it to Ferdi to at least check on her." I walked to the gate and slipped through the gap. I coughed as I entered the short tunnel leading to the second gate; that one was partially blocked, too, and the inside was heavier with smoke. I wrapped my coat over my nose, pulled off my hat, and used it to fan the smoke from my stinging eyes. I took a step, tripped, glanced down to see what I'd stumbled over, and nearly lost my lunch.

I'd never seen someone who'd died in a fire before. I'd seen people die during a fire, obviously—quite a lot of that happened that night at Clearford's—but I'd never seen the aftermath. I assumed I'd see a lot of blackened skeletons with all the flesh and skin burned off, maybe some piles of bones that had mostly turned to ash. I'd mentally prepared myself for that. At least, I thought I had. Fuck, I was wrong.

The body I'd stepped on was still recognizable as a person for the most part. Most of their body was covered in blackened chain armor that had twisted and warped but still seemed more or less intact. Their helmet had fallen off or been taken off and was a scorched mass on the floor, and their leather boots were mostly gone. That left plenty of body exposed to the fire, and the skin and flesh hadn't turned to ash and fallen away. It was still intact, black and stretched tight over their skull, hands, and feet. Their hair was gone, leaving the top of their head shiny and bald, and so were their eyes, leaving behind two empty sockets that gaped at me. Their mouth was locked open in a silent, eternal scream that revealed roasted meat where a tongue should be and shattered, blackened teeth. The whole image honestly reminded me of a pig that had been roasted too long over a fire, its skin blackened but intact, and that image was enough to make my stomach clench and heave.

I won't describe the next minute or two, but suffice it to say, I was shocked that my toenails didn't come up with the remains of my food. The resultant smell mixed with the odors of soot and roasted meat made me vomit all over again, and it took me a bit to get my stomach under control—mostly by emptying it of anything that could possibly come up.

I finally rose to my feet and staggered out through the other door. I had to get out of that tunnel; the smell was making me sick, and the smoke left me lightheaded. The worst part, though, was that the longer I stayed in there, the less both of those seemed to bother me. I wasn't sure if it was a natural response or the Hag adapting me to the situation, but I didn't care. There are some things you shouldn't be used to.

I shoved my way through the gate and froze, staring at the gruesome sight before me. I was suddenly glad that I'd emptied my stomach in the tunnel. If I hadn't, it would definitely have come up then.

"Holy shit," I muttered, wiping my mouth and feeling my stomach tremble and flutter.

Last time I'd been here, the courtyard was a mildly busy place, with halflings walking along it on their way to whatever they were doing. A few had been warriors, but most were just people, men and women living their lives and doing their jobs in the hold.

Now, it was a charnel house, a place of death and horror. Bodies lay splayed before me, far more than I'd seen before. Many still bore the armor and scorched weapons of soldiers, but the vast majority were just naked lumps of blackened meat, the gauzy fabrics they preferred to wear burned to ashes. Most were adult-sized, but the tiny, seared bodies of halfling kids dotted the ash-filled courtyard, most wrapped up in the bodies of mothers or fathers no doubt trying to carry them to safety.

The doors to the main keep hung open, and the pattern of bodies made me think that the fire had started there, and the people rushed out, trying to escape it. They obviously hadn't made it, and I wondered why. The guards behind me could surely have opened the gates—unless, of course, those were being held shut, too. But then, wouldn't the people be piled up against those gates? They looked like they'd fallen as they ran—or been killed as they fled.

I forced myself to walk forward, my eyes scanning the bodies, looking for something out of place. It only took a few seconds to spot a flash of metal on the ground, and I knelt to brush some soot and ashes away to reveal a long, wicked-looking arrowhead, its tip blunted from where it had hit the courtyard. I slipped it into a pocket and rose, looking around more carefully. Just like a person, this place had tells, clues that would reveal what happened. I just had to read them.

"It was my fault."

I spun at the sudden voice, my hand dropping to the saber still strapped beneath my coat, then froze as a dejected, ash-covered figure seemed to appear out of nowhere. I stared at Ferdi as she walked toward me, her armor and face smeared with ashes and her axe dragging behind her, leaving a trail in the soot. Her eyes were hard and bleak, and streaks beneath them showed where she'd been crying earlier. Her shoulders sagged, her head hung low, and her whole body radiated defeat.

"Ferdi," I said with a little relief. "I didn't think I'd find you here."

"Murf." She walked over to stand next to me, her eyes bleak. "I stayed in case anyone escaped. They'd come back here eventually." She looked down at my pocket. "What did you find?"

"Arrowhead," I sighed.

She nodded. "Can you see what happened?"

"Yeah," I sighed. "Looks like the fire started inside, forcing everyone out, and people were waiting for them. They killed them as they came out. Probably from inside the towers up there." I frowned. "What I can't figure out is why it spread. There's nothing out here to burn."

"Card power. Holders did this—and strong ones. Or maybe a really powerful cartomancer, one who specializes in destruction instead of divination like Azara."

I frowned, remembering the goblin cartomancer and elf archer I'd seen while being interrogated. "I think—I think the Shadow Man did this, Ferdi. His Holders did, at least."

"Me, too."

"Why, though?" I looked around. "Why would he do all this? There's no point to it!"

"Does it matter?" she asked, her voice growing angry and rising to a shout. "Look at this, Murf! What reason could there be for something like this? There is none! These were children! They were helpless…" Her voice broke, and her head hung low once more. "And I failed them," she whispered.

"What?" I asked, stunned by her response. "What are you talking about, Ferdi? You weren't even here!"

"Exactly!" she snapped, her head whipping about so her gaze met mine. "I was with you! Helping you get those fucking cards back! Stuck in the damn Labyrinth, not here where I should have been!" Her fist tightened around her axe as she spoke, but I forced myself to stay calm.

"You want to hit me, Ferdi?" I asked her as quietly and evenly as I could. "Will that help? Go ahead. It's not the first time you've hit me for no damn reason."

She hesitated, and I saw a flash of guilt in her eyes as she lowered her axe. "No, Murf. You're not the one I want to hit." She looked around. "I still should have been here."

"What if you had?" I asked, still staying calm. "Could you really have protected all these people? Fought all of Shadow Man's Holders at once?"

"I would have died with them, at least."

"And then no one would remember them. No one would mourn them. They'd just be gone. Would that be better?"

She stared at the bodies for several long, silent seconds. "When the hell did you get wise?" she asked.

"I've been through this, when my mom died," I said simply. "It was an illness, and I was the one who cared for her. I wondered why she got it and I didn't. Why she died and I had to keep on living. After she was gone, I even did my best to join her for a while, did some really dumb shit that should have got me killed but didn't."

I moved until I could look directly into her eyes again. "Until I met a dog-faced old man who told me that sometimes, living is harder than dying, but that my mom would have wanted me to keep going. He was right on both counts. And now, you have to ask yourself the same question I did: would the people who died have wanted you to die with them, or to live?"

"Kewan's blood." She swung her axe back to her back and settled it in place. "Stop talking. It's easier to think of you as selfish and shallow."

"That's because I'm both," I chuckled. "Doesn't mean I can't have my deep moments. Don't worry. That one used them up for at least a year or so."

"Good." She looked around at the bodies. "You asked why, Murf. I think I know."

"What do you mean? You know why Shadow Man did this?"

"Yes." She gestured at the corpses. "When I first found this, after I realized no one survived, I went around to the bodies, checking for cards."

"Cards?" I asked, startled. "You mean, Unity cards? There were Holders here? I thought you were the only one."

"I was the only oath-bound. A few of the others were Holders. Every hold has some to help defend it, especially in a city like this." She shook her head. "None of the corpses had any."

"They claimed them?"

"That was my first thought, too, but I don't think so. The body of a Holder that's had its cards taken feels different. There's an emptiness inside it that another Holder can feel, like a wound that won't heal. None of these felt like that."

"Maybe they didn't make it out. If the fire started inside, maybe that's where Shadow Man's Holders first attacked, and your people fought them to give everyone else a chance to escape."

Her face turned thoughtful. "That's possible, I suppose." She made a face. "There's no way to know, though, not for several days, at least. The inside is too smoke-filled to enter. I've tried a few times, and I never make it far before I have to turn back." She gave me a curious look. "What about you? Think your ability would let you adapt to the smoke in there?"

"I have no clue," I admitted. "But I'm pretty sure that I still need to breathe, Ferdi. At best, I might last a little longer than you did."

"Then we have to wait to see—but I don't think that's what happened. At least one of them would have gotten out, and I would have found their body." She shook her head. "No. I think they were taken, the same as we were. Shadow Man wants their cards."

"What would be the point of that? Why not just kill them?"

"You've drawn cards from someone, Murf. You know that it's a chancy thing at best. You don't usually get all of the person's cards, and what you get might not be what they had. In your case, it was better, but usually, it means you won't get their best cards."

She gave me a grave look. "The one sure way to get someone's cards is to force them to take them out. You'll get everything but their hole card that way, and they'll always pull what they actually have. Then, you kill them and try for their hole card. It gives you the best chances of getting all their cards."

I didn't need to ask how you could convince someone to pull out their own cards. I assumed that if you gave someone enough pain for long enough, they'd do just about anything to make it stop. If Ferdi was right, her people were probably being tortured for their cards as we spoke. In fact, with what she'd just told me, a lot of what Jerrick had said earlier suddenly made sense.

"I think you might be right, Ferdi. And I think it's even worse than that." She looked at me, and I shrugged. "They weren't the only ones who disappeared from the city while we were gone. Some Holders went missing from the Sellsword's Hall, I guess, and a Maker vanished from the Scribblers. I thought that Shadow Man took them to boost his people with extra cards for the Labyrinth he's sending them into but now..." I frowned. "Could they even use all those cards?"

"No," she shook her head instantly. "At least, it's not likely. Most Holders are like your human friend; they can bind three, maybe four cards, five if they've got great Harmony with it. Even if they rank up a lot, that number won't usually rise much higher than six or seven cards. You've gotta train your whole life to be able to get ten or more."

"Still, that's a lot of spaces for extra cards," I pointed out.

"But no Holder worth a damn goes around with a ton of unfilled spots in their deck. You fill those spots, even if it's not with the best possible cards, then replace them out as you find better ones. Maybe you leave a spot or two open, especially if you can put the right card in there to get a good stack, but for the most part, you keep your deck as full as possible. After all, you never know which ability is going to save your life, and even a weak, uncertain power is better than none."

"So, at best, Shadow Man gets these cards and lets his Holders swap them around to improve their decks." I frowned. "That doesn't sound like enough reason to piss off two Guilds and kill everyone here. I mean, no reason's good enough for that, but that one's not even good enough for a deluded villain bent on world domination."

"What are you talking about?" she sighed.

"Come on, haven't you read the stories? Some guy—or girl, I guess—has a plan to take over the whole world, and because they think they'll make the world better by doing it, they can justify anything. Flatten a Guild Hall? Awaken a sleeping monster? Fart in church? It's all good because the ends justify the means."

"That's stupid, Murf. Ends and means are separate. One can't justify the other."

"So, if I could somehow go back to when Shadow Man was a baby and stab him in his cradle to keep this from happening?" I asked. "You're saying that end wouldn't justify those means?"

"There's nothing to justify. You killed someone evil. Those are perfectly good means."

"He probably wasn't an evil baby, Ferdi."

"All babies are a little evil, Murf. They smell, too."

As I struggled to find a reply to that that wasn't hopelessly inane, a terrified-sounding scream rang out in the air, and we both spun to face the sound.

"What was that?" Ferdi asked curiously, but I knew. I swore and raced toward the gate.

That had been Millie, and I'd never heard her scream like that before.

37

I held my breath as I rushed through the twin gates and burst back onto the street. As I'd guessed, Millie stood there, and she wasn't alone. A familiar human woman stood behind her, dressed in loose, gray clothing, a soft mask concealing her eyes and a hood hiding her hair and shadowing her features. The woman stood behind Millie, a gleaming blade pressed against the redhead's throat, while her other hand was hidden by Millie's body but seemed to be pressed against the gambler. Millie's body was taut and trembling, her face pale and her eyes wide as she stared at me with tears streaming down her face.

"No closer!" the assassin snapped as I ran into view. Her hidden arm tensed, and Millie cried out in sudden pain, jerking away from the woman's hand but stopping when the knife at her throat pulled her back. "The knife I've got in her won't kill her, at least not right away, but it'll hurt like hell." She looked around. "Where's the halfling?"

"What halfling?" I asked, feigning confusion.

"The one you were just talking to," the assassin growled, rolling her eyes. "I'm not deaf."

"I'm here." I looked back to see Ferdi standing atop the wall behind me, her axe resting on one shoulder.

"Very dramatic," the assassin said drily. "Now, drop that axe. I don't know how the hell you all survived the Ochre Forest, but it means you must have some great cards..."

"No," the halfling replied coldly.

The assassin's arm shifted, and Millie's groan turned into another scream that ripped at my heart and stirred my anger. I forced myself to stay calm, though. Getting pissed wouldn't help anyone.

"I can hurt her all day," the woman said coldly. "And I can kill her before you can get off that wall."

"So?" Ferdi leaped down and landed lightly on the street. "Kill her. I don't care. I don't even like her."

"Y-you don't?" Millie gasped.

"Shut it," the assassin growled, twisting her arm so Millie screamed again. "Not another step, halfling."

"Or what? You'll torture her? Go ahead. While you're busy with that, I'm going to chop your feet off so you can't run. Then, it'll be my turn to see how much I can hurt you until you tell me who did this and where I can find them." She took another step forward.

At first, I thought Ferdi was bluffing, but a quick look at her changed my mind. She was serious. She didn't care what happened to Millie. At least, compared to the chance to find out who attacked her hold, Millie's life didn't matter much. The halfling was about to attack, and if she did, Millie would die—and the assassin might just get away.

The problem was, I wasn't sure what I could do about it. My ability might make it harder for the assassin to escape, but she'd definitely feel it as soon as it started working on her. She'd probably kill Millie at that point and run, hoping to escape whatever ability was at work on her. I had another ability, but I'd never used it, and I wasn't sure how quickly it would work or how powerful it would be. Could I calm everyone down, or would the danger and hatred here overcome my ability? Could I make everyone tired, so the assassin didn't notice my other ability? Did "sleepy" even count as an emotion, for that matter? I didn't know, and playing around with it now felt like drawing to an inside run with Millie's life on the line.

Ferdi took another step, and I realized I didn't have time to think. If I was going to do this, I was going with an emotion I knew well, and one that I was sure I could generate in someone. I'd rather draw for a flush than a run, after all. I grabbed hold of the lady in my chest, squeezing the cards. At the same time, I turned my thoughts inward. *"Charlie?"* I asked silently.

"Yes, Dad?"

I sighed in relief at the ferret's voice. I wasn't sure if I could communicate with him when he was inside me, or if he'd be sleeping or something. Apparently, he'd just been resting a bit.

"I need you to come out, buddy. Stay invisible, though."

"Okay."

I had to fight to keep my expression calm as a surge of ice rolled out of my chest and flowed up my shoulder almost painfully. A moment later, I felt tiny, icy claws against my skin as Charlie scrambled up my shoulder.

To my surprise, the assassin's eyes narrowed, and she peered at me as if looking for something. Could she see Charlie? Or did she sense him somehow? If she did, my plan might not work. After a second, she blinked rapidly to clear her vision, then seemed to relax, although suspicion still filled her gaze. I held in a sigh of relief. She couldn't see Charlie, but somehow, she'd sensed his presence. That—that, I could work with.

I tensed my grip on the cards in my chest, squeezed, and let some fly. I tried to aim them, but my inexpert grip slipped, and they sprayed out wildly. That would have to do. Hopefully, this worked the way I thought it should.

"Hold on a second," I said placatingly as the power flowed out and washed over the trio almost delicately. "There's no need for anybody to die, here." As I spoke, I sent a mental message to Charlie, who responded instantly.

"You're right," the assassin hissed, still looking around as if searching for something. "As long as you follow my directions, no one has to die. Both of you, put down your weapons, turn around, and get on your knees."

"And then what?" I asked.

She stared at me. "What?"

"Exactly. Then what?"

"What do you mean?"

"After we get down on our knees—first time I've had a woman say that to me, by the way; it's usually the other way around—then what do we do?"

"Whatever I tell you." She jerked her arm again, and Millie hissed in pain, but the movement wasn't as vicious as the last one had been, and Millie recovered quickly. "Or she dies!"

"No need for that. I'm agreeing to do what you said. Turn around, knees, no weapons. Got it. But then what? I assume you want to tie us up or something. How can you do that without letting go of Millie? And once you do, what's stopping Ferdi, here…" I gestured at the halfling. "…from whacking off an ankle or two?"

"I—do what I said!" the woman snapped. "Now!"

"I am. Really, I'm just about to. I just don't want to make any mistakes, here." I turned halfway around, facing back toward the gate. "So, we put down our weapons, kneel, and then—tie ourselves up? Tie each other up? I don't think that'll work."

"Murf, what in Kewan's blood are you babbling about?" Ferdi growled.

"Well, you heard what she said, Ferdi. We're supposed to kneel down facing away from her, right? But then, what's she going to do? It doesn't make any sense!"

The halfling lowered her axe, her gaze troubled. "You're right," she said slowly. "It really doesn't." She looked up at the assassin. "Did you think this through?"

"He's got a point," Millie gasped. "What's supposed to happen next, here?"

"I—just put down the weapons!" the woman said, her voice desperate and slightly uncertain. "Once you don't have those, I'm not worried about you!"

"You should be. I'm just as dangerous without my axe as with it," Ferdi said ominously.

"She really is," I agreed, tapping my chin thoughtfully and taking a step or two toward the woman. "You know what might work better? If you put down your weapons, instead." As I approached, she tensed, but she didn't yank on the knife. Instead, she looked at me like I was speaking gibberish.

"I—what? I'm not…"

"If you did, you could show us what you're planning," I said reasonably and walking even closer. "Then, we'd know, and we'd stop bothering you about it."

"I—wait…" Confusion flowed through the woman's eyes as she looked back and forth between Ferdi and me. "Hold on a second! Let me think! Stop moving!"

"Look, obviously, you didn't plan this well," I sighed, shaking my head and walking slowly toward her. "Maybe you should go back, think it through a bit more, then try again a little later. We'll wait for you. Won't we?"

"I…" Ferdi blinked a few times and shook her head. "I suppose we could."

"I'd like to lie down, if that's okay," Millie said weakly.

"You should let her lie down," I suggested to the assassin. "Or at least, get that ferret off your hand."

"I—what?" The woman's eyes suddenly snapped wide as Charlie popped into view on her visible forearm. He lunged upward instantly, snarling adorably as his small teeth ripped at the hand holding the dagger to Millie's throat. The assassin shouted in pain and shock and flung her arm aside, hurling Charlie from her. The little ferret shifted into insubstantiality as he flew, and I hoped that meant he'd be okay, but I didn't have time to worry about that.

In the moment that the assassin's hand left Milie's throat, I dropped my power, darted forward, and grabbed the front of the redhead's dress, yanking hard and pulling her away from the other woman's grip. She screamed as she stumbled forward, falling past me. I hoped she would be okay, too, but again, I had other concerns. The assassin's eyes were starting to clear, and once she regained her senses, she'd probably either run away or try to kill us. Before she could gather herself, I lashed out with my foot, slamming it into her stomach. She folded around the blow, which lifted her into the air and hurled her backward.

Confusion for the win. Fear wasn't really my thing, but confusion? I was an expert at sowing that in people. About the only emotion I was better at creating was irritation. Well, irritation and a healthy bit of lust, but that felt like it would be vastly inappropriate at that moment. The confusion I'd projected had been just enough to distract the woman, so she didn't notice Charlie sneaking up on her.

Before the woman even hit the ground, Ferdi slammed into her. The halfling crashed into the assassin like a raging bull, hurling her to the ground. The hooded woman slashed with her knife, but Ferdi took the strike on her armor and responded with a fist to the woman's masked face. The assassin's head slammed into the stones with a loud crack, and Ferdi's second fist crashed into her chin, dazing her. A third blow struck her forehead, and her body fell limp as her eyes glazed over.

"See what happens in a fair fight," the halfling grumbled, flipping the woman onto her face and yanking her arms behind her back. Ferdi grabbed both of the woman's wrists, twisted her arms until they were straight, then planted a foot in the middle of the woman's back and yanked, hard. I winced as both shoulders dislocated with two muffled pops, then watched as Ferdi grabbed each of the woman's ankles and twisted them until they broke. The woman stirred as the first shattered, then came awake with a scream as the second did. Ferdi flipped her back over and grabbed her fallen knife, slipping it under the woman's shirt and yanking upwards, cutting the fabric.

"What are you doing?" I asked the halfling with mingled curiosity and revulsion.

"Searching her. She's probably got cards, more weapons, maybe even some poison on her. Easiest way to find out is to strip her."

"You could just pat her down, Ferdi."

"I could. I won't."

I turned away from the warrior and hurried over to Millie, who lay on her stomach, panting and moaning, barely conscious. A slowly widening red splotch stained the back of her dress on the right side. I dropped beside her, yanking off my jacket and pulling off my shirt. I reached down and ripped open the hole in Millie's dress, exposing a deep, jagged wound in her pale skin.

"What are *you* doing?" Ferdi asked. "This isn't the time for that sort of thing, Murf. She's bleeding."

"I know," I said, folding up the shirt into a pad. I hesitated for only a moment before accepting that I'd probably lost another shirt, then pressed it onto Millie's wound. The woman moaned again and flinched away, but I held her in place. I needed to get the bleeding stopped, and this was the only way I knew how.

"Oh. That's more appropriate." I heard her rustling for a bit. "Ah. Figured she'd have one. Here, try this." I looked over and saw Ferdi holding a card in her fingers. She flipped it toward me, and it landed a few feet away. I paused, torn between keeping the pressure on Millie's wound or fetching the card. Before I could move, though, Charlie's blue-misted form swept over the ground, scooping up the card in his little teeth. He pattered swiftly to me and climbed on Millie's back, setting the card on her gently.

"For the nice lady, Dad," he said quietly.

"I'm glad you're okay, Charlie," I said with quiet relief. *"And thanks."* I used one hand to flip over the card, revealing an ace of coins. I looked at Ferdi. "She could use this for her deck, but..."

"Basic healing card. It's why I wanted to search her. Most Holders keep a loose one on them just in case. I don't want her healing herself." She didn't look up as she tore the clothing from the writhing, muttering assassin, not even trying to be gentle to her injured shoulders or legs. She reached down and slapped the woman across the face, hard. "Quiet! This is going to happen. You're just making it take longer." As she stripped the last of the woman's clothing away, her hand reached down between the woman's legs and slipped between her thighs.

"Ferdi!" I said, a little taken aback.

"What? Women sometimes hide things here, Murf." She held up her hand, displaying a slim, leather packet about six inches long and the width of my pinky. "See? Like this. Lockpicks. Now, let's check the other place..."

I turned away hurriedly, ignoring the grunted protests behind me as I picked up the card Ferdi had given me, slipped it under the compress, and channeled a bit of energy into it. Millie moaned again, but I ignored her and poured more energy into the card. I kept at it for a minute or so, until Millie's moans fell away to deep, panting breaths. I gently lifted the compress and sighed as I saw the wound scabbed over.

"Keep that going," Ferdi advised. "She's probably got a torn kidney and is bleeding inside. You'll want to stop that if you don't want her to die."

I set the card back down and again channeled energy into it, aware as I did that I couldn't do this forever. I wasn't Azara, able to channel power into cards for an hour or more if I had to. I could maybe last a few minutes, and that was pushing it. Hopefully, it would be enough.

My energy slowly flagged as the minutes passed, but I grimly kept shoving what I could into the card. My head pounded, and my fingers trembled with weakness. I felt faintly dizzy and light-headed, and that feeling grew as time crept onward. The energy came in stuttering spurts, but I kept going.

"That should be good." I almost fainted with relief at Ferdi's words, and I gratefully pulled my hand away from the card. "Her cards should heal the rest on their own."

"Thank the…" I tried to rise to my feet, but my legs folded beneath me, and I sank to the ground. The world seemed dim and distant, and as I dropped into unconsciousness, a thought popped into my head.

"Huh. I did faint with relief after all. I didn't know that was…"

38

I groaned as the comforting gray blanket that had wrapped itself around my brain rolled back. Light spilled into my closed eyes, and muffled sounds banged on my ears. Ice covered my chest, and something poked at my back irritatingly. I slowly pulled open my eyes, which stuck together as if they'd been glued shut, and blinked several times, eventually yawning to make my eyes water and clean them out a bit. I sat up, and the cold feeling slid up my chest to my shoulder, reaching out to touch my face. A blue-glowing, black-and-white head popped up in front of me, and I jumped as my brain finally started working again.

"Charlie!" I gasped. "Shit, you startled me!"

"Sorry, Dad. I didn't mean to." The guilt in that tiny voice tugged at my heart, and I reached up and petted his soft, little head.

"It's fine, buddy. It just surprised me, that's all. It didn't hurt me. No big deal." I stretched and looked around, then froze as I realized where I was. The walls were dark and covered with images of cards and ravens; the light was dim from a covered lamp overhead; a large, low table filled the center of the room, covered with black felt to keep the layouts on it from slipping.

"Azara's," I muttered, reaching down and pulling a single black feather off the couch on which I'd been lying.

"Good. You haven't broken your mind completely." I glanced up as the door to the back opened, and the woman in question appeared, carrying a wooden tray with a clay goblet and a hunk of bread on it. "Although you certainly made a valiant attempt. I'd welcome you here, but honestly, I'm not that happy with you right now."

"Nice to see you, too," I grinned.

"It's not that it's unpleasant having you here again, Murf—well, it is, but not as much as it was." She set the tray on her table and picked up the mug, walking over to stand in front of me. "It's the method of your arrival I'm not happy about. Dragged here in the back of a cart by that halfling, with a crippled, naked woman, your little slut nearly bled out…"

"Hey!" I protested, then winced as the sound and effort made my head pound.

"And you obviously suffering from magical overexertion," she pressed on. "Now, you wake up, and you're talking to someone who isn't here—and petting the air." She frowned. "Perhaps I was hasty in my judgment about your mind."

I sighed and lowered my hand. "Ferdi brought us here?" I asked, my brain still feeling foggy. "Why?"

"Because I can heal the slut better than you—and because she knew I would be able to treat you." She handed me the mug. "Drink this."

"Is it poison?" I asked hopefully, taking a sip and wincing. The drink, whatever it was, had a strong, astringent taste to it.

"In sufficient quantities, it is, yes," she said, pulling over a chair and sitting in front of me. I gave her a cautious look, and she rolled her eyes. "Murf, you've been unconscious for the past three hours on my couch. If I wanted you dead, there would have been simpler ways than poison."

"True." I took another sip and made a face. "So, what is this?"

"A tonic to help with your recovery." She reached out and touched my face, lifting each of my eyelids in turn and peering into them. "You're badly dehydrated, you've overtaxed your magical faculties, and you drained quite a bit of your body's energy reserves. Keep drinking it."

I sighed and took another sip. "Does it have to taste this bad?" I asked plaintively.

"No, probably not. I could have added some honey to it. However, if you enjoy it, you might be stupid enough to try this again just for the medicine." She leaned back, shaking her head. "It looks like you've avoided brain damage, at least. You always were lucky, Murf."

I choked on the sip I was taking, making some of the liquid spray up my nose. Trust me, that's not the best place for medicine to go. I sneezed twice, coughed again, and finally caught my breath to find Azara looking at me without even trying to conceal her amusement—and disapproval.

"Yes, brain damage," she said, clearly enunciating each word. "As in, something that your body may never heal. That sort of brain damage."

"I could have gotten brain damage? How?"

"How do you think you control magical energies, Murf?" she asked in an exasperated voice, reaching up to tap my forehead with a sharp, black fingernail. "Your *brain*. When you overdo it, you overwork that part of your brain. Cartomancers have had blood vessels explode in their head doing what you did. They've lost the ability to talk, the movement in part of their face, even the ability to walk and feed themselves."

"You never warned me about that when you taught me how to do this!"

"Because usually, it's only a danger for cartomancers. If we set up a tableau that's too powerful for us, it can suck our energy out faster than we can control it. Most normal people don't do that with a single card!" She leaned closer. "They don't because their body warns them to stop! Their head hurts; they feel dizzy and sick; their muscles start to shake. They notice those things and think, 'Hey, maybe this isn't a *good idea!*'"

She was half-shouting by the end of her sentence, but something she'd said clicked in my head. "Wait a second," I said slowly. "Is that what happened to you when you first made that shelter in the Labyrinth? Were you risking brain damage, Azara?"

She sniffed and leaned back, looking everywhere but my eyes. "Perhaps."

"So, you did the same thing I did!" I let out a snort of laughter. "The ace calling the two low!"

"It's not the same!" she insisted. "I weighed the risk against the odds of us lasting another few hours without it and decided it was acceptable. You were just being an idiot!"

"I was trying to save Millie's life," I corrected quietly. "I didn't know what it might do to me, obviously, but I was trying to keep her from bleeding to death from a torn kidney."

"Hmph. Well, she didn't. She did lose a fair bit of blood, though, and while that ace you used kept her alive, it didn't do her any great favors. Next time, use a six, instead."

"I didn't have a six."

"Then get one or find one and keep it with you. It's much better for healing. The concept of an ace is 'improvement'; using it accelerated her body's healing, but it also created scar tissue. Sixes represent 'control'. With one, you can actually guide the healing process to minimize things like scarring and clotting."

"Maybe you can. You're smarter than me, though. I wouldn't know where to start. So, is that what you used?"

"Of course not. I used a lady. Ladies are all about support, nurturing, comfort, and manipulation. I used it to essentially reset her body to its ideal state." She shook her head. "She'd picked up any number of small, lingering injuries in the Labyrinth that her cards wouldn't heal, and I repaired those." She glared at me. "Do not try that yourself! You don't have the skills for it or the energy reserves. You're likely to kill both you and the person you're hoping to help!"

"Couldn't you do that to fix my headache?"

She gave me a withering look. "Your headache is a result of too much magical energy moving through your brain, Murf. How would adding the rather substantial power flows of a noble arcana to that help?"

I sighed. Part of me thought that she hadn't bothered to heal my headache because she enjoyed my suffering, but I suppose I should have known better. Azara never did anything halfway. If she let us into her home, she'd have done whatever she could to help. If she didn't want to help, she'd have turned us away, Ferdi or no Ferdi.

I looked around the shop as I sipped the drink she'd given me. I was done with deep matters. It was time for inane banter. "How's business going?"

"There is no business, at least not at the moment," she said shortly.

"Why not?" I asked with a frown. "Is the Sage's Guild giving you trouble again? I actually have a contact there now: a halfling named Gertla."

Her eyebrows shot up. "Gertla? Senior Sage Gertla? And what, pray tell, did you do, say, or have to interest one of the top five Sages in this entire city?"

"Actually, I was going to come by tomorrow to tell you about that." I reached into my purse and pulled out a gold coin, handing it to her. "It turns out, the drop I found right before the guardian attacked us was worth quite a bit. This is your share."

She stared at the coin, her eyes hungry for it but her face clearly suspicious. "What was it, Murf?" she asked. "What was worth four gold crowns? Nothing we found except the cards would be, and if you sold her a card, she significantly underpaid you."

"It was a seed of some kind."

Her eyes grew wide, and her face paled. "A Unity seed?" she gasped.

"Yeah, one of those."

"And you simply sold it to her?" Her face grew angry, and her hands clenched around her dress, twisting it around. "She allowed you to? With your Luck—that's an outrage! I'll have her before the Guild Master for this…"

"No, no, nothing like that!" I said hastily. "She paid me to plant it in front of her! She gave us the gold, and in return, she got to ask me some questions, watch it planted, and see the result. That's all!"

She took a deep breath, but her eyes still flashed fire. "You should have called me!" she snapped. "Planting a seed without me present—it could have killed you, Murf!"

"And you could have stopped it?" I asked dubiously.

"Of course not, but I could have divined the likely outcomes. Gertla is an excellent scholar, but she's a fair diviner at best. I'm much better, and I could have warned you if the cards suggested danger, so you could have avoided it!"

"I—actually, Azara, you're right. It would have been smarter to bring you, wouldn't it?"

"Yes, it would have!" She sniffed slightly, but I saw the glint in her eyes that said that she approved of my response. "So, what did you grow?"

"Oh, this little guy." I glanced at my shoulder. "Charlie, can you show yourself to Azara?"

Azara hissed and scooted back as the ferret faded into view. "What—what is that, Murf?" she asked in a raspy voice. "Why is it attached to your soul?"

"*He* is named Charlie. And he's a ferret, Azara. Haven't you ever seen one before?"

"That thing is no more a ferret than you're a saint," she snapped. "What is it?"

"*I don't like her, Dad,*" Charlie said, fading back into invisibility. "*She's angry with me.*"

"*She's just nervous, Charlie. She's never seen anything like you before, and she gets nervous about things she doesn't understand.*" I turned my focus to Azara. "He's called a soul familiar. The seed grew him. He can turn invisible, pass through small spaces, and hide inside me when necessary." I reached up to pet him again. "He also gets upset when people yell at him, you know."

"I've never heard of such a thing." Her anger seemed to be fading, replaced by her natural curiosity. Her head cocked to the side in that oddly birdlike fashion she so often displayed when something interested her, and she leaned forward. "Wait—does it speak to you?"

"All the time," I nodded.

"Fascinating." The last traces of hostility slid away from her voice as she reached into her vest and pulled out a pack of cards, quickly shuffling through them. "A projection of your soul, given physical form and intellect! Was Gertla familiar with it?"

"Nope. Said she'd never heard of anything like it before. Of course, I didn't tell her as much as I told you."

"Smart of you. Gertla may seem harmless, but she's as dangerous as your friend Ferdi in her own way. She believes in the pursuit of knowledge with almost as much fervor as an oath-bound, and she'll do just about anything to learn more. I'm surprised she let you leave with that thing and didn't try to take it from you."

I frowned. "She did ask me to come back later to pull cards from a corpse to see if I got a better draw," I said slowly. "You think she made that up to get me to come back?"

"No, she wouldn't lie. It's likely an honest offer. However, once you're there, I could see her trying to keep you there. I'd be cautious dealing with her." She shrugged. "That's just my advice, though. The cards aren't warning me one way or the other."

"Well, thanks for it," I said sincerely.

"Thank me in a minute." She placed the cards in front of me. "Cut."

"Cut?" I asked in surprise. "You're giving me a reading?"

"Murf, you took something unknown into your soul. While you obviously think it's harmless, I don't trust your opinion. I wish to *know*. Now, cut."

I reached out and lifted part of the deck away, and she took that top section and slipped it to the bottom, then knelt on the floor and placed the deck in front of herself. She closed her eyes and began breathing, and I could feel the power rising from her and filling the room. I watched her curiously; this wasn't how she normally did readings, as far as I've seen.

"Don't you usually use a layout for this?" I asked.

"I can't," she said with disgust. "My store was looted in my absence. Someone broke in and stole every card they could find, plus all the layouts they could get their hands on."

"Someone braved your wards?" I asked incredulously. "Everyone knows that your shop is protected. Who would even try that?"

"I know who it was. I did a divination the moment I returned, of course. It was—my former employer."

"Shadow Man," I sighed. "Of course, it was. Only Holders that strong would survive your wards."

"They all didn't," she said smugly. "The cards told me that one fewer of them left alive than entered." Her face settled back into a focused expression. "It doesn't matter for this, though. There's no layout to use."

"Why not?" I asked.

"Because this is your layout, Murf. The layout of your soul." Her eyes snapped open, burning with blue fire, and she reached down to touch the top card, flipping it over. I'd somehow expected to see the familiar teal and black forest of the Hag, but to my surprise, the card turned over was totally blank. I'd never seen a blank card in one of Azara's decks before, and by the look on her face, she hadn't expected to see it there, either.

"The Hag hides herself from me," she intoned. "I cannot see the effects of her presence on your soul, but I can feel them. She works to bind you closer, to bring your goals parallel to hers, and to extend her influence over the rest of your deck, but you fight her, holding to yourself. Continue to do so, or you may be lost."

That didn't sound good, but I couldn't bring myself to speak as she placed a card atop the blank one, one that I'd never seen before but instantly recognized.

"Dad, that's me!" Charlie exclaimed, scurrying down my arm and stopping several inches from the card. His tiny nose wriggled, and his whiskers trembled as he stretched out toward it. *"I like it. It feels funny!"*

The card only showed Charlie for a moment before it shifted into something else, displaying a young man wearing a simple crown and juggling bright stars.

"Your companion is most closely represented by the prince of stars," Azara said in that same deep, echoing voice she always had during true divinations. "Prankster of the court of stars, the eternal jester with power far deeper than he displays. His tricks amuse and comfort those whom he loves but can confound and even destroy those whom he calls enemies. Treat him with care and courtesy, for he can be your greatest friend or direst enemy."

"I like that, too," the ferret practically purred. *"Maybe she's not so bad."*

Azara placed a single card facedown below the prince, then two more below that. From there, she spread out in both directions, creating a vaguely circular layout that sort of looked like a wagon wheel with only four spokes. Every card she placed seemed to resonate inside me with a small jolt, as if the cards were being drawn directly from that place deep inside me where the Hag lived. She placed a total of thirty-two cards around the hag in a somewhat asymmetric pattern, one whose mirrored sides matched one another but not the identical top and bottom halves. As the final card dropped, she looked up at me with her burning eyes.

"This is the layout of your soul," she proclaimed. "The Unity's Wheel, connecting the past and future through the present. It is a powerful tableau, one with incredible potential, but it requires equally great care." She flipped the card to the left of the prince, revealing a rather battered-looking knight of cups. The card's drawing looked smeared and blurred, as if someone wiped it with a rag before the ink could fully set, and its head faced Azara, while its feet faced me.

"The knight of cups, inverted and distorted. It has been placed poorly, and that limits its strength and recovery." She turned over the card beside it to reveal a lady of cups in much the same state. "The lady of cups, also inverted and distorted. You have played your cards badly, and they will not work well for you."

"How—how do I fix it?" I asked in a dry voice. A strange heat burned in my chest as I stared at the layout, and I could feel its rightness inside of me. I didn't know how she'd done it, but I knew that she was right: she'd somehow called forth an image of my soul deck.

She reached down and touched the cards below the prince. "Here is where the court of cups should live. You are their prince, and they are your family. They should serve as the basis for all else."

She touched the right and left sides of the layouts. "The wings of your layout are unimportant, meant to be exchanged and interchanged freely. Place that here which you do not intend to keep, as its links to your soul will be lesser, and the effects of adding and removing them milder."

She slid her hand up to the top of the layout. "Here is the true expression of your power. Place those cards here that are beyond all others, ones that display power and majesty."

She took her hand away, and her face looked grave. "Beware. The Wheel is a powerful layout, but it requires great balance, or it will become unstable. Should it flip, the base of your soul will become power, to the detriment of the entire world." She took in a deep, shuddering breath, and the light in her eyes slowly faded. As it did, she sagged, her shoulders drooping in sudden weariness. She caught herself with her hands, blinking rapidly to moisten her eyes, then looked up at me, holding out a trembling hand.

"D-drink..." she rasped, her voice dry and scratchy. I quickly handed the drink to her, and she gulped several swallows, making a face as she lowered the mug. "You might be right about the taste," she admitted, her voice sounding normal but tired. "That's bitter."

"You've never tasted it?" I asked inanely.

"Not in a long time. I rarely overtax myself." She took a deep breath. "I think that was worth it, though, to show you that you've been mishandling your deck, just like every other Holder."

"Yeah, I remember," I said, managing not to roll my eyes. "You don't like Holders."

"I don't dislike all Holders," she corrected. "Just most of them." She tried to stand, but her legs trembled so much that she sank back down. She looked up at me. "Help me to the couch, Murf."

I quickly took her arm and gently lifted, letting her get her feet under her. I guided her to the couch and sat her down, then grabbed the bread she'd left on the table and offered it to her.

"Thank you," she said, tearing off a chunk. "You should eat, too. Channeling the Unity's power takes energy from your body, and food can replace some of that."

"So, which Holders do you like?" I asked, pulling off a piece of bread myself and stuffing it into my mouth.

"The ones who know what they're doing. The ones who've asked the right questions and take care with their cards." She took a bite of bread and washed it down with a drink, then handed me the mug. "Here. You still need this, too, and it's not as bad with the bread."

As I took a sip—she was right, the bread did help—she smoothed down her black skirt and gave me a weary look.

"The problem I have with most Holders," she said, "is that they don't bother to truly learn about the cards they're sticking into their soul. They do what you did, just putting them in where they think they'll match based on how much power they think they'll garner." She looked at me curiously. "Why did you put yours there, by the way?"

"No reason," I shrugged. "Just something I heard about always going left in a maze."

"Exactly. That's how most Holders place cards: based on rumors or some random bit of nonsense they've heard. They don't care about the cards themselves or even their own souls."

"It's not that I don't care about my soul, Azara," I protested. "I just had no idea how any of this works."

"And you never asked, either." She shook her head. "Holders rarely do. They assume that because they know how to use abilities, they also know how to use cards, but the two have nothing in common. They place their cards into their souls without regard for their layouts or what they mean. When they do, they damage their soul with the cards, and they taint the cards with their souls."

"You mean, every Holder has a layout like this?" I asked, gesturing to the wheel on the floor.

"Not exactly like this, no, but yes, every Holder has a layout. So does every person, although for most, that layout is either blank or too small to hold a card. For Holders, though, that layout can be extensive, and every part of it holds meaning for their soul. If they knew that meaning, they could place their cards in a way that might not give them as much power today but would give them much more in the future. It's all about care and balance, and Holders don't seem to have much of either. They place the cards as close to their hole card as possible to gain immediate power, whereas if they placed them farther out but balanced them, they'd all be more effective."

I shook my head as a problem with her idea occurred to me. "It's a great idea, Azara, but it doesn't work like that."

"What do you mean, it doesn't work like that?" she bristled. "Are you telling me how to lay the cards, Murf?"

"No, not at all. I'm saying that we can't just put cards wherever we want. We can't even see all of our soul layout—at least, I can't see mine. Only the parts nearest to my hole card. The rest is hidden from me…" I fell silent as I pulled up my layout and stared at it in disbelief.

THE UNITY'S WHEEL

Rather than the simple distorted cross I'd seen before, the entirety of my soul deck spread out before me, revealing a layout identical to the one Azara had placed on the floor. The foggy edges of the image were gone, and Charlie's card stared up at me from the very bottom.

"What?" I asked, blinking in confusion. "Wait, I can see all the cards! How did that happen?"

She glared at me a little contemptuously. "It's your soul, Murf, and I just showed it to you. How could you not know it now?"

"Few people truly do." We both turned as the door to the back opened, and Ferdi emerged. "At least, in my experience. Most people are afraid to look that deeply." She looked at the floor, then at Azara. "You did a tableau reading for him?"

"Obviously," the avian sniffed, taking another sip. "He's putting his cards in all wrong—as most Holders tend to."

The halfling shrugged. "Being a Holder isn't like being a cartomancer. It's less about exactly where you put the cards in the layout and more about how they interact with one another. We don't even know how many cards we can fit into our deck."

"We don't?" I asked.

"How can we? If your Capacity grows, you can fit more cards in, which means your layout has to expand to accommodate them."

"That, or your layout is set by your soul, and as you grow, you gain greater understanding of it and the ability to utilize more of your potential."

"That sounds like six of one versus a half-dozen of the other," Ferdi snorted.

"Is it, Murf?" Azara asked me sarcastically. "Do you think my reading changed nothing?"

"Actually, Ferdi, I think she might be right," I said slowly as I gazed at my newly revealed layout.

"What do you mean?"

"That reading she just did? I can see my whole layout now. All thirty-three cards, and I don't think my Capacity's high enough to support that many cards. She might have a point."

Ferdi stared at me, then whipped her head around to face Azara. "Do a reading on me!" she demanded.

"I thought that you don't believe me about layouts mattering," the avian said calmly. "Why would you want one if that's the case?"

"Because if I could see my whole layout, I could plan where to put cards more efficiently, and see the best places to put stacks, of course! Can you?"

Azara sniffed, not looking at the halfling. "Of course, I can. It will cost ten golds." I spluttered as I sipped my drink, sending more of the astringent liquid shooting up my nose and starting another coughing fit.

"What?" The halfling glared at me as if it were my fault. "Is this some sort of tall-folk humor?"

"If it is, I don't get it," I wheezed. "That's a lot of money, Azara."

"And I'm worth it." The avian straightened and glared at the halfling. "I've spent decades honing my craft, halfling, and I'm very good at it. Very few diviners could show you the entirety of your soul, and none of them live in this city—perhaps not even this continent. That makes my services valuable. Why wouldn't I charge top coin for them?"

"You didn't charge Murf!"

"I know Murf. I have an interest in him not becoming a typical Holder, obsessed with power and crazed with the need for more cards, no matter what they are or how appropriate they are. And from what I just saw, the whole world shares that interest—or it should." She paused. "I'm currently ambivalent toward you."

"The feeling's mutual," the warrior grunted, twisting one partially unraveled braid thoughtfully. "Couldn't I get the same thing at the Sage's Guild?"

"You could try. There are two diviners there who could even attempt it. Neither could see your whole deck. At best, if they recognized part of it as one of the standard layouts the Guild has cataloged, they could guess the rest. More likely, they'd guess anyway and be wrong, and you wouldn't know it until it was too late." She sniffed haughtily. "Plus, they couldn't advise you how to place your cards unless you happen to have a layout the Guild has on record. You would pay maybe half what I'm charging and get essentially nothing for your golds." She shrugged. "Or you could pay me, be sure of the quality, and learn how badly you've probably mangled your layout. It doesn't bother me either way."

"I'll think about it," Ferdi grunted. "That's not why I came out, anyway. Murf, I could use your help with this assassin."

"Help how?" I asked guardedly. "Ferdi, I'm not really up for torturing anyone. I could maybe annoy her until she breaks down, but that's as close as I come."

"As annoying as you are, I don't think it'll work," she shook her head. "She's tough, and my usual methods aren't working well. I'm thinking about your ability. Drunk people like to talk, and they rarely consider consequences."

"True," I allowed. I glanced at Azara. "Would it be safe for me to do that, or would I risk hurting myself?"

Her eyes glittered with approval as she looked at me. "Finally, you ask my opinion before using the cards. About time." She gave me a little shrug. "It should be fine. The power of the cards flows through your soul more than your will, so there shouldn't be any danger. If it hurts, or you feel sick or dizzy, though, stop immediately."

"Yes, Mother," I grinned at her.

"If I were your mother, I'd take a switch to your backside," she said sharply. "You certainly need it."

"Tall folk kink is weird," Ferdi said, shaking her head. "Coming, Murf?"

"That wasn't—she didn't mean..." I sighed. "Yeah, I'm coming, Ferdi. Lead the way."

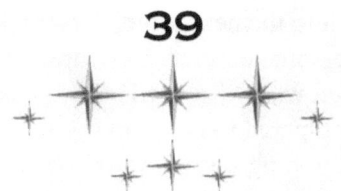

39

Leaving the front room of Azara's shop was like stepping into an entirely different building. That front room was a show, meant to impress customers and add an air of drama to the place. As she'd once explained to me, people came to a cartomancer expecting them to be aloof and mysterious, and she gave that to them. A diviner whose shop was bright and sunny went out of business fast, even if they were good at it. To some extent, she had to meet their preconceptions, or they'd assume that she wasn't what she said she was.

No matter that they might be wrong in their little prejudices. No, that never occurred to them. She had to be the problem.

The darkness and melodrama ended at the door, though. Past it, the wood was lighter, stained and varnished instead of painted. The floors were bare instead of carpeted, and much brighter lamps hung above, fully illuminating everything. It was much more cheerful and homey, which made sense because it was Azara's home.

The downstairs areas were her workspaces, I knew. Through the door lay a storage room with shelves running from floor to ceiling on both sides. Normally, she kept her supplies here: extra cards, layouts, oil for her lamps, and cleaning supplies. Those shelves lay mostly empty now, and the steel safe she'd used to store her most precious cards hung open, the door ripped free from the lock. Even with a prybar, it would have taken someone with a lot of strength to do that. It saddened me a bit to see the dusty, bare shelves. It made the whole place feel emptier, really.

Beyond the shelves, the hallway opened up into Azara's actual workroom. She had three tables set up: one for cutting fabric and card paper, one for inking new layouts, and a drawing table where she painstakingly crafted her cards. This part was a lot better lit than the rest of the downstairs, for obvious reasons. I'd seen Azara hunched at these tables for hours before, carefully and meticulously drawing out a card using her own special inks and glazing, or cautiously working out a new layout one card at a time. While she was working, I could have caught on fire, and she wouldn't have noticed. She spent most of her days here, at least back when I knew her, and from the card pinned to the drawing table, it looked like she'd been here when Ferdi arrived with us, as well.

The halfling led me into the next room, Azara's kitchen and dining room. The rest of her personal quarters were upstairs, and I'd once wondered why the kitchen wasn't, as well. Once I saw how little time she spent in her chambers compared to her workroom, though, I understood. What was the point to clumping up and down the stairs every time she was hungry or thirsty? The space was simple, with a fireplace and metal oven for cooking, a small table where she sat, and a wooden counter for preparing food.

Guilt flooded me as I looked around the room. This was where we'd spent a lot of our time together, when I'd come back from the Hall, and she'd finished her crafting and divining for the day. Now, the table where we'd sat, holding hands and laughing, had only one chair. The shelves that used to have enough food to make dinners for two were emptier. It was hard not to imagine Azara here at nights, making her small meals for herself, sitting at that table alone. She said I'd taken something from her, and I finally understood what she meant. For a while, this had been a place where she'd planned a future—our future. Now, it was just somewhere she ate.

I couldn't help but chuckle at my sudden burst of melodrama. I was being something of an idiot, I realized. I had no idea how Azara was living or how content she was with her life. She was an intelligent and beautiful woman; if she wanted company here, she could have it. If she didn't, well, that was her concern, not mine. I'd given up any right to wonder about her personal life when I walked out of it.

Besides, whatever Azara usually used this room for these days, it wasn't being used for that now. The long, low counter that usually held food—and occasionally Azara when we'd been too amorous to make it to the bedroom—had a different body on it. The female assassin lay atop the counter, ropes around her body pinning her down. Not that she could have gone far. Her arms had gone back into their sockets, it seemed, but they stuck out at odd angles that I was almost certain arms weren't supposed to be able to make. At least, not ones with fully intact bones. Her legs were twisted the same way. It looked like it hurt like hell, and I shivered just looking at her. From the paleness of her face and the way she'd bitten through her bottom lip, I was right about the pain.

Without her mask and hood, she was quite honestly average looking. She had short brown hair with a slight wave to it that curled around her ears and touched the base of her skull. Her face was slim but not overly narrow, with tanned skin and no tan lines where the mask was, despite what I expected. Her brown eyes were slightly sunken, but that might have been from the pain. Her body was athletic but not overly curvy, with slightly small breasts and narrow hips. All in all, she was someone I wouldn't have looked twice at if I passed her on the street, which I supposed was a good thing for an assassin.

At least, I wouldn't have noticed her under normal circumstances, which these were not. In the state she was in, I definitely would have paid attention.

"Ferdi, why is she naked?" I demanded. "You already searched her!"

"Too hard to put her clothes back on," the halfling shrugged.

"You could have covered her with a blanket or something, you know."

"I could have. I didn't. Besides, I don't want to ruin Azara's blankets with bloodstains."

"But you're okay with getting it on the counter where she prepares food?"

"I'm pretty sure there's been plenty of blood there. She eats meat."

I walked closer. "Couldn't you have straightened her bones back out a bit?" I complained. "It creeps me out seeing her arms and legs like that."

"Nope. If I do, her cards will heal them. They won't heal crooked like this."

The assassin watched us both, her eyes hard and flat as they darted back and forth between us, finally settling on me. "So, you're the kind guard?" she finally said with a snort. "Nice try."

"The what?" I asked, honestly confused.

"The kind guard. You're the kind guard, just here to help me." She looked at Ferdi. "She's the cruel guard who wants to hurt me. Let me guess, if I just cooperate, you'll stop her, right?"

"That's an awfully elaborate and specific scenario," I chuckled. "Is it some sort of role-playing thing? I've done that in the bedroom a few times before. My favorite is the wounded hero and the lonely priestess."

Her eyes narrowed. "The what?"

"You know. I'm the badly wounded hero, brought into the church to be healed from the brink of death after saving the city or world or whatever, and you're the priestess who's never seen a man before and didn't realize how lonely you were until you took off my clothes to heal me." I sighed. "That's a good one because I'm supposed to be barely conscious, so I just have to lie there and do nothing. Lot of fun."

"What the fuck are you talking about?" she snapped.

"Yes. That's what I'm talking about." I tapped my chin. "Of course, you're not exactly the hero here, are you? And I'm definitely no priest. I suppose we could try that guard thing you're talking about—although I should warn you that I've never been able to talk Ferdi into a threesome, and I've tried."

"It's an interrogation technique, idiot," the woman spat. "You pretend to be my friend and protect me from her, and in return, I'm supposed to feel like I can tell you things."

"Oh! Well, that's not nearly as much fun. Besides, I'm not really all that nice of a guy. Well, maybe compared to Ferdi, but still not nice."

"So, you're going to torture me, too?" she snorted. "Do your worst. You have no idea what I can endure."

"Not really my thing, sorry." I reached out and patted her knee as gently as I could. As I did, I examined the card that kept trying to pop into my vison.

Human
Rank 3 Assassin
Luck: 23 Capacity: 46 Skill: 54
Hole Card: 7 of Coins
Likely Powers: Strength Drain,
Poison, Shadow Cloak

Human
Rank 3 Assassin
Luck: 23 Capacity: 46 Skill: 54
Hole Card: 7 of Coins

"Enough with the flirting, Murf," Ferdi growled. "Get on with it."

"Ferdi, we seriously need to get you laid if you think that's flirting," I sighed.

"What was it, then?"

"An expression of my extreme discomfort with being here right now. Just seeing her arms and legs like this is giving me chills." I shuddered.

"You tall folk. No stomach for the brutalities of life. The pretty human ran upstairs the first time I broke one of this assassin's arms." She gestured at the bound woman. "You don't like it? Use your ability so we can get answers from her, and then you can go."

The assassin's gaze suddenly turned nervous, but she clamped her lips shut, and I could see the determination in her eyes. I suddenly wasn't sure that the knight's ability would work on her. Ferdi had said that Holders had defenses against cards, and the higher rank they were, the stronger those defenses. I didn't really know how strong a rank 3 person was, or what those defenses might be, but I was a rank lower than her at rank 2, and I was sure that mattered.

At the same time, the knight's base power sat at 45 according to a quick glance at it, and from what Ferdi said, that was decent for a noble arcana. The assassin had a 7 of coins as her hole card, a low arcana, and that should mean that her defenses were in the single digits, maybe the low double digits—actually, probably higher than that. The confusion I'd projected earlier worked on her, but it hadn't worked all that well, so she had to have at least partially resisted it. Of course, if I'd also used Drunken Combat on her, it might have been better...

I glanced over at Ferdi. "You might want to take a step or two back," I suggested.

"Why? Your ability never affected me before."

"I'm trying something different this time, and I'm not sure how much control I'll have over it. I'd hate to catch you with it accidentally."

"I'll deal," she said shortly.

I shrugged. "Your funeral." I looked back at the woman, but I didn't really see her. My entire focus turned inward to where my cards lay. I'd never tried using both of them at the same time before, but really, it should be no different than flicking cards with both hands. I could do that, so there was no reason I couldn't do this. Not that my reasoning made much sense, but I had a feeling that belief mattered in using my cards. If I didn't think I could do it, I wouldn't be able to do it. Confidence matters at the card table, in the bedroom, and in life in general. I saw no reason why it wouldn't affect a pair of cards lodged in my soul. I took a careful grip on each pack of cards, squeezed them gently, then let them fly.

I didn't have the best grip on the energy that rolled out from me in twin waves. I didn't care as I kept spraying the power outward, unleashing most of what I had on the woman. After the assassin sort of resisted my confusion attack from earlier, I guessed holding back would be a bad idea, so I went all in on her. Both powers slammed into her, and she shivered and shook as they sank into her and wrapped around her body.

Confusion had worked on the woman before, but I didn't want her confused. While I thought that would pair well with the knight's drunkenness, it might make it hard for her to answer questions. Arousal might have worked, too—I knew that alcohol and horniness were a dangerous combination for most people—but that would feel a lot like forcing myself on the woman. I didn't want that. Plus, if it slipped out of my control, it could spill onto Ferdi. I really, really didn't want to see an overly amorous Ferdi. So, I went with something simpler and less likely to backfire on me: friendliness. Alcohol and being overly friendly also went hand-in-hand, after all, and if it washed over the whole building, I wouldn't end up surrounded by four riled-up women and me being the only man.

Not that that would necessarily be a terrible thing, of course.

"Wh-what are you doing to me?" the assassin asked, her voice strangely thick all of a sudden as both powers washed over her. "What is that?"

"Just something to relax you," I replied conversationally. "Give it a bit to kick in. It'll probably help with the pain, if nothing else."

"I—what's happening?" Her eyes looked confused for a moment as they grew slowly unfocused, and she peered a bit blearily at me. "Stop it!" Her voice came out slightly slurred, and she blinked rapidly as if she were having trouble seeing. She looked over at me, and as she did, her expression seemed confused more than angry or frightened. "I don't understand…"

"I'm just helping you calm down a bit," I laughed softly. "So that we can have a nice, friendly chat."

"Don't—want to—chat," she said, struggling slightly, but her words came out even less coherently as my power sank in. "Can't talk."

"You can tell me your name, at least," I said encouragingly. "I mean, there's no harm in that, is there?"

"I—I go by Shadowcat," she said haltingly, her expression uncertain. "I shouldn't be talking to you."

"Why not? We're not talking about anything important. And Shadowcat's not your real name, is it? It seems less like a name and more like something you'd hear in a bad play." I crouched a bit and affected a mysterious tone to my voice. "I'm Shadowcat, kitty of the night! Beware my fearsome furball of doom!"

She snorted and shook her head. "N-no. I'm not supposed to tell people my real name, though."

"Why not?" I asked her.

"My—my organization. They don't like it when people know about us."

"What would I know? It's not like knowing your name tells me anything. Here, I'll go first. My name's Murf. Nice to meet you."

"I-I know. I heard." She worried at her lower lip, but between the drunkenness and the forced feeling of camaraderie sinking into her, it seemed that her guard was slowly lowering. "I'm—I'm Cassa."

"Hi, there, Cassa," I smiled at her. "Do you live around here? Or just visiting?"

"I-I'm here because the Guild called for Holders of rank 3 and up," she said, her words halting at first but slowly gaining momentum. "They needed stealth roles, and the pay was good. Arric and I weren't busy at the moment, so we hopped a ship here to see what it was all about."

"Arric? He's the guy I saw you with?"

"Yeah. My partner, of sorts, although we usually do jobs alone. He's better at organizing than me, though, and I'm better at figuring out ways in and out of places, so we help each other fairly often."

"You sound like a good team."

"We are," she said a little proudly. As she spoke, her words became more slurred, and her hesitance seemed to fall away.

"Tell me about this job," I suggested. "You're all running a Labyrinth, right? That sounds like a pretty standard reason for someone to hire sellswords."

"It usually is," she agreed with a faint shiver. "We knew this one wasn't right away, though, as soon as he showed up."

"He? He who?"

"Our employer, if that's what you can call him. I'm not sure any of us are getting paid, but getting stiffed is better than getting dead."

"I suppose that's true."

"It is, and that's what would happen if we tried to back out." Her words came more freely now, almost as if we were sitting at a bar having a simple conversation. "It didn't take long for us to realize that."

"He started killing you right away?" I guessed. "To prove how dangerous he is?"

"No. That came later. At first, he gathered a group of about twenty-five of us just outside the Ochre Forest. When he appeared, Arric and I both had second thoughts."

"Why?"

"You saw the way he hides his identity. Most of the others think he's using shadow powers, but he's not. I'd be able to see through those, or at least feel them. I can use shadows, you see. Did I tell you that? I can't remember if I told you that." Her voice was even thicker as she spoke, and she suddenly laughed as if what she'd said was hilarious. I just gave her an encouraging smile.

"No, you didn't. You were telling me about your boss, though."

"Oh, yeah. He's an asshole." She shivered. "He scares the shit out of me, you know, and I don't scare easy."

"Why's he so scary?"

"Well, at first there were twenty-five of us, see. I think I said that. Yeah, twenty-five of us from all over the world. Most were beastlings, of course—locals from here on Torin—but he had a few of every species. Elves, orcs, goblins, halflings, humans…" She laughed. "There was even a big troll. Have you seen them? They're huge! Ugly, too."

"I've met a couple," I admitted. "They don't usually leave Trollholme, though."

"Nah, this one wasn't there by choice. He was a slave, one of their exiles that they sell to outsiders. He worked for this goblin woman who was good with mechanical things." She shook her head. "Neither of them made it."

"He killed them?"

"The Labyrinth did. See, he gathered us at the Ochre Forest and told us we'd be running it first as a trial, to make sure we met his standards. We all went in—that whole place is orange, you know. It's the orangest place I've ever seen."

"Yeah, I've been there."

"That's right, those elves were supposed to kill you and leave you there. What happened to them?"

"They came down with a nasty case of dead," I grinned. "What happened to you all of you in the Forest?"

"Good. I didn't like them much. Alenrue, she's okay for an elf, but those two were pricks. The one guy kept looking at me like I was his next meal or something." She shivered and shook her head. "Anyway, we all got inside, and we ran the place without too many problems. It's a hunt-type, you see; you get in, and you're supposed to try to escape while the guardian hunts you." She looked around, then lifted her head toward me, speaking in a whisper. "Do you know the secret to those? You can't escape! The Labyrinth just goes on until the guardian finds you! The Unity's such a liar."

I chuckled at that. It fit well with my third Law, after all. "So, you made it?"

"Yeah. The beasts aren't too bad for people of our ranks, but we had to split into smaller groups to do it. Tight quarters in the woods, you know. That was where they lost that goblin woman to some kind of orange, hairless bear or something."

"I missed those."

"Why would you miss them? They're awful." She laughed uproariously, then belched loudly. "'Scuse me. Anyway, once his handler died, the troll was free, and he just went crazy on the rest of the group. They lost two more putting him down. They heal fast, you know."

"So I heard," I nodded. "But the rest of you got out, at least."

"Yeah. Eventually, the Labyrinth funneled us all into a big clearing, and we started setting up right away to face the guardian. Turns out, it was a giant rabbit, and I felt kind of bad when we killed it. It was cute."

That wasn't how I recalled it, obviously, but I guessed that she hadn't been riding on the damn thing, or spent any time as its chew toy.

"But we killed it anyway, and we thought that was it. Then, he said— he didn't do anything this whole time, just followed along watching us— that he didn't need all of us, but he couldn't let our cards go to waste. So, he told us that he'd only be taking twelve, and that meant we had to kill eight of our own since five had died in the Labyrinth."

"I imagine that didn't go well."

"Not even a little bit. I don't have a problem with killing." She giggled slightly as she said that. "It would be pretty stupid for an assassin to have a problem with killing, wouldn't it?"

"Kind of, yeah," I chuckled.

"Even so, there's things you don't do, and turning on other sellswords is one of them. The Guild frowns on it. Most of us just refused, and a few of the others said that they'd rather kill him." She shuddered as she spoke. "But they didn't. He killed them, instead. Boom, blast of purple fire, and they died. Never stood a chance. A couple of us tried to run at that point, and he killed them, too. He asked if anyone else felt like dying. None of us did, so when he picked out three more people and told us to kill them…" She fell silent.

"Well, that's awful," I sighed. "It sucks that you all had to do that."

"It does, yeah. You're pretty nice, you know. I wish I wasn't supposed to take you."

"Take me? Take me where?" I asked.

"Upper Kallit. Little piece-of-shit farming village an hour south of the city. That's where Arric and I took all the Holders we caught." She giggled again. "The whole place smells like a pigsty, and Tifer and Alenrue are staying there. He doesn't care—he's an oath-bound halfling, and you know how they are—but she keeps talking about how elves aren't supposed to live like that."

"Why there? Wouldn't the farmers get suspicious when a bunch of tied-up Holders show up?"

"Well, they don't stay there, obviously." She rolled her eyes at me. "It's just a stop on the way south to the Labyrinth. That's where Tifer and Alenrue take them."

"To get their cards?" I asked.

She nodded. "Yeah. He wants them, and he doesn't want to risk us drawing them. Says we might lose some or keep drawing the same ones over and over." She shook her head. "So, he tortures them into giving him their cards himself."

"Is that what happened to the missing Sellswords?" I asked. "The Scrivener?"

"Yeah. Arric and I took them, dosed them with darkbreath so they'd stay unconscious, and piled them into a wagon. We took them to Upper Kallit, gave them another dose, and tossed them into a second wagon for Tifer and Alenrue just outside of the village, where the damn farmers won't see anything. Then, they take them down to the Labyrinth."

"Why there?"

"That's where Fisya is, and she's the expert at torture." The woman shivered. "Felids are all about new experiences, and I guess giving people pain is the kind of experience she prefers."

I remembered the cat-woman and her eagerness at the idea of getting her hands on me, and I shivered. That would be a bad way to go. I forced myself to stay focused, though.

"What about the halflings? Did you take anyone from their hold?"

"Yeah, a few. We killed most of them, but we took the Holders and shipped them south." Her words were hard to follow as the drunkenness really kicked in, and I had to listen hard to hear her.

"What does your boss want with all these cards?" I asked with honest curiosity.

"Don't know." Her words were barely audible at that point, and I leaned close to catch her mutters. "Just takes them. Can't fight him. Kill you." Her voice trailed off into a mumble that I couldn't make out, and I leaned back. She'd said all she was probably going to. If I eased up on the knight's power, she'd come around, but I had a feeling she'd be a lot less friendly without it affecting her.

Honestly, I was glad she'd lost the ability to keep talking. The whole interrogation made me feel dirty. My cards had reached into her brain and altered her, making it pretty much impossible for her to resist me. The goblin cartomancer back in the warehouse said that cards couldn't compel people, and I guess technically, my cards hadn't forced her to do anything. They'd come close, though. I'd all but taken her free will from her. Granted, I thought it was better than torturing her for information, but I wondered if she would agree.

And that made me wonder once more just who or what the hell I was becoming.

40

"That was great, Murf!"

I nearly jumped out of my skin as Ferdi's voice came from right beside me. I spun to see her standing next to me, pressed closer than I could remember her standing to me. A wide, creepy smile stretched across her face, directed at me, and I knew that smile was going to haunt my dreams for days, at least.

"You got everything I needed from her! I knew I could count on you!"

"I—what?" Her enthusiasm took me by surprise, and the shock meant it took a few seconds before I realized what happened. My control wasn't that great, and I'd accidentally hit the halfling with some of the lady's ability. I quickly shut off that power, although I kept the knight running. Ferdi's face cleared quickly, and a more familiar frown wiped away that insipid smile. Thank the Unity for that. I hoped never to see that again.

"What was that?" she demanded, taking a step back from me. "Why was I feeling all nice toward you? Is that the power the lady of cups gave you?"

"Yeah. Sorry for catching you with it, but I haven't really practiced with it. I did try to warn you."

"You did. I should have listened." She walked over and glared at the now-unconscious assassin. "You got what we needed, though. She and her partner have been taking Holders and shipping them south, so that's where we have to go."

"We?" I asked. "I'm not going anywhere, Ferdi."

She looked at me, and her gaze hardened. "Murf, those are my people there. They're being tortured. I have to help them."

"I don't blame you. But I'm not going anywhere near that place," I said firmly. "I don't want to be the one being tortured for his cards, Ferdi, and that's what'll happen if we go down there and get caught." I shook my head. "Nope, count me out."

"You're a coward, Murf," she spat.

"Yes, I am. But I'm a live coward, as opposed to a dead hero, which is what I'll be if I go down to that Labyrinth."

"You think that they'll just let you be, Murf?" she demanded. "That if you just hide in the Gambler's Hall, play your little games, and have pointless sex with the pretty human, they'll ignore you? You know they won't."

"Then maybe I'll just get the hell out of Canis," I shrugged. "There'll be other tournaments. This one isn't worth my life, and once I'm away from here, Shadow Man will have no reason to bother me."

"So, you're just going to run?" she snarled, taking a step closer to me and clenching her fists. "That's it?"

"Yes, halfling, that's what he's saying." We both turned to see Azara standing in the doorway, still looking a little tired and pale. The woman's face was calm, but her eyes burned into mine. "That's what Murf does, you know. When things get difficult, dangerous, or threatening, he runs away—no matter who it might hurt."

I opened my mouth to say that running had kept me alive all this time, that I had enough problems without taking on other people's, and to ask who the hell she thought she was to judge me. Before a single one of those stupid words could dribble out of my mouth, though, I remembered the kitchen, with its empty shelves and single chair.

She was exactly the person to pass judgment on me, and in her eyes, I saw that judgment.

I could turn and walk out right now. Ferdi might get pissed, but she wouldn't attack me, and if she did, well, I'd already seen that I could take it and live. She'd work her mad out, and I'd be on my way. Azara wouldn't even try to stop me. Millie would probably go with me, happily.

But if I did that, what would happen next? The world wouldn't stop just because I wasn't there to see it turning. Ferdi would head south, where she'd run into two Holders, both of whom were probably stronger than her. She'd taken Cassa because the assassin wasn't a fighter, but I bet that the elf and halfling down there were. Ferdi would be captured, and she'd be tortured for her cards. Assuming she broke, she'd tell Shadow Man that we all lived, which meant he'd come after Azara, too, and probably Millie if she stuck around for the tournament.

Of course, I wouldn't be here to see that. If I never came back to Canis, I'd never know that Azara was gone, killed by Shadow Man since she didn't have any cards for him. I could tell myself that maybe Ferdi saved her people, and they all made it out. That maybe Millie won the tournament and was on her way to buying her way out of her family. I'd be lying, but I could say those things.

The question was, could I believe them? And if I did, what the hell kind of person did that make me? Was it worth staying alive, no matter the cost, if I couldn't look at myself in the mirror without hating what I saw? I remembered the guilt I'd felt when I left Azara; how much worse would it be knowing I'd abandoned all three of these women to their fates?

"We should help, Dad."

I glanced up and saw Charlie perched on my shoulder, staring into my eyes. *"You think so, Charlie?"*

"Yes. If we don't, they might hurt the nice lady. Don't let them hurt her. I like her."

I sighed. *"I like her too, Charlie, but…"*

Beside me, Cassa let out a single long breath as her chest fell still. As she did, a card popped up in front of me.

Unity Achievement!
You have slain a Holder of your
rank or higher.
Reward: 100 UP per Holder rank, +50
UP per rank above yours.

Rank Up!
You have reached Rank 3!
You receive:
Luck +3, Skill +2, Capacity +1

Harmonies:
Coins +3, Blades -1, Cups +1

Cassa was gone. I'd left the knight's power on to keep her from coming around, and she'd succumbed to it. I didn't feel bad about that. She was a killer. She'd taken a bunch of Holders and handed them over to be tortured. She'd probably helped slaughter the halflings. She might have killed some of those kids for all I knew. If anybody deserved to die, it was her—but I hadn't meant to kill her. I hadn't done it on purpose.

Murf's Eleventh Law: The Unity doesn't give a damn about intentions. We all make choices, and we live with the consequences, no matter what we might have wanted. Running away would be a choice, and it wouldn't matter if I thought it was justified or not, any more than it mattered that I hadn't meant to kill Cassa. She was just as dead, and fuck my intentions.

"We can't just go down there, Ferdi," I said at last. "That elf's an archer; she could kill us before we even saw her, and I'll bet that halfling's at least as strong as you. You heard her: everyone in this group is rank 3 or higher, and you're the only one of us that strong. If we just stroll up to that village, they'll take us both, and we'll be joining your people, not helping them."

"You can just do this to them," she said, gesturing at Cassa's cooling corpse. There's some morbid alliteration for you.

"Maybe. She could tell I was doing something to her, though, and if I'm close enough to do it, I'm close enough to take an arrow in the eyeball." I frowned and reached up to touch my hat, suddenly realizing I wasn't wearing it. "Wait, where's my hat? Ferdi, did you leave my hat behind?"

"No, Murf. I know how stupidly attached you are to that ratty thing. It's back in the wagon, I think."

"Does it matter?" Azara asked curiously, her head cocked sideways once more. "Do you need it to think clearly?"

"Maybe a little," I admitted.

"You're such a child, Murf."

"I've always thought so," Ferdi observed.

"Big words coming from someone who's actually child-sized," I said archly.

"And who can pick you up and throw you through that window if you keep talking like that," the halfling growled. "I'll go get your damn hat. You claim her cards." She stomped out of the room toward Azara's shop.

I grinned at the warrior before letting the smile drop from my face and turning to face Cassa's body. I wasn't looking forward to this in the slightest, but I knew it was necessary. There was no point letting cards go to waste, and who better to draw them than me? I reached out, ignoring her nudity as best as I could as I touched the skin between her breasts. A card flashed into view immediately, and I glanced over it before waving it away.

Cards Gained!

I felt the cards slip into my fingers, and I drew them out, far more than I'd ever touched at once. I held them up with a sense of awe and trepidation. Before coming to Canis, I'd considered owning eight of these cards something amazing. I'd spent years collecting them from elite tournaments, by gambling against the rich and powerful—and winning— and by occasionally liberating one from a person I felt undeserving of it. I'd never even seen a noble arcana—at least, not a noble Unity card—and I never thought that I would. Now, in one moment, I'd pulled more cards from a dead woman's chest than I'd ever owned in my life—and one of them was another noble arcana.

Queen of Cups
Likely Power: Command Emotions
Requirements:
Luck: 57   Harmony: 65
Compatibility: 20%

The queen was a regal woman seated on a throne and holding a golden goblet while servants knelt at her feet. As I stared at her, I remembered the Hag's words. *"I call my children to myself."* It seemed she was right. Since gaining her, I'd been practically flooded with damn cards. I kind of wished the old girl would shut the hell up.

"Interesting. Quite a few coins there, which I suppose makes sense."

I jumped a little again as I realized Azara stood over my shoulder, peering at the cards with her raptor's gaze.

"Makes sense? How?"

"Coins are the suit of darkness and shadows, Murf. It makes sense that an assassin would carry so many, and with your fascination with gambling, you're obviously suited for them. I also see why a killer would hold the ace of blades. The ace of staves would help with understanding things, so an assassin might use that. A four of cups would be good for sensing emotions, and the ten might be used to hide or disguise yourself. The queen, though—that, I think, is the Unity's gift to you."

"Yeah, I was thinking the same thing," I said weakly. "Any advice on what to do with these?"

"Yes. Move the knight and lady down to the base of your layout. Place the knight and lady two steps below the Hag side-by-side, then the queen in the lower spot beside the lady. Put the ten in the upper spot beside the knight. Ignore the four."

"Why not right next to my hole card?" I asked.

"Because that should be saved for the prince, the card closest to you in temperament and demeanor. The spot beside and below the knight should be for the emperor. That would give you a friendly court as the base of your layout and make everything else stronger and stabler."

I chuckled weakly. "Azara, you really think that I'm going to pull the prince and emperor, too?"

"You think you won't? You've been drawing the cups court steadily, Murf, the court that should serve as the base for your layout and your soul. The Unity will provide you the rest. The cards are sure of it."

I swallowed hard as I realized she was probably right. "Okay, so what about the rest of these cards?"

"Personally? I would ignore them. If you truly want to place the coins or blades, do so to one side or the other, but I wouldn't."

"Why not?" I asked curiously, a little overwhelmed by how much information she was offering me, especially considering the price she'd quoted Ferdi to do the same.

"Because doing so will imbalance the Wheel. The sides need to be a combination of suits and relatively close in power, or they'll overbalance one another. The best thing for those sections would likely be either a group of cards of all the same rank representing every suit, or a run of cards in each suit." She shrugged. "I would keep those until such time as you can put something more balanced in. That's just my suggestion, though."

I gazed at the cards, then set them down on the counter. "Any idea how to move the knight and lady?"

"No, sorry, but they're your cards in your soul. It seems you should just be able remove them if you wanted."

I unbuttoned my shirt and took a deep breath, then reached down and touched my chest, concentrating on the knight. I braced myself and pinched my fingers together. Something hard slipped between my fingertips, and I grasped it and pulled. Instantly, fire burned in me as what felt like a burning shard of glass slid through me, cutting and searing its way out, and I hissed with pain. Fortunately, it only lasted a few seconds before I once more held the knight of cups in my hand. The card looked no worse than it had before I put it in, despite the wavering image of it I'd seen in Azara's divination.

"Damn, that hurts," I complained, rubbing my chest.

"Of course, it does," Azara nodded sagely. "You placed them poorly and injured yourself. Now, you're removing a shard of the Unity from a wound in your soul, Murf. What did you expect? I would remove the other before replacing either."

I followed her instructions, and if anything, the lady hurt even worse coming out. Once I had them both free, I set them down, breathing heavily.

"I really don't want to do this," I muttered. "Putting cards in is not my idea of a fun time."

"I know your idea of a fun time, Murf," she said drily. "And that's not going to happen, at least not in my home, so I suggest you quit dawdling and get on with it."

"Any particular order I should go in?" I asked.

"I would begin with the knight, as it should hurt the least to put in first. Then the lady, ten, and queen in that order. The ten may hurt a little, but the lady and queen should be fine."

"Depends on your definition of fine, I suppose," I sighed, lifting up the knight. "Here goes."

I pressed the card to my chest, concentrating on placing it in the correct spot in my layout. The card touched my chest, and I winced instinctively. It slid into me, burning and stinging as it went, but the pain wasn't nearly as bad as removing it. Curiously, I lifted the lady and added her, and instead of pain, she flowed into the center of me like a rush of warm water just on the edge of being too hot. It wasn't pleasant or anything, but the lack of pain surprised me.

"That—that didn't hurt at all!" I said in amazement, staring at Azara. "I mean, it wasn't fun, but it didn't hurt."

"Because it helped balance your layout," she said. "The ten will hurt a little more, but the queen shouldn't be painful either." She shook her head. "Holders, thinking that something ripping its way into their soul is normal."

I picked up the ten and examined it. It showed a hand barely touching a golden goblet with the number ten embossed on it. Ice filled the goblet, and what looked like waves of cold radiated out from it. I took a deep breath and pressed it to my chest. As she said, it stung as it dug its way into me, but the pain was no worse than a minor cut—or being slapped in the face. It hurt, but I could easily ignore it. The queen followed, and like the lady, she flowed down easily, burning only slightly as she slid into my deck. A moment later, all four cards were in place, and my new cards popped up in my vision for me to examine.

Queen of Cups
Aura of Majesty
Rank: Noble Arcana
Attunement: 23%
Base Power: 28 **Max Power:** 122

All creatures within 30' of you will feel the desire to please you, and this effect will grow over time.

Hole Card Boost!

Your Aura of Majesty power gains an 85% bonus to effectiveness and can affect creatures protected from mental manipulation. Affected creatures may take extreme actions to please you.

TEN OF CUPS

FREEZING TOUCH

You create solid crystals of ice within any object you touch.

Low Arcana ♪ 45% ϟ13 ϟϟ29

Ten of Cups
Freezing Touch
Rank: Low Arcana
Attunement: 45%
Base Power: 13 **Max Power:** 29
You create solid crystals of ice within any object you touch.

Hole Card Boost!
Your Freezing Touch power gains an
85% bonus to effectiveness, can
affect creatures immune to cold, and
accumulates faster.

Layout Boost!
The abilities of your 10, Knight,
Lady, and Queen of Cups are
boosted by 15% to range and
effectiveness, and their Harmony
requirements are reduced by 5 due to
their advantageous position in your
layout.

"Huh. It worked, Azara," I said in mild astonishment as I read the last card. "I got a 15% boost to all those cards just for being in the right places in my layout."

"I don't know why you sound surprised," she replied, seemingly unimpressed. "I know cards, Murf. You should know that by now."

"I do. I just didn't realize that it would have that much of an effect."

"It does. And it should increase as you add cards to that base."

"Wait," I said slowly, my eyes narrowing. "It *should* increase? You mean, you don't know?"

"It was just a theory," she said nonchalantly. "I've never had the chance to put it into practice to see, though. It's comforting to be vindicated."

"You didn't know? You mean, you had me change my cards all around on a *guess?*"

"Not a guess. An educated hypothesis. It works with tableaus; it should work the same with soul decks." She shrugged. "And if it hadn't, you could have changed them back. It did, though, so there's no need to be upset, is there? After all, a 15% bonus isn't something to sneeze at, is it?"

"Kewan's blood!" Ferdi's curse saved me from having to decide if I wanted to hug Azara for helping me or throttle her for using me as an experiment. "15%? How did you get that kind of boost to your cards?"

"Following her advice," I muttered after glaring at the avian for a second or two, something that seemed to bother her not at all. "About layouts. Turns out she's right. At least, my cards said so when they gave me that boost."

"Seriously?" Ferdi stomped over to Azara, her eyes wide and fierce. "I want a reading, too!"

"As I said. Ten gold. Do you have it?"

"No," the halfling muttered. "I don't have any at the moment."

"Actually, you have one," I said helpfully, pulling a coin from my purse and handing it to the halfling. "Your share of what I got selling something I found in the Labyrinth."

"What did you...no." She shook her head. "I don't want to know. Fine, bird-woman. I'll get your gold somehow, and you'll give me that reading—and advise me the same way you did Murf?"

"Of course. That's part of the service."

"Good." She stuck my hat out toward me, her face discontented but resolute at the same time. "Here. Your security blanket."

"It's a security hat, thank you very much," I said, feeling a sense of relief as I slipped it onto my head. As it settled into place, I looked at the woman curiously. "Did you keep her clothes, too?"

"Whose?"

"Cassa's. Her hood and mask. Did you keep those?"

"Yes. I thought if I left them behind, it would be evidence that she's been captured. They're in the wagon, as well. What do you want with them?" She looked back and forth between us. "Is this another one of those sex things? Like the hero and the priestess?"

Azara's eyes narrowed instantly, and she glared at me. "How does she know about that?" she asked in a hoarse whisper.

"He told the assassin. I think he was flirting with her."

"I wasn't flirting with her," I said quickly, stepping back from the avian as her head-feathers began to fluff up in anger. "I was trying to get her to calm down so my abilities would work on her."

"It worked," Ferdi nodded, poking the corpse with a finger. "She's very relaxed. Why do you want those clothes if not for a sex thing, then?"

"I think that with them, we might be able to do this." I looked upstairs and grimaced. "We'll need Millie to go along, though. I might have to talk fast to get her to agree."

"You already talked her into your bed," Ferdi shrugged. "How much harder can anything else be?"

"You really do need that hat to think clearly," Azara said wonderingly. "There's something deeply wrong with you, Murf."

"There's something deeply wrong with all of us, Azara, or we wouldn't be thinking about doing what we're going to do."

"We?" the avian asked archly. "I don't recall agreeing to anything."

"If you weren't going to help, you never would have let us into your shop, and you know it," I chuckled. "And you never do anything halfway."

She grimaced. "Damn you, Murf. Fine. I want to pay my former employer back for betraying and stealing from me, anyway. What do you need from me?"

I glanced back upstairs once more, considering how I was going to get Millie to go along with this. "I have a feeling I might need some healing in a bit," I muttered.

"I can do that—unless the pain is deserved, of course. Then, you're on your own."

41

Upper Kallit was pretty much exactly as Cassa described it. It was a farming village, and it seemed to have a higher-than-average concentration of pig farms in the area. To make things worse, someone had built a rendering plant just outside the village. Don't get me wrong, I'm appreciative of things like soap, wax, tallow, and glue. I just don't want to smell them being made. The smell of rotten eggs mingled with that of pig crap and animal manure to produce an odor that I felt certain was going to linger in my hair and clothes for weeks, if not forever.

"Another set of clothes gone, once I have to burn these," I thought darkly. *"I need to find a card that gives me the ability to clean and repair clothing. I'd save dozens of silvers the way things have been going lately."*

The wagon creaked along the dirt road. The horses had to go slowly to keep from damaging the wagon on the uneven surface, which made the trip take half the damn day. I wished we could have just taken a boat—we would have been there a lot faster—but we didn't really have much of a choice. Cassa had always gone by wagon, so we did, too.

"This isn't going to work," Millie muttered from her spot beside me on the wagon's seat. She looked distinctly uncomfortable in Cassa's loose, gray clothing, and even more so with the soft mask covering her face and hiding her features. With the hood up hiding her coppery ringlets, though, I wouldn't have recognized her, at least not from a distance. Hopefully, the elf and halfling wouldn't, either.

Getting Millie to go along with this plan had actually been shockingly easy. She'd apparently heard everything downstairs and had wisely chosen not to get involved, but she'd been swayed by Ferdi's arguments.

"You could just leave town, you know," I'd reminded her.

"You're forgetting something, Murf," she sighed. "That other assassin is still somewhere in Canis, and he might be watching the harbor gate. Trying to leave the city might get me a knife in my back, and one of those is more than enough for me." She shook her head. "No, my grandfather taught me that the only good enemy is one who's dead." She laughed weakly. "That could be one of your laws."

"I've always kind of hoped to never have enough enemies to need a law like that, personally."

"So did I, but here we are. We either have to all try to run together and hope for the best or try to make sure your Shadow Man isn't a problem anymore."

"My Shadow Man? When did he become mine?"

"The day you dragged me into this." She kissed me gently on the cheek and smiled wanly. "I still blame you completely, by the way, and you owe me big."

In fact, the hard part had been getting her to take the ace and two of blades and four of cups and try to put them in her deck. The ace had been so painful it knocked her out, and Ferdi pronounced that she'd pretty much reached the limit of her current capacity. Azara looked less convinced, and part of me wanted to try and convince the cartomancer to give Millie a reading to see how she could lay out her deck more effectively, but I doubted the avian would go along with that—at least, not without being paid for it. So, I kept the two and four, along with the other, higher cards, and slipped them into the card holder that I'd never gotten around to selling.

There had been one little hitch in my plan. Originally, I'd thought to have Millie dress in Cassa's clothing while the rest of us hid in the back of the wagon, then surprise the Holders the way I had Alerion and Taveroth. Sadly, that wouldn't work for one simple reason. Millie had no idea how to drive a wagon. Neither did Azara, as it turned out. That left me or Ferdi, and of the two of us, she was the more visibly dangerous. She also would have had to take off her armor, and I wasn't about to ask the warrior to do that. I was pretty sure she slept, bathed, and answered nature's call without ever taking it off. How she managed that, I didn't know, and I wasn't going to ask her.

So, there I was, sitting in the wagon seat, driving the two horses along the rutted road that was really barely more than a path toward a village that was noteworthy only for its horrific stench. And to keep up the disguise, Millie had one of Cassa's long daggers resting against the side of my neck where one really good pothole in the road could jam it deep into me. Yeah, I was definitely not a fan of this plan, and apparently, I wasn't alone.

"They'll know I'm not her," Millie fretted for perhaps the fiftieth time. "They'll kill us—or worse!"

"Relax, Millie," I muttered soothingly, trying not to think about the fact that a woman on the verge of a panic attack was holding a knife against my neck. "Remember, it's just a bluff. You've done it a thousand times before. They're nothing more than players at the table. You're just convincing them that you've got a hand you don't really have. You can do that."

"Right," she said, taking a deep breath. "Just a bluff. They're just players…" She took another deep breath. "You know, Murf, if you turned the wagon around now, we could probably make the city gates before sundown. We could spend the night doing what those elves stopped us from doing in the Royal Lamb, then start out nice and fresh in the morning."

"You really think it'll be any better in the morning?"

"No, but I thought that maybe I could distract you then, too, and eventually, it would all sort itself out."

I forced myself not to chuckle. I didn't know if or when we might be watched, but I had to assume we were. If Cassa's former partner was the one following us, the game was probably up. He'd know right away that Millie wasn't the assassin; she didn't quite move correctly, she held her knife differently, and he could probably get close enough to hear her voice. Anyone else, though, would have to get closer to see. At least, that was my hope: they'd get close enough to be in range of my abilities. At that point, I hoped that I could overcome any particular suspicion they might have.

That was why Charlie now hid in my soul, Millie's knife had been pressed to my neck the entire trip, and our conversations had been quiet and furtive. I'd kept a defeated look on my face and drove with my shoulders slumped in despair. I hadn't looked directly at her once, and I'd kept looking around as if hoping to escape. With Millie's mask and hood concealing her face, I hoped that anyone watching us would see exactly what I wanted them to see: Millie—or Cassa—had captured me and the others and was forcing me to drive myself and her cargo to my own demise.

"It's a tempting offer," I finally said quietly, keeping my lips as still as possible as I spoke, "but I think it might be too late. Unless I miss my guess, that's Upper Kallit just ahead—and that's our welcoming committee."

She had the good sense not to look—it would have been out of character—but I let my eyes drift up to the road ahead. Upper Kallit was a village only in the roughest sense of the word, I guessed. It was probably more accurate to call it a collection of hovels surrounded by pig farms. Everything was wood, and while it was still too far away to really tell, I guessed it was probably held together by mud and snot. If you think that's an exaggeration, you've never seen a troll "village" before. They really are built that way. Upper Kallit looked better than that, but not by nearly enough, and it smelled just as bad. I couldn't see the renderer's from where I was—at least, I didn't think I could, although it was hard to tell since everything looked like it might be filled with boiling pig fat—but I could smell it. The stench of rotting eggs was thick enough that I could practically taste it on my tongue, in fact.

However, none of that mattered as much as the armored halfling standing in the road up ahead. He'd chosen to take the high ground, although it wasn't really high ground so much as the highest part of an incredibly gentle rise of maybe a foot or two over a hundred. Still, he stood on it like he owned the place, dressed in gleaming steel plate that had to be hot as hell and holding a long spear in his hand. I didn't think he expected trouble since his helmet hung from his belt rather than covering his pale green hair, but then, for all I knew, he just didn't think he'd need it to deal with the likes of us. And he would probably be right, all things considered.

The elf wasn't visible, but I figured she was nearby. After all, a person with a bow or crossbow is a lot more dangerous when you can't see them. The fields around us didn't offer a lot of places to hide, really, but the ramshackle buildings did. I didn't know the effective range of an elven longbow, but I was pretty sure it was more than a hundred feet or so. That meant she could be hiding behind one of the buildings with bow in hand, ready to drop an arrow on my face if I so much as twitched funny. That thought made the center of my forehead itch, as if in anticipation of a sharp steel arrowhead sinking into it, and I had to fight not to reach up and scratch it.

I expected the halfling to hold up a hand dramatically and say something like, "You may go no further!" or, "None may enter!" or, "I'm suffering from swamp crotch in all this armor!" but he just stood there watching us as we got closer. I did my best to keep up my look of defeat and let a little of the fear I truly felt slip through as we neared, trying to ignore the itchy feeling on my forehead and my hammering heart. There were so many ways this could go wrong, and really only a few where it could go right.

We rolled forward slowly, and when we got within what I judged to be a good range, I reached inside myself and grasped the stack of cards representing the lady of cups and her power. As it turned out, Azara's advice had another benefit: the cards being in a more balanced and appropriate position made them easier to use, which I suppose was why their Harmony requirements dropped by 5. My mental grip on the cards felt surer and more comfortable as I squeezed the deck, and when I relaxed to let the cards fly, only a handful flipped outward. The halfling frowned as a barely perceptible ripple of power flowed from me, filling the air out to a bit less than fifty feet with a palpable feeling of apathy.

I'd argued with myself for a while about what feeling to use when we finally reached the village. I'd thought about fear—combining that with the queen's power to encourage people to do what I wanted might have let me cow the Holders into dropping their weapons, surrendering, and maybe finding us some decent food in this pigsty—but Ferdi convinced me that scaring a pair of armed Holders probably wasn't the best idea. I'd considered going the friendly route, the way I had with Cassa, but that took a while to really work on her, even combined with the knight's drunkenness. Azara was the one who suggested apathy; she pointed out that the Holders in Upper Kallit didn't want to be there and probably hated their job already. If they already didn't care about doing it, it wouldn't take much to push them into not caring about us, either. Then, even if they had suspicions, they'd probably just ignore them.

The halfling's frown faded into a neutral expression as I slowed the wagon horses to the barest walk, then reined them in twenty feet from the man. At that point, I took a moment to glance at the card that kept trying to stick itself in front of my eyes.

Halfling
Rank 4 Warrior
Luck: 35 Capacity: 51 Skill: 53
Hole Card: 7 of Blades
Likely Powers: Improved Armor,
Damage Resistance, Improved
Endurance

Halfling
Rank 4 Warrior

Silence reigned between the two groups for a bit before the halfling shifted his grip on his spear, holding it across his chest and staring directly at me. The silence grew, and it suddenly occurred to me that there might have been some kind of passcode involved, here. What if Millie was supposed to greet him with some predetermined phrase like, "The eagle flies at midnight" or, "The stupid eagle crashed into a tree because eagles can't see in the dark"? Apparently, I was terrible at the whole "interrogation" thing because it had never even occurred to me to ask Cassa how the handoff was supposed to go.

The halfling's frown returned, and he walked closer to us, sidestepping the horses to come up on Millie's side. His spear slid forward, pointing at me.

"I know you," he said calmly. "You should be dead." The spear drifted over to point at Millie. "Who are you, and what have you done with Shadowcat?"

My heartbeat suddenly pounded, and I stared at the man for a moment in shock. Millie had been right; he'd seen through our little charade. My mind raced for something to say or do, some bluff I could run, but I drew a complete blank. Fortunately, Ferdi's reactions were a lot faster than mine.

The canvas covering the back of the wagon exploded upward as the halfling leaped out, her new axe flashing as it slashed at the man holding his spear on Millie. She moved quickly enough that her form was little more than a blur, no doubt using some sort of speed ability to boost herself. Her axe rippled with power as she activated an attack power. Her strike was swift, brutal, and seemed unstoppable, and I braced myself to get splattered with bisected halfling bits.

The clang of metal on metal rang in the air as the man leaped backward, moving as swiftly as Ferdi. His spear swept sideways, intercepting her blow and knocking it out of the way. She let him push her weapon aside and whipped it around in a sideways slash that clanged against the apparently metal shaft of his spear, then knocked his return thrust out of the way with the buckler strapped to her left forearm. The two stood facing one another, their weapons ready and their eyes hard as they gazed at one another.

"Ferdi," the man spoke in a calm, emotionless voice that reminded me that my power was still running. "Glad to see you didn't die. How did you manage that?"

"Tifer," she nodded, her voice just as relaxed. "Ran the Labyrinth, of course."

"Impressive. You've gotten stronger, it seems."

"I have. Does your oath give you the option to stand down, here?"

"No, it doesn't. I agreed to the contract; I have to fulfill it. Yours?"

"He's got my people, Tifer," she shook her head. "You know I can't."

"Too bad." He lunged forward again, stabbing with his spear, but Ferdi's shield batted it aside, and her axe swept toward him. The two exchanged a rapid series of blows, their weapons clanging against one another or sliding off each other's armor, attacking faster than I could easily follow. I just stared at them; I'd never seen two oath-bound halflings go at it before, and it was frankly kind of amazing. They moved like their weapons and armor were weightless, and the whole thing honestly looked like a perfectly choreographed dance, one that I could only watch in awe. At least, until Azara's voice hissed in my ear.

"What are you doing? Don't just sit there! Help her!"

I jumped to my feet as I remembered where we were and what we were supposed to be doing, and that movement probably saved my life. The arrow that should have taken me in the throat instead slammed into my left shoulder. I screamed as the pain of it exploded through my body and grabbed the arrow, yanking at it instinctively. It didn't move, and the pain increased dramatically, so I dropped it and fell to my knees. That meant that the next arrow sailed over my head instead of killing me.

Millie let out a strangled cry as she dove into the back of the wagon and ducked down, while Azara dropped out of sight just as quickly. I tried to scramble to cover myself, but my left arm didn't want to move, and that slowed me down enough that the next arrow caught me in the back of my right thigh. I roared as it ripped into me and fell backward off the wagon as my leg buckled beneath me. I screamed again as I hit the ground, and suddenly an arrowhead erupted from the front of my leg, driven completely through me by the impact with the ground. I reached down and grabbed the shaft, pulling it up, and it slid out of my leg easily enough. The gash still throbbed, and blood spread quickly along my pants, but it hurt a lot less without the arrow in it.

I quickly scooted sideways, ducking underneath the wagon, and as I did, another arrow slammed into the wooden wheel, punching completely through it and jutting out the other side. I kept moving, trying to put the wagon and horses between me and that damned elf archer. Another arrow plunged into the ground a couple feet from me, and I stumbled back even faster. Once I felt reasonably safe, I stopped and took a deep breath, collecting my thoughts and analyzing my injuries.

My leg wasn't as bad as I'd first thought. It burned and throbbed, but I could still move it, and while the wound was bleeding, it wasn't gushing. My shoulder was probably worse since I couldn't move my left arm at all. The arrow might have cut the nerves running through my shoulder, and I wasn't sure if those would heal. I pushed down the moment of panic and forced myself to focus. I'd healed quite a bit of damage over the last week or so; I could probably heal this, too. As it was, the pain in my leg was easing, and the blood seemed to be slowing by the second. The same would eventually happen with my shoulder, but probably not until the arrow was out. I supposed I could try to jam it through my body the way the other arrow had, but I couldn't bring myself to deliberately suffer that kind of pain. The arrow would have to stay; maybe Ferdi would know what to do about it.

The thought of the halfling made me remember that she was in the middle of a fight. I ducked low and peeked out below the wagon. The two halflings were still at it, but it was obvious that Ferdi was getting the worst of their exchange. Her armor had a couple of rents in it where his spear had tagged her, and she slowly backed away from him, unable to close with him to put her weapon to use. I wondered why for a moment until her arm swept up like she was swatting a bug. An arrow exploded against her buckler with a loud crack, but in that moment, the man's spear darted forward and plunged past her guard into her thigh. She stumbled and fell back again, and I knew that without help, she was going to lose this fight.

"Charlie, go find that elf who's shooting arrows and bite her," I instructed. *"Hard!"*

"Yes, Dad." A surge of ice rose up from my chest as the ferret surged out of me, flowing in his misty blue form down my chest to the ground. He raced outward, scampering around the horses' legs and vanishing.

"And make it hurt, Charlie!" I thought a little spitefully. I took a deep breath, trying to ignore the pain of my wounds, then reached down and triggered the knight's ability, pouring it forth. I didn't want to blast it all out, just in case, but I was worried that the oath-bound might have some sort of resistance to it. Plus, with as much pain as I was in, I didn't have the best focus. The power just kind of sprayed out, rushing across the battlefield in a wave before I could rein it in.

If Tifer had any kind of defenses against my power, my probably over-the-top blast of it must have overcome them. The man stumbled in his next lunge, his spear going wild and missing Ferdi completely as he shook his head in sudden confusion. She batted the thrust aside and darted in, and her axe crunched through the armor over his stomach with a loud grinding sound. He staggered back, whipping his spear down to drive her away, then stood, swaying on his feet, looking confused and unsure.

Another arrow sped out of nowhere, but Ferdi batted it aside almost contemptuously and rushed the man again. The two battled fiercely, but their combat lacked the finesse that it showed earlier. Ferdi's wounds slowed her down, and as my power crept its way into the man's body, he staggered and stumbled more often. Their battle shifted about back and forth, drawing closer to the wagon, and as it did, I crept forward, getting near the edge and watching. The battle raged closer, and as it did, I reached inward and grabbed the ten of cups, flexing the stack of cards and holding it ready. I'd never used the ability before, but I knew that I had to be touching something to make it work.

"Ferdi! Bring him closer!" I shouted at her.

She nodded and shifted about, her axe whipping about like a toy as she battered at the man. He tried to avoid being moved toward me, but as Drunken Combat sank deeper into him, he seemed to be fighting just to stay standing, much less to resist Ferdi's blows. He stepped back, almost in range, and I pushed with my good leg, lunging out to touch his back, the power ready to leap forth into him.

To my shock, the halfling whipped about, faster than I could track, and the haft of his spear slammed into the side of my skull, knocking me backwards. I lost my grip on the cards, and the power rushed out of me, surging in a wave into the spear through the contact with my head. I fell to the ground, my head ringing and stars swirling in my vision. I recovered swiftly, though, just in time to see the halfling's smoking, frost-coated spear lash out to block Ferdi's axe—and shatter into pieces in his hands. Her axe plunged into his side, and he crumpled up around the blow, dropping to his knees. She swept the weapon around once more, and the flat of it slammed into the side of his head. His eyes rolled up, and he dropped to the ground, unconscious.

"Get down, Ferdi!" I called out as I scrambled beneath the wagon. "The elf…"

"Taken care of," she shook her head, staring sadly down at the fallen man.

"Taken care of?" I asked. "How?"

"The pretty human and bird-woman—and that ferret of yours. Get out here, Murf, so I can look at that shoulder."

I crawled out from beneath the wagon and sat back against a wheel. Ferdi walked over to me and crouched down, pulling my torn coat and shirt aside around the arrow shaft. She tugged on the shaft, and I groaned in pain.

"Barbed arrow," she nodded solemnly. "I'll have to cut it out." She pulled out her knife, her eyes grim. "Brace yourself. This is going to hurt."

Ferdi, as it turned out, had quite the knack for understatement.

42

Cutting the arrow out hurt a hell of a lot worse than the thing did going in. It involved her slipping her knife into the wound, working it around a bit on both sides, and slowly sliding the arrow out. I screamed several times while she worked and nearly passed out from the pain twice. Once it was free, though, the pain began to ebb almost immediately, and I sat there, panting, covered in sweat, wondering if it would be okay to pass out for a bit or not. Apparently, the answer was "not", as Ferdi reached down, grabbed me under my good arm, and hauled me to my feet.

"That was a terrible plan, Murf," she said flatly. "It didn't work at all."

"Didn't it?" I asked as I leaned against the wagon. My leg still throbbed, although the burning had eased, and I felt faintly lightheaded. I gestured at the fallen halfling. "They're down. We're still here. How is that not a success?"

"It only worked because we got lucky. If that archer had put the first arrow in your eye, we'd all be gone right now. You should learn how to take cover."

"Maybe," I shrugged. "She didn't, though, and worrying about things that didn't actually happen seems pretty pointless, doesn't it?"

"It's not called worrying, Murf. It's called learning."

"And we learned that my plans work," I grinned at her. "See how it all comes together?"

The halfling grumbled, then moved back to the wagon and pulled out her pack from it. She withdrew a set of chain manacles and began strapping them to the unconscious halfling, locking his hands behind his back and his feet together, then attaching a collar around his neck and tying it to the wagon. I watched her in curious silence.

"Do you always carry manacles and a collar around, Ferdi?" I finally asked. "That seems pretty kinky, even for you."

"I got these for you," she said shortly.

"Me? I'm flattered, Ferdi, but I'm not usually into that sort of thing. You know, whips, chains, elven variations…"

"Not for sex. I told you, I'm not interested in that with you." She paused. "Although you could borrow them for the pretty human when we're done here, if you want."

"I'll consider it," I chuckled. "It might take some fast talking for Millie."

"You think? She seems to be into everything." She shrugged. "In any case, I got them for when I caught you in the city. I'd hoped you'd come there for the tournament—that's why I came to Canis in the first place—and I figured I might have to break into the Gambler's Hall and drag you out. So, manacles and a collar."

"You were going to break into the Hall?" I asked dubiously.

"That was the plan. At least, until you walked up to the hold yourself." She seemed upset, and I had a feeling I knew why.

"I take it you and this Tifer guy know each other, then?" I asked gently.

"Yes. We took our oaths together." She began searching him, rummaging through his pockets and pulling out a number of weapons and cards. "He's my oath-brother."

"And he fought you?" I asked a little incredulously. "Over the money from a contract—one he's probably never getting paid for anyway?"

"No." She stood up and gave me a flat, hard look. "He fought me over his oath. Standing aside would have broken it, just as walking away would have broken mine. He won't break that, no matter what—even if it meant killing his oath-sister."

"What happens when he wakes up, then? Won't he try to kill you again?"

"It depends on his contract. Most sellsword contracts have a surrender clause in case you're captured that either suspends or voids the contract entirely. If his does, then being bound like this will be enough for him to help me."

"And if not?"

She didn't reply but knelt back beside the man and kept rifling through his belongings. I watched her in silence for a few moments, not saying anything. I understood, and I really hoped it wouldn't come to that.

"Little help, here?" I turned to see Millie walking toward us, dragging what looked like a large, leaf-covered bush behind her—a very heavy one, by how she was walking backward and the strain in her arms. To my surprise, Charlie was riding invisibly on her shoulder. "Murf?"

"What are you doing?" I asked her curiously. "Why did you pull that bush out of the ground?"

"It's not a bush, you ass! It's that elf. Come on, Murf! She's heavier than she looks!"

"I'll do it," Ferdi said, rising to her feet. "He's too wounded to be useful. Is she dead?"

"Yes," Millie said quietly, her face pale even beneath her hood and mask. "I—I killed her."

The halfling grabbed the brushy elf with one hand and hauled her onto her shoulder almost effortlessly, carrying her over and dumping her beside me. "Here, Murf. Claim her cards—if you can find them in that mess."

I looked down at the elf's corpse. It really was a mess. Not that Millie had shredded her or anything; her body was just covered in a tangle of vines, leaves, and branches that made it look like a humanoid bush of some kind.

"I take it this was some kind of camouflage?" I asked.

"Yeah," she said weakly, her face pale beneath her hood. "She was tucked up against a bush, and I couldn't see her at all, even with Azara telling me where she was. If it hadn't been for Charlie popping into view and biting her face, I might not have found her before she spotted me."

"I made sure it hurt, Dad," the ferret said proudly. *"Just like you asked! She said bad words and everything!"*

"Good boy, Charlie," I grinned at him. I knelt beside the body and reached for my knife before realizing that I wasn't wearing it; I thought being armed would be a dead giveaway. I had to borrow Millie's, then began sawing and hacking at the branches one-handed in an amazingly ineffective fashion. The branches the elf had used were green and springy, and they resisted my blows, sliding away from the knife without parting. If I'd had my other hand, I could have held them in place, but as it was, I was accomplishing a whole lot of nothing.

"Here, let me do it," Millie sighed, taking the knife from me. She began cutting with swift, sure strokes that slid through the tough branches with ease, and I eyed her curiously.

"New cutting ability?" I asked.

"Deep Cut. Came with the ace of blades," she said shortly.

"You okay?" I asked her quietly.

She paused, and I saw the trembling in her hands and the tenseness of her body. "No, not really," she said in a ragged voice. "I—I killed her, Murf. I mean, I know I had to—she would have killed us if I hadn't—but I did it. I snuck up behind her while Charlie was biting her, stuck my knife in her, and—oh, fuck!"

She dropped the blade and turned away, and I heard the sound of her retching over by the wagon. I ignored it and picked up the knife, cutting the branches away as best I could with one hand.

"I'll help, Dad." Charlie flowed down onto the body and began gnawing at the branches, his sharp little teeth far more effective than my blade. I watched him for a moment, then turned to look at Millie. I felt nothing but sympathy for the woman. It wasn't long ago that I was that person, emptying the best meal of my life out into the Labyrinth over Taveroth and Alerion. I couldn't exactly judge Millie. I glanced at Ferdi, expecting to see disapproval in her eyes, but to my surprise, she looked at Millie with understanding. As I watched, she walked over to the redhead and crouched beside her, ignoring the vomit splattered nearby as she rubbed the woman's back almost tenderly.

"It's not easy, is it?" she asked simply. "Killing another person, that is. It's different from killing a beast in the Labyrinth." Millie didn't respond, and the halfling just kept talking. "I remember the first time I had to do it. I'd killed plenty of beasts, so I thought that killing an orc—one who was trying to kill me—would be easy. I was wrong. I responded the same way you are."

"How—how did you get over it?" Millie gasped, coughing and spitting.

"I didn't. At least, not for a long time. When it happened, though, I told myself that I had no choice. I kept saying that until I sort of believed it, which let me keep functioning. Then I found a drinking hall, drank myself into a stupor, and woke up with a tattoo."

"A tattoo?" I looked at the woman in disbelief. "You have a tattoo, Ferdi? I didn't know that!"

"There's a lot about me you don't know, Murf."

"What is it?" I asked with a spreading grin. "And where?"

"A dripping axe on my lower back. Bad place for it, it turns out. It hurts like hell when you put pants and armor on for the next couple of days, and if you leave it uncovered, males seem to think it's an invitation to stare at your ass. I found out later that a tattoo there is called a 'harlot's mark' and is considered a proclamation of promiscuity. I ended up having to break a lot of wandering hands over it, and now I make sure it's always covered." She shook her head. "I recommend the drink. Not the tattoo."

"Thanks," the redhead breathed, seeming to have recovered herself. "I can finish that, Murf."

"I will deal with it," Azara said, slipping down easily from the wagon and pulling out a handful of cards. "Move, Murf." I stepped back and watched as she set up the cards, laying them around the body. At last, she placed one atop the corpse. For a moment, it seemed like nothing happened, but after a few seconds, the leaves began to shift colors from green to yellow and then to brown. The branches seemed to shiver as they shrank and dried out with a rustling sound. Half a minute later, Azara picked up the card and nodded. "There. They should come free easily, now."

I reached down and grabbed one of the branches, pulling hard. To my surprise, it tore loose easily in my hand, practically crumbling to sawdust in my grip. I ripped away the rest of the branches and nodded at Azara.

"Thanks. I've never seen you use that layout before."

"Yes, you have," she corrected. "It's just the inversion of the one I use to keep my plants alive when I've forgotten to water them for a while."

"Oh, yeah, I'd almost forgotten that. Still can't keep a plant alive?"

"I've had much better luck in the last few years. It's easier when there's no one around to distract me."

I winced but didn't say anything as Charlie and I cleared away the last of the branches and examined the elf woman. She was darker than most elves, with lightly tanned skin that looked like pale gold rather than the nut-brown of halflings or humans. Her hair matched, and she looked vaguely pretty in a haughty, contemptuous sort of way. Of course, that describes 99% of elf women. Or men, for that matter. Both genders tend toward the "pretty" side. Her body was unmarked, which made sense since Millie had gotten her from behind.

I reached down and touched the woman's chest, pinching my fingers together and reading the card that flashed in my vision.

Cards Gained!
You have claimed the cards of
another Holder.
Luck check success! You have
drawn a card with a high Harmony!

I held up the three cards, staring at the image of the noble card I'd pulled. It showed a youngish man with a rakish appearance holding a simple golden cup in his hand and wearing a rather plain crown. The man looked sort of like he knew something I didn't and was willing to use it against me the first chance he got.

Prince of Cups
Likely Power: Charm
Requirements:
Luck: 51 Harmony: 47
Compatibility: 25%

"That's you, Dad," Charlie observed in his piping little voice.

"You think so, Charlie?"

"It feels like you."

"Another noble of your court." I looked back to see Azara looking calmly over my shoulder. "The prince this time. You know where to add it."

"What about the others?" I asked curiously. "With the three and four, I've got a run, all off-suit, ace to four. I just need a five of coins to fill it out."

"And what will you put opposite them, to balance them out?"

"I've got the six, seven, and nine of coins…"

"Which won't balance anything, as you know. You'll have a four-flush in coins. What would you do in a game with that hand?"

I sighed. "Hold it and wait for the next card to drop, hoping for another coin."

"Then, that's what I would do."

"What are you telling him, bird-woman?" Ferdi demanded, walking over to stare at the two of us. "Murf, what did you get?" I held up the cards, and she threw her hands up in the air. "Kewan's blood! The damn prince! I assume you're going to bind it?"

"I suppose," I sighed. "We were just talking about the rest of the cards I've got and what to do with them."

"Rest of them? How many do you have?" I dutifully pulled out the stack of cards I'd gathered and handed them over to Ferdi, who examined them with wide eyes.

"Fuck me, Murf," she breathed, fanning out the cards.

"I didn't think we had that kind of relationship, Ferdi," I chuckled weakly.

"I'm not interested in you that way, Murf—but if you keep pulling cards like this, I might be." She looked at me almost accusingly. "You can't bind any of these? I know you can handle the cups, and I'm sure that you can manage the coins, as well. Even if you've got no harmony for them, the two and ace will be useful; the two will give you a better defense, and the ace will make your mind work better or improve your senses. And that six will help you heal even faster!" She held them out to me. "You should bind as many as you can!"

"And then, his entire layout would unbalance," Azara said caustically, "and everything would function worse. It's not worth damaging his soul and tainting the cards just for a quick boost of power!"

"It's not about power, woman, it's about surviving!" Ferdi said, raising her voice as she spoke. "What's the point of having a perfect layout if you die to an elven arrow before you can get it?"

Azara opened her mouth to retort, but before she could say a word, Millie stepped between them, raising her hands. "Wait a second," she said, shaking her head. When Azara drew a breath, the redhead repeated, "I said, wait a second! Enough! You've both said your piece. Azara, you want him to wait and place his cards carefully. Ferdi, you're worried that if he does, he might not live to do it." She looked at me. "The real question, Murf, is what do you want? Not what does Azara want, or what does Ferdi want, but what do you want?"

I grimaced, but there was only one answer I could give. "I want to get by while binding as few cards as possible," I admitted. "I hate being a Holder, and every card I add feels like I'm stepping closer to becoming a real one." I took a deep breath. "At the same time, those arrows fucking hurt, and so did Ferdi's axe when she cut me. I really don't want to keep getting hurt, so if adding a couple cards can help me, I'll do it."

I looked at Ferdi. "Of these cards, what do you think the most important ones to add are?"

She frowned, but she shuffled through the cards and held up two, the ace of staves and two of blades. "These two. The extra mental boost from the ace will help all of us so you come up with better plans than this one, and the defense from the two will help you live longer. And the prince, obviously."

"Azara," I said, turning to the cartomancer, "if I added those two to one side of my layout, could I put something on the other side to balance it? What if I put one on one side and one on the other?"

"That would be balanced," she admitted. "Or you could put them both on one side and the three of cups on the other. That would balance, as well."

"Do that, then," Ferdi said quickly. "The three will give you some form of attack power, and that's always useful."

"Only if you plan to spend all your time fighting," Millie observed, "which I don't think Murf does." She made a face. "It would be useful in the short term, though."

"Fine," I sighed. "I'll do those, then." I closed my eyes and took a deep breath, holding up the prince. "Here goes."

I touched the card to my chest. To my shock, it simply flowed into me like a cool, refreshing stream of water. There was no pain or discomfort at all, and I stared at Azara as the card trickled merrily into the space I'd chosen for it.

"That—that actually felt kind of good!" I said in astonishment.

"What?" Ferdi asked, glaring at me. "It didn't hurt? How many cards do you have, now?"

"That's the fifth."

"You have to be getting close to your capacity," the halfling said almost accusingly. "That should have burned like hell!"

"He placed it in the perfect position in his soul," Azara sniffed. "And it's the card that his soul has the most connection to." She gave me an even expression. "I would add the ace and two with the ace closer to the center and the two one rank outward, then the three. The two should hurt the worst of the three, but it shouldn't be too bad."

I followed her advice, and as she said, the two stung significantly going in. The ace hurt a little, but the three barely burned at all. When I finished, I found the others watching me, and I gave them a hesitant look.

"What?" I asked.

"That didn't hurt?" Ferdi asked dubiously.

"No, not really. The two burned, like Azara said it would, but the others weren't bad at all."

"The last card I put in hurt so much that it knocked me out, Murf," Millie complained. She turned to Azara. "Can you tell me how to do that? Please?"

"Of course. I charge five gold for that kind of reading."

"Five?" Ferdi demanded. "You told me ten!"

"You demanded a reading. She asked politely. I always charge rude customers double." She looked calmly at Millie. "Do you have five gold?"

"Not yet," she shook her head. "I'll get it, though. If it can keep the cards from hurting, it's more than worth it. And thank you."

"Thank me with your coins, and I'll be satisfied."

I tuned out their argument and focused on the images of the new cards I'd gained.

PRINCE OF CUPS

GOLDEN TONGUE

Creatures see your words as trustworthy, and this effect grows over time.

👑 Noble Arcana ♪27% ⚡33 ⚡⚡124

Prince of Cups
Golden Tongue
Rank: Noble Arcana
Attunement: 27%
Base Power: 33   **Max Power:** 124
Creatures see your words as trustworthy, and this effect grows over time.

Hole Card Boost!
Your Golden Tongue power gains a 125% bonus to effectiveness and affects both your words and actions. This effect can cause others to be enraptured by or enamored of you.

TWO OF BLADES

THICK SKIN

Your skin is resistant to being pierced or cut, and
this resistance grows while the power is active.

👑 Low Arcana　♪11%　⚡2　⚡⚡6

Two of Blades
Thick Skin
Rank: Low Arcana
Attunement: 11%
Base Power: 2　**Max Power:** 6
Your skin is resistant to being
pierced or cut, and this resistance
grows while the power is active.

Hole Card Boost!
Your Thick Skin power gains a 105%
bonus to effectiveness and can
protect you from card-enhanced
attacks. Regular blades have an
increasing chance to shatter on your
skin.

THREE OF CUPS

GAZE OF DESPAIR

You can instill despair and defeat in any creature with whom you make eye contact. This inflicts a penalty to all actions they take while afflicted.

♛ Low Arcana　♪78%　⚡7　⚡⚡9

Three of Cups
Gaze of Despair
Rank: Low Arcana
Attunement: 78%
Base Power: 7　**Max Power:** 9
You can instill despair and defeat in any creature with whom you make eye contact. This inflicts a penalty to all actions they take while afflicted.

Hole Card Boost!
Your Gaze of Despair power gains a 125% bonus to effectiveness and can affect creatures protected from mental effects. The sense of despair can overwhelm and cripple a target.

ACE OF STAVES

IMPROVED PERCEPTION

Your senses are mildly increased, and this increase grows the longer the power is used.

Low Arcana · 67% · 4 · 6

Ace of Staves
Improved Perception
Rank: Low Arcana
Attunement: 67%
Base Power: 4   **Max Power:** 6
Your senses are mildly increased, and this increase grows the longer the power is used.

Hole Card Boost!
Your Improved Perception power gains a 125% bonus to effectiveness and allows you a steadily increasing chance to penetrate illusions or disguises.

Layout Boost!
The abilities of your Ace of Staves, Two of Blades, and Three of Cups

are boosted by 5% to range and effectiveness, and their Harmony requirements are reduced by 2 due to their advantageous position in your layout.

Potential Stacks Built
Type: Flush Run
Cards: 10, Kn, La, Pr, Qu, Em of Cups (Eldritch Hag).
Benefit: +51% effectiveness to all cards, all cards gain an additional effect at 71% power, activating multiple cards in the stack improves all effects by 15% per card active.

Do you want to form this stack?

Type: Run
Cards: A of Staves, Two of Blades, Three of Cups, Four (Eldritch Hag)
Benefit: +17% effectiveness to all cards.

Do you want to form this stack?

"Hey, Ferdi!" I called out, interrupting whatever conversation the women were having. "What happens when you form a stack of cards?"

"It depends on the stack," she said absently. I looked at her and found her leaning over the still-unconscious Tifer, holding my six of coins against him.

"What's wrong?" I asked her.

"I think I hit him too hard. He should be coming around by now."

"That'll work better if Azara does it, you know," I pointed out.

"I know. She won't."

"I'm not about to heal an enemy who will likely wake up and attempt to kill me on sight," she said stiffly. "I'm not quite as durable as you, halfling."

"No, you aren't." The warrior looked up at me. "What kind…?" Her eyes widened. "Kewan's blood, Murf, you can make a flush run in the court of coins, can't you?"

"Yeah. Plus a run out of the ace, two, and three."

"Two stacks? Hell, yes, do it!"

"Okay, but what happens if I do?" I hedged. "I mean, what if I get the Emperor later on? Can I add it in, too?"

"As long as you don't meld the cards, then yes, you can. You can always add to and remove from a stack—although I wouldn't add anything lower than the ten to that one, and you shouldn't go higher than a six with the other."

"Why not? Isn't more, better?"

"Not always," she shook her head. "A run's strength is determined by the middle cards. All the cards add their strength to the others, but only to a point, usually about five to seven cards. If you keep adding cards to it, you dilute out the power and will actually make it weaker overall. Same goes for a flush run."

"What does a run or flush run do, though?"

"It makes the cards in it stronger." She shifted to face me more fully. "You can stack cards four ways: a run, a set, a flush, or a flush run. They're made just the way they are in your silly card games, except that technically, you can make a stack as big as you want. That's a bad idea, though, since they max out at some point and get weaker from there. More than that, and the benefit actually decreases. You're better splitting long stacks into two smaller ones.

"As I said, a run makes every card in it a little stronger, just a few percent usually. A flush, on the other hand, expands the powers of the card in it. If you've got a blades card that makes you better in combat, adding it to a flush might also give you an earth or metal-based ability at really low power. Again, though, if your flush is too long, those extra abilities will get weaker, not stronger."

She shook her head and made a disgusted sound. "A flush run is the best of both worlds. The power boost is greater, and the extra abilities are stronger. They're still best around six to seven cards long, but those six cards can become really powerful. A run in a noble court—well, like I said, noble dynasties have been built around one of those. So, yeah, make the stack, Murf. It'll make all your abilities more powerful and versatile. Like you need it."

I chose to ignore that last, muttered part and thought, *"Yes"* twice at the hovering card. It vanished from my vision, and I waited to feel the stack happening. I assumed it would be a buzz of power, or maybe a feeling of joining in my chest. Perhaps some sort of fanfare denoting my awesome achievement. Instead, what I got was—a whole lot of nothing. Not even a tingle in my chest or the toot of a single horn. I'd have been satisfied with a decent burp to commemorate the moment at that point, to be honest. Instead, all I got was a new set of cards popping up in front of me, showing their new abilities.

Eldritch Hag Activated
The Eldritch Hag has duplicated the powers and harmonies of cards needed to form a stack. These cards cannot be attuned and do not receive adjacency or layout bonuses but do receive normal stack bonuses.

Emperor of Cups
Crown of Authority
Base Power: 21 **Max Power:** 103
Any creature or person hostile to you within 40' receives a steadily increasing penalty to all actions, reactions, and resistances. All creatures friendly to you in the same range receive a similar bonus.

Four of Stars
Know the Deck
Base Power: 3 **Max Power:** 5
You learn the rank, suit, and ability of a single card in a Holder's deck if they are within Base Power x 2 feet of you. You gain knowledge of additional cards the longer the power is active.

Stack Powers

You gain additional powers to the cards of your flush run.

Ten of Cups
Alter Self
Base Power: 13 **Max Power:** 30
You can change your outer appearance to resemble another person of your race and gender.

Knight of Cups
Living Nightmare
Base Power: 36 **Max Power:** 80
All enemies within 15' see you as their greatest fear or deadliest enemy and suffer a growing fear reaction.

Lady of Cups
Sanctuary
Base Power: 32 **Max Power:** 97
You disguise yourself to look like part of the background, causing others to struggle to see you.

Prince of Cups
Bereft of Sense
Base Power: 34 **Max Power:** 127
You shut down a single sense for a group of people within 20'. This group can be allies, enemies, neutrals, or all at your discretion.

Queen of Cups
Mentor's Words
Base Power: 28 **Max Power:** 125
You appear as someone to be inherently obeyed to all within 20'.

Emperor of Cups
Vision Mastery (71%)
Base Power: 15 **Max Power:** 73
All creatures within 25' will see only what you wish them to see.

I whistled at the new abilities, all of which seemed to be about shifting or changing what people saw or sensed. Sanctuary looked the most useful to me—I could think of a few dozen times I'd have loved to be invisible—but being able to disguise myself with Alter Self seemed pretty valuable, and Living Nightmare to scare off bounty hunters and the like could be useful. I could also see plenty of utility in Bereft of Sense; blinding a group of enemies or deafening some guards so they couldn't hear me could be handy. I wasn't sure about Mentor's Words since it sounded a lot like putting myself in charge of things, and I hated being in charge. Vision Mastery felt too complicated to use. Did I have to decide everything that people were going to see? What happened if I forgot to include the sky or the ground in that? How detailed did I have to make the image? There were too many questions, and unless I played around with it, I'd probably never get an answer.

Which, of course, meant that I was totally going to play with it. Ferdi would make a great test subject. She'd bitch about it, of course, but what would she do if she couldn't see me to hit me? Probably just lash out blindly with her axe, so I'd have to be careful how I messed with her.

I put that idea on hold and looked at my new abilities. Seeing those surprised me. The Hag's description said that she could fill in for any card in the deck, but I thought that meant taking their place to create a hand. Apparently, she could actually mimic the powers of that missing card, as well, although without the adjacency bonuses she provided, they weren't anywhere near as strong as the rest. What was it that she'd said?

"All magic is within my purview…"

Apparently, she meant that in a literal fashion.

I dismissed the cards and pulled up my layout to see how the stacks were represented in it. As it turned out, it wasn't that big of a deal.

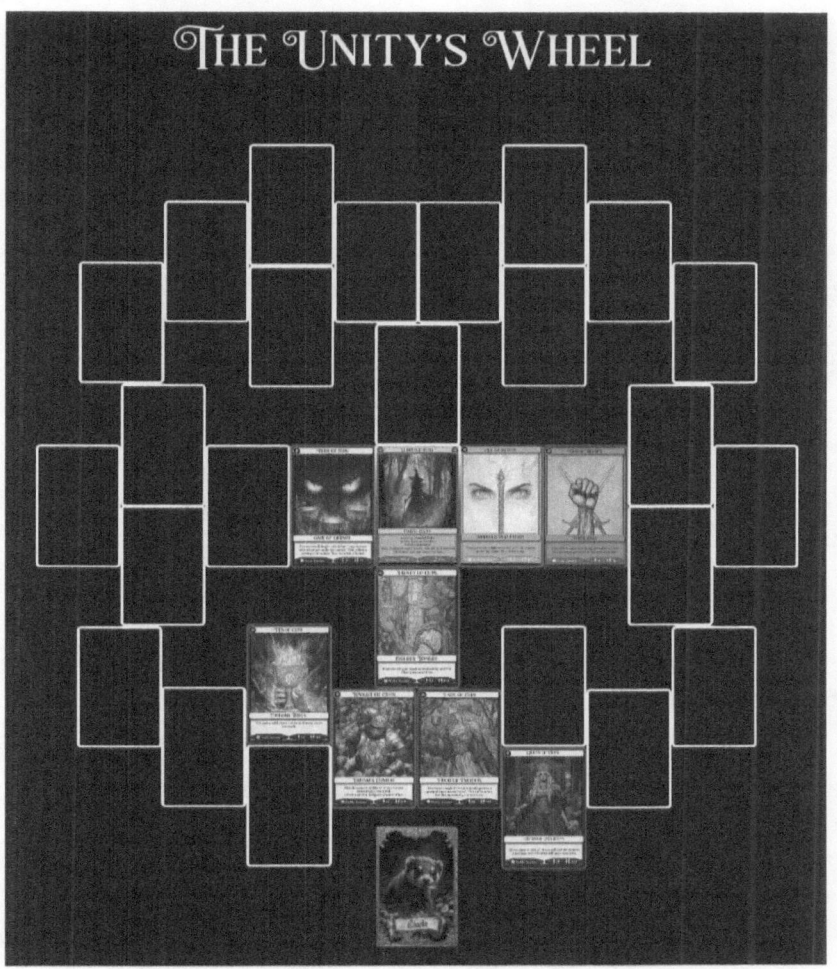

The only difference I could see was that the white frames around the cards had changed color. The cards of my flush run were outlined in purple, while red bordered the outside of my basic run. The border around the Hag was purple at the bottom, near the prince, and red to the sides, where it touched the three and ace. I assumed that was because the Hag was taking the places of cards in those stacks, and the colors meant they were all linked together. That was nice and all, but I'd expected something more, like an actual stack of cards. Of course, that might have changed things in the rest of my layout, leaving gaps in places there weren't supposed to be any, so it might have been a bad idea. Plus, this way, I could still see what cards were close to my empty spots.

"I need that drink," Millie sighed, looking back at the village behind us. "Think there's a drinking house in this place?"

"There almost has to be," I snorted, waving away my layout a little grumpily. "Look at this place—and smell it. There's no way everyone here doesn't drink themselves into a stupor each night."

"I certainly would," she nodded, looking back at the others. "Azara, would you like to come with us?"

I assumed the avian would decline, probably in a nasty fashion, but to my surprise, she nodded. "That would be welcome, yes. The smell of this place..." She grimaced. "I'll need something strong to clear it out, I'm afraid."

"Ferdi?" I said, glancing at the halfling.

"I need to make sure he's okay," she shook her head. "And someone should be near him when he wakes up in case he can get out of the manacles."

Azara sighed, walked over to the fallen man, and placed a card on his chest. "He has bruising to his brain and a minor fracture of the skull. No bleeding, and no fluid seems to be leaking. His cards should heal him soon enough." She lifted the card and slipped it back into her vest.

"Good," the halfling grunted, lifting his prone body and placing it gently in the back of the wagon. After a moment, she hefted the elf's corpse and tossed it in, far less carefully. "They have to be staying somewhere in this place. I'll find out where and meet the rest of you there in an hour or so."

"Works for me," I nodded, then turned to the other two. "Coming, ladies? First round's on me."

"I can pay for my own drinks, thank you," Azara sniffed.

"Well, I won't turn down a free drink," Millie winked at me.

"I imagine you rarely turn down much," Azara observed drily.

"You should try it sometime," Millie grinned at her. "It's a hell of a lot more fun!"

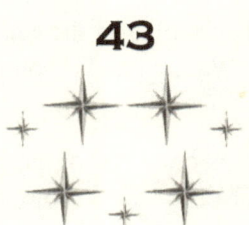

43

Upper Kallit's "drinking house" wasn't even a house. An enterprising brewer had placed a bunch of benches next to a couple long tables, propped a sheet of canvas over it to keep off the rain, and that was pretty much it. The choice of drinks included his local ale or well water, neither of which were all that great. The stench of the rendering plant seemed to have made its way into the water, giving it a faint taste of eggs, and the ale probably should have been aged longer than the day or two it felt like it had been.

"How do the people here drink this?" Millie asked in a low voice, staring into her wooden mug distastefully.

"No doubt the odor of the place has altered their senses of smell and taste," Azara observed with sour expression.

"So, you're saying that compared to the smell of boiled pig fat, this is probably delicious," I grinned.

"Yes. Exactly." She sniffed slightly and winced. "Although that isn't much of a standard to set."

"Murf, you—have you gained a rank as a Holder yet?" Millie asked me in a slightly reticent voice.

"Yeah," I nodded, then grimaced as I realized what must have happened. "You got enough points from that elf to rank up, didn't you?"

"Yes," she sighed, looking glumly down at the table. "It says that I have to pick a profession."

"I had to, as well. All I can tell you is what Ferdi told me: choose the least common profession that sounds like something you want to do. I guess it's easier to rank up a profession that you'll enjoy."

She made a face. "That doesn't help much. I've got three choices. One is common, but I like to do it. One is uncommon, but I hate the thought of it. The last is common, and I'm not interested in it."

I held my hands out helplessly. "I don't know what to tell you, Millie. You now know as much about this as I do. Maybe talk to Ferdi later?"

"Maybe." She looked disgruntled as she stared down into her ale, then looked up at me shrewdly. "Wait, what did you pick? And are you happy you picked it?"

"I picked the least common one. As for happy…" I shrugged. "I'm not happy about any of this, Millie. The whole Holder thing makes me about as happy as that erecting thing that Gertla was talking about."

"Erecting thing?" Azara asked quizzically. "Senior Sage Gertla wanted you to build something?"

"It was a question she asked him," Millie said with a bit of a giggle. "About whether or not he was able to function—you know, in bed."

"Ah. Erectile dysfunction." She gave me her curious look, with her head cocked to the side. "Are you having difficulty with that, Murf? I don't recall it being an issue previously."

"No, I'm good on that front," I said quickly as Millie let out a quick burst of laughter. "The point it, I can't say I'm happy, but it did give me an interesting ability."

"Oh?" Millie asked, quickly settling down. "What ability?"

"Something called Suppress Cards. It makes all cards harder to use and less effective within about twenty feet of me."

Millie's eyes narrowed slightly. "So, why didn't you use it during that last fight? It might have made the whole battle a lot easier!"

I paused for a moment before shaking my head. "Actually, I didn't think of it," I said apologetically. "Although, I'm not sure if it would have made a difference. It works against all cards within that radius, so I think it would have affected Ferdi, too—and maybe even you and Azara."

The avian sniffed. "Better that you didn't use an ability that you don't understand in a dangerous situation, actually. Your forgetfulness might have aided us."

"It might," I nodded, then took a drink, letting the conversation lapse into silence.

"So, Azara, what brought you to Canis rather than setting up in Avis?" Millie asked in the tone of someone making conversation but not really interested in the answer.

"Why would I live in Avis?" the cartomancer replied flatly.

"Well, I know that it's the avian capital city…"

"So, all avians must live there? We can't travel? Be born in other cities?"

"I wasn't saying that," Millie protested. "I—help me here, Murf!"

I chuckled. "You know she's right, Azara. Of all the beastlings, avians are the least likely to travel far from their homes."

"Of course, but some of us still do."

"And did you?" Millie asked a little desperately. "Or were you born in Canis? That was what I was asking."

"That's a better question, at least. It's somewhat personal, though. I might ask why you left your obvious life of wealth and privilege to become a gambler, as well."

Millie made a face, took a long drink of her ale, and made another, even sourer face. "Actually—I didn't leave it so much as I was cast out of it," she admitted. She looked at me, and her eyes held a deep pain and sorrow that I'd never seen in them before.

"Murf knows this, but my family is the Deepwaters, rulers of the Plutarchy of Deepwater," she told the suddenly silent cartomancer. "I'm not in the immediate line of succession, but I'm in the main family, so my family considered me to be something of a commodity."

"A commodity?" Azara echoed. "Meaning?"

"Meaning that once it became apparent that I look the way I do, my father immediately began making plans to use that for the family's benefit," the redhead said a little angrily. "I was raised to become a merchant, just like all my siblings, but once I began—developing, my education shifted. I had tutors come in to teach me manners, etiquette, and 'wifely' duties like caring for a household and a husband. I protested, and my father sat me down and explained very clearly why my protests didn't matter.

"'With your features and assets, Millicent, I'll be able to marry you to nobility, if not royalty.'" Her voice deepened as she spoke, as if impersonating the man, but it didn't mask the anger in her words. "'You'll give him an heir, inherit his lands and estates, and bring those into the family. You could expand the entire plutarchy, and all you have to do is learn to be a good, little wife.'"

"I'm guessing you didn't respond the way he wanted?" I said drily.

"Not at all," she chuckled. "There was no point in arguing, of course, and running away wasn't an option. If I'd been a distant cousin, maybe, or less valuable to my father, but as it was, I'd never have made it out of the city. So, I decided to devalue myself as a commodity. After all, what noble or merchant would want a good, little wife who's spent more time on her back than a courtesan in the Avenue of Roses? I made it my mission for every new ship in the harbor to consider me a friendly port, so to speak."

"So, he kicked you out when he found out?" I guessed.

"No. He sent me to my grandfather. Grandfather told me, 'Millicent, there's a place for someone who's chosen the path you have in the family. It's not as pleasant as the one your father had in mind, but it's not as stifling, either.' So, my third education began." She pulled out her knife and twirled it on her fingers. "This one was a lot more interesting than the first two. I kept learning about manners and etiquette, but no more wifely duties. Instead, I got to learn about wines and food, clothing, how to fight—and how to seduce a man and keep him seduced." She gave me a wan smile. "And how to gamble, of course. Those were my favorite lessons."

"That doesn't sound like an ominous sort of education at all," I sighed.

"Ominous?" Azara asked in a confused voice.

"Yeah. Think about it, Azara. Seduction, how to be a high-class lady, and weapons—especially small blades like that? What sort of thing could he have been training her for?"

"Oh," Azara said after a moment. "He was raising you to kill, then."

She nodded. "You understand. I didn't. I didn't realize what Grandfather had in mind for me at first until I happened to see a letter he was writing to my father, updating him on my progress as one of the family's assassins." She shivered slightly. "I confronted him about it, and he just confirmed it.

"'The family is going to use your assets to its best advantage, Millicent,' he told me. 'You ruined yourself for your father's purposes, and no granddaughter of mine will become an ordinary whore, no matter how accomplished. This is the way you'll serve.'"

"And you went along with that?" Azara asked, her voice slightly outraged.

"It's not exactly 'going along with it' when you have no choice," Millie replied hotly. "My grandfather controls an entire nation and is one of the five wealthiest men in the world, Azara. No place is out of his reach."

"Then how did you get away?" I asked.

She shrugged. "I stopped learning my lessons. I put no effort into any of them. Grandfather punished me, of course, but it didn't matter. I wasn't going to do that. Eventually, he gave up trying, and I slipped out of his house and down to the docks. I thought I'd gotten away, but he met me on the ship I'd booked passage on.

"'You're a stubborn girl, Millicent,' he told me, 'but that can be useful, too. You want to see the world? Go, see it. But one day, you'll repay me for what I've given you, one way or the other. Until then, you're still part of this family, and I never lose sight of family.'"

"That guy sounds creepy as hell," I muttered.

"He is." She shivered. "Mostly because he never gets angry or upset. He's always perfectly calm, no matter what. I've never even heard him raise his voice." She shook her head and looked at me. "I told you that I'm an investment that went bad, and I need to buy my way out. Now, you know why. If I don't, eventually, Grandfather will find another way to make me pay off my debts, and I'm afraid I know what it'll be."

"Fuck," I whispered, shaking my head. That was a lot worse than I'd thought. I'd imagined that Millie had simply refused to be a merchant and had to pay her family back for the education she received. I never imagined they'd tried to turn her into a damn killer. I didn't really know what to say, so I didn't say anything. Instead, I reached out and placed my hand on hers. She hesitated for an instant before clutching it tightly, and I could feel the near-panic flowing through her. Silence reigned for long moments before Azara broke it at last.

"Normally, I envy people their families," she said slowly. "In this case, I don't." She looked up and met Millie's gaze. "Thank you for sharing that. My story is far more prosaic, I'm afraid."

"I—I'd still like to hear it," Millie said, reaching up and wiping her eyes. "If you'd like to share, that is."

"I'd be rude in the extreme not to after that." The black-haired woman shrugged. "You were correct in your assumption. I am from Avis originally. I grew up there with my father. My mother was a human, but she left us soon after I was born." She gave me a flat glance, and I couldn't help but wince beneath it. She went on without commenting, but I understood her point. I wasn't the first to abandon her. I hadn't known that, obviously; if I had—well, it probably wouldn't have changed anything, sad to say.

"Father raised me on his own as well as he could. When I was old enough, I even apprenticed with him, as he was also a cartomancer—although only barely one, to his great shame."

"Shame?" Millie asked.

"Yes. You see, I come from a line of diviners, one that extends back over a thousand years. The gift has passed from generation to generation, stronger in some, weaker in others." She smiled sadly. "In Father, it was weak, although I didn't know this until I was much older. I thought it was amazing when I lost my doll and he found it in minutes with the cards, or how he could tell what the weather would be most days. I thought it was magical, and I idolized him."

She smiled wistfully. "He was much like Murf in many ways, determined to wring joy and happiness out of every situation and to make the most of what meager talents he had." She gave me a steady gaze that I couldn't quite manage to return as guilt flared in me again. I'd never known that, either—I knew about her father, but not that she thought we were alike.

"He recognized my talent early on," she went on. "He insisted that I learn the cards, and that I would go on to do great things with them one day. So, I learned the secrets of the deck, how to speak with them and hear their words, how to arrange them to channel the Unity's power. And as time passed, I realized he was right. I was talented. I could do things easily that he could only do with great effort, and the cards spoke to me like old companions when he struggled to hear them shouting at him. As word of my talents spread, more people came to his shop not to see him but to see me."

"That must have been hard on him," Millie noted.

"If it was, he never showed any signs of it," she shrugged. "I never saw anything but his pride in me. And my skills brought in more money, which we needed." She looked down, and her expression fell. "Eventually, he died, as we all do. Avians are short-lived compared to humans, and he'd been getting older. His memory was failing, and he couldn't hear the cards anymore. Then, one day, he went to sleep—and never woke up."

"I'm sorry, Azara," Millie said sympathetically.

"There are worse ways to lose a parent," she replied, flashing me a look that I understood. "At least he died peacefully and knowing that he'd left me something so I wouldn't be on my own. I'd reached my majority by that point, so I inherited the shop and could have kept running it—only, I couldn't stay there. It hurt too much. I woke up each morning and remembered that he was gone. I'd work out a new layout and go to show him, but he wasn't there. Every time I walked past his room or picked up his cards, I missed him."

She straightened. "So, I sold his shop and cards, kept his equipment, and made my way to Canis. It's the biggest city in Torin, and I had some vague idea that I'd become famous and be the diviner for the meritocrats. It didn't happen quite that way, of course, since the meritocrats only trust and uplift their own kind, despite whatever protests to the contrary they make, but I can't complain. I do well enough, better than most, and being detached from the city's politics and power structure gives me more time to develop new layouts and hone my craft." She offered us a wan smile. "And that's how I ended up in Canis. As I said, it's not much of a story, but as you shared with me, it's only fair that I do the same."

"Thanks," Millie smiled at the avian. "I'm glad you did. It's kind of nice, actually. Your father sounds like a wonderful man, and it seems like he genuinely cared about you."

"He was, and he did," she nodded. "I'm glad you recognize it." She looked at me. "Is it your turn, now?"

Thankfully, before I had to answer, Ferdi barged into the drinking house, shoving patrons out of the way if they didn't move quickly enough.

"Come on, Murf," she said, walking up and grabbing my arm. "I need you."

"Ferdi, seriously, you've gotta stop sending me mixed signals," I said with a touch of relief in my voice. "Are we getting naked together or not? Make up your mind!"

"Not. Most definitely not. That's not what I need you for. Ever." Her voice was firm as she spoke. "Tifer woke up, and there's no exit clause in his contract. I need your help."

I nodded and rose to my feet. "Do you want to come along?" I asked the others.

"No, thank you," Millie shuddered. "That ability of yours—I only caught the edge of it back there, and it still made me feel like I just didn't much care about anything. I'll pass."

"As will I," Azara agreed. "At least until you've gained control over your abilities, Murf. The apathy didn't bother me, but the forced feeling of camaraderie that I felt in my shop was unpleasant."

"Don't worry about us," Millie said, giving me an arch grin. "The two of us will just stay here while you're gone and talk about what we have in common. Mostly you."

I froze in the act of stepping away from my chair. "You're going to do what?"

"An excellent topic," Azara nodded. "I can tell her of all your flaws, Murf—and there are any number of those. She can tell me if she's noticed them or not yet. It'll be quite entertaining."

"I can't wait," Millie chuckled, shooing me away with a hand. "Go on, now. We need to make you as uncomfortable as that damn ability made both of us."

I walked away from the pair, half-dragged by Ferdi, with a sinking feeling. Don't get me wrong. I was happy that the two were sort of getting along. I just didn't know if I was comfortable with critiquing me being their bonding moment.

And more to the point, I wasn't sure what the hell I could do to stop it.

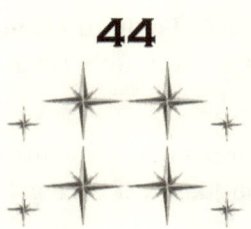

44

The house that Tifer and his elf friend had either purchased or taken over in the village was one of the nicer ones. That meant that the straw roof was intact enough that there were no signs of water damage inside, and the walls fit together well enough that the draft blowing through was tolerable. The windows lacked glass and were covered with leather hides, which didn't do much to keep out smells or small insects but probably prevented larger animals from crawling inside and tearing up the place. Not that it really would have made much of an impact. The floors were bare, packed dirt, and the furnishings inside were mostly furs and blankets tossed on the ground. The main room was little more than a brick stove for heating the place and cooking, a set of wooden shelves to hold cooking supplies, and a central pole that I imagined supported the roof. Two smaller rooms to the sides each held a flat-topped wooden chest and a straw-filled mattress that lay on the ground, and Tifer lay on one of these.

The clanking of chains echoed through the small house when we entered, and I followed Ferdi back to the second bedroom to find Tifer on his side, his hands behind his back and his feet pulled up so that the manacle chains linked his wrists and ankles behind him, keeping him from straightening his legs. Ferdi, it seemed, had also tied the collar's lead to the chains, so if the man did try to escape, he'd probably choke himself. It was a pretty effective way to immobilize the man, and for a moment, I imagined myself in the same position, waiting for Ferdi to remove the organ for which she'd set the bounty. I shuddered and hastily pushed that thought away.

"Go ahead," she said, gesturing at the bound man. "Do what you did to the assassin."

"Do what you must," Tifer said in a calm voice, glaring at the both of us. "I will not speak, Ferdi."

"What did you want to know?" I asked.

"Where my people are, how to get to them, what kind of guards they have, and if there are any passphrases or signals to get them."

"I can't tell you those things, Ferdi. If I could, I would," the man said. "The contract forbids it, and my oath forbids me from violating the contract."

I hesitated, looking at Ferdi a little dubiously. "Are you sure about this?" I asked quietly. "I don't know if I can get him to break his oath, Ferdi."

"If I don't try, I've broken mine," she said tiredly. "He knows that. One of our oaths is going to break today, and I don't intend for it to be mine."

"If you say so." I looked back at the man, then turned my thoughts inward toward my abilities. I began by activating Drunken Combat, flicking a few cards at the halfling. He shuddered as they struck him and shook his head.

"If you think—making me intoxicated—will loosen my tongue," he said slowly and carefully, "then you don't understand the nature of the oath-bound, human."

"I'd love for it to be that easy," I chuckled, sitting down beside him and pulling up the card I'd seen earlier when I looked at him.

> **Tifer**
> Rank 4 Warrior
> Luck: 35   Capacity: 51   Skill: 53
> **Hole Card:** 7 of Blades
> **Likely Powers:** Improved Armor, Damage Resistance, Improved Endurance

I dismissed the card after a glance, as I realized the numbers really didn't mean anything to me. His Capacity was a little lower than mine and his skill a lot higher, but I didn't know exactly what that meant. How much better was five points in a stat, really? Ten? Twenty? Could I handle an extra card compared to him? Two extra? Three? Or was it more complicated than that? I didn't know, and I'd never bothered to ask because, quite frankly, I also didn't much care.

Instead, I flexed the next card, the lady, willing the man to feel friendly and talkative. The power flowed out, and as it did, I felt a small surge roll out of the knight, as well, boosting the lady's energy. Tifer blinked and looked confused for a moment, staring at me blankly.

"What are you doing?" he asked warily, his speech faintly slurred. "What's this?"

"Nothing special," I assured him.

"Won't—work," he said, shaking his head and blinking rapidly. "I won't—won't speak."

I ignored him for the moment and reached for the next power in the stack. The prince's energy flexed easily in my mental fingers, feeling almost comforting in my grasp. I'd never used it before, which meant that I was likely to overdo it, but I assumed that having him find me too believable wasn't really that big of a deal. I let the cards fly, and they slid like silk from my fingers, washing over him and plunging into him. As the cards flowed out of me, I could feel twin surges from the knight and lady, as if the prince drew power from them, as well. All those mingled energies washed over him, wrapping around him and sinking into his body, and his expression swiftly grew alarmed as he stared at me.

"What's going on? What are you doing to me?"

"Don't worry," I said reassuringly. "I'm not going to hurt you. I'm just trying to make you feel a little more—relaxed."

"No. It won't work." Even as he spoke, though, I could see the effects of my abilities on him. He relaxed against his restraints, laying back on the flimsy mattress. He stopped struggling, and while I could still see the tension in his face and eyes, it flowed out of his body. Still, he wasn't quite ready to talk yet, so I reached down and touched the last noble in my stack, flicking a surge of the queen's power out at the man. As the energy rushed out, I felt now-familiar flows from the rest of the nobles, along with a powerful rush of energy from the Hag at the core of my being. A card popped up in front of me, and I read it in surprise.

Unique Stack Ability Activated
A Noble Master
Base Power: 65 Max Power: 218
While all Court of Cups powers are
active:
All abilities use this ability's base
power instead of their own.
Resistance to your cups abilities is
halved.
Resisting your will causes increasing
pain and cold damage.

Following your will gives increasing
pleasure and euphoria.
Enemies see you as a trusted friend
or confidant.
Anyone following you gains
increasing bonuses to all actions.

Tifer shuddered as a sudden wave of power washed over him. At rank 4, he was stronger than me and probably had solid defenses, but that Noble Master thing had a 65 base power and halved his resistance. That meant that he'd have to have triple digit resistance to hold the ability out. Unless he had some ability or card specifically designed to shield him from mental attacks, he probably didn't stand a chance, and even then, if it wasn't a noble, it probably wouldn't matter. As I watched his expression glaze and his eyes go vacant as all the fight went out of him, I decided that he probably didn't have that sort of card, or if he did, it wasn't anywhere near strong enough to resist the Hag. He gazed blankly at nothing, and I watched him for a few seconds, refocusing my thoughts.

The whole Noble Master thing was a little ridiculous, really. Obviously, the abilities of the court of cups all complemented one another, and I assumed the same was true for the other courts, too. It was how they came together that shocked me, and I wasn't sure I liked the result. Halved resistance was nice and all, but the idea that resisting me caused him pain and damaged him seemed a lot like torture. Plus, what exactly did "pleasure and euphoria" mean? Was Tifer going to get turned on by answering my questions? I didn't think I was ready to deal with a horny halfling warrior bound in chains. I don't think it's possible to be ready for something like that, to be honest.

"Are you okay?" I finally asked the man.

"I—I don't know," he said slowly. "I feel strange. My head is foggy." He looked at me with that same blank expression, then gave me a wide smile. "Ah, it's you. Why am I restrained?"

I didn't know who he thought I was, but the card said he'd see me as a trusted confidant, which explained why he smiled when he saw me. That might make all this a lot easier.

"It's for your own good," I told him with a friendly smile. "You know how touchy Ferdi can be. This way, she won't hurt you by accident."

"Ah, yes. Ferdi always was the most emotional of us." I blinked in surprise at that; Ferdi was the emotional one? For that to be true, all the other oath-bound had to be carved from solid ice.

"Okay," I said, drawing the word out. "I'm going to ask you a few questions, Tifer. I'd like you to answer them for me."

He frowned at me slightly. "It-it depends on the questions," he hedged. "I can't say anything that'll break my oath. You know that."

"I understand. All I want to know is: where are Ferdi's people? Can you tell me that, Tifer?"

"I—I can't." His back arched as a sudden flash of pain washed across his face, but he shook his head. "I can't tell you. I want to—I want to tell Ferdi, too. I can't. My oath won't let me."

I sighed. Of course, it wouldn't be that easy. "Okay. Let's find something you can tell me. Is everyone else down at that Labyrinth that you're all supposed to be getting ready to run?"

"I—I shouldn't say," he hesitated, grimacing in pain once more. A chill pallor crept up his neck and down his arms as he resisted; that, I assumed, was the cold damage the card mentioned. I hoped it wouldn't really hurt him or even kill him before he told me what I needed to know. Asking his corpse questions promised to be a lot more awkward.

"It's okay. You can tell me. I've been there before once, actually. It's down inside a big ravine, and the path leading into it has steps cut into the stone. You're not telling me anything I don't know."

"You have been there," he sighed and relaxed as the pain seemed to wash out of his body. "When did that happen?"

"A while ago. It doesn't really matter."

"I suppose not. And you're right; if you already know about it, then talking about it won't hurt anything. Yes, they're down there."

"What are they doing?"

"Stalling." He shivered slightly as he spoke. "Trying to avoid *his* attention."

"His?" I couldn't help but notice the emphasis the warrior put on that word.

"My—well, my employer, in a manner of speaking. The man who organized all this, and with whom I signed a contract, most foolishly I'm afraid."

"Why was that foolish?"

"Because there's a strong likelihood that he won't live up to his end of it, and we'll all be lucky to escape this with our lives, much less the promised compensation."

"What did he promise to pay you, then?"

"Ten gold crowns for entering the Labyrinth, twenty more for completing it, plus a card suited to my Harmonies."

I couldn't help but whistle in amazement at that. "And he promised that to each of you? How many are there of you all now?"

"I'm not entirely sure. Maybe ten of us in total. For such a simple job, it's had an extremely high mortality rate, and we haven't even started."

"What do you mean?"

"The Labyrinth is supposed to be virgin and untouched—although that might not be true—and first clears are always deadlier. We haven't even gone past the entrance, yet, and already Alenrue is dead, I assume Shadowcat is, as well, plus the two elves he sent to throw Ferdi and her companions into the Ochre Forest. Mogaki, the female orc, died looting the cartomancer's shop when her wards turned out to be too much for Zeric to handle." The man chuckled a little evilly. "He made a mistake, there, you know."

"Did he?"

"Yes. You see, no one wants to go into the Labyrinth because they don't know anything about it, and going into a Labyrinth blind—especially a virgin one—is suicide. He thought that Zeric would be able to divine information about it, but he can't. It's too high-ranked for him." He laughed again. "It's justice for how he betrayed that avian cartomancer. I've heard about her, and I'll bet she could divine a lot more than Zeric can."

"I've heard of her, too, and I wouldn't take that bet," I laughed easily. "What happened to her, by the way?"

"He threw her into a Labyrinth with Ferdi and two others. We assumed that they died, but they were all in the wagon with Ferdi, so they obviously didn't. I don't know how they survived, though. It must have been the Unity's will."

"Or sheer dumb luck," I suggested.

"Maybe, although Ferdi is very skilled, and Zeric still believes that the man ran the Labyrinth solo. If he did, then the Ochre Forest wouldn't be a challenge for him."

"You don't sound like you agree."

"I don't. Anyone powerful enough to run an ancient virgin Labyrinth solo wouldn't have been taken by those elves and might have been able to kill us all in that warehouse. Plus, he'd have to be a Holder, and the avian didn't sense any cards in him." He paused. "Of course, she might have been lying, especially if she suspected she'd be betrayed, and a strong diviner might know that. If that's true, they'd have been able to fight free."

He shook his head ruefully. "Either way, they came out, and the elves didn't, which means that they might have been useful in dealing with the Labyrinth. If instead of kidnapping them and betraying the avian, he'd recruited them all, we might already be in the Labyrinth. Instead, the four of them are responsible for the deaths of at least five of our number, six if they found and killed Deathroot, as well."

"Deathroot?" I asked with a low laugh. "Who's that?"

"Shadowcat's partner. That's not their real names, of course. They're part of some assassin's order that gives its members absurd names. I think it's supposed to be tall folk humor, but I don't get it."

"Neither do I." I paused as a troubling idea occurred to me. "Are they Black Roses?"

"I doubt it. If they were, I think they'd be stronger, and I don't think their organization would let them do this sort of work. Black Roses are supposed to be elite killers, and they work hard to keep that reputation. If they were, though, it would make things easier since he could just send them into the Labyrinth for information. I understand that the Black Roses have ways of getting into and out of Labyrinths, so they're never trapped inside them."

"That sounds useful."

"Very."

"So, how are they getting more information, if this Zeric guy can't give it to them, and they don't have any Black Roses to send in?"

"They aren't, not really. They go in through the entrance, look around while they can't be hurt, then get back out before it closes. From what I've heard, they've learned all they're going to. Trying to find out more is just an excuse. No one wants to go into a Labyrinth without information, and there's none to be had on this one. Like I said: they're stalling."

"Why aren't you down there? And your elf friend?"

"Alenrue? She's no friend. I can't stand her. She's conceited, even for an elf, and she likes to hurt people. Not as much as her cousin Alerion did, but she still enjoys it. It would have been better if I'd been put here with Taveroth."

"Taveroth? I met him. He's not that great of a guy."

"He's a murderer and a butcher," the halfling said simply. "However, one of his cards stills his emotions. It makes him easy to deal with, and it's why he partners with Alerion. He's always calm and rational, and without him, Alerion isn't trustworthy." He paused. "Although, I don't think that's an issue anymore. I'm pretty sure he betrayed the elves and locked them in the Ochre Forest, too—or had those assassins kill them. They were turning into a liability and drawing more attention than he wanted from the Meritocracy. I doubt they're still alive."

"That seems like more reason for you two to be down at the Labyrinth," I reasoned.

"No, he's gotten replacements for them. We're here because the others are higher-ranked, and he thinks we're too weak to help in the Labyrinth."

"And that doesn't bother you?" I asked curiously.

He shrugged. "As I said, going into a virgin Labyrinth without information and a team of at least twenty is suicide. The others are rank 5 or 6, but I don't think it'll be enough. I'm glad to be here instead of there."

"If I wanted to go help them," I said slowly, "how would I get there?"

"Help them?" he asked quizzically. "Why would you help them?"

"Well, as I said, I've been there, and I have some information about the Labyrinth that might help them out. I could trade that information for something valuable."

"Information?"

"Yes. See, I haven't just seen that Labyrinth. I've been inside, and I got out."

His eyes narrowed. "Then it's not a virgin Labyrinth anymore?"

"No, it's not. Your boss should know that, don't you think? It might change his mind about sending people inside."

"It might." He sighed. "If you have that sort of information, I suppose I could tell you. There's a trail to the Labyrinth from here. Leave on the southern river road and look for a tree with a red blaze cut into the trunk. Follow the blazes, and you'll find the Labyrinth."

"And are there guards around it?"

"Of course. They make sure that no one gets too close. Zeric says that it's not necessary, that his layouts are watching the area, but he doesn't trust the goblin anymore, I don't think. Zeric's a combat cartomancer, not a diviner, and his skills there aren't much to speak of."

"Is there a way past them? I'd hate for one of them to kill me on accident before I could get the information to your boss."

Tifer frowned. "I suppose you could go down the river instead of through the jungle. There's another path marked with blue blazes that leads to the top of the ravine, and you could make your way down from there. That's not really watched."

"Thanks," I said with a smile. "Hey, what if Ferdi wanted to say goodbye to her people? Where would she find them?"

"Say—say goodbye?" he frowned again, but his expression relaxed a moment later. "That's fair. She should be able to do that. They're up there at the top of the ravine. The others don't like listening to the screams of Fisya's victims, and the canyon walls muffle those. She's got a place near the path down to the base encampment, in the jungle a bit. She keeps the captives there."

"And is she the only guard they've got?"

"No. The orc is usually up there since he's the only one who can stomach what she does. No one else wants to be near her."

I patted his leg and stood up. "You did good, Tifer," I said approvingly. "Can you think of anything else I should know about?"

"Maybe. Shadowcat's partner, Deathroot. If Ferdi and her companions haven't killed him already, then he's still in the city, scouting likely Holders to be forcibly recruited into joining us. I should probably tell Ferdi to watch out for him. If he finds them, he'll probably kill them." He sighed. "I'm glad I could help you. It feels really good to help out."

"It does, you're right." I turned and looked back at Ferdi, only to see the halfling woman on her knees, clutching her ribs and doubled over. "Ferdi!" I said, half-shouting in alarm. "What happened?"

"Turn—off—damn—power," she grunted. "Hurts—hell."

I blinked as I realized that she'd been fighting my abilities this whole time, and while she did, A Noble Master caused her pain. I quickly shut off everything but Drunken Combat just to keep Tifer under control, and the woman let out a deep, shuddering breath, placing her shaking hands on the floor.

"Are you okay, Ferdi?" I asked.

"No," she grunted. "That felt like my heart was freezing solid. What the hell was that?"

"Stack power. When I use all the abilities in the stack at once, resisting them hurts. I didn't realize it would hurt that much."

"It didn't. Not at first, at least. You were saying things, and some part of me really wanted to listen to you, like what you were saying was the most important thing I could think of. I knew it wasn't, though, so I stuck my fingers in my ears and started humming. That's when the pain started." She shivered as she spoke. "At first, it was just uncomfortable, like I ate something that didn't agree with me. It kept getting worse, even though it got easier and easier to ignore you."

That, I assumed, was the Crown of Authority ability boosting the woman's resistances, even to my own powers. Sadly, it didn't work against the stack power, it seemed—or maybe it did, and without that resistance, it would have been a lot worse for her. That was a sobering thought. Ferdi was tough, and if that Noble Master thing hurt her that much, I probably wanted to be really careful using it against people. It really was like a form of torture, and that thought made me more than just a little ill.

"Sorry about that," I said sincerely. "All these powers are new to me, and I don't have a good handle on them yet."

"You need to get one." She rose unsteadily to her feet, brushing aside my attempt to help her. "You have to learn to control them, Murf."

"I'm happy to, Ferdi," I shrugged. "How? Practice? You want to be my practice dummy? You think the others do? Maybe we could keep Tifer tied up and try it on him until I get it right? These abilities don't really lend themselves to practice without hurting people."

She grunted. "Fair point. Maybe start with your lower arcana, then. Practice with them and get a feel for how much power you put out and where you target it. Once you've got that under control, use those lessons with your noble arcana." She straightened, leaning back as if to stretch out her stomach muscles. "In the meantime, did you get anything?"

"You weren't listening?" I asked, surprised.

"Were you? I just told you. Fingers in ears. Humming. After that, trying not to scream. What did he say?"

"Your people are down by the Labyrinth, along with the rest of the captives. We'll be taking the river south and cutting across to the top of the ravine to avoid the patrols. They've got two guards, that felid torturer and one of the orcs. That's all I could get."

"That's more than enough." She walked over to Tifer, who seemed to have passed out once I let the other powers lapse on him. Or maybe they were keeping him awake and alert; he hadn't seemed especially incapacitated while we spoke. I didn't really know how it all worked, which, I supposed, was the whole point. I needed to learn, and fast, before I accidentally did something to one of the others that couldn't be undone. Ferdi was tough, but what if that had been Millie or Azara on the floor? Would they have shaken it off as quickly as the halfling? I wasn't sure, and that meant I had to get better.

"Did anything happen to him while he told you all that?" she asked quietly.

"Happen to him? What do you mean?"

"You'd have recognized it if it happened." She stared at the man for several seconds. "Do you know what being oath-bound means, Murf?"

"Not really," I shook my head. "I mean, I know that it's more than just making an oath, and that it gives you extra strength and toughness…"

"Not always," she cut me off. She reached to her side and, to my surprise, began unbuckling her armor.

"Ferdi, is this really the time and place for this?" I asked a little nervously.

"Yes, it is. Remember what I said about giving trust to get it? You gave me trust by telling me about your card. I haven't repaid it. My cards and abilities are easy to figure out, and anyone with half a brain could guess them. Knowing yours puts your life in danger. This is only fair."

She pulled the locks on her breastplate free and slid it open to reveal a padded shirt beneath. She reached up and yanked it down, exposing the tops of the rising mounds of her small breasts—which I'd never seen before, honestly, and which I wasn't completely sure actually existed—and what looked like a rectangular burn scar in the center of her chest. The scar was raised and red, and it looked to have some sort of pattern to it that I couldn't quite make out.

"What happened there? That looks painful."

"It was. That's the mark of the oath-bound." She let her shirt slip back and began re-buckling her armor. "You're right. It's not just an oath. An oath-bound swears their soul to a principle, and that oath is witnessed by a card. Not just any card, either; it's sealed by the Magus."

"The Magus? I've never heard of that one."

"No reason you would have. Few who aren't sages or delvers have. It's from the deck of powers, the Worldly Sage. It's the binder of compacts, and the Unity keeps any oath sworn with it."

"Then that burn…"

"Is the mark of the Magus. I swore an oath of justice, Murf. When I see an injustice, I have to do my best to right it. That's why I couldn't let you go for all those years, and it's why I have to try my best to get my people back. In return for that, the Magus granted me a measure of power, the extra strength, speed, and durability to be able to seek out injustice and right it."

"Why'd you become a delver, then?" I asked curiously. "Why not something like a guard or bounty hunter?"

"Because I'm hoping to right another injustice—the one that drove me to take the oath." She shook her head. "That's another story, and not one for right now.

"The point, Murf, is that there are all sorts of oaths, and they aren't all combat related. I have an oath-sister who took an oath of perfection. She's oath-bound to do her best to create perfect clothing, so the Magus gave her extra dexterity, coordination, and eyesight. The oath is a little different in all of us, but it always grants us some power to follow the oath—at a cost."

"I take it the cost is that you can't do anything to break it?"

"Exactly. The oath is burned into my soul, and if I break it, the Magus' power will turn on me. It'll break my layout and probably eject every card but my hole card—for good. I've seen it happen once, and the man who did it died from the pain. Just the pain of breaking his oath." She gestured at the sleeping Tifer. "Like I said, you'd know if it happened."

"What was his oath?"

"It's not my place to say. Telling you what he did probably broke it, though, and once he realizes that, the Magus will turn on him."

"What do you mean, once he realizes it? Isn't it just—broken?"

"It's not that simple," she sighed. "A lot of our oaths are about our perception. For example, if Miedla—the perfectionist I was telling you about—did her best with a weaving but accidentally wove a flaw into it, her oath wouldn't be broken. She tried her best, and we all make honest mistakes. If she got tired or lazy, though, and deliberately left a mistake in, it would be broken. You see the difference?"

I nodded. "In one case, it was accidental; the other was on purpose."

"It's more that in one case, she didn't know that she'd broken her oath, and in the other, she did. If I walked past an alley where a crime was happening, and I didn't see it, I wouldn't break my oath by not interfering. If I saw something happening but knew that trying to interfere would get me killed, I wouldn't have to step in. But if I thought that I could help and didn't, for whatever reason, then I'd break my oath.

"Perception is the key. We have to believe that we broke our oath to break it. Sophistry and clever words won't work, but honest belief will. Sometimes, I have to ignore small injustices in pursuit of a larger one, or because trying to fix it would be the work of a lifetime." She gestured at the walls. "Like this place. That people have to live like this is unjust, but fixing the entire system is beyond me. I can't do anything about it."

"So, if Tifer couldn't help himself because of my power, does that mean he didn't break his oath?"

She shrugged. "It depends on him. It doesn't matter if he intended to break his oath or not. All that matters is if he thinks he did—and he'll think he did. Tifer's very strict about his oath. The only way to convince him he didn't would be to tell him about your hole card."

"Why would that help?" I asked.

"Because it's the reason you affected him—and me—so strongly." She turned and glared at me. "You remember what I told you about inherent defenses against abilities?"

"Yeah. We all have them, and higher rank means a higher defense."

"It does, but it's more complicated than that. Any Holder has a base defense based on their hole card. For most of us with low arcana as hole cards, that's just the card's rank. Mine is a six of blades, so my base defense against an ability is 6. I've got other abilities that modify that, and I've trained my resistance, which improves it, and so does my rank. You get a boost to your defense for every rank higher you are than the person using an ability on you.

"Your defense directly opposes the base power of an ability used on you. If the defense is higher, then the power just doesn't work, or you have to maintain it for a while to make it work. If your pretty friend out there used her blade skill on my bare skin, I doubt she'd even cut me. If she had the knight, it might have made Tifer a little dizzy, but that's it. That hole card of yours gives you a ridiculous base power for all your cards, though, which means it gets through our defenses when it probably shouldn't. If he knows about it, he won't blame himself. Are you willing to tell him?"

I stared at the man, then shook my head. "No, I'm not. Sorry."

"Don't be sorry. I'd say the same. I told you to keep that from people. I meant it." She reached out and laid her hand on the sleeping man's chest almost affectionately. "In that case, the kindest thing to do might be to keep that ability on him until it's over. It'll be better than letting him wake up and dealing with a broken oath."

"Ferdi, are you sure? I know he's a friend of yours…"

"Oath-brother. Not a friend. We trained for our oaths together. We were close, once. Now?" She shrugged and looked at me. "If you had his oath, one that wouldn't let you break any contracts, what would you have done if his boss told you to be part of the attack on the hold? My hold?"

I frowned. "I mean, I'd have to see the contract, Ferdi, but I'd probably take Shadow Man's orders, agree to them, and just take so long to carry them out that it didn't matter. Or let you know first, so you could clear everyone out, then attack the empty hold."

"Exactly. That's how a friend thinks. You look for a way to keep your oath without harming the person you claim is a friend. Tifer always put his oath above everything, even the people he cared about, and now, he's paying the price for that." She patted his chest and stepped back. "Don't forget to claim his cards afterward."

"You aren't going to stay?" I asked in surprise.

"My oath-brother has to die, Murf. I don't have to watch it happen." She blinked rapidly and touched two fingers to her forehead, lips, and throat. "Bardona's blessings, Tifer. Shelter in her embrace."

She turned and left the room. I sat there, thinking about what she'd said. Ferdi took an oath of justice. That had to be an incredibly hard oath to follow. The world wasn't a remotely just place, and she had to see all that around her. The halfling hold in the slums was surrounded by examples of injustice; how could she live in the middle of it and do nothing? How could she justify that to her oath?

After a few seconds, I realized I was making some broad assumptions. Maybe she did do something. Maybe that hold was in the slums for that exact reason, in fact. I'd noticed that there weren't many thieves and beggars in the southeastern part of the city; what if the halfling warriors were the real reason for that? Hell, for all I knew, her people fed the hungry and starving on a daily basis and protected them from the wealthier people who'd beat, rape, and murder them without worrying about legal repercussions. That would be a sort of justice.

The more I thought about it, the more I realized that I'd vastly underestimated Ferdi and her oath. I'd always assumed she'd sworn her service to some power or another in return for her abilities. Instead, she'd sworn to a concept, an ideal of how she wanted the world to be. She had to know she'd never actually fix anything—the world was set up so that people like the meritocrats and Millie's grandfather would always have power over the masses, and there wasn't much a single halfling could do about that—but the fact that she still held her oath meant she kept trying.

I wouldn't have. I was honest enough with myself to admit that. I'd have given up a long time ago. Actually, I never would have sworn an oath of justice. I might have sworn an oath of no cheating, but even then, I didn't cheat mostly because it wasn't worth the risk of getting caught, not out of lofty principles. I couldn't remember ever caring enough about anything to dedicate myself to it, at least not since my mom died. That taught me a valuable lesson: the Unity can take anything from you at any time, so be ready to let it go or walk away from it at any moment. That was why I'd left Azara; it was why I would part ways with Millie after the tournament; it was why I'd never really made much effort to get Ferdi her cards back. The more you care, the more it hurts when the Unity decides to take what you care about.

Ferdi had to know that. She'd lost her siblings to a Labyrinth, the halfling hold to Shadow Man, and no doubt countless other things over the years. She hadn't lost her oath, though. She'd chosen to persevere when I would have run.

Somewhere during my ruminations, Tifer let out a single deep, shuddering breath and fell still. As he did, a card popped up in my vision.

> **Unity Achievement!**
> You have slain a Holder of your
> rank or higher.
> Reward: 100 UP per Holder rank, +50
> UP per rank above yours.
>
> +450 UP

Tifer died, and I'd profited from that death in some small way. His death was just another sign that the world was a massively fucked-up place. A man who was probably decent and honest simply ended, never knowing it and without any real chance to fight back, and someone like me just kept on going. Where the hell was the justice in that?

45

For once, my Luck stat failed me when I drew the halfling's cards from his chest. Instead of pulling cards more suited for me, it seemed like I'd pulled three of his actual cards, leaving six behind. I got the seven of blades, his hole card, plus a three of stars and ace of cups. I gave the ace to Millie, just in case she could add it at some point; Azara asked for the three; and Ferdi almost reluctantly took the seven. That left me with nothing, but that was fine with me. I already had more cards than I wanted or probably needed. In fact, I planned to sell some to the Scribblers or Sages when I got back to Canis; I needed coins more than I needed cards, to be honest.

The village had a single riverboat that could carry all of us plus the horses, and it probably should have cost an arm and a leg to hire it to take us upstream. Thanks to my Golden Tongue ability, though, it only cost an arm. The boat wasn't much to speak of. Dark patches of mold streaked the white paint on its sides. It had a noticeable list, nothing alarming but enough to make the whole world feel tilted slightly to the right. Its captain was an old canid who always seemed to have a bottle of some sort nearby, and its crew looked like a bunch of beggars who'd become sailors because thieving was too hard. Its single bedraggled sail didn't do much more than help the rowers fight against the current, and the whole vessel creaked and groaned alarmingly as it navigated the sluggish waters.

Fortunately, we didn't need to go far. The captain knew the spot that Tifer had mentioned, the beach with a blue blaze on one tree to mark a trail into the jungle. In fact, he knew a lot more about what was happening than I thought he probably should, such as the fact that all those Holders were camped out near a deadly Labyrinth. That made me suspicious for a bit, at least until the man explained under the effects of my abilities.

"The city folk, they think we're blind, deaf, and stupid, milord," he told me expansively, the reek of alcohol on his breath clearly showing that I didn't have to use Drunken Combat on him to get him in a talkative state. "We're not, though. We can see lightning and hear thunder, and we know when a storm's blowing in. People have been vanishing into that draw for as long as anyone remembers, and you think none of us noticed a horde of Holders passing through?" He laughed wheezily.

"So, has anyone checked on them to see what they're doing?"

"Now, why in the hell would anyone do that, milord? I told you: we know a storm's coming in, and when a storm comes in, you find shelter and wait for it to blow over. You don't stick your head out to see if lightning in the face hurts or not."

"I certainly wouldn't," I grinned at him.

"Kind of seems like you folk are doing that right now," he observed.

I shrugged. "Sometimes, Captain, the storm's about to blow down your house, and staying inside is worse than going out. I'd much rather be sitting in a nice room with a cold bottle and a warm woman right now if I had the choice."

"Makes two of us, milord," he grinned at me, displaying a smile missing a few teeth and with several more stained and discolored badly.

I didn't recognize the beach where the captain dropped us, but the giant blue streak painted onto one of the larger trees suggested that it might be the right place. We disembarked the boat and headed into the jungle, tying the horses near the beach but out of sight of the river. Ferdi set out almost immediately, her eyes grim and her axe in her hands, with the rest of us in tow, but we hadn't gone far before Azara pulled us all up short.

"Stop!" the avian hissed loudly, her voice urgent. "Halfling, stop!" she repeated when Ferdi only hesitated.

"What, bird-woman?" Ferdi demanded irritably. "We're close to my people. I can feel it!"

"And I can feel danger ahead of you." Azara pushed past the rest of us and stopped a couple feet before Ferdi. She pulled out a single card and held it in the air. A surge of energy washed out from it, and a moment later, a thin, gauzy plane of energy shimmered into being maybe five feet in front of her. The wall of power looked weak and translucent, like it would be easy to push through, but I had a feeling doing so would be a bad idea.

"If you had continued, you'd have set off this ward," the cartomancer said flatly, giving Ferdi a hard look. "And then, the people you hunt would know you're coming."

Ferdi stared at the ward for a second before grunting. "Good catch. Can you do something about it?"

"Yes. It's obvious that goblin did this, and he's not very good." She pulled out another card and held it out. I could almost see streams of energy roll out of the card and wash over the barrier. A moment later, the center of the barrier flickered, faded, and vanished, leaving a hole through it large enough for us to pass.

"There. That should do it," Azara said with a cold smile. When nobody moved, she flashed us an irritated glance. "Quickly, please. This isn't easy to hold open."

"I thought you said he wasn't that good," Ferdi observed.

"He's not, but he's powerful—no doubt thanks to the strength of the cards he's placed in his soul. It takes energy to hold this open. Either go through, or I'll close it, and we can turn around and leave. I don't care either way."

The halfling strode quickly through, and the rest of us followed behind. Azara came through last, and the hole slid shut behind her. As she rejoined us, Millie gave her a curious look.

"I'm assuming you could have just undone the entire ward, right?" she asked the cartomancer. "Wouldn't that have been easier than holding it open?"

"I might have," Azara agreed in a surprisingly calm voice. "However, that would have taken far more energy, and he likely would have noticed it. I doubt he sensed the tiny disruption that hole made, and it was much easier to do."

To my surprise, the two women had gotten along pretty well the entire trip here. It seemed that they'd bonded a bit over the foul ale in the village. They weren't being friendly, exactly, but Azara had lost some of the iciness in her attitude toward the redhead, and Millie seemed more comfortable talking to the cartomancer. While I appreciated their sudden camaraderie, it also made me nervous. Despite their threats, I was fairly sure that they could find something more interesting to talk about than me. Fairly sure wasn't totally certain, though, and Azara had plenty of stories about me that I'd rather not have been spread around too much. The hero and priestess thing was just about the least embarrassing of them.

I didn't really recognize the path we were on, despite the fact that I thought it was where the elves had dragged me to toss me into the Labyrinth. Of course, it was night back then, I was bound and gagged and struggling just to keep up, and I hadn't exactly been marking my trail. I definitely didn't remember the three separate wards that Azara had to part for us to pass, but again, I had no idea how she was finding them in the first place. For all I knew, I'd walked through them without knowing back then. Hell, they might not have been there if the Holders hadn't yet set up camp around the Labyrinth.

When the jungle opened up into a clearing that ended abruptly a couple dozen feet ahead of me, though, a shock of recognition made me pause.

My heart beat faster, and my feet didn't want to keep walking as I stared at the cliff edge.

"Are you okay?" Millie asked quietly, standing beside me and placing a hand on my arm. "What's wrong, Murf?"

"I—yeah, I'm fine." I shook off my moment of paralysis and walked into the clearing. My feet seemed to carry me forward of their own will until I stood at the edge of the cliff, peering down into the ravine below.

"Murf, get back!" Ferdi hissed. "They'll spot you from below!"

"I don't think so," I shook my head, gesturing into the ravine that opened below me. "Come look."

The halfling slipped cautiously forward, stopping well short of the edge. Her head darted out and back, giving her a quick glimpse below, then she froze. She walked forward and stared down into the chasm, her face puzzled.

"What the hell is that?" she asked.

"The Labyrinth," I said heavily, gazing at the shroud of darkness that filled the ravine. That night, I'd thought that the darkness shrouding the place was a result of the general darkness all around, it being night and all. It turned out I was wrong as usual. The late morning sun hung just above the trees behind us, bathing the opposite side of the ravine in light. It was only a hundred feet or so across, so I could see the other side pretty clearly. At least, I could see the top thirty feet of it clearly. Below that, shadows that the sun's light couldn't pierce swathed the stone, and after a couple feet, a pall of darkness covered the entire ravine, hiding anything below.

"I've never seen a Labyrinth like that," she said suspiciously. "Are you sure it's really one?"

"I'm sure," I laughed weakly. "Trust me. It's a Labyrinth, and one that makes the Ochre Forest look as easy as cheating a blind orc at cards."

"So, you have been inside. I figured that was where you got that card." She looked at me curiously. "What was it like?"

"Traps. Lots and lots of traps. It was the inside of a tomb or temple or palace or something, and every door and every passage was filled with traps. And not the nice kind like shallow pits filled with poison spikes. It had walls that slammed shut on you, floors that opened up beneath your feet, poison darts that shot out of the walls—there were even passages filled with jets of fire or clouds of acid."

"Kewan's blood," she breathed. "Wait. If it's so dangerous, how'd you survive?"

"Sheer, dumb luck. Nothing more. It was meant to keep people out, and I was leaving." I shook my head and stepped back from the edge. "Plus, there were no monsters inside it to make my life harder since I'd already completed it."

"You finished it? Then why not just leave through the exit?"

"I didn't know there was one. There were two doors, a big fancy one and a small one, and I assumed the small one led to a closet or something. I took the big ones, instead."

"So—you went back through the whole damn thing rather than stepping out the exit door?" she asked disbelievingly. "Murf, that's the dumbest thing I've ever heard of!"

"Yes. It was stupid. I didn't know better." I shrugged. "Besides, it worked out. I'm still here, right?"

"I suppose. Still dumb, though."

"So is thinking someone betrayed you just because you couldn't find their hat, Ferdi."

"That wasn't dumb. Is it really so hard to believe that you'd do that, Murf? Really?"

"Yes." I turned and gave her a hard glare. "I'm a liar, a thief, and a coward, Ferdi. I'm not a cheater, and that would have been cheating. You should have known that." I shifted my hat on my head, ignoring her startled expression as I turned around and looked at the others.

"Okay, so what's the plan, here?" I asked.

"Plan?" Millie echoed. "Wait, is there a plan? I don't remember anyone mentioning one."

"The plan's simple," Ferdi growled, stalking away from the edge and pointing to her left with her axe. "My people are over there somewhere. We go that way, find them, kill whoever's holding them, and bring them out the way we came in."

I cleared my throat and pointed the opposite direction. "Ferdi? The Labyrinth's entrance is that way. Pretty sure that's the way we need to go."

"Fine." She slipped her axe back onto her shoulder. "Then let's go that way."

"And when we're seen approaching—or that ridiculous armor of yours lets everyone within a mile hear us coming—what then?" Azara asked coolly. "When those holding your people raise an alarm? Are you prepared to join them in captivity? Because I'm certainly not."

"I can be quiet," Ferdi protested.

"You might, but your armor can't," I shook my head. "Azara, can you locate the other halflings?"

"Of course," she nodded. "However, doing so might alert that goblin to our presence, especially if he's put a ward around them."

"Which he probably has," I sighed, lifting my hat up to rub my eyes tiredly. "And that means that Millie or I can't just go sneak off and find them, either. We'd all have to go together, so you can get us through any wards—and that means no sneaking, thanks to Ferdi's armor." I glanced at her. "Unless you could take it off, of course."

"I could. I won't. Only an idiot goes into battle without wearing armor, Murf."

"You know you're the only one of us wearing armor, right?"

"Of course. That's pretty much my point."

"What about Charlie?" Millie broke in as I opened my mouth for a scathing reply. I stopped and looked curiously at the woman.

"What about him?" I asked.

"Could he go scout out the halflings?" She glanced at Azara. "Would wards detect him?"

"It depends on the wards," the avian responded, her head cocking sideways in thought. "And how they're constructed. If they're designed to detect anything living going through them, then maybe, yes. If it only detects a member of one of the intelligent species, though, then no, probably not."

"Can you tell which it is?" I asked curiously.

"Not without doing a reading on them, which runs the risk of triggering them." Azara stood for a second, her eyes distant, then shook her head. "I don't think it would, at least not in its insubstantial form. First, only an idiot would set wards against the living in a jungle; they'd be going off all the time. Second, the wards around my shop didn't register it, and I believe they're of much better quality than these."

"And then what?" Ferdi asked. "That thing goes out and finds them. We still have to get to them to do anything about it since the animal can't do more than bite someone. We're in the same situation."

"Well, technically, that's not true," I said slowly. "He can use a weaker form of any of my abilities. I've just never had him do it before."

"He can?" Millie asked, her voice surprised and a little sharp. "I didn't know that."

"I didn't want to say it in front of Gertla, and afterward, I kind of forgot," I admitted.

"Wise of you to keep it from her," Azara nodded. "Had she known that your familiar could use card abilities, it's likely that she would have tried to keep you in the Sage's Hall to run experiments on it."

"That's what I was worried about," I nodded. "Plus, it never hurts to have a hole card that people don't know about."

"You know that could have been very useful in dealing with that archer," Millie said in a clipped tone, crossing her arms over her chest. "If Charlie could do the drunk thing to her, I might have been able to capture her instead of killing her."

I froze in a moment of realization. "Yeah, I guess it would have, wouldn't it? I honestly forgot all about it until now."

"It might have, it might not have," Ferdi shook her head. "It depends on how much weaker its powers are than yours—which is kind of important now, too. How strong is it, Murf?"

"Half base power, I think."

"And does that include the boosts from your hole card?"

"No clue," I shrugged.

"That seems like an important thing to know, doesn't it? Those Holders are likely at least rank 5, and you're what? Rank 1?"

"Rank 3," I corrected.

She stared at me, her eyes wide. "Wait, you're *what?*"

"Do I seriously need to repeat it, Ferdi?" I sighed. "You heard me just fine."

"I did. I hoped I was wrong." She shook her head, muttering what I assumed were curses in her native tongue for a few seconds. "Fine. You're rank 3. A rank 5 Holder has their resistance doubled against you, more or less. And is the beast the same rank, or is it stuck at rank 0? Someone who's rank 5 has their resistance boosted more than ten times against a rank 0 Holder. Even your noble arcana at full power would struggle to overcome that. Without that hole card of yours to boost its abilities, it might not be able to affect them at all."

"As the familiar is part of Murf's soul, where his cards are stored," Azara said with a sniff, "then it should have access to every card he does, including his hole card."

"Should and does are two different things, cartomancer. We need to know, not guess."

"Then let's find out," I said with a sigh, turning my thoughts inward. *"Charlie, can you come out here?"* I did my best not to wince as the ball of ice under my heart flowed up my chest onto my shoulder, swirling into the misty blue ferret in an instant.

"I can do it, Dad," Charlie said in his little, piping voice.

"Do what?"

"I can help! I can find the short people for you."

"Can you have it manifest, Murf?" Azara asked, interrupting our conversation. "It's troubling watching you stare at your own shoulder like that."

"If it makes you feel better," I chuckled. "Hey, Charlie, mind letting them see you?" The ferret's misty aura faded as its weight settled onto my shoulder.

"Hi, Charlie!" Millie said, taking a step toward the ferret. I expected him to zip over to her, but to my surprise, he skittered away from her, ducking behind my back. I could feel him peeking out over my shoulder, and I felt a surge of nervousness and guilt flow out from him. Millie froze, her face hurt and surprised. "Charlie, what's wrong?"

"I'm sorry I didn't help the nice lady, Dad," he said in a morose tone. *"You didn't tell me to, though. Tell her I'm sorry."*

"I think he heard you talking about how his powers could have helped you," I sighed, reaching over my shoulder to rub his head and nose. "It's okay, Charlie. It wasn't your fault."

"No, it wasn't," Millie agreed, glaring at me and taking another step closer. "And I'm not upset at you, Charlie, I promise."

"The nice lady's not mad at me?" he asked meekly.

"No, she's not mad. At least, not at you, buddy." The ferret's weight vanished as he flowed through the air in his misty form, flashing over to Millie and scampering up onto her shoulder. She giggled as he solidified on her, nuzzling his nose into the side of her face.

"Charlie, that tickles," she laughed, petting his head.

"Can you have it use one of its abilities?" Ferdi asked. "I want to judge how strong it is."

"Can you do that, Charlie?" I asked.

"Sure, Dad. Which one?"

I stopped and considered the abilities I had. Freezing Touch was out, obviously; I didn't want him actually hurting anyone, and I doubt he wanted to, either. Drunken Combat only worked on enemies, and since he couldn't talk, I wasn't sure if Golden Tongue would do anything. Aura of Majesty might work, but it would be hard to tell, and the same with Flood of Emotion and Crown of Authority, the power that the Hag gave me by taking the role of the emperor of cups. There was one ability I had, though, that was sharply targeted, and we'd know pretty quickly if it worked or not.

"Try Gaze of Despair," I suggested. *"On Ferdi."*

"Okay. I don't really like her anyway." The ferret shifted his head to stare at Ferdi, and as he did, I felt a sudden tug in the center of me, where my cards lay. Power flowed out of me, a smaller flow than I usually used. Charlie's eyes brightened for a moment, then turned utterly black as the power rolled into him and washed out at Ferdi.

The power darted out and struck the halfling—and nothing happened. Ferdi stood there, unmoved and apparently unaffected by the ferret's unsettling gaze. Seconds passed without a change, and I began to fear that Charlie really couldn't affect the halfling. I glanced at my card and realized that it only had a base power of 7, meaning Charlie's attack probably had a strength of 3 or 4. Ferdi told me she had a resistance in the teens, meaning she could shrug off a low-power ability like that. Maybe Charlie really couldn't affect such strong Holders...

I paused as Ferdi suddenly shivered, a faint tremble passing through her body as she stood. She blinked rapidly as if to clear her eyes, looking away from the ferret, but Charlie's clear gaze never wavered. Another tremor passed through her, and she swallowed hard. Her fingers began to tremble, and she gripped the haft of her axe hard enough to make her armored gauntlets creak. Her shoulders hunched slightly, and the trembling spread down into her legs. After nearly half a minute, her skin paled, and she took a step back. She almost hesitantly drew her axe, holding it out in front of her protectively, at which point I figured she'd had enough.

"That's good, Charlie. You can stop now."

"Okay." The flow of power coming from me cut off, and the ferret's eyes returned to their normal shade. *"That was fun! Can I do it again?"*

"Maybe in a bit," I grinned at him. *"For now, just keep playing with Millie."*

"Okay!" He went back to scampering around the redhead's head and shoulders, and she laughed as he nuzzled her hair and neck affectionately.

"That…" Ferdi took a deep breath. "What was that?"

"Gaze of Despair. Power I got from the three of cups." I shrugged. "I haven't used it yet, but it seemed like a good choice. Single target, and it doesn't really hurt you."

"That depends on how you define hurt," the halfling said, taking a deep breath.

"I take it that it was effective against you, then?" Azara asked drily.

"To an extent. At first, I didn't even feel it, but it sort of crept up on me." She shivered and clutched her axe. "It was as if the beast's gaze touched on my worst fears and forced me to think about them. Something in its eyes just kept telling me that there was no point to fighting, that I was never going to get my people back, and trying would just get us all caught. The longer it stared at me, the more I wanted to drop my axe and give up before I dragged you all down with me." She shuddered again. "That a potent and dangerous ability for a simple three, Murf."

"Potent enough to affect the Holders guarding your people?" Azara asked.

"Maybe. Probably, in fact. It wasn't much to start, but like your abilities, Murf, it kept getting worse the longer it lasted as it wormed its way through my resistances, and even though I knew it was affecting me, I couldn't just shake it off." She shook her head. "That hole card of yours is ridiculous, Murf."

"Trust me, I know," I nodded, feeling a little bad. Charlie's ability looked like it had a deeper and more profound effect on Ferdi than I thought. I'd hoped to make her a little sad, but she looked genuinely shaken up. And it had kept working when she looked away from him, meaning it might work even when he was insubstantial and impossible to see or hurt. I wondered if he could use all my abilities the same way. If he could, that opened up some very interesting possibilities…

Ferdi straightened and seemed to shake the lingering effects of Charlie's gaze off, turning to look at me. "It worked, which means the beast should be able to affect whoever's holding my people. Have it do whatever it is that you did to Tifer, then we can go get them out."

"That might work," I agreed, glancing at the ferret frolicking on Millie. Currently, he had his nose poked down the front of her shirt, and she seemed unsure if she should be annoyed at what he was doing or happy that he was playing with her. As I watched her struggle to tell the little guy calmly that some parts of her were off-limits while he did his best to ignore her. Like me, the little guy was good at being annoying, and that gave me an idea for how I could use his abilities to do more than just free the halflings. I sent him a silent command, and he gave me a pleading look before somewhat grudgingly shifting back into his misty form. He swiftly flowed down Millie's body, speeding off into the jungle far faster than I could have run.

"Thanks for that," Millie murmured to me, adjusting her clothing so that it rested normally again. "He's sweet, but that curiosity can be a little annoying."

"I hope so," I grinned at her.

"What do you mean?"

"I mean, I've got an idea of how we can save Ferdi's people and hurt Shadow Man all at the same time, and Charlie's the key to it."

"Another plan?" Ferdi said disapprovingly. "We should keep it simple, Murf. Let's save my people and get the hell out of here."

"And then what?" I asked. "What will you do with them, Ferdi? Where will they go where Shadow Man and his people can't just grab them again? Do you think he'll ignore us killing a couple of his Holders and stealing back his captives? That he'll let all those witnesses return to the city to tell people what happened to them? That other assassin is still in the city, remember. There's no point in saving them just to have their throats slit the first night they're back."

"What do you have in mind, Murf?" Azara asked calmly. "We should hear your idea before pointing out how absurd and complex it is."

"For your information, it's really simple," I chuckled. "And it all depends on Charlie being able to be annoying and disruptive."

"Since it's an extension of your soul, I'd count on that," she said with a thin smile. "I'd like more details, though, if you don't mind."

I began to explain my idea to them, and as I did, their expressions went from doubtful to curious to considering. I couldn't help but smile as they slowly came around. If this worked, I was about to toss a wild card into the Shadow Man's deck, one that would bust his hand—or at least give us a few more cards to play with.

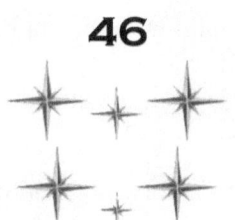

46

As it turned out, we'd been worried about Ferdi's armor for nothing. At least, mostly for nothing. We could have marched up to the torture shed talking loudly and banging cymbals together, and we wouldn't have been heard. All that worrying and arguing was totally wasted. Although, to be fair, to me, any day not spent gambling, drinking, and entertaining attractive women with only loose ideas of morality was wasted, so this whole week was pretty much a bust as far as I was concerned.

Charlie returned thirty minutes or so later to lead us to where the halflings were being held. At first, I thought he'd gotten confused as he led us down a path that seemed to just trail off into nothing—at least, I did until Azara stiffened beside me.

"That—that bastard!" she hissed, clenching her hands into fists as she stared at the forest.

"Charlie?" I asked in confusion. "What did he do?"

"No. That goblin!" She closed her eyes, and her lips began moving, although no sounds came out. A moment later, she pulled a card from her dress and lifted it up in front of her face. The card began to glow with the same eerie blue light that her eyes sometimes got when she did a reading. A moment later, an answering glow lit up a wavering, hazy wall hovering about ten feet in front of us. The wall shimmered in the azure light, then seemed to harden and clear, revealing the path continuing onward beyond it.

"What's that?" Millie asked nervously, her hands on the daggers at her waist.

"My ward," the avian said in a tone like ice.

"Your ward?" I asked in confusion.

"Mine, Murf! The one I made to hide myself! The one I used to conceal us all in the Labyrinth! That damn goblin stole it from my shop and turned it into a tableau!" She practically quivered with rage as she glared at the wall like it had personally offended her. "How dare he?"

"Can we get through it?" Ferdi asked impatiently.

Azara just glared at the wall for a moment before taking a deep breath and seeming to master herself. "Yes. My ward doesn't hold anything out. If it did, it would be detectable from the outside. We can simply walk through."

"Good." The halfling strode forward, stopping the moment she breached the wall. She seemed to tense up, then kept walking, practically stomping forward. Millie followed her a second later, looking nervously around, while I reached out and patted Azara's shoulder commiseratingly. She turned and looked at me, and to my surprise, I saw tears shimmering in her eyes.

"He's using my layouts, Murf!" she said, her voice trembling. "Some of those—some of those came from my father. They've been in my family for generations, and he's using them!"

"I'm sorry," I said, not really sure what to say. "At least you know where they are, though. All you have to do is kill him to get them back."

"Yes," she hissed, her voice hard and intense. "That's what I'll do. I'll teach that filthy Holder what being a true cartomancer is, then I'll retrieve my layouts from his mangled corpse!"

I blinked as she stalked forward. I'd never really seen a bloodthirsty side from Azara before. I'd seen her angry, sure, but never actively looking forward to killing someone. Those layouts, it seemed, meant a lot more to her than I knew. I kind of felt bad for the goblin if she got her hands on him. Well, only a little. He did have it coming.

As Azara said, the ward didn't offer the faintest resistance to walking through it, and when I stepped to the other side, I immediately realized why Ferdi had paused when she passed it. The moment I cleared the wall, a long, agonized scream assaulted my ears. The voice was deep and fluid as it cried something that I didn't understand in the trilling halfling tongue. When I saw how Azara's face paled when the cry reached her ears, I was glad I'd never taken the time to learn Ferdi's language.

We left the path shortly after slipping through the ward and circled around until a building appeared before us. It wasn't much of a building, to be honest. It looked like it had been tossed up in a hurry by an arthritic carpenter drunk on really crappy whisky. It was long and low with a flat roof. Whoever built it had obviously scrounged up the materials for it, meaning the walls were made of a mishmash of different types of wood, some painted, others stained, and some raw planks that had never been sanded. The whole thing leaned slightly to the right and looked like a swift kick to it would send it crashing down. That made its windows slightly angled, as well, leaving gaps between the poorly fitted glass and the frame that let sound pour through.

We'd found the torture shed. If the intermittent screams coming from the building weren't proof of that, the orc warrior standing in front of the door would have been. He stood a bit shorter than me but bulked much wider. Armor made of bands of metal riveted to hardened leather covered his chest, arms, and legs, and a helmet of the same design shielded his head but left his face open. He gripped a weapon that kind of looked like an oversized dagger atop a seven-foot pole with a wicked hook sticking out the blunt side, and swirls of ochre decorated the green skin of his face. As I looked at him, a card popped up in front of me.

Orc
Rank 5 Bloodsworn
Luck: 53   Capacity: 62   Skill: 61
Hole Card: 8 of Blades
Likely Powers: Wide-area strike,
Ranged slash

"Ferdi, any idea what a 'bloodsworn' is?" I asked her quietly as I read the card.

"What?" she replied irritably.

"Bloodsworn." I gestured at the orc. "He's a rank 5 bloodsworn, whatever that is."

"Shit," she muttered. "That's not good. It's an Uncommon profession. The Bloodsworn are a group in the Orcish army. They've sworn never to leave combat until their enemy's blood stops flowing, or theirs does." She glanced at me curiously. "Wait, how do you know that?"

"I just do. It's a card thing. I know his stats, that he's a rank 5 bloodsworn, that his hole card is an eight of blades, and that he's most likely got some sort of area or ranged attack."

She stared at me, her eyes wide. "Wait, you can tell all that just from looking at him?" Her gaze narrowed. "Do you know all that about me?"

"Yeah. Millie, too."

"You know my stats?" the redhead whispered. "I was going to pay for a divination to get them! What are they?"

"Is this truly the best time for this discussion?" Azara asked waspishly.

"She's right," Ferdi grumbled. "We will be talking later, though, Murf. Some things are private, and a Holder's stats are one of those things."

The waiting was the hard part. Well, technically, the fighting would probably be the hard part, and I felt sure there'd be some fighting. Getting punched, crushed, and stabbed is never a good time unless you're really into that sort of thing. I try not to judge, but if you are into that sort of thing, part of me can't help but wonder how you got there.

Ah, well. Not my deck, not my hand to play.

In any case, the waiting sucked. I'd wanted to go with Charlie down to the main encampment so I could watch him do his thing, but Ferdi and Azara both pointed out that it might be a bad idea.

"There are a bunch of Holders down there, Murf," Ferdi reminded me. "All it takes is one with a four of blades that lets them sense metal or a four of coins that just improves your senses, and we'll be spotted if we get that close."

"Plus, the closer we are to that bastard cartomancer, the more likely he is to detect us," Azara added. "His wards will be stronger and harder to bypass the closer we are to their source."

So, we waited. I knew Charlie was okay and doing his thing because I could feel the power he was drawing from me flowing out of my chest.

Plus, I heard him giggle and laugh every so often in my head, which was both creepy and distracting. I guess distance and wards didn't really keep us from communicating. Not being in my sight seemed to make him a little rebellious, though, since he ignored me when I asked what he was doing and just kept snickering every so often. I suppose that kids are kids, even when they're insubstantial hunks of your soul given life.

That probably wouldn't make a good law. A bit too specific, really.

While we waited, we crept as close as we could to the piece-of-shit torture hut, moving during the occasional screams so that we wouldn't be heard. Ferdi tensed each time, and I could practically feel her seething the longer we stood around with nothing to do.

"We should just take them, Murf," she gritted at me. "We hit the orc hard and fast, then go in and deal with the felid. There's no reason to wait!"

"Sure, Ferdi," I snorted. "We charge the orc. He shouts out an alarm. The felid lady signals the camp, then starts killing your people so we can't rescue them—or holds them as hostages. The rest of the Holders show up and capture us. We join your people instead of saving them. Is that what you're going for?"

"You don't know that she can signal the others!"

"I don't know that she can't, either, and it's smarter to assume she can. That's a rule in gambling, Ferdi. Always assume your opponents are just as good as you are. Murf's thirty-third law: If you're the best player at the table, you're playing solitaire."

Millie giggled beside me. "I like that one."

"Me too," I grinned. "It keeps me humble."

"Then it's failed miserably," Azara noted. "He's correct, though, halfling. Attacking now will jeopardize your people, not save them. We have a plan; we simply must be patient."

The warrior clenched her fists around her axe. "Easy for you to say," she growled. "Those aren't your people in there."

"Yes, it is easy for me to say. That doesn't make it incorrect."

I opened my mouth to speak, but before I could, a pulse of power rippled from the hut. The orc straightened instantly and spun, flinging open the door and leaning inside.

"That was the camp alarm!" he growled in a deep, guttural voice. "Something's attacking them!"

"Or something panicked Zeric again," a languid voice from inside the hut replied. "That goblin is the most easily startled person I've ever met. I'm sure everything's fine."

"It's our duty to assist them, Fisya!"

"It's my duty to extract the cards from these halflings, Argak," she purred in reply. "And that duty's far more enjoyable."

The orc growled and lifted his weapon. "I'm going to help them!"

"If you wish. They're no danger to me at this point. Return when the bear or whatever scared the little goblin into activating the alarm is dealt with."

The orc glared at her and fingered his weapon as if he wanted to use it on her, then turned and rushed down the path leading into the jungle. As he vanished into the brush, the felid continued speaking, apparently to the captives.

"Well, with that distraction out of the way, let's continue," she said in a sultry purr. "Come now, my delicious morsel. You've seen what happened with the others. They broke in the end, and so will you. Why put yourself through this when the result will be the same?" A sound of someone spitting came from the hut, followed by a weak moan. "Ah, still obstinate? Fine with me. That lets me enjoy this longer."

Another scream rang out from the hut, and as it did, Ferdi exploded into motion. She burst from the foliage and charged into the hut with a roar, her axe held back as she readied herself to swing. Her reaction left the rest of us startled for a moment before we tore ourselves free of the bushes and raced after her. Millie got there first as her speed ability carried her ahead of us, but I was only a couple steps behind her as I charged into the room, where I froze in mingled shock and disgust.

The hut didn't look any better from inside than it did from outside. In fact, the construction looked even worse from this angle, as I could see light gleaming through gaps in the boards of the walls and roof. The floor was dirt, not wood or stone or even clay, and rain leaking through the roof had left much of it a muddy and slippery mess. Of course, that wasn't what really made the hut awful.

I'd prepared myself mentally for a pretty terrible sight. This was a torture shed, after all. It wasn't going to be fun. I imagined instruments of torture, metal cages, whips hanging from the walls, the felid in a leather teddy—well, I wasn't sure about that last part, but I was trying to be hopeful that there'd be something good in that room. I was wrong. It was horrific, and I wasn't remotely prepared for it.

The smell hit me first. The room reeked of feces, urine, and vomit. The coppery scent of blood lay atop that, and so did the sweetish odor of rot and decay. It was as if someone had taken just about every terrible smell imaginable and squashed them together, then stuffed them up my nose.

The sights of the room assaulted me next. Metal cages did line one wall, but they weren't anything like jail cells. They were more like animal kennels, too small for even their halfling inhabitants to do more than crouch in. They held three listless, broken captives. That was the only way to describe them. Each had been badly disfigured, missing fingers, toes, ears, and an eye each. Burn scars creased their bodies, most of which looked like they'd gotten infected and were slowly killing their victims. None had hair or clothing, and each looked like their genitals had been terribly mutilated. None of them so much as glanced up at us as we entered the room. Their eyes stared at nothing as they crouched in their own filth, too broken to even realize what was happening around them.

The walls of the room were bare. A table stood in the middle of the room, heavy, solid, and big enough to fit even an ursid on it, and a figure lay strapped to that table. She was a girl, barely old enough to be called a woman, and she was obviously the current target of the felid's attentions. Bleeding burn wounds creased her nude flesh. Someone had taken a knife to her genitals and breasts. Half of her fingers were missing, leaving bleeding stumps behind. A bloody hole remained of one pointed ear, and one eye dangled from its socket and rested against her cheek.

My ears registered their input next, and compared to the rest, they were a blessing. The sound of retching filled the room as Millie dropped to her knees beside me, while Azara stumbled back with a sharp curse in the Avian tongue. The clash of metal on metal rang through the air as Ferdi slashed her axe furiously, roaring her fury at the totally nude felid woman. The felid, in response, chuckled merrily as she danced away from the halfling's powerful blows, parrying and sliding them with a pair of serrated, hook-pointed daggers that dripped blood and worse. The bound halfling sobbed quietly, her one remaining eye streaming tears that ran over bloody cuts and burns.

For a moment, I simply stood there, numb from the instant sensory overload. My brain refused to process what it took in, and my thoughts just froze in my skull. It couldn't be real; no person could really do all this to another. What I saw didn't mesh with my view of the world, with the laws I'd carefully worked out over years of cynical observation. People were selfish, stupid, and horny. They made bad decisions. They missed obvious opportunities or refused to take them out of fear or laziness, and they blamed the world for their failures. They ignored what they didn't want to know and embraced what they did. They were awful, by and large, but this...

This was evil. This was something that shouldn't exist, something outside my laws. And as I watched the felid duck beneath one of Ferdi's blows and slash at the halfling with a knife that sparked and crackled with electricity, I decided that it wouldn't exist anymore. Not if I could help it.

"Help me." I sent the thought spiraling inward toward the Hag nestled in the center of my being. I felt her silent agreement. In this, we were one. This was something that didn't belong and needed to be gone.

The felid blurred, slipping behind Ferdi and jamming her dagger low into the halfling's back. Ferdi cried out as the blade pierced her armor with ease and plunged into her. The warrior's body shook as lightning surged from the blade into her, and when the cat yanked the blade free, the halfling dropped to a knee.

"You're strong," the felid purred, lifting up the blade and licking it sensually. "You'll make a fine subject for..."

Power flooded my body as I charged at the felid. She spun as I moved, her motions impossibly fast, and lifted a hand that sparkled and arced with electricity. Her other hand whipped up, flinging her knife at me as swiftly as a bolt from a crossbow. To me, it all happened in slow motion. The knife rotated gently through the air, and I slapped it aside without effort. Electricity leapt from her fingers toward my face, but just as I had the knife, I brushed it aside. The felid's eyes widened as I reached her and lashed out with a fist, slamming it low into her stomach. I felt resistance as her cards tried to protect her, but the Mother of the Fucking Deck had my back. Her wayward kid wasn't going to stand in my way.

The felid gagged and choked as my blow crumpled her defenses and lifted her into the air. Vomit sprayed from her mouth as she flew backward and slammed into one of the walls with a thump. She bounced off and hit the floor in a crouch, raising her head and flinging another arc of lightning at me. I let it crawl harmlessly over me and responded with a kick. She tried to dodge, but she was slow, far too slow to escape me. I felt her ribs crunch as my boot slammed into her lower chest, and she crashed into the wall again, curling up around her shattered bones.

"W-wait!" she cried out, lifting a hand as she fell to her knees, but I didn't want to hear what she had to say. My fist lashed out, catching her on her chin, and her jaw crumbled beneath the blow as her head cracked into the wall. She slumped to the floor, but I wasn't letting her get away that easily.

Fury filled me; rage at this woman and what she'd done screamed in my brain. I reached down and hauled her up by the back of her neck, throwing her backward into the wall and holding her there with one hand. My fist slammed into her, crumpling more of her ribs. My knee flew up, and whatever was left in her stomach spewed out on my arm as I knocked every last bit of air from her body. Blows slammed into her face and body, pummeling her flesh.

She reacted like the trapped beast she was. She slashed me with knife and claws. Electricity crawled along my skin. Her knees and elbows slammed into me with brutal strength. I endured it all, letting the Hag adapt to her attacks. I ignored the lines of blood she drew in my face, arms, and chest. I paid no attention to the lightning tingling like ants scurrying across my skin. I didn't even grunt beneath the impact of her powerful blows. With each strike, the pain grew less as the Hag changed me to weather the felid's attacks. Sadly, she had no such protection from me.

Her head jerked sideways with a loud snap as my fist crashed into her cheek, and her body went limp in my grasp. I didn't care. I rained blows upon her, pummeling her unresponsive flesh. Somehow, that woman became everything that was wrong with the world, everything terrible and awful I'd ever seen happen and that had ever happened to me. Rage filled each blow as I beat her body, pulverizing her bones and tearing her skin. It felt good to let go like that, to let the anger flow, and she was a perfect target for it.

Something grabbed me and yanked me backward, and I fell away from the felid as a powerful force hurled me away from her. I landed hard on my back but scrambled to my feet, ready to release my rage on whatever else was attacking me. I froze as Millie stepped in front of me, her face pale and her hands raised between us.

"It's over, Murf!" she said, her voice trembling. "It's done! She's dead!"

"I—what?" I asked, confused.

"She's gone. You killed her. It's over." The woman took a trembling step toward me, placing a hand almost tentatively on my arm. "The hand's done, Murf. It's time to step away from the table."

I blinked, struggling to understand what she was talking about. As my anger faded, though, the power flooding me drained back into my chest. With its retreat came clarity, and I stared past her at the wall—and the ruin of a person I'd left behind.

The felid barely looked recognizable. Her chest was sunken in, the bones there crushed. Her head hung at an impossible angle, and her arms twisted around her corpse like limp noodles. Her face was crushed inward; her jaw hung from her skull, partially detached; the side of her head was pulped and mashed. It looked like someone had taken a massive hammer to her body and flattened it out. I glanced down at my bloody knuckles and realized that, in a sense, I'd done exactly that.

I dropped to my knees, shaking and trembling. Once more, rage had taken over, and with it came savagery I didn't know I had inside me. I'd enjoyed pulping the woman. It had felt good!

"What the fuck is wrong with me?"

47

I didn't mean for the words to come out in a whisper, but they did, and they hung in the room for long seconds as the other stared at me.

"Nothing, Murf." I looked sideways to see Azara crouching beside me, her eyes stricken but her expression compassionate. "Nothing's wrong with you."

"How can you say that, Azara?" I half-scoffed, half-sobbed, holding up my blood-smeared hands. "Look what I just did!"

"And look what she did to bring you to that place," the avian replied intensely. "Look at the cruelty she inflicted for her own enjoyment. She was evil, Murf. If anyone deserved this, it was her." She reached out and touched my cheek, forcing me to meet her eyes.

"I told you that there's a darkness in you, Murf, and it's true. There is. There's darkness in all of us. Yours just runs deeper than most because your most fundamental truth came from watching an evil take someone you loved from you. That doesn't make it wrong." She lowered her hand, and I took a deep, shuddering breath.

"She's right, Murf." I looked over at Millie, who squatted down beside the cartomancer. Her eyes shone with tears, but I could see the pain and rage in her gaze. "If I'd been able to, I would have done the same thing you did. This woman was twisted. She deserved everything you did to her and more."

"That was justice," Ferdi proclaimed from behind Millie, pointing her axe at the fallen woman. "You did good, Murf."

"It doesn't feel that way," I muttered, wiping at the tears that flowed from my eyes.

"Good," Millie said. "It shouldn't. Trust me. Some of my former teachers would have done that and wouldn't have cared in the slightest." She shivered. "You don't want to be like them, Murf. Be glad that you hate what you did."

"Millie's showing great wisdom for someone who looks like she does," Azara nodded. "You should listen to her. And if you don't like what you've done, well, just don't do it anymore."

"Just don't do it?" I chuckled, rising to my feet. "That's your advice?"

"Yes. You lost control. You let yourself fall into your darkness. If you don't like what happened, don't do that. Remember my reading, Murf." She placed a hand on my chest, over my heart. "Hold your heart close, or the Hag will snatch it away." She rested her forehead against my chest for a moment, and I just stared down at her, startled. She used to do that all the time, and the familiar gesture brought with it a flood of emotions, most of which were tinged with guilt.

"Good advice, cartomancer," Ferdi said. "Now, if we're done making Murf feel better about doing the right thing, can you help me look at my people? I think they're beyond my ability to heal."

"Yes," the cartomancer replied, stepping back away from me and giving me a weak smile. "I can do that."

As she walked away, I caught Millie eyeing me speculatively. The redhead took a step closer, then poked her finger into my chest.

"I told you: no harems," she said firmly. "Keep that firmly in mind, Murf. I like Azara, but I'm not good at sharing."

"No harems," I chuckled weakly. "Got it."

"Good." She stood up on her tiptoes and kissed me gently on the cheek, cradling my face with her other hand. "Are you okay?"

"No, not really," I shook my head. "I will be, though." I looked around the room with a grimace. "Maybe. I'm going to have nightmares about this for months."

"The same," she sighed. "They're going to have to get in line behind all the other nightmares, though." She shook her head. "You really need to work on how to show a girl a good time, Murf."

"Our dinner date hasn't exactly had the best results, has it?" I chuckled. I took her hand. "Once this is done, we'll have a nice dinner in the Guild Hall, where nothing like this will happen. Deal?"

"Deal," she sighed, taking my arm and resting her head against my shoulder.

"Murf, don't just stand there," Ferdi said. "Go claim her cards. We don't have a lot of time, here."

I sighed, releasing Millie, then walked over to the crushed body of the felid. I tried not to look at the ruin of her face as I touched her chest, pinching my fingers and pulling free a stack of cards.

Cards Gained!
You have claimed the cards of
another Holder.
Luck check success! You have
drawn cards with a high Harmony!
Skill check failure. You fail to
recover most cards.
Cards Gained: 4/9
4 of Coins, Ace of Cups, 3 of Stars,
Emperor of Cups

I lifted up the emperor, the only card missing from my court. As I did, Millie walked up beside me and looked at what I held.

"What did you...another noble?" Millie asked with an exasperated sigh. "The last one from your court, right? I assume you'll add it?"

"Yeah. I've got a spot set aside for it." I pulled open my shirt and placed the card against my chest. It felt slightly uncomfortable as it slid in, but it didn't burn or feel like jamming flaming glass into my heart. That was definitely an improvement. As it slipped in, new cards flashed in my vision, adding to ones that had popped up earlier.

Unity Achievement!
You have slain a Holder of your
rank or higher.
Reward: 100 UP per Holder rank, +50
UP per rank above yours.
+50% for Uncommon Profession
+1,050 UP

Card Attunement!
You have increased your Harmony
with your hole card, the Eldritch
Hag, from 10% to 20%, giving you
Lesser Attunement with this card.
Benefits

Adjacency Bonuses +50%.
All abilities are +50% stronger.
Adaptive and Needful Body abilities
respond 25% faster.

EMPEROR OF CUPS

CROWN OF AUTHORITY

Any creature or person hostile to you within 40'
receives a steadily increasing penalty to all actions,
reactions, and resistances. All creatures friendly to
you in the same range receive a similar bonus.

♛ Noble Arcana ♪30% ⚡73 ⚡⚡244

Emperor of Cups
Crown of Authority
Rank: Noble Arcana
Attunement: 30%
Base Power: 73 **Max Power:** 244
Any creature or person hostile to
you within 40' receives a steadily
increasing penalty to all actions,
reactions, and resistances. All
creatures friendly to you in the same
range receive a similar bonus.

Hole Card Boost!

Your Crown of Authority power
gains a 110% bonus to effectiveness.
Penalties and bonuses associated
with this ability increase more
rapidly. Penalties can become fatal
over time.

Potential Meld Built
Type: Flush Run
Cards: 10, Kn, La, Pr, Qu, Em of
Cups
Benefit: All card benefits +141% to
strength, range, and duration.
Ability: A Noble Master can be used
at will.
New Ability: Fool of Senses

Do you want to form this meld?

I read the cards over several times in surprise. I'd expected the
emperor to simply give me the power that the Hag had before, and it had,
although that ability now had a 110% bonus to its strength and a base
power of 73, way better than the Hag's replacement thanks to her and the
other cards boosting it. However, I also had the opportunity to meld those
cards, which it looked like meant combining them into a single card. That I
wasn't sure I wanted to do. Would I lose the powers of the other cards?
And what was this Fool of Senses ability? I didn't know, and while I'd ask
Ferdi later, she was a little busy at the moment.

"What about the rest of them?" Millie asked when the emperor
vanished. "Will you add any of them, too?"

"Not without talking to Azara," I chuckled, slipping the rest of the
cards into my pocket. "Did you want any of them?"

She shuddered. "Not until Azara's done that divination for me. They
hurt way too much to put any more in." She sighed and glanced upward as
a rumble of thunder rolled through the sky. "And it's going to storm.
Because of course it is."

I didn't reply; instead, I watched Azara and Ferdi go around to check
on the other halflings. The warrior tore their cages open and freed them,

but they simply huddled inside, refusing to leave. Ferdi had to physically haul each one from their cages, and as they exited, Azara touched each with a card. Her face looked bleak, and her expression darkened with each person she touched. The weather seemed to agree with the stormy look on her face, as after a few minutes, the sky opened outside, and rain shuddered against the roof with a roar, letting streamers of crystalline water stream through the holes to splatter against the dirt floor. Eventually, Azara laid her card on the chest of the woman lying on the table, then pocketed the card and gestured for us to follow her outside. I only hesitated for a moment before stepping into the pouring rain. I didn't like being wet, but it was a lot better than being inside that place. Besides, I wasn't exactly cleaned up for dinner, and the rain would hopefully awsh away the felid's blood.

"There's little I can do for them," the cartomancer said bluntly as we exited.

"You can't heal them?" Ferdi asked suspiciously.

"I can heal their bodies to some extent, yes. Given time, I can regrow lost appendages and even things like eyes." She shook her head. "That's a matter of days or even weeks, though. We don't have that kind of time. At best, I might be able to drive out the infections plaguing them. I won't be able to replace their lost digits or the genital scarring, and without that, they won't make it through the jungle."

She took a deep breath. "However, the deeper issue is that the torment they've suffered has damaged their souls, as well. There's nothing I can do for that, halfling."

"Heal what you can, then, and we'll worry about the rest once we get them back to Canis."

"Can we do that?" Millie asked nervously. "Pretty soon, that orc will come back, Ferdi, and when he does, he'll sound the alarm. Will we even be able to get them back to the river before they catch us?"

"No," Azara shook her head. "They won't be able to move faster than a slow walk at best, and it's likely that none of them will willingly follow us—especially in this storm. They don't have that much awareness right now."

"If he catches up to us, then I'll kill him," the halfling said flatly.

"And if he's bringing other people?" I asked. "What if there are two of them? Three? Five?"

"Then you can do whatever you did in there."

"I'm not sure if I can, Ferdi," I shook my head. "That wasn't on purpose. And if I did, I don't think it'll work against that many people."

"Even if you succeed, they may never recover," Azara said calmly. "Souls are slow to heal—and the scars often never fade. They may not thank you for your rescue."

"So, what are you suggesting?" the warrior demanded.

"Nothing. I'm simply telling you the reality of the situation. You have to decide what you'll do about it—and quickly. The longer we wait, the less healing I can give them before we have to be gone."

Ferdi glared at the woman, then looked back at the hovel, biting her lip. "What about Jidra?" she asked after a few seconds.

"Who?"

"The girl on the table. It looks like she hasn't been tortured as long or as much as the others. What if you only healed her? What could you do?"

"I could make it so she could walk back to the boat with some help," Azara shrugged. "And perhaps repair her eye, as it's still mostly attached. She'll still move slowly, though. We'll likely be caught."

"I can carry her." The halfling took a deep breath, then looked at me. "Can you give me some more time, Murf?"

"What do you mean?" I asked.

"Can you go with that beast of yours and help it keep the camp busy while I…" She took another breath. "While I do what I have to? If you can, we might be able to get out of this in one piece."

I looked at her, understanding what she meant to do, and nodded. Sure, I didn't really want to go put myself in more danger, but that was nothing compared to Ferdi's task. The other halflings couldn't make it out of the jungle, and she wasn't going to leave them for Shadow Man. There was only one solution. Yeah, compared to that, trudging through the rain toward the possibility of death was a regular walk along the beach.

"I'll go with you, Murf," Millie volunteered. "They don't need me here, and you might."

"Fine. The two of you go make sure we aren't followed, then catch up to us." Ferdi looked back at the hovel, her expression bleak. "Shadow Man's going to pay for this somehow. I promise you that."

Getting down to the camp wasn't as simple as just walking down a trail. The path led through the jungle, and while the trees did shelter us, they didn't keep the rain off completely. The path swiftly turned into slippery mud, and we slipped and slid down it as much as we walked, coating ourselves in orange clay that didn't wash off easily in the rain. The worst was when mud lay thinly over smooth rocks, and both of us fell on our asses. Millie went down almost gracefully, landing with a cute little, "Oof!". When I slipped, my ass nearly slid off the path, which would have sent me tumbling down into the ravine and presumably the Labyrinth below. I managed to catch myself by grabbing onto a bush—one covered with thorns that pierced my palm, of course—and after that, we moved a bit more carefully.

"I'm not sure we need to do anything to keep them from coming after us," I muttered, pulling a thorn out of my thumb with my teeth and spitting it into the bushes to one side. "Nobody in their right mind is going to take this path in a rainstorm."

"Except us," she noted.

"Which proves my point, I think."

She snorted. "Well, one of us is a little questionable, to be sure."

"It's good that you can admit that about yourself," I grinned at her. "Knowing there's a problem is the first step to fixing it, after all."

"Go talk to a mirror, Mister 'I-sometimes-talk-to-the-invisible-ferret-on-my-shoulder'," she snorted.

"That's a really long name. I would hate to have to sign it over and over again."

"So would I. It's bad enough having to sign things as 'Deepwater' and get all the questions about it." She glanced curiously at me. "You know, that reminds me. I don't know your last name."

"You're right," I nodded solemnly. "You don't."

She stared at me for a moment. "I believe the standard response to that observation is to offer your last name, Murf."

"I've always been above the standard," I said airily. "Quite a bit above, really."

"I won't argue that. Is there a reason you don't want to share your last name?"

I grimaced. "It's my father's name," I sighed. "My mom insisted that I have it. I don't like using it, though, so I don't. It's that simple, really."

"Why not change it, then? Or make up a name? No one would know."

"I would know. See, my mom wanted me to have it. I argued with her, but she told me, 'It doesn't matter if you like the cards the dealer gives you, Murf. You still have to play them.'" I shrugged. "So, I just keep that card close to my chest and do my best not to play it."

"I can see that," she nodded. "Okay. I won't press."

"Thanks."

"I'll just make one up in my head for you. How about, 'Murf Wankpants' or, 'Murf Diddlecrotch'? Either of those could work."

"Whatever you wish, Lady Deepwater," I grinned at her, bowing low.

"Stop that. Fine. Just Murf it is."

We heard the camp long before we saw it. The sound of shouts and arguing rang out over the rumbling of the storm and the roar of the water. Someone screamed, and a sharp crack snapped through the air. We nervously slowed down and crept forward, trying to stay out of sight as much as possible. As the path widened out into a clearing, we slipped behind some wide-leafed bushes and took in the results of Charlie's handiwork.

"Damn," Millie said softly.

"Damn is right," I muttered back. Really, that was all there was to say.

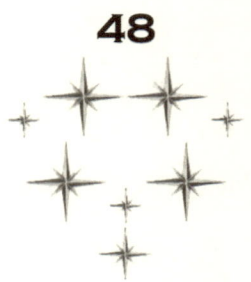

48

"Charlie did all that?" Millie asked, staring at the wreckage before us.

"No. They did all that, I think. Charlie just encouraged them to."

When I'd left the Labyrinth, the stone steps leading out of the ravine opened directly onto a barely visible path surrounded by the jungle. That wasn't the case anymore. The Holders had either cleared a large campsite themselves or conscripted some locals to do it. It looked like they'd hacked down the big trees, then used fire to clear out the smaller bushes and reduce the stumps to ashen protuberances jutting out of the soil. A bunch of tents stood around the edge of the clearing, the different sizes and styles of them suggesting that each Holder had erected their own. A large firepit steamed in the middle of the camp, extinguished by the storm.

And the whole thing looked like someone had swept a giant axe through the middle of it, then set fire to what remained just to be safe.

Half the tents lay on the ground, knocked over or slashed to pieces. Two of the ones that still stood smoldered, and flames still licked at a third despite the downpour, which made me think that magic was involved somehow. A large iron pot that had probably been for cooking lay dented and ruined twenty feet from the firepit, and smoking holes the size of a fist dotted the ground. Blood splattered most everything, swiftly washing away beneath the rainstorm. The place was a disaster, and it looked like it was getting worse rather than better.

Shadow Man had gotten himself some more Holders, it seemed. I supposed that was necessary since between us we'd removed Alerion, Taveroth, Tifer, Cassa, Fisya, and the elf woman whose name I couldn't remember from his employ—plus whoever he'd lost breaking into Azara's shop. At most, he'd have had the bloodsworn orc, female ursid, and goblin cartomancer remaining from the ones I'd seen in the warehouse. Oh, and Cassa's partner, but he was presumably still up in the city. Whatever the case, Shadow Man probably didn't have enough Holders to run the Labyrinth anymore, so he got some more. I didn't know if they were the ones who'd disappeared from the Sellsword's Guild or not, but really, it didn't much matter to me. The important thing was that once more,

Shadow Man was down a few Holders, and it looked like he was in danger of losing a couple more.

The ursid female lay next to the dented iron pot, the caved-in side of her head showing what had dented the thing in the first place. A male elf with dark blue hair plastered to his skull knelt near the fire, clutching a bleeding gash in his right forearm. A canid woman with the fur on the left side of her face burned off stood at one side of the camp, swaying as she leaned on a bladed staff of some sort. A blonde felid woman crouched behind one of the fallen tents, fingering a crossbow while a nasty cut in her shoulder bled furiously, as did another in her back. Another woman, this one a crane avian, knelt on the ground near the axe-wielder, her hand pressed across a wound in her stomach. Two more bodies, a canid man and a human woman, lay near the center of the camp. The goblin cartomancer, I noticed, was nowhere to be seen.

Only two of the Holders looked more or less uninjured. A burly human with a heavy beard and a heavier axe stood at one edge of the camp, shouting at the tattooed orc we'd seen before standing on the other side of the place. The orc yelled right back, gesturing furiously with his polearm.

"...killed them, treacherous human shit!" the orc roared.

"They attacked me first, orc dog!" the bearded man shouted back. "I had no choice! They all started killing one another!"

"I should gut you where you stand!"

"Try it, and we'll see if losing your head makes you any less ugly!"

"Hi, Dad!"

I jumped slightly as Charlie's somewhat tired voice spoke in my head and his tiny body swarmed up to my shoulder.

"Charlie!" I thought with a sigh of relief. *"What happened here?"*

"I did what you wanted. I made them all not like each other. They started yelling, so I started biting them to make them madder. Pretty soon, the big lady who's not moving anymore punched the guy with the hair on his face, and he threw that pot at her. Then, they all started fighting." He laughed, a merry little sound that was oddly disconcerting considering all the death and violence. *"Did I do good?"*

"Yeah, Charlie," I laughed silently. *"You did great."*

"Yay!" He sent me a mental yawn. *"I'm tired, though. That was hard."*

"You can rest, buddy. I'll take it from here."

"Thanks, Dad." He paused. *"Oh, I also found something that I think the lady with the feathers will like. There's a box with a bunch of those things she likes over there. I dragged it away so it wouldn't burn."*

"Things she likes?" I asked in confusion.

"Yeah. The things that show the spots for her to put cards on. I remembered she was mad that she lost some."

I chuckled; apparently, Charlie had found some layouts, hopefully the ones Azara was missing. How we would get them out was another story, but there was a much more pressing issue to deal with.

"It looks like we don't have to do much," Millie whispered to me, pointing at the camp. "They aren't going to be coming after us anytime soon."

I shook my head. "I'd agree with except for something that Ferdi said after that bunzelle tried to cook you and eat me. For Holders, if it doesn't kill you, you'll heal from it, and I'll bet most of these guys have healing cards."

"But even so, by the time they get those working and figure all this out, we'll be long gone!"

"And then? If we go back to the city, what's stopping Shadow Man from sending these people after us there? After Ferdi and Azara?" I took a deep breath, scarcely believing what I was about to say. "We need to deal with them here and now."

Millie's eyes widened as she stared out at the camp. "There are still six of them, Murf!" she hissed. "Six!"

"Four of them are wounded, though."

"That still leaves two, and both of them look like warriors! They'll kill us!"

I frowned. "I—might have an idea."

"Oh Unity, not another of those!"

"Hey! My last one worked out great! And for this one, you don't have to do much at all."

She sighed. "So, what's this idea?"

"You go around and deal with the wounded ones. I'll have Charlie distract the one with the crossbow. I'll handle the two in the middle and keep people from noticing you."

She frowned. "Do you think you can?" she asked doubtfully.

"No idea, but it can't hurt to try." Except, of course, that I knew it could. It could hurt a hell of a lot. "Besides, I got a bit of a power upgrade a while back, and I think it'll be handy here."

She stared at me, her face astonished. "Wait—you mean the emperor?"

"No, I got some new abilities from making my flush run. Thanks to the emperor, they're even stronger now, though. If they work, they won't even see us coming."

She sighed. "Fine. We'll try—but if something goes wrong, I'm getting the hell out of here as fast as I can!"

"That's fair," I grinned at her, then leaned over and kissed her wet, muddy cheek. She gave me a wan smile, seemed to hesitate for a moment, then slipped sideways, vanishing into the jungle. I turned my focus outward and grasped hold of my cards. I felt their normal powers filling them, but if I concentrated, I could also sense their secondary abilities. Those were significantly weaker, ranging from a base power of 21 for Alter Self up to 63 for Bereft of Sense. Plus, the energy inside me felt seriously diminished, down to maybe half of normal, no doubt thanks to Charlie. Even worse, I'd never used these secondary abilities before, meaning they probably wouldn't work the way I wanted them to and might fail on me entirely. I didn't really see much choice, though; I wasn't about to try and take the Holders on in an actual fight, and I really didn't want them healing up and coming after me.

Taking a deep breath and mentally begging the Unity to stop being a bitch for just the next few minutes, I flexed the lady in my deck, willing her Sanctuary power to roll forth. A shimmer surrounded me a moment later, the only sign that the card might have worked. Crossing my fingers for luck, I rose slowly to my feet, prepared to turn and run like hell if someone spotted me. The crossbow-wielding felid's eyes narrowed briefly in my direction, but the human warrior shouted at the orc again, and her gaze snapped back to him. I reached down and grabbed the emperor next, this time activating its actual power. Energy rolled out from me, and the felid's head darted my way again, but I froze and waited until her attention shifted back to the other two Holders arguing across the clearing.

I crouched low and moved forward slowly, guessing that the card's power would work better if it didn't have to shift quickly to hide me and trying to give it as small of an area to conceal as possible. Moving that way, it took me a minute to make the trip into the middle of the camp, where I activated my next ability, one I'd never used before. I could feel it coiled up inside me, though, and all it took was a touch for Suppress Cards to wash out from me. The ability wasn't great, making all cards within 30' of me 15% harder to use and 15% less effective, but combined with the ever-growing penalties from Crown of Authority, it should make the other Holders' cards a lot less powerful.

I moved until I was about halfway between the orc and human, pulled out my saber, and triggered Drunken Combat. The ability spread across the camp, and the felid's eyes swiftly darted back to me, this time widening as whatever ability she had apparently saw through my weakened card disguise. Her crossbow snapped up, but she screamed and swore as Charlie appeared on her head, his small but sharp fangs biting and digging at her face. Before anyone could react, I dropped Sanctuary and triggered the knight's secondary power, Living Nightmare.

"Holy shit!"

"Aah! What's that?"

The screams that rang out gratified me, but the fire and fury that exploded a moment later were a lot less exciting. The felid lady's crossbow twanged, and a bolt that burned with bright white flames shot outward blindly, slamming into a tent that wasn't in flames and igniting it instantly. Beard-guy slashed with his axe, and a sparkling, insubstantial blade like a ghostly axe whipped out from it toward me. The orc did the same, thrusting with his polearm, and a thicket of spears erupted in my direction. I dropped to the ground and triggered Sanctuary again, then rolled quickly sideways. Both attacks surged past me, rolled through one another, and slammed into the other Holder. The orc screamed as the glittering axe slashed across his chest, while beard-guy roared in pain as several of the spears punched through his armor and into him.

I rose to a crouch as the two slightly injured warriors charged one another, then ducked again as a blast of fire surged out from someone behind me and swirled around them. The fire washed over them but didn't seem to be all that effective, rolling over Beard-man's armor and Orc's skin without doing more than singeing a few eyebrows. I rose back up again, then shouted and fell backward as a burning pain stabbed into my left arm. I looked down and saw a flaming crossbow bolt buried in the meat of my arm, and I looked over to see felid lady cranking her weapon back for another shot, her eyes fixed on me. No one else seemed to be looking my direction, so I assumed she had a power to see through my concealment. Charlie was nowhere to be seen, but I could still feel him, so I assumed she'd flung him off her.

I pushed myself to my feet and ran toward her, dropping Sanctuary. Her eyes widened as the still-active power of Living Nightmare washed over her, and she flinched backward, nearly dropping her weapon. More screams came from behind me, and I felt a sense of power welling up, so I dropped flat again no more than ten feet from the felid. She shouted in alarm as a blast of crackling lightning arced over me, some of it crawling along my back and tingling but doing no damage. The same couldn't be said for her. The electricity buzzed into her, and her limbs shook and trembled as it raced through her nerves. It cut off a moment later, and I leaped to my feet. The woman recovered swiftly, dropping her bow and pulling out a short sword. She slashed with it, the blow lightning-fast, and I winced as her blade cut through my jacket and sliced my chest. Even as she struck, though, she stumbled clumsily for a moment as either Drunken Combat or Crown of Authority hit her, the sword suddenly seeming awkward in her hands. I stabbed very ineptly with my weapon, and had she been ready for it, it probably wouldn't have hurt her in the least. Off-balance and still recovering from the lightning blast, though, she couldn't move in time to avoid me, and my blade plunged into her throat. Her eyes widened as she gasped and gagged on the weapon, and her hands came up to grab at it, but I yanked it free and stepped back to avoid the gush of blood that sprayed from the wound. Her eyes rolled up in her head, and she dropped to the ground.

I spun and activated Sanctuary again, feeling an ache in my chest as I realized the power there was swiftly draining away and seeing that the base power of the ability was down to only 33. Even so, the chaos of the camp worked in my favor, and no one was looking in my direction. The avian with the wound in her belly was down with a bleeding hole in the back of her neck; so was the burned canid with the staff. Millie stood across the camp, fighting with the wounded elf whose rapier danced about, trying to spear her while she parried desperately with her daggers and nimbly dodged about. Even as I watched, though, the emperor's power continued to grow; Millie's strikes became surer and swifter as the card supported her, while the elf's blade grew slower and clumsier. He stumbled during a lunge, and she reacted instantly, slashing his hand with one of her knives while the other plunged low into his stomach. He cried out and dropped back, clutching the wound, but she spun past him like a dancer and buried her first dagger in the back of his neck, killing him swiftly.

I turned my focus from the woman to the center of the clearing, where the orc and human warriors still battled. It was a close thing, but as I watched, I realized that Beard-guy was going to win. He had better armor, and my card didn't seem to be affecting him as much as it did the orc. Still under the veil of Sanctuary, I slipped toward him, moving slowly so as not to catch the orc's attention—or to get caught up in the storm of battle surrounding them. Both of the Holders used their cards freely despite my ability suppressing them, and while they seemed concerned by how little effect those cards had on one another, they didn't stop hurling blasts of force, ghostly axes, and forests of spears at each other.

When the moment came, it came quickly. Beard-guy blocked a blow from the orc, who stumbled backward, dropping his guard for a moment. Beard-guy lunged forward, and the orc cried out as the axe buried itself in his stomach. Beard-guy shouted in pain a moment later as I lunged forward, a surge of power rolling up my arm as I thrust my saber at the man's lower back. His armor shimmered as my blade struck it, and I could feel a card resisting my attack, but the Hag's strength was undeniable, and the weapon pierced the steel plate and plunged into Beard-guy's spine, breaking in half with a loud snap as it did. He dropped to the ground, his legs unmoving as he dragged himself around to face me and his eyes widening as he saw only whatever the dregs of Living Nightmare showed him. Apparently, my attack had canceled Sanctuary's effect; either that, or I'd run out of power for it at last.

"Y-you!" he gasped, dragging himself backward. I didn't know who "you" was, but I was pretty sure it wasn't me. Although that might have been kind of flattering. Most of the time, when I'm someone's nightmare, it's because they're worried about what I might be doing with their wife, daughters, or the coins they'd kindly donated to me at the card table. Being legitimately feared would be interesting.

The orc roared again, and I spun toward him. He reached for his fallen polearm, but I ran over and grabbed it, yanking it from his weakened grasp. He snarled at me, but his complaints cut off as I raised it overhead and slammed it down toward him. He managed to get an arm up to block, but the power flowing through me as the Hag strengthened my body made me far stronger than a regular human. The blade sliced through his upraised arm and plunged downward, deflecting away from his neck toward his head. A bit more of my swiftly dwindling power rolled down my hands as the blade struck, and it swept through his skull at an awkward angle, cutting into his jaw and exiting the other side. It wasn't quite the neat decapitation I wanted, and I had to fight to keep my lunch down as the top part of his head fell off, leaving his tongue and lower jaw behind to twitch and flap about in a way that I knew was going to haunt my dreams for the next lifetime or so.

Pain seared a line down my back, and I stumbled forward as I remembered that I'd left Beard-guy lying behind me. I staggered around to face him just in time to see him sweep his axe in an awkward one-handed movement while propped on his other elbow. A curved arc of force streaked toward me and caught me across my chest and stomach, slicing through my clothes and cutting a gash in my skin. Another sweep of his weapon sent a smaller arc burning into my stomach. I bent over from the impact of the blow, but while the slash hurt, the pain wasn't as bad as when Ferdi cut me open, and I guessed that meant I'd adapted to it—or ignored part of it with my Arcana Resistance. Eyes wide, the man slashed again, and pain flared in my shoulder as a much smaller ghostly axe blade splashed over me, but this time, it felt less like a slash and more like a minor cut. A final arc of power struck me in the face, feeling no worse than a slap, and when I touched my throbbing cheek, my fingers came away clean; the blow hadn't even cut my skin.

"H-how are you doing that?" he gasped in obvious fear, scooting backwards even faster. Well, it probably would have been faster if he hadn't been trying to drag himself away one-handed while waving his axe at me with his other hand and splashing me with smaller and smaller axe blades that didn't even sting my skin as they struck. It's a lot harder to be fast when your legs don't work, after all.

I caught up to him in two quick steps. He raised his axe again, but before he could attack me, I slashed downward with the polearm. The blade at the end of it crashed into his forearm and kept going, shearing through his armor and severing his hand a few inches above his wrist. He cried out as the weapon dropped, his severed hand still clutching it. He reached for the axe with his other hand, but he had to roll to do it, and I stopped him with a quick jab to his chest. The power that rolled out was a lot weaker than it had been, but it was enough to punch through the armor of his shoulder and plunge the weapon into the joint. That had been an accident—I was aiming for his chest—but as his arm dropped lifelessly at his side and he rolled onto his back, I decided I'd take it.

I flipped my weapon over, snagged the axe clumsily with the hook on the back of it, and yanked it out of his reach just in case he healed quickly. He simply lay on his back, his eyes losing focus as the last vestiges of the power of the knight and emperor together sank into him. I quickly released the abilities as the ache in my chest grew sharper, and he shuddered as the effects of them vanished from his body.

"Is—is he the last of them?" I looked over to see Millie approaching me cautiously, quite deliberately not looking at the sort-of-decapitated orc. Her eyes were wide, her face was pale, and streaks of blood stained her hands and clothes. Her hair was in serious disarray, and her hands kept twitching and jerking nervously. She was at the end of her rope.

Honestly, so was I. I felt at least as rough as she looked. More nightmare fuel for the next few years, I supposed.

"I think so," I replied, looking around before sending out a mental call. *"Charlie! Are you okay?"*

"I'm fine, Dad." The little ferret appeared atop one of the tents, his form misty and blue as he flowed across the ground. He ignored me and raced up Millie. The redhead screamed slightly as he suddenly materialized on her shoulder, then relaxed as she saw who it was—and the glittering gold coin in his mouth.

"I found this for the pretty lady, Dad," he told me silently. *"There's a whole bunch of them. Should I get them for her?"*

"In a minute," I told him with a smile before looking at Millie. "Charlie says that's for you."

"Oh, Charlie," she whispered, pulling the ferret close and stroking his head affectionately. He practically purred with joy as she snuggled him, and from the tears streaming down her face, she needed the hug badly.

I turned away from the pair and lowered my stolen weapon at Beard-guy, checking out his card as I did.

Beard-Guy
Rank 6 Dire Axeman
Luck: 56 Capacity: 48 Skill: 63
Hole Card: 8 of Stars
Likely Powers: Magical Attack,
Light-based Area Attack

Beard-Guy
Rank 6 Dire Axeman
Luck: 56 Capacity: 48 Skill: 63
Hole Card: 8 of Stars
Likely Powers: Magical Attack,
Light-based Area Attack

I couldn't help but chuckle tiredly as I read the card. Apparently, even the Hag decided he should be called "Beard-Guy". Either that, or the card reflected whatever I thought they should be called. I preferred to think that the first one was right. That way, the Hag shared my sense of humor. Otherwise, I would have to picture her standing in her forest, rolling her eyes at me.

"Dire Axeman. That sounds like a pretty dangerous profession, huh?" I asked, trying to trigger some of my abilities. All that happened was a sharp twinge in the center of my chest. Apparently, I was tapped, which meant this probably wasn't going to go well. To my surprise, though, he didn't try to fight or even look at me.

"How do you know that?" he asked in a hoarse whisper. "Did he send you? Are you here to clean up this mess?"

"You mean Shadow Man?" I shook my head. "No, he and I aren't exactly on speaking terms. In fact, I'm here to toss a wild in his deck, so to speak."

"That's a good name for him." He shifted uncomfortably, still staring at the sky and not me. "And you're his enemy. Good. You'll want me to tell you what I know. I can do that—for a price."

"Well, that depends on the price," I shrugged. "I don't have all that much money on me, I'm afraid."

"Not money. I'll talk—if you promise to kill me afterward."

I let my obvious confusion show on my face. "Wait, what? You mean, you want me not to kill you, right?"

"No. You have to kill me. Don't leave me for him. I can't go back to him."

"I could just heal you if you promised to get the hell out of here and never come back."

He shook his head. "He has someone—someone I care about. I can't leave. If I disappear, he'll kill her, then me. If I die, though…"

"Then he'll have no reason to hurt them," I sighed, feeling the weight of his words in my chest and another spike of anger at Shadow Man. "I understand. Tell me what I want to know, and I'll kill you afterward, and I'll make it as quick and painless as possible."

That was an awful bargain as far as I was concerned. Yeah, a quick and painless death is probably better than one by torture, but it was a lot worse than no death at all. At least, that was my opinion, but it seemed that Beard-guy disagreed. He nodded once, his body relaxing slightly, then looked up at me with a solemn expression marred by the pain that he had to be in.

"What—what did you want to know?"

Part of me wanted to draw this out—I didn't really want to execute him at the end—but the pallor in his face and the blood dripping from his severed forearm convinced me otherwise. I wasn't sure how long he would be alert or even awake, and I had no good way to heal him. That meant I needed to get to business.

"First and most obvious. Do you know anything about him?"

"No," he shook his head. "Except—I'm pretty sure he's a noble, and a powerful one."

"Why do you think that?"

"Came early to a meeting with him one time—hoping to catch him off-guard and see his face. Instead, I saw a meritocrat sneaking out of the building. Nobody but a noble with lots of power and money could get a meritocrat to come to them like that."

I nodded. "That's good. How did you end up working for him?"

"I told you. He has someone I care about. He came to me one night in the Blade Hall with a couple Holders behind him and told me. Described her in too much detail for it to be fake. Told me I worked for him now. He did something like that to most of the people here, and the ones who were with him already obviously hated and feared him."

"Were you part of the attack on the halfling hold?"

"No. I came after. I never helped him take anyone." He took a deep breath. "I didn't try to stop it either, though, and I could have. That Fisya…" He refocused on me, his eyes turning hard. "You should kill her, too. She deserves to die. She and those halflings are up…"

"She's taken care of," I cut him off. "And the halflings are free."

He sighed. "That's something, at least."

"What about the Scribbler he took? Are they around here, too?"

"No. I think he's got them closer to him. I don't know where. I think that damn goblin does." He looked around. "Is he dead, too?"

"No, sorry. I think he ran when you all started fighting."

"Typical. He's terrified of everything." He snorted. "He's convinced some raven cartomancer is going to hunt him down and torture him."

I didn't mention that his fear was probably entirely justified. "Were you guys really going to run the Labyrinth?" I asked.

"No choice. We were stalling as long as possible, but we knew that would only last until he came back, and then we'd have to. None of us probably would have survived it, but probably dying is better than definitely dying at his hands." He laughed. "Looks like we just died a little sooner, is all."

"Why don't you think you'd have survived it?"

"We sent a few people in as scouts, just to see what happened. Some of the captured people who gave their cards to Fisya. They went in first, then we went in a minute later to watch what happened when their invulnerability wore off." He shook his head. "They all died. Instantly. Traps, then undead."

"Undead?" I asked quizzically. I'd heard Ferdi mention those before, too, but I'd never asked her about them.

"Dead bodies that move around and fight. They're hard to kill; they don't feel pain or fear; you can't hurt them with poison or anything like that. The only way to end them is to cut off their heads or destroy their whole bodies with something like fire. Otherwise, they just keep fighting."

"And you just sent people in to die to them?" I asked in a cold voice. "That's pretty brutal."

He flinched at my words. "You don't understand. They—they weren't people anymore. Not after she was done with them. They were like shells that walked around. Killing them was a favor, and we just did it in a way that helped us, too. None of them even knew what was happening to them." He shuddered. "It was awful. Those undead had to be at least rank 10 from how fast they moved. None of us would have stood a chance, assuming we survived the traps. We'd need at least twenty Holders, all prepared to deal with the Labyrinth, and even then, most of us wouldn't make it."

I nodded, recalling the broken halflings. I did understand, but what they did was still pretty awful. I pushed that thought aside; they'd certainly paid for it.

"Anything else you can think of to tell me?"

"Don't—don't try to fight him," he muttered. "Shadow Man. He'll kill you—or worse. He's a demon…" His eyes rolled back as his wounds or blood loss finally overcame him. He'd told me all he could, and it was time for me to live up to my end of the bargain. I grabbed his axe, feeling its weight and heft for a moment. I lifted it high overhead and brought it down, trying to aim a lot more carefully than I had with the orc. It either worked, or I got lucky, and the blade sliced through his neck with only a bit of hesitation. I was nearly out of power, but it looked like he was, too. A moment later, a card flashed into my vision.

Unity Achievement!
You have slain Holders of your rank
or higher.
Reward: 100 UP per Holder rank, +50
UP per rank above yours.
+50% for Uncommon Profession
+100% for Rare Profession
+4,900 UP

Rank Up!
You have reached Rank 4!
You receive:
Luck +3, Skill +1, Capacity +1

Harmonies:
Coins +2, Blades +3, Cups +2, Staves
+1, Stars -1

I swiped away the cards, my heart heavy as I looked around the camp. It looked like I'd taken the axe that Charlie swept through it earlier and followed it with its older brother, the sledgehammer, then lit most of it on fire for good measure. The rain pouring down kept the whole place from going up, but it couldn't quite extinguish the magical blazes. No tent remained standing; no one but me stood in the clearing, with even Millie down on her knees, nuzzling Charlie. The boat captain had said that a storm was coming, and he'd been right.

He'd just been wrong about who was bringing it. The Holders weren't the storm; they were the flimsy trees being swept away by it. Charlie, Millie, and I were the wind, thunder, and lightning that devastated this place.

"Can we go now, Murf?" I looked over at Millie as she rose slowly to her feet, gazing around at the destruction with haunted eyes. "I think it's over. Please say that it's over."

"Yeah, it's over," I agreed heavily. "We can't go just yet, though. We should claim their cards, just to keep Shadow Man from having them if nothing else. Oh, and Charlie found a couple interesting things, including some of Azara's layouts that the goblin stole."

"He can show me to those," she sighed. "Azara should have them back."

"She should." I gave her a weak grin. "He also said that there's more coins like that. I'm sure he'd be happy to show you those, as well."

"It almost seems wrong to profit from all this, but…" She nodded. "Go ahead and show me, Charlie."

"This way, pretty lady!" He leaped off her shoulder and scampered across the ground, stopping to wait for her as she plodded after him. I knelt over Beard-guy's body and pulled, beginning what promised to be a long and morbid experience.

Five minutes later, I slipped the last card from the ursid with the caved-in head. I hadn't gotten all that many, all things considered. My Skill checks failed more often than not, so I only got a card or two from most of the Holders, but my Luck checks usually succeeded, so the cards I got were fairly suited for me.

Cards Gained!
You have claimed the cards of
another Holder.
Cards Gained (12):

4 of Cups	8 of Stars
10 of Coins	Ace of Coins
5 of Blades	7 of Cups
6 of Cups	4 of Blades
2 of Coins	3 of Staves
2 of Cups	5 of Stars

In addition, I'd gotten two more noble arcana, this time in a new suit.

Millie came up to me while I was looking at the new cards, shaking her head. "More nobles?" she asked in an exasperated voice. "In coins this time? Are you trying for a second full court, Murf?"

"I'm not trying for anything," I chuckled. "It just keeps happening. If you don't like it, take it up with the damn Unity."

"I should. In fact, there's a hell of a lot I'd like to take up with it, while I'm at it." She looked sadly around the clearing again. "One hell of a lot."

"Yeah." I glanced at her and pulled up her stats once again as I remembered a question she had earlier.

Millie
Rank 2 Darkblade
Luck: 27   Capacity: 33   Skill: 38
Hole Card: 3 of Coins
Likely Powers: Wind Strike, Rapid
Attack, Blinding Attack

"By the way, your Luck is 27, Capacity is 33, and Skill is 38. Oh, and you're up to rank 2 already?" I paused. "And you picked a profession. What's a darkblade?"

"It's—it's an assassin type," she sighed. "I think I got it because of my training. I could have picked gambler, and I wanted to, but then there was all this." She swept her hand out toward the bodies littering the ground, her eyes shimmering with tears as she did. "I love gambling, but I—I didn't want to die, and it's Uncommon instead of Common…"

"You don't have to explain anything to me, Millie," I said firmly. "I'm not judging you. Your cards are yours to play, not mine, and I've got no business telling you how to play them." I laughed. "I told you, I picked the rarer one that I didn't really want, too. It's something called cabalist, and I'm fairly certain I got it because of my hole card. I didn't pick gambler, either."

She sniffed and looked around the clearing, shivering. "This is terrible, Murf. People shouldn't have to do things like this just to survive."

"Yeah. Hopefully, though, it's the last time either of us will ever have to, though."

"I'm not one for praying to the Unity—but that might be something to ask for." She looked at me. "It's ironic, you know. I ran away from my family so I didn't have to do this sort of thing, and here I am, doing it. I killed those people, Murf, and I didn't even hesitate."

"I thought you ran away from your family because they were forcing you to do this sort of thing, whether you liked it or not, to whoever they decided."

"Well, yes, that's true." She sighed again. "And I see your point. This was my choice, to use my training this way. I still don't have to like it, though."

"I don't blame you. I hated it." I took a deep breath and shook my head. "Enough of that. Did you find anything good?"

"Oh, yes," she smiled, holding up a long, wooden box. "Azara's layouts are in here—at least, somebody's layouts are in here, and I think she should have them."

"Agreed. Anything else?"

She held up a bulging leather purse with her other hand and shook it, producing the jingling of coins. "Quite a bit of coins, as well. Six crowns, thirty-one wands, ninety-five discs in all. Not enough to make us rich, but not bad."

"Not at all. Especially when I search you for the rest later," I grinned at her.

"Murf!" she gasped. "You don't trust me?"

"I know you," I laughed. "Plus, searching you sounds fun."

"It could be, depending on how thorough you are."

"Well, I found a dozen cards in addition to the knight and lady," I told her, fanning out the rest of what I found. "Obviously, you can take half if you'd like, but I'm thinking that we could probably sell quite a few of these for good coin. Enough to finally roll around in, maybe."

"What about the others?" she asked. "Ferdi and Azara?"

"The way I see it, we came down here, and we did the fighting. So, this belongs to us." I made a face. "Although I'll probably offer a card to each of them, just to be nice. The rest are ours, though—and so are the profits we get from selling them."

"You do know how to talk to a lady, Murf," she laughed weakly before looking around and sobering quickly. "Let's get out of here," she said, grabbing my arm and pulling it close. "I'm ready for a hot bath, a hot meal—and a warm bed." She rested her head on my shoulder.

"I can't imagine anything better right now," I agreed, summoning Charlie to my shoulder once more. I turned my back on the Labyrinth for the second time and began the long, slippery trudge up to the top of the ravine. Hopefully, this time, it would be for good.

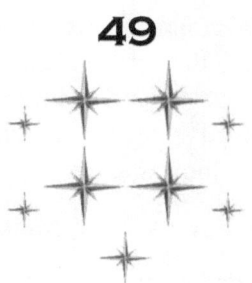

49

The rain stopped soon after we began our trudge uphill, and Millie and I caught up to Ferdi and Azara pretty quickly after we slipped and slid our way to the top of the muddy path. As she'd promised, the halfling held the lone survivor from the hold in a princess carry, but although she was strong enough to run with the woman without effort, she had to move slowly and carefully to keep from aggravating the captive's injuries. As it was, Jidra moaned with every step in obvious pain.

"Murf," Ferdi said as we returned, her voice bleak and strangely emotionless. "How long do we have?"

"As long as we need," I sighed. "They won't be coming after us."

"Are you sure?"

"They won't be," Millie said with a slightly sick voice. "They won't hurt anyone ever again, Ferdi."

The halfling glanced between the two of us and nodded. "Good. Did you get their cards?"

"Yeah," I replied, pulling out the four and five of blades and holding them up before her. "You want one of these?"

"I'll take the four," she nodded. "Blade sense is useful, and I've got a five already."

"Can you only put one of each card into your deck, then?" Millie asked curiously.

"No, you can have duplicates. If you do, you either get a new ability with the second card, or your first ability gets stronger. For most people, though, it's a waste of a valuable slot in your deck, and if you make a set out of those cards, the results aren't as good as if you mix up the suits."

"Makes sense." I turned to Azara and held up the three of staves and five of stars. "Either of these interest you?" I asked.

"The five, yes. Threes are too aggressive." She held out her hand, and I handed over the card. "Thank you."

"Don't thank me, yet. We found something else you might like."
Millie walked forward holding the box and held it out for Azara. The
cartomancer's eyes looked puzzled until she lifted the lid and pulled out a
roll of green fabric. She gasped as she unrolled it to reveal a layout, and
her eyes teared slightly as she looked at me.

"You—you returned my layouts to me, Murf," she said in a quiet voice.

"Well, Charlie found them," I shrugged. "Once he did, we figured we
had to get them back to you."

"Thank you. This layout…" She took a deep breath and smiled at it
fondly. "It was one of my father's favorites. It was one of the first ones he
taught me, and I've got lots of memories of the two of us doing it together.
The thought of that goblin pawing at it…" She took a deep breath, then
leaned over and kissed me gently on the cheek. "Thanks aren't enough,
Murf. You gave me back part of my heart, and you risked your life to do it.
Whatever you did—the man you once were—it's all forgiven." She looked
at Millie. "And for your assistance, I'll be happy to do your soul reading
free of charge, Millie."

"Thanks, Azara!" Millie said happily but tiredly. "I'd really like for
cards to stop hurting. I don't really care if that means they're not as
strong."

"Which is why I'm happy to help you. The best Holders seek balance
within themselves, not power." She gave the redhead a shy smile that
Millie happily returned.

"I'm just glad you got those back, Azara," I smiled at the avian. As she
turned away, I saw Millie glaring at me. The woman's lips moved, and
while no sound came out, I understood her words perfectly.

"No harems!"

I simply chuckled and turned to Ferdi, who was still carrying the
halfling girl. "Is she going to be okay?" I asked quietly.

"I don't know," the warrior replied tersely. "There's no way to say.
The avian says her soul is still slightly damaged, and I don't have any cards
to heal that."

"Are there cards for that?" I asked curiously.

"Who knows? The cards give slightly different abilities to everyone,
and when you meld cards, you get unique abilities." She hesitated.
"However, if there's a card that can do that, it's a power, not an arcana."

"Why do you say that?"

"Because arcana only deal with the physical, not the spiritual. Powerful ones like yours can affect the mind, as well, but that's different from the soul. Only powers can mess with that." She gave me a sideways glance. "And those above them, of course."

Her words reminded me of the option I'd gotten when I drew the emperor, and I glanced at it curiously. "What's melding, exactly?"

"Melding? It's when you take a stack of cards and combine them into one. When you meld a stack, it creates a new, unique card with any equally unique power."

"So, all the other cards just—go away?"

"No, their powers are wrapped up in the melded card—and they're usually stronger. It just gains a new one in addition to whatever it had." She gave me a sideways glare. "You pulled the Emperor, didn't you?"

"Yeah, from Fisya," I nodded. "I added it, and when I did, it gave me the chance to meld them all. I was wondering what the downsides were. I'm sure there have to be some."

"Oh, there are. First, once you meld a stack, you can't take it out of your soul. Where you put it is where it stays, and when you die, that card is lost forever along with whatever cards you melded to it. Second, once you meld a stack, you can't add to it or combine it with other cards. It's locked how it was when you melded it, and it can't grow from there." She snorted. "Not that you need to. Your cards are as good as they're going to get."

"What if your hole card is part of the stack?" I asked curiously. "Does that meld, too?"

"Yes, and then that card becomes your hole card, which is why so few people do that. If you meld your hole card, it won't combine with anything else—well, not unless you're lucky enough to meld other cards into something compatible. The only people who do that are those with extremely low Capacity who know they'll never get more than three or four cards; for them, melding to their hole card frees up the rest of the space in their deck, so they can add more cards. Nobody else would do it, though."

"So, it sounds like something I should do," I nodded. I glanced at Azara, who was listening carefully. "Should it go right next to my hole card?"

"It depends on the final card," the cartomancer hedged. "If the result is something that you feel doesn't truly represent you, then you should place it at the bottom of your layout, close to the center. If you feel it's something very like you, then you should place it next to your hole card." She shrugged. "Until I know more, I can't truly advise you."

I looked at the card, and taking a deep breath, I chose to make the meld. Unlike forming a stack, I felt the melding happen. Heat rose in my stomach as power roiled and churned, and pressure filled the middle of me. I could feel the cards squeezing together within me, their energies compressing and joining. It wasn't painful, but it wasn't comfortable, either. It felt almost like I really had to burp—and burp fire, at that—but couldn't. The pressure and heat built and built within me until it was almost painful before I felt something collapse and crumple inward. The bulging core of power in my stomach flattened and condensed, becoming a heavy layer of energy that hung inside me a little uncomfortably. As it formed, a pair of cards popped up in my vision.

> **Meld Formed!**
> You have melded the stack: 10 of Cups, Knight of Cups, Lady of Cups, Prince of Cups, Queen of Cups, and Emperor of Cups! This forms the new card:
> Rake of Cups!

> **Rake of Cups**
> Melded Court of Cups
> Likely Powers: Multiple
> **Requirements:**
> Luck: 62, Harmony 64
> Compatibility: 45%

"Rake of cups," I said, staring at the card that looked like a handsome, careless-looking young man with golden hair, holding a goblet of the same hue and several cards while surrounded by grape leaves. He looked both trustworthy and utterly unreliable at the same time, as if he'd promise you anything—but he might not see it through.

"What?" Ferdi asked.

"That's what it made. The rake of cups."

"I've never heard of that card," Millie laughed.

"You wouldn't have," Ferdi growled. "When you meld a stack, you get a new card that's never existed before. Of course, it's not usually a noble arcana of its own. Your Luck is ridiculous, Murf."

"It sounds like it would suit you," Millie offered.

"It does," Azara nodded. "What's more important, though, is what it feels like. How does it feel, Murf?"

"Like an old friend," I chuckled, staring at the image. "Someone I've known for a long time."

"Then place it below your hole card," she nodded. "That's where it belongs: attached to the center of your soul."

I did so, and immediately, two new cards popped up.

Rake of Cups
Fool of Senses
Rank: Unique Arcana
Attunement: 47%
Base Power: 142   **Max Power:** 427
Use all Cup Court abilities at +156% power; use A Noble Master freely. You can create illusions indistinguishable from reality to fool any sense you choose for all within 20'. This ability can reproduce any of the illusory abilities of the Court of Cups at normal power.

Hole Card Boost!
All abilities tied to the Rake of Cups
get a 150% bonus to effectiveness,
can ignore resistances or immunities,
can become crippling or fatal, and
grow 150% faster than normal.
Fool of Senses can create lethal
illusions.

"That—that's incredible," I breathed.

"Good ability?" Ferdi asked.

"Yeah." I swallowed hard as I examined the card. "It's—it's got a base power of 142, Ferdi."

"A three-digit *base* power?" she demanded, spinning to face me fully. "Out of what?"

"427."

The halfling stared at me, her face stunned and her mouth agape. "Wh—over 400 power? That's ridiculous, Murf! That's power-level strength, not arcana!"

I shrugged. "I wouldn't know. It makes the other cards in the court a lot stronger now, too, though."

She snorted. "As if you need them to be. That's insane, Murf. I'm surprised that the Unity hasn't reached out and slapped you down after giving you something like that. Whatever happened to its balance?"

"Well, it did saddle me with you," I grinned at her. "That kind of evens out."

"Hardly. Without me, you'd be dead several times over. That's hardly a balance to such a powerful card."

Once more, she'd missed my sarcasm and ruined a perfectly good insult. I sighed and turned back to Azara, pulling out two more cards and holding them up for her. "Azara, would I be able to place these two cards safely without unbalancing anything?" I asked.

"What are those?" Ferdi asked, craning her neck to see what I held. "Are—those are more noble arcana, aren't they? What the hell did you pull, Murf?"

"The knight and lady of coins," I sighed.

"The lady of coins? Are you serious? Do you have the Harmony for it?"

"I'm close, yeah."

"Good enough. You need to bind that one, now!"

"He needs to see where it can be bound safely," Azara sniffed. "Not just throw it into his soul without care."

"Look, avian, I get that you're trying to help him," Ferdi growled. "But this time, he really needs to bind that—and the knight won't hurt either."

"Why, Ferdi?" Millie asked curiously. "Why is that card so important?"

"Because the lady of coins is probably the most sought-after arcanum in the whole damn deck, woman!" She took a deep breath and looked at me. "Do you know what it does?"

"Something about storage," I nodded.

"It's not just storage. It's the perfect storage! It's invisible, it goes with you everywhere, and with it, you can store things without having to carry around their weight. Best of all, only someone with a card like the prince of coins can get to it."

"The prince of coins?"

"It gives you the ability to steal things from a distance. That doesn't matter, though. You need to add that card to your deck, now. It's too useful not to!"

I looked at Azara. "What do you think?"

"It's possible," she nodded. "With the meld you just made, your base is now open, and unless you hope to find the court of cups once more, the court of coins is most suited for that area. Place the knight and lady where the knight and lady of cups were before, just below your new card, and they should balance. They'll be less comfortable than the cups court was, though; they aren't as good a fit for your soul. I would place the knight first; it will hurt somewhat, but the lady should then be easier."

I reached down to pull open my shirt before realizing that, thanks to Beard-guy's axes, it was already open. It was also somewhat bloodstained and probably ruined, meaning I'd need to go shopping when we got back to the city once more. I touched the knight to my chest and winced as is slid in, burning slightly and feeling like a hot splinter slipping into my chest. It wasn't pleasant, but it still wasn't as painful as the knight of cups had first been. Once it was in, I added the lady as well. She also burned slightly sliding into me, but the sensation was more discomfort than pain, and once she settled into place, that turned into a rather pleasant warmth in my chest. I quickly examined the cards that appeared before me.

KNIGHT OF COINS

MELEE MASTERY

When fighting in melee combat, you gain a steadily increasing bonus to combat skill and speed.

♛ Noble Arcana ♪36% ⚡27 ⚡⚡75

Knight of Coins
Melee Mastery
Rank: Noble Arcana
Attunement: 36%
Base Power: 27   **Max Power:** 75
When fighting in melee combat, you gain a steadily increasing bonus to combat skill and speed.

Hole Card Boost!
Melee Mastery gains a 130% bonus to effectiveness. Any weapon you

wield has an increased chance to overcome defenses. You gain basic combat skills quickly and can advance those skills to near-mastery in time.

LADY OF COINS

PHANTOM PORTER

You gain a hidden storage area, accessible only by you. Volume available equals Base Power in cubic feet.

♛ Noble Arcana ♪30% ♭27 ♯♯90

Lady of Coins

Phantom Porter

Rank: Noble Arcana

Attunement: 30%

Base Power: 27 **Max Power:** 90

You gain a hidden storage area, accessible only by you. Volume available equals base power in cubic feet.

Hole Card Boost!

Phantom Porter gains a 130% bonus
to effectiveness, including volume.
Your Storage is resistant to other
abilities that might penetrate it.
Items in Storage experience a vastly
slower passage of time.

"How was it?" Millie asked curiously.

"Not that bad," I shook my head. "The knight burned a bit, but the lady felt okay."

"As I said," Azara pointed out.

"Exactly as you said, yes. Thanks again for the advice."

"Continue to follow it, and I'll be happy. Do you have any other questions about your deck?"

I frowned and pulled out the cards I'd collected. "I've got quite a few of these," I noted. "I'm wondering if I shouldn't try to bind some of them."

"Kewan's blood, Murf!" Ferdi swore, staring at my hand. "How many cards do you have there?"

"Fifteen, I think," I said with a grimace. "It's a ridiculous amount, really."

"It is, especially when you aren't binding them! You must have some potential stacks in there!"

"Well, with what I've already got in my deck, I've got a couple of 3-sets," I said dubiously. "Aces and twos. I could also make a long run from ace all the way to ten in multiple suits, although you said it would be better to split that into two, I think."

"And why would you do that?" Azara asked calmly.

"Because he can!" Ferdi said in an exasperated voice. "Murf, a 3-set of aces would give you another combat power! And a 3-set of twos would give you a sensory ability. Both would be weak, but with your hole card boosting them, they'd still be as powerful as most higher arcana! You need these!"

"Is that true, Murf? Do you want to add those cards just because you can? Do you need them? What will they give you that you don't already have?"

I almost answered, "Power" until I stopped and thought for a second. Would those lesser arcana really help me stay alive? I already had three of them bound; how often did I use them? Not very. My court cards and the Hag combined were so strong that the lesser cards just didn't seem to do much for me. And if the Unity was about to start feeding me the court of coins as well, I'd be getting plenty strong off those without needing a bunch of lesser arcana filling up my deck unnecessarily.

"If I'm being honest?" I sighed. "Probably nothing."

"Murf, with those cards..."

"What, Ferdi? I might gain a few extra abilities that I'll probably never use. I have trouble remembering the ones I have now, in fact." I shook my head. "I don't really want any more of these things in me than I need, to be honest, and adding them just to do so seems—well, kind of greedy."

"It is," Azara nodded. "Some people are so greedy for power or strength that they'll do anything for them, no matter what. They lord it over others and use that strength to get whatever they want."

Ferdi sighed, shaking her head. "Yes, avian. That's true. Some people add cards simply for the strength. Some people use their abilities foolishly or evilly." She glared at the woman. "But then, some cartomancers do the same thing, don't they? They pretend they have powers they don't and lie to people just for coins or to impress others. They give people terrible advice and ruin lives rather than admit that they don't know because they don't want people to realize that they're basically charlatans. Isn't that right?"

"Yes, it is," Azara agreed coolly. "And if you're saying that I shouldn't judge all Holders by the actions of a few, I feel I should point out that I never judged all Holders. Just the ones who lust for strength."

"I'm not as good with words as you," the warrior shook her head. "But do all cartomancers lie for the same reasons? Is it always because they're greedy?"

"Obviously not..."

"And it's the same for Holders. Some of us are greedy. Some are cruel." Her face hardened. "But all of us are hunted. People will happily kill us for our cards, and we all know it. That's why even the most peaceful of us get stronger; if we don't, we die. Yes, some people revel in that power, but most of us are just trying to survive. And for Murf, that's an even bigger problem."

She pointed at my chest as she continued, with Azara watching in silence. "You know what he's got inside him, avian. If people find out about it, they'll do their best to kill him. Archers will wait for him whenever he walks outside. People will try to break into the Guildhall to get to him. Nobles will send Black Roses, and not just for him. They'll target anyone close to him, looking for leverage. Those greedy people you mentioned before would burn a damn city down for a chance at the card in his chest, and to hell with who dies."

She looked at me, and I saw real worry in her eyes as she spoke. "You've got two choices, Murf. Hide away and never use that thing, or be so damn strong that people are afraid to cross you. Fools will still try, but you'll be able to handle them. It's your only chance to be safe and still have a life worth living. That's why I keep pushing you. Not because that's what everyone does, but because if you don't, you'll die, and while you piss me off sometimes, I don't want you to die."

I didn't say a word, but Ferdi's diatribe matched far too closely with the Hag's for me to ignore her. She was right; I did need to get stronger, and I couldn't stop just because I didn't like it. I didn't think Azara would want to hear that, though, and I had no intention of getting into the middle of the argument between the two. To my surprise, though, rather than angry, Azara's face turned speculative, and she seemed to calm down a bit.

"You raise a good point," Azara finally nodded. "There are many reasons a person might seek power, and not all are motivated by selfishness and greed. If I misjudged you, I apologize."

"Accepted," Ferdi grunted.

"And I accept that Murf, more than most, needs to be as strong as possible, just to shield himself from those kinds of dangers. However, the card in his soul offers an additional danger that you might not be aware of. Right now, Murf controls it, more or less, and keeping his layout balanced helps with that. However, the less balanced his layout is, the harder it will be for him to resist the card's influence, and if it takes control, it could spell disaster for everyone."

"I think you might be overdramatizing," Ferdi snorted.

"You think so?" Azara's voice turned hard once more as she spoke. "Imagine Murf being able to adapt to anything, instantly. Any attack. Any card power. Nothing could harm him; no force could touch him.

"Plus," she continued grimly, "Murf's card draws the deck to it. I can hear her calling to them, summoning them, and they can't help but obey. You've seen it; cards simply come to him when everyone else has to fight and scramble for even a single one. He's already got two cards of the court of coins, and he'll have the rest soon enough. The other courts will probably follow, and eventually, he'll draw the powers of the deck.

Imagine him with every court of the arcana and multiple secrets, all stacked and linked to that hole card of his, all wielded by a man who can't be killed, no matter how hard you try."

She leaned closer to the halfling, who stared at her with wide eyes, frozen in place. "Now, imagine all that power held by someone like the Shadow Man, one who craves power and cares nothing for how he gets it. That's what will happen if Murf loses his ability to resist the Hag, and his layout flips to one based in power instead of his heart."

She leaned back, and her voice lost some of its iciness. "That's why I keep telling him to stop and think about the cards before he places them. If he loses his heart, the whole world loses with him."

Ferdi stared at the avian in silence for long seconds. "Do you know that?" she asked quietly. "Or are you guessing, the way you did with his layout?"

"I did a divination on him and his soul. His card hides from me, but I saw enough to know that it wants him to be stronger, no matter the cost. It wants him to help it gather its children."

Ferdi shook her head. "It's a card. Cards don't want anything."

"Spoken like a typical Holder," Azara sniffed. "You're wrong, halfling. Even the least of arcana has a voice if you're able to hear it, and the greater cards are as aware as any of us."

"She's right, Ferdi," I broke in softly as the warrior opened her mouth to retort. "My card's got a mind of its own."

"What do you mean?" the warrior demanded. "How do you know that?"

"I've talked to her. She told me how my stats work and what the different types of cards are, arcana and powers. She's alive, and she's a hell of a lot smarter than me."

"That's not the hardest bar to reach," she muttered, shaking her head. "Did you hit your head right before this?"

"No," I chuckled. "And even if I had, too much of what she told me has turned out to be true for me to have imagined it. She's alive and aware, Ferdi, and she says the other cards are, too—if not quite the same way as her."

"That..." The woman took a deep breath and began marching down the path again. "You know what? It doesn't matter, and honestly, it's easier just to believe you." She looked at Azara again. "And if he's right, then you must be, as well. He could be that dangerous?"

"The Hag said that arcana affect the Holder and the area around them," I offered. "Powers affect a wide area. Cards like her, though? They affect the whole world."

"I'd call you a liar, but honestly, you're the strongest Holder I've ever seen, and you're barely starting," she sighed. "Fine, avian. If you admit that he does need to keep getting stronger, I'll admit that he needs to be smart and safe about it, for all our sakes. That work for you?"

"I can agree to that," Azara nodded.

"Good. Then it's settled. Murf, you have to get stronger, but be smart about it. Got it?"

"I can hear, you know, Ferdi," I chuckled.

"You can. Sometimes, you choose not to."

"That…" I paused. "Is actually kind of fair."

"I'm glad that's decided," Millie said lightly, stepping up beside us with Charlie still nuzzled on her shoulder. "However, if he's not going to bind those cards—what should we do with them? He can't just go around carrying them, can he?"

"It's probably not a good idea," Ferdi sighed. "There are cards and abilities that let people sense loose cards, and a lot of Delvers and treasure hunters have them. Carrying around a few extras is normal and even useful. With that many, someone will try to rob him."

"I can feel them, as well," Azara agreed. "Any decent diviner could."

"We could sell them," Millie suggested hopefully. "Some of them, at least."

"That's not a bad idea," Ferdi agreed. "If no one can use them, that is. Money is always useful."

"I don't recommend trying to sell that many cards at once," Azara suggested. "At least, not to the Sages. It'll raise too many questions, and Sages are as susceptible to greed and a lust for power as anyone."

"The same for merchants," Millie agreed. "If we sell them, we'll have to do it in bits and pieces, sell a couple to the Sages, a couple more to different merchants, and maybe a couple to the Scribblers."

"You won't get a good price from them," Ferdi shook her head. "I could sell a couple in the Blade Hall without raising eyebrows, though."

"Sounds like we need to split these up, then," I said. "Azara, you and I can take some to the Sages and sell them; Ferdi, you can do the same with the Sellswords, and Millie, you can take a few to the Merchants."

As I spoke, Charlie's head popped up from Millie's shoulder, his eyes fastened on the cards in my hand. He suddenly turned misty and flowed away from Millie, landing on my shoulder and gazing down at the cards with a strange intensity.

"What are those, Dad?" he asked in his tiny voice.

"They—they're cards, Charlie," I replied, slightly startled. *"Unity cards. You've seen them before."*

"Cards. I like them." He ran down my arm and sniffed at the cards, his little whiskers tickling them. He peered back over his head at me. *"Can I have one?"*

"Can you—wait, what? You want a card?"

"Yes. They smell…" He paused and sniffed the cards again. *"They smell good. Can I have one?"*

"Murf, what's going on?" Millie asked me in a concerned voice. "You've got a strange look on your face."

"It's Charlie," I answered slowly. "He says he likes the cards and wants to know if he can have one."

Millie giggled. "Can he bind one? Maybe you should give it to him if he can."

"No," Azara shook her head firmly. "That creature is an extension of Murf's soul. It has no soul of its own to bind cards with. It has no layout or deck."

"Why would he want a card, then?" Millie asked.

"I'm not sure. Think I should let him have one and see?"

"Don't be ridiculous," Ferdi snorted. "Even the least of those cards is worth gold, Murf. They're not a toy for your fuzzy little thing."

"Fuzzy little thing?" I asked in mock offense. "Who have you been talking to, Ferdi? I'll have you know that while it's fuzzy…"

"Not your genitals. The creature," she cut me off. "You're entirely too obsessed with genitals, Murf."

"That's sadly true," Azara sighed.

"I don't know about sadly," Millie grinned. "It does seem pretty true, though."

"I don't remember either of you complaining—hey! Charlie! Stop!"

As we spoke, Charlie crept closer to the cards, and the moment I was distracted, he snatched one from me and leaped off my hand, running a few feet away from me.

"Charlie! Give that back!" I demanded.

"Can he hurt it, Murf?" Millie asked curiously.

"No," Ferdi shook her head. "Nothing can damage or destroy a card."

"Charlie, bring that back," I sighed. "It's not a toy…" I froze as Charlie opened his mouth, sank his sharp little fangs into the card—and tore off a chunk of it. The chunk he bit off flared into the same misty blue energy that seemed to make him up and flowed down his throat, and as it did, I felt a tiny pulse of ice in the center of my chest.

"The card!" Millie gasped. "Is he…?"

"He's eating it," I said grimly, watching as he took another bite of the card.

"Impossible!" Ferdi gasped, staring at what to her had to look like a card vanishing one chunk at a time. "Nothing can destroy a card!"

"Shadow Man did," Azara reminded her.

"Okay, yeah, but that thing's not Shadow Man!" She looked at me. "Murf, stop it!"

"There's not much point, now," I shook my head, gesturing at the thieving little ferret. "He's halfway done with it."

The woman took a step toward the ferret. "If you won't stop it, I will."

"How? You can't touch him right now."

"Besides, Ferdi, Murf's right. There's no point to stopping him," Millie added. "Do you really think that the card will still work with it being half-eaten?" She looked at me. "I'd put the rest away, though, if I were you."

I quickly stuffed the other cards into my holder and made sure it was secure in my pocket, then watched as Charlie devoured the last of the card. As he nibbled it, more power flowed into me, gathering in the tiny, icy core at the center of my body where he slept. When he finished, letting out a tiny burp of misty, blue energy, a new card appeared before my eyes.

"Damn," I whistled, staring at the card in front of me.

"What?" Millie asked.

"That card—it made Charlie a little stronger. It boosted his abilities by an extra 5%, in fact."

"What?" Ferdi demanded, spinning to face Azara. "I thought you said that thing can't bind cards!"

"It shouldn't be able to," she shrugged. "Everything I know about cards, Holders, and the soul says it shouldn't be possible."

"He didn't," I cut in before the two could start arguing again. "He absorbed its energy. It didn't give him an ability; it just gave him a power boost."

Charlie burped again and looked up at me, his face a study innocence. *"That was good, Dad! Can I have another one?"*

"No, you can't have another one," I said aloud as sternly as possible. "You took that one without permission!"

His head sunk low, and he curled up a bit, backing away from me. *"I just wanted it, Dad. I'm sorry I made you angry."*

"That's quite interesting," Azara said thoughtfully, cocking her head sideways as she peered at the spot where the card had been, even though I didn't think she could see Charlie. "It took the ace of stars, yes? That card typically boosts the strength of layouts and can make other cards' powers stronger. It seems that it took the essence of the card into itself and used it to grow." She nodded. "It might be worth giving it more cards, Murf."

"What?" I demanded, glaring at her. "You want me to give the little thief more cards?"

"Of course, it's a thief," she said evenly. "You're a thief, Murf, and it's an expression of your soul. How could it not be a thief? If you want it to gain a sense of ownership, you need to learn one yourself, first."

"Plus, Charlie would be even more useful if you made him stronger," Millie suggested before hesitantly adding, "Of course, the gold we could have gotten for that card would be nice, too."

I sighed and rubbed my head, then looked at Charlie. Azara was right; it wasn't really the little guy's fault. I had a tenuous grasp of the idea of property ownership at best, and he was just a projection of me. The poor little guy never really stood a chance, and it wasn't right to get pissed at him for it—especially when I'd praised him for taking stuff in the past. Of course, that didn't mean I couldn't set up some ground rules.

"Look, Charlie. I know you didn't mean any harm," I said soothingly. *"But from now on, you can't take things from me without asking—or any of my friends. Okay?"*

"Okay, Dad," he nodded. *"But from other people?"*

"As long as you don't get caught, I don't much care," I laughed. *"And in the future, when I find cards, I'll share one or two with you if I can. But if you start taking them, then I'll stop sharing. Deal?"*

"Deal!" he said happily, racing back up my body and settling onto my shoulder, where I reached over and began to scratch his head and under his jaw, listening to him purr happily.

"I told him not to steal from any of us," I told the others. "And that I'd share cards with him in the future if he promised not to take any more from me. He agreed."

"You're going to feed more cards to that abomination?" Ferdi demanded.

"He's not an abomination," Millie said firmly, glaring at the halfling. "He's adorable, smart, and useful. And you owe him for finding your people! Consider the card a fair reward for his help."

Ferdi glared at the woman before grunting. "Fine. But if it touches any of my cards, it's ending up on my axe."

"I don't like her, Dad," Charlie said, glaring at the halfling. *"Can I bite her?"*

"Maybe later," I chuckled before looking at the others. "Come on. Let's get the horses and ride back to the village. I need a hot bath and a soft bed."

"You're soft, Murf," Ferdi growled.

"Yes, Ferdi, I am, and if becoming un-soft means sleeping on the ground, eating that nasty stew the Unity gave us, and tromping around in armor all day, I'm happy staying soft, thanks."

50

The rest of the trip passed easily enough. We sold our horses in Upper Kallit and hired the drunken captain to take us all back to Canis, which was much faster than a trip on horseback would have been. I kept my eyes peeled the whole way for the goblin who Beard-guy said had run when the fighting started, but I didn't spot him, and I assumed he'd either taken the chance to run for the hills and get away from Shadow Man, or he was too far ahead of us to catch.

Azara did Millie's reading on the boat, revealing a layout she called the Bladed Lotus. It didn't look like a blade or a flower to me, though. It was smaller than mine and kind of looked like a three-pronged trident of nine cards set on a flat base seven spaces wide, with an upside-down triangle of six cards beneath it.

"The Lotus is split into three parts," Azara told the eagerly listening redhead. "The blade at the base is your capacity for violence; place the cards that aid you in violent endeavors there, with the strongest close to your hole card and the weakest at the tip. The petals reaching up at the top are your beauty and passion; your coins and cups should go there, again with the lowest at the tips and the greater ones toward the base. That base is the joining between those two, the place where you exist; save those for the cards most like you, the ladies of coins and blades, and eventually their queens."

"You think she'll ever see a lady or queen?" Ferdi snorted.

"With Murf around, you think I won't?" Millie laughed. Ferdi grumbled but didn't argue more.

"Your cards are poorly placed, as expected," Azara continued, ignoring the halfling. "The ace should be the tip of your blade, with the three above it, not touching your hole card. The two of coins should be the end of your central petal, and you should build down from there, growing your flower until it reaches the root."

"You'll lose any bonuses you might have from your hole card," Ferdi predicted.

"I don't care if it means adding cards doesn't hurt so much," Millie shivered. "I guess I have to pull the rest of them out, right?" Azara nodded, and the redhead took a deep breath. "Here goes…"

Apparently, Millie's cards hurt a lot more coming out than mine had when I pulled the knight and lady at Azara's direction. At least, judging from the groaning, screaming, and writhing on the deck of the ship she did, they must have. Once she recovered, she hesitantly took Azara's advice and placed the ace of blades, wincing before the card even touched her chest. She hissed in pain as it slid into her, but she didn't scream, thrash around, or pass out, so I called it a win.

"That—wasn't that bad," she admitted after the card sank into her. "It hurt, but not that much."

"Your connection to the Unity isn't as strong as Murf's," Azara shrugged. "That means that cards will hurt you more than they do him, I'm afraid." She looked at me. "Murf, you have an ace of coins, don't you?" I nodded. "Give it to her. Millie, place it at the tip of the central petal, then put the two beneath it. You should find those hurt a lot less."

I handed her the card, and Millie took it with only minor hesitation. She touched it to her chest and winced. When it vanished, though, she let out a sigh of relief. "That really was better, Azara. It still hurt, but it was like a burning splinter going into my chest instead of a red-hot knife."

"Good. Add the two next, then the three of blades. Murf, do you have any more low coins or blades?"

"The four of coins. The five is my only blade, though."

The cartomancer shook her head. "Too strong. It'll drag her layout down into violence. Keep an eye out for the two for her; it will fit nicely next to the three." She looked at Millie. "Go ahead and add that one, then the four that Murf's going to give you. Right, Murf?"

I handed over that card, as well, and Millie added the three and four. She hissed in pain again from the three, then groaned as she added the four.

"Okay, that one hurt," she gasped.

"You're running into the maximum of your Capacity," Ferdi snorted. "No matter how much you play with your layout, you're still at the mercy of your stats." She paused. "Although, I'm impressed that you got that many into your deck. Avian, are you sure you won't consider doing the reading for a bit less? Maybe three crowns?"

"Because of the pain you suffered offering mercy to your people, I'll take five," the cartomancer sniffed.

"Fine," Ferdi sighed. "I think I can get you five."

"It's worth it, Ferdi," Millie said, her eyes wide as she stared at something only she could see. "I got a ten percent bonus to all my cards because of their placement, and my coins cards got another ten percent for being placed together. Plus, that felt incredibly good compared to how they did the first time." To my surprise, she reached over and hugged Azara. "Thank you. I really appreciate you helping me."

Azara looked shocked for a moment before she awkwardly patted Millie's shoulder. "Yes, well, it seems a fair repayment for helping return my layouts. Come to me when you have more cards, and I'll advise you how best to place them."

"I will."

We entered the city without issue, where the four of us split up once more. Ferdi headed to the Sellsword's Guild with Jidra since the halfling hold was pretty much uninhabitable, while Azara returned to her shop, and Millie and I went to the Gambler's Hall.

When we reached the Hall, Millie and I did exactly as we'd said, grabbing some food, a hot bath, and dry clothing before falling into bed together. Neither of us got any sleep that night, but it wasn't for the reasons I wanted. Oh, we made love a couple times, but we both suffered from nasty nightmares. Each time one of us woke up in a terror-filled sweat, we dragged the other from their own bad dream, and as soon as either of us drifted off again, it started all over. We both eventually crawled out of bed exhausted, cranky, and miserable all day.

"I think, Murf, that tonight, I might sleep in my own room," Millie yawned as we ate a late breakfast that was really lunch by that point in the day. "I don't mind sleepless nights with you, but I prefer the screaming in them to come from a wholly different source."

"I don't blame you," I said, stifling a yawn of my own. "Last night was—difficult." I gave her a sly grin. "Of course, just because we're sleeping alone doesn't mean we can't spend some time testing out the workmanship of my bed beforehand."

"And do the walk of shame each night, as more and more gamblers arrive for the tournament?" she asked archly. "I think not." She flashed a grin that matched mine. "You'll simply have to come to my room, instead."

"So, I'm the one doing the walk of shame?"

"Let's be realistic, Murf. No one in this guild would be surprised to see you walking out of a lady's room at the third hour after midnight. In fact, they're probably shocked every night they don't."

I chuckled. "That could be true."

"Exactly. I'm glad that's decided."

Once we headed downstairs, we found a note from Gertla at the Sage's Guild waiting for us. I read it through, confirming that it said she had a body for me to trying drawing from, then handed it to Millie.

"What do you think?"

"I think you're looking at a few more gold crowns, Murf," she replied. "Plus, you can sell a bit of what we got down south. I'm still hoping for that roll in coins you promised me."

When we arrived at the Guild, we sent a message for Gertla, and she appeared quickly to lead us into the back offices.

"I was starting to worry that you'd reconsidered our arrangement," the halfling told us as she guided us deeper into the hall. "I left that message days ago. I assume there was a reason for the delay?"

"We were otherwise occupied outside the city," I told her blandly. "We arrived yesterday afternoon and got your message this morning."

"That seems to be a satisfactory explanation." She looked up at me. "Do you still have the creature that the seed gave you?"

"He's back at the Gambler's Hall," I lied. Charlie was safe in my chest; I didn't really want to worry about the Sages trying to steal him.

"A shame. I was hoping to examine it again. Perhaps next time." She opened a heavy door, and a blast of cold air washed out from it and struck us in the face. I shivered and pulled my coat more tightly around me.

"Why's it so cold in there?" Millie asked with a touch of suspicion in her voice.

"This is our cooling chamber, where we store things that need to be kept at a low temperature. That includes bodies, as the chill inhibits the process of decomposition." She walked inside, and after a moment, we followed. The room beyond wasn't just cold; the freezing air struck my face and hands like a thousand tiny needles digging into my skin. However, that sensation passed quickly as the Hag adapted me to the cold. Millie, who was dressed far less warmly than me in another of her elaborate dresses, wasn't so lucky. She clutched her arms around her shoulders and shivered as she entered. Gertla led us past rows of shelves to a metal table holding the body of a nude canid female.

"This woman is a convicted felon," she began. "She murdered…"

"I don't care if her crime was farting on the meritocracy," I cut the sage off. "It's too cold in here to matter. Let's just do this."

"Very well. I've performed a divination, and she holds…"

I ignored her and stepped over to the metal table, touching the dead woman's chest and pulling out some cards. "Got them. You can explain more when we're out where it's warm."

Gertla stared at me, blinking in surprise, then shrugged. "As you wish. After you."

We left the frigid room, and once we were out in the much warmer hallway, I took a glance at the card that popped up when I pulled the cards.

> **Cards Gained!**
> You have claimed the cards of another Holder.
> Luck check success! You have drawn cards with a high Harmony!
> Skill check success! You recover all of this Holder's cards.
> Cards Gained: 3/3
> 8 of Cups, 7 of coins, 9 of Cups

"Here's what I got." I held the cards up and showed them to Gertla, who examined them in silence for several seconds.

"This—this is unexpected," she finally said in a slightly quavering voice.

"Oh?" I asked.

"Yes." She cleared her throat. "You see, as I was telling you earlier, I performed a divination on this Holder before you arrived. She had three cards, a 3-set of aces. With your Luck, I presumed that you would draw something higher—threes or fours perhaps."

"I do believe I told you you'd be pleasantly surprised," Millie purred at the halfling sweetly.

"Yes. Yes, you did. I supposed I should have listened." The sage tapped her pursed lips. "Especially as my failure to do so has placed me in a bit of a quandary."

"How so?" I asked tiredly, suspecting I knew the answer.

"Well, had we performed a standard claiming of the woman's cards, we would have drawn one-and-two-thirds of them successfully."

"Two-thirds?" Millie echoed curiously. "Can you draw part a card?"

"Only as a useful approximation of value. As you are both gamblers, I assume you're familiar with statistical analysis?" We both nodded, and she continued. "To determine the base value of a draw, I first assign odds to each possible result. We typically average around half of a Holder's cards, meaning that a result of two is fifty-percent likely and a result of one is half as likely. With such a small number of outcomes, though, the chances of getting all or none of them have to be factored in, with a fifteen percent chance of getting all three and a ten percent chance of none. Summing those, we reach a result of approximately one-and-two-thirds cards.

"The standard value of an ace is two gold crowns. Thus, I adopted a base value of this draw of three crowns, six wands, thirteen brass. I believed that at most, you'd draw three fours with a value of fifteen crowns, meaning I would owe you approximately eight crowns. To be safe, I procured almost double that amount, fifteen crowns." She lifted the cards I'd drawn. "These have a total value of forty-six crowns, meaning I owe you twenty-nine crowns, seventeen wands, and six brass, seventy percent of the difference."

"These are worth more almost fifty crowns?" Millie gasped.

"Yes. Typically, we value any rank of low arcana as a third higher than the rank below, with aces beginning at two crowns. The market varies somewhat, and sometimes you can get more or less selling to the Scriveners or Merchants, but the values usually fluctuate around that price point, and we of the Sage's Guild do prefer exact numbers to fickle supply and demand forecasts."

"What about noble arcana?" the redhead asked almost idly. "Does the pricing system extend to those, as well?"

"Yes, but with a different baseline. Noble arcana are both rarer and far more powerful than low arcana, and the sale price of a knight usually starts at a hundred crowns, with the values rising from there." She hesitated. "Why? Do you have one such for sale?"

I was tempted. Oh, I was sorely tempted. If a knight was worth a hundred crowns, a lady should be worth 133, and I had both in my deck. 233 crowns was a small but not insignificant fortune, and with it in the Swindlers' vaults, I could live modestly for years without worrying about money. Of course, if I handed the sage the cards, I'd have to explain where

I got them, and while I thought that I'd mentioned that I had some nobles in my deck the last time we'd talked, I didn't want to remind her of that fact. Now that I knew it was possible to torture someone into removing their own cards, I wasn't precisely eager to experience it myself. I didn't think Gertla was the type for that, but I didn't really know anything about her. Plus, she wasn't the only sage in the Guild, and the Sages didn't keep the power they had by being gentle and sweet.

Pushing the thought of so many crowns from my mental vision, I shook my head. "No, we don't. It's nice to know the value in case we run across one, though."

"Normally, I would say that the odds of that are vanishingly small, but considering your luck, it's a possibility. Should you bring one to us, we'd happily pay the full price for it. Such cards are rare, and the chance to test them is very valuable." She hesitated. "However, in all fairness, I should tell you that you might be able to make significantly more if you find a particularly wealthy Holder with a high compatibility for the card."

"We'll keep that in mind," Millie said. "Can I assume that the difficulty you're facing is that you don't have the money that you owe us?"

"Precisely, and with such a significant amount, it will take me several days to get it. I will, of course, give you the fifteen crowns I have in my possession, but for the rest, you can either wait until I can gather it…" She paused. "Or I could let you choose one or more items from our collection that have a similar value."

I didn't even hesitate. "Do you maybe have a coat like this?" I asked, touching mine. "One that won't shred the first time something tries to eat me?"

"I…" She froze, her expression startled as she blinked at me in confusion for a few seconds. "Perhaps? We do have socketed clothing. Do things often try to eat you?"

"More often than you'd imagine. What are socketed clothes?"

"Quite useful things, really. Socketed items have a layout built into them. Placing a card in or touching it to the socket, the initiation site of the layout, charges the layout and creates a magical effect. Socketed armor usually offers the sort of protection you seek. I presume clothing does, as well." She began walking down the hallway. "Let me take you to our vaults. The archivist there can provide you with more information."

The archivist was an older felid man with gray and black striped fur who eyed Millie appreciatively the entire time we were at his desk. He didn't have a catalog that we could browse, so we each told him what we were looking for, and he showed us his offerings. After I told him what I wanted, he vanished into the back and returned carrying a coat similar to mine but much nicer, with a brushed black shine to it, decorative ebony buttons, and touches of silver thread at the collar and cuffs.

"This is a socketed coat," he explained. "Placing a card in the left inner pocket improves the material's resistance to damage by around 15% and its overall durability by 25% per rank of the card. Also, if the card is left inside, the coat repairs any damage it suffers at a slow rate of a few percent per hour. It's worth two crowns."

"That's a lot," Millie whistled.

"Yes, but with a card of sufficient rank, it can grant a defense similar to plate armor and restore itself to a perfect state in a day or two. Assuming it isn't totally destroyed, it's the only coat and armor a person might ever need."

"Do you have something similar in a leather vest?" she asked after a moment. "Or perhaps an undergarment?"

He seemed to stumble slightly as she mentioned undergarments, and his eyes flicked down over her body as he licked his lips faintly. "I—I do believe I have a vest like that, yes."

"And maybe something that we could hold additional cards in?" she pressed. "Something that I could keep hidden beneath a vest, or slip into here?" She motioned toward her cleavage, and he swallowed hard as he stared into that creamy valley without even trying to conceal his interest.

"Y-yes, I do have something like that. Give me a moment."

As he disappeared into the back, Millie turned toward Gertla. "Since you're going to be making arrangements for the remaining crowns anyway, would you like to purchase some cards at the same time? Say, a couple low arcana?"

The halfling had been watching the woman with an expression of amusement, her gaze thoughtful, but she roused herself at the woman's words. "Do you have cards to sell, or is this just more curiosity?"

I reached into my card holder and pulled out two cards at random that turned out to be the seven of cups and five of blades. "We do, actually."

She pulled a card from her own pocket and held it up, and I felt a surge of energy wash over me. Her card lit up, and she slipped it back into her pocket with a nod.

"They're real. Yes, the Hall would be interested in purchasing them."

"Do people actually try to sell fake cards to the Sages?" Millie asked with a light laugh.

"Fairly regularly. Most of the time, they themselves were deceived by an unscrupulous merchant or Holder, but occasionally, someone attempts to defraud us." She shrugged. "We always detect it, and if we believe that it was intentional, they're banned from the Hall and the authorities are alerted."

"Good thing that these are real, then," I chuckled.

"Yes, it is. The value of those two cards is seventeen crowns. I can add it to your total, if you'd like."

"That's fine," I nodded, slipping them back into a pocket.

"I will need them first, though," she pointed out.

"And I'll need something in writing that you've agreed to buy them for seventeen crowns," I laughed. "Along with the remainder of the debt you already owe me."

She frowned for a moment before nodding. "That's fair and actually somewhat wise. I'll go write that up while you complete your dealings here."

The archivist returned less than a minute after Gertla left, and Millie resumed her combination flirting and haggling with the man. She kept touching her chest, leaning forward, and walking about strapping knives to her thighs beneath her dress, and he got more and more flustered as she spoke. At the end, he was walking a little funny as he went to fetch the rest of what she wanted, and I was surprised that he hadn't ripped a hole in the front of his pants from the way he couldn't seem to catch his breath. We ended up walking away with my coat, a similarly armored corset for Millie, a pair of fancy whitesteel daggers, a sealable coin purse that would only open for its owner—or a very sharp knife—and a similarly sealed card holder for a total of ten crowns. Gertla returned after a few minutes and just watched silently, then shook her head as we walked away from the counter with our new acquisitions.

"That was enlightening," the halfling said as she led us back through the hall.

"How so?" I asked curiously.

"The Hall has a policy of no haggling. We set one price based on our evaluation of an item, and you can either purchase it or not. Ketyor back there is one of the biggest proponents of this policy, in fact." She glanced at Millie. "And yet, you convinced him that all those items that he'd valuated at twenty-seven crowns total were worth less than half of that. And I recall that you convinced me that his services were worth more than I believed."

"I've always been rather persuasive," Millie said airily.

"And no doubt whatever mercantile training your family gave you amplified that talent, along with a willingness to use your appearance to get your way," the halfling nodded. "Between your silver tongue and his Luck, the two of you make quite the formidable pair."

She flashed me a wicked grin. "Yes, we do, don't we?"

"I think so," I grinned right back.

"Then we're all in agreement. Good." The halfling stopped before the door leading out into the main lobby and held up a piece of paper and a small pouch. "Here are the fifteen crowns I promised you, plus the written acknowledgement of the debt the hall owes you that you asked for. The cards, please?" I handed the two cards over, and she nodded. "Excellent. I'll send word to the Gambler's Hall once I've procured the rest of the coins." She ushered us out into the lobby, then closed the door behind us. As she did, Millie grinned at me eagerly.

"Well, that was fruitful," she purred. "We walked away with all this plus fifteen crowns and the promise of twelve more. With my half of Gertla's purse…"

"Wait, your half?" I asked archly. "I believe I pulled the cards, didn't I?"

"Yes, but I brokered the deal, plus I got you a nice discount on that coat and card holder." She grabbed my arm and favored me with a pout. "Surely, that's worth half of that purse!"

"I suppose I could offer you a couple of brass," I mused, rubbing my chin. "I mean, you have been help…oof!" I laughed as she punched my arm lightly. "Okay, okay. Half it is. No need for the rough stuff—at least, not until later."

"Oh, that could be interesting," she said, leaning up against me. "Shopping first, though."

"Fine. Shopping first."

We walked out of the hall, but as we did, I felt an icy surge in my chest. I blinked as Charlie flowed out of me and leaped to the ground, racing back toward the Sage's Hall. "Charlie!" I hissed. "Where are you going?"

"Be right back, Dad!" he called out to me as he slipped through the doors of the hall and vanished.

"Charlie?" Millie asked, staring back the same direction I was looking. "Did he go back into the Hall?"

"Yes," I sighed. "I'll bet he's looking for more gold for you."

"Good Charlie," she purred. "What a good boy!"

"You probably shouldn't encourage him," I noted.

"Why not? It works when I do it to you." She kissed my cheek. "With a little encouragement, you do all sorts of amazing things for me."

"I could say the same for you," I grinned at her.

"Yes, you could, so keep encouraging me."

We waited for about ten minutes before the blue form of the ferret reappeared. He climbed back up my shoulder, holding a gold coin in his mouth as expected—and a single Unity card, the seven of coins that I guessed was probably the one I'd just pulled from the corpse.

"Charlie, where did you get that?" I asked as I took the coin from his mouth and handed it to Millie.

"You said it was okay to take from other people, Dad," he told me happily. *"And I don't like that lady—but I do like cards."* He began to munch on the card, and once more, I felt a trickle of icy energy flow into me. When he finished, once more letting out a tiny burp that wafted across my face, a card flashed in my vision.

> **Card Absorption!**
> Your Soul Familiar has absorbed the
> energy of the card: Seven of Coins.
> It has gained:
> **Health Absorption:** 12% of all bite
> damage inflicted heals you.

"Did he get something again?" Millie asked, slipping her coin into her purse.

"Yeah," I sighed. "When he bites someone now, it heals me a little."

"That sounds useful. You do seem to get hurt a lot, Murf."

"Can I go try it on that short woman, Dad?" he asked me eagerly. *"Please?"*

"No, you can't go bite Gertla to test it," I chuckled, reaching up and petting him while Millie giggled. "Don't worry. I'm sure you'll get to try it on someone soon enough."

We headed to the merchant's square, where most of the reputable merchants set up shop. I bought two more sets of clothing to replace the ones I'd ruined on the trip south. I also reluctantly visited a weapon shop and purchased a short, straight sword to replace the saber I'd broken, a second dagger, and a small collapsible hand crossbow. The conversation Azara and Ferdi had by the Labyrinth still rang in my mind. I was going to attract danger, and I'd be stupid not to be ready for it. Now, I just needed to learn how to use the damn things. Maybe I could convince Ferdi to help me. She owed me pretty big as it was. Of course, I wasn't sure I'd like having Ferdi as a teacher, but beggars couldn't exactly be choosers.

I didn't really want to carry those weapons around, though, which seemed like a perfect excuse to try out my new storage ability. I led Millie into a nearby alley where I felt we probably wouldn't be seen, then gripped the lady of coins and tensed, trying to spray out the smallest amount of energy I could. As I did, a shimmering oval haze appeared in the air in front of me, looking almost like heat rising from an oven.

"What's that?" Millie asked nervously, stepping back from the wavering disc. "Is something wrong?"

"It's my storage ability. I was hoping to put my weapons in there, so I don't have to carry them around." I frowned. "I'm not really sure how to do it, though."

"Try sticking the sword in, and see what happens."

I lifted the blade and pushed it point-first into the shimmering air. To my surprise, the tip of the sheathed blade vanished, leaving me holding what looked like a severed sword only a foot or so long. I kept pushing, then pulled the blade back out. It looked fine, so I tossed it inside and did the same with the crossbow.

"How will you get them back out?" Millie asked curiously.

"No clue," I shrugged. "I might have to reach in there and pull them out."

"Maybe ask Ferdi first."

"That's probably a smarter idea."

We returned to the Guild Hall to find old Aggie's orc messenger waiting for us again. The moment he spotted us, he stepped in front of me and held up a piece of paper, shoving the thing directly in both of our faces.

"Look. Orders from the Guild Master. Signed by him. Go to his office right now and wait there until he calls you. Got it?"

"He's getting better at this," I noted to Millie as the charter twinged in my chest, urging me to head toward Jerrick's office.

"Jerrick, or our friend, here?" she asked.

"Both." I grinned at the orc. "Of course, there's nothing in here that tells us what route we have to take to get to his office, is there? I vote we choose a route that includes the dining hall and both of our bedrooms. What do you think?"

"Please," the orc said, his voice almost sobbing. "Please, just go straight to his office and wait for him. I'm begging you."

"He's begging us, Murf," Millie said in a stage whisper. "I kind of feel bad now."

"Me, too," I whispered back, then looked at the orc. "Okay, friend. We'll go straight there."

"Thank you," he sighed, his shoulders sagging.

"No problem. And if he makes us wait again, well, we can just do what we were going to in our rooms right there in the office. Those chairs look plenty sturdy. Besides, it might entertain old Aggie."

"What?" he croaked. "You—you can't do that!"

"I assure you, we most certainly can," Millie smiled at him. "It wouldn't be the first time I've bent over a chair like that."

"No, I mean..." He looked around like a trapped animal, then leaned closer. "You can't give her—ideas!"

"Who, Aggie?" I asked.

"Yes! Ever since the last time you were in her office, she's been looking at me like—like a piece of meat she's about to devour! She keeps reading trashy human romance books in front of me and quoting them aloud. If I hear about one more quivering member..." He shuddered. "If you do that in front of her, who knows what she'll do to me?"

"You know, you could fix that problem in about ten minutes," I pointed out.

"Ugh. Human genitalia are just so—hairy. It's disgusting." He shuddered again, then looked guiltily at Millie. "No offense."

"How is that not supposed to be offensive?" she asked primly.

"I didn't mean you. I'm sure yours are great..." He stopped and turned beet-red. "I need to stop talking."

"That's probably a good idea," I chuckled. "Come on. Let's go see if we need to entertain Aggie or not."

Unfortunately, when we reached Jerrick's office, Aggie ushered us right in. We stepped inside and saw Jerrick sitting at his desk with Eegla sitting in front of him. The Guild Master pointed to the seats, and the two of us sat down. Jerrick simply glared at us for several long seconds, his anger palpable. At last, he leaned forward and folded his hands in front of him.

"What did I ask you to do, Murf?" he growled at me.

"When, Jerrick?" I replied. "You've asked me to do a lot of things over the years."

"Three days ago. I asked you to stay in the hall. Do you remember that?"

I rubbed my chin thoughtfully. "I have a vague recollection that you said something like that," I nodded before looking at Millie. "What about you?"

"I think he might have mentioned it," she shrugged. "I wasn't really listening at the end."

"It seems you might have said something along those lines," I shrugged. "Why, Jerrick? Is something wrong?"

"That same day, a wagon left through the Jungle Gate," Eegla said in a quiet voice. "The man driving it looked an awful lot like you, Murf. A masked woman with red hair wearing all gray sat beside him. They left the city and didn't return that day. Then, yesterday, you both returned to the city on a river boat with three people: a halfling that sounds a lot like Ferdi, a raven avian who's a cartomancer here in the city, and a badly wounded halfling."

"Where were you, Murf?" the Guild Master growled. "And does it have anything to do with those disappearances we were talking about before?"

I remained silent for a few seconds, then leaned back in my chair. "Do you really want to know, Jerrick?" I asked quietly. "I mean, do you really, truly want to know? Because once you know, you can't exactly un-know it."

He hesitated. "Is it something that can come back and hurt the Guild, Murf?"

"Honestly? No clue. I don't think so, but..." I spread my hands helplessly.

"Then I have to know. What's going on, Murf?"

I glanced at Millie, who gave me a weak shrug, then gave the pair a heavily edited version of the past few days. In it, Ferdi and Azara did most of the heavy lifting, while Millie and I played some minor roles. I told them that the Holders had already been fighting when we arrived, and we just convinced them to turn on one another completely. Jerrick listened to our story silently, then took out a sheet of paper and handed it to me.

"Recognize this?" he asked. "It should feel familiar to you."

I took the paper and glanced down at the image of me drawn across the front, along with the words:

Wanted: Dead or Alive
Name: Murf
Last known location: Gambler's Hall
For the Crimes of Murder and Theft
of Unity Cards
Reward: 5 Crowns for his capture or
death, 3 crowns for information
leading to his arrest.
Please report any sightings of this
man or his accomplices to the
Meritocracy.

"Huh," I said, handing the paper to Millie. "That's not a bad reward. Three golds just for information on me? Pretty tempting."

"I received this from the Meritocracy this morning, along with a demand to turn you over to them," Jerrick said flatly. "A very strongly worded demand."

"Are you going to?" Millie asked.

"What, turn him over?" He snorted. "I'm considering it."

"No, you're not," I chuckled. "Half the members of the guild have arrest warrants on them somewhere. That's why the charter guarantees us sanctuary in a guild hall. If you broke that to toss me to the meritocrats, you'd be telling every gambler here that they aren't safe in your hall. You'd have a general uprising in a day."

"And since it was over a breach of the charter, you wouldn't be able to stop them," Millie added in a slightly cold tone. "In fact, the guild would have to either remove you as Guild Master or shut down this entire branch since the charter wouldn't apply with you in charge here anymore."

"Besides, this isn't the Meritocracy," I said, tossing the paper back onto his desk. "It's Shadow Man."

"What do you mean?" Eegla asked.

"He's obviously got a meritocrat or two in his pocket from what Beard-guy told me. He's pissed that we busted the hand he was building down there. He arranged this to get his hands on me—and the cards we took from his Holders after they killed each other."

"Cards?" Jerrick asked. "How many cards, exactly?"

"More than a few," I hedged. "Enough that I could see why someone would go to this much trouble to get them."

"How would he know it was you?" Eegla questioned.

I grimaced. "There was a goblin cartomancer who stole a layout that lets him hide invisibly. He might have been in the camp watching without us seeing him, then made it back to the city and reported what happened." I'd given that a bit of thought, and once I remembered that the goblin had Azara's hiding layout, I realized that he might have been hanging out at the camp watching the fiasco without me seeing him. He might not have, but it was smarter to assume he was.

Jerrick grunted, picked up the paper, and ripped it in half. "Just so you know, I already sent them my response. No guild is required to turn over a member to the authorities of any city for any crime below treason, and no city or nation can forcibly enter a guild hall to remove a member. So, as long as you're in the hall, you can't be touched." He glared at me. "So, this time, please stay in the damn hall, Murf!"

I hesitated. "I would, Jerrick, but if they've got a bounty out for me, they've probably got one out for Ferdi and Azara, too…"

"Ferdi's fine in the Sellsword's Guild," Eegla said quickly. "They won't hand her over any more than we would—no matter what fool-ass thing Jerrick might say in a moment of anger." She briefly glared at Jerrick, who had the good grace to look sheepish for a moment, which was a startling expression on a dog-man, to be sure. "As far as the cartomancer, she could seek the safety of the Sage's Guild…"

"She won't," I shook my head. "She's not a fan of them."

"We can contact her and move her here," Jerrick said heavily. "She's not a member, so technically she can't claim sanctuary, but I don't think the Meritocracy will fight us over one avian. At least, not with the tournament on."

"How are the preparations for that going, by the way?" Millie asked innocently. "I assume the Meritocracy realized that they have to work with you or cancel the whole thing."

He glared at her sourly for a second, then smirked. "Yes. Your advice was sound. The tournament is on, it will be here, and with all the brouhaha, it promises to be larger than we imagined." He took a deep breath. "Look, Murf, Millie, I know that you were just worried about your halfling friend. That's admirable." He gave me a look. "And somewhat out of character, really. I think you're having a good influence on him, Millie."

"I do my best," she said airily.

"Well, keep doing it. However, please, *please* just stay in the hall until the tournament. Afterward, I'll figure out a way to get all of you out of the city without the Meritocracy knowing—assuming the bounty's even still active."

"What if someone needs me again, Jerrick?"

"Then you let me or Eegla know, and we'll arrange to bring whoever it is here to talk to you. If you have a friend in danger, we'll shelter them. If you want to go shopping, we'll send a runner to do it for you. If you absolutely have to have your favorite flavor of chilled wine, tell me, and I'll go get a damn bottle myself! But keep your asses in the damn hall. Please."

"He did ask nicely," Millie murmured.

"Yeah, he did," I sighed. "Fine, Jerrick. If something comes up, I'll let you know." I paused, and he groaned.

"Seriously? Already?" he asked in an exasperated tone.

"Sort of, yeah. Gertla at the Sage's Guild owes me a lot of money, and I'd like to collect it."

"How much?"

"Enough that I'm going to collect it, one way or the other."

"You were gambling with the Brainies?" Eegla laughed. "That's ballsy even for you, Murf! They never gamble unless they know the odds are in their favor. What was the game?"

"Single draw, I bet that I could pull higher cards than she predicted," I lied with a shrug. "I won."

"Of course, you did," Jerrick sighed. "I'll let her know to send it here by messenger. Is there anything else?"

"Yes," Millie said. "You need to hire a male courtesan for Aggie."

The canid stared at her in shock for a long moment. "I—what did you just say?"

"She's been overly aggressive with your orc messenger ever since Murf suggested that she let him bend her over her desk," Millie smiled. "I guess she took the suggestion seriously, but it's making him uncomfortable. The orc, I mean. Probably Murf, too."

"He…" His gaze whipped to me. "You told her to *what?*" To the side, Eegla burst out laughing, and he gave her a fierce glare that she totally ignored.

"She's too uptight, Jerrick," I shrugged calmly. "I've found that a quick romp like that is an excellent stress reliever. Trust me, you'll thank me for it later."

"I—I can't just send her a prostitute!"

"Well, you wouldn't tell her that he's a prostitute, of course," Millie laughed. "You'd tell her to expect a messenger, then have him come in and seduce her. It's a simple solution, really."

"I'll look into it," Eegla said. "Do you think she's partial to orcs?"

"Maybe," I shrugged. "She might also just be partial to anyone at this point. She seems pretty deprived."

"I can take care of it."

"Eegla!" Jerrick said in a shocked tone.

"The tournament's coming up in less than a week, Jerrick, and you have a million things you have to do. We don't have time for your assistant to be distracted. If letting her take one on her desk will help her do her job, I'll strap a false one on myself if necessary." She looked at me, her eyes twinkling. "Or get Murf to do it. From what I hear, that way, you'll know it's done right."

"I'm not listening to this," the Guild Master said, waving his hands in the air. "You two, get out of here. Oh, and for the week, all your expenses in the hall are waived."

I froze in the act of rising from my seat. "Wait, all expenses, Jerrick? Drinks? The good food? All of it?"

"Yep. But only as long as you stay in the hall. Leave it, and the deal's off."

"I could rack up a lot of expenses in a hurry that way, you know."

"Yes, but if it keeps you here, it's worth it. Plus, thanks to Millie, I know I won't have to pay for any special sessions with the servers."

"How little you know me, Guild Master," Millie purred.

"No, how well I know Murf. He doesn't like to share. Now, go on. Leave. Eegla's right about how busy I am."

Millie and I walked into the office, then froze as we saw Aggie leaning over her desk, her face mingled with pleasure and embarrassment. Her dress was hiked up around her waist. The orc stood behind her, his hands around her hips and his eyes firmly closed as he thrust his hips against her with an impressive ferocity. Aggie slapped a hand over her mouth as her eyes widened and her body trembled. A moment later, the orc pressed hard against her, grunting deeply. Apparently, he'd set aside his distaste for furry humans in favor of being left alone for a while, and Aggie looked tremendously happy that he had.

I turned and leaned back into the office. "Cancel the prostitute!" I called out. "It's handled!"

"And handled so well," Millie murmured approvingly. "Well done, both of you!"

51

I shot from bed as my door burst open. I'd been dreaming, a particularly nasty nightmare this time, and it took me a second to realize that I was awake. As my heart pounded in my chest, I grabbed at my waist, realizing a moment later that I was stark naked, and my weapons were on the other side of the room entirely. I reached down without thinking for the cards in my chest and flicked them outward, spraying the room with a blast of A Noble Master.

"M-Murf!" Millie gasped as she staggered back from the doorway, putting her hand on her head and shaking it in confusion. "T-turn it off!"

I quickly released the ability, and the woman stood in the doorway, grabbing the frame to steady herself as the power swiftly wore off. She took a deep breath and straightened, blinking several times before stepping into the room and closing the door behind her. "Whoa. That was intense."

"What was that, Millie?" I asked a bit irritably, swinging my legs out of bed. "Why'd you barge in like that?"

"Sorry. I was hoping to surprise you a bit." She made a sour face. "Which we now know was a bad idea. Are you okay?"

I leaned forward, taking a few deep breaths and letting my racing heart calm down. "Yeah. Bad dream, as usual. You get it."

"I do," she nodded, sitting on the end of the bed. "Want to talk about it?"

"I was in a Labyrinth," I said slowly. "One that kept going deeper into the ground, layer after layer, and each layer was harder than the last. There was a white-furred felid there helping me, but she was honestly more cat than person. She could shoot magic bolts from her eyes, and she called me her pet." I shook my head. "Oh, and I couldn't find a pair of boots, no matter how hard I tried. A voice that I think was supposed to be the Unity kept making fun of me about that."

"That—sounds disturbing, really."

"Yeah, it was." I took another deep breath. "But it was just a dream, so no biggie." I rose to my feet and walked to the wardrobe, where I pulled out some clothes and began dressing. "I take it it's almost time?"

"Yep," she said with a smile that beamed from her face. "The roster just got posted, and they'll start in a couple hours. I'm seeded, Murf!"

"I told you that you would be," I chuckled. "I know all the top seeds, and you're as good as most of them."

"Yes, but you might have been saying it so I'd keep doing that thing you like," she grinned. "You know, the one where I put my legs back behind my head…"

"Oh, I remember," I laughed, ignoring the way my body inevitably reacted to that memory as I leaned over and kissed her. "I'll never forget that!"

"Good. Then I'll remember to do it again sometime." She stood up and helped me slip into my clothes, buttoning up my shirt for me and fixing the collar before smoothing the chest and shoulders out. "Very nice."

"Thank you. You aren't so bad yourself." In truth, the woman practically sparkled in another shimmering emerald dress with golden trim. The dress left her shoulders bare and exposed her plunging cleavage, and it looked like a good sneeze might reveal her assets for all to see. Her hair lay elaborately atop her head, with a cascade of curls running down the side of her smooth neck and coiling just above her breasts to draw even more attention to them.

"Not so bad?" she pouted.

"Stunning." I kissed her again. "Ravishing." Another kiss. "Delectable."

"Oh, Murf, you do say such nice things," she said with a moan as my last kiss trailed down her neck.

"My pleasure." I stood up and offered her a hand, which she took as she allowed me to pull her gently to a standing position. I grabbed my armored coat and slipped it on, hesitating only a moment before slipping the ten of coins into the inner pocket. Power flowed over the coat in a ripple, settling quickly so the fabric simply glowed brilliant black once more. To my surprise, a card popped in my vision as it did.

Armored Coat
Base Power: 17   Max Power: 17

"Expecting trouble?" she asked in a slightly subdued voice.

"Cassa's partner's still around somewhere," I shrugged. "So's that goblin—and Shadow Man might have gotten himself some new Holders. Murf's Fifteenth Law: Trouble comes the moment you stop watching for it."

"There are an awful lot of those. How many do you have, anyway?"

"As many as I need." I flashed her a grin.

"So, would you like to see where you're seeded?" she asked.

"No need. I'm sixth."

She stared at me in surprise. "How did you know that?" she asked suspiciously. "Did the Guild Master leak the roster to you? And you didn't tell me?"

"No, nothing like that," I chuckled. "I just know who's here, and which ones are going to be ranked higher than me. Horstya, Carcrick, Xilla, Bargish, and Trendon are the top five, although Bargish and Trendon might swap places."

"Then you all know one another?" she asked.

"Yep. I've known them all for years, and I've played all of them at one time or another all over the world." I shrugged. "For most of us, this is just another game, really—just a big one with a nice prize."

"Well, it's more than that for me," she said, smoothing her dress down. "Any tips you can give me?"

"Let's go check out the roster," I sighed, grabbing my hat and slipping it onto my head. "Then I can tell you who you're facing and what I know of them."

The Guildhall was obviously extremely busy as we stepped out into the hallway. Men and women of every species walked along, some chatting amiably while others trudged in silence. I recognized many of them and exchanged greetings, introducing Millie to the ones I thought worth knowing and simply tipping my hat toward the rest. Millie was her usual effervescent self, charming men and women alike without much effort, speaking to them like they were old friends rather than new acquaintances and touching them subtly on the arm or hand to reinforce a perceived connection. Several men watched her as we walked away, as did more than one woman. Not that I blamed them, of course. Millie was quite the sight to behold.

The gaming hall was just as crowded, although for once, no one gambled. All but eight tables had been cleared out, and those stood in a staggered line across the center of the room. Seating ringed two of the walls, while a second bar had been erected along the third. This would be the heart of the tournament, the place where the seeded players would play, those guild members who'd earned enough rank and notoriety or won enough at the tables in the past two weeks to be considered the elite of the tournament. There were thirty-two of those, with another 128 unseeded players who had to pay to enter and who'd be playing in the outer room. The top winner of that room would join the top four seeded players for the final round to determine the champion. Typically, they were also the first person out in the final round, but sometimes a nobody would come out of nowhere. In fact, that was how I'd gotten the attention of Jerrick all those years ago: I'd won the unseeded round, gaining a one-crown bonus for doing so, then made it to the final two at the last table. It wasn't common, but it did happen.

The two of us stopped at the bar and grabbed some drinks—still free since the tournament hadn't started yet—then turned and began walking around. I scanned the room, noting some of the more important players and pointing them out to Millie.

"See that guy?" I said, gesturing with my drink at a round-faced man with loose black hair and a cherubic expression.

"The one with the baby face?" she asked.

"Yep. That's Trendon, either the fourth or fifth seed. Don't let the smile fool you; he's a demon at the table. Never bets big but just hammers away at you until suddenly, you're out of chips and you don't know how it happened."

I turned her gaze toward a distinguished-looking male canid with tan fur along the sides of his head and sleek, oiled black fur along the top that ran up his sharply pointed ears. "There's Bargish, the other one who'll be seeded fourth or fifth. He's got sharp eyes, and he rarely makes mistakes."

I pointed her toward a laughing goblin woman with turquoise hair wearing her typical white dress that didn't really show off much of her body. "And that's Xilla, probably the third seed. She seems playful, like she's not taking the game seriously, but she'll go all-in on her own mother without missing a beat."

I shifted her attention to a brown-feathered male avian with hawklike features. "There's the number two seed, Carcrick. He's incredibly smart and a big fan of playing the odds. He's also won more tournaments than any other player here."

"Then why isn't he the top seed?" Millie asked.

I gestured toward a crowd of people with a rueful grin. "That's why."

"What? Who are you talking about...oh."

"Yep. Oh."

Her attention was focused on a felid woman who could only be described as "voluptuous". Or maybe "volumptuous" considering the exceptionally large protuberances on her chest. Light tan, almost white fur covered her face. A darker stripe ran down the middle of her face, down the center of her throat, and spread out to disappear into the ample valley of her barely contained cleavage. Her movements were smooth and impossibly graceful, and every expression and gesture demanded attention.

"That's Horstya, the top seed," I told her. "She's not only good, she's incredibly lucky. I've seen her blind draw into a flush run and hit it or win a tournament by pulling a 5-set. People accuse her of being a Holder with a luck power, but all the tournaments have tableaus to detect that sort of thing. As far as I can tell, she's just really lucky and has the skill to take advantage of it."

"And the looks to distract other players," Millie sighed.

"Yes, but don't rely on that sort of thing," I admonished her. "At least, not here. The top ten seeds are used to ignoring those sorts of distractions. If you're going to win, you'll have to do it on your own, not relying on your—more visible assets."

"So, who will I be playing in the first round?" she asked nervously.

"Let's take a look at the roster," I sighed. She walked me over to the large board listing the seeded players, and I scanned it for her name, finally locating "Millicent Deepwater" in the twenty-seventh spot.

"Not bad," I admitted.

"What do you mean?" she asked.

"Well, typically, the bottom five seeds in a tournament are reserved for newcomers, people who haven't played before but who deserve to be ranked. You took the spot above that, which means you pushed out a regular seed to get in. Good job!"

She beamed at me, then looked at the board. "So, who will I be playing?"

"Eight tables," he replied, glancing around. "That means the first table will have the first seed, ninth seed, seventeenth, and twenty-fifth; every eight places. That puts you up against Xilla, the goblin woman I showed you earlier; Yamag, an orc guy; and Burgrank, who I don't know but who sounds like an ursid from the name."

"What can you tell me about them, especially Xilla?"

I began to tell her what I could of the goblin woman, which wasn't as much as she'd probably like. I knew a couple of Xilla's tells that I could share, but the woman was a solid player and rarely gave much away. The simple fact was that Millie was going to be on her own, and there wasn't much I could do to help her once the tournament started.

"The big thing to remember is that the top players here are going to be looking for someone who looks like you to try and distract them. If you want to fluster them, you're going to need to be a lot subtler."

"Subtle," she nodded. "I can do subtle." I gave her a doubtful look, and she laughed. "Granted, I usually choose not to, but I *can* do it, Murf. Trust me." She looked around and sighed. "My chances of winning aren't that good, are they? These are some of the best players in the world!"

"The chances of either of us winning are pretty much shit," I laughed. "And nobody here is among the best in the world, Millie. Trust me. Not even close."

She gave me a startled look. "Really? I thought a tournament like this would attract the top players in the Guild!"

"Nope." I gestured at the milling gamblers surrounding us. "What you're seeing here are the younger gamblers, the up-and-comers still trying to make names for themselves. The truly great players don't bother with things like this. The prizes are too small, and they consider playing against people like us a waste of their time. They wait for the private invitationals, ones held by royalty or guild courts. We never hear about those, and they're rarely open for the public to watch. They're held for the entertainment of the elite, the prizes are supposed to be ridiculously large, and they get paid hundreds of crowns just to show up."

"So, how does a girl get an invite to something like that?" she asked with a grin.

"Easy. Win. Win often, but more importantly, win in a way that people remember. Go to tournaments like this and walk away with the prize again and again until people take notice. It's as simple as that." I shrugged. "And it'll take years, decades even. Most of the players in those invitationals are old enough that their wrinkles have wrinkles, and the dealer has to shout the bets so everyone can hear them."

She laughed softly. "Sounds like I've got time, then." She made a disappointed face. "Although it would be nice to get paid to come to a tournament."

"I imagine it would. I'm hoping to experience it myself one day." Movement caught my eye, and I looked past her to see the door leading into the upper reaches of the guild begin to open. "And speaking of money, looks like things are about to get started."

52

Most eyes turned toward the door as Jerrick, Eegla, and a male canid I didn't recognize emerged from it and walked out onto the balcony of the steps leading into the main room. The stranger had mottled black and white fur that gleamed glossily with oil to slick it against his body. He was dressed impeccably in black silk with a white overcoat and a narrow-brimmed hat that had been brushed until it glowed. Gold and jewels glittered on his fingers, around his throat, and from his ears, and everything about him screamed, "I'm rich! Rob me blind!" Of course, no one would try that thanks to the pair of ursid guards following behind the trio, both armed with wicked polearms and both shimmering with the hidden power of Holders. As I glanced at them, a pair of cards tried to pop up in my vision telling me about them, but I willed them away without even looking. I didn't much care how powerful those guards were; I wasn't planning on fighting them or anyone anytime soon. Which meant that I'd probably end up with both of them trying to kill me at some point, at least the way things had been going lately.

Jerrick moved to the edge of the railing, looking down on the mass of professional gamblers, and tried to clear his throat for attention. That didn't do anything, of course, so he tried again, a little louder. He glanced sideways at the fancy canid, who arched one eyebrow expressively.

"Everyone, settle down!" Jerrick called out in a voice I could barely hear and that had pretty much no effect on the people around him. "Settle down!"

Eegla rolled her eyes, took a deep breath, and shouted, "Everybody, shut up, now!" at the top of her lungs. For such a small person, she had a powerful voice, and the room quickly fell silent. She grinned at the flinching Jerrick. "Guild Master."

"Thanks, Eegla," Jerrick sighed, once again glancing nervously at the canid beside him. "Guildmembers, welcome to the twenty-third Triannual Tournament of Canis!" Polite applause rose around the room, and he waited for a moment for it to settle before continuing.

"For those of you who don't know, I'm Jerrick, Master of the Gambler's Guild here in Canis. This is Eegla, my lieutenant." He paused for more polite applause. "We're excited to have so many talented gamblers in our hall for this event. The rules are simple: we'll be playing standard noblesse; spread, cross, and fool; no wilds. Ante is one and blind is three. You'll each start with chips worth a thousand brass. If you're out of chips, you're out of the tournament; there are no buy-ins.

"The winners of each table in the first round will advance to the semi-finals, where the winners of the even-numbered tables will play one another while the winners of the odd-numbered tables do the same. Top four in the semifinals will go to the finals with the winner of the non-seeded players."

"That means we won't play one another unless we both make the finals," Millie said brightly. "You're on an even-numbered table, and I'm on an odd one."

"You sound happy about that," I noted.

"I am. I don't want to put you out too early, after all." She flashed me a grin, and I chuckled at her.

"Glad to hear it. Although, if I am out early, I can sit around, drink, and watch everyone else worrying about how the cards fall. It might be nice."

"Feel free to forfeit to find out," she said slyly.

"You could do the same and tell me how it went."

"As Ferdi would say, I could. I won't."

I turned back as Jerrick continued speaking, his tone flat and his expression suddenly hard. "Every table is equipped with layouts to detect cheating and Unity card usage, and anyone caught doing either will be ejected from the game, forfeit their winnings, and face a Guild hearing that I guarantee won't go well for you, so save us all some trouble and don't do it." He glared at everyone for a couple seconds before his eyes softened once more.

"Most of the tournament this year will be exactly as you expect. There will be some differences, however. To explain those, let me introduce Karrth Grodwulf, Meritocrat of the city of Canis." He gestured at the finely dressed man and stepped back, allowing the meritocrat to step up. The man straightened, waiting for some sort of applause. Only steely silence met his rather pompous gaze.

"Doesn't seem like many people like the meritocrat," Millie noted in a quiet voice.

"Jerrick probably let it be known that the Meritocracy was pressuring him," I shrugged. "We gamblers don't like being pushed around, and most of us have problems with authority. I know I do."

"Really?" she gasped in mock surprise. "I never would have guessed that, Murf!"

"I know. I'm pretty subtle about it, but if you watch closely, it's there."

The meritocrat apparently realized that no one was going to applaud him. His face darkened slightly, in anger or embarrassment I wasn't sure, but he plastered a smile on his face and took a deep breath.

"Honored gamblers…"

He broke off as I and a few others began to clap for him, loudly and excitedly, a burst of applause that quickly spread across the room and drowned him out. He stared at us all, his expression pleased and startled, then waited as the applause rolled on for a good thirty seconds. That was long enough that it was starting to get awkward, and the man shifted a little uncomfortably as he stood there. He lifted a hand, and the applause quickly died out.

"Thank you," he smiled. "Honored gamblers…"

He fell silent once again as another round of applause swelled up, this one accompanied by occasional hoots and cheers of approval. His face reddened a bit as he realized what was happening, but he couldn't do much but endure the ovation for another half a minute before he motioned for silence. Behind him, Jerrick pinched the bridge of his nose with his fingers, while Eegla grinned openly.

"Yes, yes, much appreciated," the politician said. "As I was saying…"

He broke off again as more clapping drowned him out, and this time people started screaming his name. Some enterprising young woman even tossed her underskirt up at the man, hitting him square in the face with it. He yanked it free, spluttering and clearly pissed, which of course only drove the applause to new levels. He lifted his hands for silence, but people just hooted and shouted even louder. That lasted until Jerrick stepped to the rail, and silence descended at once.

By this point, Grodwulf seemed both pissed and completely disconcerted. "Honored gamblers…" He spoke the words quickly, then stopped, waiting to be drowned out again. When only silence met his words, he sighed, took a deep breath, and plowed on. "The city of Canis welcomes you…"

At which point, cheering and screaming cut him off again. His face turned so red I thought it might stain his fur, and his entire body trembled with rage and embarrassment. That got even worse as the enterprising lady apparently decided to follow her underskirt with the underwear beneath it and once again caught him clean in the face. He snatched the somewhat soiled garment away from his open mouth, spitting and wiping his face, his expression utterly furious. At last, Eegla stepped forward, cupping her hands over her mouth.

"All right, that's enough, you jackasses!" she bellowed. "Shut it!" The crowd fell silent instantly, and she nodded at the disconcerted politician. "They're all yours, Meritocrat. I'd keep it short, though. They get like this when they're all riled up. Like children, gamblers are, really."

"Yes. Umm...thank you." The man seemed totally thrown, and he gazed out at us with an air of suspicion. "Honored gamblers, the city of Canis welcomes you to this tournament." He said the words as quickly as possible, then paused, obviously waiting to be shouted down. When nothing happened, he cleared his throat and plowed on, speaking rapidly as if trying to get through his speech as fast as he could.

"It's an honor to have so many talented gamblers in our fair city. We look forward to a grand display of skill and talent, one unparalleled in recent memory. Indeed, this tournament promises to be different from any in recent memory in any number of ways, not merely the skill of its contestants.

"The city of Canis has been troubled by a number of disturbances lately," he continued. "While these are under control, we of the Meritocracy wish to keep the city calm, and to make sure nothing untoward occurs during the tournament." He gestured toward the two ursids behind him. "To that end, we will have guards stationed throughout the hall during the tournament, watching for signs of outside trouble. Please be assured that their presence is only to ensure that the tournament proceeds without disruption in an orderly and fair manner."

A few people muttered about this, but no one complained openly. Not that I expected them to. Most of the people here probably didn't much care about guards since they weren't planning to get into a tussle. I noted the few who seemed upset and saw Eegla doing the same; anyone pissed about extra security was likely to be a security risk.

"In the matter of fairness," the meritocrat continued, "in addition to the standard detectors attached to the tables, we will have diviners from the Sage's Guild present throughout the tournament, looking for signs of cheating or Unity card usage."

That provoked a much larger response from the assemblage. After all, while I didn't cheat, the same couldn't be said about every gambler out there. Those who did cheat had worked out ways to bypass standard detectors, and those ways might not work against active divination quite so well. I didn't bother trying to remember who this news upset, although I did catch a tiny flash of chagrin on Horstya's face that vanished so quickly I doubted anyone who wasn't watching for it even saw it.

"The Meritocracy is aware that these changes are unexpected," the man went on, speaking loudly to be heard over the mutters and protests. "To help offset your discomfort and displeasure, we've agreed to supply an extra prize for this year's winner!" Most of the crowd fell silent at that. Nobody there really planned to lose, after all, and winning a little more was always nice. "I'll leave that disclosure to the Guild Master, however, as is proper. Once again, welcome to Canis, and good luck to all of you!"

The man stepped back, and Jerrick resumed his place up front. "As you can see, there are some minor differences this year, but nothing that should really affect any honest gambler—and I'm sure all of you are honest gamblers." A few chuckles spread around the room as Jerrick continued. "Hopefully, the prizes will make it all worth it. As usual, we're awarding cash prizes for anyone finishing in the top half of the seeded tournament or better. The top sixteen will receive an award of ten silver wands each, while the top eight will receive a prize of a gold crown. The five finalists each receive ten crowns as a prize, and the second-place finisher gains an extra twenty crowns as a bonus. Finally, the champion will receive a prize of fifty gold crowns—plus a chance to draw from a full and complete Unity deck, complements of the Meritocracy."

Startled and excited murmurs rose around the room at that, and Millie looked around, her expression confused. "I don't understand," she admitted. "Why is a draw from a Unity deck such a big deal?"

"Because typically, a big prize in a tournament like this is a single low arcanum," I said with a sigh, rubbing my forehead as I felt a minor headache coming on. "With a draw from a full deck, though, you could get any card, not just one of the low ones. Remember how much Gertla said court cards were worth? Imagine pulling an emperor from that deck."

Her eyes brightened instantly. "That could be worth five hundred crowns, Murf!" she gasped.

"Yeah, and while I'm guessing most people here don't know that, they know that a high card has to be worth a lot more than the cash prizes being offered. A really lucky draw could let someone retire for life."

She pursed her lips. "Something like that could get me a lot closer to buying my way out of my family." She glanced at me curiously. "So, why do you seem so unhappy?"

"Because this is the sort of prize that I'd expect to see in one of those invitationals I was talking about earlier, not something like this. It's too much for such a small tournament."

"And that's bad?"

"Well, the last time I played in a tournament where the prize was too good to be true, the whole place burned down, most of the players died, I had people hunting me for weeks, and I ended up with Ferdi's bounty on me. You can imagine that I'm a little nervous, now."

"I can see why." She looked up at the smiling meritocrat. "And isn't he the one who was protecting Shadow Man?"

"Yep. No way this can go wrong, is there?"

She shivered. "Maybe that whole forfeiting thing isn't such a bad idea after all, Murf."

"And now, we'll open the hall to the public," Jerrick announced. "The tournament will be starting in ten minutes, so grab one last drink, find your tables, and get ready to begin!"

"Probably best to do what he said," I sighed again. "Once the crowds come in, this place will get noisy fast." I leaned over and kissed her cheek. "Good luck, and don't worry too much. Just because you can't flirt your way into Xilla's head doesn't mean you can't get in there."

The two of us made our way to the bar and grabbed new drinks—again, still courtesy of the hall—then made our way over to stand by the tables. As we reached them, the main doors opened, and people flooded in. These weren't just any people, of course. There were no ragged thieves slipping in hoping to steal from the wealthy onlookers, no prostitutes looking to comfort the losers as they exited the game, not even any simple laborers or farmers. The entrance fee for the non-seeded tournament was a simple brass disc, but it cost silver to get into the main hall to watch the big game and multiple silvers or even gold for the front seats where you could see the players up close and personal. Wealthy merchants, successful artisans, and nobles of the city filled the stands, and as I watched them pour in, it occurred to me that Shadow Man could be among the crowd. In fact, if he knew I was alive—which it seemed he did—there was a decent chance that he was. I would have been there if I were him and knew that we were alive.

"Murf!"

My shouted name drew my attention, and I looked around, quickly spotting a short figure in blue waving her hand to get my attention. I simply stared; I'd never seen Ferdi in anything but armor before. In the Labyrinth, she even slept in it. Seeing her in a sky-blue doublet and matching hose was like seeing the Unity suddenly appear before me and do an erotic dance. It simply seemed impossible, and if I weren't witnessing it, I'd have called anyone who said they saw it a liar.

"Ferdi?" The halfling couldn't approach thanks to the ursid guards keeping people away from the tables, so I hurried over to her with Millie at my side. I glanced down at the warrior, looking her up and down. "Wait—are those breasts, Ferdi? I didn't know you had those!"

"Of course, I do, but since you're never going to see them, there's never been a point in drawing attention to them." She shrugged. "They're nothing like hers, though." She stared openly at Millie's exposed cleavage. "Those things are really impressive, you know."

"So you've mentioned," Millie said, blushing slightly. "You should see the ones on the top seed, though."

"The felid over there? Yeah, I see them. They're big, but really, they're too big." She shrugged. "It seems like more than a mouthful is really too much, you know."

"A—a mouthful?" Millie asked in a faint voice.

"Of course. There should be enough to get hold of and stick in your mouth, and anything extra is just wasted." She gave the woman a curious look. "Isn't the whole point of breasts: feeding babies? Why would you want more than you need to do that?"

"Oh, *babies!*" Millie breathed. "Thank the Unity. Yes, I suppose you have a point, Ferdi."

"No, she doesn't," I chuckled. "And there are a lot of good reasons to want them bigger, Ferdi."

"Oh, you mean for sex? I've never understood that. I mean, you can't actually have sex with them or anything."

I opened my mouth, but Millie elbowed me hard in the side. "Not. A. Word," she hissed at me.

I laughed but let the matter drop. "Why are you here, Ferdi?" I asked. "Something tells me that you aren't here to watch the game."

"I am, but not because I care all that much," she shrugged, then jerked her head backward. "She came and got me and told me to be here."

I looked past the halfling and saw Azara standing back toward the edge of the room, wearing one of her nicer black dresses, watching everyone but carefully not looking at us. I glanced back at Ferdi.

"Is she not speaking to me again?" I sighed. "What did I do now?"

"Probably several things, but that's not why she's over there. She's one of the diviners the Sage's Guild hired for this, and she thought it wouldn't look good to be seen talking with the contestants before the tournament."

"Smart," I nodded. "So, she brought you along?"

"Yep. Said the cards told her there was danger." She shrugged. "I wasn't doing much else, so I came."

"Isn't there an arrest bounty on you?" I asked.

"Not that I know of. There's one on you, though. This one's not my doing, though, so don't blame me for it."

"We think it's from Shadow Man," Millie said quietly.

"That's what I think, too, which means he knows we're alive. Probably best to get the hell out of this city when this is over, just in case."

"That's the plan," I smiled. "You should come with us."

"I should. I won't. Someone still has to care for Jidra."

"How is she?" Millie asked delicately.

"Physically? Mostly recovered. All her parts are back, at least. I can't heal the way the bird-woman can, though, so she's got some scarring that'll fade in time but won't ever go away." She grimaced. "Her mind's not all there, though, and I'm not sure anything will fix that but time. She needs someone to watch her, and right now, that someone is me."

"Last call for players to take their seats!" a voice rang out, and I glanced back before giving Ferdi an apologetic look. The halfling just waved a hand at me.

"Go. Play your silly games. Just know that I'm here, so if the avian's right, I've got your back." Her eyes softened slightly. "Least I can do for a friend, right?"

I smiled at her. "I suppose so," I agreed. "Wish me luck!"

"You don't need more luck, Murf. Just keep your eyes open in case the bird's cards weren't lying to her—and she's not just a crazy woman hearing things."

I turned away and hurried to my table. It was time for the tournament to begin at last.

53

I settled into my seat at the far right of the table and quickly looked over my soon-to-be competitors while my fingers idly counted my chips, making sure they were all there. It probably wasn't necessary since the hall wasn't about to ruin the tournament by shorting someone, but accidents did happen sometimes—and sometimes, they weren't really accidents. The organizers of non-guild tournaments occasionally had favorites, and I was never one of those.

The tournament had attracted a pretty cosmopolitan crowd. There were more beastling players than any other type, obviously, considering where we were, but every major species was represented a little. There weren't any trolls, though. As far as I knew, they didn't play cards, and I'd never met one with the mental equipment to understand the game. Plus, no one with a nose wanted to sit at a table with one.

An orange-haired halfling female I recognized sat to my left; a gray-and-white mottled avian man I didn't know sat beyond her. A felid woman with calico fur rounded out the group, flashing me a playful smile as she caught my eyes on her. I smiled back, then looked at the halfling.

"Darlyn," I nodded to her.

"Darling?" the avian quite literally squawked, his eyes narrowing suspiciously. "Wait, are you two attached? That seems like a conflict of interest! Dealer…"

"'Darlyn'," I corrected. "D-A-R-L…" I looked at her curiously. "Is it Y or I?"

"Y-N," she finished tersely. "My name. Darlyn. Idiot."

"What did you call me?" the avian demanded, his voice rising in volume.

"Sir, please calm down," the canid woman acting as dealer said quickly, leaning over the table. "You don't want to be ejected from the game before it even starts."

The man's feathers fluffed out a bit, but he snapped his mouth shut and simply grunted, his lips moving as he no doubt berated Darlyn silently.

"So, how've you been?" I asked the woman.

"Well. You?"

"Nothing to complain about. Not that anyone listens when I do."

"Doesn't seem to stop you from talking," she noted idly.

"No, not really. I'm not sure anything can. I'll probably speak up at my own funeral." I looked past her at the felid woman. "Hi there. My name's Murf."

"I know," she purred, lowering her eyes to gaze up at my shyly. "I'm Reiew."

"Nice to meet you, Reiew," I said, pronouncing it ree-yoo.

"You, as well. I'm looking forward to seeing if you're as good as they say."

"He is," Darlyn supplied.

"Well, that depends on who 'they' are, and what they say I'm good at," I laughed. "I'm much better at some things than others, after all, and cards aren't the only things my fingers are talented at." I gave her a slight grin, and she blushed and looked down at the table.

"Can we start?" the avian demanded irritably.

"Of course, sir," the dealer said amiably. "Game is standard noblesse, no wilds, spread, cross, and fool. One to ante, three on blind." Her fingers danced as she shuffled the doubled deck, while her eyes fastened on me. "Blind's on you, sir."

I slipped three white coins out into the middle, while the others pushed out one each. The dealer's hands flew as she deftly slipped the cards out to us. I flipped through mine rapidly before focusing my attention on the others. Darlyn I knew from other games; she was a good player but not a great one, prone to overbidding on bluffs and giving herself away with small tics that I don't think she knew existed. The avian I didn't know, but from how quickly he'd gotten upset, I wasn't too worried about him. Angry people bet poorly and were easy to manipulate. To get into the seeded part of the tournament, he had to have some mastery over his emotions, but I was both expert and uniquely talented at being annoying. The felid actually concerned me a bit. She came off as shy and playful, but I got a feeling that was an act to make her seem less dangerous than she was. Fortunately, all the time I'd spent with Millie lately made me very aware of how dangerous a pretty face could be.

The betting started with me, and I quickly checked. I didn't have anything, just a three and eight of cups and a five of staves, but since I'd bet the blind, folding made no sense. Darlyn beside me folded immediately, while Reiew and the avian whose name I'd never gotten but who I decided to call Cockhead since his plumage sort of resembled a rooster's both called, tossing in two coins each to stay in. The spread came, an eight of stars that helped me, but I still checked. The avian thought for too long before folding, while Reiew tossed another coin in that I matched. The cross dropped, a two of cups, and Reiew quickly upped her bid to two coins. I folded, and she claimed the pot. A 2-set of eights just wasn't enough to hang in, not this early in the game when I was still learning tells.

I folded quickly the next few hands until one came that I liked, a 2-set of tens with an ace of staves. I bid modestly on it, feeling the others out more than anything. Darlyn stayed in, as did the felid, while the avian dropped out quickly. The spread and cross fell, a nine and eight of stars respectively, and each time, I bid a little more, just a few coins to test the waters. Darlyn dropped out at the cross, but Reiew pushed the bid a bit farther. I didn't think she had anything; the odds were that she was bluffing to see if she could push me out the way she did the first round, so I called, and the fool appeared for the first time that game. It was another ten, which meant it was possible that she had a run with a six and seven, seven and knight, or knight and lady in her hand. I checked, and she immediately tossed in a red chip.

"Ten," she practically purred, looking at me shyly through lowered lashes. I gazed at her, examining her closely, noting how she idly stroked the fur of her left arm, and how the tip of her tail twitched behind her. I'd seen those gestures before in the game when she had a decent hand, but as my gaze darted back to her eyes, I noticed a flash of cunning in them.

"You little minx," I chortled silently.

"Twenty," I countered, tossing in a pair of red chips and flashing her a grin. I saw the look of regret flash in her eyes as she realized I'd figured out she was deliberately showing tells to try and fool me. It was a clever tactic, but a good gambler never relies on one set of tells. They always look for more, just in case. This was that case. She sighed and slid her cards into the middle.

"Fold."

I collected the pot and slid my ante into the middle. The cards fell, and as the minutes turned into an hour, I got a better feel for the other players. Cockhead was an insecure player who tended to fold at the first sign of trouble. Darlyn was competent but tended to lose big when she lost, which was why she'd never been a top ten seed. Reiew had stopped showing me false tells once she realized I was on to her, and that let me pick up on her real ones quickly enough. Coins slowly but steadily drifted into my pile as I ground away at the others, chipping away at them—pun totally intended—whenever I could.

The hours passed, night fell outside, and my winnings grew steadily larger. As I called bluffs, went in hard on good hands, and gently lured the others into overbetting on hands they probably should have folded, Darlyn looked steadily more resigned, Reiew seemed disappointed by her losses, but Cockhead got more and more irritated. His bids grew larger as desperation set in and his temper got the best of him, and his play turned erratic. That in turn made bluffing him easier, and his pile dropped precipitously until he had only a hundred or so chips left.

Murf's 22nd Law: If you play angry, you'll lose even angrier.

I flipped through my cards quickly; the blind was on me this hand, so I simply checked, allowing the blind to stand as my bid. Darlyn folded, but Cockhead looked at his cards for a little too long, a sign that he had something but wasn't sure how good it was. At last, he nodded and tossed two coins out.

"Call."

"Fold." Reiew pushed her cards into the middle, leaving the birdman and me alone at the table. The spread came, an eight of coins, and I checked once again. Cockhead examined his cards for a second time as if they might have changed somehow, finally tossing two chips into the middle.

"Two."

"Three more," I countered, throwing a blue chip into the pot.

He glanced at his cards again, no doubt confirming they hadn't shifted magically on him, then nodded. "Call."

I watched the cross flip to reveal a lady of stars, and my eyes darted almost involuntarily over to Azara, standing against the wall with cards in her hand. Stars were the suit of magic and power, as I recalled, which meant if that card represented anyone in this room, it was her. I refocused quickly and looked at the bird.

"Check."

"Five." The man didn't hesitate this time, tossing a blue chip into the middle.

"Call." I matched his chip, and the dealer slid the final card out for us. I checked again, and Cockhead stared at it, tapping a finger almost idly against his cards.

"Ten," he finally said, flipping a red chip into the middle.

I chuckled and shook my head. "I'll see your ten and raise you another five, Cockhead."

He reached for his chips, then froze, his eyes widening as Reiew suddenly snorted in laughter. "Wh-what did you call me?"

"Cockhead." I shrugged. "You didn't bother to give me your name, and you kind of look like a cock."

"I look like a *what?*" he demanded, his voice rising angrily.

"A cock. You know. A rooster. A great big, walking, talking cock. Thus, the name."

"My name," he growled, "is *Quaroth!*"

"That's nice," I shrugged. "I like Cockhead better." I gestured at the pot. "Bet's on you, Cockhead."

"I—you..." He sputtered, then grabbed his last two red chips. "Twenty!" he snapped, flinging them both into the middle and knocking the others around.

"Please refrain from splashing the pot, sir," the dealer said reprovingly.

"What she said, Cockhead," I agreed with a grin. "And I'll see your fifteen and raise you five more."

"Fifteen? I bet twenty!"

"The bet was on you for five, sir," the dealer explained. "You called it, then raised fifteen more."

"I meant to raise twenty!" he snarled.

"Then you should have seen me first before raising," I shrugged. "But the bet's on you again. Think you can handle it this time?"

"You son of a whore," he snarled, tossing a blue chip into the middle followed by four stacks of white ones. "Raise twenty!"

"That's a big raise, Cockhead." I grinned at him. "That's something you don't hear a lot. I'll bet no one's ever been able to say your cockhead's had a big raise before, have they?"

Reiew snorted again in laughter, while Darlyn simply eyed the avian curiously, glancing down toward his pants before shrugging disinterestedly. Halflings. Just no sense of humor at all.

"Shut up!" he spat at Reiew, who pointedly ignored him as he whipped back to face me. "Are you going to see my bet, or don't you have the balls for it?"

"It's nice that you're interested in my balls, Cockhead," I said lightly. "I'm afraid you don't do it for me, though, so I'll take your money instead. I'll see your twenty and raise you five more."

"Another twenty!" he snarled, shoving five stacks of white chips forward. "No, twenty-five!" He tossed a blue chip that bounced off the table and smacked into the dealer's left breast—well, one of them. Canid ladies have four in total, after all.

"Sir!" she gasped.

"Be quiet!" he snapped back before glaring at me. "Well?"

"That wasn't nice, Cockhead," I said, shaking my head as I tossed four chips of my own into the middle. "Your problem's with me, not her. Well, your problem's with how poorly you play cards, not her. I'm just taking advantage. Raise five."

"Five! Five! Always fucking five!" he snarled. "I'll raise fifty!"

"Sir, you only have forty-two chips remaining," the dealer said coolly.

"Fine! Then I bet forty-two!" He shoved the last of his chips in, spilling them everywhere.

"Cockhead is all in," she replied in an even tone, drawing another curse from the man. "The bet's on you, sir."

"I'll call," I nodded, sliding a few more chips into the pot. "What do you have, Cockhead?"

"3-set of ladies!" he said triumphantly, flipping two of his cards over to reveal the pair of court cards he'd been dealt. It was a decent hand, to be sure, but not really one worth betting everything on. And sadly, it wasn't quite good enough.

"Run," I said calmly, turning my cards over to reveal a nine, ten, and knight that matched with the eight and lady in the middle of the table. "Eight to lady." Cockhead just stared at my cards, his mouth open.

"The gentleman wins with a run," the dealer said in a neutral voice before looking at the avian. "Well played, sir, but I'm afraid you're out of chips, and that means you're out of the tournament."

"But—I..." The man stammered, his eyes widening as he realized what happened. "You!" He whirled to face me. "You tricked me!"

"I did," I admitted, not even looking his direction. "And just a word of advice, Quaroth: work on that temper of yours. It's too easy to manipulate, and nobody plays well angry."

"Fuck you!" he snapped, pushing away from the table hard enough that his chair caught on the carpet and tipped backward. It spilled him onto the floor with a loud and embarrassed squawk, and he scrambled to his feet to the sound of laughter from the crowd. His feathers fluffed out even more, and he glared furiously at me before stomping off and vanishing into the crowd. People clapped and cheered as he vanished, but I simply gathered his coins, restacked them, and slid them into my pile.

The 22nd Law. Ignore it at your peril.

Cockhead wasn't the only person to lose their temper that night, of course, and his departure wasn't the only one that was less than dignified. Shouting rose from the tables every so often, usually ending quickly as the dealers calmed people down. More than one person cried as they left the tables, both men and women. Particularly jolting was seeing a large ursid male staggering away from a table sobbing loudly, snorting into his furred arm and bawling at full volume. I just shook my head as I watched him. I felt bad for the guy, sure, but the fact is, if you can't afford to lose, you shouldn't play the game.

And that wasn't even the least dignified way someone left a table that night. At one point, an ursid warrior appeared at the table to my right and laid a paw on the shoulder of a human woman with short, dark brown hair sitting there. To my surprise, Azara stood next to the ursid, her face a mask and her eyes unreadable.

"Ma'am, come with me," the ursid growled.

"Wh-what?" she said, her eyes wide and her voice high-pitched. "What's the meaning of this?"

"You've been cheating," Azara said in an almost bored tone of voice. "Palming cards."

The dealer frowned. "The detectors haven't caught anything, ma'am," he pointed out.

"I'm better than a detector. Check her vest pocket, halfway down. She's got a card case in there that hides the cards in it, and she slips one card in first then takes another out, so the detector never picks up the extra card."

The player screeched in protest as the ursid yanked open her vest and pulled out a slim case. Opening it revealed a handful of cards.

"You bitch!" the canid man sitting two over from her growled, half-rising to his feet. "You've been cheating us?"

"Sir, please remain seated," the ursid growled. "Ma'am, either come with me willingly, or I'll carry you."

The woman looked at the dealer, who refused to meet her eyes, then sighed and rose to her feet. The ursid grabbed her arm and half-dragged her to the stairs leading up into the higher offices while everyone watched with expressions of anger, contempt, and nervousness in a few faces. The dealer collected her chips and distributed them to the rest of the table, and play continued without her. I couldn't help but shake my head. Being caught cheating in a tournament like this was a death sentence for a gambler. Even if Jerrick didn't toss her out of the Guild—which he had every right to do—it would be years before she was allowed at another Guild-sponsored tournament, and no reputable gambler would want to play with her. She'd have to settle for the lesser games in the common area or frequent gambling dens outside of guild control, which were much more dangerous and usually far less profitable. It was a stupid risk she took, and it left her busted.

She wasn't the only one to get caught, either, just the only one to go quietly. A commotion far to my left caught my attention as a male felid was dragged away from the table, yowling, screaming, and clawing at the ursid bodily carrying him. The bear-man didn't even acknowledge the man's assaults as he hauled him to the door leading upstairs and tossed him through it. Once again, Azara stood beside the guard, watching impassively, and I couldn't help but shake my head.

Cheating is part of every card game. It's not really right, but it's true. People have cheated at cards since the first person drew the first card on a hunk of stone, then probably wiped his ass with it or threw it at someone he didn't like since you can't really play cards with just one. So, I guess, people have cheated at cards since the first time someone made enough cards to have a game. Everyone expects some cheating from time to time.

However, cheating in a tournament where there are not only layouts but actual diviners trying to catch you? That's just stupid. And desperate. Maybe the only thing worse than an angry player is a desperate one. Of course, if you're playing against either of them, they're great. So, in short, don't be the desperate player; be the person taking all their money and making them even more desperate. At least, if at all possible.

After Cockhead—excuse me, *Quaroth* left, the game proceeded fairly predictably. Reiew fell a couple hours later when her run dropped to Darlyn's, and an hour after that, I called the halfling's bluff and took her pile with a 2-set of sixes. It wasn't much, but it beat the nothing hand she'd had, and that was all it had to do. Just like that, the game was over, and I was into the semi-finals. I rose to my feet to a decent amount of applause—winning by calling a bluff wasn't as exciting as winning with one great hand beating another, after all, but it was still fun to watch—then strolled over to table two to see how Millie was faring.

The answer? Pretty damn well.

The table was down to two players, Millie and Xilla. I'd known Xilla for a while, and I liked her a lot. She was a happy sort of person, someone who laughed often and liked to make fun of life. We'd had some good times drinking and gambling together, and no matter what, she always wore a huge smile.

She wasn't wearing it then, though.

In fact, her face was more serious than I'd ever seen it before as she stared at Millie—and more to the point, at the rather large pile of chips in front of the redhead, one much larger than her own. The goblin was losing and losing badly, it seemed. As I watched the game progress, I understood why. Millie had taken my advice and done what I did to Cockhead. She'd gotten into Xilla's head, only she'd done it a lot more nicely than I had—and in a way I wouldn't have expected.

"Well, five coins!" Millie gushed vapidly, touching her hand to her chest as she looked down at the spread, fool, and cross, a six and four of stars and a prince of coins. "That's so many! I'm not sure I can afford a bet like that, Miss Xilla!" She giggled slightly. "Of course, it's only money, right? I'll see yours and maybe add two more." She placed a pair of red chips in with a blue one.

"That's twenty, ma'am," the male canid dealer said in a long-suffering voice.

"It is? Oh, well, I guess I bet that, then. I'm not sure if my cards are worth it, though!"

"I'll see your twenty and raise ten," Xilla practically growled.

"Ten? Is that one of those red ones? I like those. Let's add—six more of them to the pot! Won't that be fun?" I had to fight not to laugh; Millie sounded like the most empty-headed person I'd ever met, but somehow, she'd obviously kept winning. That had to drive someone like Xilla utterly crazy. Losing was bad enough, but losing to someone who seemed like they had no clue what they were doing? That would drive a competent gambler mad!

"You'll have to go all-in to call, ma'am," the dealer informed Xilla.

"I know," she sighed, staring at the redhead. "Fine. Call." She pushed her chips into the middle and flipped over her cards. "Flush in stars."

"Is that good? That sounds so good!" Millie gushed, then sobered instantly, all the vapidness dropping from her at once. "It's a shame it doesn't beat my full hall, princes over fours." She flipped her cards over to reveal a pair of princes and a four of staves. She smiled gently at the goblin. "Good game."

"Oh, thank the Unity," Xilla breathed, tossing her cards down and slumping in her chair as applause erupted all around them. "You're not really as dumb as a malformed troll!"

"I'm afraid not," Millie laughed. "Although I've never met a troll to compare myself to."

"You don't want to, believe me. They smell." Xilla's grin reappeared on her face. "I'm just glad that you were playing me, and I didn't really lose to someone with wind between their ears. I couldn't have shown my face in a Gambler's Hall for a year if that happened!"

The two shook hands as the applause continued, and Millie rose from her seat, spotting me quickly. Her eyes sparkled and color flushed her cheeks as she approached.

"One win down," she said breathily. "Two more to go!"

"So, you chose to get in her head by pretending there was nothing in yours?" I asked archly. "That was mean, Millie."

"It worked, though. I'm in the semi-finals, Murf!" she said excitedly. "Can you believe it?"

"Congratulations!" I laughed. "And honestly? Yeah, I can believe it. I told you that you're better than you think you are."

"I could make top four," she breathed. "It's possible!"

"It is," I nodded.

"So, who else made it?" she asked, looking around.

I glanced at the tables. Three more were finished and empty; the other three were still playing, but the winners looked to be all but determined. At table seven, Taegen, a brass-haired elf male and the guy seeded below me, looked like he was about to win. And, to my surprise, at table four, Bargrish the canid was losing badly to a platinum-haired elf woman I didn't know but who looked vaguely familiar. I walked over to the boards listing the players and read through them, noting the crossed-off names.

"Looks like my table will be me, Carcrick, a goblin male named Zureg, and that elf girl over there—it says her name's Cewri. Yours will be you, Trendon, Taegen—that elf over there..." I made a face and pointed to the first table. "And Horstya."

As I watched, the felid woman flipped up her card to reveal a 4-set of threes, an excellent hand that beat her opponent's full hall handily. She gave the man, a grey-furred canid, a winsome smile as she raked in the last of his chips. Since doing so gave him an excellent view down the valley of her cleavage, he didn't seem too upset about the whole losing thing.

Millie's face took on a sour expression that quickly shifted back into one of delight. "It doesn't matter. I don't have to beat her; I have to keep her from beating me and take out the others. That'll get me into the final round, where the real money is!"

"Absolutely," I nodded.

"So, what now?" she asked a little breathlessly.

"Well, the others will finish up, and then there'll be a two-hour break so the players can rest and eat before the semi-finals." I smiled at her. "We could grab a bite if you'd like—of food, or anything else that catches your eye."

"A bite sounds amazing," she breathed, leaning heavily against me. "Although I'm not sure if two hours is enough time."

"I'll make it work," I promised her with a chuckle.

"You'd better. I plan to celebrate again when I make it to the finals, and if it stops working, I'm going to be very disappointed."

We began to walk toward the back area for a well-earned rest—of sorts. As we passed the main doors leading into the common hall, though, I glanced through them. My feet froze to the floor without my active consent, which meant that when Millie kept going, still holding to my arm, I nearly toppled over. I caught my balance, but that jerked her backward, and only her grip on my arm kept her from tumbling, as well. She flashed me an irritated glance as she fixed her dress.

"What the hell was that, Murf?" she muttered, lifting up her bodice to resettle some things that had apparently gotten slightly tweaked. I barely noticed. My entire focus was on the table closest to me, where eight people sat playing cards. Most of them, from the look of things, were playing pretty damn badly—at least, I assumed that was the case since the last player seemed to have almost all of their chips. As I looked at the man, I felt twin surges of anger and fear swell in me, and I tore my gaze away from the man, scanning the crowd of the inner hall for a familiar, blue-garbed figure.

"Murf, what's wrong?" Millie asked in a quiet voice, the irritation gone from her voice to be replaced with mingled curiosity and nervousness. "What are you doing?"

"Looking for Ferdi," I said irritably. "Why's she have to be so damn short? If she grew a couple feet, this would be easier."

"Next question, then. Why are you looking for Ferdi, Murf?"

I took a deep breath and forced down my anger. "I just saw an old—well, not friend exactly. More like, 'deeply hated enemy who I'd love to personally strangle but won't get a chance if Ferdi gets to them first'."

"And you want to tell Ferdi they're here?" Millie asked dubiously. "Are you trying to get her thrown out for fighting?"

"I know, I know. And actually, Ferdi's not the one who needs to know. Jerrick is." I made a face. "Except that there's no way he'll see me right now."

"Why not?"

"It's the middle of a tournament, and you and I are both serious contenders for the win. If we're seen talking beforehand, it'll look like he colluded to help one of us."

"What about Eegla? Could you see her?"

"Same problem. However, Eegla knows Ferdi, and Ferdi could talk to her no problem…" I paused as a flash of blue with golden braids caught my eye. "There she is." I pushed through the crowds, half-dragging Millie behind me as she scrambled to keep up. As Ferdi emerged from the crowd, she glanced up at me, her face curious.

"Murf," she said, inclining her head. "Problem? You look upset."

"Yeah, there's a problem," I said, bracing myself for the halfling's reaction. "You remember that guy I told you about, Ferdi? The one who burned down that other tournament and killed everyone inside?" Millie gasped at that and gripped my arm tighter.

"Yes…" the halfling said, drawing out the word.

"Well, he's here." I jerked my thumb back over my shoulder. "Old Lord Bloodfane's sitting in the common room, winning chips hand over fist."

54

It wasn't exactly easy calming Ferdi down after that. In fact, "calming her down" was something of an understatement. It was probably more appropriate to call it, "stopping her from charging after the man like a bull that had been kicked in the stones." She'd wanted to barrel out into the main room with her fists swinging, but I managed to convince her otherwise, mostly by refusing to tell her exactly who the man was. She could have tried to guess, but there were sixteen tables out there, someone was winning at each of them, and probably around half of those were men. She'd only get one shot at attacking the man before the guards nabbed her, and without armor or weapons, she wasn't going to be fighting them. Once she realized that—and stopped threatening to maim me if I didn't point him out—she calmed down enough to agree to pass a message to Eegla telling her who Bloodfane was and what he'd done the last time we met. Hopefully, that warning along with the extra guards present would be enough to make sure the same thing didn't happen twice.

The two-hour break passed far too quickly. Millie and I ended up back in my room, but both of our moods had soured a bit with my discovery. Our clothing stayed on for much longer than I'd originally hoped, and we passed the time talking, mostly me telling her the story of that tournament, how it ended, and where I'd gone from there. That led to a discussion about what we would do if the worst happened again, a discussion that mostly focused on the concept of, "getting the fuck out without getting killed." Only after we'd hashed that out did we strip down, and the lovemaking at that point was short, fierce, and frenzied. Both of us had been through enough pain and violence lately that the thought of more triggered our survival instincts, and we enjoyed one another like it might be the last time either of us would ever be able to.

Considering how things went last time I'd seen the man, that seemed at least a little likely.

I found Ferdi before the semi-final round started and confirmed that she'd spoken to Eegla, then made my way to my table for the semi-final. I deliberately shoved all my thoughts and concerns out of my head. I'd done what I could, and letting those thoughts distract me would only make me play badly. I still wanted to at least place in the top four in the tournament, and that wouldn't happen if I lost this round.

As I approached, Carcrick rose and greeted me enthusiastically.

"Murf," the hawk-faced avian said, reaching out and shaking my hand. "Good to see you again."

"You as well, Carcrick," I grinned at the man. "You seem to be in a good mood."

"Yes, well, it's always a pleasure to play against you. You have an interesting playstyle that's hard to predict, and I love things that are hard to predict."

"No, you don't," I laughed. "You hate them."

"Fine, yes, but at least it's interesting."

"Well, then, I'm glad to be of interest." I looked at the other two players. Zureg, I knew from other tournaments. He was the number eight seed, a goblin male with gray skin and their typical overlarge head and features. Oddly enough, he perpetually sported a monocle that made one of his tiny eyes look huge, although I didn't know if that was because he needed it or because he liked how it looked. The elf woman, though, I didn't know, even though I felt like I recognized her or had seen her before somewhere.

The four of us took our seats, and play began normally enough. I forced myself to stay focused on the game and ignore the sense of unease filling me. The cards fell, and I slowly took the measure of my fellow players. Carcrick, I already knew well. The man knew all the odds, and his swift mind could calculate when to bet, when to bluff, and when to fold almost instantly. Playing the odds as he did wasn't always a winning strategy in the short term, but in the long run, it had carried him through more tournaments than the rest of us at the table had probably played all together. I'd played Zureg a time or five, as well, and I knew that he tended to play a bit too conservatively. That made it harder to get him to go all-in or to overbet on a weak hand, but it made it easier to bluff him. The elf I didn't know, but I had to assume she was a solid player to have made it this far.

The minutes slid into hours, and I played conservatively, getting a feel for the table. It wasn't an easy task. Carcrick I'd always struggled to read; the man was an excellent player and rarely gave anything away. Zureg was a little easier, but the man's extreme hesitance to make large bets made taking his chips a matter of attrition.

The elf woman Cewri, on the other hand—honestly, at first, I had no clue how she'd gotten to this table. She was a terrible player. Her face showed her cards plainly, her eyes reflecting disappointment or excitement whenever she picked them up. It was easy to tell when the spread or cross worked for her or hurt her. She bet too much and too often, staying in when she had nothing and risking far too many chips on cards that didn't support that sort of aggressiveness. She never seemed to bluff and lost frequently.

And strangely, she was actually ahead at the table.

"I'll see your three and raise you two," she told Zureg in an excited sort of voice. Her face reflected her glee as she stared at the layout on the table: a two of cups, a three of staves, and a nine of coins. It was a terrible layout, but obviously, it worked for her—and for the goblin, who hesitated a bit before tossing two more chips in.

"Call," he said tersely, flipping over his cards. "I've got a 3-set of nines." That was a low hand, too low to have lasted until the fool, really, but I knew why he'd hung around. It was the best hand someone could reasonably expect to have from the displayed cards. The odds of someone holding a run or full hall were tiny, especially with him having two of the five nines out there—but unfortunately, tiny wasn't zero.

"Run, two through six," the woman said promptly, flipping over her cards to reveal a four, five, and six. Carcrick snorted in amazement, and I couldn't help but shake my head. That was how the girl had made it this far. She had the best luck of anyone I'd ever seen. The fool had saved her from big losses countless times at the table, and those huge wins offset all of her smaller losses. It meant that despite being a truly awful player, she was slightly ahead of the rest of us in chips.

The hours slipped by, and chips moved slowly but steadily toward Cewri. I was holding my own against her, mostly by capitalizing on her losses and not going in against her when she seemed excited. Zureg was losing to everyone else slowly but steadily. The big surprise was that Carcrick was currently low stack at the table, though. His style of relying on the odds and counting on them to hold up over the long run didn't really work well when someone at the table kept defying those odds. That, in fact, was why he was ranked second to Horstya: she usually beat him the same way more often than not. He grew increasingly frustrated as the cards kept flipping over in the elf's favor, turning what should have been a pat hand for him into a bitter loss.

For her part, Cewri seemed to be enjoying herself; that is, she did except when she looked at me. Then, her eyes hardened, and her gaze went flat and cold. Apparently, she had a problem with me, and I wondered what I'd done to piss her off in the past. I hadn't slept with her; that much I was sure of. I was an ass sometimes, but I remembered everyone I'd lain with. She did look familiar, though, so maybe I slept with her sister or cousin or mother or something at some point. She wasn't a half-elf, so at least I knew that if I had boinked her mom, she wasn't my kid. Plus, judging from her age, I would have had to have been about ten when she was born. I was a precocious brat, but not that precocious.

It might have also been some other grudge; maybe I'd beaten her at cards somewhere or left her father destitute or something. Hell, maybe she just didn't like the way I looked or heard something bad about me, and it wasn't anything personal. Whatever the case, though, she was obviously not a Murf fan, and it showed whenever we interacted. That actually gave me a minor advantage with her because she obviously wanted to hurt me, and even her luck didn't help when she bet big on a 2-set of twos or something similar.

The cards fell again, and I flipped through mine quickly. They weren't phenomenal—a decent 2-set with an ace of staves—but they were enough to stay in. Carcrick had the blind this time and checked. Zureg dropped out, but the elf immediately called as she usually did, and so did I, tossing two chips in to match the blind. The spread flipped, and Carcrick checked again. Cewri bid two, and I matched it.

"I'll see that," Carcrick said, tossing two pairs of chips into the middle. "And raise you two more."

"Call," Cewri said instantly. I did as well, although only with a bit of hesitation. The spread wasn't anything great, a seven of stars, but I guessed that Carcrick either had a 2-set of them in his hand or a 3-set of something else. He couldn't have been trying to bluff her; the elf showed herself to be amazingly ignorant of attempts to trick her into folding early. That meant he had something, and the spread must have helped him.

The cross turned over to reveal a lady of staves, and once more, I couldn't help but glance up at Azara, standing well back and watching the game impassively. Staves were the suit of knowledge, and once again, that seemed like it suited the avian woman immensely.

"Five," Carcrick said, tossing a blue chip into the middle.

"Call," Cewri answered immediately, adding her own blue chip.

"I'll see that," I agreed. "And raise you five more, Carcrick."

The old bird stared at me, his gaze raking across me for long seconds. I met his eyes with a flat, emotionless stare, letting him see nothing but confidence. Eventually, he slid another blue chip into the middle with a nod. "Call."

The fool turned over, and I glanced at Cewri. A big smile spread across her face, which meant she had something good. Carcrick saw it, too, but to my surprise, he tossed a red chip into the middle. "Ten."

"Twenty—no, fifty!" Cewri said eagerly, flipping out a red coin and pushing a red stack out behind it.

"I'll raise that another ten," I added, sliding a stack and two red chips into the middle.

Carcrick looked at the woman, then at me, and nodded. "All in." I could only stare in shock as he slid his coin pile into the middle.

"Ma'am, sir, you'll need to bet four-hundred-eighty-six to call," the dealer informed us after quickly counting the chips.

"I'll call," Cewri said quickly.

"So will I," I sighed. I knew how this was going to end, after all, and it wasn't going to be fun for Carcrick.

"I've got a full hall!" the elf proclaimed, flipping her cards over even though it wasn't her turn. Three tens gleamed in the light of the oil lamps above. "Tens over ladies!"

"A nice hand," the bird smiled at her, turning his cards over as well. "It's a shame that it won't beat a 4-set of sevens." Three sevens shone on the table, and Zureg whistled in disbelief as the crowd around us clapped and roared appreciatively. I didn't blame them; a 4-set was a great hand, with only a flush run and a 5-set beating it.

"What the hell kind of shuffling are you doing over there?" the goblin demanded of the dealer, who looked equally surprised. "How did that happen?"

"The odds of being dealt a 3-set are calculable," Carcrick proclaimed. "In fact, they're about three times the odds of getting a flush run. So, two people receiving a 3-set in the same hand is still more likely than a flush run."

"And if you'd shown one of those, I'd still be asking the same question," Zureg growled. "Especially when I had nothing."

"Sorry, Zureg," the avian shrugged. "But just because something's unlikely doesn't mean it's impossible."

"True," I agreed. "However, some things are much more unlikely than others—say, two people getting a 4-set in the same hand." I turned my cards over to show the two ladies I'd drawn that matched the lady of staves and lady of stars showing on the table already. "4-set, ladies. Sorry, Carcrick."

"Holy shit!" Zureg snarled as Carcrick leaned back, his face slumping. Around us, the crowd's cheers and exclamations grew even louder as people saw the hand I'd flipped over. It was the highest possible hand for that round, and if Carcrick hadn't gone all in, limiting what I could bet, I would have gone all in myself when it came back around to me. I'd expected Carcrick to up the bid again, assuming he had a full hall with his sevens and ladies, but if I went all in, he'd have dropped out. Cewri wouldn't have, and that would have been a sweet triumph, doubling my chips while sending her to low stack on the table where she belonged. His bet caught me by surprise, and instead of crippling the elf, I'd taken someone I respected out of the tournament.

I guess her luck was still working in her favor.

"I'm out," the man said heavily, shaking his head. He took a deep breath and smiled at me. "At least you're the one who put me out, Murf. I—I can live with that." He rose and walked over to me, resting his hand on my shoulder. "Especially if you win this whole thing in the end."

"I'll do my best," I smiled back, resting my hand on his for a moment. He nodded to the others, then turned and walked away to loud applause. One thing I had to give the man: he had dignity, and nothing would take that from him, even such a heartbreaking loss. I, on the other hand, had been looking at the tail end of dignity for years and doubted I'd ever catch up to it. And really, I was fine with that. I'd take coins, cards, and women over dignity any day.

My win catapulted me to the top stack on the table, and I used that leverage to slowly whittle down the other two players. Zureg was simple enough; I just had to keep my bets low enough to keep him in until the fool, then bet big to drive him out. I didn't even need great cards; the more chips he lost, the less willing he was to risk that I was bluffing until I was getting him to fold when I literally had nothing. Cewri was harder to deal with; she didn't bluff, and I couldn't bluff her, so the only way to beat her was to have better cards and stick around until the end. She won a lot of pots where Zureg and I simply folded, not willing to wait until the fool to find out if we lost or not. When I did stick around, though, I tended to win pretty big since she didn't know how to control her bets, so I stayed well ahead of her.

In the end, the game ended fairly anticlimactically. Zureg was down to less than fifty chips and stuck around with 3-set of fours, two in his hand and one on the table. As it turned out, Cewri had a 2-set of knights that matched the fool that flipped at the end, giving her a higher 3-set. He'd gone all-in, knowing that if he didn't win that hand he was sunk, and that loss put him out of the game. I'd simply sat back and watched; just like that, the round was over. I'd ended up as high stack; Cewri took second, and we both were headed for the finals. I tried to congratulate the elf, but she simply rose from the table, giving me a black glare as she strode off. I shrugged, thanked the dealer, and stood up to watch the rest of the other game.

As I'd expected, Horstya had high stack at the table. The felid's chips were piled before her, significantly more than what anyone else had, and she purred happily as she raked in yet another pot, showing a flush in coins that beat Trendon's small run. What I honestly hadn't expected was that Millie was second-high, with a respectable stack of coins only somewhat smaller than Horstya's. As I watched the two women flirt, touch, and deliberately almost expose themselves to the two men, though, I supposed I shouldn't have been all that surprised. Sure, top gamblers were used to dealing with that sort of thing, but there was a limit to what anyone could ignore. It almost seemed like the two women had decided to work together to take the men out since they flirted with one another as much as with the guys, and every time they touched the other or made barely disguised innuendoes, the men looked more lost. Between the two of them, they were a sex-laden force of nature, and it looked like that force had washed over the elf and human with the power of a tidal wave. They were both losing badly, and neither seemed able to dredge up enough focus to care.

Honestly, I'd never seen gamblers so content with losing before.

"She's cheating."

I spun toward the voice at my elbow and saw Azara standing beside me, staring at the table.

"I thought you weren't supposed to speak to me," I noted.

"I didn't think it would be a good idea before, no. I'm not one of the diviners assigned to the finals, so it won't hurt, now."

"You aren't?" I asked, honestly surprised. "Aren't you one of the best diviners in the Guild, Azara? It seems that they'd want you on the final round most of all."

"The best," she sniffed, and I saw the pleasure on her face at my acknowledgment of her talents. She nodded toward the table. "And I have no clue why I was excluded. I assume it's a matter of guild politics, and I don't play those." She shrugged. "I am certain of one thing, though. She cheated."

"Who, Millie?"

"No, the elf at your table. She cheated."

I blinked in surprise. "Wait, you know that? Why didn't you send guards after her, then?"

"Because I don't know how. I can tell she cheated; the cards were changing as she played, shifting to favor her. I simply don't know how she did it."

I frowned. "That sounds like a card power to me, Azara."

"Yes, but I don't detect any cards in her possession." She glanced at me. "Don't you see what cards someone carries when you look at them, now? Did you see any in her?"

"No, I didn't." I sighed. "So, we know she's cheating, adjusting the cards, but we don't know how. That's not going to hold up if she wins the tournament and I lodge a protest, you know."

"She won't win. Whatever she's doing won't work against the cartomancer. It barely worked against you."

"Cartomancer? What cartomancer?"

"The felid." She inclined her chin toward Horstya.

I gaped at the number-one seed for a moment before turning back to face Azara. "Wait, she's a cartomancer? Are you sure?"

"Of course. I can feel her communicating with the cards. She's quite talented." The avian sniffed. "Not as much as I am, of course."

"Obviously," I chuckled, then shook my head. "Azara, would you be willing to tell Jerrick—the Guild Master—about this?"

"If he asked, I suppose. Why?"

"Because cartomancers can't gamble," I chortled. "It's against the rules. It could get her kicked out of the tournament!"

"She's not a true cartomancer, though," Azara said dismissively. "At least, not the way you're thinking of it. She's an untrained talent, that's all."

"Meaning what?"

"She has a natural ability to sense the cards, Murf. That's how she plays so well. She knows what cards are coming up, and she can sometimes convince them to appear the way she wants. However, she can't use the cards or create layouts. I don't feel any power in her, just latent talent going unused, and I don't think you can kick someone out of a tournament just because they *could* be a cartomancer." She glanced at me. "Which is good news for you, by the way."

"For me? You think I could be a cartomancer?"

"Of course. You have the talent. It's not all that strong, but it's there. I remember you told me that sometimes, when you're playing, you can just feel how the cards are going to fall and what everyone's hands are. That's the cards speaking to you, and every so often, you're able to hear them. If you trained that skill—or just listened harder—you could use it a lot more frequently, you know."

I stared at her, then looked back at Horstya with a sigh. If Azara was right, then I couldn't exactly act on what she'd just told me. At least, not if Horstya was just doing something similar to my ability to feel the cards. Granted, I only had Azara's word that that was what I was doing, but then, that was all I had to say it was what Horstya was doing, too. It would be stupid to believe part of what she said but not all of it.

"Did Ferdi tell you about Bloodfane?" I asked her quietly.

"Yes. It explains why the cards predict danger."

"It might. Are you staying for the finals?"

"I might." She gave me a look that looked oddly vulnerable for a moment. "Will you be leaving after?"

"Not the moment they're over, no," I chuckled. "I do plan on leaving the city, though. What with the arrest bounty on my head, I think getting out of Canis is a good idea." I paused as something Millie had said earlier occurred to me. "However, I have a couple days, I imagine. Maybe we could have lunch together sometime, so I could say goodbye properly this time."

Her gaze became startled for a moment, then turned suspicious. "Are you hoping to replace your harlot with me when she leaves, Murf?"

"No," I laughed. "I just think I owe you a better farewell this time, is all."

"Hmm." She looked back at the table, where the men's chips continued to flow towards the women. "I'll consider it. I believe you owe me considerably more than that."

"I do," I agreed.

"And I think I owe Millie, as well," the avian sighed. "That was her idea, wasn't it?"

"…maybe a little."

"I thought so. She's not quite as insensitive to other people as you are. Close, but not quite." She looked back at me, her face serious. "I'll be here for the finals, Murf. Ferdi and I will be watching in case trouble comes." She made a face. "No, for *when* trouble comes."

"You seem confident that it will."

"You're around, aren't you? Trouble always seems to find you, Murf." She reached up and touched my cheek tenderly for a moment before letting her hand drop away. "And I would prefer it be dinner at my home. I'll make something, and we'll catch up. Then, I'll have a fond memory of you leaving, at least."

As she walked away, I turned back to watch the table. It was pretty clear who the winners were going to be. Barring some major turnaround, Millie and Horstya would be advancing with Cewri and me to the finals. The only real question was: who would be joining us from the non-seeded tournament? I had a pretty good feeling I knew the answer to that, too.

I watched silently for several minutes until loud cheering erupted from the outer hall. I quickly walked through the doors and moved around until I could see the final table there. An older man with a pleasant face, muttonchop sideburns, and slicked-back dark hair streaked with gray stood from the table, waving to the crowd and shaking hands with a canid woman beside him. As I watched him, the man slowly turned, his gaze sweeping the crowd until his eyes met mine. As I stared into his dark brown eyes, I saw recognition in them, and a moment later, he flashed me a wide grin and made a sweeping bow.

Bloodfane was in the finals. Yeah, no way this could go wrong.

55

"How long do we have?" Ferdi asked when I told her what I'd discovered.

"Before what?" I asked.

"Before the last game starts. How long?"

"An hour. They'll be moving it out into the common room where there's more space for people to watch, but that also means they'll have to clear the rabble to make a space for the people who paid to watch the game from the front."

"That's plenty of time for me to run to the Blade Hall and grab my equipment, then."

"They won't let you back in here with that axe of yours, Ferdi," I reminded her. "Or with any of your weapons, for that matter."

"I know. I need you to meet me just outside of here in thirty minutes. You store my stuff with your ability, and then if I need it, you can give it to me."

"Actually, that was something I was going to ask you but forgot. How do I get something back out of there after I've stuck it in?"

"How should I know, Murf? I don't have that ability. Have you tried reaching in to grab it?"

"No. That seems a little risky, sticking my hand into something like that."

She rolled her eyes. "It's your ability, Murf. It won't hurt you. Meet me outside in thirty."

She stomped away, and I watched her go, trying to still my whirling thoughts.

"You could just forfeit, Murf," Azara said quietly. "You and Millie both. Walk away from the game, and you'll walk away from danger."

"Not at this point, we can't. A finalist dropping out would hurt the tournament, so there'd be hard questions. I'd have to go before the Guild

Master and explain myself, and if he didn't like the answers, I could end up facing a fine, a temporary ban, or both."

"Surely, having to play against a known murderer who destroyed the last tournament he was in would be explanation enough."

"You think?" I looked at her with a raised eyebrow. "Ferdi passed my information to Eegla, who's definitely told the Guild Master. He knows who Bloodfane is and what he's done. He could have had the man tossed out already. He hasn't, which means he won't, and that means he either doesn't believe me, or something else is making him keep Bloodfane in the tournament—or someone else, like a pushy meritocrat."

She nodded. "Are you ready for when something like that happens again?"

"As ready as I can be." I gave her a serious look. "If things do go wrong again, I intend to get the hell out. Millie and I talked about it, and we're both in agreement. If things go to hell, we're running. You should do the same thing."

"I intend to. I don't care who wins this tournament, after all. I'm only staying to help you and Millie, nothing more."

"Millie, too?" I asked with faint surprise.

"Yes. It's hard not to like her, especially knowing what she's running from. How she manages to stay so open after all that is beyond me, but it's admirable." She shrugged. "Besides, after all the effort I spent helping her layout, it would be a waste to let something happen to her."

I laughed at that. "And me?"

"That would also be a waste—but for far more reasons." She leaned over and gently kissed my cheek. "When danger comes, I'll shield you as best I can, Murf. However, the cards are warning me that the danger is great, and I might not be able to help you. You may need to turn to what's inside you to get through this."

"Let's hope it doesn't come to that."

"I'd rather plan for when it does, personally."

"I think I'd rather you do that, too."

I watched as Millie's game ended exactly as expected, with Horstya as high stack, Millie in second place, and both men losing. Just like that, the players for the finals were set. Millie rushed over to me, her eyes bright and sparkling.

"I did it!" she said happily. "I made it to the finals! That's a guaranteed ten crowns right there!"

"How much do you need to buy out of your family?" I asked curiously.

"A lot more than that," she sighed, then brightened once more. "Still, that's ten crowns closer, and with that, I can afford to join bigger games and win even more!"

I smiled at her enthusiasm. Azara was right; it was hard not to like Millie. She somehow stayed positive no matter what came her way, and she seemed determined to be happy despite how the world seemed to work against her. I leaned over and kissed the top of her head, and she gave me a curious look.

"What's that for?"

"Just for being you." I straightened and gave her a smile that faded to a serious look as a familiar-looking pair made their way through the crowd toward us. I recognized the black-spotted white fur of Meritocrat Grodvulf immediately, of course, and the face of the dark-haired man beside him was burned forever into my memory. I felt my fists clench as the pair neared, but the sight of the two ursid guards following behind them convinced me to relax and forced a pleasant expression on my face. Privately, I thanked the Unity for Ferdi having left before this; she didn't always have the control I did, and I really didn't want her tossed out on her ass for punching Bloodfane in the face hard enough to send his teeth flying out his ass. I did kind of want to see her do that, honestly, I just didn't want her getting thrown out over it.

"Mr. Murf," the black-haired man said in a pleasant, jovial voice. "And Miss Deepwater! I understand we'll all be playing one another soon!"

"So, I hear, Bloodfane," I said in a voice that only held a trace of the icy anger filling me.

"Bloodfane? I'm afraid you've mistaken me for someone else," he laughed. "My name's Thibald Lanly, recently of the city of Harborage." He gestured to the side at the meritocrat. "And this, as I'm sure you know, is Meritocrat Grodvulf, my very good friend."

"Meritocrat," I said a little distantly, inclining my chin at the man. "A pleasure."

"I wish I could say the same, Mr. Murf," the politician said coldly. "However, I find it difficult to speak politely to a known thief and murderer!'"

"You seem to be doing fine with Bloodfane, here," I shrugged.

"You dare to accuse Baron Lanly of such vicious crimes?" the meritocrat spat, taking a step toward me. "I should have you dragged from this place and executed!"

"That would be a terrible idea, Meritocrat," Millie said coolly. "The guild's charter prevents you from taking action against a member within its hall, and if you violate that, then they're free to do the same—say, by refusing the pay the city its share of the profits of this tournament. Plus, no gambler would ever come back here to play again, and the guild would demand your head on a platter as recompense. You'd lose a fortune—and probably your life. Is it worth it?"

The man's nostrils flared, but he quickly composed himself. "You're right, Miss Deepwater. My apologies for the outburst, but the sight of this—this filth frankly sickens me." He turned to Bloodfane. "I'll go make certain that the arrangements for the final match go smoothly, and that everything is done fairly and correctly." He eyed me angrily. "We wouldn't want the Guild Master's favor for one player or another to be reflected in the final game."

"Of course, Meritocrat," Bloodfane said with a slight bow. "Please, see you what you must. I'll be along shortly."

The politician paused. "Should I leave one of my guards with you?"

"Oh, I don't think that will be necessary. It seems Mr. Murf simply confused me with someone else, someone for whom he seems to hold a great deal of anger. Now that he's aware of the misunderstanding, I'm sure things will be fine."

"As you say, Baron." The meritocrat turned away, and Bloodfane looked back toward me, his amiable expression not slipping for a moment.

"Well, Mr. Murf, long time, no see," he said in a friendly voice.

"So, we're done pretending that you're not Bloodfane?" I asked calmly.

"Well, technically, I'm no more 'Lord Bloodfane' than I am 'Baron Lanly'," he chuckled. "But it does seem like there's little point in pretending. You've obviously told your companions who I am, and I'm sure they're more willing to believe you than me." He turned toward Millie and bowed low. "Miss Deepwater. Please give my fondest regards to your grandfather."

"I'd be happy to," she said with a smile. "What name, exactly should I give him?"

"He and I worked together when I was Count Dunstow," the man chuckled. "I doubt he remembers me all that fondly, though."

"I doubt anyone remembers you fondly, Bloodfane," I replied.

"Very few, it's true." He looked at Azara. "Miss Khillia. A pleasure to meet you. I've heard quite amazing things about you."

"Indeed?" she asked, cocking her head toward him. "Interesting. I've heard nothing about you. In fact, I've never even heard of a place called 'Lanly'."

"That's likely because it doesn't exist. Claiming the family name of an actual family can be difficult, especially if a member of that family shows up unexpectedly. I learned that lesson the hard way, long ago." He chuckled. "I do try to learn from my mistakes."

"And was Clearford's tournament one of those?" I asked calmly.

"Oh, very much so. I'd intended to walk out with all of the cards; instead, I got about half of them, and the local authorities became involved. I learned something important that day: never take a risk like that unless you're absolutely certain the payoff is worth it." He grinned at me. "That sounds like one of those laws of yours I've heard so much about. Is it?"

"No," I shook my head. "I think the Twelfth Law will apply most to you, actually."

"And that is?"

"A drawn blade beats a 5-set."

He laughed heartily, smacking himself on the leg. "I like that one! You're right, that principle has guided much of my life—and continues to do so." He gave me a friendly stare, but when I met his eyes, I saw a coldness there that no amount of forced joviality would touch. I also felt something else, a shimmer of something that wasn't quite the same as what I felt with a Holder. I withheld a frown; there was power there, I could tell, but the type eluded me, and the fact that the Hag didn't say anything about him suggested it wasn't the power of a card.

"Well, I'd wish you both luck in the coming match, but frankly, I rather hope you'll both lose," he chuckled. "You understand."

"I feel pretty much the same way," I nodded.

"I thought you might. Goodbye, Mr. Murf. I look forward to finding out which of us is truly better."

"I don't think you'll enjoy learning the answer," I shrugged.

"Oh, one way or another, I'll enjoy it. Trust me." He turned and walked away, and I took a couple deep breaths, pushing the anger aside so my thoughts stayed clear.

"Are you okay, Murf?" Millie asked me quietly.

"Not remotely," I sighed.

"You should go to your Guild Master," Azara told me in a flat voice.

"Why?" I asked.

"He openly admitted to being this Lord Bloodfane, Murf! That should be enough to get him thrown from the tournament!"

"It won't be," Millie shook her head. "Not on Murf's word, or yours, or even mine with my family name. Not with the meritocrat in the man's pocket. If Jerrick tried to have him removed, Grodvulf would throw a tantrum."

"Which is why he made a point to introduce him as his 'very good friend'," I agreed. "He wanted us to know that we couldn't do anything about him."

"What will you do, then?"

"What we planned. Prepare, and hope for the best. I'll go meet Ferdi outside and pick up her stuff, and we'll play the best we can."

"Hopefully, we won't need it," Millie offered.

"We will. He just told us that we will. A drawn blade beats a 5-set; that's his guiding principle, even today." I grimaced. "I have a feeling this is going to get bloody."

56

"Murf," Horstya said warmly as I approached the table for the final round. "It's so wonderful to see you again."

"Horstya," I smiled at the felid, taking her extended hand and lightly brushing it with my lips. "The pleasure's all mine."

"It could be," she purred at me.

"It will—the pleasure of seeing your coins in my stack, that is," I grinned at her, releasing her hand and straightening. "You should know better than to think your flirting will work with me, Horstya."

"The one gambler whose appetites and conquests rival my own," she sighed. "Our time together would be amazing, you know."

"And a little dangerous," I chuckled. "I'm not sure the Hall could survive the encounter."

"You might be right," she said throatily. "I do tend to get a little—feral, at times."

"Feral can be fun. I've got a pair of handcuffs and a riding crop somewhere."

Her eyes glittered. "Tease."

"Absolutely."

She looked at the others as they gathered. "What can you tell me of the elf?" she asked calmly. "I didn't get to watch you play."

"She's like you," I shrugged. "But without the skill. Pure luck and nothing more. Lots of luck, though."

"And the newcomer?" she asked. "The mysterious baron who swept through the unseeded rounds like a storm?"

"What about him?"

"I saw you speaking with him earlier. It seems you know one another."

I nodded. "I played him in a tournament a long time ago. I don't know how good he really is; I was pretty sure he was cheating, but I never caught him."

"Hmm. That's unfortunate. Do you think he cheated his way to victory?"

"Probably. I'm not sure he'll be able to do it here, though. There's a lot more detection on him."

"There's always a way to cheat, Murf," she laughed. "You just have to be cleverer—and more creative—when you do it."

"Not an issue for me," I shrugged. "I never cheat."

"Of course, not. Neither do I."

"Unless you count being able to hear the cards talking to you as cheating," I said slyly, enjoying the sudden look of stunned panic that swept across her face before she schooled it back to a neutral expression.

"I'm not sure what you mean, Murf. Cards don't speak."

"My mistake," I chuckled. "Anyway, best of luck to you, Horstya—not that you need it."

Meeting back up with Ferdi and storing her axe, a sword, and a handful of daggers had gone smoothly. She'd had me practice pulling one of the knives back out to be sure I could do it; as she suggested, all I had to do was reach into the shimmering wafer of air, think about the knife I wanted, and I felt its handle in my grasp. The air inside the storage place was cold, almost icy, and it left my hand slightly tingly, but it didn't seem to do any real damage. I wouldn't want to leave my hand inside there for a long time, though; I didn't know if the Hag would adapt to my own abilities.

After that, Millie and I grabbed a drink together—paying for them like all the other peasants for the first time in a while—and chatted while we waited for the next round to start. Azara spent that time moving around the room, cards hidden in the palms of her hands, looking for anything out of place, while Ferdi did the same thing without cards. I'd told them how Bloodfane had somehow hidden fighters in Clearford's place, and Azara assumed that meant they'd used something like her hiding layout, or that they all had an ability that let them blend in. She felt confident she could find something like that, but I wasn't so sure. Bloodfane seemed to know her, and that meant he'd have taken precautions against her snooping.

At last, the call went out for the players to gather, and the two of us made our way to the table and took our seats. We were placed based on we'd been seeded in the tournament, so Horstya had the rightmost seat, with me on her left, Millie next to me, and Cewri beyond her. Bloodfane, as the unseeded champion, took the low spot at the table to the far left.

I took a moment and looked around. The common hall had been cleared of tables in the last hour and extra seating added near our table, so the high-paying guests could sit and watch in comfort while the peasants and commoners crowded around the outside on raised benches. The second bar from the inner hall had been moved out, as well, and servers roamed the crowd, focusing mostly on the innermost seats, where the wealthier guests watched, the ones more likely to tip well. The place was packed, and I couldn't see Azara or Ferdi in the mass of people.

"Ladies and gentlemen!" I stopped looking around to see Jerrick climbing up on top of one of the bars, holding his hands out for order. "Welcome to the final round of the Triannual Tournament!" Applause rose at his words, and he paused for a bit to let it pass.

"We have with us today five of the finest gamblers you're likely to meet," he continued. "Each of them played their way to the top, earning a spot at this final table! Allow me to introduce them, beginning with the winner of the unseeded tournament, Baron Thibalt Lanly!" Bloodfane raised a hand to a smattering of applause and a number of boos, most likely from people he'd beaten in the tournament.

"Next, recently from the elven city of Dornangar, Cewri Orilan!" The elf got more applause than Bloodfane as she waved a hand at the crowd, smiling broadly.

"From the Plutocracy of Deepwater, Millicent Deepwater!" Jerrick proclaimed. As the redhead turned and curtsied to the crowd, she got a much more substantial ovation than Cewri or Bloodfane had, especially from the men in the audience. She looked at me and rolled her eyes as she took her seat.

"The first of our two semi-final winners and overall chip leader from the semi-finals, originally from…" Jerrick paused. "Hell, I have no idea where he's from. Murf!"

I rose and tipped my hat to the crowd, receiving a sizeable round of applause and a few blown kisses from women. One even held up a hand to reveal a number on her palm that I assumed was her room number in the guild. I winked at the woman and resumed my seat.

"And last, but certainly not least, winner of countless tournaments, the number one seed, originally from the city of Felis, Horstya Mishio!"

The applause that Horstya got as she rose and bowed to the room was thunderous, and men and women both cheered and screamed for her. It lasted for a full minute before Jerrick could restore order enough to continue speaking.

"The game we're playing is noblesse, with the spread, cross, and fool, and no wilds," he proclaimed. "Ante is three; the blind is five. The table winners of the seeded tournament will each begin with 1,250 in chips, while the rest will start with 750, as usual. Players, good luck, and let's begin!"

I'd expected the larger ante and blind for the game; doing so made it go a little faster, as did giving fewer chips to the second-place finishers at each table and Bloodfane. After all, those were the people most likely to bust first, so putting them closer to that point made the most sense. I'm sure some people thought it was unfair, and really, it was, but then, nobody ever promised fair. The tournament was about entertainment and making money for the Guild, not being totally fair and giving everyone an equal shot at winning.

I fanned through the first cards given me and saw that I had a decent hand, a prince of cups, a ten of staves, and a seven of coins. Horstya checked, and I called, tossing two coins in to stay in the round. Millie folded beside me; Cewri stayed in as usual, and Bloodfane folded as well. The dealer flipped the spread to reveal a knight of stars. Horstya checked again, as did Cewri and I. A prince of staves turned over on the cross, and I bid two this time, making Horstya fold. Cewri predictably raised me, and I called her to get to the fool. A seven of blades gave me a double set, princes and sevens, and from the disappointed look on Cewri's face, that hadn't helped her. I bid twenty, going in on her hard, and she reluctantly called, turning her cards over to reveal a lady of coins, queen of cups, and four of staves, an emperor short of a run.

It was a good first hand, but I folded the next several. As the game progressed, I tried to get a feel for the table, but it wasn't easy. Cewri's tells were ridiculously easy to see, of course, and I'd already learned Millie's. Both of them slowly but steadily bled chips to the others, as Cewri's luck failed her, and Millie's distracting tricks only worked on Cewri. Sadly, I wasn't doing a whole lot better. Horstya and Bloodfane gave me very little to work with, and both were good players. Bloodfane played conservatively but not timidly, winning rarely but winning well when he did, and Horstya's luck held out as usual—although I couldn't really call it luck, assuming that Azara was correct.

I frowned slightly at that thought. If Azara was right, I had the same sort of luck, in a way; it just came to me a lot less often than it did to Horstya. What had the avian told me? If I trained that skill or just listened better, I could do it a lot more often. I didn't know how to train it, but listening—that was worth a shot.

As the cards fell, I reached out to them, trying to capture the feeling I had of being connected to the table. I let my thoughts wander across the cards, trying to hear what they had to say. I lost the next two hands in my distracted state, but on the third one, as the cards fell, I could swear they were telling me what they were. I folded quickly that hand, sensing that I wasn't going to get anything good, but the next hand, I stayed in until the fool. I was certain that Bloodfane was bluffing, and when he folded against my bet of twenty chips, I realized I was right.

The feeling grew stronger as the hours passed. It wasn't the same as my usual sense of the table; it wasn't anything that strong, really. It was more of a general idea of how the cards were falling and when they would turn my way. I folded when I had a decent hand, feeling that the next cards wouldn't go my way; I stayed in with nothing when my gut told me that there was something there. I called people who I knew were bluffing, going in hard on them and forcing them to fold. I bluffed people with decent hands, convincing them that what they had wasn't quite enough to stay in the game.

I stopped losing chips and started winning them back, doing my best to take them from Horstya and Bloodfane when possible to narrow her lead and get him out faster. My easiest target, though, was Cewri; as my sense of the cards expanded, I could feel whatever she was doing trying to change them, and whatever it was seemed to stop working whenever she went up against Horstya or me. I could feel her frustration as her chips drained away, until she had no more than a couple hundred left before her.

The cards slid out before us, and I knew even before I flipped mine that I had an okay hand but not a great one. Millie's was good, though, and Cewri's was decent. Millie checked, and Cewri quickly called. Bloodfane folded, as did Horstya, and I followed suit. The dealer turned over the spread, an ace of stars that Millie obviously liked but Cewri didn't. Millie bid five, and Cewri, who should have folded, stayed in. A nine of coins flipped next, and Millie bid ten more. Cewri hesitated a moment before calling, taking it to the fool.

I frowned as the dealer reached for the last card. I could tell what it was, a three of staves that would give Millie the winning hand. At the same time, I could feel—something reaching from the elf woman out to it, trying to convince a different card to appear. I focused on the card, concentrating on it staying as it was. I felt the card pushing back at me, and as I concentrated, I thought about what Azara always said, how the cards spoke to her and did as she asked, not as she commanded. It was worth a try, at the very least.

"Hey, do you mind staying the way you are?" I asked it, feeling like an idiot even as I did. *"I'd really appreciate it."*

The last card turned over, and I couldn't help but smile at the six bluish wands glowing on its face. It wasn't the card I'd wanted, but it would do. I glanced at Cewri and saw puzzlement on her face; whatever she'd been doing hadn't failed, but it also hadn't worked completely, and she clearly didn't understand why.

Millie took one look at Cewri's face before smiling. "Well, it looks like we've got about the same amount. What say we put it all on this hand? I'm all in."

People muttered at the redhead's words, but the dealer held up a hand for quiet. "To call, you'll have to go all in, as well, ma'am," he advised Cewri. The elf worried at her lip before nodding.

"I'll do it. All in." She flipped over her cards triumphantly, revealing a seven, eight, and ten, all off-suit. "Run, six to ten." The crowd applauded behind her; a run was a good hand. I just happened to know that in this case, it wasn't good enough.

"Flush," Millie said sweetly, flipping her cards over to reveal the two, knight, and queen of staves. "Sorry about that."

"The lady wins with a flush in staves," the dealer proclaimed. "I'm afraid you're out, ma'am." The crowd clapped and whistled approvingly; it was always fun to see a good hand get beaten by a better one, after all. Cewri looked to be far less impressed.

"I—what?" she said, rising to her feet and slamming her hands on the table. Her face purpled, and her eyes narrowed. "That's not possible! How did you beat me?"

"You see, a flush is a higher hand than a run," Millie said lightly. "So, I won. That's how the game works."

"No, I—you shouldn't have done that! That..."

"Why not?" Millie asked with a frown. "I've got just as much chance of drawing a good hand as you do, right? Or did, I suppose. Unless there's some reason the cards are supposed to be better for you, that is."

Cewri's face blanched, and she quickly shook her head. "N-no. Of course not. I just—I was surprised, that's all."

"I understand. It was a well-played game, and at least you're walking away ten crowns richer. That's nothing to sneeze at!"

"No, it's not. Thank you." The elf turned away and walked past us, but as she neared me, she suddenly paused. A sense of danger ran up my back as the woman suddenly yanked a dagger out of who-knows-where and lunged at me with a scream.

"Die, murderer!" she screeched, stabbing the blade at me. I reacted quickly, pushing myself aside so the knife missed and falling to the floor in the process. She leaped onto me, straddling me and pressing one hand against my chest to hold me down. Normally, I was happy when a woman in a dress did that to me, but the knife in her hand and the wild look in her eyes sort of dampened any enthusiasm I might have normally. She slashed downward, but I reached up and caught her wrist, stopping her attack cold and holding the knife at bay. I bucked beneath her, lifting my hips upward, and her eyes widened as my pelvis slammed up between her legs. She flinched away reflexively, and I used the moment to lunge upward and slam my fist into her jaw. She fell backward, her wrist still gripped in my fist, and I rolled onto her, grabbing the knife and twisting it out of her hand before pushing myself to my feet.

I stared at her as she lay on the floor, panting and holding her cheek. I hadn't hit her hard; I'd basically given her enough of a tap to get her off me but not enough of one to knock her out or break anything. I'd wanted to hit her harder, mind you, but with the Hag empowering me, I was worried I might accidentally kill her. I stepped back a bit and glared at her.

"What the hell is your problem?" I demanded.

"Murderer!" she snapped at me, still rubbing her cheek.

"Who, exactly, did I murder, lady?"

"My brother!" she screamed, and as she said that, it clicked. I realized why I recognized her. She looked just like a female version of Taveroth, the elf I'd stabbed to death in the Ochre Forest what felt like years ago but was really just a few weeks. That meant that technically, she was right. I did kill him. She didn't need to know that, though—not that I thought she'd listen to anything I said anyway.

"You killed him!" she hissed. "And now, I'll kill you! With what I've received from…oof!"

I really didn't think that "Oof!" was who she'd gotten something from. That, I felt certain, was Shadow Man, who'd probably used his tame goblin cartomancer to let the elf influence the cards and ensured that she'd end up close enough to me to stick a knife in my ribs. That felt like something he'd do, at least, and I guessed she had something else up her sleeve. She never got to use it, mostly because "Oof" was the sound she made when the ursid warrior who'd come up behind her smacked a cudgel across the back of her head. At least, that was the sound her mouth made. Her head made a sort of muffled thumping noise that sounded distinctly unhealthy. As if to verify that, her eyes rolled up, and she collapsed like a pile of limp noodles to the floor. The ursid looked at me and held out a meaty paw.

"I'll take the dagger, sir," he growled.

"Oh. Sure." I flipped the knife around and handed it to him, and he nodded to me before grabbing Cewri's hair and dragging her unconscious body into the suddenly silent crowd. They parted around the pair, and I watched them go for a moment before the sound of someone clearing their throat drew my attention back to the table.

"Sir, are you injured?" the dealer asked in a concerned voice.

I looked myself over, then brushed myself off, stooped down to pick up my hat from where it had fallen when I hit the floor, and planted it firmly on my head.

"I seem to be fine," I smiled, pulling out my chair and sitting back down. "Although that was pretty tense, wasn't it?"

"It's the first time I've seen a man thrust a woman off himself like that, to be certain," Millie observed in a sly voice. "Usually, he prefers to keep her in place."

"I always imagined that you had well-developed pelvic muscles," Horstya purred, looking me up and down like a side of beef. "It's good to see my imagination bear fruit."

"That sounds like a conversation for later," I grinned at her. "For now, maybe we should just finish the game."

"Spoilsport," Millie pouted.

"Tease," Horstya added. I couldn't help but roll my eyes at the two women before turning my focus back to the game.

The cards fell, and as my sense of the table grew, so did my stack of chips. Horstya managed to hold her own with me—I could feel her changing the cards every so often, just as Azara said, but they tended to listen to her instead of me when I asked them to stop. Bloodfane was down a bit, with around 500 chips or so, but Millie was struggling. She was low stack at about 300 chips, and I could feel the desperation growing in her. I knew that desperation would push her into a bad decision at some point, and sadly, I was right.

The cards dropped, and I flipped through mine to confirm that I had a 2-set of tens plus a nine of stars. Horstya, beside me, had nothing, and neither did Bloodfane. Millie, though, had a good hand, and when I checked, she quickly called. The spread turned over to reveal a prince of stars, and I checked again. Millie bid five, and I called, taking us to the cross. It was another card that helped Millie, a star that led into the flush she was building, and she bid twenty. I raised her another twenty, and she called. The fool flipped, and I bid fifty, hoping to drive her out.

"Do you have something, Murf?" she asked idly. "Or are you just hoping to bluff me?"

"Only one way to find out," I shrugged.

"That's true. You know what? All in." The crowd gasped as she leaned back in her chair, deliberately giving me an excellent view of her ample bosom. I couldn't help but smile as I pushed several stacks forward to match what she had.

"I'll call."

She turned her cards over with a smile, revealing a pair of stars that matched with the three showing on the table. "Flush in stars," she said simply. Instead of turning my cards over, I slid them silently to her. She lifted them up, her face stricken as she saw the two tens and nine then glanced at the ten of coins and nine of staves showing as the cross and fool, respectively. A full hall, one hand above a flush—enough to win the pot.

"I—I lost," she said softly. "You put me out of the tournament, Murf!"

"I did," I nodded. "Sorry about that."

"You..." She took a deep breath and smoothed down her dress. When she spoke, her words were crisp and formal, not her usual playful self. "Well-played, Murf. Congratulations."

"To you, as well. You made the top four, just like you wanted."

"You're right. I did." She rose from the table and curtseyed at everyone. "Baron. Horstya."

"Miss Deepwater," Bloodfane nodded.

"You played amazingly, dear," Horstya said encouragingly. "I'm quite impressed."

"Thank you." She turned and walked away, leaving me to collect her chips to enthusiastic applause. I hoped that she was just angry, and that once she calmed down, she'd understand that it was just the game. I wasn't sure about that, though. She'd gone from having a chance at winning the whole thing to being out of the tournament, and it was my fault. That wouldn't be an easy thing to simply forgive.

I pushed those thoughts away and sank myself into the cards. I could feel them, and that awareness kept expanding as whatever they were supposed to be saying or doing washed through my brain. The hands passed, and with each one, I could feel that connection to the table growing stronger. I sensed Horstya's similar connection to the cards and felt how she shifted and changed them, and I worked to stop her where I could, begging the cards to stay as they were instead of obeying her. Sometimes it worked; sometimes it failed spectacularly. Overall, though, I kept whittling at her stack until she was low at the table by a fair margin. As she grew more desperate, she played more aggressively, pushing her luck and rapport with the cards to try and score big wins.

The dealer slipped another hand before us, and I knew right away that Horstya had a potentially good hand this time. Not only could I sense it from the cards, I could feel it radiating from the woman. Bloodfane, who had the blind, checked, and without pausing, Horstya pushed one red and two white chips into the pot.

"Ten."

"Call." I didn't hesitate either as I matched her chips.

"I'll see that," Bloodfane agreed, then tossed two red chips into the middle. "And raise you ten more." Since he had three small cards off-suit, I assumed that he was either bluffing, or he was counting on whatever he was doing to cheat to win the hand for him.

Horstya hesitated for a moment, then smiled at us and slid her stack a bit forward. "All in." The crowd behind us gasped and muttered in appreciation of the rather gutsy move. Going all in early in the hand was extremely risky—at least, it was when you couldn't feel what cards were coming up, the way she could. Sadly for her, so could I.

"How much to call?" I asked the dealer.

"523, sir," the man nodded, and I pulled the stacks aside and slid them into the middle.

"I'll call, then." I glanced at Bloodfane, whose stack was between mine and Horstya's. "What do you say, 'Baron'? Want to see the fool with us?"

"I feel like I'm looking at a 2-set of those already," he chuckled, tossing his cards into the middle. "I'm out."

"Turn your cards over, please," the dealer instructed, and we both flipped our cards over to show what we had. My cards looked like nothing: an ace, three, and ten, all off-suit. Horstya, on the other hand, had the seven, eight, and nine of stars, the center of a flush run, and with her legendary luck, it wasn't such a stretch to imagine her drawing it. People oohed and aahed in amazement as they saw what she had, and I saw more than a few heads shaking at my hand, which quite frankly looked pathetic.

"You bet five-hundred on that?" Bloodfane chuckled. "Murf, I'm disappointed in you! I had a better hand!"

"The hand's not over, is it?" I asked calmly, gazing at the man. "Not until the last card falls."

"Spread." The dealer's voice drew my attention as he flipped over a card and placed it on the table. The ace of stars stared at me, giving me a 2-set and Horstya a four-flush. People muttered and laughed; while the hand wasn't technically over, it was a lot more likely at that point that Horstya would win. After all, she just needed one of the next two cards to flip as a star, and she had her flush. It would be a lot harder for me to make anything.

"Cross." The dealer waited several seconds to give the onlookers a chance to place bets if they wanted, and to heighten the drama. He slipped the next card over to the middle of the table and flipped it, and a ten of stars gleamed in the overhead lights, the array of stars on it dazzling. People whooped and cheered; Horstya had made her flush, and while I now had a double set, her victory was all but assured.

"Ooh, bad luck, Murf," she purred happily. "Sorry about that."

"There's still one card, Horstya," I chuckled. "I still have a chance."

"I never knew you were such an optimist, Murf."

"I'm a realist. The hand really isn't over. Let's wait and see who the fool is—sorry, what the fool is," I chuckled.

"Fool," the dealer intoned, moving the card facedown to the center of the table and holding it there for a couple seconds to heighten the drama. At last, he turned it over, and the crowd gasped, then burst into applause at the ten of cups shining in the light of the oil lamps. Horstya hissed in surprise, her eyes wide, and Bloodfane hooted and clapped.

"By the Unity!" he laughed, leaning back in his chair. "Talk about luck!"

"The gentleman wins with a full hall," the dealer said with a slight smile. "Tens over aces. I'm sorry ma'am, but you're out."

"Well, well, well, Murf," the felid purred, her eyes narrow. "That was quite the lucky draw. Someone might think you borrowed my luck for this game."

"That's the thing about luck, Horstya," I laughed. "You can never count on it when you need it." I held my hand out to her. "Good game."

"Indeed, you're right. She's a rather untrustworthy lady." She placed her hand in mine, and I lifted it to brush with my lips. "Well played." She looked at Bloodfane. "Baron. I'd wish you luck, but honestly, I'm not sure there's much point. Murf seems to be unbeatable tonight."

"Anyone can lose, Miss Horstya," the false noble chuckled, looking at me. "And I have a feeling that Murf's luck is about to change."

As he spoke, I felt a surge of the same energy I'd sensed before. This time, instead of hiding within him, that power rolled upward and flowed out and around him. I barely managed to conceal a wince as I sensed the energy; unlike the hidden fire of a Holder, Bloodfane's power felt—foul. That really is the best way to describe it. It felt like the inside of your mouth after a night of way too much drinking, far too much spicy halfling food, and maybe a couple attempts to rinse it all out by gargling sewer water. It felt like I imagined the inside of a troll's underwear smelled, like how the soul of one of the Swindlers must look, or like the feeling of being tossed into the cesspool outside an orcish slum. Yes, that one I can attest to. Long story.

In other words, it felt utterly nasty in every sense of the world

The moment the power washed out, though, my sense of Bloodfane cut off completely. I could feel the table, the deck, and the cards in my hand, but as the dealer tossed cards Bloodfane's way, my sense of them vanished, cut off completely as if a wall of silence surrounded him. It didn't much matter, as I could feel the cards while they were still in the dealer's hand, and I knew he didn't have much, a low 2-set and a middling card like a six or seven as a kicker. I checked; he called, and the spread flipped to reveal an eight of blades. I checked again, and to my surprise, so did he. The same thing happened on the cross, a knight of cups, and the fool, a four of staves. I didn't have much, just a double set of fives and knights, but that was enough to beat his small 2-set. I flipped the cards over with a smile.

"Double set, fives and knights."

"An okay hand," he nodded, revealing his cards. "Doesn't beat a 3-set of eights, though, does it?" I stared in confusion at the two eights and ten showing on the table. Those hadn't been the cards he'd been dealt; somehow, he'd changed them.

"Like I said," the man chuckled, raking in the admittedly small pot. "I have a feeling your luck's about to change."

57

I quickly pushed away my confusion as the next hand fell. Once again, I could feel the cards being passed to Bloodfane by the dealer, but now I suspected that my senses weren't going to be much of a help in telling what he had. At least, they wouldn't if he could keep shifting the cards in his hand somehow.

Fortunately for me, I didn't exactly rely on that sense to play. Oh, it was helpful, to be sure, but I was a gambler, not a cartomancer or whatever Azara thought I was. I could play without feeling the cards just fine. I just had to rely on my other skills, and those still worked excellently.

The cards fell like rain, and as they did, I played with as much skill as I could. I read Bloodfane's body language, noting the way he arranged his cards after looking at them, the set of his jaw, the narrowing of his eyes. No matter how hard a person works, it's impossible for them to completely shut off all their tells. At best, you can hide and mute them so that only someone who's really skilled can see them, but they're always there. Bloodfane's were faint and difficult to read, but they existed, and I used them to my advantage.

Of course, his seeming ability to shift the cards in his hand changed things quite a bit. He stole several pots from me that way, when every sense I had assured me that the man was bluffing, and then he'd flip over his cards to reveal a winning hand. There wasn't much I could do about that, especially if he was shifting the cards at the last second so that I'd have no warning. I still won those pots occasionally, usually when he didn't shift his hand into one that was quite good enough to beat mine, but I lost more of those than I won.

All he had to do was shift his cards like that each hand, and he would eventually be guaranteed to win. I knew it, and I'm sure he did, too. That didn't happen, though. Most of our hands played out normally, without any trickery involved. I didn't know the reason for that, obviously, but I had a couple of ideas. The first was that whatever power he held was limited, and he didn't want to use it all up too quickly. The second was that if he used the ability too much and too often, it would draw suspicion and might get detected. I couldn't feel what he was doing, but there were actual diviners here, and they might be able to if he used it too much. Plus, if every hand was a flush run or 5-set, everyone would suspect him of cheating, and even his pet meritocrat wouldn't be able to argue with that. Occasional flashes of luck were one thing; a constant stream of it was another.

So, we mostly played a standard game, and it quickly became apparent that he couldn't keep up with me there. I bluffed him out of decent pots when I had nothing. I called his bluffs and forced him to fold. I pushed hard when he had a good hand but I had a great one, and I dropped early when I knew that his hand was going to beat mine. He won a few large pots with his ability, but in between those, I hammered away at his stack, and as the time passed, the chips sluggishly flowed my way. He tried going all in a couple times in desperation, but I avoided those, knowing that he'd use his ability to secure a win and recoup his losses, and continued to chip away at him, pun absolutely intended.

As we played, I sank myself into the game. Nothing else mattered; not the crowd cheering around us, not the glowering meritocrat watching his meal ticket lose, and not even the disaster at Clearford's tournament all those years ago. Only the cards, my opponent, and me existed. I couldn't feel the cards in Bloodfane's hand, at least not at first, but as I poured myself into the game, that slowly changed. I still couldn't quite sense them, but I felt little nibbles of them here and there, enough to feel the moment when his cards shifted. The first time I sensed it, I had to suppress a wince; it felt wrong and unnatural, as if it were something that shouldn't be. I felt the same way the first time I saw a male goblin naked, in fact; those little guys have some funky-looking equipment down there, and the lack of hair makes it all the more surreal.

I still have no clue how goblins manage to reproduce, but they do excel at it. More power to them, I guess. If I were a goblin woman, I'd swear an oath of celibacy first chance I got.

The point is that there was a sense of wrongness in what Bloodfane was doing, and that sense grew stronger as the game progressed. His ability was like a sore tooth throbbing at the edge of my awareness or a bit of indigestion that I knew was going to turn into something extremely unpleasant eventually. It wasn't enough to disrupt my play, but the discomfort it caused steadily grew. As it did, an odd feeling stirred in the center of my chest, that place where the Hag and my deck rested. It wasn't a feeling of power or energy like I was used to; instead, it was almost like the Hag was trying to talk to me. I'd felt that once before, when I fought Fisya and sensed the Hag's agreement that the felid was someone who needed to stop existing. The feeling wasn't quite the same, but I could sense that the card was trying to tell me something.

Bloodfane's ability triggered again. I could feel his cards well enough at that point to know that a second ago, he'd been holding three cards of different ranks and suits, and those shifted into something more compatible.

"3-set," he said smugly, displaying a pair of sixes that matched the spread, a six of staves. "Can you beat that, Murf?"

I couldn't. I had a double set, princes and fives, enough to beat the hand he'd had but not enough to beat the one he switched to. At the moment, though, that didn't matter to me. As the power activated, the strange feeling from the Hag seemed to solidify in my brain. It was a word and a concept, and the moment I understood it, the word slipped from my lips without my intent.

"Warlock," I said, my voice little more than a murmur.

Bloodfane's eyes suddenly widened, and I saw a flash of mingled panic and anger race across his face before he swiftly schooled it and laughed.

"I don't believe I know that hand, Murf," he chuckled. "Are you making cards up, now?"

I didn't bother to flip my cards over; instead, I flashed him a grin. "I wondered how you were changing the cards," I said in a quiet voice that only he, I, and the dealer could hear.

"Sir, an accusation of cheating without proof..." the dealer began in a shocked voice, but I powered over him.

"That's what it is, isn't it?" I asked Bloodfane as the knowledge the Hag fed me crystallized in my brain. "You're a warlock. You've made a deal with the worlds below for power, and you're using it to change the cards."

"I don't have the faintest idea what you're talking about," he chuckled, although I saw his eyes dart quickly toward the dealer for a moment. "Is this some strange type of bluff? A mental game? Are you hoping to get me to forfeit?"

"I don't need to," I said easily, gesturing to my stack. "I'm winning already, and we both know it, even with you shifting the cards around."

"That's twice you accused me of cheating," the man said, his voice turning cool as he spoke. "Do you have any proof? Any evidence? Or are you just making random accusations?" He looked at the dealer. "Is he allowed to do that?"

"He's right, sir," the dealer told me in a firm voice. "Accusing someone of cheating without proof is reason to be ejected from the tournament. If you can't prove what you're saying, you need to stop."

I shrugged. "It should be easy enough to prove. We've got diviners here; I'm sure one of them could detect your little arrangement."

"By all means," the man said, spreading his arms wide and grinning. "Let them check! I've got nothing to hide!"

"Sir, you know that if I ask for a divination, and nothing's discovered, you'll have forfeited the game," the dealer told me nervously.

"That's true, Murf," Bloodfane nodded. "Is it worth the risk?"

"I think so," I nodded, then paused for dramatic effect. "Especially considering that Azara's still here. What say we have her perform the divination rather than whichever one you've already paid off?"

I saw the concern race through the man's eyes as I said that. "She's not an official diviner for this round," he shook his head.

"So? If you're not a warlock, it shouldn't matter who does the divination, should it? She's a member of the Sage's Guild; she's probably the best diviner in the city; she doesn't care about the outcome of the game, so she won't lie for either of us; she can't be bought, so you can't pay her to cover for you."

I flashed the man an evil grin and leaned forward. "Except that it does matter, doesn't it? I wondered earlier why you'd done research into Azara. After all, she's not really anyone important in the city. The only thing notable about her is how good she is at divining, so why would a minor noble who's in the unseeded part of the tournament care about her?"

I shook my head. "He wouldn't. Someone who planned to cheat their way to the final round would, though, especially if that person had a pet meritocrat and enough money to make sure that a talented, incorruptible diviner wasn't brought in for that round." I chuckled. "I thought that the guild kept her out over politics, but that wasn't it at all. You arranged for her to be excluded, didn't you?"

"I have no idea what you're talking about," the man said in a dangerously lazy voice.

"No? Well, in that case, you shouldn't mind if Azara does the reading, right?" I looked at the dealer. "Could you have her brought over here? I know she's in the crowd…"

"Damn you, Murf," Bloodfane said with a sigh, leaning back and rubbing his forehead. "You know, I was really, really hoping not to have to do this again, but you're leaving me no choice, here." He leaned forward and fixed me with a hard gaze. "This is on your head. You're going to have to live with it—not that I expect you will for very long."

A sudden surge of that greasy, disgusting power that I now knew was infernal energy rolled up from him and surged outward. It blasted past me, washing over the room. The oil lamps above flickered for a moment, and the whole crowd seemed to pause to take a simultaneous breath.

Which is exactly the moment that all hell broke loose, in the most literal sense of the word.

58

Screams and curses rang out as black-armored figures suddenly popped into view all over the room, shedding whatever cloak they'd been hiding beneath. Each bore some sort of wicked-looking weapon, from axes to swords to polearms, all adorned with various hooks, spikes, and serrated edges that made them look extra cruel. The entire room sort of froze as the figures stood there, menacing but silent for a moment. That lasted only until Bloodfane flicked a hand negligently, and the warriors sprang into action.

Screaming rose anew as one of the figures slashed outward, and their axe blade ripped through a woman's throat with a spray of blood that splattered everyone around them. People shouted and shoved, trying to get away, but the armored figures struck out implacably, thrusting at slashing at bare flesh. The hapless citizens of Canis had no chance, and the evil-looking weapons cut them down without mercy.

A sense of danger flared in my skull, and I shoved back from the table without thinking. My chair tipped backward, spilling me onto the carpeted floor, and my head cracked painfully into the wood beneath it. I didn't regret it in the slightest, though, as a weapon that looked like half of an axe blade attached to a six-foot-long pole slammed into the table where I'd just been sitting, lodging itself in the wood for a moment before the armored figure ripped it free and spun toward me. The weapon swept down, and I rolled sideways to avoid the blow—right into a kick from a metal-clad boot in the chest that crumpled me up and flung me a couple feet backward.

"Murf, you've been a right pain in my ass." I looked up, clutching my aching ribs as Bloodfane walked calmly into view, looking around at the carnage and mayhem with one of the armored figures standing at his side. "Why do you persist in screwing with my plans? Why can't you just let well enough alone?" The man gestured, and the armored figure lashed out again with a foot that caught me in the ribs with awful force. I heard my bones creak as I slid backward another foot, but nothing seemed to break, and I silently thanked the Hag.

"None of this had to happen," the fake noble continued to expound. "If we'd just kept playing, eventually, I'd have turned it around and taken you, and then I'd have had access to that deck. But no, you had to turn out to be more perceptive than the vain, selfish lecher I've always assumed you to be."

"Or maybe you're just a typical wannabe villain with shitty plans," I croaked, receiving another boot in response. It hurt, but not as much as it could have as the Hag began to adapt to the blows.

"You really don't understand just how much went into this, do you?" he continued, apparently unfazed by my insults. "Do you know how much money it took to bribe a meritocrat? To bring that silly elf girl in and grant her the power to shift the cards in the hopes she'd beat you and keep you from the finals? To arrange for the diviners watching my tables to ignore me?" He paused. "No, really. Take a guess. You won't even be close."

"The souls of a dozen unborn babies?" I guessed. "That feels like your style."

"Ha!" he laughed. "Sadly, no. If I could have paid for all this with souls, the way I pay for the powers I hold, this would all have been much simpler." He sighed. "And it's all wasted. If I was going to do this, I could have done it from the start and saved myself a ton of time and money."

"And kept old Grodvulf from bringing all those guards," I added, rising to a sitting position and looking around. "I'll bet they're making things harder for you."

"You mean those guards?" he asked, pointing behind me. I looked over my shoulder and saw Grodvulf standing near the back wall, surrounded by most of the guards I'd seen walking around before. The clash of steel on steel, grunts, and shouts showed that the Guild's guards were fighting Bloodfane's warriors, but there weren't many of them, and I wasn't sure if they could take all the armored figures. Apparently, Grodvulf was fine standing back and letting all those people die.

"Idiot," I shook my head. "You're just going to kill him afterward. You can't have anyone reporting what happened here, can you?"

"Not at all," Bloodfane laughed. "You see, our dear meritocrat and I are going to emerge from this as heroes! Mysterious assailants attacked the tournament, killed everyone, and stole the deck that was supposed to be the reward, but Grodvulf's guards fought them off before they could spread out into the city. It's a terrible tragedy, of course, but it just shows the need for a stronger, more centralized rule here in Canid."

"You mean, by someone like Grodvulf," I guessed sourly.

"Exactly! I get my prize, Grodvulf gains more power, and by letting him live, I gain a powerful ally who might be able to assist me in other endeavors in the future. Really, it's a win for everyone." He paused. "Well, except for all the people getting killed, of course. And you, Murf. I'm afraid I can't let you live again. Doing so last time was a mistake, and I do try not to repeat my mistakes, as I said earlier."

"That's a shame," I shrugged.

"Yes, it is—for you." His grin turned vicious.

"No, not for me. For you. See, you're about to be disappointed, Bloodfane. You should never bring mercenaries to a halfling fight."

The armored warrior beside Bloodfane shouted in a strange, alien language as a blue-armored figure slammed into the back of it, hurling it forward past me. I'd seen Ferdi making her way toward me, fighting through the crowd, and I'd timed my little quip to coincide with her attack. The halfling spun and slammed a fist into Bloodfane, knocking him backward across the table to crash to the floor behind it, then spun toward me.

"Murf, my axe!" she bellowed.

I quickly activated Phantom Porter and plunged my hand into the shimmering disc of air that appeared before me. I hauled out Ferdi's axe and tossed it to her. She snatched it up by the center of the handle and launched herself at the staggered armored warrior with a bellow of rage.

I glanced around and saw Millie crouched down, ducking away from another armored figure. Her skin had an odd ashen tint to it, as if she was sick, but she didn't move like anything was wrong with her. She danced around the warrior's attacks with superhuman fluidity, and one time when its blade slipped across her arm, the gray there darkened briefly, leaving behind nothing but a thin scratch. She was holding her own, but without a weapon, I wasn't sure if she could do more than dodge. I shouted her name, then pulled out a pair of knives and tossed them her way. She scooped one up without looking at me, slipped around an attack, then rammed her blade into the center of the warrior's back with a loud clang and a screech of shearing metal. The armor collapsed beneath her card abilities, and the warrior arched its back in pain as it dropped to its knees.

I pulled out my own short sword, closed the storage portal, and reached down inside myself, grabbing the Rake of Cups. I could feel the powers radiating from it like the edges of cards in a tightly stacked deck, and I thumbed a few, spraying them outward. Drunken Combat washed over the room in a wave of power, followed by Crown of Authority and Living Nightmare. My senses sharpened as I touched the ace of staves and activated Improved Perception, and my flesh tingled as my mental fingers slid over the two of blades and triggered Thick Skin. Lastly, I reached down to the knight of coins and flexed it, as well, using Melee Mastery for the first time.

An armored shape charged at me, swinging a heavy, hook-pointed sword nearly as long as I was. I jumped backward, letting the blow slide past me, then triggered Gaze of Despair in response. The warrior staggered as the power struck them, and icy energy poured down my sword as I stabbed with it. Even as I did, I realized that my form was terrible; I thrust the blade like it was a stick, and I was poking the guy in the stomach with it. I shifted my feet a bit and relaxed my grip on the weapon, allowing the power of my legs to drive the blade. It plunged into the warrior like I'd stabbed a pile of feathers, and frost quickly spread out from the wound as Freezing Touch washed out into the person's body. They dropped instantly, and I whirled to find myself standing in a moment of calm for just a moment. I took that chance to turn my thoughts inward.

"Charlie," I sent to the tiny ferret, *"I need you to come out and find Azara. Keep her safe and bring her here."*

"You got it, Dad!" The chilling sense of the ferret burst from my chest as his misty form leaped out of me and hit the floor.

"Use whatever abilities of mine you need to."

"I will! Can I bite them?"

"Charlie, these are very bad people," I told him in a deadly tone. *"I don't care what you do to them—or if they survive it. Got it?"*

"Yep! I'm on it!" He raced into the crowd, weaving around people and vanishing almost instantly from sight. I turned toward movement in my periphery and tried to dodge as a heavy, spiked hammer flew toward my chest. I managed to twist so it hit my side, bracing myself for the pain of the spikes ripping into me, but the blow just knocked me sideways into the table. I'd forgotten about my armored jacket, and I silently thanked Millie for getting it for me—even if it was with my money.

I ducked the next hammer blow, sensing that trying to stop it with my sword would be futile, then spun and slashed low at the knight. My blade clanged as it cut through their ankle, severing their foot easily. I almost froze as thick, black blood poured from the wound and immediately turned into a rancid vapor that stung my nostrils before vanishing. I'd never seen blood like that, but it didn't matter; whatever these things were, they needed to die. I wasn't a great guy, but I wasn't about to stand aside and watch a slaughter, not when I could do something about it.

Another warrior lunged at me, stabbing with a serrated spear that slammed into my armored coat like an orc's fist. I grabbed the spear right behind the shaft, and they yanked backward, trying to pull it free. I let myself be pulled with them, using that momentum to ram my blade into their chest. I twisted the sword and pulled it free, then kicked them backward away from me. Another slashed at me with a scythe-like weapon that dragged across my jacket and made me stumble forward, but as it passed, I grabbed the shaft and yanked. I wished I could see the shock on the warrior's face as it staggered toward me, pulled by the strength the Hag sent flowing through my body. That shock lasted only a moment before I slashed it across the throat, cutting through the front half of its neck and twisting to avoid the spray of black, volatile blood.

Behind me, Ferdi's axe flashed and spun, tearing through black armor with ease and lopping off limbs left and right. Literally, she lopped off left arms, right arms, left legs… You get the idea. To my right, Millie slowly retreated toward me, dodging a fighter wielding a wicked axe that chopped mercilessly at her. I took a chance and triggered Fool of Senses, willing it to mask the redhead's presence from sight and sound. Her attacker staggered and looked around wildly, unable to see her, and in that moment, she rose up and jammed her dagger into the bottom of its chin. It dropped as he blade sliced its brain, and she backpedaled toward me, her eyes wild and her face pale.

"Dammit, Murf, why does this happen every time we get together?" she shouted at me.

"It's probably something you're doing," I shouted back. "It never happened before we met!"

"Me? I don't think so! This is all you!" Another warrior lunged toward me, and I parried its strike while she slipped to its side and stabbed it in the back. She stared at it in surprise as it died without even trying to dodge her attack for fight back. "What the hell?"

"Didn't I tell you?" I grinned. "They can't see you or hear you."

"What? How?"

"New ability of mine. I'm not sure how well it works, though, so it's probably best if you stay close to me."

She gave me an unreadable look, then smiled at me. "Yes, I guess that probably would be best, Murf." She leaned over and kissed my cheek. "Thanks."

"Not the time, people!" Ferdi shouted as she moved to my flank. "Flirt later; fight now!"

"Hey, you got it right, Ferdi!" I called back.

"Got what right?"

"Flirting! That actually was flirting that time. Way to go!"

"Shut up and kill something, Murf!"

Armored warriors threw themselves at us and died swiftly. Ferdi's axe cut them to pieces; Millie's unseen daggers crippled and wounded them; my sword stabbed through their hearts or slashed their throats. More and more of them turned their focus to us, and while I wasn't happy to be the object of their attention, while they fought us, they weren't killing a bunch of innocents.

As we fought, a loud crack and a flash of light burst out of the back of the room. I felt surges of power roll out of me, and I knew that Charlie and Azara were fighting, as well. I could feel the little ferret drawing closer, and after a couple minutes, Charlie appeared at the edge of the crowd. He flew through the air as he flung himself at an armored warrior, then vanished as his body slipped through the gaps in its armor with ease. The warrior stiffened and flung its hands up to its throat, and a moment later, ice spread across its armor as Charlie used Freezing Touch on its neck. A sudden surge of energy slammed into the thing, and its head flew from its body with a loud snap as Azara appeared, holding up a glowing card. Charlie emerged from the headless body and led the woman toward the three of us.

"Azara!" I said with relief as she appeared. "Are you okay?"

"Well enough, Murf, thanks to your companion, here." She nodded at Charlie. "It's quite effective—and very dangerous."

"Only when he doesn't like you," I grinned. "Right, Charlie?"

"Right, Dad!" The little ferret ran up my body and perched invisibly on my shoulder. *"Did I do good?"*

"You did great, buddy. I'm proud of you!"

"Thanks!"

"Do you know what these things are, Murf?" Azara asked in a voice filled with dread.

"What they are?" I echoed, stabbing another warrior in the chest and kicking it away. An arc of lightning flashed past my shoulder and slammed into the one behind the person I'd just ended. "Don't you mean, 'who they are'?"

"I know what I said, Murf. Those aren't people. They're demons."

I paused at her words, and that let the next armored figure jam a sword into my chest. My coat turned it aside, but it still throbbed painfully and made me step backward. "Wait, are you being figurative? As in, 'those are really bad people, and we should kill them Murf'?"

"No, I mean, those are literal demons. Spawn of the infernal realms." She shivered. "The cards are screaming at their presence."

"They die like anything else," Ferdi shrugged, beheading a warrior with a sweep of her axe.

"No, they don't. Killing them simply banishes them, nothing more. Their summoner can bring them back, so long as he has the power."

"They were right about you, avian. You truly are a gifted diviner."

I whirled to see Bloodfane rising a little unsteadily from behind the table. A purple bruise covered his face where Ferdi had hit him, but even as I watched, the discoloration began to fade and drain away. He touched his face rather gingerly, then nodded at Azara. "She's right, by the way. That's exactly what those are—and no matter how many you kill, there'll be another to take its place."

"I'll bet they'll stop if I kill you," Ferdi said in a cold voice, hefting her weapon. "The punch didn't do it. Maybe this will work better."

"Not very likely. Better have tried. For example…" He turned as a huge ursid warrior lumbered toward him, wielding a huge axe and roaring in fury. Bloodfane lifted his hand and pointed at the bear-man, and a jet of purple fire shot from his palm and slammed into the warrior. The bear lurched and stumbled as the fire sank into him, then spurted out the center of his chest. He dropped to his knees and collapsed, lifeless, on the floor with violet fire blazing from his chest. Bloodfane just shook his head.

"What a waste," he sighed, then clapped his hands together. Four more warriors, these larger and more heavily armored than the rest, suddenly appeared between us and him. "Ah, well. I still have a whole deck awaiting me. Take them."

I barely managed to register it as several figures appeared from nowhere and moved toward us. The only thing that my brain really processed was that purple fire. I'd seen it before, and I knew what it meant.

Bloodfane was Shadow Man, and suddenly, I realized that we were in a whole shitload of trouble.

59

"Get down, Murf!" A strong hand grabbed my jacket and yanked me down, just as a blast of flame washed over me. I looked up and saw a familiar-looking goblin standing beside and behind Bloodfane, holding up a card in his hand. He lifted another in his hand, and a blast of light shot from it, racing toward us. The light struck a sparkling shield and faded out in an instant, and I looked back over my shoulder to see Azara standing behind me, her hands outstretched and her eyes blazing. Every feather on her body stood fluffed out, and her nostrils flared furiously.

"You think to use the cards against me, goblin?" she asked, her cold voice laced with fury.

"You're no Holder, bird!" the goblin shouted back. "You don't stand a chance!"

"And you are no cartomancer," she hissed. "The cards revile you. I can hear them screaming in your grip. They will never serve you as well as they do me, no matter what you have buried in your soul."

"Look out!" Millie's slightly panicked shout drew my attention back to the four figures that rushed toward us, lifting massive weapons, their armor clanking as they ran. Ferdi met the first with a battle cry, swinging her axe at it furiously, but the creature dodged nimbly aside and responded with a slash by its curved sword that Ferdi barely avoided.

The second demon charged at me, and I shook off my shock and confusion as it swung a wicked poleaxe in my direction. I tried to dodge, but the blade caught my shoulder, and I hissed as it cut through the protection of my jacket and drew a burning line along my upper arm. I ducked under the blow and stabbed at its leg, but it stepped back and kicked at my sword, forcing me to pull it back to keep from having it knocked from my grasp. Millie began to slip around behind it, but the third creature rushed her, clearly able to see her despite the rake's power. She leaped back, avoiding a sword slash, then twisted sideways, barely dodging the following thrust.

The warrior charged me, trying to drive me backward with its axe, but I knew I couldn't retreat. Azara was behind me, and if I moved, it would have her. I did my best to block the blow, sensing that it was better to use the sword to guide the weapon than to try and stop it, but the sheer force behind it was enough to knock me off-balance. It thrust with the weapon, and the spearpoint on the tip of it caught my shoulder, punching through the jacket and stabbing into me. I jerked backward, then knocked the axe upward and dove under it, slashing with my sword. The knight leaped back, giving me a little more room to move, then struck at me again. This time, I felt more comfortable sliding the blow; apparently, Melee Mastery worked better when I actually had to do things over and over rather than just putting the knowledge in my brain or whatever it did. I spun beneath the blow and slashed, and my blade cut through the armor on the warrior's thigh with a screech of twisting metal. It stumbled back, favoring that leg, but before I could pursue it, a spear stabbed at me, forcing me to jump backward as the last knight joined its partner, teaming up against me.

"Now, that's totally unfair," I grunted as I blocked another thrust and grabbed the spear, trying to pull its owner toward me. "Ferdi's the fighter! Gang up on her!"

"I'm having enough trouble here, Murf," the halfling shouted back as she ducked a sword slash and leaped over a low cut. "I don't need more!"

"Don't even think about pawning them on me, Murf!" Millie panted as she danced around her enemy's heavy sword, unable to get close enough to use her knives. "I'm barely holding my own!"

"Fine," I grumbled. "I'll do it myself." I let go of the spear as a poleaxe swept toward me, forcing me to twist sideways to dodge. I blocked another spear thrust, then ducked an axe blow. The two knights attacked me viciously, and while my card made it possible for me to hold my own— or at least not get stabbed instantly—it wasn't enough to let me actually attack them. Their blows got past my defense, but each one did less damage as the Hag adapted to them. We were at an impasse. I couldn't attack them, but they couldn't really hurt me, and soon, they wouldn't be able to hurt me at all. I reached down and pressed the knight of coins harder, pouring more of its power into me. I just needed to be a little better, a little faster, a tiny bit more skilled...

Pain flared in my lower back, and my legs went numb as something cold slid through my coat and armored skin and plunged into my spine. I dropped, my legs no longer working, and caught myself on my hands. I looked back and saw a man in gray clothing standing behind me, his slim dagger dripping with my blood pressed against Azara's throat. He glared at me, his eyes hard behind his mask.

"You killed Cassa, you fucker," he growled. "Now, I'll return the favor." His arm tensed as he prepared to cut Azara's throat, but before he could, a blue flash leaped from my shoulder and slammed into him. The man cried out as Charlie appeared on his face, snarling and biting. He swept a hand at the ferret, but Charlie turned insubstantial and let the blow pass through, then solidified instantly and resumed his furious assault.

A foot slammed into my chest, knocking me on my back and pinning me to the ground, and I groaned as I saw one of the armored knights standing above me, one foot on my chest while the other pinned my arm to the ground. Bloodfane walked up beside the demonic knight and peered down at me, his face curious.

"That's quite the trick, Murf. You obviously have cards in you, but I can't feel them. How are you doing that?"

"Unborn baby souls," I grunted. "Lots of them. Plus a little lemon zest. Helps them go down easier."

He chuckled and shook his head. "I really do admire your humor, Murf. The ability to laugh at what you know is your imminent death—and the deaths of your friends—is an admirable trait." His face hardened. "However, play time is over. Tell me how you're hiding your cards, and maybe I'll let your friends go."

"Sorry, Bloodfane," I shook my head. "You tried that one once already, remember? Right before you tossed us into the Ochre Forest. Fool me once, shame on you. Fool me twice, I kick you in the nuts."

"I seem to recall that saying a little differently. One of your laws?"

"Nope. Just a promise." My foot lashed up and slammed into the man's crotch, and he cried out and fell backward, clutching his stones. Poor Bloodfane had given me far too much of the one thing I really needed: time. Time enough for the Hag to adapt to the wound in my back and return feeling to my legs. I still hurt, and my back screamed as I kicked upward, but at least I wasn't paralyzed anymore.

That woman could do wonders. I supposed I should start being nicer to her. Or at least consider it.

Power roared down my arm as I yanked upward, and the knight above me staggered as I tore my arm free of its foot. My blade slashed across the knee pinning me down, and the weapon sliced through it with a screech of metal. The off-balance and now one-legged knight crashed backward to the floor, its ass slamming onto my foot before I yanked it free and scrambled up to stand. The other knight leaped toward me, stabbing with its spear, but I twisted to the side, grabbed the weapon again, and yanked, hard. This time, the power roaring through me jerked the knight off-balance, and it stumbled toward me.

I lunged forward, ramming my blade through its neck, then took the spear and swept it outward, slamming the haft into the knight facing Millie. It staggered backward, and Millie lunged forward, past its blade to plunge her knives in the side of its neck. It dropped, and I reversed the spear before jamming it down into the chest of the knight I'd crippled.

I readied myself to go help Ferdi, but an arc of lightning ripped past me and tore into her opponent, stunning it for a second, easily long enough for Ferdi's axe to whip out and cleave its head from its shoulders. I looked past where Bloodfane had been and saw the goblin on the ground, shivering and shaking, its flesh burnt and frozen. Behind me, Azara stood, swaying slightly, her dress torn and her face slightly burnt, but with power glowing from her like a damn bonfire.

I spun to check on Charlie and saw that Azara had helped him first; the assassin lay on the floor, shivering and trembling with a scorch mark on his chest. Charlie stood atop him like a victorious hero. The ferret vanished for a moment before flowing across the floor. He raced up my body and appeared on my shoulder, clutching a gold coin in his little teeth.

"I got him, Dad!" he said in his piping voice. *"Did you see? I stopped him from hurting you, and I got a present for the pretty lady!"*

"Good job, Charlie," I replied with a chuckle, taking the coin from him. *"Keep an eye on him, though. If he tries to get away or hurt anyone, bite him somewhere it really hurts."*

"You got it, Dad..."

"Enough!" I looked back to see Bloodfane stagger to his feet, his expression a mask of pain. "You think that means anything, Murf? You defeated my knights. Guess what? I've got more, and I'll call them back over and over again until they've killed your friends." He lifted a hand and pointed it toward me. "Too bad you won't be around to see it."

His palm flared purple, and suddenly, a jet of violet energy screamed from his hand and slammed into me. The energy surged down into my chest, ripping and tearing as it went. I gagged and dropped to a knee; the power felt vile and unclean, like someone poured a cesspool down my throat, and I wanted to hurl it back up. It sank into me, though, surging toward the cards in my chest, burning with terrible power...

And in return, power rose within me, crashing into that violet flame and driving it backward. I could feel the Hag's fury as she hurled the hideous energy from my body with terrifying force. The fire winked out, and as it did, I rose unsteadily to my feet, meeting Bloodfane's suddenly terrified gaze.

"What?" he gasped, taking a step backward. "That—that's impossible!" He stepped forward, and another blast of purple fire streaked toward me, crashing into my chest. Once more, the Hag rose to meet it, holding it out and shielding me from its touch. Bloodfane lifted a second hand, and more fire bathed me, wrapping around my body and diving into me, but the Hag's strength and rage protected me, and I took a step forward, lifting my sword. Bloodfane's eyes widened, and he stepped backward, fear showing on his face. That was when Charlie struck.

The little ferret leaped from my shoulder and sailed through the air, not needing the ground to run across as he dodged around the purple flames. I'd instructed the little guy to attack Bloodfane, thinking that he'd bite him in the eye or something and distract him. After all, I'd seen that whatever powers the fake noble had, resistance to damage wasn't one of them. With his fire not an issue, we could swarm him and kill him, and I don't think any of us would have hesitated to do that.

I almost fell as Charlie instead scrambled over the man's arms, leaped toward him—and plunged into the center of his chest. Bloodfane gasped, and his fire guttered out as he clutched his chest, staring at me.

"What—what are you doing?" he asked in a hoarse voice.

"Honestly, I have no clue," I replied sincerely. "This is new to me, too."

Bloodfane suddenly cried out and dropped to his knees, screaming in pain. A moment later, Charlie emerged from the man's back, coming out tail-first. His little feet braced on the warlock's skin as he pulled his head out, seeming to drag himself from the man's chest as Bloodfane screamed in pain. His ears and little whiskers came next, followed by his pink nose. All four legs tensed, and the little guy jerked backward, flinging himself off the warlock's back and landing on the ground. All I could do was stare at the card clutched in his mouth.

Bloodfane was a Holder. And somehow, Charlie had ripped a card from his deck.

The moment the card came free, a ripple passed through the room, and I looked around to see the remaining armored warriors boil away to nothing. Screams and curses quickly quieted into sobs and moans as the carnage ended. I stared in shock as Charlie ran back, darting around Bloodfane and swirling his way up my arm to my shoulder, where he presented me with a card. I picked it up and got a quick glimpse of a hooded figure in a graveyard before the card crumbled to ashes in my grip and flowed away on a breeze.

"H-how?" Bloodfane gasped, rising back to his feet. "That's not possible!"

"How doesn't much matter," I shrugged, brushing off my hands nonchalantly despite the fact that I was a bit freaked out. I'd never had a card just disintegrate on me, after all, and I had a lot of questions about what that meant. They would just have to wait; I was a bit busy at the moment. "What matters is that without your little demons, I'm pretty sure Ferdi, here is going to kill you. A lot."

"I can. I will," the halfling said grimly.

"If I don't first," Azara hissed, lifting up a card. "You betrayed me, Warlock!"

I eyed Millie, who simply shrugged. "I'm not really all that worried about who kills him," she admitted. "As long as he's dead."

The man's eyes narrowed slightly, then widened. "The Labyrinth!" he gasped. "You entered it and completed it! Zeric was right!"

"Guilty as charged," I nodded.

To my surprise, a grin creased Bloodfane's face. "Then you still have some use to me," he laughed. "I'll see you around, Murf." Ferdi lunged for him, but fast as the halfling was, he was even quicker. A brilliant light exploded from his hand, followed by a blast of dark energy that picked us all up and flung us backward. My head slammed into something far too hard for heads to crack into safely, and darkness flooded my vision as I sank into unconsciousness.

60

I blinked my eyes as the darkness shattered around me. I sat up, expecting to see the Guildhall—at least, whatever was left of it after Bloodfane's assault. Jerrick was going to be pissed about that, I knew. Granted, a bunch of people died, but more importantly, at least to him, cleaning up the mess and repairing the damage would probably cost a huge chunk of the gold the Guild made from the tournament. Of course, it all happened because Grodvulf and his guards stood back and did nothing, which meant that the Meritocracy should probably bear at least some of the cost. Maybe all of it. I'd have to make sure Jerrick talked to Millie about that; she could probably help him figure out how to convince the meritocrats…

I paused as I realized that what I was seeing didn't exactly match my expectations. At least, not unless Jerrick had done some massive renovations while I was out. If he had, it was probably time for him to step down as Guild Master. Anyone who redecorated a gambling hall by filling it with inky black, leafless trees and turquoise dirt beneath a cyan sky had obviously lost it and couldn't be trusted to dress themselves, much less manage a guild. Of course, there was another possibility, but I liked it even less than the idea that Jerrick had lost his mind and turned the Guildhall into a magical forest of some kind. Sadly, it was the only option that made sense, especially considering the deep, endless power that flowed through the air and bloomed in the ground beneath me.

"You've gotten better at sensing that," a lyrical, mellow voice said in an amused tone.

I sighed as I recognized the voice and rubbed my forehead. "I don't know if I've gotten better at doing it, or if I'm just paying better attention," I countered morosely.

"Does it really matter which is true? The result is the same."

"True. And either way, I don't much like it." I rose to my feet and turned around to see the beautiful, turquoise-haired, extremely poorly named Eldritch Hag seated at a table made of twisted tree roots. A steaming pot of tea rested on the table, with a cup next to the empty chair that was obviously meant for me. "I'm not really a fan of being here, either."

"Really?" She looked around and took a sip of her own tea. "I'm finding your soul to be quite a pleasant place, myself. Very relaxing."

"You know that there aren't a lot of people who'd find all this…" I waved at the mystical forest around me. "…very relaxing. I think most people would find it downright terrifying."

"But you aren't most people." She gave me a coy wink. "Do I terrify you, Murf?"

"Frankly, yes. Of course, that's because I know who you are and what you can do if I piss you off." I pushed myself to my feet and brushed the dirt and leaves off myself. Not that I probably needed to, I supposed. I didn't think that anything there was real, which meant I wasn't really dirty. Still, appearances had to be maintained, and brushing myself off made me feel a little better.

"So, how exactly did I get here? I thought I had to be in a cathedral, touching a Unity star for this to happen."

"No, although it helps. I can use a symbol of the Unity as a bridge between us, but I can also reach you when you're deeply asleep—or unconscious." She smiled. "Which you are right now, obviously."

"Why haven't you before now, then?"

"There hasn't really been a need," she shrugged. "Doing this takes energy—more when you're asleep than when you're touching a symbol of the Unity—so I tend to save it for times that are important." She grimaced. "This is important."

"I take it that it's about Bloodfane? And him being a warlock? Thanks for the tip about that, by the way." I paused. "That was you, right? I wasn't just imagining things, was I?"

"No, it was me," she laughed. "I'm glad you heard me; I wasn't sure I was getting through for a while, there. I'd been basically screaming at you for the past hour, trying to warn you." She sobered quickly. "And you're right: I wanted to talk to you about him. Actually, we *need* to talk about him, and a few other things."

I lifted my cup, noting that it was suddenly full of steaming tea, and took a sip, enjoying the warmth and heat of it. I closed my eyes, inhaling the scent of the beverage and basically putting off whatever she was going to say. I knew I wouldn't like it. Of course, I wasn't going to like it in a minute, or ten minutes, or a year, so there wasn't much point to stalling. As

I thought that, though, I remembered that I had a question I'd never asked her the last time, one that was actually important and couldn't really wait.

"Before we do that, I have to ask you something," I said, putting down the cup and leaning forward to glare at her. "How do I use you? For my other cards, I just reach inside, and they're there, waiting for me to grab—in a metaphorical sense, at least. How do I do that with you?"

She sighed and gave me a slightly regretful look. "Well, at the moment—you can't, Murf. You can't use me."

"I can't?" I leaned back and gave her a suspicious look. "Why not? Aren't you supposed to be my card?"

"You could say that," she admitted. "It would be just as accurate to say that you're my human, of course, but we'll let that pass for the moment. What matters is that those other cards are arcana. They aren't really aware, not the way you are, so they don't have any say in how they're used. They just sort of exist, and that lets you use them however you please.

"Obviously, I'm different," she shrugged. "I decide how and when I'll be used, and for the moment, that means that I'll lend my power where I think you need it. If you want to have more control over how I use my power, you'll have to keep attuning yourself to me and me to you." She grimaced. "Although no matter what, you'll never be able to use me the way you do those arcana, I'm afraid. I'm not just an object of power to be called upon, Murf. I'll always have my own thoughts and opinions, and even at our closest, we'll be willing allies, maybe even friends, but never servant and master."

I nodded slowly. "That's actually fine with me," I said after a few moments to consider her words. "I'm not really into the whole 'master' concept, to be honest. Plus, you've been doing a decent job so far. At least, I'm still alive, and really, I shouldn't be. Bloodfane's power burned out the cards of every other Holder he hit it with. Obviously, he couldn't do the same to you."

"No, he couldn't, and that's part of what we need to talk about." She sipped her tea again, her eyes hooded as she gazed at me, and I waited patiently. I had a feeling she wanted me to ask her more questions, but I couldn't think of any that mattered. At least, not until she'd said whatever she was going to. Then, I'd know what questions to ask. Maybe. Assuming I understood whatever she was going to say at all, which, judging from past experience, wasn't all that likely.

She set her tea down and rested her hands somewhat primly on her knees. "You see, Murf, the man you call Bloodfane, even though I think we both know that's no more his name than 'Baron Lanly'…"

"It's the name I knew him as the first time he tried to kill me," I shrugged. "While it wasn't the first time someone tried that, it was the closest anyone ever got—at least, until the last few weeks—so it feels sort of memorable."

"I can see that," she chuckled. "Be that as it may, he's not a typical warlock."

"No? He kind of seemed like one, especially as Shadow Man. Villainous mastermind, hidden in darkness, can't take a kick to the crotch…" I shrugged. "Seems fairly normal to me, really."

"He's not, though." She shook her head. "To understand, you have to know how a warlock or zealot gains their powers."

"Unborn baby souls?" I asked hopefully.

"What's with you and the unborn baby souls, Murf?"

"They just seem so typically evil. 'Devouring the souls of the unborn' feels like something any good villain should be doing. I'm kind of disappointed Bloodfane wasn't into it."

"It doesn't even make sense. How would they even gather unborn souls in the first place? They haven't been born yet."

"I refuse to let logic get in the way of a perfectly good idea," I grinned at her, and she rolled her eyes in response.

"Well, oddly enough, you're close. Souls do matter. You see, to get anything from the other worlds, first, a warlock or zealot has to get in touch with one of the powers of those worlds. Once they do, they offer something that power wants—and yes, souls that have actually been born already are a currency that those powers accept—and in return, they get a little bit of the energy of that power. Do you remember what I told you about how this world is in balance? And how that balance affects the powers of the worlds above and below?"

"It weakens them, right?"

"Correct. The whole point of the Unity is to diminish the influence of those powers to the point that they can't affect this world, even through an agent. Most warlocks or zealots can perform a few small tricks similar to what a low arcana might provide a Holder—throw fire, shield themselves from normal attacks, maybe call some unintelligent creature from the other worlds to serve them for an hour or so, that sort of thing."

I frowned. "Bloodfane was obviously stronger than that, though. I take it that's why he's not normal—besides whatever's wrong with his mind, that is?"

"You actually might be right about his mind," she laughed. "Prolonged contact with the other worlds isn't healthy for a mortal's sanity. And yes, compared to most warlocks, he was almost ridiculously strong. Being able to summon a single azdrast warrior is an impressive feat; to summon that many and keep summoning them when they're killed is something even I've never seen."

"Is that what those things are called? Ass-hat warriors?"

"Azdrast," she corrected. "The foot soldiers of most of the worlds below."

"I like ass-hat better," I grinned, then sobered quickly. "Okay, so he was strong. He still lost and ran away like a goblin lass at an elf orgy. So, why do you seem so upset?"

"Because he was a Holder, Murf. That's what makes him so powerful. He was channeling infernal energy through his cards, boosting its effect. That card you took from him? It was the Reaper, the Infernal Guide. It's part of the deck of powers, and normally, it allows someone to draw infernal energy or maybe summon a powerful creature. He poured infernal energy through it to call that many warriors, and once he lost it, he lost the ability to keep all of them in our world at the same time."

"Hey, why did it crumble to ashes like that?"

"Cards are expressions of the Unity, Murf. Infernal energy isn't good for us. It must have been leeching power from his soul to stay intact, and once it was out, it ran out of energy and dissipated."

"So, that card's just gone?" I asked, startled.

"No. Its energy was returned to the Unity. Besides, powers aren't unique, remember? There are other Reapers out there."

"Got it," I nodded. "Okay, he's a Holder. I still don't see the issue."

"Exactly, Murf. You didn't see." She leaned forward and glared at me, placing her hands on the table. I leaned back a little nervously from the intensity of her stare. "When you looked at him, did you see his status? His hole card? Probable abilities?"

"No," I shook my head, suddenly realizing that she was right. "I didn't. Why didn't I?"

"You didn't because I couldn't sense them myself," she sighed. "And there's only one way he could hide his cards from me. He has to be like you, Murf."

"Like me? Like me, how?"

"He has a Cabal card. He's got it as his hole card. That's the only way he could shield his cards from me."

I stared at her in shock for a few seconds. "He—wait, what?"

"It's true. I recognized the power he holds. It's the Cabal of destruction. I can't tell you more about it, but I can tell you that it's a powerful card, and it took most of what I had to shield you from it."

"I—no," I shook my head. "The odds of that—just running into another Cabal Holder—they have to be practically zero!"

"By accident? Maybe, although you forget that I call the others to me, and that includes my younger siblings. Those odds will rise over time. However, this was no accident. Bloodfane was here for me."

"For you? How would he know about you?"

"I misspoke. He wasn't here for me, personally. He was here because after pulling one Cabal, he probably hoped to pull another from my Labyrinth. It's exactly what someone looking for a Cabal would hope for: a pristine Labyrinth, one that's been tried but unbeaten for a century or more, would gather enough of the Unity's power for a Cabal to be a possible reward. If he can pull one, he can pull another. That's why he wanted to clear my Labyrinth; he hoped to find one of us and add them to his deck." She shivered. "And that makes him very, very dangerous, Murf."

"Considering how powerful you alone are? I can imagine how strong someone holding two of the Cabal in their deck would be."

"Yes, but that's not the danger." She paused. "I can't tell you much, Murf. The Unity forbids it. However, I will say that bringing all of us together—me and my siblings—is a very, very dangerous idea. If a man like Bloodfane manages it…" She shuddered again. "It could be the end of this world, Murf. Of all life on it."

I stared at her again in shocked amazement. "Please tell me you're exaggerating."

"With all of us together, Bloodfane could hand this world to his masters, whoever they are. It would be the end of the Unity, and probably the end of life as you know it. Even if he didn't, all of us in the hands of a man so hungry for power could be just as bad." She shook her head. "It would be worse than anything you could imagine, Murf, trust me."

"Let me guess: you expect me to stop him," I groaned. "I'm no hero, lady. I don't want the world destroyed, obviously, but I'm not the guy to save it."

"I don't think you'll have a choice," she laughed. "I told you: I call the others to me. They'll find you, eventually, one way or the other." She grimaced. "Plus, it's likely that Bloodfane suspects you have one of us. Any lesser card, even something as powerful as a triumph of powers, would have at least been damaged by his ability. You surprised him this time, but if you meet him again—no, when he finds you again, he'll be more prepared."

She reached across the table and poked my chest. "Which means you have to be, as well. You've got a good start with that rake, but you need to keep building out your deck. Follow Azara's advice, but listen to Ferdi's, too. You need balance and strength in equal measures to survive what I fear is coming."

"And what's that?"

"You'll see soon enough. You're about to wake up, so we're out of time. Goodbye for now, Murf." She stood up, and I felt a force lifting me away from the table.

"Wait!" I said loudly, fighting against that force without any effect. "I still have some questions!"

"Sorry!" She shrugged, and the entire world around her seemed to shrug with her. "Oh, last thing! Get a Unity medallion! It'll make it easier…"

The eldritch forest spun away, and light poured into my eyes as pain flared in my face.

61

"Murf! Murf!" The voice that spoke my name in a deep, familiar growl sounded like it was a mixture of truly pissed and slightly worried. Something smacked my cheek, rocking my head sideways a bit. "Wake your ass up, damn you!"

"Jerrick," I growled, fluttering my eyes open and squinting at the sudden light stabbing into them. "Do you really think it's a good idea to slap around someone who got knocked out like that?"

"Told you!" a familiar voice laughed, and I looked over to see Eegla standing behind the Guild Master, a tense smile plastered on her face.

"I don't have time for nice, Murf," the man growled, hauling me to me feet. I swayed a bit as the world spun around me, but it quickly stabilized. My head pounded; my neck and back throbbed; my mouth tasted like I'd made out with a syphilitic orc grandmother; my chest burned and stung from where Bloodfane's fire hit it. In other words, I felt like shit, but when I looked around at the wreckage of the outer hall, I realized that I was definitely one of the lucky ones.

Bodies lay everywhere in the hall, dozens of them scattered all over the place. Fancily dressed nobles and merchants lay in pools of their own blood beside eviscerated commoners. Elderly grandparents had fallen clutching their helpless grandchildren, all of them still and unmoving. Heads and limbs were flung everywhere like debris after a bad storm. The smell of blood and worse filled the room, and the sounds of weeping, moaning, and sobbing served as a grim melodic background for the horrid scene.

About all I could think was, *"Well, at least it's not on fire this time."*

"What the fuck happened, Murf?" Jerrick demanded. "What did you do to my Guildhall?"

"Me?" I laughed, shaking my head. I winced as I realized that was a bad idea. The Hag would heal me soon enough, but she hadn't quite gotten around to it yet, and the motion felt like someone stabbed a pick just behind my right eye. "How in the hell do you think I did all this?"

"Because the damn meritocrat is screaming that you're to blame," Eegla said grimly. "What happened, Murf?"

"Exactly what I warned you would happen. Bloodfane. Or Baron Lanly, I guess he was calling himself." I gestured at the carnage. "He did this."

"How?" Jerrick growled.

"Same way he did the last time. Called a bunch of demon warriors and set them to killing people." I looked at him curiously. "You saw them, right? The black-armored people with swords and axes?"

"We didn't see anything, Murf," Eegla sighed. "We were trapped up in the higher offices. Grodvulf's people wouldn't let us out. Said it was for our own safety."

"Start at the beginning, Murf," Jerrick sighed, rubbing his head. "What happened, here?"

"You want the short version or the long version?"

"Start with the short one, and we'll go from there."

"Short version? I made Bloodfane as a warlock, someone who draws power from the worlds below, and called him out on it—and the fact that he was cheating. He demanded proof, and I said we should call Azara for a divination. He either knew or at least suspected she might see through him, so rather than being kicked out of the tournament and kept from getting his hands on that full deck the meritocrat put up as a secondary prize— probably at Bloodfane's suggestion—he unleashed hell on the Guild. Literally."

"How did you know he was a warlock?" Eegla asked.

"I've felt it before," I lied. "It's something unnatural inside of them. He had it well, though. Took me a while to realize what I was feeling."

"And then?" Jerrick pressed.

"Then? A bunch of people died, Jerrick. I would have, but Ferdi had snuck a bunch of weapons in, and she gave some to me and Millie. The three of us plus Azara managed to keep from being killed until the warriors just kind of vanished." I shrugged. "And then Bloodfane said something about seeing me again, disappeared, and threw us all backward. I must have hit something hard because the next thing I knew, your dumb ass was slapping me awake and shouting in my face." I looked around. "Speaking of them, are they okay?"

"They're fine," Eegla assured me. "Millie and Azara were both out, like you, but Ferdi wasn't, and she took them into the hall to let them rest. Said they needed protection more than you did." Her eyebrows rose quizzically, but I didn't answer her unspoken question. After a moment of silence, Jerrick spoke again.

"Okay, that was the short version. Now, for the long..." The man cut off as a bellow roared out over the room with a voice that was sadly all too familiar.

"There he is!" Grodvulf shouted, making my head pound from the sheer volume of the noise. "The man who did all this! Arrest him, immediately, and prepare him for execution!"

"You know that you can't take him from the hall, Grodvulf," Eegla said with a faint sneer as she looked at the speckled canid. "Not without violating our charter."

"So? After he's executed, we'll draw up a new charter, one that will treat the guilds like the subservient entities that they are..."

"And then we'd have no guilds, and without them, Canis would become a backwater within a handful of years, Grodvulf," a sharp, acerbic voice spoke. We all turned and saw a female canid enter the room, surrounded by a dozen heavily armed guards, her golden fur gleaming in the light of the oil lamps. She stepped delicately around the hall, avoiding the bodies and puddles of blood, no doubt worried about staining her green silk clothing and matching leather shoes. "Is that what you want?"

"What are you doing here, Kurrgetha?" the meritocrat asked in a voice dripping with venom. "I don't recall summoning you."

"I'm here as a representative of the Meritocracy, of course, Grodvulf. I received an anonymous tip that something like this might happen tonight, so my guards and I rushed here to stop it." She made a sorrowful face and shook her head sadly. "Sadly, we arrived too late. Truly, a horrific act, perhaps the worst slaughter this city's ever seen—and at the tournament that you alone organized." Her sorrow faded to evil glee as she looked at the black-and-white spotted canid. "Someone's going to have to be blamed for this, you know."

"I have the perpetrator right here!" Grodvulf snarled, pointing at me. "He claims the sanctuary of the guild, but considering the awful nature of this atrocity, I'm denying it to him!"

"And how do you know that he did this?" she asked, then looked around. "Indeed, how could one man do all of this? That hardly seems possible, Grodvulf."

"I saw him with my own eyes, Kurrgetha. I witnessed the whole thing."

I couldn't help but snort, and both meritocrats turned and looked at me, one curiously and the other with open hatred. Jerrick flashed me a warning glance, but I ignored him as I stepped toward the pair.

"That has to be the single dumbest accusation I've ever heard," I said, chuckling as I spoke. "Seriously, Grodvulf. That's the best you can do? You're not even trying!"

"You dare to mock me, Murderer?" he growled.

"Not you, Meritocrat. That stupid thing you just said: that I did all this. It's idiotic." I waved a hand at the room. "First, she's right. How could I do all this? Kill all these people and fight the guild guards, just little, old me?"

"You hired a band of mercenaries. I saw them..."

"So did I," I cut him off. "And more to the point, so did every single person still alive here. They all saw the 'mercenaries'—and I'm sure plenty of them saw me fighting against them."

"Obviously, they turned on you. Your depravity must have sickened even them..."

"And those same people," I kept going, rolling right over him, "also probably heard them taking orders from someone: your old buddy, Bloodfane. Oops, I mean, Baron Lanly. The man who confessed that the whole thing was his idea, that you were part of it, and that you intended to let all these people die and then try to install yourself as the sole leader of the city afterward."

"You lie!" the man snarled, taking a step toward me, but Kurrgetha's guards stepped forward ominously, and he froze, realizing that her fighters outnumbered his own. The female canid stepped between the two of us, her eyes bright and her expression hopeful.

"You heard this confession, then?" she asked me. "Would you be willing to testify about this before the Meritocracy?"

"Happily," I shrugged.

"This man is a known liar, thief, and murderer!" Grodvulf thundered. "His testimony would never stand!"

"Perhaps mine would, then." Another voice spoke, and I saw Carcrick hobble toward me, favoring a leg that had a long gash down it. "I also heard the mercenaries receiving orders from the human noble."

"And I heard him confess his plans to Murf," Horstya purred, sashaying into view, somehow untouched by the carnage and bloodshed. "I'd be happy to tell the Meritocracy about it."

"I'm sure his companions did, too," Eegla added. "One of whom is a cartomancer of this city well-known for her honesty. Another is an oath-bound halfling who I don't believe can lie." She flashed the man a wicked grin. "And the last is Millicent Deepwater, in the direct line of the Plutarch of Deepwater—who, I imagine, is going to be very, very unhappy to hear that his granddaughter was put in harm's way. Pretty sure he's going to be looking for someone to take his displeasure out on, and I doubt a scapegoat's going to satisfy him." She tapped her chin thoughtfully. "You think he's got enough money to hire the Black Roses to remove the whole Meritocracy? I'm betting he does."

"And if that's not enough," I chuckled, "all we have to do is look at your guards, Grodvulf. Half the Guild's guards are dead, but yours don't have a scratch on them. It's almost like you kept them from fighting." I shook my head. "Once word gets out that you let all these people die just to keep yourself safe, you'll be lucky not to have rioting in the streets."

"That's enough for me," Kurrgetha said, her voice gleeful as she spoke. "Grodvulf, I place you under arrest for murder, false accusation, and conspiracy to commit treason. Guards, seize the accused traitor and have him placed in the prison…" She hesitated and grimaced. "In the tower cell, of course. It wouldn't do to throw a meritocrat in with the murderers and rapists—at least, not until he's been properly tried and found guilty, of course."

"No!" the man screamed as the ursids who'd had his back up until a moment ago grabbed him and hauled his arms behind him. He struggled vainly against their strength as one of them clicked a set of manacles into place around his wrists. "Stop this! You can't do this! I'm a member of the Meritocracy!"

"Not for long, Grodvulf," Kurrgetha purred. "Once the others hear the testimony of how you intended to supplant us—and, of course, how you not only allowed this terrible tragedy to occur but actually actively assisted the perpetrator—they'll sentence you to death." She pursed her lips. "Perhaps we could send your head and some small portion of your fortune to the Plutarch as an apology for allowing his granddaughter be placed in danger. I'm sure you'd make an excellent trophy."

"NO!" the former meritocrat screeched, kicking and thrashing as two of the guards hauled him away. "You can't do this! Let me go!"

As the ursids dragged the man out of the Guild hall, Kurrgetha turned toward me, her expression clearly delighted as she held her hand out toward me. "Well, this was certainly an unexpected windfall," she said throatily. "I hoped to use this tragedy to discredit Grodvulf and weaken his position—he demanded to be in sole charge of the plans for the tournament, after all, which gave him sole responsibility—but I never imagined it would lead to his utter disgrace. And I have you to thank for it, Mister..." She paused. "Forgive me, I don't believe I ever got your name."

"Murf, milady Meritocrat," I bowed to her, taking her hand and brushing it lightly with my lips, ignoring the feeling of fur against my skin. "Just Murf."

"Mr. Murf. You've done me quite a favor today. What could I possibly offer you in return for this gift?" She took a step toward me, her expression sultry and her voice lowering as she spoke. I kept a bland expression on my face as I straightened, still holding her hand lightly.

"Well, it would be nice if the bounty Grodvulf laid on my head happened to go away," I smiled at her. "It does make traveling about the city—inconvenient."

"A mere trifle," she said airily. "I'm certain that any bounties the former meritocrat placed will be rescinded by the end of the day, no matter who they target. Is that all that I could do for you?"

I looked around at the ruins of the Guildhall. "I suppose the guild could use some help cleaning up and repairing the damage from this, milady." I flashed her a sly grin. "The sort of help that a large portion of Grodvulf's fortune might offer, in fact. You know, just so it doesn't go to his heirs."

"That does seem reasonable," she chuckled, her grin matching mine. "Surely, though, you can think of something else I can do for you—or perhaps to you?"

"I can think of any number of things, milady. Sadly, while my spirit is willing, my body's somewhat battered at the moment—far too battered to handle someone with your obvious skill." I brushed her hand with my lips again. "Maybe we could say that you owe me a favor once I'm in better shape?"

"I could agree to that," she laughed, her voice low before she turned to Jerrick. "Guild Master. It seems that there'll be an opening in the Meritocracy soon. Perhaps you'd consider applying for it?"

"With all due respect, Meritocrat, I've got enough trouble just running the Guildhall," he said in a tired voice. "A whole city might be a bit much."

"It's a challenge, to be sure, but it can be quite rewarding." She laughed again. "And speaking of challenges, I need to go see how I can leverage Grodvulf's disgrace before the others hear about it and pounce on his holdings like vultures."

"You seem to have a highly developed sense of self-interest, milady," I laughed with her. "I can appreciate that."

"Yes, I could tell you would. You played the game excellently today, yourself, Mr. Murf."

"I simply played the hand I was dealt," I shrugged. "That's all any of us can do."

"Indeed. You might make a good meritocrat yourself—if only you weren't a human." She shrugged, then nodded toward us. "Good day, gentlemen."

"Milady." I bowed toward her, lifting my hat slightly. As she moved away, Jerrick grabbed my arm and hauled me backward toward the stairs leading into the upper offices.

"My office, Murf," he growled. "Now."

"In a hurry, Jerrick?" I asked calmly as he pulled me along. "If you're looking for the same thing as the meritocrat, my body is definitely too battered for that—and it always will be, I'm afraid."

"Don't flatter yourself. It's time for the long version—the very long version. This town's had disaster after disaster from the moment you stepped foot in it, and I want to know why—so I can decide how far up your ass to plant my foot."

"I told you, Jerrick, I'm really not in the mood for that sort of thing," I shook my head. "And to be clear, I never will be."

"Good, because I definitely don't want you to enjoy it. Now, let's go have a nice, long chat, Murf, and you can tell me what the hell's really been going on in my Guildhall."

62

As I followed Jerrick back to his office, I took the moment to glance at some cards the Hag apparently had waiting for me.

Unity Achievement!
You have defeated agents of the Infernal! Reward: +200 UP per creature slain.
+2,000 UP

Unity Achievement!
You have slain powerful agents of the Infernal! Reward: +1,000 UP per creature slain.
+2,000 UP

Unity Achievement!
You have defeated a mortal agent of the Infernal! As this agent is also a Holder and possesses an Incredibly rare profession, UP rewards are tripled!
+4,800 UP

Rank Up!
You have reached Rank 5!
You receive:
Luck +3, Skill +2, Capacity +2

Harmonies:
Coins +4, Blades +5, Cups +1, Stars +2
Infernal -1, Worldly +2, Divine +1

New Ability!

For reaching Rank 5 in Cabalist, you
gain the ability Flip the Card!

Flip the Card
You can attempt to shut down a
single active card ability. Always
works against any arcana. The
chance for success against a power or
cabal is equal to an attack at base
power equal to your rank x 15 against
the ability's base power. Once
successful, both the ability and the
card negated may not be activated
again for 1 hour.

I wasn't sure how useful the new ability would actually be, especially since it wasn't guaranteed to succeed, but I supposed being able to turn off another Holder's defenses or stop them from tossing lightning at my face could be handy. That would be a worry for another day, though. At least, I hoped so. I really wasn't up for any more fighting, at least not for the next year or two. Or ten.

The best part of the next hour or so was seeing Aggie. The woman was barely recognizable when I entered the outer office. Her hair was down and styled, she had a light layer of cosmetics on her face, her dress had an actual bodice, and most of all, she smiled at me when I entered.

"Mr. Murf," she said pleasantly. "So nice to see you again."

"You, too, Aggie," I replied, tipping my hat toward her. "You're looking—very well, actually."

"Why thank you," she said demurely, touching her chest without covering it. I was pretty impressed; it felt like she'd relaxed immeasurably, and I was sure that made Jerrick's life easier. As we entered the office, I jerked my thumb back toward the woman with a wide grin, and Jerrick rolled his eyes and grunted.

"Yes, she's been easier to get along with, Murf. Apparently, your idea worked. Congratulations. Now, sit down and tell me what the hell's going on—and start at the beginning."

"The beginning?" I tapped my chin. "Well, I'm not up on al the creation stories, but I think the beastlings say that the world started as the fruit of a giant tree, don't they? And then another tree grew out of the fruit, and a monkey lived in the tree and ate the fruit and got wise…"

"Not exactly, and not what I meant. Start when you came to Canis. How did we get from there to here?"

I paused. "Okay, but there are going to be some things I'm not going to be able to tell you, Jerrick."

His eyes widened in surprise. "What do you mean? What things?"

"Things that I have to keep secret for my own safety—and yours. If you don't know, people like Bloodfane can't torture the information out of you."

"I think you're being a bit dramatic, Murf," he snorted, but I shook my head in denial.

"No, I'm not," I said seriously. "I've seen him torturing people to get their cards. I saw what was left of them—it wasn't pretty. He'd do the same to you—or Eegla—in a heartbeat if he thought you had information and were withholding it. If I don't give you that information, though, there's no reason for him to do that."

"Jerrick, he killed almost sixty people and was willing to kill two hundred," Eegla said quietly. "Maybe we should accept that Murf's telling the truth this time."

The canid grunted, then looked at me. "Fine. Tell me what you can, then."

I launched into a much more detailed explanation of the events of the past few weeks. I told him about my descent into the Labyrinth and revealed that I'd become an accidental Holder. I talked about Alerion and Taveroth, and how I'd killed them in the Labyrinth. I didn't say anything about Millie being a Holder, but I did tell him that she had some pretty extensive weapon training thanks to her grandfather, and he seemed to accept that.

As I spoke, the door opened, and the orc messenger appeared, leading Ferdi into the room. I looked the halfling up and down; her armor was dented and rent in places, her face had dried blood congealed on her cheeks and neck, and her braids were loose and matted. She looked exhausted, but I saw the fierce look of triumph in her eyes as she strode into the office. Jerrick gestured at one of his chairs, but she shook her head firmly.

"I prefer to stand, Guild Master," she told him in a voice like iron. "I can react faster that way."

"You're not in any danger here, ma'am," he said deferentially. "You have my word that you can relax."

"I can. I won't." She looked down at me. "You look like shit, Murf."

"Same to you, Ferdi," I chuckled. "How is everyone?"

"Sleeping. You should really all start wearing armor, you know. Or helmets, at least."

"My coat is armored," I protested. "And I was wearing a hat!"

"Not the same thing. Did it stop you from being knocked out when you hit me?"

I blinked in surprise. "Wait—I hit you?"

"Yep. Head slammed right into my back, and you were out like an oil lamp. Made an impressive sound, though."

"I'll bet. I assume you were fine?"

"Of course. I was wearing armor in a fight like a sane person, so it didn't hurt me at all. Well, except for being knocked down and having a couple hundred pounds of gangly human sprawled all over me. You're too tall, Murf."

"Can we get this back on track?" Jerrick sighed. "I really do have a lot to do today."

"Hey, I'm happy dropping the matter here," I shrugged. "You're the one who wants all the details."

"Need, Murf. I need the details. I'm going to have to report this to the Guild Court, and I need to know what to say. Now, talk."

I continued my story, with Jerrick and Eegla interjecting every so often with questions while Ferdi jumped in to clarify things every so often. Millie entered the room ten minutes later, her face pale but otherwise seemingly in good shape, and Jerrick halted the interrogation to inquire about her health, offer her something to eat, and ask if she wanted to go rest in her room.

"You never gave me those choices, Jerrick," I complained. "You didn't even ask if I'm okay!"

"I like her better," he growled.

"Meaning he's more worried about what my family's going to say about all this," Millie sighed.

"It can be both, Miss Deepwater."

"It can, but it isn't, and if you don't start calling me 'Millie', Guild Master, I swear that I'll send a letter to my grandfather telling him that you tried to molest me while I was unconscious."

He looked startled but nodded and gestured at me to continue.

The story went that way, in bits and pieces. Azara joined us a few minutes after Millie arrived, looking remarkably healthy for having been knocked the fuck out, which I assumed meant she'd healed herself. I told the main part of the tale, with the others adding bits I missed or answering questions. It took a full hour to tell that way, and my voice was dry and scratchy by the end.

"And you know the rest," I finished. "Bloodfane didn't want Azara to reveal him, but he knew that she could, so he struck before she had a chance to. He and Grodvulf planned it: he'd slaughter everyone, Grodvulf would take the credit for 'saving' the upper echelons of the Guild and driving off the attackers. Grodvulf is the hero and takes over the Meritocracy; Bloodfane keeps the full deck that was being used as a prize. We stopped him, and he ran away when his demons vanished and his Holders were beaten." I frowned. "What happened to them, anyway? The goblin and the assassin?"

"They vanished when Bloodfane did," Ferdi grunted. "Both of them faded out of sight, and by the time I'd untangled myself from you, they were long gone."

The man leaned back and rubbed his face with his hands. "This—this is a lot to take in, Murf. How the hell am I supposed to write all that into a report?"

"You don't, Guild Master," Millie shrugged.

He shook his head tiredly. "I have to report this, Miss—I mean, Millie. The Court would have my head if I didn't."

"You mean, you have to report about the plot between Grodvulf and Bloodfane to steal the tournament prize? And how they tried to falsely blame it all on a Guild member in good standing? Yes, you probably should report that."

Jerrick's eyes narrowed. "What are you getting at? I'm too tired for subtleties right now."

"It's pretty obvious, Jerrick," I laughed. "And kind of brilliant, really. You see, what really happened here is that Bloodfane and Grodvulf plotted to use the tournament for their own ends. To do that and get away with it, though, they needed a patsy. Since Bloodfane and I have a history, they chose me."

"And then worked to make him look guilty," Millie added. "They kidnapped him—and all of us because we might ask questions about his disappearance—and held us outside of the city while they caused all sorts of mischief. His absence made it seem plausible that he was involved."

"What he didn't count on was us escaping and making it back to the city. When he saw us, he got afraid that we'd implicate him, so he attacked the tournament." I shrugged. "Your guards fought them off, and then I heroically talked Meritocrat Kurrgetha into arresting Grodvulf and helping finance the repairs to the Guildhall."

"Heroically?" Jerrick asked doubtfully.

"I missed that part," Millie laughed, looking at me with open admiration. "How did you do that?"

"He gave her plenty of ammunition to use against Grodvulf," Eegla answered. "Then, he flirted with her until she agreed to use Grodvulf's money to pay for the repairs."

"Do you ever stop flirting, Murf?" Ferdi asked with mild exasperation.

"No, he doesn't," Azara said flatly. "Ever."

"Charming a Meritocrat into getting what you want?" Millie asked archly. "I'm impressed, Murf!"

"Thank you." I frowned. "I have to wonder how she responded so quickly, though. Any ideas about that, Jerrick?"

"Oh, after I got your message, I sent a warning to her that I suspected one of the players planned violence at the tournament—and that Grodvulf might be involved. She and Grodvulf hate one another, so she hurried down just in case I was right so she could blame him for it. I'm fairly sure she was just waiting outside for the screaming to stop."

"She let this atrocity happen, while she had a dozen guards right outside who could have intervened?" Ferdi demanded in a shocked voice.

"Probably, yes. I doubt she wanted to risk herself." The man shook his head.

"The Meritocrats are all like that," Eegla added. "They're hungry for power and influence and mostly lacking in morals. I've always said that anyone who wants power badly enough to join the Meritocracy is probably the wrong person to have it." She paused and looked at Jerrick. "Which is why you should probably seriously consider Kurrgetha's offer, Jerrick."

"Are you out of your mind, Eegla?" the man snorted. "I'd be a terrible meritocrat!"

"No, you'd be an honest one. Wouldn't it be nice to have one honest person in charge of the city? Someone who'd stop something like this just because it's the right thing to do, and not because it benefits them in some way?"

"Leaving you as Guild Master, I suppose."

"Me? Not on your life. Only an idiot would take the job—or any job where you're the one in charge of anything. Especially a whole city. I'd nominate Murf."

"And then the whole Hall would clear out as people tried to get away before he wrecked it."

"Sure, but it would be fun while it lasted."

"I wouldn't take it anyway," I chuckled and pushed my chair backward. "Is there anything else, Jerrick?"

"Yes, Murf, there is," he sighed. "Your ceremony."

"Ceremony?"

"You won the tournament. At least, you will have once Grodvulf's conviction happens and Lanly's officially blamed for attacking the Guild. You've earned your prize."

"Just have the gold put on my account," I shook my head. "Or deposited with the Swindlers."

"Even if I were willing to do that, which I'm not, there's still the matter of the card draw."

I winced and shook my head. "You know, I think we can just skip that, Jerrick. I'm fine with just the money."

"Murf, the ceremony isn't for you," Eegla said seriously. "It's for everyone who went through that carnage downstairs. People lost loved ones. They're scared, hurt, and angry. We'd normally have a ceremony, and they could use some normalcy."

"Plus, Murf, you could just sell the card you draw," Millie pointed out enthusiastically. "If you draw one of the nobles—even an emperor—you could sell it for thousands!"

"That's not likely, Miss—Millie," Jerrick snorted. "The regular rules don't apply when you're drawing from a Unity deck, and neither do the laws of statistics. I've seen a dozen or more draws like this over the years, and while I should have seen at least a couple nobles in that, no one's ever pulled one."

"And those rules don't apply to Murf, Guild Master," Ferdi grunted in reply. "If he draws, it'll be something good. Trust me. However, if you do this ceremony, you know you're just asking for Bloodfane to show up and try again for the deck, right? You'll get a lot of people killed."

"I hadn't thought of that," Eegla said with a wince before her eyes brightened. "Wait. What if we did the actual draw first, in private, then had a fake draw for the ceremony? If there wasn't a real deck, Bloodfane wouldn't have any reason to disrupt things, would he?"

"Assuming he can tell the difference between a fake deck and a real one," Jerrick muttered.

"He can," I nodded.

"If he can't, his pet goblin can," Azara spat. "He's a pathetic diviner, but his skills are sufficient for that."

"Then, that's what we'll do," Jerrick decided. "We'll take a couple days to clean up and let people heal a bit, then we'll have the ceremony for the top four winners. Tomorrow, though, we'll let you draw from the deck."

"Fine," I sighed. "Is that it?"

"I think so, yes."

"Good." I pushed my chair back and stood up. "I think we could all use some rest."

"Will you put the avian and I up in the Guildhall, Guild Master?" Ferdi asked. "Somewhere close to Murf and the redhead?"

"I suppose it's the least we could do after the two of you helped stop all this. Why not go to your own guilds, though?"

"Because Murf's here, so it's where Bloodfane is likely to come back if he's still in the city." She fingered the axe strapped to her back with a smile. "I owe him an axe to the face."

"And on that note, I think this meeting is over," the canid said. "Thank you all for your assistance. Eegla will make the arrangements for your accommodations. Murf, Millie..." He paused. "Is there even a point to asking you two to stay out of trouble?"

"You can always ask, Jerrick," I shrugged.

"And will you do it?"

"Probably not, no, but you can always ask. It's your time; feel free to waste it however you'd like."

63

I headed back to my room and immediately passed out. I considered asking Millie to join me, but with Azara taking the room a few doors down from mine, I thought that might be a bit heartless. I'm an ass sometimes, but even I'm not that self-absorbed. Usually. Okay, I am, but I have my good moments, too.

I slept for hours, and when I awoke, the sun was low in the sky outside, and evening was drawing closer. I lay in bed for a bit, thinking over the past few weeks, all the changes that I'd undergone, and what they meant for me in the long term.

It had been a chaotic time, to be sure. I'd faced death—actual death, not being accidentally beaten to death by an angry husband or father—more times than I had over the rest of my entire life. Even then, lying in bed in the Guildhall, I felt on edge, as if danger might be just outside the window or door. I'd hung my sword on my bed with the hilt in easy reach when I went to sleep, and I reached out to touch it, feeling a tiny bit of comfort in the contact. I'd never had a weapon feel relaxing before; of course, I'd never had to rely on one to stay alive so often, either.

Not only had I faced death, I'd visited it on others. I'd killed before, of course, but that was an act of self-preservation. It was a last resort when I couldn't talk, bribe, or flee my way out of a fight. That wasn't the case anymore. I hadn't really had to kill Cassa, Tifer, Fisya, or any of Bloodfane's Holders, really. None of them had been immediate threats to me. I killed them so they wouldn't become threats in the future—or in Fisya's case because she seriously needed to die—and that wasn't something I'd ever done before. I'd never needed to. If things were getting that hot for me, I just ran and found some other place to occupy for a bit. A year ago, I'd have said to hell with the tournament and taken the first ship out of the city; instead, I'd fought to be able to stay there. More to the point, I'd fought so that Ferdi, Millie, and Azara could stay there. I'd killed for them, not just for me. It was a weird feeling, and I wasn't sure I liked it. Knowing that I was making decisions based on other people instead of myself felt a lot like being tied down, and I hated being tied down.

To top it all off, I no longer had any interest in sticking around Canis. I'd come for the tournament, and with that over, I could already feel the city pressing in on me. I felt restless and antsy, ready to move on and see new places. Other games awaited me, with different players and different challenges. There were other sunsets out there to see, and new women to love, and I was eager to do both. I'd fought to be able to stay here safely, but in the end, I was leaving, and soon. I'd stay for the ceremony, but no longer than that. As I considered that, I realized I had something I needed to do that day, something important, and I needed to do it right away.

I rose from my bed and dressed quickly. I walked to the door and yanked it open, then jumped backward and grabbed for my sword as something leaped through the door at my legs. I settled as I recognized the blue-armored figure that fell through the door, landing on her back and gazing up at me through sleepy eyes.

"Ferdi," I said, touching the brim of my hat as I gazed with amusement at the halfling. "Fancy meeting you here. Isn't your room down that way a bit?"

"Murf," she grunted, sitting up and stretching before rising somewhat noisily to her feet. "I was keeping watch on your room."

"With your eyes closed?" I chuckled. "That's quite the trick, even for you."

"I fell asleep. It's been a long day." She twisted her head from side to side and looked up at me. "Where are you going?"

"I have to talk to Azara."

"Fine. I'll go with you."

"She's right down the hall, Ferdi. You don't have to come."

"I don't have to. I will. I'm not letting Bloodfane get another shot at you without me being there."

"It's a little private, Ferdi," I said delicately.

"A sex thing? That's fine. I'll wait outside."

"No, it's not a..." I sighed and shook my head. "Fine, Ferdi. Do what you like."

"Naturally."

Azara took a full minute to respond when I knocked on her door, and when she pulled it open, her head feathers were disarrayed, and her eyes peered at me a little blearily.

"Murf," she said shortly. "What can I do for you?"

"I was hoping we could get that dinner that I promised you," I said with a smile.

"Now?"

"I'm planning to leave right after Jerrick's ceremony. Tomorrow, I'll be busy getting ready for the trip—and drawing that stupid card." I shrugged. "So, it kind of has to be tonight."

"We could simply skip it, Murf."

I shook my head. "This is important to me, Azara. Please. This time, I want to leave the right way: as your friend."

She stared at me for a few moments, then nodded. "Give me ten minutes to get dressed. We'll go to my place..." She paused and looked past me. "What is the halfling doing here?"

"She invited herself. She's worried that Bloodfane's going to attack me while she's not around."

"That's an absurd conclusion. The warlock already tried to kill you and failed, Murf—and lost a card in the process. He's far more likely to try and take someone close to you, like Millie, and use her as leverage."

My heart jumped a bit at that, but Ferdi grunted approvingly behind me. "You're right, avian. He would. I'll go watch her instead." She clomped off down the hall, and I turned and mouthed my thanks to Azara, who smiled in reply.

"Ten minutes, Murf."

Dinner was a simple affair. Azara made a plain meal of fish, rice, and vegetables, and the two of us sat, talked, and caught up a bit. I told her of some of the places I'd been and gave her more details about Clearford's tournament and my first meeting with Bloodfane, and she shared with me her attempts to become the diviner to the Meritocracy—attempts that were ultimately doomed to fail.

"No matter what it claims, the simple fact is that the Meritocracy is less concerned with ability and more concerned with your species," she told me, shaking her head. "They only hire canids to be their assistants, no one else. They claim that it's practical to avoid interspecies and intercultural conflicts, but it's nothing more than base politics and speciesism. All those assistants are also members of wealthy or powerful families, and taking in their non-heirs gives the meritocrats influence with those families."

"That sounds about right," I nodded. "Everyone's always looking out for themselves first, after all."

"One of your laws?"

"Just a statement of fact." I reached out and placed my hand atop hers. "This is nice, you know. I missed talking with you."

"It is, and so have I," she sighed. "It can't go back to the way it was, though, Murf. I'm sorry."

"I don't expect it to. I told you: I'm heading out in a couple days. I'd still like to be your friend, though."

She hesitated. "You could ask me to travel with you, Murf."

I looked at her, letting my surprise show on my face. "What?"

"You could ask me to go with you. There's no need to leave me behind."

"Your shop is here, Azara. Your life is here."

She sniffed. "My life is my cards, and they'll be with me wherever I go. This shop is just a place." She looked around a little sadly. "And sometimes, a rather lonely one. I've been thinking about selling it and returning to Avis anyway—the oligarchs there don't have the same prejudices the meritocrats do. I could travel with you instead." She smiled. "Besides, you need me. Without me, you'll destroy your layout again by listening to people like the halfling, and that would be a disaster for everyone."

I swallowed hard, and when I spoke, my voice was low and hoarse. "Azara, like you said, it can't be the way it was. I've changed a bit, it's true, but I'm still who I am. If you're with me, would you be able to handle me being with other women?"

"I don't know," she admitted honestly. "And you're right. That might be—difficult." She shook her head. "I'll think about it."

We chatted for a while longer, then Azara walked me to the door. I gave her a hug, then she rose up and kissed my cheek softly. "Thank you, Murf. Thank you for the memory."

"Aren't you coming back to the Guildhall?"

"No," she shook her head. "There's no need. With Grodvulf arrested, Bloodfane no longer has any reason to stay in Canis. He doesn't have the forces he'd need to forcibly take the deck thanks to your destroying his card, and he doesn't have the time to find new Holders to do it for him. My guess is that he went straight to a ship heading out of the city the moment he heard about Grodvulf. I'll be fine here."

"I'll miss you, Azara," I smiled at her.

"There's a simple solution for that. Return and visit me—and don't wait so long this time."

"Deal."

I returned to the Guildhall to find Millie waiting for me with Ferdi close by. The redhead took my arm as I stepped inside and walked with me toward the inner hall. "How was your dinner?" she asked lightly, although I could feel the tension in her body.

"Nice," I said honestly. "We caught up a bit. It ended on a happy note, at least."

"Oh? How happy, exactly?"

I chuckled. "Millie, are you jealous?"

"No, Murf. I told you: I'm not going to be part of any harems. If I wanted that, I would never have left my family in the first place."

"They wanted you to be in a harem?" I asked, startled.

"Not directly. They wanted me to marry royalty, which is pretty much the same thing. I'd either be the first wife of several, or I'd be the wife of a man with concubines and lovers. Either way, I'd be sharing, and I hate sharing. So, how happy?"

"Nothing like that happened," I assured her. "Just dinner and talking." I leaned down and kissed her cheek, then laughed. "Besides, it's not like it matters. I'll be leaving the city after the presentation, and I assume you'll be doing the same, right?"

"Yes, but…" She stopped walking and bit her lip. "Where will you be going?"

"Honestly? No clue. I was thinking of heading south to Felis for a bit, then maybe jump around the Kine Isles. They're fairly fun."

"I've never been to either of those. Maybe—maybe we could see them together?"

I glanced down at her in surprise. "I thought you'd be looking for the next tournament to help buy your way out of your family."

"Murf, I made more crowns incidentally with you than I did at the tournament. And if we sell more of our cards, I'll have much, much more."

"You also almost died a few times."

"True, but if I don't buy out of my family, I'll be facing the same thing but against my will." She gave me a wan smile. "Plus, you promised to teach me to be a better gambler, remember?"

"That I did." I sighed, and my voice turned serious. "And when we get tired of one another? Find someone else more interesting? It's going to happen, you know."

"Then we part ways," she shrugged. "I'm not looking for forever, Murf. I just want to enjoy the world—and you're the most fun I've ever had." She smiled at me again, a more genuine one this time. "What do you say?"

"I say that you're your own person, Millie," I finally answered. "You can do or go wherever you want to. You don't need my permission. I'd be glad to have you along, though—at least for the time being."

"Good enough." She rose up and kissed my cheek.

I shook my head and looked back at Ferdi. "What about you? You planning to join me, too?"

"Maybe, if Bloodfane doesn't try to kill one of you before you leave," the halfling shrugged.

"Seriously? Ferdi, the last time we tried to be friends, it really didn't end well, remember?"

"I remember. This time, listen to me when I tell you something's a bad idea, and I won't have to hunt you down after. Besides, the pretty girl's right. You're interesting to be around—and lucrative."

"Lucrative?"

"I've gained three ranks in the past few weeks, Murf. Three. That's more than I got my whole life up to this point."

"It's the Holders," I shrugged. "They're worth a lot of points."

"No, it's you, Murf. Do you know how you get UP? It's not by completing Labyrinths or killing things. It's by getting the Unity to notice you. When it thinks you've done something noteworthy, it rewards you. I've killed Holders before and never got any UP from it. The Unity pays attention to you, though, so when I'm with you, it notices me, as well." Her voice turned firm. "I'm coming with you."

"What about Jidra?" I asked a little desperately.

"She's being cared for until the Prelacy sends another group to take over the hold, and they'll watch her as long as necessary."

"Prelacy?" Millie asked.

"The government of Khuker, the halfling nation," I said with a sigh, rubbing my head. "What the hell is happening, here? Why is everyone suddenly so interested in traveling with me?"

"Because you're an interesting man, Murf," Millie laughed, kissing my cheek again.

"Things are exciting around you," Ferdi added.

"And because the Hag draws us all in her wake." I turned back and stared in confusion as I saw Azara walking toward us, her eyes a little sad but determined as she approached. She had a large pack on her back, and her expression looked hesitant, as if she weren't sure how I'd react to seeing her.

"What?" I asked. "Azara, I thought we decided…"

"You were wrong. I was wrong. There's nothing for me here, Murf. My place is with you. I can't fight it any more than these two can." She gave me a wistful smile. "Don't you remember what I told you in my divination? 'No place will be your home, and those who follow in your path will wander forever, never knowing what drags them down the endless roads.' We're pulled along behind you, Murf, and we'll follow as long as we can. I'm afraid you're stuck with us." She walked over and kissed my cheek, then looked at Millie with a smile. "And yes, Millie, I know. No harems."

"You might as well give in, Murf," Ferdi said. "The more you argue, the more foolish you'll look when you lose."

"Fine!" I said, throwing my free arm up in the air. "You can all come along! While we're at it, let's invite Jerrick, and Eegla, and half the damn city!"

"You can't afford to pay for all that passage," the halfling shrugged. "Now, we should all get some rest. We're going to spend a long day preparing for this trip to wherever the hell Murf is dragging us—plus, there's still the chance of Bloodfane showing up tomorrow or the next day."

"You sound far too excited about that prospect, halfling," Azara noted.

"I am. I have a lot to pay him back for."

"I hope I never see him again," Millie shivered. "Or any of his Holders."

I felt the same, but I doubted it would be that easy. If the Hag was right, and Bloodfane was trying to collect the Cabal, he'd eventually have to find me again. Considering it that way, I actually felt a little grateful that the others would be with me. They might cramp my style a bit, but then, so would being captured and tortured for my cards. It felt like a reasonably fair trade-off.

We spent the next day shopping, and Gertla called me to the Sage's Guild to pull the cards from a few bodies, mostly guards who'd died in the battle the day before and had no one to leave their cards to. I felt a little morbid standing in the icy room in the Sage's Hall, yanking cards from men and women who'd been protecting me the day before, but a deal was a deal. I pulled a total of 14 cards, most of which were mid-range arcana with a few nines and tens.

"Well above what I predicted, once more," the sage said morosely, shaking her head.

"Does that mean we have to wait for our payment again?" I asked a little irritably.

"No. A good sage accepts their mistakes and learns from them. I learned from mine." She pulled out a silver card embossed with the symbol of the sages on it. "Take this to the Usurer's Hall. By the time you reach it, it will have the requisite 116 crowns and four wands on it, available to be transferred into your account there—I assume you have an account there?"

"I do," I nodded, pulling out a few more cards. "By the way, would the Guild be interested in purchasing these, as well?"

Gertla took the cards I'd offered and examined them. "Nine and seven of coins, and six of cups? You have no use for them?"

"Not really. I could use the money more."

She shrugged. "Very well. They're worth an additional forty-four crowns. I'll add it to the card. Is that all?"

"That's more than enough, thanks."

"160 crowns, Murf!" Millie muttered as we left. "I could kiss you! To hell with tournaments; cards are the way to make money!"

"Sure, but remember what we had to go through to get them," I reminded her, and she grimaced.

"True. Fine, I'll stick with gambling. Besides, with a stake like this, I'll be up over a thousand crowns in no time!"

As we left the Sage's Hall, I once again felt Charlie slip out of my chest, but this time, I ignored him. I wasn't really worried about him after having seen him handle the demonic warriors, and I knew he'd catch up. He did, a few minutes later, carrying a gold coin for Millie as usual and chewing on another card, the five of stars I'd pulled from one of the ursids. I didn't say a word as he nibbled the card, watching until it vanished, and a card flashed up before me.

Card Absorption!
Your Soul Familiar has absorbed the energy of the card: Five of Stars. It has gained:
+9% resistance to detection

The day flew by, until eventually, the time came for me to pull the card I'd been awarded. The four of us headed up to Jerrick's office, where I found the Guild Master, Eegla, a half-dozen guards, and, to my surprise, Kurrgetha all waiting for us.

"Milady Meritocrat," I bowed to the woman, taking he hand and brushing it lightly with my lips once more. "To what do we owe the pleasure of your company?"

"Ah, Mr. Murf. So nice to see you once again." She gestured to an ursid at her side, who held a flat wooden box about the size of two of my fists in his hands. As I gazed on the box, I could feel the energy within it. I'd felt something similar before in the Ochre Forest, when I'd opened the box holding the cards we got as a reward. It was a feeling of potential, of untapped energy, although this time, it was much stronger than it had been then. It was strong enough, in fact, that I felt it drawing me toward it. I ignored it, though, and kept a light smile focused on the canid woman.

"As you know," she continued, "the prize is being offered by the Meritocracy, not the Guild, so I'm here to oversee the drawing and record the results."

"And to make sure I only take one card?" I chuckled.

"Not how it works, Murf," Ferdi spoke up, shaking her head. "A full Unity deck isn't just a pile of cards. It's a separate kind of beast, and once you draw from it, you can't draw from it again."

"The halfling is correct," the meritocrat nodded. "When a full set of Unity cards is combined into a deck, it can't be thought of as a collection of cards anymore. It's more like a lottery—reach inside, and you never know what you'll get. It's in the Unity's hands: you could get a simple ace or a noble, depending on how much it likes you—although I've never actually seen one of those pulled from it. Once it's been drawn from, though, it becomes inert for a time."

"For how long?" Millie asked curiously.

"It depends on what's drawn from it. The higher the card pulled, the longer it remains inert. Typically, though, it remains inert for around a year. In fact, it just reactivated from its last draw a few weeks ago, which is why it was decided to use it as a prize for the tournament."

"And probably why Bloodfane chose this tournament to join," I added.

"These can't be all that rare, though. I know cards are hard to acquire, but I'll bet my family could buy enough to make a few."

The meritocrat smiled. "It's not quite that simple, Miss Deepwater. Creating a deck like this is the work of several lifetimes. It requires not only the presence of at least one of each of the seventy-five cards in the deck, it also requires a supremely talented cartomancer who knows the proper methods to bind them together. Plus, two of them can't exist too near to one another, or they'll both go inert. This, to my knowledge, is the only one of its kind on this continent. I know that the elves and goblins each possess one, and I assume the Empire has one or two. And I wouldn't be surprised if your grandfather owns one, as well, as you surmised. They're far too useful for someone with his money and connections not to take advantage."

"Okay, so it's rare," I said slowly, "but why would Bloodfane—sorry, Baron Lanly want it so badly? If he can only draw a card from it every year or so..."

"What one cartomancer can do, another can undo," Azara said quietly. "And destruction is always easier than creation."

"So, if he had it..."

"His pet goblin might be able to unbind it and release the cards from it, yes. It would give him one of every card in the deck of the arcana."

"So, why not do that? Wouldn't it be a lot more useful in the long run?"

"Not at all, Mr. Murf," the meritocrat chuckled. "If the deck is unbound, once a card is taken from it, it's simply gone. While the deck is bound, though, it can provide the same card multiple times. The only limit to what can be taken from it is how long it remains inert between drawings. This deck has existed for over a century, and it's given out many more cards than it should contain. Many, many more."

"I think that's enough questions," Jerrick interjected. "I'm sure the meritocrat has other things to do today, and she's eager to return this deck to the Meritocracy, where it's safe."

"Quite so," the woman nodded. She gestured at the ursid holding the box, and he stepped forward. She reached over and flipped the lid, and as it rose, I glanced inside. I expected to see cards laying facedown within, but instead, a shadowy darkness filled the inside of the box. Power rolled up from it, almost as much as I'd felt from Bloodfane and the Hag when they fought using my chest as their battleground. I couldn't see the bottom of the box; in fact, it kind of reminded me of the darkness filling the Hag's Labyrinth.

"Go ahead and make your draw, Mr. Murf," the meritocrat urged me. "You've earned it."

I took a deep breath and reached inside. As soon as my hand hit the darkness, a card flashed up in my vision.

> **Unity Deck**
> You have drawn a card from a Deck of the Arcana.
> Luck Check is successful!
> Skill Check is successful!
> Harmony Check is successful!
> You have drawn a card of a higher-than-normal rank with a high Harmony!

I felt the edges of a card in my fingers and pulled it up with a feeling of dread. I wasn't sure what the message meant, but I assumed it couldn't be a good thing. A higher-than-normal card had gotten me into this mess, after all. The card slid up with a surge of power, and as it flowed out, the box shuddered briefly. The power within it suddenly winked out, and the shadows inside it faded, leaving an empty box behind.

"That—is different," the meritocrat said, frowning as she looked into the now-empty box.

"What is, Meritocrat?" Jerrick asked a little nervously.

"Usually, after a draw, the darkness in the box thins but remains. I've never seen it vanish so completely." She looked up at me with a combination of suspicion and sudden nervousness. "Can we see what you drew, Mr. Murf?"

I held up the card and turned it around for the room to see. Azara and Ferdi both gasped, while Jerrick and Millie simply seemed puzzled. The color drained from Kurrgetha's face as she saw the card displayed before her. The image showed a person seated at a poker table, cards and chips spread out before them, their face hidden in the shadow of a hood. The card's name was written on a wooden plaque across the top, a name that popped up in the card in my vision.

The Gambler
Power: Worldly Performer
Likely Power: Chaos
Requirements:
Luck: 64   Harmony: 66
Compatibility: 100%

"A—a power," Kurrgetha gasped. "How? That—that's an arcana deck! There are no powers in it!"

"I can tell you how, Meritocrat," I said with a grimace. "It's Murf's First Law."

"Murf's what?"

"Murf's First Law: if you can draw a bad card, you certainly will."

EPILOGUE

✦ ✦ ✦ ✦
✦ ✦ ✦

The ship rocked and churned on the sea, but the man crouched down in the bilges barely noticed. He didn't feel the motion of the vessel; he didn't hear the creaking of the timbers; he didn't smell the reeking bilgewater splashing around him. Every sense focused keenly on the diagram he painted carefully on the wooden hull of the vessel, knowing that if he got even a bit of it wrong, it could be catastrophic. At best, it would shatter that part of the hull and no doubt doom the ship. At worst—well, he didn't want to think about the worst.

Baron Lanly, also known as Lord Bloodfane, Count Isekelia, Sir Dirrik of Tanarka, and a dozen other names none of which were any more correct than the last, dipped the brush into the bowl of warm blood at his side and carefully drew a long, curving line. He'd done this hundreds of times, but he never let himself get overconfident. The one who'd taught him this art made that mistake and ended up inside the belly of something that still gave the man nightmares. He'd always resolved not to make the same mistake, not to assume that his skills were infallible...

"You did, though, didn't you?" a voice echoed in his head, a voice that he couldn't tune out or ignore no matter how hard he tried. *"You assumed your plans were perfect, but they weren't, and random chance shattered them."*

He didn't bother arguing with the voice or even acknowledging it. For one, the more attention he paid it, the stronger it became. For another, it was correct. He had let his arrogance blind him, assuming his superiority over mere Holders thanks to the powerful card in his soul and the dark powers granted him. And in the end, he'd been bested by a buffoon, a gambler who thought the world was a game and who'd probably never had a serious thought in his life.

"For the second time," the voice reminded him. *"Who's the buffoon?"*

He pushed his thoughts aside and refocused on his task. The blood he'd taken from the sailor was cooling quickly, and only warm blood would serve him. The sailor himself was drifting in the ocean somewhere far behind the ship, his death unnoticed by the rather lax crew. They'd miss him eventually and no doubt assume he'd fallen overboard, but no one would ever link his disappearance to the warlock. He'd made sure of that.

He completed the final stroke, examined his creation carefully, then reached down into himself and grasped at the dark power roiling within him. Few warlocks could hold as much energy as he could; only the powerful card at his heart gave him the strength of will and mastery over the Unity to gather that much power. Of course, when he turned to that power, the card refused to fully serve him, but that was fine. He could still use it to channel his energy, and his infernal abilities weakened the card's resistance enough that he could tap it in a very limited fashion. That power flowed down his arm and into the elaborate diagram he'd forged, and the side of the ship suddenly seemed to burst into flames. Blood-red fires roared toward him for an instant before being sucked down into a red-glowing hole in the hull. Time froze for a moment as the power of the worlds below reached through the hole in reality he'd made forged a region where neither world truly existed.

Some part of him still rejoiced in his accomplishments. His mentor had been considered a powerful warlock and had only created a small window with this ritual, not the gaping hole in the fabric of everything that he tore. That, he knew, was partially due to the card in his soul and partially due to his native talent and skill. In that moment, the realm of the infernal had a tiny foothold in the world, a small place where its energies flowed freely, and he drank of them deeply, replenishing much of what he'd lost in the battle with the damned gambler. He wouldn't be able to fully recover without his patron's approval, but he restored enough of his lost energy to feel confident dealing with any nosy guard or passing Holder who might recognize him.

Of course, that wouldn't replace the Reaper the gambler had somehow stripped from his deck, also stealing his ability to summon more than a single azdrast at a time. That was a major blow; powers weren't easy to find, and infernal powers were even harder to locate. The Unity favored its own, making worldly powers far more abundant than divine or infernal ones, and he doubted that he had enough of its favor anymore to randomly draw one just because he had the Luck and Skill to. He'd have to hunt for more Labyrinths to raid, powerful ones that hadn't been tapped in decades or centuries, and even then, it would probably take years to replace it.

He stopped absorbing energy as a presence spilled through the doorway, one vaster and far greater than the man and his powers. He lowered himself instantly, dropping his head to the floor and closing his eyes in obeisance. The presence was terrifying and thrilling, horrifying beyond the man's comprehension and exciting beyond all measure. If it chose, it could obliterate him with a thought, but it could also grant him terrible powers that the pathetic Unity simply couldn't or refused to match.

DID YOU ACQUIRE THE CARD?

The voice that spoke wasn't a thing to be heard. It was a thrumming in the world, a shifting of power that spiked directly into the man's brain and poured its intent inside. He didn't hear what was said; he simply knew what his master wanted to communicate. He took a deep breath, knowing that his hesitation and fear answered the question far better than he could have.

"I—I failed, Master," he said in a meek tone.

HOW?

"Another penetrated the Labyrinth before I could and stole the card. I found them and tried to take it from them, but they resisted my powers. I need more strength…"

I WILL KNOW THE TRUTH OF THIS.

Pain suddenly ripped through the man as the infernal being's presence plunged into his thoughts, riffling through them like the pages of a book. Its power shredded his mind and will, tearing through his consciousness. For a moment, he stopped existing; then, the pain withdrew, and his battered and broken mind collapsed back into something that vaguely resembled a whole. It wasn't the first time it had done this, and each time it happened, he wondered what he'd lost. The voice appeared in his thoughts after the second time; his memories of his birth and original name vanished after the fourth. Eventually, he knew, there wouldn't be enough left of him to put back together, and he'd be as insane as most warlocks. Part of him thought that was what his patron wanted, at least, once he'd fulfilled its mission for him.

THE GAMBLER HAS ONE OF THE CABAL.

"Are—are you certain, Master?" the man gasped, jerked out of his errant thoughts. "Perhaps it was one of the greater powers…"

NO. ONLY ONE OF THE CABAL COULD RESIST MY POWER CHANNELED THROUGH YOUR CARD. HE HOLDS A CABAL.

"Then—then I'll take it from him. I'll rip it from his chest and make him watch as I claim it…"

YOU WILL FAIL. HIS CARD SERVES HIM WILLINGLY, WHILE YOURS STRUGGLES AGAINST YOU AND IS WEAKENED BY MY PRESENCE. YOU WILL NEED MORE POWER.

"Y-yes, Master! Give me more power!"

NOT MINE. YOU WILL SEEK THE OTHERS OF THE CABAL AND JOIN WITH THEM. THEY WILL GRANT YOU THE POWER THAT YOU NEED.

"How will I find them, Master? I spent years locating this Labyrinth…"

FOLLOW THE GAMBLER. WATCH HIM. THE CARDS WILL COME TO HIM. TAKE THEM WHEN THEY DO.

"What do you mean, Master?"

The presence's voice battered his mind and soul as it swelled to a roar.

DO AS I INSTRUCT! FOLLOW THE GAMBLER! WATCH HIM. CLAIM THE CARDS AS THEY COME. DO NOT FAIL ME AGAIN!

"Yes! I'll do as you command! I won't fail you!"

GOOD. I WILL LISTEN FOR SIGNS OF THE OTHERS AND INFORM YOU AS I DISCOVER THEM. DO NOT CONTACT ME WITHOUT SOMETHING TO REPORT AGAIN.

The flames whipping into the hole before him exploded outward, washing over him in a blast of power. The unholy fire plunged through his skin and seared its way into his soul. He screamed in agony as pain beyond anything he'd ever felt ripped through his body, torment beyond his mind's ability to comprehend it. Just as quickly, the flames winked out and the hole before him collapsed, plunging him into darkness. His body shook uncontrollably, and he had to fight not to burst into sobbing tears at the very memory of the pain.

That, he knew, was his master's warning. It was a taste of the tortures awaiting him should he fail. It was the stick designed to goad him into action and obedience, but as the shaking left his body, he couldn't help but grin triumphantly.

His master had made a mistake. The man had been forced into this bargain, one he had no intention of keeping. Alone, he would never have found the other cards of the Cabal, no matter how much money and influence he accumulated. They hid from one another, afraid of what would happen if they were rejoined with the decks of arcana and powers, and since he held one, the others would do their best to avoid him. Only the vast network of infernal agents that his patron possessed had the abilities and talents to pierce the veils hiding those cards—or, he supposed, an equally potent divine network. Whatever the case, he'd been reliant on the terrible power to find those cards, and he hadn't been sure how he would keep their strength for himself. Now, though, he knew exactly how to find them, and that meant he didn't need his "master" anymore—at least, he wouldn't for long. All he had to do was wait for that idiot gambler to bring the cards to him, claim them—and then, last of all, rip the final card from the man's soul while he screamed in torment.

That—that would be a revenge worth waiting for.

A gray-robed man knelt in a basement room below one of the nicer sections of the city. His heart hammered in his chest as he kept his head bowed low. Death surrounded him, reached for him from every angle, and he stood closer to it than he ever had before. He and his brethren were the arbiters of it, doling it out as deemed necessary by their elders. Well, his brethren and sistren, assuming that was a real thing. He felt like it should be since the females of the order were just as deadly as the males, if not more so...

He pulled his wandering mind back into focus. He knew why it went off on strange tangents. That was a common response from his victims when they knew that they were going to die and couldn't do anything to stop it. They laughed; they joked; they spoke of irrelevant matters; they bargained and pleaded. They did anything to take their minds off their imminent demise. And now, he was doing the same thing, letting pointless thoughts distract him from his likely end. Sadly, that couldn't last long.

"You failed, Deathroot."

It was a stupid name. Deathroot. He'd always hated it. Oh, he understood it, obviously. Deathroot was a plain-looking flower whose roots concealed a deadly toxin that slowed the heart and lungs to the point of paralysis within a couple of hours. There was no antidote besides card abilities; once someone ingested it in sufficient quantities, they were dead. He appreciated the lethality of the name, but he wanted to be something more active, like "Deathfang" or "Deathviper". Cassa's pseudonym, "Shadowcat", was a little better, implying that she was quick and deadly— which she was—but it still sounded juvenile to him. He always felt the order would be better served with simpler, less dramatic code names, something like "Jez the Axe" or "Dakota". He couldn't exactly call out the name "Shadowcat" across a crowded tavern, after all...

The silence that stretched out reminded him that his elder was waiting for an answer. He gathered his scattered thoughts and considered what would serve him the best. He could list any number of reasons why he'd failed. He was betrayed by his employer. The Holders set to guard and secure the Labyrinth let themselves be killed. His partner disappeared, leaving him to try and complete a two-person mission alone. The elder wouldn't want to hear any of that, though, so he went with the simple truth.

"Yes, elder. I failed."

"You admit this? No excuses? No explanations? Even knowing that it will mean your death?"

"Yes, elder. I can only control my own actions, not those of others. My failure is my own." He glanced up at the elven woman standing over him and saw vague approval in her silver eyes. He'd said the right things, at least, parroting back the order's teachings. It was all a pile of shit, obviously. He'd been working as part of a team, and he had to rely on the others to do their parts for his to work. No one had, and that made it impossible for him to succeed despite having done everything that was asked of him. He'd infiltrated the halfling hold and paralyzed its Holders so they couldn't offer a defense to the invasion; he'd slipped into the Sellsword's Guild and learned the secrets of powerful Holders to force them to work for his employer; he'd even managed to kidnap a Scribbler right out of their Guildhall. He'd completed every mission given him; the others let him down. The order didn't believe in things like that, though, mostly because it encouraged its members to work alone specifically to avoid those sorts of entanglements.

"Hmph. I wonder if you believe that, or if you're simply repeating your lessons." He tried not to wince at her words as she guessed his true intent, but fortunately, she kept speaking, either not seeing or ignoring his sudden discomfort.

"Not that it matters. You failed, true, but you were failed, as well. Because of that, there may be some room for leniency—if you speak the truth without dissembling further. The truth is your only shield, Deathroot. Do you understand this?"

"Yes, elder."

"Good. Then tell me how such a simple job went so dreadfully wrong. How clearing a Labyrinth led to mayhem and chaos in the city, not one but four entangled guilds, a massive power shift in the city, and the loss of one of our more promising members."

He swallowed hard as her last words confirmed a truth he hadn't wanted to face. "Then, Cassa—I mean, Shadowcat..."

"Is dead, yes," the elf nodded. "Her body was found in the harbor, likely washed down the river. Her limbs had been broken, but there was no sign of how she died beyond that, so we assume poison—or an ability. Hers is a grievous loss. Explain how it came to be."

The man lowered his head and began to speak. He told of meeting his new employer, the trial run in the Ochre Dungeon that ended in the first betrayal of several. He talked about the sadistic pair of elves who decided to kill a random gambler who happened to win against them, setting off this whole chain of events. His employer then botched that same gambler's death again, placing him in the Ochre Forest and assuming it would kill him. Obviously, it hadn't, and the man and his companions emerged far stronger than they'd gone in. The travesty continued with the pointless slaughter of the halflings, the kidnappings around the city, and Cassa and he taking the loved ones of powerful Holders to force them into their employer's service. It turned into a debacle when their people in that pathetic village south of the city went silent, and the cowardly goblin appeared, telling a ludicrous tale of the gambler and his redheaded harlot slaughtering the Labyrinth camp in a storm of power and abilities. At least, it seemed ludicrous until Deathroot watched those same two and their companions fighting his employer's mercenaries and cutting them down like blades of grass. His story ended with the man sending a summoned monster after him, one that ignored his every attack and ability, sapping his strength and will with its gaze and befuddling his mind while its sharp teeth shredded his shadow armor.

"I watched as my employer's flames bounced off the gambler without effect," he said in a wooden tone. "Then, somehow, one of my employer's cards was torn from his body and floated into the gambler's hand, where it burst into flame and was destroyed. When that happened, I knew that it was over. We'd failed, and all I could do was escape with my life to report all this. So, I did; I shrouded myself and slipped out during the aftermath of the carnage."

The elf hadn't spoken through all of this, and when he finished, she simply nodded her head. "Your words track with the reports I've gotten, Deathroot, and answer many questions I've had about this affair. Did you know that after your employer's rather dramatic exit, the gambler orchestrated the fall of not one but two meritocrats?"

"I-I did not, elder."

"And that he's been associated with one of the Senior Sages in the Sage's Guild? That he seems able to ignore the commands of his Guild Master as he pleases? Do you know what all this tells me?"

"No, elder."

"You should. It tells me that this man is no mere gambler. He is a member of the Gambler's Court, a powerful one—and a hidden one, kept out of sight of the world at large. No doubt the Guild got wind of your former employer's plans and brought him in to foil them, and he did so quite effectively."

"Are—are you certain, elder?" he asked dubiously. "Begging your forgiveness, but he seemed like a rakish fool…"

"And do you allow the world to see how deadly you are, Deathroot? Or do you hide your depths behind an ordinary mask?"

He frowned at that; it was true that he did his best to seem ordinary in between jobs, to draw no more attention to himself than necessary. Was this gambler, this Murf, doing the same? Did he hide his power and lethality behind a mask of bravado, arrogance, and debauchery? It seemed impossible—but he'd seen the man shrug off a dagger to his lower spine, one covered with paralytic venom that should have rendered him comatose, then go on to casually slaughter a pair of armored knights. Perhaps the elder was right.

"Then, what will we do?" he asked after a moment. "If the gambler is a member of a Court…"

"Normally, he would be untouchable," she nodded with a sly smile. "However, in this case, the mask he wears serves us, as well. None know him as a member of the Court, so none will speak up against us should he fall."

"Elder, his skills and abilities—I am unsure that any of us can bring him down."

"Even the greatest tree can be felled, Deathroot. One simply needs a sharper axe—and a stronger arm. You will be that axe, and I will be the one wielding you. I will personally sharpen your blade until it can cut through even the toughest wood, and when the time is right, I will wield you myself to fell this gambler—this 'Murf', or whatever his name truly is." She straightened, and her smile turned vicious. "And with his death, we will take our rightful place as equals to the Roses—or even betters. All it will take is the removal of that single tree…"

He listened to her belabor her metaphor beyond all reason with a steadily sinking heart. She seemed confident, but then, she hadn't seen the gambler in action. He had. He doubted it would be a simple matter. There would be blood, and lots of it—much probably his own.

Of course, he'd seen someone cutting down trees before, and it never looked fun for the axe.

The wind ruffled my hair and blew the scent of the ocean into my nostrils. I breathed deeply, then let out a loud sigh before looking at Ferdi standing beside me. The halfling stared at the harbor dourly, but I ignored her sour expression. Ferdi hated boats and sailing and had as long as I'd known her, which just made the coming voyage that much sweeter for me.

"Do you smell that?" I asked her expansively.

"What? Dead fish? Yes, I smell the dead fish, Murf."

"No, Ferdi. Freedom. That's the smell of freedom!"

"Freedom never smelled like dead fish to me."

Millie giggled as she held onto my arm. "I know what you mean, Murf. After the last few days, getting out of the city feels—invigorating."

As it turned out, the card I drew was a much bigger deal than I'd guessed. Kurrgetha hadn't been expecting that, and she claimed that the card rightfully belonged to the Meritocracy, not to me. She'd only offered me a draw from an arcana deck, after all, not a power. She raged and screamed, threatened and cajoled, one moment offering me vast amounts of wealth for the card while at the next threatening to toss me into jail beside Grodvulf if I didn't give it back. It wasn't until the next day that I learned why she'd been so upset.

"That card you took is a treasure almost as valuable as the whole damn deck, Murf," Jerrick explained to me. "And she's on the hook with the other meritocrats for its loss. They didn't want to honor Grodvulf's offer, but she convinced them that doing so would show their good faith—and that they weren't like him. Now, the deck they have is more unpowered than they've ever seen and might not be active for years, you're walking away with something as valuable as half the damn city, and she's set herself up to take the fall for it."

Unfortunately for the meritocrat, I didn't much care. Besides, by then, I'd already stuck the thing in my soul.

"The Gambler is obviously your presence in the Deck of Powers," Azara told me when I asked her about it. "It will be the card you build your future on. Place it directly above your hole card." She paused. "It's going to hurt, though. It's a powerful card, and there's no way to add something like that to your deck without pain, I'm afraid."

She was right, of course. The card burned like boiling acid going in, and I almost screamed with the pain of it. It slid into place with a burst of power, and I staggered a bit as the energy surged into my core. When it settled at last, a card appeared in my sight to explain what I'd gotten.

The Gambler
Luck of the Draw
Rank: Worldly Performer
Attunement: 30%
Base Power: 179 **Max Power:** 398
When this power is active, all acts of random chance within base power x 30 feet of you tend to favor you. This effect will grow the longer the card is active. Beware! Luck is fickle, and this power can turn on its wielder!

Hole Card Boost!
Luck of the Draw gains a 150% bonus to effectiveness, and it grants increasing chances of random unfortunate events happening to

anyone in the radius hostile to you.
The chances of the ability turning on
you are lessened, but effects when it
turns are magnified.

Power Deck
The Deck of Powers is a more
powerful and potent one than the
Deck of Arcana. Rather than suits,
it has three secrets: Worldly, Divine,
and Infernal. It holds nine ranks of
cards: Supplicant, Performer, Guide,
Sage, Pair, Priest, Warrior, Ruler,
and Avatar, in order of power.

Arcana Dominion
All arcana-based abilities are halved
in effectiveness against power-level
abilities. This does not include
inherent resistance to abilities.

That was a potent and dangerous ability, and I wasn't even sure how it worked. How would a random event a mile away from me—like a coin flip, for example—turn out in my favor? I didn't know, and it wasn't a power I was sure I wanted to experiment with. It ran totally against my First Law: If you can draw a bad card, you certainly will. Using this felt like a prime opportunity to draw a really terrible card.

I couldn't help but grin as I realized that meant I'd absolutely be using that power at some point. It was just a gamble, after all, and what good was a gambler who was afraid to take his chances?

Once that was dealt with, the fake presentation ceremony went fairly smoothly. A larger crowd than I expected gathered in the Guildhall, especially considering what happened last time, and while there was a definite edge to the people there, they seemed in relatively good spirits. Millie, Horstya, and I came up to claim our prizes one at a time, each to a decent round of applause. Honestly, the fifty crowns were nice, but I already had more in the Swindler's vaults than I needed. I'd have to find a way to spend some of it in a fun way soon. The whole point to money was to spend it, after all.

After the ceremony, we were stuck in the city for a couple more days while Kurrgetha tried to find a way to get the Gambler back from me. Eventually, Jerrick had to threaten to bring the Guild Court and Millie's family into the matter before the meritocrat let it drop.

The day after, news went out all over the city that there would be nominations for two vacancies in the Meritocracy. I guessed that the other meritocrats hadn't taken the loss of the card well. Some people are just better at fixing blame than fixing problems.

That should probably be a law.

In any case, we finally arranged for passage on a ship, said our goodbyes to Jerrick and Eegla, and got the hell out of the city as fast as we could. I felt a sense of excitement as we neared the ship we'd chosen, a slow but comfortable vessel with three available cabins. The ship was a hive of activity, with sailors moving about the decks, loading last-minute cargoes, checking various ropes and sails, and otherwise looking like a group of halflings drunk on sugarcane rum. Halflings are normally a dour bunch, but when they're three sheets to the wind, they're a lot of fun. As long as they're not armed, that is.

Despite the activity, though, a spot of calm stood at the top of the passenger gangplank. A human male with graying hair dressed in a fancy emerald suit stood with four large, armored humans arrayed behind him. I felt Millie stiffen as we approached, and my burgeoning sense of danger flared as I looked at the group. According to the Hag, each of them were rank six or seven Holders with various professions like "warrior", "swordsman", or "uptight asshole." Okay, maybe not that last one, but they all looked dangerous and felt the same way. The man in the middle, though, felt a whole lot more so, and the Hag quickly agreed with my assessment.

Unknown Man
Rank 11 Devoted Courtier
Luck: 74   Capacity: 62   Skill: 85
Hole Card: Prince of Stars
Likely Powers: Nullification, Magic
Resistance, Power Resistance

Unknown Man
Rank 11 Devoted Courtier
Luck: 74   Capacity: 62   Skill: 85
Hole Card: Prince of Stars
Likely Powers: Nullification, Magic
Resistance, Power Resistance

The man was rank 11 and had a noble for a damn hole card. In other words, he was probably extremely dangerous.

When we reached the top of the gangplank, the silver-haired man bowed low to Millie.

"Miss Millicent," he said in a respectful voice.

"Caldwell," Millie said in a faint voice filled with nervousness. "Fancy meeting you here. Did you come to congratulate me on the tournament?"

"Indeed, your grandfather did wish to send his regards and admiration for your finish—not that he would expect anything less from a true Deepwater, of course."

"Of course," she smiled weakly. "Tell him thank you very much, and I hope to continue to impress him with my accomplishments."

"I'm certain that you will, Miss Millicent. However, that isn't the only reason he sent me to meet with you."

"I didn't think it would be," she sighed. "Spill, Caldwell."

"First, your grandfather was most displeased to hear of your unfortunate betrayal in the Royal Lamb, and he made his displeasure very clear to the owners of that establishment. I give you my personal assurances that the felid in question is now inhabiting the bottom of the harbor and deeply regretted his actions before his untimely end."

"I—thank you, Caldwell," the redhead said weakly.

"But of course, miss. I serve your family as best as I'm able, even when its members choose to be a little wayward." He gave her a smile that didn't reach his eyes. "Which brings me to the main point of my visit. Your waywardness, Miss Millicent, has taken you into some rather dangerous areas, places where your grandfather would greatly prefer that you not go."

The woman's eyes narrowed. "Have you been following me, Caldwell?" she asked in a slightly heated tone.

"I, miss? Of course, not. However, you should know that your grandfather wouldn't allow someone as precious to him as yourself to wander the world without minders. Yes, you have been watched."

"You mean, a valuable investment to him," she snapped, fire filling her words. "I'm no more precious to him than you are, Caldwell—or one of his prized hounds, for that matter."

"To the contrary, miss. You've developed some unique talents and skills that your grandfather would find extremely precious, and he doesn't want those to be lost in the depths of some Labyrinth or a back-alley scuffle."

"Are you intending to take me back, Caldwell?" she asked in a quiet voice. "Because I'm not going quietly."

"I suggested that would be the case, so your grandfather has offered you a choice, Miss Millicent. Return with me and resume your training—including the new skills you've gained—or prove to him that it isn't necessary."

"Prove to him how?" she asked, her voice cold.

"This ship has been rerouted from your chosen destination of Felis to the goblin city of Sharg. An enemy of your family lives there, one quite powerful and influential. End that threat to the family, and your grandfather will know that you're capable on your own, and he'll give you the time you need to acquire the funds you desire. Fail or refuse, and I'm to take you back to him—by any means necessary."

"That doesn't sound at all threatening or ominous," I snorted. "Do they pay you to be creepy and vaguely intimidating, Caldwell?"

"I'm paid to be effective, Mr. Murf."

"I wonder how effective you'll be with my axe buried in your chest," Ferdi growled. "Try to take the redhead, and you'll find out."

"I would greatly prefer to avoid violence, Oath-bound," the man replied urbanely. He gestured over his shoulder. "However, I did come prepared for it, as you can see."

"I think we all would, Caldwell, but if you try to take Millie, you're going to have it," I sighed. "And while there's only four of us, I'd put better than even odds on our chances to take you. We've dealt with an awful lot of Holders over the past few weeks, plus we fought an actual warlock and his summoned demons just a few days ago. These six aren't exactly scary to us."

"I heard about the demonic incursion," he nodded. "And I'm aware of your group's recent exploits, Mr. Murf. It's possible that you're right, and that should violence descend, you might be victorious. However…"

He fell silent as I touched Fool of Senses and flicked it out at the group, willing us to vanish from their sight and hearing. The warriors jumped and reached for their weapons, looking around with dangerous expressions, then fell still as Caldwell lifted a hand with a sigh. To my surprise, he turned back and looked directly at me, apparently seeing easily through my ability. I thought back to the Hag's description of him and guessed that his hole card made him able to nullify my card, or at least weaken it enough to be able to see us.

"I amend my statement. It's likely that should this descend to violence, you would force me to become involved personally, which I would prefer not to do. However, even if you overcame me somehow, that would simply encourage the Plutarch to send a larger and more dangerous group—or perhaps a dozen or so Black Roses. As well, I'm certain that should violence prevail here, his offer to grant you a chance to prove yourself would disappear, Miss Millicent."

I looked over at Millie, seeing the indecision on her face. "What do you think, Millie?"

She glanced at Caldwell, who hadn't reacted. "Can—he can't hear us, can he?"

"I'm not sure. I think he can see us..." I began before Caldwell interrupted.

"I can hear you, yes, Miss Millicent," he informed her. "However, the others cannot, and I shall endeavor not to listen to your discussions."

"And you certainly won't report all of them back to your boss, will you?" I chuckled.

"The plutarch will know all that happened here today, one way or another, of course," the man shrugged. "I will certainly include everything I hear in my report to him."

"Even if I were to call him a doddering old buffoon of a man who can't get it up anymore and so lives his sick fantasies through his granddaughter? Would you tell him that?"

"I would, and I'm sure the description would amuse him. He has been called far worse by far better, Mr. Murf."

"Sounds like I need to try harder, then."

"Murf, this isn't helping," Millie interrupted me, gripping my arm fiercely. "We have to decide what to do."

"I say we dispose of the Holders and forget about this," Ferdi suggested. "If they can't see us, it should be easy, and while the old human is obviously powerful, I don't think he's a match for all four of us."

"And then, we might find ourselves being hunted wherever we go," Azara sniffed. "Even more so than we are. I would prefer not to try evading Black Roses, halfling."

"Then we take the old human with us and use him as leverage to keep them away."

"I assure you that Plutarch Deepwater would not hesitate to act out of concern for any threats you might offer to me, Oath-bound," Caldwell interjected.

"Hey, I thought you weren't supposed to be listening," I protested.

"I assumed you knew that was a fiction to make you comfortable, Mr. Murf. Surely, you're bright enough to know that I am most certainly listening."

"I—maybe I should just go with them," Millie interrupted with a sigh.

I looked away from the infuriatingly calm courtier and put my hand on her shoulder as I turned her to look at me. "Hey. You wanted me to help you be a better gambler, right?"

"Well, yes, but…"

"Then here's some free advice. Never fold when you haven't even seen your hand."

"What do you mean?"

"I mean, you don't have the faintest idea what cards you hold, or how strong your hand is." I gestured at Caldwell. "So far, he's just told you that there's a game to be played. You have to decide: are you going to fold without even seeing the cards, or will you ante and see what comes up?"

Her jaw firmed, and she straightened. "You're right, Murf. Thanks. What kind of gambler would I be if I walked away from the table without even knowing the game?"

"A shitty one."

"Exactly."

"I see that you have you reached a decision, Miss Millicent," the courtier nodded. "And I believe it is the wiser one—and the safest for everyone in the long run."

"I hope you're right, Caldwell," she said with a hint of ice back in her voice. "Either way, though, I'll show my grandfather that he doesn't need to meddle in my life. Who's my target?"

"Discovering that is to be part of your test, Miss," the man smiled, bowing toward her. "I'm instructed to tell you that you have one month to prove your ability, or I'll have to find you once again—and this time, I'm afraid I won't be able to grant much leniency. Miss."

The man bowed again, then brushed past us with his warriors in tow. I watched them go, then looked back at the ocean stretched out before me. It no longer smelled like freedom. Now, it smelled like we were about to sail into a massive pile of shit.

The First Law still held. We'd drawn a very bad card, indeed.

Thanks for reading One Bad Card! I hope you enjoyed it.

Murf can get by on women and cards, but for an author like me, reviews are lifeblood. Please take a moment to review or rate this book!

To find more of my work, check out my Amazon Page.

To learn more about LitRPG, talk to authors, and just have an awesome time, please join the LitRPG Books group!

If you love Gamelit and want to read more series like this, or to hear about the newest releases and best series, check out the GameLitRPG Society!

Murf
Rank 5 Cabalist (18,825/37,375)
Stats
Luck: 112   Capacity: 60
Skill: 40 (+5%)

Harmonies (37 to add)
Coins: 57   Blades: 26
Cups: 62   Staves: 33
Stars: 39
Divine: 67   Worldly: 70
Infernal: 64

Hole Card
The Eldritch Hag
Rank: Cabal
Attunement: 20%
Abilities
Adaptive
Arcana Defense
Needful Body
Rootless

Cards
Rake of Cups
Rank: Unique Noble Arcana
Attunement: 59%
Stack Bonus: 156%
Placement Bonus: 15%
Adjacency Bonus: 150%
Base Power: 120   Max Power: 544
Abilities
A Noble Master
Aura of Majesty
Crown of Authority
Drunken Combat
Fool of Senses
Freezing Touch
Golden Tongue

Ace of Staves

Rank: Low Arcana
Attunement: 78%
Stack Bonus: 17%
Placement Bonus: 5%
Adjacency Bonus: 150%
Base Power: 5   Max Power: 6
Ability: Improved Perception

Two of Blades
Rank: Low Arcana
Attunement: 31%
Stack Bonus: 17%
Placement Bonus: 5%
Adjacency Bonus: 120%
Base Power: 2   Max Power: 7
Ability: Thick Skin

Three of Cups
Rank: Low Arcana
Attunement: 72%
Stack Bonus: 17%
Placement Bonus: 5%
Adjacency Bonus: 150%
Base Power: 8   Max Power: 10
Ability: Gaze of Despair

Knight of Coins
Rank: Noble Arcana
Attunement: 55%
Stack Bonus: 0%
Placement Bonus: 0%
Adjacency Bonus: 130%
Base Power: 42   Max Power: 77
Ability: Melee Mastery

Lady of Coins
Rank: Noble Arcana
Attunement: 46%
Stack Bonus: 0%
Placement Bonus: 0%
Adjacency Bonus: 130%
Base Power: 43   Max Power: 93
Ability: Phantom Porter

Gambler

Rank: Worldly Performer (Power)

Attunement: 45%

Stack Bonus: 0%

Placement Bonus: 0%

Adjacency Bonus: 150%

Base Power: 179   Max Power: 398

Ability: Luck of the Draw

Other Abilities

Know the Deck

(Wild Ability)

Stack Bonus: 17%

Base Power: 3   Max Power: 6

Suppress Cards

(Profession Ability)

Flip the Card

(Profession Ability)